BLOODMARK

By Jean Lowe Carlson

The Kingsmen Chronicles, Book Two
Copyright 2017 Jean Lowe Carlson
First Print Edition

COPYRIGHT

First Print Edition, 2017
ISBN 978-1-943199-19-8

Edited By: Jean Lowe Carlson and Matt Carlson.
Proofread By: Matt Carlson and Anders von Reis Crooks.
Cover Design: Copyright 2017 by Yocla Designs. All Rights Reserved.
Maps: Copyright 2017 Jean Lowe Carlson, edited Matt Carlson. All Rights Reserved.
Chapter Graphics: "Typo Backgrounds" by Manfred Klein: http://www.dafont.com/ Free Commercial Use.

ACKNOWLEDGEMENTS

To everyone who made this labor of love come true, you are awesome! Special thanks to Ben Rayack for helping craft languages, and to Anders Reis von Crooks for his proofreading. Love to my family Steph, Wendy, and Dave for their encouragement. Thanks to my friends Marco and Claire, Josh and Lela, Sam and Ben, Anders and Nadine, and Amber for their constant support. Thanks to the amazing author J. Thorn, who teaches me more everyday about being generous in this world, and to author Nick Stephenson, marketing brilliance extraordinaire.

Special thanks to my amazing Launch Team - Anders von Reis Crooks, Kim Taylor, Brad Reynolds, Marco Cabrera, Rob Alspaugh, Tonja Carlson, Amber Byers, Sue Twiss, Gabrielle, Matthew J. Yancik, Jules Green, Brian Robinette, Valerie Jondahl and Kathryn Kelly - you guys rock!!

But most of all, thanks to my incredible husband Matt Carlson. I honestly could not have done this without all your plot twists, fight scene suggestions, editing details, mapmaking abilities, heaps of encouragement, and so much more! You are the best, baby, and I love you more everyday!

OTHER WORKS BY JEAN LOWE CARLSON

The Kingsmen Chronicles
Blackmark
Bloodmark
Goldenmark
Crimson Spring

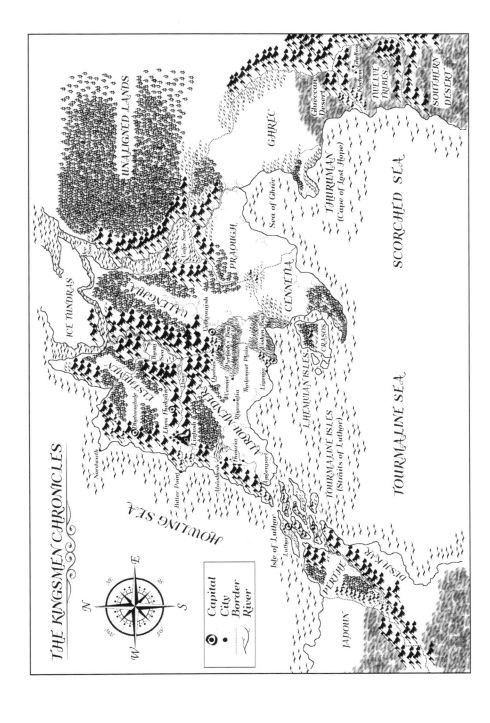

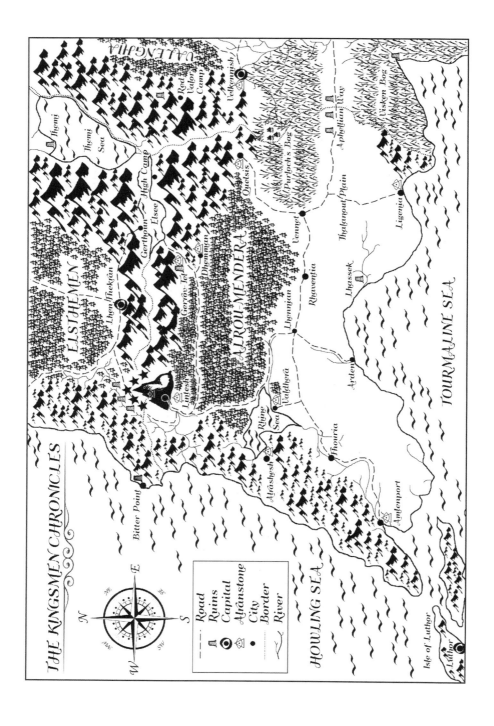

THE KINGSMEN CHRONICLES

Legend:
- Road
- Ruins
- Capital
- Aranstone
- City
- Border
- River

VALINGHIA

ELSTHEMEN

ALROU-MENDERA

Themi
Themi Sea

Red Valor Camp
Valkennish

Gertholm
High Camp
Elsee
Lhen Thekan

Purloch's Bog
Aphelliani Way
Lisheen Bog

Quelsis
Dhennian
Gerov Tel
Agheniian

Vennet
Thalanout Plain
Ligenia

Rhaventia
Lhngssek

Lhennian

Ilesh
Valesh

Arden

Valdhen

Fhouria

Rhine Sea

TOURMALINE SEA

Bitter Point

Ayasheshi
Ardenport

HOWLING SEA

Isle of Luthor
Luthor

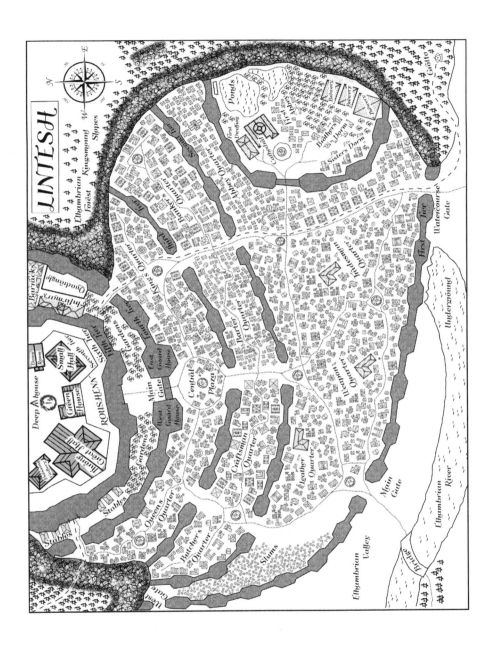

LINTESH

Labels on map:

Elthambrian Forest
Kingsmount Slopes

N
E
W
S

Ponds

First Brethren Dwelling

Brothers' Dorm

Brothers' Barracks

Sister's Dorm

Barracks

Quadrangle

Infirmary

Deep Abyrose

Small Hall

Dining Room

Green House

ROUSHENY

Home Great Hall

Thristan Practice

Stables

Stables

West Gate

Queen's Quarter

Butcher's Quarter

Slums

Elthambrian Valley

Main Gate

Bridge

Elthambrian River

Underground

Watercourse Gate

Grotto

First Tier

Hammered Quarter

Western Quarter

Leather Quarter

Craftsman Quarter

Central Plaza

Barter Quarter

West Guard House

First Guard House

Main Gate

Seventh Tier

Sixth Tier

Fifth Tier

Gardens

Fourth Tier

Third Tier

Banker's Quarter

Upper Quarter

Second Tier

First Tier

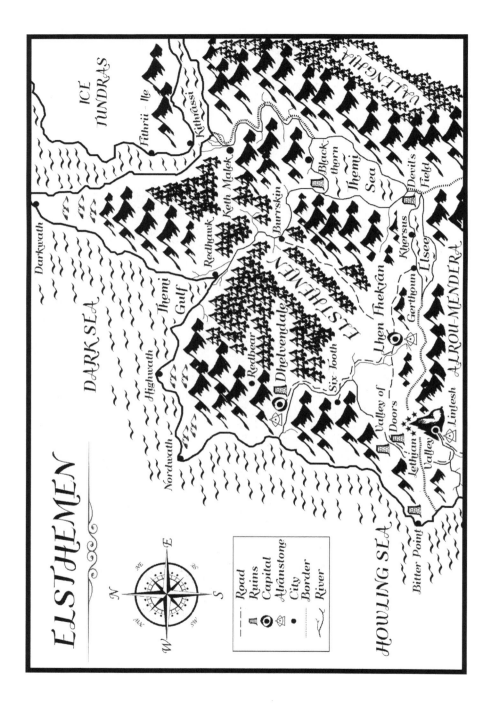

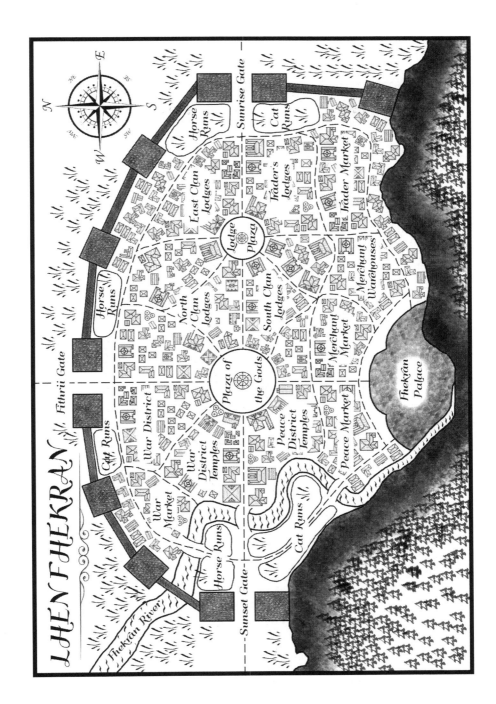

THE TWELVE TRIBES

AJ NAAB

SCORCHED SEA

SOUTHERN DESERT

GJUREC

TWELVE TRIBES

Chirus
Ghellen
Kheßem
Vénoußem
Asyana
Etrü
Aj Naab
Ongani
Revenßim
Beßáa
Lukßaan
Drásßgaan
Nürm

Road
Ruins
Capital
Aßänstone
City
Border
River

N
NE
E
SE
S
SW
W
NW

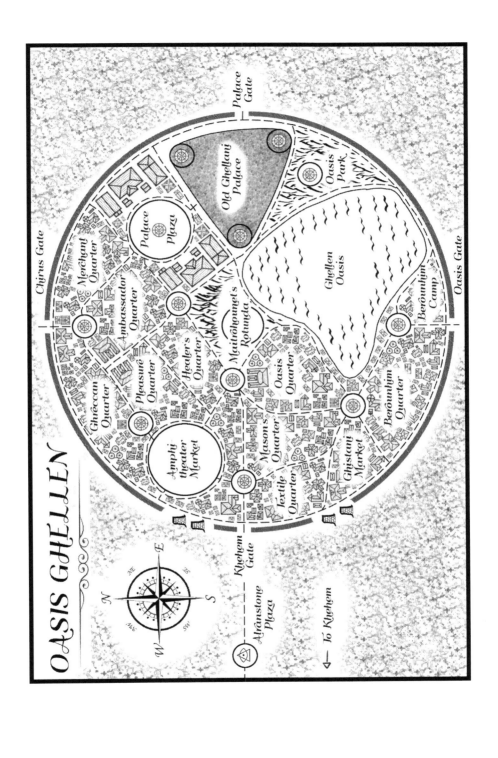

OASIS GHELLEN

N

E

S

W

NE

SE

SW

NW

Chyrus Gate

Palace Gate

Oasis Gate

Khehem Gate

Afranstone Plaza

To Khehem

Merchant Quarter

Palace Plaza

Old Ghellani Palace

Oasis Park

Ambassador Quarter

Ghellen Oasis

Ghéccan Quarter

Healer's Quarter

Pleasure Quarter

Maitrôhomet's Rotunda

Beóunhim Camp

Amphitheater Market

Oasis Quarter

Mason's Quarter

Beóunhim Quarter

Textile Quarter

Ghystany Market

PROLOGUE – TEMLIN

When men call for blood, nothing else will do.

Surveying the throng from his perch atop the wagon's ale-barrels, Brother Temlin den'Ildrian's belief in humanity plummeted. Humidity smothered the noon hour as the mob surged beneath the summer sun, roaring for bloodshed. The plaza before Roushenn Palace's main gate reeked of acrid sweat. Feet stamped in unison, voices brayed. Rhythmic clapping knifed his ears.

The entirety of the King's City of Lintesh, turned out to watch the spectacle.

Sweat slid down Brother Temlin's neck beneath his black robe, his cowl up in the hopes that he wouldn't be associated with this madness. Taking a swig of ale from his pewter tankard, he tried to quell the sickness that clenched his gut. A cabbage went sailing over his perch toward the hangman's scaffolding under the blackiron teeth of the palace gate. From his vantage, Temlin watched Palace Guardsmen in their cobalt jerkins jostle the seething crowd back, keeping the barrier before the scaffold.

A clarion fanfare sounded.

At last, it was time for the entertainment.

Paraded out by Guardsmen from the palace yards, the hooded and manacled accused shuffled forward along the cobbled promenade. Booing surged as the Elsthemi captives from the Queen's assassination one week ago were marched up the stairs into a row upon the platform, then turned to face the gallows.

The crowd roared, eager for blood. Another cabbage went soaring over Temlin's head, followed by wilted summer kale. They hit a Guardsman. He scowled, pointed past Temlin's cart toward the nuisance. Two Guardsmen in cobalt leather began shouldering their way through the roaring ocean. But they might as well have been minnows fighting the tide for all the good it did them.

From the shade of his hood, Temlin gazed up to the parapet

above the gate. And there they were, the two-bit ringleaders. Conniving bastards, the King's Chancellate. Clad for state function in black velvet doublets with draping cobalt robes, they stood serene before the thunder. Temlin cussed, gave his ale another deep swig. He'd lost count of how many tankards he'd had, furious at this sham justice.

Furious that innocent men and women waited on those gallows today.

Temlin's old limbs filled with vigor, fueled by hatred. Four of the seven King's Chancellate members were suspected Khehemni Lothren, the smug bastards, though none of the Alrashemni Shemout's suspicions could be confirmed. Sticking a knife in the Alrashemni for generations, deep in the shadows, the Lothren were the central organization that led the Khehemni, bitter enemies to the Alrashemni. Rage blistered Temlin despite his advancing age as he stared up at them, and he drank off the rest of his ale in a rush.

Surveying the Lothren's ringleaders, he noticed Chancellor Rudaric den'Ghen, the golden-maned pretty boy. A rose-scented git, though the man's political record was as immaculate as his artfully-sculpted hair. While Chancellor Jhik den'Cammas, he had the stature of a thug, now didn't he? Black hair, dark eyes, one might have mistaken him for Alrashemni had he not had a list of crimes a half-league long behind his family. All cleverly disguised, of course.

And Chancellor Theroun den'Vekir had been a Khehemnas for years, Temlin was certain of it. Upright and wiry, with iron streaks at his temples and in his military-short beard, Theroun had the stature of a hard man of battle. His gaze of cold disdain could have decimated the throng below. The once-General had been resurrected into politics after his murderous disgrace upon the Aphellian Way ten years ago. Slaughtering Blackmarked Alrashemni, he'd not spared even those within his own army, though he'd claimed madness at the time from a dire wound. He'd been recalled personally from the battlefield by his King. And for some ungodly reason had been given a royal pardon.

Which left their ringleader, Chancellor Evshein den'Lhamann. His white hair wafted like dandelion fluff in a breeze that touched the ramparts but not the crowd below. So innocent he seemed, with his frail, grandfatherly charm. But he was the worst of the lot. One of the hydra's heads who had brought down not only a King, but his son, and now his daughter and last remaining heir.

And today was a farce, a fiction, all because of these men.

But Temlin had no proof.

Raising skinny old arms beneath his black robes, Chancellor Evshein's gilded embroidery caught the sun. "People of Alrou-Mendera!"

A trick of Roushenn's acoustics made the Chancellor's reedy voice slice the air. The crowd settled, attentive, even the inebriated like Temlin. "We are gathered here today to witness punishment for the most heinous of crimes! The assassination of our Queen upon the very day of her coronation!"

The crowd surged in booing, curses. Voracious as wolves, they crowded close, eager to tear the flesh of those hooded upon the platform. Guardsmen pushed back, holding the line.

"This is a serious offense to our nation!" Chancellor Evshein continued, not bothering to soothe the rancor below. "And for this offense, judgment has been swiftly passed! Let all ears hear the decision of the King's Chancellate, who act in stead of the Crown until a suitable heir to the throne can be found. Chancellor den'Ghen, if you would."

Golden-maned den'Ghen stepped forward, unrolling a scroll with due solemnity. "For the crime of plotting against the crown of Alrou-Mendera, we as a nation hold the Highlands of Elsthemen responsible! For the actions of Elsthemen's First Sword Devresh Khir, now deceased, we as a nation hold King Therel Alramir of Elsthemen responsible! For the attempted and successful assassination of Queen Elyasin den'Ildrian, we as a nation hold the late Devresh Khir responsible, and by proxy to King Therel Alramir. For the theft of the Queen's body as an Elsthemi war-trophy, we hold King Therel Alramir responsible. And for the duplicity and crimes of Elsthemen, we hold these Elsthemi and the two spies they placed in the palace to be personally responsible! The punishment for these crimes, done by Elsthemen unto our nation, is to be hanged from the neck until dead."

Chancellor den'Ghen stepped back, rolling up his scroll to a fresh wave of noise. The deafening roar was muted by the booze ringing in Temlin's ears, but not by much. The crowd surged forward. Guards scowled and pushed back, but the frenzy was reaching its peak.

Temlin turned, disgusted, filling his tankard afresh at the topmost barrel upon the wain. He tried to catch Abbott Lhem den'Ulio gaze, sitting next to him upon the barrels, but the fat walrus was riveted to the scene. Combing his plethoric white mustachios with thumb and forefinger, a vicious fervor riveted Lhem's posture. Temlin scoffed, swigging his ale. He'd known Lhem was eager to see history turn today, but all the same, it was sickening.

"Can you believe this horse shit?" Temlin gestured toward the platform as the prisoners were unhooded, allowed to see their death coming at last. The crowd roared.

"This is how justice is done, Temlin." Abbott Lhem spoke, fingers combing his mustachios.

"Justice! Bah!" Temlin snorted, swigged his ale. "This is a circus. Any sensible idiot should be able to see that, Lhem. This sham, this blame of Elsthemen for an atrocity they didn't commit."

"Elsthemen's First Sword ran our Queen through, right in the middle of her coronation." Abbott Lhem turned to Temlin, giving him a stern eyeball. "There's no evidence that killing her wasn't an Elsthemi plot."

"Crap and bollocks." Temlin growled. "No sensible King would try to kill his bride *during* their wedding ceremony! If he'd wanted to control Alrou-Mendera, King Therel Alramir of the Elsthemi Highlands would have waited until they made their nuptial tour through Elsthemen to do that deed."

"Men have rash deeds done to garner power, Temlin."

"This was no power play, Lhem. Why would King Therel take my niece Elyasin's body while he was being pursued? Because she's not dead! War-trophy my ass. Any King worried about his skin after an assassination would have dumped the body and saved his own hide!"

Temlin's gaze flicked back to the platform, where the Elsthemi accused were being urged by guards to step up onto cendarie benches and thread their heads into the nooses.

"Careful, my friend." Lhem boomed low at Temlin's side. "Rumor has it Queen Elyasin died."

"Rumor put out by *them*," Temlin nodded up at the ramparts, where the King's Chancellate gazed down upon the proceedings with fervor in their eyes. Though that old war-General Chancellor Theroun den'Vekir simply looked stony. "We know a number of them are secretly Khehemni, Lhem. That they plotted this. Maybe not all the Chancellate, but enough to make *this* come to pass. Usurping the throne to put their own lily-white asses in control of the nation in lieu of any rightful monarch."

"In the absence of a direct heir to make claim upon the den'Ildrian throne, the King's Chancellate rules by law." Lhem intoned. "You know that."

"But they're Khehemni Lothren, dammit!" Temlin gestured to the ramparts with his ale. "And all this happened because you and I and the rest of the Alrashemni Shemout were too slow to protect my niece!"

"Shut it, Temlin!" Lhem's thick hand gripped Temlin's arm, fierce. "We're Jenner Penitents representing the First Abbey! Close your drunken mouth, man!"

Temlin shut his mouth. He'd not meant to admit to being Shemout Alrashemni in public. A faction of Alrashemni that wasn't supposed to exist. But the roaring crowd was so fierce now as the nooses were cinched tight, that he doubted anyone had overheard such sensitive information. His gaze flicked to the wide gallows platform. Roushenn's gate yawned like teeth above the accused, jaws wide and ready to snap.

Ready to claim innocent lives, just like that bloody palace had done for years.

Temlin's attention returned to the platform, to the prisoners now ready for the drop. Only ten Elsthemi had been caught alive. All had the look of Highland warriors, fur-clad and weather-beaten. Except for the spies. That well-built youngster in the cobalt jerkin with hard grey eyes and bluebottle Alrashemni curls. And the impressively beautiful blonde woman in colorful Tourmaline silks, now besmirched with bluestone grit and blood. Both seemed surprised to be where they were, standing out among the Elsthemi.

Temlin narrowed his eyes, perusing the haughty face of the blonde. Something about her seemed familiar. A fanfare sounded above. Temlin looked up, just as Chancellor Rudaric den'Ghen stepped forward with another scroll.

"The names of the guilty will now be read. Ghersus Mennir. Claydi Hafthein. Urso Hemmen. Petre Fuhss. Gerta Bashti. Lekki Heim. Reingalt Cladir. Shara den'Lhoruhan. Gherris den'Mal. Let justice be done."

Temlin blinked, startled to hear Menderian names of the two spies. But he had no more time to ponder as the executioner started down the line, kicking stools out from beneath feet. Like a series of pounded pegs in a workbench they dropped, a sudden punctuation to the screaming fervor. One by one, they strangled, twitching, shuddering, faces purpling. Bodies trying to stave off their final journey with the grim desperation of fish caught on a line.

And one by one, they all came to stillness.

The roaring of the crowd hit its zenith, bloodlust satisfied at last.

"Justice." Temlin spat, scathing. "Mass murder of innocents is what it is. Mass murder that is going to start a goddamned war."

"The sentence has been carried out." Chancellor Evshein's reedy voice sliced down through the plaza like garroting wire. "Let the Highlands of Elsthemen know that the great nation of Alrou-Mendera will suffer no injustice. Let King Therel Alramir know that we call for his surrender, and that any and all blood shed today, or over the course of our reprisal upon Elsthemen, is his to bear. As of today, we declare war upon the Highlands. Until such time that King Therel Alramir of Elsthemen is caught or killed, or voluntarily surrenders his throne. This is our verdict, this is our law."

The old man lowered his spindly arms. With a flourish of hunting-horns, the Chancellate turned and departed from view upon the parapet. Temlin narrowed his eyes, watching the King's Castellan Lhaurent den'Karthus go. The tall, dismissive man had been in silent attendance in his regular grey silks, and now moved languidly away to attend the Chancellate's needs. He served them now, rather than serving any King.

"No one to claim that fucking deathtrap of a throne but me." Temlin murmured into his ale.

"Temlin, old man, don't make it worse." Abbott Lhem turned, attentive to Temlin now that the show was over. "We can't have you coming out of the woodwork now and laying claim to the throne."

"Well why the fuck not?" Temlin slurred. "I don't see the

problem with it. I'm the last den'Ildrian left, dammit! Don't imagine I'd last long in the position, anyhow, shoddy job as the Shemout have done protecting the rest of my family."

Milling away from the scaffold, people had begun to crowd the wagon, calling for drink in the sweltering heat. "Ale's out! Go find a tavern!" Temlin snapped in irate response. It was partly true. The lower barrels had already been emptied into the gullets of the throng earlier. Only the topmost barrel had a bit left, and Temlin was doing a fine job on that one. Temlin began to clamber down to the driver's seat, making shooing motions. "I said go, dammit! We've got none left!"

"Temlin, old man, don't be a grouch." Lhem settled his ample bulk next to Temlin, the old driver's bench protesting with a groan. People were getting the hint, and had begun to clear from the sides of the wain. Temlin took up the reins for the draft horses, when someone odd suddenly caught his attention, thirty paces away by the shops.

A frightfully tall fellow, he was dressed entirely in black, not Alrashemni charcoal greys but a true, flat black that ate the summer sun. His jerkin's deep hood shrouded his face as he leaned at an apothecarist's shop, arms crossed, watching the crowd. His leathers had a weave in a foreign herringbone pattern, and as he lifted his gaze to the ramparts, Temlin's blood ran cold to see a terrible scar ripping across his neck. Not a clean scar like a blade might have done, but torn like he'd been mangled by some frightful creature.

The man's attention moved to Temlin, as if he felt Temlin watching. The man tensed. Reaching up, he lifted his hood, drawing it back to reveal his face. Dark eyes bored into Temlin. Black like onyx, not grey like the Alrashemni. Straight dark brows and an unruly shock of thick black hair gave the man a brooding look, though his handsome face with its high cheekbones was exquisitely aquiline. Temlin had a moment to think he looked northern Greccan, or perhaps from the Unaligned Lands, when he suddenly felt lightheaded.

Something slid into Temlin's mind, cold like a snake, as the fellow in herringbone leathers gave a small smirk. *See me not, old man. Or I'll make you loose your bowels.*

"What the devil?" Confusion washed over Temlin as he fought

sick cramps suddenly, the horse's reins forgotten in his hands. Guts cramping mercilessly, he doubled over, losing eye contact with the stranger. Temlin dropped the reins to grip his middle, fingers digging into the soft cloth of his black Jenner-robe. Taking long, deep breaths, he fought off nausea and agony. Pain was familiar, he could manage it; his old body gave him plenty. Gradually, the pain calmed and he gulped air, as Lhem gripped him by the shoulders to keep him from falling off the wagon.

"Temlin, old man! Enough drinks for you! Let's get you back. Lenuria's going to give me an earful, dammit!"

Lhem took up the reins and slapped them over the horses' backs. The wagon lurched. Confusion filled Temlin as his pain abated. He'd been looking at something, before these cramps took him. What was it? His gaze scoured the square as the wagon rattled toward the eastern avenues. He was certain he'd been looking at something, or someone, just a moment ago. Someone unusual in the searing heat. But as he gazed at an apothecarist's shop now, nothing seemed amiss. Just folk of Lintesh coming and going, with satisfied glances to the ten Elsthemi swinging in a breeze now sighing down from the Kingsmount.

"The hell was that...?" Temlin said as the wagon lurched away from the plaza, parting the mid-afternoon throng.

"Temlin, old man, are you hallucinating?" Lhem glanced around, chewing his white mustachios.

"A fellow over by the apothecarist's just disappeared to thin air!" Temlin growled, finally remembering what it was that had eluded him for so many minutes. "A man in black herringbone leathers. He had an Unaligned look to him. Didn't you see him? He was looking right at us."

Lhem scowled, white brows frowning. "Temlin. You are drunk. Ever since your niece was killed, you've been on a bender. How many have you had this morning?"

"Fuck you." Temlin soured, crossing his arms and tucking his hands into his voluminous sleeves. Heat rose in his body, a ferocious temper that had nothing to do with the scorching day or the ale.

"As your elder and your Abbott, I have cause for concern." Lhem glanced over, a stern sympathy all over his plethoric jowls. "If you can't get it under control, old man, I'll have to remove you from your station in the Shemout for a while. You're no good to us all boozed up, Temlin."

Heat blistered Temlin's sinews, the bitter fire of a life un-lived. With an unsteady lurch he stood, then set a hand to the wagon and launched himself from it. He surprised himself by landing upon his feet on the dusty bluestone cobbles, an astonishingly agile move from younger days. Lhem's white brows shot up as he sawed the draft horses to a halt.

"Get back in, you old goat!"

"Make me." Temlin threw up his black cowl, though nothing could cover his rage.

"Don't make me get down off this wagon and come get you!"

"It's not your business if I shit and piss myself right back into the gutter!" Temlin snapped, yelling now. "Let me grieve for my niece, Aeon-dammit!"

"It is my business, Temlin!" Lhem boomed back, their scene commanding attention now in the middle of the avenue. "You're my friend and I'm responsible for watching over you!"

"No one asked you to be my caretaker." Temlin snarled.

"No one told you to be a belligerent, cantankerous drunk. Be *smart*, man. Let the booze go. Let the rage go."

Something about Lhem's plea sobered Temlin. Here they were, yelling at each other in the middle of the street, friends for over forty years. Ever since their teens when everything had gone so disastrously wrong for Temlin. Temlin's older brother Uhlas falling in love with Molli. Molli beginning to go insane. Uhlas sweeping in to be her white knight, spiriting her away to the Abbey so she could rest. Courting her in secret, even after he became King. Temlin away marshaling armies on the field, unable to wrest their attentions apart. Coming home to find she was Uhlas', bedded to him in secret.

Rage. Countless blank months drunk in the gutter, whoring and forgetting his life. Being dragged back to sobriety by Lhem only to find his father had disowned him from House den'Ildrian. His military career in shambles, his life a ruin, his woman stolen, Temlin had come to the Abbey in shame and had been living that way ever since.

Temlin's eyes prickled with tears, staring at the wagon's cartwheel. He'd lost everything. A family, a kingship, a brother, his

19

love, a nephew and now a niece. "You can't imagine what this feels like for me."

"No, I can't." Lhem boomed softly, people passing by now that the spectacle was no longer notable. "I came to the Abbey by choice. While you… your choices were taken from you. Be smart, old man. Come on home."

His rage cooling, Temlin felt an empty hole in his chest. "I think I'll walk back."

Lhem gave him a critical eye, but at last nodded. "Take your time. Stop at Helene's Bitters for a cold mint tea. Or go buy a whore for the afternoon if you need to. Just stay off the ale. And make it home tonight."

The unspoken plea was plain between them. *Don't make me come get you out of the gutter tomorrow.*

"I don't need a whore." Temlin waved a hand. "But tea would be welcome. I'll see you back at the Abbey."

Lhem's raptor-sharp gaze perused him a moment more, then released him. "The way is the life, Brother. Remember that. Walk on." He snapped the reins over the horses' backs, and the cart lurched forward. Temlin watched it go, his view of Lhem soon obscured by barrels. And then the cart was swallowed altogether by the busy city. Temlin stood in the road, people milling past. Some nodded to him, showing respect for a Jenner.

At last, Temlin took a deep breath. "I don't need an ale right now." He murmured, trying for resolve. "Just right this moment, I can do without. Maybe some shade. And some licorice taffy."

His mind firmed around a destination, one that wouldn't put him in the gutter tonight. Helene made licorice taffy to gut a man for, and her cold blackmint tea was just the thing for the heat. Best of all, her shop had a shady little arbor out back. He could sit for hours undisturbed, listening to the sway of willows that secluded her patio from Lintesh's noise. Temlin picked up his feet, his mind fixed upon his destination. But with every taproom he passed, his attention sharpened upon the sour acidity of ale reeking through the air.

Suddenly, Temlin felt a creeping sensation, like he was being watched. Glancing over, he saw another man in herringbone black leaning upon a bluestone building, by an open tavern door. Hood thrown back, he watched Temlin with clever dark eyes. More slender than the first man, his tall frame still towered over the ants of Lintesh. This one had no scar, but wore a scruff of beard, his sleek black hair pulled half-back. Gold Ghreccan hoops were pierced up both ears, and he'd unbuckled his herringbone jerkin in the heat, baring a pendant made out of a scorpion's tail upon his chest above his shirt.

Come inside, old man. Temlin felt the thought slide through his mind. *Come have a drink with me. We need to know if you'll be a problem, Scion of den'Ildrian.*

Problem? Temlin thought it back, as if it was the most normal thing in the world to speak by mind across fifteen paces of busy street.

Yes, a problem. The man reached up to touch his pendant, fingering it almost lovingly. *We need to know if we have to eliminate you. Or if you can go on unharmed, under the Abbott's watchful care.*

Something went cold inside Temlin. *What is this about? Who are you?*

The man gave a small smile. *This is about nations crumbling. Come inside. Drink with me.*

Temlin felt it then, the urge to drink creeping up his throat. Like a silver wave of pleasure, the memory of cool ale slid down his gullet. The fresh smell of lemon and hops, the bite and prickle of bubbles upon his palate. The sweetness of that languid oblivion where nothing mattered, none of his failures, none of his sins.

He could drink and just be, entirely in the moment, come Halsos' Burnwater.

Temlin stumbled a step forward, then another. And then was walking to the man by the tavern door, extending a hand as if they were old friends. The man took it, clasping wrists with a welcoming smile before he gestured in a gentile fashion toward the door. Temlin took the deep breath of his training, trying to fight it. The pull. The need, drowning him like a silver ocean in his mind.

But all he could smell was the reek and promise of ale.

Temlin stepped into the dim tavern and out of the afternoon dust, followed by the man in black herringbone leathers.

CHAPTER 1 – ELOHL

A man lives hard on the road.

Elohl could feel it in his aching shoulders, in his back and legs from so many days traversing rocky mountain paths on horseback. He'd grown accustomed to trekking in the High Brigade, but riding a horse was another curse entirely. It was a relief to be in camp now, his limbs stretched, his horse browsing scrub-grasses beneath the highland pines. A soft chirring came from the alpine meadow as Elohl brought out the cendarie pipe he'd been whittling from his leather belt-pouch. Evening's gloaming spread out over the meadow. A summer wind rippled knee-high grasses beyond the semicircle of makeshift canvas awnings propped up into crude tents.

Lintesh was a week behind. King Therel Alramir's retinue were deep into the Highlands now, Elsthemi territory. They had ridden hard again today, climbing up around the Kingsmount through the wilds. Towering cendarie had given over to highland pine and snowbark birch as they wound their way northeast toward the Elsthemi capitol of Lhen Fhekran.

Their camp blazed with bonfires tonight, deer roasting over two of them, fat hitting hot coals with a sizzling hiss. The evening held a raucousness now that they were in Elsthemi territory. Penny-whistles had been produced and rhythmic clapping kept time, as King Therel Alramir's Highswords bellowed hearth-songs of giants and *shouak-ten*, the soul-eating wights of the tundra.

Tonight's bonfires were typical, entire saplings hacked down with pack-hatchets, then piled high to ward off the seeping glacial nights. The Elsthemi worshipped flames nearly as much as they worshipped belching, sex, and contests of strength. Roars went up as another pair of fur-clad men sat across a large stone in the field adopted as an arm-wrestling table. Cheers split the thin air as the two of Therel's best, redheaded trees of men named Lhesher Khoum and Kesh Tawny, began to wrestle with growls and curses.

A smile touched Elohl's lips as he whittled in the descending gloom. Though his life had been turned upside-down when they had fled Lintesh as fugitives after saving Queen Elyasin den'Ildrian from her attempted assassination, he found himself strangely calm. As an ex-Brigadier, the life of a soldier was familiar, even though he had to leave Eleshen, Olea, Ghrenna, and any kind of a normal life behind yet again. Elohl blew away curls of wood, examined the claws of the beast he created upon the curved pipe. It was nearly finished. The likeness of the vicious black creature was precisely as Elohl remembered it from the halls of Roushenn a week ago.

One corner of Elohl's awning buckled. He glanced up, to see King Therel Alramir pressing a hand upon the line. The King of Elsthemen still wore his finery from his Queen's coronation, crimson and black, though all was filthy with week-old bloodstains from carrying the stabbed Elyasin during the flight from Roushenn. And yet, the Highlander King made even ruined finery seem rakish, his grey wolf pelt about his shoulders, twin longknives with silver hilts in his buckled black boots.

"Elohl. May I join you?" Therel crouched, his pale blue eyes piercing in the violet evening. His ruff of thick blonde hair shone alabaster in the fire's light. A pale beard from a week of hard travel graced his angular jaw.

Elohl nodded, his whittling paused. Therel ducked beneath the overhang and settled. Elbows around his knees, he gazed out at the roaring bonfires, their luxuriant heat caught by the canvas lean-to. Other awnings popped up nearby like fae-caps, a semicircle of protection in the night.

Therel glanced back, watching Elohl carve. "That's a good likeness of the creature that attacked us in Roushenn."

"Thank you," Elohl examined the pipe where the beasts' long talons curved around the bowl.

"I still don't know how Lieutenant den'Kharel managed to kill that beast single-handedly." Therel's gaze rested upon the sleeping Fenton den'Kharel. Elohl glanced over also, to see the compact Roushenn Guardsman still out upon his oilcloak spread atop a pile of cendarie boughs.

Lean and trim, with unassuming brown hair and average stature, Fenton was still pale from the injuries he'd taken at the beasts' talons a week ago, but he had ridden these many days without complaint, jaw set and gold-brown eyes determined. He was healing surprisingly fast, only a jagged red scar across his abdomen to tell of his battle now. Unlike the Queen, who dove in and out of consciousness as they rode. Her wounds from the assassin's blade were healing under the care of her King's Physician, golden-handsome Luc den'Lhorissian, but riding opened them up again each evening.

"I don't know how he killed that creature, either." Elohl commented. "But he'll not say a word about it, other than asserting it trapped itself between the shifting walls."

"That I don't believe." Therel grunted. "How is he? Better?" Concern drew the King's golden-white brows in a line.

"He's a survivor." Elohl worked his knife into the pipe's wood, etching final contours on the beast's fanged snout. "Fenton den'Kharel had an unsurpassable record in the High Brigade. My sister Olea appointed him First-Lieutenant of the Roushenn Palace Guard for a reason."

"He's a Kingsman, isn't he? Alrashemni." Therel nodded at Fenton. "And so are you."

Elohl made another careful shave with his knife. "You spoke High Alrakhan the day we fled Roushenn. We recognized it. You knew us for what we were, and we knew you."

A pause stretched between them. After a week of travel, the Elsthemi King finally sought answers. Elohl knew he'd do it eventually. Any good commander would take stock of his men after such a calamitous event. Measure their strengths, weaknesses, secrets. Those lupine blue eyes were locked to Elohl, seeing if he'd squirm under a king's gaze. Though he was a good five years younger, only in his mid-twenties, Therel was no fool.

"Here in Elsthemen we Alrashemni call ourselves Highswords. You didn't think you Kingsmen were all alone, did you?" Therel chuckled, his smile amused by the firelight. "You may have suffered a purge, but your brothers in Elsthemen have been watching. What would Alrou-Mendera do after their King broke the force that keeps them safe at night? What would a young Dhenra do?"

Therel's gaze drifted to his large canvas awning, to where Queen Elyasin den'Ildrian, his newlywed bride, had been settled for the evening with the healer Luc.

"Your family line is Alrashemni?" Elohl asked.

One corner of Therel's lips quirked. "And no one lets me forget it."

"So you knew my sister Olea den'Alrahel was Captain-General for Elyasin. A Kingsman kept openly close to the throne."

"My father put two and two together," Therel nodded serenely, "that your sister and the Dhenir were intimate, close as they were all the time. He once thought my older sister Merra would wed the Dhenir, but after that heinous Summons, it was better for the Dhenir and his Kingsman protectorate to remain close. I was told to ready myself to marry Elyasin after that. She showed sympathy to the Alrashemni, a boon to our nation, just as her brother had."

"So your marriage was arranged?" Elohl wondered why the young King spoke so openly tonight.

Therel chuckled, his smile wry but soft with true care for his bride. "After my father passed, I could have engaged my own hunt for a wife. More than one woman has come to my bed seeking the privilege. But I knew, *knew*, that to see the Alrashemni rise once more in Alrou-Mendera, that Elyasin and I had to wed. Every Alrashemni has a duty. Mine is to protect her, almost more than it is to hold my lands. My sister, High General Merra Alramir, does a decent job intimidating other nations all on her own."

Elohl nodded, whittling, still wondering where this was going. "Merra is older? She abdicated the crown to you?"

Therel leaned back on his hands, stretching out long legs. "She's a year older. Elsthemen should have a Queen, not a King. But Merra doesn't like being tied down. She'd rather be out marshaling armies and fucking her Captains than sitting a throne listening to petitioners. Which brings us to why I've come. I've told you some of my history. In the truth-sharing customs of the Highlands, I invite you now to tell me some of yours."

Elohl didn't respond, his hands stilling upon his woodworking.

"How did you move like you did at Roushenn?" King Therel watched Elohl closely. "You were lunging to attack my First Sword *before* he moved. And when the walls shifted, how did you know where to lead us out?"

Elohl stared the King down. "I saw your First Sword shift his feet."

King Therel narrowed those blue eyes, his demeanor silent like a wolf hunting. "Horseshit. You watched any number of men shift their stance for over an hour, and didn't draw your sword. Did you conspire in the assassination attempt upon your Queen? With a twin close to the throne where unfortunate accidents happen? Do I face a Khehemni agent in this tent?"

"Why would I kill him if we supposedly worked together?" Elohl simmered at the accusation.

"Convenience." Therel's blue eyes were glacial. "To look the hero, so you could travel with my party, hoping to win my confidence, hiding the fact that you're a bloody spy."

Therel massaged his knee, but it put one hand near the hilt of his boot-knife. The gesture was not lost upon Elohl. It demanded a gesture in return. Slowly, Elohl unbuttoned his cobalt jerkin with non-threatening movements, then unlaced his travel-worn shirt. Holding Therel's gaze, he bared his new Inkings, golden script that curled in lines cascading over his chest and up the sides of his neck. As well his original Kingsman Inkings, the stark black Kingsmount and five crowning stars over his sternum.

"Do you see what you hoped to see?" Elohl murmured.

"I see golden markings other than your Kingsmount, Brigadier. Strange ones I don't recognize."

"Then your ignorance is the same as mine."

The King blinked. His gaze roved Elohl's markings, his hand uncertain near his blade. "You don't know what the gold means? The script? Those sigils? Did you not have them inked upon yourself?"

"No." Elohl said. "The Goldenmarks were given to me by Alranstone, just three weeks ago. I was trying to find out anything I could about them at the First Abbey in Lintesh, when Olea dragged me into all this mess."

A grim smile spread across King Therel's face. "You tell a good tale. Good as any Highlands fae-yarn. Very well. Keep your secrets about your golden Ink. But I will know by what means you knew my First Sword would attack. And how in Hadro's Caverns you navigated that palace."

"By my own gift. I can sense things before they happen."

Therel's blue eyes went flinty. "It is unwise to lie to me, Brigadier."

Letting out a slow breath, Elohl sat tall, trying not to let his own anger show. It would solve nothing to enter a dispute with the King of the Highlands. Shucking his cobalt jerkin, he pulled his shirt off over his head. Therel lifted one pale eyebrow, his gaze roving over Elohl's goldenmarks. Elohl took his shirt and bound it over eyes, blindfolding himself.

"Try to hit me." Elohl's hands relaxed into his lap.

"You're blinded!" The Elsthemi King scoffed. "What will this prove?"

"That I'm telling the truth to my King."

Therel paused, and then Elohl felt energy with a sharpness to it rip into his sensate sphere a moment before the King moved. Therel lunged with his boot-knife. Moving ahead of that flow, Elohl avoided the cut, then struck out, landing a stout punch on the Elsthemi King's jaw. He heard a grunt. The knife whipped again, a quick slice toward his throat. Elohl slipped it. He dodged Therel twice more, then hit the King again, a compact punch to his chin. Elohl disarmed Therel with a flick of his hands. He thrust Therel's boot-knife into the earth behind his back.

"Are we done?"

"*Fhenrir rakhne!*" The Elsthemi king barked a short laugh. "I suppose so!"

Elohl pulled his blindfold off. King Therel was rubbing his jaw, his demeanor entirely changed, open with camaraderie.

"It seems I owe you an apology," Therel grinned, his wolfish eyes irreverent with delight. "You've got the *wyrria*, inborn Alrashemni magic! Instinct like I've never seen. But tell me now that we are acquainted, how can I repay the thanks I truly owe? You did me a great service in Roushenn, getting us out. Saving the life of my sweetgrape. So. What can I do for you?"

Elohl rubbed a hand over his chest. Ever since the King of the Highlands had entered his tent, Elohl's golden Inkings had been throbbing like an old wound. They had been doing that, on and off, ever since the party's escape from Roushenn. Reminding him of mysteries unsolved. An image surfaced in his mind, of a hard-eyed wilder king with tattoos of red and white over his chest and shoulders.

"You can help me figure out what these goldenmarks mean." Elohl spoke. "You can help me send word back to Olea about where I've gone and why. And you can keep Queen Elyasin alive."

Therel cocked his head, keen. "You really don't know what they mean, those marks?"

"Do you?"

"Fuck *rakhne*, no. Wherever you had those done, friend, the fellow was either a genius or was crazier than a shithouse rat." Elohl held Therel's gaze, until the smirk was wiped from the Elsthemi King's face. "They were really Inked by Alranstone, weren't they? You told me no lies."

"I never lie." Elohl plucked the King's dagger from the earth, proffered it back hilt-first.

"No. You don't, do you?" Therel took his knife, head cocked with level seriousness. "But you're solitary. A man of stillness, and depths that hide much. A ronin keshar can survive the wild, my friend. But life is better when you hunt in a pride. As you are oath-pledged by your Blackmarks to my Queen's service, and saved our lives, I will do as much as I can, looking into your mystery. But you'll have to tell me the full story of those golden Inkings at some point, Kingsman."

Therel stood, ducking out of the lean-to. He turned back, regarding Elohl with a face uncommonly hard for his young years. "And Elohl. If our Queen dies, you can have my head, blindfolded or no. A blade through my heart, if Elyasin comes to harm. Goodnight."

Therel Alramir exited the lean-to, stalking off into the deepening night. Elohl watched him go, then picked up his knife, whittling into the gloaming.

* * *

Three more days brought them up through the rocky moors and scrub-pine of the Kherven Valley and deposited them upon the doorstep of Lhen Fhekran, capitol of Elsthemen. Nestled into a defensible niche between two towering mountains, the city was fed by glacial meltwater cascading down between the peaks. The air was brisk with a bite of autumn. Furs with oiled leather were the garb of villagers on the road leading toward the city. Thatch houses of masoned river stones were common, villages surrounded by berms of sharpened pine poles for defense.

Lhen Fhekran stood higher than the valley, on a hill between the sheltering mountains. The streets were busy in the morning hours as the King's party rode through a cedar-beam palisade and gate painted bloody red, decorated with arcane sigils. The sun was well up as they moved through the sprawling, dirty city. Vendors of every sort rolled carts down rutted muddy avenues to wherever they would make berth for the day. Carts were drawn by oxen, but now and again someone had a keshar in the traces. Horse hooves clattered over white volcanic bonerock. Thatch and pine dominated here, and everything had the look of a barn. Now and again, larger structures of bonerock or masoned river stones would rise from the street, decorated in sigils.

"What are these buildings?" Elohl enquired as they rode past a soaring structure of white pine hung with streamers of red silk, erect red phalluses painted upon the timbers.

"Tha's a temple." Their self-appointed guide, Lhesher Khoum, rode to Elohl's left. One of King Therel's Highswords, the enormous Lhesher with his thick red braids and braided beard had taken to Fenton and Elohl. "See the carvings?" Lhesher gave a booming laugh, gesturing to the stout double-doors sporting bulls with enormous genitalia. "Temple of Kotar, god of stamina in bed!"

"Highlanders have a temple for just about everything, so I've heard." Fenton smiled with a calm ease as they rode through the busy city.

"Aye. Those temples ye see," Lhesher gestured to a soaring structure carven with prowling cats, "are where our women pray to Berlunid for strength in battle. These ones here," Lhesher gestured to a strong structure decorated with arrows, "are where hunters pray to Lheshoni, goddess of the hunt. We've got temples where men pray for a feisty wife, and temples where women pray for bloody retribution. We've got temples an' gods fer just about everything! Damnable business keepin' it all straight, I tell ye."

They proceeded past a group of Highlanders, three men and

two women with a wildness about them. All were bare to the waist in the midsummer sun and positively covered in whorls of tattooing, their eyes flinty and suspicious, their red manes unkempt. Two tawny cats pulled a battle-chariot of raw pelts behind them. The cats gave a snarl, causing nearby horses to shy away.

"Ach! Hate the traces, doan' they?! Surly rogues. Stay back a pace from those cats, nasty things. Can take down a bear, though, and make no mistake!" Lhesher saluted with a palm to the heart as they rode past, and to Elohl's surprise the group did the same.

"Who are they?" Elohl glanced back. One of the women stuck her tongue out at him in a cat-yawn that showed her tongue, pierced three times. She had bars through her nipples and rows of piercing upon her cheeks. Her chest sported a black-Inked mountain and stars in the strong Elsthemi fashion, nearly lost to other colorful tattooing in white, red, and a silver pigment that caught the sunlight.

"That's Clan Blackthorn. Some of Therel's most loyal, no matter how they look. They're fierce. Patrol the Valenghian border far up the Bhorlen mountains." Lhesher grinned at Elohl. "Gishla thinks yer a good-lookin' conquest."

"She what?" Elohl glanced back. The woman shook her breasts at him, then laughed, returning to her business.

"Haha!" Lhesher slapped Elohl upon the back. "Got some pleasure if ya want it, lad! I'll tell ye where ye kin find Blackthorn's tents later."

Fenton chuckled in his smooth tenor, and Elohl flushed.

"Watch this, now," square-jawed Lhesher beamed, "Highlands women in action." His face was filled with roguish delight as he leaned far over in his saddle to smack a pretty blonde in rough-spun red wool on the ass. The woman yelped, then slapped Lhesher's face hard before he could right himself. But before Elohl knew it, she had a foot slung in Lhesher's stirrup, and was lifting up to plant a deep kiss upon his lips. Elohl blinked as Lhesher squeezed her close with one arm. It went on a while, a good, solid kissing with groping included. And when they were done, she jumped down from his stirrup with a cheeky wink, and was off about her business.

"Did you know her?" Fenton gazed off after the woman, his eyes agog.

"Nah!" Lhesher burst into raucous laughter. "Such are the

Highlands, lads! Never a moment to lose, never a hearth to deny, never a night alone in the cold. So say I, and so say most! And so do we pray to our gods. For you never know which blizzard is going to end it for you, or which battle might spill the last of your ruby-choked blood."

"But I thought Elsthemen was at peace with Valenghia and the tundra tribes," Fenton inquired.

"Yes, of course!" Lhesher continued. "We'll have no part of your bloody wars! But you don't take into account clan feuding. King Therel has his hands full of warring clans, day in and day out."

"But the clans unite when it comes to war." Fenton pressed.

"Aye, so. But after the war's up... back to squabbling over sheep and pasture! A Highlander would have it no other way. Live for the moment, and steal a man's thatch just for the thrill of it!"

Elohl's mouth quirked. "Sounds like you've enjoyed your share of raiding."

"Aye, so," Lhesher's grey eyes were merry. "But I prefer women, lads! Let others raid their neighbors for milk and honey. I'll woo the stable-lasses in the barn, while the lads are out for sport! Ha, ha!"

Lhesher leaned over, swatting another woman on the ass. This woman was quite something other than the first. Clad in tight-buckled brown furs like she lived out in the mountains, her white-blonde hair was intricately done in a myriad of small braids. A longknife was in her hand almost as fast as Elohl could blink, swiping.

"Whoa, now!" Lhesher jerked out of the way, kicking his leg up near his horse's neck so she didn't slice his thigh. She gave him a glower, and Elohl saw danger in her river-ice eyes. She yanked up a patched hood of fur and sheathed her knife into its thigh-strap, striding off through the throng.

Elohl and Fenton shared a look.

Lhesher laughed, gazing off after the woman's daring sway. "Ahh... keshari women! One of Merra's outriders, from the tundra ye kin tell, white hair an' all. What I wouldn't give to take one of those snowy bitches to my bed! Too bad they're tougher than the claws of their mounts and thrice as mean. We have a saying in the Highlands: *take a tundra lass to bed, wake with claw-marks on your head!* If ye know what I mean!" Lhesher made an unmistakable cutting motion across his groin with a grin.

Fenton laughed, a startled bark. "That swipe. She gave you a warning!"

"Didn'a she just!" Lhesher rumbled. "And what more warning does a man need? Look at those hips! Just look at them! Slay me with those hips, lads, and I would die a blessed man."

Elohl watched as the woman mounted a massive cat at the edge of the busy market plaza. Snow-white, the enormous keshar had black paws, and a black-marked face. Settling upon its high-canted saddle, a polearm with a long blade resting in her stirrup, the woman stared back at them with veiled eyes. One hand twitched the reins of a bridle that laced the cat's neck and ears. The big beast angled away, whispering smoothly through the crowd.

"That's Mikka Khuriye. First Scout of the Bhorlen Rangers, up north." A woman's voice came near Elohl's shoulder. "Takes a real bitch to tame that big tesh-tir she rides. An' I can confirm fer ye, Mikka's a bitch."

Elohl blinked over. A woman had slipped up so silently that his senses had barely felt her. The tallest woman he had ever seen, she rode a tawny cat, a polearm set into her saddle stirrup. Her fiery orange hair was braided back like Lhesher's, one ear pierced with an eagle's talon. White tattoos wisped across her cheeks like smoke beneath ice-white eyes. A sword was slung across her back, a black keshar-pelt buckled around her shoulders with a leather halter and gauntlets, and pants of black fur. She reined up, pacing next to Lhesher.

"Jhonen Rebaldi!" Lhesher boomed as they clasped wrists.

"Lhesher!" The woman Jhonen laughed in a strong alto, ferocity and merriment in her every move. "We heard ye had some trouble in Alrou-Mendera. Our keshari scouts engaged a party of Menderians in the Valley of Doors, sent to kill our lookouts. Somebody didn't want Therel to make it back to Elsthemen. Not alive, anyhow. General Merra's furious. It's good you took to the wilds around Mount Veldir."

"Mount Veldir?" Elohl murmured to Fenton.

"The Kingsmount." Fenton returned.

"Aye, so." Lhesher's basso was a rough growl. "Filthy Menderian bastards! We barely got outta that palace alive. Were it not fer these lads here, we'd be mincemeat. Sturdy Brigadiers, hey?"

Jhonen's eyes turned appreciatively to Elohl and Fenton. "Quite sturdy, though they could stand a bit more meat on their bones. In any case, rooms have been made for ye in Fhekran Palace. I'm ta show ye where. There'll be discourses on war in the next many days, so says General Merra."

"Lead on, Jhonen. We'll follow." Lhesher nodded.

Jhonen edged her cat into the King's procession before Lhesher's horse. As they neared the south end of the city, the buildings grew denser, though still interspersed with gardens and paddocks of livestock. Their procession wound its way at last up an upheaval of white bedrock nestled in the mountain's cleft, topped with a brutal palisade of sharpened logs surrounded by a wicked telmenberry thicket.

At last, the procession moved through an enormous gate of cendarie five feet thick, the doors pushed back to either side. The Fhekran Palace grounds were given over to gardens, not ornamentals but foodstuffs. Sprawling cat-paddocks could be seen past the gardens, reminding Elohl not so much of a palace, but a well-organized farm. And indeed, the building rearing up out of the bonerock foundation was not so much a keep as it was a very ornate barn.

And yet, Elohl had never seen any structure so elegant. Massive red cendarie trunks formed the palace's support, beams wider than three men could reach. Extending up five tremendous stories, they supported arched gables created by trees curved in bows, like the vaults of a ship. Supporting thick thatch given over to moss dotted with little white flowers, the roof-timbers ended in fanciful dragon's heads, snarling wolves, and keshar-cats with fangs bared. Between the support-timbers, the bonerock had been hewn into massive blocks that gave over to timbers above. The stone was thoroughly carven with sigils, basketweave scrollwork, and images of warriors spearing tundra-wights and foes of all sorts. Massive pearled-glass windows shone from every arched vault, depicting heroes of legend, ancient stories from the north.

Grooms rushed out from nearby stables to take the horses as they rode up the crushed-gravel causeway and into a broad plaza bordered by the gardens. Highswords dressed in motley furs and

leathers rushed out to greet King Therel Alramir and his company.
Therel greeted each by name, clasped a number of arms before
turning to lift Queen Elyasin down from the neck of his mount. She
was awake today, had been alert all morning as they rode.
Highswords rushed in to help, but Therel shook his head, lifting his
bride into his arms and carrying Elyasin up the bonerock stairs
himself.

A contingent of women clad in furs and weapons rounded the
side of the palace at a trot. The one at the front was hard-eyed and
battle-vicious, her long red-blonde hair done back in braids. Dressed
in tight-buckled leathers, she wore a white keshar pelt about her
shoulders, set with a silver Mountain-and-Stars pin. Piercings dotted
up the sides of both ears. Therel greeted her with a kiss upon the
cheek and a brief press of foreheads, and they walked through the
carven doors side-by-side. Elohl could only assume she was Therel's
older sister Merra Alramir. They had the same wild look, though she
was shorter by a head and fiercer thrice over.

Fhekran Palace had a subtle grandeur, like a barn-turned-
cathedral, Elohl noticed as he followed Jhonen and Lhesher up the
grand ingress. The white stone inside the palace was polished to a
high gloss, carven with intricate runes and woven scrollwork.
Pearled-glass windows in arching gables colored the light, making
the red cendarie beams glow with warmth. Every door was
ironbound hardwood, fully carven with sigils. Servicemen and
women wore buckled furs and leathers bristling with weapons rather
than silks or finery. Elohl and Fenton were led aside by Jhonen as
Lhesher clasped wrists and departed after his King. Up a grand
staircase of lacquered red wood carven with snarling dragons, they
were shown to a pair of adjoining rooms.

"There'll be a tray and wash-water brought up," Jhonen
pushed in through the double-doors. "Make yerselves at home.
Lhesher an' I must parlay with our lieges, but if ye need either of us,
we're just three rooms down the corridor. Ye've been summoned to
meet with King Therel and General Merra soon as yer settled. Ask
anyone fer directions to the Throne Hall. Ta!" Jhonen whisked out,
shutting the door.

Elohl glanced around the comfortable room. A sturdy pine bed
occupied one wall, stuffed with wool and a topper of goose-down. A

breakfasting table occupied a vaulted gable with pearled-glass windows, and a stout pine desk sat by a riverstone stone fireplace. The fireplace was enormous, large enough for five men to walk into. It dominated the room, and as Elohl approached the windows with their floor-to-ceiling white wool drapes, he saw that the pearling was merely a pane latched in front of finger-thick glass, sturdy insulation for hard winter nights.

Fenton walked through the side-door to the adjacent room. His boots made a soft swish over lambswool carpets as he re-entered from the pass-through. "I suppose we should settle in."

Elohl glanced around, feeling a pang of loss for his High Brigade gear and his Kingsmen greys, left back in Lintesh. "What's there to settle?"

A knock came at the door, and Fenton answered it. A housecarl in buckled leathers with archer's vambraces wheeled in a trolley of food, with a steaming basin and twill towels. He left with a nod, closing the door behind him with the grace of a woodsman. Fenton went for the trolley, picking out hot brown bread and slathering it with butter, while Elohl reached for the basin and a towel, stripping to the waist and stepping into the fireplace to wash.

"Shaper be holy!"

Elohl glanced around. Bread and butter were abandoned in one hand, Fenton was staring at his back, at the markings that ran the length of Elohl's spine. The man was riveted, his gold-brown eyes wide. A tremor took him from head to heels. Elohl thought his eyes flashed red, but it was just a trick of the colored light flooding in through the windows.

"Where on this side of Undoer's Abyss did you get those?" Fenton set his bread aside, staring.

Elohl blinked at the strange phrase, then turned back to washing. Splashing water on his face, he rubbed sweat away with the cloth, combing out his short beard. "An Alranstone Inked them upon me. I don't remember it."

Silence held court behind him. Elohl curried steaming water scented with rosemary through his hair, then sluiced his chest, neck, back, and underarms. It was a hasty bath, but better than he had gotten in weeks. At length, he felt a presence beside him. Fenton was bare to his waist also, a fresh towel slung around his neck.

"Let me in at that?" Fenton nodded to the washbowl. Elohl nodded and stepped back, briskly wiping dry with his hands, a habit of the High Brigade. Fenton stepped in, his gaze flicking over Elohl's chest and collarbones. Fenton's wiry frame, Elohl noticed in return, was all roped muscles and stark white scars, of both blade and burn variety. But the Shemout Alrashemni was curiously absent of Inkings. And for the first time, Elohl saw that Fenton was missing the ends of the two smallest fingers on his left hand.

Elohl nodded at the fingers as Fenton washed. "Frost blight?"

"Wild keshar, actually. During my time in the High Brigade. I plunged my knife down its gullet. The last thing it did was bite those bits off. Better those than other bits, I suppose." Fenton chuckled.

Elohl lifted an eyebrow. "You said you were Shemout Alrashemni. A hidden Kingsman. Why don't you have the Mountain and Stars?"

"Technically, the Shemout are not supposed to exist, Elohl. So we can't have Inkings out in plain sight." Abruptly, Fenton pulled a dagger from his belt, pricking the center of his sternum with the dagger's tip. As blood began to seep out, Elohl saw a Kingsmount and Stars done in crimson appear, starting from the blood and spreading out like tendrils of ink in a water glass.

At last, the entire Inking came clear.

"Blood-ink," Fenton wiped his knife and sheathed it. "Some call it the Bloodmark. It will fade when the wound knits. The deeper wound I take near the Ink, the faster the Bloodmark triggers, the more slowly it will fade." He pressed the towel to his chest, compressing the nick.

"So you really are part of a secret network of Alrashemni." Elohl commented, fascinated.

"Buried in all walks of life. We're trained in secret, we live in secret, and we die a secret."

"Except you're telling me."

"The time has come to tell." Fenton shrugged. "I'm not the only one unveiling. We had to protect you Kingskinder until you were old enough to make our vows live once more in Alrou-Mendera. You've made quite an impression on King Therel, you know. Saving Elyasin, and all of us, like you did."

Elohl narrowed his eyes. "You killed that beast in the halls.

Your actions allowed us to get away."

A quick smile flitted over Fenton's placid features. "It got itself killed. I got lucky."

"Why don't I believe you?"

"Believe what you will." Fenton checked the cut, then set the towel upon the hearth. "You see, Elohl, to the world I am Fenton den'Kharel, First-Lieutenant Guardsman of Roushenn. Secret tasks are given to me by the Shemout, in amongst my daily life, and I do them. My task for the past ten years was to protect your sister Olea. But my task has shifted given recent events. Now, it is to protect you."

Fenton eyed Elohl's golden markings. "The Shemout have a saying. *Protect the wyrric, for in them lie our Great Peace.* Your twin is *wyrric*, blood-born with innate magic. Beloved by a Dhenir, trusted by a King and his daughter. Considering the way you move, and to have been touched by an Alranstone, blessed with markings made by no hand of man? If that's not *wyrric*, then I don't know what is. So my sword is yours."

Elohl held Fenton's level gaze, pondering his words. Fenton's eyes seemed to flash red again in the stained light through the windows. Suddenly, Elohl's golden Inkings surged. With a hard throb like he'd been bludgeoned, they gripped his body in heat, prickling like an army of ants. Upon the heels of that sudden fire, twin pools of midnight surfaced in Elohl's vision, a wash of cerulean bottomless as glacial lakes. Ghrenna's eyes. She had found him again, this connection between them that came and went as suddenly as the night wind. Elohl's equilibrium gave a lurch and he reeled. Setting a hand to a nearby chair, he blinked, breathing slowly to keep from passing out.

The vision faded, back to a sunlit room.

"Elohl? Is everything all right? What happened?" Fenton den'Kharel watched him carefully, brows knit in concern.

"The golden marks," Elohl managed, spots still dancing before his eyes, "they've been... surging, recently. Ever since the battle at Roushenn."

Fenton's brows drew together. "Like I said. *Wyrria*, my friend. You've got it. Whether you want it or not, I suppose."

"I have no idea where this *wyrria* is leading me, Fenton," Elohl managed to stand up straight again. "But if you wish to follow me on my quest to figure it out, I'd be glad to have you."

"With any luck, we may be able to find out more here." Fenton spoke, concern still etching his placid face. "Alrashemni rule in Elsthemen, and have for a very long time. They keep old tales. But we should go. King Therel has summoned us, and I doubt he'd wish us to dawdle."

Elohl glanced at the table, at the meal. "I suppose we'll not find any peace here, will we?"

"Peace." Fenton gave him a strange smile, soft and wry, like Elohl had told him a sad joke. And then the look cleared, and Fenton clapped him upon the shoulder. "No. No peace for us. Not yet, at least. The tides of Kings and Queens are ever thus. We soldiers move through their ebb and flow as best we can. Get dressed. Let's go see what they want."

Elohl moved off to don his gear. His fingers slipped into his leather belt-purse, alighting upon the pipe he'd been whittling. "Fenton."

"Yeah?" Fenton turned around, completely dressed in a new white shirt and leather-buckled jerkin, with a white rabbit pelt slung around his shoulders from the open bureau.

Elohl offered the pipe. "I thought you might want a memento."

Fenton moved up, sliding one longknife away in his gear. He reached out, taking the pipe with slow fingers. A kind of reverence shone in his eyes as he perused the carvings. His gaze missed nothing, from the beast's fanged snout to the long talons sharp as razors, to the bristled mane down its bony back, like a boar.

"You've done the Khets al'Roch justice. Thank you." He murmured.

"How do you know what it's called?" Elohl asked, wondering.

"It's a long story. I'll tell you another time. Ready?" Fenton tucked the pipe in his own pouch with a small smile.

"When is a Brigadier not ready?" Elohl gave a wry smile, and Fenton returned it with a chuckle. Stepping back to the table, they snuck a hasty bite, then pushed out the door toward the summons of a King.

CHAPTER 2 – OLEA

They were two weeks in the desert. And still, no one would tell Olea what in Halsos was going on. From her perch halfway up the alabaster amphitheater's beautiful ruin in the center of Oasis Ghellen, Olea contemplated the ancient desert city, the largest jewel in the nation of the Twelve Tribes. The Alranstone near Lintesh had sent them through just a week ago, escaping turmoil at Roushenn in the wake of the Queen's disastrous coronation, and dumping them out in this magnificent land.

Olea thought about that desperate day, feeling as if it had faded, almost like a terrible dream. Time moved slowly in this place of endless sun, sand, and curling wind. Olea had ample time for contemplation, since her escort, spear-captain Lourden al'Lhesk, would say nothing of import to her, Aldris, Vargen, or Jherrick. They were waiting for a meeting with the citadel's wise woman, the *Maitrohounet*, before the Ghellani would say anything about their mysterious emergence through the Alranstone, or even speculate upon why it had brought them here.

A wise woman who had been in trance and unavailable since before they arrived.

Adjusting her white silk *shouf* head-wrap against the sun, a gift from their host's wife, Olea gazed out over Ghellen. Looking through a crumbled section of the vast amphitheater, she took in the desert beyond, then glanced down into the bustling market inside the amphitheater's ring. Enchanted by the busy market, Olea's gaze lingered. Bustling at the high-noon hour, the market exploded with slender Ghellani in their colorful silk wraps, their blue-black curls glinting in the sun. Soaring silk awnings with hot colors rippled in the desert breeze. A crimson bird-seller's stall caught her eye, with a brilliant saffron border. A booth of medicinal elixirs glinted from vials inlaid with tiny mirrors and squares of colored glass. At a glassmaker's stall, flutes of multi-colored glass hung on iron chains, lit votives making the elegant lamps sparkle when the wind coursed. An astrologer's silk awning was woven with white stars and the phases of the moon.

From her spot two hundred feet up the rows of stone seats, a smile lifted Olea's lips, watching the vivid life of Oasis Ghellen. It was an ancient city, she knew that much. Their host Lourden estimated it to be over three thousand years old. Gazing through the break in the amphitheater, Olea could see life and destruction in every direction. Along the causeways, plinths and arches were viciously pitted, crumbling from the harsh eons of desert life. Alabaster columns topped with carvings of water lilies and herons were broken, marred. Some stood in long rows, supporting aqueducts that sparkled blue as they snaked from the palm-engulfed lake at the center of the oasis, out to every part of the city. Mounds of white sand gathered in the streets, showing the direction of the prevailing wind from the west.

But a terrible war had torn this citadel apart once, in addition to the ravages of time. Grand arches showed blasted edges, as if they had been damaged by some immense force long ago. Entire sections of aqueduct had fallen and not been rebuilt. Ghellen's enormous wall, tall as thirty men, had been completely demolished in places. And beyond those breaches lay the desert. White and bleak, the desert blinded Olea with wind-sculpted dunes and cracked plains. Arroyos and canyons split the land further to the north, and purpled mountains dominated the far northern horizon.

Nearer, just beyond Ghellen's broken wall, lay the white avenue of tumbled columns they'd traversed into Ghellen the day they'd arrived. There was the alabaster Alranstone they'd come through, in its circular plaza of sand-swept stone.

Further to the west, a league beyond the Alranstone plaza, a haunting shadow hunkered upon the land. A city bleak and barren, black rather than white like the stone all around it. Abandoned, the desert was taking it back. Pulling its formidable walls down, a stronghold once made to defy time. But time cared not for the protection created by some long-dead king. Sand swept over the buildings beyond the breaches in the wall, licking everything into obscure mounds. Sand piled in sculpted drifts against broken black towers. Sand filled shattered domes, softening some terrible destruction wrought eons ago.

A shiver passed through Olea as the breeze curled her hair around her cheeks. That first day, when she'd come here in private conversation with their host Lourden, he'd pointed out that curse upon the horizon. And told her its name.

Khehem.

Olea's gaze shifted, back to Ghellen. Though it had seen nearly as much destruction as Khehem, this city was fluid, alive. Tumbled columns had been reclaimed, their blocks fitted into new dwellings. Wash-lines stretched between abodes, fluttering like colorful flags.

Near an arch at the base of the amphitheater, Olea saw the citadel's guards. Idling in warrior-attire of white *shouf*, leather breastplate, gauntlets, knee boots, and short leather-paneled skirt, the guards laughed and joked as people passed from the market. Leaning upon tall spears tipped with blades of obsidian and strung with a *shakha*-tassel of crimson bristles, the guards would shake their spears at anyone who needed a warning.

One such man now climbed the broken blocks to Olea's perch. Their host and guide, spear-captain Lourden al'Lhesk, was all sinew and strength. Moving with lean effortlessness, his desert-honed beauty would have commanded attention in any land. Like most Ghellani, he was slender and tall, tan as an almond soaked in brandy. His silver-worked helm shone in the afternoon sun, his crimson crest reminiscent of war horses and signifying rank. He was of exceptionally high rank, Olea knew that much. But still, Lourden would tell her little, even of his own duties. Planting his spear, he vaulted over a tumble of blocks, landing near Olea with light grace, silver shin-guards winking in the sun.

He swept a firm bow, one palm to his crimson reed-woven breastplate. Olea had seen Lourden's ornate Mountain and Stars Inkings beneath that breastplate. Cascading over his chest and shoulders, they were done in twelve vivid Inks with twelve stars. Tendrils scrolled down his abdomen and down his spine. Lourden's white *shouf* with its silver-and-red geometric border wrapped about his shoulders to keep off the sun. At its edges, Olea could just see the last curls of ochre, saffron, and a vivid cobalt Inking where they ran up the sides of his neck. Quartz in the pigments caught the sun.

Lourden's pearl-grey eyes were arresting as he swept the silver helm from his head. His high cheekbones cut like daggers, emphasizing his stern impeccability as he settled to a seat next to Olea. Staring out over the market throng, he brushed a hand through his short shock of black curls, limned blue in the sun.

"I find you up here again, *Olea-gishii*. Pondering our fair city."

Lourden's rolling baritone was easy with camaraderie. A rich accent curled his tongue, made his Menderian ripple and slice like a stirred ocean. Lourden was nearly fluent in Menderian. And Olea was learning a few phrases of Khourek, the native tongue of the Twelve Tribes, which was a bastard version of Ghrec with a musical lilt. *Olea-gishii* was what Lourden called her, which meant *branch of the olive tree*, a symbol of peacekeeping among the Ghellani.

And part of an ancient lore Olea had yet to hear.

She glanced over at Lourden, meeting his gaze. "Your lovely city has much to see. I would learn of it, and of your people." It was the same reasonable reminder she had spoken every day. A reminder that Lourden was stalling. Keeping her and Aldris, Vargen and Jherrick completely in the dark about why they might have been sent through that Alranstone in Lintesh to the one here beyond the citadel.

Lourden's lips twisted into a subtle humor. But his eyes sparked today with pleasure rather than apology. "And so be it. The Maitrohounet has surfaced from her trances. She will see you and your Guardsmen. If you would come with me. The others are being gathered by my *Rishaaleth* and will meet us at the Maitrohounet's rotunda."

Lourden rose to his graceful height, cradling his helm beneath one arm. He gave a crisp beckon with his spear. Olea rose, eagerness lifting her steps as she followed Lourden down toward the market. She was glad of the soft knee-boots Thelliere had given her, their scaled cream *loa*-leather a kind of smooth lizard hide. Her short wrap of white silk with its brilliant saffron, red, and gold border had also been a gift, her heavy Roushenn leathers abominable in the heat.

Leaping down tiers of stone, they entered the teeming zigzag of the marketplace, winding through booths toward the tumbled exit. Tugging her *shouf* closer, Olea avoided stares. She looked Ghellani with her lean height and bluebottle curls, but still, her pale skin stood out. She had learned that her garb with its saffron, red, and gold border meant she was an important diplomat, and as a foreign commander, she had also been allowed to wear weapons in the market. Only the city guard were allowed a blade here; Olea had been given special privilege. She had also been allowed loa-leather gauntlets and a harness for her longknives.

Stepping through the broken vaults of the amphitheater's once-grand entrance, Lourden nodded to the guards. They nodded back. More guards supervised a wall of stone cubbies where commoners deposited weapons in exchange for pieces of jute paper written with numeric sigils. Lourden marched briskly away from the amphitheater, into the well-lived city. He gestured up an avenue, and Olea stepped to his flank, the two commanders having an easy routine now that they had abandoned the stiff protocol of the first few days.

Olea gazed around at Ghellen's people as they walked. Most looked Alrashemni, tall with grey eyes, black curling hair, and almond skin. But some had brown hair, or russet red to complement caramel golden skin. Many wore a garment similar to Olea's, a tunic of colorful silk wrapped about their person, affixed with ornate stone or bone pins, occasionally with precious gemstones. Some men went bare-chested, wearing no tunic, but trousers tucked into *loa* boots, combined with a short vest and silk sash binding short knives to their person. Women wrapped their silk into long gowns with deft twisting and tucking, draping and pinning.

Color sated the eye at every turn. The Ghellani stood out like flowers among the ruins. Bold colors were fashionable, edged in geometric patterns, often with gold or silver thread. Their sheer silk fabric billowed in the light wind, leaving little to the imagination. Women strode by with baskets or brightly-painted clay urns atop their heads. Gracefulness blessed these people, every movement flowing with milk and honey. Their Khourek language was no less graceful, bubbling like fountains with long vowels, slapping with clipped consonants and guttural rolls.

Two men and one woman strode by in black fighting garb, their fitted silk shirts and trousers cinched tight with silk cords. Their weapons harnesses had black loa-scales rather than tan, their boots and bracers the same. Black silk *shoufs* were wrapped into deep hoods that shrouded their faces. As they approached, Olea saw hard grey eyes upon the two men, though the woman's eyes shone a vivid sienna ringed in gold. The three wore dual sickle-swords upon their backs. Daggers, throwing-knives, and blow darts were lined up on their harnesses, their black gear prickling with danger.

Lourden gave a subtle nod to the trio. The trio nodded in turn, the woman placing a palm to her chest as they strode by. Her eyes flicked to Olea, widening. But she recovered quickly as the trio ducked past on their errand, lithe and graceful and utterly deadly.

"Who are they?" Olea nodded as they moved on.

"Caravanserai for the Tribes." Lourden turned to watch the trio go. "The desert is a harsh place, fraught with countless dangers. The *berounhim* are our most elite warriors. They protect and guide the caravans."

Lourden and Olea wove through close buildings, up and over a white bridge of stone and down into a tight alley. "You do them honor. Acknowledging them."

"My own skill is as nothing to theirs." Lourden glanced over, harsh honesty in his sand-swept visage. "They are born in the desert, and they die there, sacrificing their lives for ours, so that the trade of the Oases can thrive. So that we can make it across the mountains to exchange goods with Ghrec. And to trade with the *Ghistani* nomads of the Southern Desert, past Oasis Bel'raa. And the black-eyed *Ajnabiit* beyond Oases Etrii and Aj Naab, over the eastern mountains, at the far eastern edge of the peninsula. To the *berounhim*, we owe all our lives."

"I saw a few in the market," Olea commented. "They wore full weaponry."

"The *berounhim* have earned that right." Lourden gestured past a few smaller buildings, homes of re-purposed stone mortared with a white paste, punctured with bundled red reeds for beams along the rooflines. "They may go armed where they please, in any of the Oases. Even among the *Chiriit* of the northern crevasses at our most sacred Oasis Chirus. Who are known for killing on sight if you come to plunder their garden paradise without a *berounhim* to negotiate trade."

"Do *berounhim* help you and your *Rishaaleth* protect the Alranstone?" Olea asked. *Rishaaleth* were Lourden's hand-picked spearmen and women, the most elite fighters of Ghellen. Olea had learned that the Alranstone between Ghellen and Khehem that Olea's group had come through had been quiet for eons, but had suddenly woken ten years ago. Brigands had been coming through ever since, brigands that spoke Menderian, Ghreccan, Thurumani, and sometimes the guttural *galhuk* of the Unaligned Lands.

Lourden turned his head and spat with rage, as he did whenever the topic was mentioned. He scowled. "No. The *berounhim* are land-striders. My *Rishaaleth* have the duty of fighting back the coarse men that have been trying to steal Ghellani through the Stone and force them into slavery. *Rishaaleth* honor the prowess of the *berounhim*, but so also do they bow to us, for keeping the citadel safe for their return."

"The *berounhim* sound like the Alrashemni." Olea said, walking through the shuttering shade of palms. Well-tended gardens with benches and crushed stone paths surrounded them now. This wealthier quarter of the citadel enjoyed the shade of high-arching *alahda*, the native Ghellen date palm. Smaller lace-palms in clay pots flanked mansion ingresses along the avenue. Mats of woven reeds dyed astonishing colors were let down for privacy in the heat of the day over doors and windows.

Lourden glanced over, sad, honest. "The *Alrashemnari* were once aligned with the *berounhim*. But I may say no more, until after you have spoken with our Maitrohounet."

Olea nodded. Her time to get answers was nearing. She chose a different topic as they walked, hoping it was one Lourden could answer. "So does Ghellen have a ruler? You speak of your Maitrohounet with reverence, yet I have the feeling she's not exactly your Queen."

Lourden trotted down stairs in a narrow alley, deep depressions worn in every alabaster step. "The Ghellen Council rules in matters of law and daily activity, a circle of twelve with our Maitrohounet as consult and tiebreaker. She is the one we consult when unusual events occur."

"Unusual events. Like when I came through your Alranstone."

He glanced over, made a flicking motion with one hand. "You come with a dire name, *Olea-gishii*. A name from legend. It speaks of things we once held in high hope. The return of the *Alrashemnari*,

45

heralded by *Olea dihm Alrahel*, the Olive Tree of the Dawn. The return of a golden age. A return of *wyrria*, the magic of the Alrashemni, to our lands. For this we pray, as long as we have lived since Ghellen's ravishing and Khehem's fall a thousand years ago."

Halting her stride to gaze around at the citadel's ancient destruction, Olea noted a man draw near to one dwelling, conducting a ritual she'd observed before. Pausing on the threshold of his abode, he reached up, brushing his fingers over a potted vine with delicate heart-shaped leaves and white starburst flowers. Set into a niche in the lintel, the vine was shaded by lace-palms in ceramic urns upon either side. The lintel was worn deeply over time. After the man touched the plant, he rubbed the stone. Olea could make out sigils carven upon the stone, and the relief of the same vine, just below the live greenery.

"Was it one war that broke your city, or many?" Olea asked, watching the man. "And how long has it been this way?"

Lourden glanced at her, a soft smile touching his lips. "Forgive me, *Olea-gishii*. I have been instructed by our Council to offer little of our history until after our Maitrohounet meets you. I know you have been frustrated. Persevere but a few hours more. All will be answered, soon."

Olea nodded at the vine over the lintel-stone, at the man now slipping inside his abode. "Can you tell me what he was doing?"

"Ah. This I can answer." Lourden gazed at the house. "He gives thanks as he enters his home."

"To whom does he pray? I've seen stones like that over every dwelling."

Lourden gave a soft laugh, his eyes amused. "So many questions. But this I can answer. This man honors Chiron, the Growing Vine, our god of knowledge and green land. The Tribes have lived in our desert for thousands of years. Chiron brought us learning; numbers, letters, plants for medicine. And how to harness our *wyrria*, our inborn magical gifts, to grow peace and prosperity. Because of him, we became so much more than warring nomads and herdsmen."

"Was he a man, Chiron?" Olea asked, intrigued.

"Perhaps." Lourden gave an elegant shrug. "But when a legend is five thousand years old, how can one tell the truth from the…

swelled truth?"

"Exaggeration?" Olea offered. "Myth? A truth made untrue by retellings?"

Lourden smiled gently. He reached out, settling his thumb to Olea's lower lip in a surprisingly intimate gesture, his desert-worn fingers cupping her jaw. "Yes. A truth that one never expects will come true... One that seems only legend, until a man is faced with it in the flesh."

His touch lingered. Olea's breath caught, feeling a pull deep within her body, something she'd felt with no one since Alden's death two years ago. The Ghellani were familiar. Caressing each other's faces was common among casual friends, but Olea was unused to it. A flush flamed her cheeks. She pulled back, a shiver taking her despite the vicious heat.

"Forgive me." Lourden's smile was wry. His fingers slipped away. "Come. We have arrived."

The spear-captain gestured, ushering Olea toward a massive building surrounded by lush gardens. A white dome ringed in columns, it had a wide colonnaded porch topped by an imposing triangular lintel carven with flowering vines and sigils. The sprawling garden around the structure was contained by a ring of date palms, as if the bustle of the city didn't wish to disrespect the dome by crowding too close.

Idling in the shade of the gardens with a few of Lourden's spearmen, were her Menderian fellows at last. Young Jherrick den'Tharn rose from his seat upon the desert crabgrass with his usual awkward stumble. He'd lost his spectacles in the flight from Roushenn after the Queen's assassination, but he didn't need them for distance, hailing Olea with a merry flash in his grey eyes and an upraised hand before he tousled sweat from his sand-blonde hair. Clad in a white embroidered vest with a white *shouf* about his shoulders, a crimson sash, and tan silk trousers tucked into loa-boots, Jherrick had been allowed a longknife stuck in his sash as he was escorted about the citadel.

The Alrashemni silversmith Vargen den'Khalderian had been leaning against one white column, and he pushed away from it now, putting a thick bear-paw to the open center of his dark grey vest, over the mass of scarring that had once been his Kingsman Inkings.

He bowed, his other hand upon the Guardsman's sword at his side. Vargen had opted for charcoal silk attire, the color of Kingsmen greys, not even his *shouf* in any garish pigment. A dark shadow in the bright day, his garb soberly devoured sunlight but for the gleam of his pulled-back curls.

Aldris den'Farahan was his usual cheeky self, lifting one blonde eyebrow and smirking as Olea neared. He didn't bother to push away from his casual swordsman's slouch against one column. Regal in white, Aldris had received a sash from their host's wife Thelliere in a bright hunter green that made his eyes piercing in the noontide sun. Recognized as Olea's Second-in-Command, he'd been allowed his longknives in the city. His only sign of respect to Olea as he idled was a brief touch of his fingers to the center of his chest.

"Finally!" Aldris called out. "And here I thought you actually wanted answers out of these blasted Ghellani?"

"Have some respect, Lieutenant." Olea countered as she neared.

Aldris grinned, pushing away from the column and extending his hand so they could grip wrists. "Get a good eyeful of the market this morning?"

"No more than the past few days." Olea replied, clasping his wrist.

"Great. I had a lovely time sleeping in."

Olea turned to Vargen, lifting her eyebrows. "And you?"

"Jherrick and I were with the children, helping Thelliere in the garden. They taught us a number of new phrases in Khourek." Vargen rumbled in his rolling basso.

"*Salish-te ah'khanek houret na hathne, ips hathne na houret salish-e, bithii.*" Jherrick's pronunciation of the Twelves Tribes' Khourek was impeccable, whispering with desert winds and guttural twists. Lourden suddenly broke into a roll of deep laughter. He reached out, clapping Jherrick upon the shoulder, who grinned though he also flushed. Jherrick reached up, rubbing the bridge of his nose as if fiddling with spectacles that were no longer there.

Olea lifted her eyebrows, missing the joke. "What did he just say?"

Lourden laughed again, a good, free sound. "He said, *we wile away the sundial's curve, as you while away your curves upon the sundial.* And then he used the honorarium for a female warrior, *bithii*."

Olea blinked, glancing to Jherrick. Who went positively puce, shuffling his boots in the dust. "Explain."

Lourden coughed, suppressing a chuckle. "It is an old Tribes saying. Meaning that a warrior woman may go where she pleases, and do what she will. And her men stay at home like dogs, waiting for her return. My Thelliere has a sense of humor in the things she teaches your men."

"Implying that I'm out *fucking* my way through town, and that you three are my harem?" Olea began to smile, getting the joke at last.

"Maybe not *harem*," Aldris smirked. "But Thelliere clearly thinks the three of us are strung on your line. Captain."

Lourden slapped a white column, vast amusement in his opal-grey eyes. "I will have a talk with my wife. She can be..." he gestured to Aldris, "like your man here."

"A cheeky bastard?" Aldris supplied helpfully.

"In so many words, yes." Lourden smiled wide. His love for his entertaining wife beamed from him. Something twisted inside Olea, feeling his previous caress upon her lip. "In any case. We must not keep the Maitrohounet waiting. Let us enter."

The building had an enormous mat of crimson reeds rolled down over the towering doorway. Lourden moved forward to pull a set of saffron silk cords that rolled up the mat. Before striding in, the spear-captain touched a trailing vine in a niche beside the doorway, then set his palm to the lintel post. He ducked in, waving the four Menderians in behind him.

Olea went first, pausing to put her palm to the post. The others followed suit. Inside, the vaulted alabaster dome was luminous. Silver censors ringed the room, trailing blue-white smoke, which wafted up through a circular oculus cut into the highest vault of the dome. The upper reaches of the dome were shrouded in gloom, slit with slanting sunshine lighting lazy dust motes that shifted down from the oculus.

There was no ornament in the room other than the censers, not a pillow nor table, no effigies of any kind. The polished alabaster floor was swept clean of sand. A white-haired woman sat in the hazy noon sunshine beneath the oculus. She occupied the center of a golden circle, inlaid into the floor and lit with the afternoon sun, flaming with thirteen fiery golden spokes. Olea blinked in surprise, recognizing the Jenner Sun, though stylized with flourishes of minuscule script and flowing sigils.

Cross-legged, the old woman sat with hands folded in her lap. Spine straight and eyes closed, she was swathed in crimson silk with a saffron border worked in gold and silver sigils. She did not move as they entered. Lourden quietly set his spear, helmet, and breastplate on the floor by the door. He nodded to Olea's weapons, mimed removing them. Olea did, leaving her harness and knives by the door also. Vargen did the same, then Aldris and Jherrick. Lourden's spearmen waited outside. One pulled the silk tassels, letting the reed mat fall back into place, drowning the chamber in a solemn hush. Lourden moved forward, taking a seat at the rim of the wheel's spokes, facing the meditating Maitrohounet.

Olea followed. The rustle of people sitting finally died. A breathing silence pervaded the chamber, stretched with expectation. At last, the white-haired woman took a deep inhalation. She opened her eyes with a serene smile.

"*Taile arabine welekhoum.*" The woman's somber voice held no infirmity. Resonant, it made the arching walls thrum. Her opal eyes were clear, sparkling with knowledge. Rather than old, she seemed ageless, as if she had somehow stepped out of time. The Maitrohounet's grey eyes flickered over her guests.

Lourden cleared his throat respectfully, laying a hand upon his multi-hued Inkings, his chest bare. "*Taile scherram Menderian, Maitrohounet. Ne Khourek.*" Lourden informed the Maitrohounet her guests spoke Menderian, not Khourek.

"*Menderian?*" The woman's gaze passed over them again, suddenly sharp, angry. "*Taile elepsios sayan. Kirthe elim lhe'ghavanesh nhis Lhaurent den'Karthus!*"

Most of this was unknown to Olea, but what she had picked out made her bristle. Castellan Lhaurent's name had struck her ears like a sour gong. Her heart sped, her chest gripped. He'd been here. Somehow, the Eel of Roushenn had been here, and had slimed his way into the severe ire of Ghellen's populace.

And then Olea understood. Lourden and his spearmen had been threatening when Olea's party had arrived through the

Alranstone, telling them to *go back to the eel you serve.* Olea had been confused, not knowing why the spear-captain was so venomous, nor how he'd known the Menderian language in this desert bastion so far south and east. But now, all Lourden's hints fell into place. How he spit every time the slavers that came through the Stone were mentioned. How he carefully avoided details, telling Olea it would be discussed once they obtained audience with the Maitrohounet. How fluent Lourden was with Menderian, educated to be, as a protector of the Stone.

Olea's gut clenched, worried that the Maitrohounet had just assumed her guests were ambassadors of Lhaurent's from Roushenn. But their spear-captain growled and shook his head, his grey eyes fierce as he argued low with the Maitrohounet.

"*Ne, Maitrohounet! Taile ne elepsios sayenti! Ne elim! Ne ghavanesh nhis Lhaurent den'Karthus. Taile Alrashemnari. Menderian Alrashemnari.*" He glanced at Olea and for her benefit, spoke in Menderian. "They are of the *Alrashem.* To the Tribes, they have returned, to make right the ancient wrongs. These do not serve the eel Karthus. I am certain of it."

The woman blinked. Her eyes flicked to Lourden. "*Taile fherroum lhis Alran-beihn?*" She asked him, her body displaying a sudden tension.

Lourden nodded again. Eagerly. "*Sahverya, Maitrohounet.*"

"*Alrashemnari...*" The woman's eyes flickered over them again, infinite and wondering.

The spearman cleared his throat. He gestured to Olea, then laid his palm upon his multihued Inkings. "*Sei Olea brethan khoum tantha Alrahel! Sei Olea dihm Alrahel.*"

Olea sensed the Maitrohounet needed proof of what her guests were. She reached up, pulling down her silken tunic so her black Mountain and Stars Inking could be seen upon her chest. A startled sound escaped the woman's lips. Her eyes fluttered wide. A tremor took her, lifting her chin in a deep breath. Something tense inside her crested and broke, and suddenly the energy in the room felt gentle, rather than strung tight. Her grey eyes shone with a film of tears. The lines in her face eased as a smile beamed from her.

And then she responded in a language Olea did understand. "*Alrashemnari.* Be welcome in Oasis Ghellen." The Maitrohounet bowed her head, laying a palm over her thin chest. And Olea had no doubt that she wore Inkings like Lourden's beneath her silk garment.

CHAPTER 3 – THEROUN

Chancellor Theroun den'Vekir slammed one sword-calloused palm down upon the stout table, wrathful. The sound ricocheted around the vaulted Chancellate meeting-hall inside Roushenn Palace, thunderous like a war-drum. The other six Chancellors standing around the map of Elsthemen upon the wide table jumped, quieting their bickering. Golden sunlight filtered in through high-arching windows set in gables of plain blue byrunstone. The sound of Theroun's palm boomed off the granite, startling a flock of pigeons out upon the balcony, which took wing beyond the open glass doors with a whir, off into the sweltering afternoon heat.

White-whiskered Chancellor Evshein den'Lhamann had the balls to fix Theroun with a deprecating glare. Brushing his gnarled old hands down the gilded edge of his black robe, he harrumphed a reprimand in his throat for the aggressive disturbance.

"What we're contemplating in this upcoming conflict," Theroun growled, his customary glower deeper than usual, "will be a rout! We can't just send in Brigadiers and Fleetrunners to face Elsthemi keshar legions! The keshari will flay them alive!"

All eyes were upon him. Chancellor Rudaric den'Ghen combed his golden mane back from his forehead, an exasperated gesture in the fierce late-summer humidity. "You have a better idea, Theroun?"

"I have ten better ideas." Theroun crossed his arms over his sinewed chest, still strong as when he'd once commanded armies in battle. "If we want to wage war upon Elsthemen and follow up that awful spectacle last week with anything useful, then we need heavy cavalry lancers protecting heavy bowmen to combat those Elsthemi cats."

"We don't have the cavalry to spare." Rudaric objected, his blue eyes colder than icewater. "They're all on the Valenghian front."

"Because you goddamn well put them there! And now all of

you are lusting for yet another war our nation can't afford!"
Theroun's shout sent another wave of pigeons careening away from
the balcony. He gestured roughly around the table in fury. "Bristling
for battle without even a shred of knowledge about what such a
thing would cost! Without substantial evidence that our Queen is, in
fact, dead!"

"Now, Theroun." Chancellor Evshein broke in calmly, his
rheumy eyes sharp. The ancient man with his flyaway white hair and
bushy brows never raised his reedy old voice, though it pierced like
daggers. "We all saw Queen Elyasin get mortally wounded during
the coronation. That was a fatal wound, and you know it. Even if
King Therel managed to get her back to Elsthemen alive, she would
still be a prisoner of war in the Highlands."

"She's his bride, dammit. It's his right to take her wherever the
hell he pleases." Theroun growled.

"Are you *quite* forgetting what the Elsthemi First Sword did to
our Queen?" Evshein's tone held warning, entirely for Theroun. For
him to get in line or get cut to ribbons himself.

Theroun simmered. This meeting was a sham, a farce. The
Khehemni Lothren controlled the majority of this Chancellate, and
he knew the voting would go wherever Evshein, the Lothren's most
senior member on this council, wanted it to go. And the Lothren
wanted this war in Elsthemen. All Theroun could do was influence
how the fucking mess would play out at the northern border in the
coming months.

"Gentlemen." Theroun continued with a growl that out-
blistered the heat, ignoring Evshein's warning. "I am not about to let
good soldiers die needlessly. Those bladed pole-weapons of the
keshari legions have a seven-foot reach, and can take off the leg of a
horse. Keshar-cats leap eight feet in a short stride, fully fifteen at the
maximum. We cannot afford to allow them in close, and we *cannot*
send in battalions with thin armor against them! We need heavy
plate, lances, longbows! Brigadiers and Fleetrunners are swordsmen,
lightly armored or not at all. And though they are both uniquely
suited for difficult terrain such as the Highlands, I *must* insist upon
using them *only* for reconnaissance."

Evshein was scowling, vastly displeased. Theroun and Evshein
both knew the majority of the surviving Kingskinder and Kingsmen-

in-hiding were in the High Brigade and Fleetrunners. Hence, the Khehemni Lothren's desire to use those factions in the first push of the Elsthemi war and get them killed off. But most of the Chancellors did not know that. Only Evshein, golden-maned Rudaric den'Ghen, and swarthy Jhik den'Cammas, who scowled like a thug where he leaned in one corner against a pillar, sipping bloodred wine from a chalice.

"Legions are currently on their way to the lower Lethian Valley, Theroun." Evshein argued in that rickety-iron voice of his. "Ten battalions of foot, six of light cavalry, and every man who can be spared from the Fleetrunners and High Brigade. A full fifteen thousand men, all told. A camp is already being set on the border of Elsthemen, just south of the Valley of Doors."

Theroun shot Evshein an especially dark glower. He knew men were on the move. After the Chancellate had given preliminary approval for war-preparations, Evshein had taken it upon himself to send the first orders to the nation's Generals, without the Chancellate's approval. The old man was getting too comfortable, presuming that he led the Chancellate and the Khehemni Lothren. Theroun didn't know for certain how high up the old man was in the Lothren, but to make moves like that, it was right near the top.

And now, one could hardly see for the amount of dry dust being kicked up along the King's Road. Soldiers had been pouring into Lintesh the last two days for supplies and a last good whoring at brothels in the lower city. The whole fucking city smelled like sex and sweat and vomit when the wind blew just right off the plains.

"This will fail. And we'll be facing an *invasion* after our men fall." Theroun scowled around the table. "If you want to wake with your heads in a keshar's maw, then by all means, pursue this course. A keshar can run from the Elsthemi border to Lintesh in a day. Send footmen and light horse to do a heavy cavalry job, and you'll have keshari terrorizing Lintesh by dawn. Yet another reason we've always pursued *trade* with Elsthemen, not war. Uhlas and his forefathers knew that."

Theroun fixed Evshein in his glower. The man was making a vast mistake that would cost them the entire nation when it went sour. Chancellor Rudaric den'Ghen stroked his golden mustachios, then mopped a fine sheen of sweat from his brow with a white kerchief. He had never been afraid of Theroun's glower, and he wasn't now. "Sounds like you want to come out of retirement, First-General," he joked mildly.

"I would, if I could." Theroun's gaze still menaced Evshein, but he found the old man was watching him curiously now, his head cocked like a hunting owl.

"Indeed." Evshein stroked his white beard. "Give us your opinion, Theroun. Whom would you send to manage this campaign?"

"General den'Kharnis or General den'Albehout, from the Valenghian border." Theroun snapped at once. "They're the only two with experience of keshari."

"General den'Ulthumen has already been offered and accepted the post." Evshein warbled.

"Den'Ulthumen's versed in the phalanxes of Ghrec and Thuruman," Theroun's gaze was as withering as the late-summer sun outside. "Elsthemi fight Highlands-style, wraiths sliding through the woods with tricks up their furs. When you see them in the open, you can bet keshari will be the dominant force, but in the woods, they hunt like wolf packs. Taut-wires to bring down horses, screens for ambush, rope-snares, poisoned darts. They have the terrain to their advantage, and they'll taunt you from the trees until you come in after them. Your mistake. They may not be numerous, but those who survive in the Highlands are skilled adversaries."

Mutters went around the table. Chancellor Evshein took control of the group with an upraised hand. "Den'Ulthumen's tactics will be more than adequate to rout the Highlanders."

"In the Lethian Valley." Theroun crossed his arms over his chest. "But that valley is long and narrow, gentlemen, little more than a river canyon the Lethian Way follows up through the forested foothills. Open space for phalanxes? Not until you get thirty leagues up into the plains of the Highlands, past the Valley of Doors."

Chancellor Rudaric was gazing at the map, stroking his mustachios. "I agree with Theroun. But what about a sea-strike? We're not using our fleets much against the Valenghians, with only three harbors as they have."

Theroun gave him a withering look. "Have you seen the Elsthemi coast?"

A flush across the man's cheeks gave the answer. Lothren or not, Rudaric was a politician, not a tactician.

"There is a reason," Theroun continued, "Why the Elsthemi don't trade by sea. Their coastline drops off in sheer cliffs that dive straight to the ocean. Rivers cut bitter gorges before they hit the coast. The few villages that fish do so by basket-and-net contraptions they lower down the cliffs. Just as our northern coastline rises in elevation, so theirs does start where ours leaves off, and is so incredibly unassailable, they don't even try to defend it."

Rudaric was chagrined and it showed. He reached out for a chalice of watered wine, and had a deep drink to cover his embarrassment. The man was intelligent, but sometimes he spoke before his wits caught up with him. "Well, then. It seems Theroun has this war entirely planned out, gentlemen! I would like to offer a movement before the Chancellate. To send our most reliable asset, Theroun den'Vekir, to the front personally to act as war-counsel for General den'Ulthumen."

The motion was a slap of surprise to Theroun. He blinked, staring at Rudaric. But before he could say anything, Chancellor Evshein suddenly raised his reedy voice. "I second that motion. It is obvious that Theroun's gifts are wasted here, and may better serve us at the war-front. Shall we put it to a vote?"

The six other members of the Chancellate nodded and mumbled. Evshein held the vote. Two fingers went to each man's lips around the table, unanimous. It was odd for the King's Chancellors to use a Jenner affirmation, but it noted a tradition of agreement and peace they were supposed to uphold. Except now, this den of thieves was backed by a secret order, stealing a Queen's rule and starting a second war. Theroun was in the adder's den, and where once he had been an adder, now he was a viper in the wrong nest.

Evshein peered at him through rheumy eyes. "It seems you are needed at the front, General."

"I'm not fit. You know that." It was all Theroun could do to not flicker an eyelid.

"Yes, there is that," Evshein eyed him critically, taking in his twisted right ribs, his old war-wound. "But all the same, we have come to agreement. A new post shall be created for you, as Counsel-General, a non-combat supervisory role to General den'Ulthumen.

Your duties as Chancellor will end, naturally, with you so far from the palace, and a suitable replacement shall be found. But I'm sure that will be quite satisfactory to you. So. Are you ready to return to war, Counsel-General?"

It was a prospect Theroun couldn't refuse. In his deepest heart, he wanted to return to the battlefield, and this was his chance. It was also his chance to seize any available men or resources, if he could, for his Queen. But something slipped uneasily within him, wondering if the Lothren had planned this to get him out of the Chancellate. Because they suspected him of disloyalty. Because it would be easier to kill him off at the front, rather than keep him here at Roushenn, causing trouble.

His moment of thought sparked something in Evshein, for the wizened old man murmured low, "*Thouliet dannoua Khehem, yethan chelis.*"

Remember you to Khehem, with your heart.

Rudaric's eyes narrowed on Theroun, mopping his brow. Jhik perked from his disinterested slouch, his swarthy face breaking into a smirk. They knew Theroun had just been reprimanded. But Old Khehemni was not a language the other Chancellors knew. They cocked their heads, bemused, thinking it perhaps a line of ancient poetry.

"I will take the post." Theroun growled.

"Good." Evshein nodded decisively, a smile creeping across his wrinkled face. "I will send a rider to General den'Ulthumen at the front."

Theroun scowled harder. Seizing command from a Khehemnas might be an issue. "The boy better do as I say, or I'll tan his hide and send him yelping home."

Chancellor Evshein smiled broadly as the other Chancellors laughed. "I'm sure you will find him *quite* agreeable to your presence. Congratulations, Counsel-General, in your new post." Evshein proffered one withered old arm from beneath his gilt-threaded black robes. "I will have my scribe write up the appropriate documents and deliver them to your quarters. Make ready to depart for Camp Lethia at once. The Chancellate look forward to your first report from the field. Let us adjourn for today, gentlemen. It is hot, we need rest, and I'm sure Counsel-General Theroun has much to do."

Theroun took the adder's hand and shook it, harder than he should have. But Evshein was Khehemni, stronger than he looked, and bore it well. His old eyes glinted with cunning, and when Theroun turned to stride from the hall, he felt those eyes boring into his back.

* * *

The hated knock came late that night. Theroun had just finished his evening sword routine, and was sluicing off in a pan of water by the cold fireplace in his sparse rooms. It was too hot for a fire, crickets and bullfrogs chorusing in the thick humidity of the summer night. Theroun's water was tepid and brisked his skin with a fine chill, just like the hasty scrubs he had been used to as a commander at war. A standing branch of candles illumined the darkness near his red cendarie desk, throwing an uneven light as an evening wind sighed through the open windows. Theron threw on a quilted crimson dressing-robe and cinched the sash, then hid a knife in the inner breast pocket as he bellowed, "Come!"

Castellan Lhaurent den'Karthus slid around the door. Clad in his usual spotless grey silk doublet, breeches, soft boots, and open sleeveless robe, he closed the door with one ruby-beringed hand. His silver-streaked black hair was carefully oiled back from his brow, his short beard silvering and neatly trimmed on his lightly-lined face. A servile stoop bent his tall shoulders, making the grey silk hang off his gaunt frame, and his silver chains of office dangled from his doublet's high collar.

Theroun had the thought suddenly that Lhaurent must have countless suits of identical grey silk. Theroun had never thought about that before, and it made him chuckle. His chuckle caught Lhaurent off-guard, and the man raised dark eyebrows as he entered, a bottle of wine in one hand.

"Do I amuse you, Counsel-General?" Lhaurent slid forward to place the bottle upon the desk and gather two goblets from a side trestle. He cracked the seal on the wine and pulled the cork as if they were the best of friends.

"Endlessly." Theroun allowed his chuckle to last, enjoying the way it irked the Castellan.

59

"Because?" Lhaurent poured the goblets with a deft, elegant manner, long-used to waiting table at court. Despite his smooth, irksome manner, the man had been Castellan to three generations of den'Ildrian royalty, after all.

"Because all that perfume and silk belongs on a pleasure-boy, not a grown man."

Lhaurent's smile was oily but tight upon his lips. "Just because you've never enjoyed the finer pleasures in life doesn't mean others can't, Counsel-General." He lifted his goblet in a toast. "To you and your much-anticipated new post."

Theroun lifted his goblet also, taking a deep draught. Lhaurent took only a demure sip, as he ever did. The man never had taken much drink. Theroun put his goblet down upon the desk. "And what do the Khehemni Lothren wish me to do with my post, pray tell?"

"Ah! May I sit?" Lhaurent flowed into an overstuffed chair without being invited, crossing his legs at the knees like a pompous turd and swirling his wine. "We are pleased with your post, naturally. We enjoy placing our agents where they are most needed. Did you like your raise in salary?"

Theroun chuckled, and watched Lhaurent try not to fidget, enjoying this new game. "Very generous, I'm sure. I had wondered about my placement. Rudaric isn't smart enough to have come up with that motion today all on his own. What are my objectives for the Lothren?"

Lhaurent sipped his wine, more a nervous twitch than his regular ease. "The usual. Use your best knowledge to rout the Elsthemi. Find and interrogate any with the Blackmark. Draw out their ties within our ranks and the Highlanders. Place any with the Mark in positions of danger, citing their superior ability to handle rigors of battle. You will not have any opposition from General den'Ulthumen, nor his top four officers. Their orders are the same."

"So many eels the Lothren have, all in one stew-pot," Theroun growled.

"Eels have been breeding in the lake, my friend, because the black pike grow too numerous."

Theroun snorted. "The black pike haven't been numerous since the Summons. The eels in Alrou-Mendera strangle them out."

Lhaurent's sea-grey eyes glittered dangerously. "Precisely, my dear Counsel-General. Strangling is something we excel at. You'd do well to remember it."

Theroun's eyes hardened. "Threatening me again, Lhaurent? I thought we grew tired of that game."

Lhaurent flowed to standing, setting his goblet upon the desk, his wine barely touched. His eyes glittered, watchful. "You may be out of my palace, but my domain doesn't end there."

"*Your* palace?" Theroun snorted.

"*My* palace, sir." Lhaurent slid closer. "I have watched you pull your desk to the center of the room, I have seen you write so small and so secretly. If the Khehemni Lothren didn't have such grand plans for you, I would have had you by now. And I may yet, if you step wrong, Theroun. Step wrong, for me. Get yourself sent back to my loving embrace. And then learn what true pain is."

Theroun chuckled, watching Lhaurent. "You don't like it that I'm being sent off by the Lothren. Out of your clutches, is it?"

Lhaurent's eyes glittered, slick as eel-flesh underwater and thrice as deadly. "The *Lothren* need to learn their place."

"You don't fear them at all, do you, eel?" A dark spear of unease pierced Theroun's gut.

Those cold grey eyes were upon Theroun, and it was like gazing into the face of Death. "There is only one Uniter, Theroun, not an entire Lothren of them."

Theroun growled, but beneath it was confusion at Lhaurent's words. He had no idea what those words meant, nor to what they referred. But Lhaurent did, and apparently he thought it gave him power over the Khehemni Lothren. A lot of power.

"More threats?" Theroun sneered. "I've made peace with my death, eel. Have you? What will the Khehemni Lothren do when they find out what you've been up to behind the walls of Roushenn? Since before Uhlas, wasn't it? When you came to the palace and found out what Roushenn really is?"

His empty guess was apparently correct. Lhaurent twitched violently. His grey eyes were searing, murderous. "You know nothing, fool!"

"Don't I?" Theroun growled. "All that power behind the walls, a network of spies? People go missing from the palace all the time, don't they, Castellan? How much of it do the Khehemni Lothren truly know? And would they be pleased, I wonder?"

Lhaurent said nothing, but his eyes glittered ruthlessly.

Theroun leaned in, whispering by his ear. "Want to run that blade you hide in your doublet through my gut? You could cover it up, you know. Easy. No one to hear me scream except for those spies you've got stashed in the walls. Counsel-General Theroun just disappeared, they'd say. But then who's going to win your war, so you can continue playing King here? Pull your knife. Come at me. You know I'll send you straight to Halsos."

Lhaurent's face was red as a beet when Theroun finally pulled away, chuckling. Theroun thought for a moment the eel would hiss and be gone. But the man cocked his head, his anger shifting like coils underwater to something else entirely.

A small smile spread over his face. "You think I want to be King of Alrou-Mendera. Quaint."

Theroun blinked, suddenly feeling his battleground was nothing but quicksand.

"How utterly quaint, General." Lhaurent took a greasy slide closer. He smiled again, self-possessed. "I don't need you to win any war, Theroun. I need you to kill. I need men to die like fallen leaves around you. For that's what you do best, Black Viper. The Lothren mistakenly think you are an asset to their cause. But you are not necessarily an asset to my cause. You are useful because death follows you. And although Halsos will welcome you with a kiss, you will find that I am your master, cur."

Theroun scowled. "Your aims run counter to the Lothren's."

Lhaurent's oiled lips smiled. He leaned in. "Smart, Thaddeus. Very smart."

Theroun went icy to the tips of his toes. He only used that phrase with Thaddeus in private conversation. Lhaurent could only know it from spying, listening behind the walls of Theroun's chambers. Theroun's knife was in his hand before he could even think. But suddenly, he felt the pressure of someone else's knife in his ribs, digging in from behind him. A cold voice said, "Stop."

Theroun froze, his eyes riveted to Lhaurent. Lhaurent hadn't even moved, his hands still clasped servilely before him, his grey silks undisturbed. His eyes shone with dark pleasure by the flicker of the candles.

"Put down the knife," the empty voice behind Theroun spoke.

Theroun had no choice. He dropped his knife with a clatter upon the bluestone floor of his suite. "I've swept this chamber twenty times for any entry-access since I found out about your treachery behind the walls, eel," Theroun growled, his eyes pinned to Lhaurent, furious. "How do you get your fucking spies in here?"

Lhaurent's eyes were exquisitely pleased. "Someone told you about the secret passages behind Roushenn Palace's walls, but they didn't tell you everything, Theroun. I should probably kill you for knowing what you do. But it's so much more interesting to see how much chaos you'll create knowing just a little, but not enough. Just like you did on the Aphellian Way."

Theroun strangled with rage, despite the man with a knife in his ribs behind him. "What's that supposed to mean?!"

Lhaurent smiled wider, a cat in the cream, an eel escaped from the barrel. "Do you really think all those men and women you caught so *easily* and strung up on the Way were Alrashemni?" He shook his head, making a little tsking sound. "Poor Theroun. Someday I'll show you how simple it is to convince someone to Ink whatever you like upon their bodies. Or a whole village full of someones."

Theroun's heart dropped like a stone. "Thelkomen's Crossing were all Alrashemni, dammit! Them and the assassin who knifed me!"

"Were they?" Lhaurent lifted an eyebrow. "Well. You can believe that if you want to. Goodnight, Theroun. Safe travels to the front tomorrow. Khouren. Leave him."

Lhaurent turned his back and glided from the room, shutting the iron-bound door closed behind him. The man at Theroun's back finally released the knife. Theroun turned, slowly, to see whom it was behind him, sensing that the man was not sent by Lhaurent to actually kill him this night.

The fellow had stepped backwards a pace, toward a wall with a massive tapestry in a hunting scene. He wore Kingsman greys so ancient, they would have been rotten had they not been so well-cared for. A charcoal hood was up over his hair, and a wrap obscured his lower face. But as Theroun regarded him, the man reached up and pulled the facewrap down, baring strong features with high cheekbones and smooth lips that were utterly Alrashemni in lineage.

"You've been spared this night, Black Viper," The man's grey eyes flashed in the flickering candlelight. "But if you threaten the Rennkavi, I won't hesitate next time."

Theroun blinked. "Rennkavi? What in Aeon's fuck is that?"

The man lifted his facewrap back in place, his flat grey eyes empty of emotion. His next words were muffled. "You'll know soon enough."

Walking backwards, he moved toward the tapestry upon the byrunstone wall. And then disappeared *through* it, his visage wavering like smoke upon the wind before it was gone. Theroun gaped, his heart hammering his chest like he'd just fought a battle.

He'd just come face-to-face with the Ghost of Roushenn.

"What the flying fuck is going on…?" Theroun murmured to the empty room, trembling in a cold sweat. He gazed around the fire-dark room, wondering who was watching from behind the byrunstone walls.

And how many of them Lhaurent had.

Theroun was suddenly eager to be leaving for the front tomorrow. He turned and swiftly scooped his knife up off the floor and slid it back in its sheath, not even caring at the lancing protest from the old battle-wound in his ruined side. Eyes darting to every shadow, he strode to the bureau and hauled it open, dressing hastily in a white shirt, black leather jerkin, boots and trousers. Half his mind was upon the short list of items he always brought on campaign, but the other half still scanned the shadows. His old war-gear was packed in short order, his routines still sharp. And when there was nothing left, Theroun began to pace by the cold fireplace, his mangled ribs aching with every lurching step. Rage mixed with a cold fear roared within him, and it did nothing for the constant pain in his lungs.

A knock came. Theroun barked for entrance. Theroun's lanky, tow-haired scribe Thaddeus den'Lhor peered around the doorframe, then came in. He dumped today's recordings upon Theroun's desk from a leather satchel, then began shuffling through them studiously, with nervous glances though his wire-framed spectacles at Theroun's pacing.

"Thad," Theroun spoke so suddenly the slender young man jumped.

"Yes, Chancellor," Thaddeus spoke, his green eyes wary.

"Take a ride with me. Scurry to the kitchens and pack us a good amount of food with plenty of water and some ale. Get a large blanket for a late snack, and some fire starter. I have a need for the dark and solace of the woods. Put it all in a pack, lad, and meet me at the south stables. Bring that map, there, of Elsthemen. I need to think over strategy while we eat. And bring your parchment and a nib."

"Sir, it's very late. Wouldn't you rather…?" Thaddeus' protest was careful, concerned.

"Hustle, lad, now!" Theroun barked.

"Yes, Chancellor!" Thad's eyes widened behind his spectacles, clearly confused. But he seized his parchment, a nib, the map, and stuffed them into his satchel. He rushed out, hauling the door open with lanky arms.

Theroun sighed and glanced around his chambers. If someone was watching him, he couldn't help it. This had to be done. He buckled his leather jerkin as he snatched up his baldric and sword and buckled that on also. Sliding a hunting knife into the breast of the jerkin, he strode through the door, breathing into the gripping pain that twisted his right side rather than shy from it.

Thaddeus was a nimble lad. By the time Theroun had woken grooms to saddle and equip two horses, Thaddeus came running across the dark yard from the lights of the south palace kitchens. They mounted up, Theroun clambering up a far gentler horse than he had ever maneuvered in war.

Thaddeus peered at him as Theroun angled their horses up the rise of the mountain out of the West Stables and into the dark trees. Theroun simmered with dire thoughts as they rode, feeling his old battle-scar pulling at his lungs and right side. Jaw set, Theroun ignored the pain as they traversed the well-worn hunting path through the Kingswood, a lantern upon his saddle-horn illuminating the way. Bullfrogs chorused in the night. Two owls took up a call-and-response between the towering evergreens.

At last, Thad cleared his throat. "Where are he headed, sir? What's this about?"

"How well do you love your Queen, Thad?" Theroun growled low.

"Queen Elyasin is the most beautiful woman I've ever seen, sir." Thaddeus coughed.

Theroun glanced over. The lad was blushing furiously in the lamplight, adjusting his spectacles. "That will do." Theroun chuckled softly. "Would you die for her?"

Thad's eyes widened. "Are you going to kill me, sir? Is that what this is? Because of what I suspect about the Kingsmen Summons?"

Theroun chuckled again. "No. I'm not going to kill you, Thad. But you might get killed doing what I hope you'll do next. Tell me, Thad... why did you begin asking me questions about the Kingsmen all those weeks ago?"

And though the young man's eyes were wary, there was a light in them now. "My passion is history, sir. The true stories of our people. That's why I wanted to apprentice under you. You've seen it all. A leader of campaigns, mired in politics, friends with a King, involved in the power that runs nations. You have more influence than just about any man I've ever met or even read about. All of it worthy history. Sir."

"And yet, the stories that truly make history are never known. Thad, I'd like you to be a part of one of those stories, right here, right now."

The lad's eyes widened. "Yes, sir."

"Don't agree so easily." Theroun shot him a warning look. "It could cost you your life. And if you fail, I'll most certainly lose mine. Well, I'll probably lose mine no matter what."

Thaddeus went very still, and his animal sensed his unease. It shied to the side, then halted upon the narrow track. Theroun reined in also.

"What do you want me to do, sir?" It was barely a whisper from Thaddeus in the lantern-lit dark, but still, Theroun saw courage there.

"I want you to take a message to King Therel Alramir for me. Can you do that, lad?"

The young man swallowed hard, his eyes darting around the midnight forest, then over the saddlebags on the horses. "I have to go right now, don't I?"

Theroun dismounted, pain making him grimace. He led his horse to Thad, then handed up the reins, winding them around the pommel of the young man's saddle. "Thad. Listen to me. These horses have everything you need for a journey north. Get out your parchment. I need you to take down a letter. Deliver it to King Therel or Queen Elyasin, if she lives. *Insist* to see them in person. Stay off the road and travel cross-country, up over the west flank of the Kingsmount. If you are taken prisoner by Highlanders, say you bear an important message of amnesty from the Menderian Chancellate. Memorize what I put down. If they threaten to kill you or take the document, burn the parchment and tell them only you know what it says. Mystery keeps men alive, Thad. Any king would be furious for killing a messenger before the message is heard."

Thaddeus was ready with charcoal and parchment, spreading it upon the horse's withers in the lamplight, his eyes hard with determination. "What do you want it to say?"

"Write this: To King Therel and Queen Elyasin. The Chancellate of Alrou-Mendera are infiltrated by Khehemni agents called the Lothren, a secret sect of men who desire power behind thrones, and have it. They are bent upon war to annihilate all remaining Alrashemni in Elsthemen and Alrou-Mendera, most of whom hide in the military ranks, as they are currently doing in Valenghia. I give the gift of what few names I know to you now. Chancellor Evshein den'Lhamann, Chancellor Rudaric den'Ghen, Chancellor Jhik den'Cammas, Castellan Lhaurent den'Karthus, and myself, to my utter remorse. Expect battalions of lancer cavalry in the Lethian Valley, and Brigadiers and Fleetrunners with knowledge of your tactics, which I unfortunately must provide. Be especially wary of the Castellan. Know that Roushenn Palace is his domain, to what end I know not, but that he holds secret passages and spies behind every wall. I also suspect him as the perpetrator of the Kingsman Summons and subsequent disappearance. Elyasin," and here Theroun's voice cracked, though he did not mean it to. "I was your father's man, to the end. I did not mean for any of this to happen. I seek only to make amends for my many wrongs. Although I am not fond of Alrashemni, I cannot support the destruction of our nation and of your noble House. Yours in clean conscience,

First-General of Alrou-Mendera, Theroun den'Vekir."

Thaddeus' hand was trembling as it finally came to rest, his eyes red-rimmed. "Anything else, sir?"

"No, Thad. Here, let me sign it." Passing it to Theroun, Thad watched as Theroun affixed his signature, then accepted it back.

"Carry it well," Theroun continued. "Do not return to Roushenn. Remain in the Elsthemi court where you will be safe. You weren't built for war, lad. I hope we'll meet again, but I doubt it. There's an ample bit of gold in that pouch," he nodded to a leather purse slung from the saddle. "So watch that. And take this," he unbuckled his sword, wrapping the scabbard with the leather of his belt and tucking it up beneath the saddle-flap within Thad's reach. "It might come in handy."

Thad nodded, rolling the parchment and tucking it into his leather doublet. Theroun was about to give his horse a slap, but Thad reined it, gazing down, spectacles reflecting the lamplight. "You're a hard man, sir. But you have a good heart. History will remember it, in the end. I will write the truth of it, someday."

Theroun snorted. "My story is nothing but woe and death, Thad. Write something else. Write of the triumph of Queen Elyasin, if she lives. Don't waste words on a fool of a General. Go, hup!"

He slapped the horse upon the rear. It surged forward, pulling the other beast into a quick, neck-high walk. Theroun turned and moved down the incline, back the way they had come. He still had his knife, tucked inside his doublet. He'd make a few convincing gashes once he was closer to the palace and fake a deep limp, say that Thad died in an accident while they were riding out in the woods.

The body and horses would never be found, and he'd say it was wolves.

"I will do what I can to save your daughter's nation, Uhlas," Theroun spoke to the thick darkness beneath the trees. "Lhaurent and the Khehemni Lothren will learn they do not own the Black Viper of the Aphellian Way."

CHAPTER 4 – ELOHL

Fenton had surprised Elohl early upon their third morning in
Fhekran Place, by busting into his room and throwing a knife at
Elohl's head. His sensate sphere always alert, Elohl had snatched the
knife out of the air practically from a dead sleep. Fenton had
grinned at him. After dressing and a quick bite of hardboiled eggs,
they'd ambled to the practice yards as crimson light blushed the tops
of the mountains in a chill, misty dawn.

Elohl found a practice sword in the armory-racks much like the
sword he had trained with in his youth at Alrashesh. Alrashemni-
made, it was a slender, swift weapon with narrow grooves in the
blade to lighten the weight, longer than a Brigadier sword by a hand.
And though Fenton had eschewed practice the past three days,
settling instead into long hours of meditation and breathwork to
mend his injuries, today he was lithe as a keshar. With a spring in his
step and a competitive glint in his eyes, the shirtless Fenton ambled
close, selecting a blade that matched Elohl's.

Together, they stepped to an unused white-sand practice circle
in the thin sunshine. A number of bouting Highlanders stopped to
watch, and Elohl felt a press of eyes roving his Inkings. Black Inkings
in the Elsthemi style limned the men and women in the circles,
Therel's elite Highswords. But Fenton's Bloodmark had already
disappeared, only a small nick marring his chest today as they
squared off.

Elohl brought his blade up. Fenton's attack came like liquid
music, swift. Elohl slid his blade down Fenton's, like stroking silk,
taking the center line. But Fenton recovered in a strong upward cut
that caused Elohl a sharper blade meeting than he would have liked.
Shivers jarred his arm. Elohl countered, sliding steel down and
around, locking Fenton's elbow in close to hammer the man under
the ribs with his shoulder, right in his wound.

Fenton went down with a huff. Elohl's blade flicked to his neck.

"Good strategy, Kingsman, pummeling my wound." Fenton grinned, on his back in the sand.

"You should have expected that." Elohl felt a smile twitch his lips.

"Touché." Fenton chuckled, that eager darkness in his eyes again, as if the man lived to battle. Elohl extended a hand, hauling Fenton up.

They bouted all morning, first with swords, then staves, and lastly the *avari*, a lightweight polesword that was the favored weapon of the keshari riders. Which Fenton wielded with surprising ability. Their practice quickly gathered a crowd, both men sweat-slicked and bruised but fighting like water eddies in a river, without either actually besting the other. At last, Fenton signaled a halt, reaching down to massage his scar.

Elohl leaned on his polesword with a pleasant exhaustion. "Where did you learn the *avari*? You fight like it's something you've known for decades."

Fenton chuckled, but did not answer. Striding to the weapons rack, he put the polearm away, his fingers walking over a pair of curved daggers. He picked them up, a delighted glint in his eye, then selected another pair and tossed them across the sand to Elohl.

"Want to fight *jherra*-style?"

Elohl knew his eyes glinted like Fenton's, eager. "I haven't danced the *jherra* since I was twenty in Alrashesh. You sure you want to? You look tired enough to lay down."

Fenton's slight smile was secretive. "I'll lay down when Halsos pulls me down. And not a moment before."

With that, Fenton rushed in, faster than a keshar. It was all Elohl could do to stop the man from slicing his guts open. Shocked, Elohl countered as best he could. He'd felt nothing from his sensate sphere. No warning, no flare, no surge. It was as if Fenton was a phantasm without substance, and Elohl fought hard to counter in time. Blood pounded Elohl's veins, alarmed as he fought. The *jherra* knives were sharp, and Elohl ducked one blade to his throat while taking a quick block upon his forearm. Blades shivered, and Fenton's slid up, hilts locking. There was a brief struggle as he whisked the other blade in to slice Elohl's underarm. Elohl spun out, dropping into a backwards roll to catch his breath.

Fenton was cool, his brown eyes placid, piercing. "Got you on the run already?"

"How the hell? Why didn't I feel you?" Elohl gasped, tested far more than he'd been in a long while. This was a different man fighting him. Fenton had been holding back before, in every way.

But he wasn't now.

Fenton's smile was subtle. "I have my secrets and you have yours, Elohl. Olea was the same. But she and I never pried into each other's pasts, so we got along fine. I offer the same to you. If we're going to work together, I get to keep my secrets and you yours."

"Why?" Elohl's eyes narrowed.

"Because I don't like talking about my past."

Suddenly, Fenton attacked again, faster. But this time, Elohl felt it. He blocked, then spun in time to catch the next bout. Knives whipped at his neck, his middle, his wrists and inner arms. Fenton was a blur, slicing at the back of his knees while rolling, angling attacks up towards the groin. Elohl worked hard, barely fending the smaller man off. Matching blades was rapid and furious, in which Fenton used his wiry frame to his advantage. A number of times Elohl had to rely upon his gift rather than his eyes.

Fenton den'Kharel was simply too fast.

His energy flagging, Elohl slipped sideways to avoid the next slash at his neck, but moved too slow. Fenton's blade whispered over his skin, silk-smooth like a lover. Fenton instantly pulled back in alarm, tossing both knives into the sand point-first. Elohl touched his neck; his hand came away bloody. It was a worthy cut, but it had missed the vein. Blood spilled in a small trickle, pooling behind his collarbone.

"First blood," he nodded to Fenton, who nodded back, relief upon his features. Elohl threw his knives into the sand, then knelt, palm to his Inkings. "I concede. You're fucking fast, Fenton."

Cheers went up around the ring, ragged growls, hollers, and battle-roars from Highlands men and women. Bare-chested men stepped forward to thump Fenton and Elohl upon their backs. Women in furs pressed close, and suddenly Elohl was gathered into a deep kiss, a woman's firm hand to the back of his head. He pulled back, startled, and the honey-braided woman's green eyes flashed. She slapped his chest, then stuck a finger in his blood, sucking it off and turning away with a merry glint.

Lhesher approached through the crowd. He strode to Elohl and Fenton, beckoning. "Yar! Kingsmen! There you are. King Therel wishes to see ye both fer war-parley."

Elohl nodded, quickly gathering up his shirt and cobalt jerkin. He strode off, following Lhesher, Fenton shrugging his shirt on a step behind. It was a quick trek through the buttressed halls of stout timber. The throne hall was lovely, though not ostentatious. Like the rest of the palace, stout ribs of high-arching pine supported the ceiling, coming to a peak at the center that ran the length of the hall. Pearled-glass scenes of hunts and heroic deeds and odd sigils let the light in to cascade across the white bonerock floor. Man-sized hearths marched the length of the hall upon both sides, long wooden trestle-tables lined up in rows for feasting, currently bare except for silver candelabrums.

King Therel was at the front, seated upon his throne, a modest affair of carven pine decorated judiciously with Elsthemi fire-opals. One throne sat to either side of his, all of equal stature. On the right sat his sister, High General Merra Alramir, clad in her white fur and buckled leathers. With one leg slung over the arm of her throne, she perked as Fenton and Elohl entered the long hall, then rose, King Therel doing the same. There was no carpet for processions, so Elohl and Fenton simply walked forward between the rows of tables, to the dais raised only three steps above the rest of the hall. Therel beckoned to Elohl and Fenton, and they stepped up.

"Loyal Kingsmen," he clasped wrists first with Elohl, then Fenton, "to whom I owe my life. Such a debt is repaid in the Highlands, as long as it needs repaying. I wish to hold council with the two of you, and have you meet my sister, formally. High General Merra Alramir, please meet two Alrashemni Kingsmen of caliber. First-Lieutenant Brigadier Elohl den'Alrahel, and First-Lieutenant Guardsman Fenton den'Kharel."

Merra had a lioness' grace as she clasped each man's arm, her grip strong as mountain pine. Petite and curvaceous in a rugged, battle-hardened way, the top of her head barely reached Elohl's collar, but no man would ever have called her dainty. A fire burned in her clear blue eyes. Her smile was sharp as she flicked thin red-blonde braids back over one shoulder.

"Gentlemen. I heard what happened. You brought Therel home safely, and I am in your debt. If his ass doesn't sit that throne there, then I have to." She laughed, bright and merry. "In any case, Therel and I have bruised our asses on these damn things all day, so we will adjourn to my quarters to have our discussion."

"How is the Queen?" Elohl asked, catching Therel's gaze.

Relief showed upon Therel's features. "She's finally healing. Luc den'Lhorissian is still attending her, on and off. The strain of sitting the saddle kept opening her wound. But it's knitting nicely these past three days, and her fever is gone."

"I am relieved." Elohl inclined his head, one palm to his chest.

"As am I. Very much so. This way, Kingsmen. Let us adjourn."

They followed the Elsthemi King and High General from the hall through a side door, down a vaulted corridor with towering panes of colored glass depicting ancient battle. General Merra pushed through a set of white pine doors, into a graciously lit space. The General's apartments were strangely fluffy for such a hard woman. Furs of white alpine-goat with a luxuriant nap had been made into massive rugs before every hearth, colorful pillows strewn about them for lounging. Wool carpets woven with ornate sigils joined the hearth-areas. Merra unbuckled her boots and instantly made herself at home, lounging upon a set of pillows near one roaring fire. She gave Elohl and Fenton a thoroughly scandalous look while wine and sweetmeats were brought by a battle-ready housecarl.

"Your housecarls," Fenton commented as the man left, while Therel poured them all a goblet of wine, "they wear weapons. Why?"

"Every man and woman who works inside this palace is trained for battle," Merra answered from the pillows, "and conducts themselves appropriately. I feel far more at ease when I know every maid could hold off an enemy should I be wounded."

"Indeed." Therel handed goblets around, sinking to the pillows. "You may have noticed that our customs are... more relaxed and yet more vicious then you are used to. In the Highlands, death is ever near. A soft man or woman is turned away from life within these halls. One of the many reasons your Queen will be an excellent fit here. She may be young, but she is rugged."

Elohl sipped his wine and settled to the pillows. Fenton fetched the tray, setting it between the four of them. Merra opened her lips to speak, when the double doors suddenly boomed open. Queen Elyasin stood upon the other side, one hand to her ribs but standing tall in a high-necked quilted dressing gown the red-wine color of telmenberries.

"My King! She wouldn'a stay put!" Lhesher Khoum was on Elyasin's heels, towering above her, a pleading set to his square jaw.

"I am Queen here." Elyasin's tone was imperious, filling the room. "A war-council should not be held in my absence."

King Therel stood smoothly, and all the men followed suit, though Merra remained reclining. Elohl noted the viciously pleased glint in the Highlander King's eyes. "My thanks, Lhesher. My Queen knows her body. If she feels well enough to be present for this meeting, she should be. Leave us."

The big Highlander gave a conceding nod, then backed out, shutting the doors. Elyasin moved toward the pillows slowly, then lowered gingerly down upon a large cushion near Merra.

Fenton poured her a wine, handing it over with deference. "My Queen."

"Thank you, First-Lieutenant." She sipped, then glanced to Therel. "So. Where were we?"

The men re-sat themselves, Therel beside his wife. "We were just beginning." Therel smiled. "You've missed nothing."

Therel smoothed a hand over her temple, brushing back waves of her golden hair, then took up her hand, skating his fingers over her knuckles as if he couldn't bear not touching her. Elyasin seemed pleased at the attention, but Elohl noticed a flush bloom over her pale cheeks as she shivered, smiling.

"Alrou-Mendera brings war to our doorstep," Merra resumed their discourse, blue eyes flashing wrath. "We have received word that your Chancellors have declared emergency rule. They are putting out rumor that you are dead, Queen Elyasin, that Therel killed you and fled, stole your corpse. They call for my brother's head. All our Elsthemi who were caught at the coronation have been hung. An edict has been issued that Therel surrender. Their military is massing in force. My outriders report a camp has already been established at the border in the Lethian Valley, just south of the

Valley of Doors. Light cavalry and foot soldiers are trickling in. The preparations are hostile. They're digging in, erecting pavilions, assembling supply lines. It's going to be war. Soon. Within three weeks we may see the first skirmishes to test our defenses. In a month, we may see an all-out push into our lands."

"That's madness," Fenton commented smoothly. "Alrou-Mendera is currently at war with Valenghia. What nation surrounds themselves with enemies?"

"One that doesn't want to last long," Therel growled. Elohl glanced over, to see Merra's hot wrath simmering in Therel's eyes also. Elohl glanced to Elyasin, and though he'd expected to see fury in her, what he saw in his Queen made him consider her character again. She was motionless, her green eyes filled with the chill retribution of avalanches.

"That will not be my nation's fate." Elyasin's soft words brought the room to stillness.

"Nor ours." Merra waved one hand, taking up the conversation again. "I trust the clans to come together when needed. No offense to your fighters, Queen Elyasin, but we are tempered by northern climes. Weaklings die out in the snow. To your nation's challenge, I will bring the full force of my keshari riders."

"Any news from your agents at Roushenn, Therel? Messengers? Ravens?" Blood drained from Elyasin's face, though she kept her posture. "Have they tried negotiations?"

"No." Therel's wolf-blue eyes were hard, a scowl upon his chiseled face.

"Does my Chancellate even know I'm alive?"

Therel sighed heavily. "I've sent two fast envoys across the border to Lintesh, to tell your Chancellate as much. Neither has returned. I don't dare send a third."

"My men *killed* your messengers?" Elyasin was shocked.

Therel rested back upon his pillow. A crease in his brow made him seem tired. "They're not your men right now. And they're bent on war, Elyasin."

"There is a force that opposes Alrashemni at every turn," Fenton spoke suddenly. "They call themselves Khehemni; their ruling group is known as the Lothren. I believe they are behind this movement. They live in secret amongst us. I myself was part of a select, secret group of Alrashemni known as the Shemout. And for a while, my organization has suspected a number of your Chancellate of being Khehemni Lothren."

Elyasin lifted a blonde eyebrow. "I've heard of your clandestine alliances, First-Lieutenant."

"Forgive me, my Queen," Fenton placed a palm to his chest, sincerity radiating from his gold-brown eyes. "But please believe me when I say it was safer at the time for you to not know of us. Of me. Being unknown allowed me to observe much in my duties, to maneuver people close to you who were absolutely worthy of trust."

"I suppose I should thank you. I have my life because of your astute judgement." A wry smile twisted Elyasin's lips. Her gaze flicked to Elohl. "Your sister said that I am of Alrashemni lineage, this Line of Kings, Linea Alrahel, whom the Khehemni oppose. Your bloodline."

Elohl placed his palm over his heart. "My Queen. I seek not your throne; not any throne. Olea is the same. You are our liege. You are our Sovereign. And Kingsmen do not forswear their oaths."

Elyasin's bitter smile softened. "You are very much like her…" She took a deep breath, winced. Her hand moved to her side and her eyes closed briefly in pain before opening again. "Kingsman den'Alrahel. I have seen proof of your oath. I saw you move in the Small Hall. The speed of your blade made Therel's First Sword miss his mark. You saved me when I would otherwise be dead. Olea said my brother Alden died because of the same shadowy forces, and I will never again gainsay her word. If I live long enough, I intend to bend my knee to Olea in humblest apology. I regret confining her as I did."

"We know of the Khehemni Bloodmarked here in the Highlands." Therel commented. "They're a thorn."

"In the Highlands, perhaps," Fenton spoke again, "but in other nations, a bed of spikes. We have reason to believe Khehemni agents close to the throne issued the Kingsman Summons ten years ago, resulting in the Purge in Alrou-Mendera."

"Olea said much the same thing," Elyasin spoke. "But she had no proof, no names. What do you know of our mutual assailants?"

Fenton took a deep breath. "Olea and Alden learned dangerous information, I could not stop them. Uhlas was on a secret mission to Valenghia at the time of the Summons, a last effort to salvage the situation there before the war began. We have a Kingsman eyewitness to the event inside the palace."

"Olea said she had a witness." Elyasin sighed. "Would that I had listened to her and heard his testimony. Things might have turned out differently."

Fenton shook his head. "Do not be hard on yourself. Even if you had postponed the coronation, the Khehemni would have found a way to move against you."

"Dammit!" Therel sank back into the pillows, glowering. "My own First Sword! Do you believe the Khehemni have other plants secreted among our keshari, our Highswords?"

Fenton nodded. "I have no doubt of that. I suspect a war between Alrou-Mendera and Elsthemen has been intended for years."

"But why engage a war on two fronts?" Merra waved her hand again. "Madness! They'll annihilate their military and leave themselves vulnerable to invasion from Valenghia!"

"The last of the Kingskinder are still in the military," Elohl said.

"And a small number of older Kingsmen who were away from Alrou-Mendera at the time of the Summons," Fenton continued. "Many are Shemout, like me. We believe the Lothren's maneuverings are based entirely upon killing off Alrashemni hiding in the ranks."

"Brilliant. Ghastly, but brilliant." Therel's blue eyes were icy as he swirled his goblet. "What nations have the strongest Alrashemni presence that we know of? The Isles, Perthe, Elsthemen, and Valenghia. Valenghia had a purge of Alrashemni fifteen years back. And Perthe had a civil war. Alrou-Mendera engages Valenghia for ten years after their Purge. And now us. The Khehemni have been swatting down Alrashemni strongholds like a toad does flies, for decades."

Merra's scowl was vicious. "Fully half of my keshari riders are Alrashemni. A decent third of our clans bear the Ink."

Silence stretched upon the cushions.

King Therel broke it. "We *will* defend ourselves. Merra, begin to move your legions to the southern border. Evacuate all townships within thirty leagues of Alrou-Mendera. I won't have our people slaughtered. I will get Lhesher to send riders to each of the clans, have them begin gathering at the Valley of Doors."

"What other allies do we have?" Elyasin asked, glancing to Therel.

"King Arthe den'Tourmalin remained for our wedding." Therel stroked her wrist. "Alliances are strong between all our houses."

"Indeed." Elyasin's gaze went long. "But Arthe has ships to harry the coasts, not men for a border-war. We could ask him to raze the Menderian ports, cause a distraction. Make it too costly for these Khehemni to engage Elsthemen."

"They would attack the Highlands anyway." Fenton's smooth baritone was frank. "The Khehemni's only objective is Alrashemni annihilation, an enmity that has been sustained for generations. If they think their goal is within reach, they'll obtain it however they can, my Queen."

Therel's gaze rested upon Fenton. "Any ally is welcome. I will send a trio of ships down from Nordwath to King Arthe of the Isles, and see what he might be willing to do for us."

"And our other resources?" Elyasin broke in.

"There is a rogue Alrashemni contingent," Fenton spoke again, "in the bog that stretches north of the Aphellian Way, led by a man named Purloch. They number some thousand, last I knew. They were once allied with Vicoute Arlen den'Selthir. He's the leader of the Shemout Alrashemni. A very convincing man, excellent at commanding armies. Back in the day, he was Second-General of the Realm, when Theroun den'Vekir held the title of First-General, before his atrocities upon the Aphellian Way. Arlen holds Vennet, and could probably persuade the entire eastern bloc of provinces to stand for you. He's not gone to battle in a long while, but he might be willing to do so again. With the right… persuasion. We could muster an army of perhaps two thousand Kingsmen, bring it in from Alrou-Mendera's eastern border. March upon Lintesh and rally the First Abbey to put pressure on our enemies."

Elohl blinked at the man, wondering just how high up in the Shemout Fenton was. The man was proving full of surprises, and secrets. "The Jenners? They're all Kingsmen?"

"Not all of them." Fenton gave a wry smile. "But a number of the ones who matter. The Abbott, the Abbess, their Master Brewer, a man by the name of Sebasos. And…" Fenton's gaze flicked to Elyasin. "Your uncle. Temlin den'Ildrian. Uhlas' younger brother."

Elyasin's green eyes went wide. "I have an uncle?"

Fenton's smile was soft, sad. "You wouldn't remember him. He was confined in the Abbey in his twenties, before you were born. Struck from his titles, the line of succession, and the family genealogies in disgrace by your grandfather. Not to mention dishonorably discharged, all because of a problem with drink and a rash temper. But he's a strong warrior, my Queen. He once led the Roushenn Guard and held the title of Third-General of the Realm. He marshaled armies with Arlen den'Selthir in the Karthian Raids, assisting the Tourmaline Isles. King Arthe would remember Temlin. They were close as brothers, at one time."

"I have an uncle." Elyasin's eyes had filled with tears. "My father never mentioned a brother."

"Uhlas and Temlin were ever at odds. But Temlin would fight for you," Fenton spoke, "if given proper motivation. If we can get someone through to Purloch and get his fighters to Vicoute Arlen den'Selthir, we could send a force to take the city with Temlin's help. If Lintesh is sieged, the armies would come home. And if the armies retreat, we can get you through, alive. To take your city back in person."

Elyasin was speechless. Tears still flowed down her cheeks. She brushed them away with a deep, steadying breath. "How do we get ambassadors down to the bog?"

"The easiest way to that bog is via the Elsee." Merra spoke. "I could have ambassadors delivered across the border by cat in a week's time."

"They'll have agents watching the Elsee." It was out of Elohl's mouth fast. He and Fenton shared a look of mutual understanding. "I had a number of assassination attempts during my years as a Brigadier. I didn't know about them at the time, but it makes sense now, that the Khehemni have agents there. Talented ones. And by now, the Chancellate has likely sent fast riders up to alert the High Brigade and Fleetrunners to be on watch for Elsthemi movements."

"Can you confirm this?" Therel's icy eyes flicked to Fenton.

Fenton nodded. "Some. I've seen a few reports on Khehemni activity on the Elsee and in the Brigade, though most of those go to the Vicoute."

"Dammit!" Therel growled.

"I could get them across the Devil's Field." Merra lounged expertly, alert to the conversation. "Smuggle them into Valenghia. From there, it would be a two-week trek down the Eleskis south, through the Long Valley and into that bog. But two talented ex-Brigadier Kingsmen like yourselves could manage it. Stealthily, I imagine."

Merra and Fenton shared a long look. A subtle smile lifted Fenton's lips. Merra returned that smile. Something passed between them, sleek with fur and claws. Elohl saw Fenton's gaze darken, saw him weighing the Elsthemi war General with curious interest.

And something more.

"I imagine you are *quite* capable." Merra's gaze was fixed upon Fenton.

"Indeed, milady." Fenton gave a small nod.

Elohl was certain suddenly that they were no longer discussing battle. Not exactly.

Therel cleared his throat, deraling the tension. "Fenton. If you carried Elyasin and my's seals through to this Purloch, could you rally the Kingsman support we need?"

"I believe so." Fenton stated, glancing back to the King. "I have not met Purloch personally. But they will know me by my Shemout Bloodmark. I believe I could rally them. Persuade them to march."

"Are you certain you are so very persuasive?" Merra's lecherous eyes roved Fenton's frame.

"You might be surprised at my skills." A dark heat simmered in Fenton's gaze as he glanced back to the High General.

"Indeed." Merra's smile had grown rapacious. Her gaze flicked to Elohl. "But such an endeavor is best accomplished with two men."

Elohl discouraged her innuendo with a frank steadiness. "General. I will serve my King and Queen in whatever manner they require of me."

Merra gave a liquid shrug, and a completely unapologetic smile.

Elyasin interrupted, pinning Elohl with her fierce gaze. "I hear you have a record nearly as fine as my First-Lieutenant. I would be trusting my throne to the two of you in this. I need the Kingsmen to help me win it back, but we must also win the people."

Fenton's gaze was steady. "The Jenners could do that. Also your Second-Lieutenant, Aldris den'Farahan. He's Shemout, like I am."

"Another one of your plants in my Guard?" Elyasin gave a small smile.

"Aldris earned his promotion directly from Olea." Fenton grinned. "But I may have said a thing or two so she took note of his promise."

"Can we send a raven through to the Abbey?" Elyasin looked to Therel. "Get them to rally Lintesh directly?"

He shook his head. "Keshari scouts are reporting that ravens and hawks are being shot down along the border. Hunters are being paid in silver to bring in any birds that have messages."

"In any case," Fenton continued, "the First Abbey couldn't hold against the Roushenn Guard without help. They could survive a siege for a while, but if they're locked in, they wouldn't be able to rally the populace for you."

"Then you must go across the passes to the bog, at once." Elyasin sat tall. "You and Elohl. I must have ambassadors I trust to get word through the nation that I am alive. We *must* get my populace to rally against this foolish war."

"My riders can take you as far up the Devil's Field as Lodresh Glacier." Merra broke in. "I'll lead them myself, deliver you safely to the Valenghian border. But cats don't do well in the thin air. From there, you'll be on your own."

"Where does that leave your promise to me? About my golden ink?" Elohl held Therel's gaze, wanting answers.

Therel gave a hard sigh, apology in his eyes as he re-crossed his long legs before him. "I know a seer who might be able to tell you something about them. But she is far up on the tundras. I cannot summon her in time, before you travel out. But I can get her here by the time you return."

Elohl sighed. Even if he made if back to Lhen Fhekran, it was a tenuous thread at best. "I understand. Fenton and I will make ready to travel immediately."

"Stay out the week, or two." Therel's gaze was sorrowful. "Supplies need to be made ready, and getting the both of you used to riding by cat will take time. There will be feasting, once my Queen is recovered, to celebrate our nuptials. Even if I cannot honor my promise right away, I can still show you both the hospitality of the Highlands. Please, my house is yours."

Elohl nodded. It was a gracious offer, all things considered.

"Well." Elyasin broke in, gathering her feet beneath her, one hand holding her side. "I must recover my strength so I can actually *stand* at this upcoming feast, and not be carried around like an invalid."

Therel stood abruptly, reaching down to help his Queen to her feet. He stroked back a lock of her hair. "I will carry my sweetgrape in the chalice of my arms, wherever she wishes to go."

"You will *not*." Elyasin turned on him, testily. "I will walk on my own, and greet my new people as a Queen must. With dignity." But all the same, she did not relinquish Therel's supportive arm.

"I must tend to my Queen. Gentlemen, until tomorrow." With Elyasin upon his arm, Therel gave a smile, then nodded to his sister. Together, the King and Queen pushed through the doors.

"Milady." Elohl and Fenton gave curt bows to General Merra Alramir, palms to Inkings. Elohl turned for the door, Fenton upon his heels. But as they moved away, a mischievous call came from the pillows.

"Fenton den'Kharel!"

Elohl glanced back, to see Fenton turn.

"I require further information from you. Stay." Merra pinned Fenton with her ice-blue eyes. Alluringly dangerous, she lounged upon the pillows in such a way that her curvaceous hips angled sharply down to her slender waist. She had unbuckled the white pelt across her shoulders, displaying a generous swath of chest above her leather binder, the stars of her Inkings clearly visible.

Fenton glanced at Elohl.

"Go," Elohl smiled. "We'll meet up later."

Fenton nodded, took a halting step towards General Merra. And then another that was not halting at all. Elohl smiled, turning from the room and letting himself out into the hall.

CHAPTER 5 – KHOUREN

Khouren Alodwine stood at attention behind his Rennkavi in the shadowy hall of blue byrunstone. Shrouded in his assassin's garb with the charcoal hood up, his dark-gloved fingers lingered near fly-blades in his leather harness, ready. Fey blue globes floated in the cavernous vaults of the Hinterhaft, their eerie light writhing like sandwater swirled in a glass chalice. Curious about the negotiations taking place in the suffering darkness below, they writhed about columns, illuminating carvings of vines and desert lotus. One wafted close to the heavy ironwood table in the center of the ancient hall, lighting the two men sitting at corners from each other.

This was the true seat of power in Roushenn Palace. These secret vaults, these catacombs with their lost heights. And Castellan Lhaurent den'Karthus was the true owner of that power, the austere planes of his long face currently set in a benign smile. It was a mask, Khouren knew. That was his Rennkavi's blankest face. Seemingly at his ease in his impeccable grey silk robe and doublet, the Castellan leaned back in a carven throne that would have been the envy of any royal hall.

Lhaurent reached up, combing long fingers through his carefully oiled, silver-streaked black waves. Khouren could see his magnanimous profile, the slight twist of lips that meant his Rennkavi was vastly displeased. Lhaurent lifted a gold chalice, a ghastly glimmer in the fey light, and sipped a dark wine. He set the chalice down, tapping the rim with one ring-bedecked finger.

The finger that bore the pale star-metal ring of Leith Alodwine, the ring that controlled all of Roushenn and its deadly churning walls.

The ring that now controlled an entire city, the city of Lintesh.

"So." Lhaurent continued in his smooth, aristocratic cadence, "Khorel Jornath. You'll not go to the Elsthemi border as I've asked?"

The man sitting at the table, caddy-corner in the blue darkness, had his carven chair angled towards the Castellan. The Kreth-Hakir High Priest leaned it back upon two legs, black buckled boots crossed beneath the table. Thick, sword-calloused hands were laced in his lap, elbows out upon the chair's velvet armrests. His black armor was made entirely of studded leather with blackened iron buckles, artfully crafted in a herringbone weave. His silver-streaked brown waves were curried back from his forehead, lending him a cutting elegance like a lord of mercenaries. Stern and solid, his gaze beneath heavy dark brows held the hulking pressure of vultures. And yet, there was something taunting in it, like a scorpion arching to sting, testing its foe.

Arrogant, certain of himself. Certain that Lhaurent was nothing to fear, no matter any threats the Castellan might level. The man's thick lips turned up in a genial smile, an amused glint in his dark eyes. He brushed away a limpid blue globe that tried to land upon his black gauntlet.

"Now, Lhaurent." The leather-clad High Priest laced his fingers together. "I never said I wouldn't go to Elsthemen for you. Only that what you ask of me is impossible."

"Then we have no options." Khouren watched Lhaurent stiffen almost imperceptibly, something he would have missed had Khouren not known his master so very well. His Rennkavi was ever-uneasy around the Kreth-Hakir. With good reason.

"We have some options," Khorel Jornath spoke, recrossing his massive boots beneath the table, completely at ease.

"Such as?" Lhaurent asked.

"Such as, I invite a few more of my Brethren into your territory. And we get your errand done."

Lhaurent shifted, a gesture anyone else would have missed in the airy darkness of Roushenn's breathing halls. "How many?"

"Nine of us should do." The man examined the torn fingernails of one hand. "In total."

Khouren's Rennkavi visibly startled. "Can you not accomplish this feat on your own?"

Khorel Jornath chuckled in a low rumble. "My, my, Lhaurent. You think much of me. My abilities are formidable. But to subdue an entire army of Elsthemi? I think not."

"Metrene speaks of a time when she could subdue a thousand

men in battle."

The Kreth-Hakir's smile rippled with snarl. His dark grey eyes went flat, flinty. "Metrene al'Lhask was a legend in her time. She was the first woman to accept our god Leith's *wyrric* gift, and the most powerful wielder of it our Order has ever known. You know not what you hold in that Kingstone at the center of this palace, Lhaurent. Metrene is a force to be reckoned with. Were it not for her righteous sense of justice, she would have done our Brethren proud. Even punished as she was by the Order for supreme disobedience, she still managed to destroy the minds of thirty of our best before Leith Alodwine personally sequestered her here. I still do not know by what means you have yoked such a force of nature to your command, Lhaurent. But in these days of dwindling magic, feats as Metrene's are no longer possible in our world. Even the best of us require other Brethren to channel through, to snare thousands of minds at once."

"Nine is rather more than a handful." Lhaurent shifted. He tapped a finger upon his gilded goblet. "How many will you use at the first battle? To enliven your… charms."

"That is for me to decide." Khorel Jornath's lips lifted in an amused smile. "Call my Brethren's ability what it is, my friend. We smash minds. We break people. The Kreth-Hakir are the waves that pound the cliffs of Khosh-Nianti, and we never fail."

"You failed at the Twelve Tribes."

The big man sneered. For the first time, Khouren saw anger flash through that arrogant visage. "*That* was unexpected. Anyone of Alrashemni bloodline, with even the barest hint of *wyrric* power, breaks before my Brethren. Elsthemen will fall. Its bloodlines are rampant with Alrashemni weakness."

"And if I want you to break Elsthemi ranks, I need nine of you."

"Nine or none." The arrogance was back.

Khouren heard his Rennkavi draw a soft breath. "Nine will do."

The man lifted his wine goblet, sipped with a soldier's decorum. "Then let us speak of payment."

"Last time I requested your services, you wanted children. A full hundred under the age of seven. Do you wish so again?"

Lhaurent asked, taking another sip of wine. A blue globe eased past, lighting the goblet glimmering gold.

The big mercenary's smile was condescending. "The Kreth-Hakir have a healthy crop of Brethren now, thanks to our endeavor ten years ago. Seventeen of those hundred Alrashemni children survived the training and have swelled our ranks. But no. Children have been easy to come by of late. Due to your faux-war with Valenghia, there are plenty of wandering orphans. Our thanks for that." Khorel Jornath gave a salute with his goblet.

Lhaurent nodded, but he did not drink when the vulture did. "So what is it you want? Emeralds are within my grasp. Slaves from Jadoun and Perthe. Uncountable provisions, poisons, medicinal herbs."

"No, no." The man shook his head. "The steppes and forests of the Unaligned Lands will provide. In truth, our Brethren need very little. No. We want something else."

"Ships? Caravans?" Lhaurent sat very still, tense. The negotiations were going badly. Lhaurent didn't enjoy being manipulated, and he didn't like surprises. Khorel Jornath was giving him a taste of both, and Khouren knew his Rennkavi had nothing to oppose the man with.

The hulking Kreth-Hakir shook his head, a smile creeping about his thick lips. "You sully my Brethren's reputation, Lhaurent. Such things we can acquire easily. No. What we want, are the *wyrria*-dead."

Lhaurent lifted his eyebrows, so great was his surprise. "Only men and women of the Twelve Tribes are immune to your vast gifts. Whyever would you want them for slaves?"

"You misunderstand me, my friend." Khorel Jornath's smile grew teasing, as if suffering a child's idiocy. "The Kreth-Hakir do not need more slaves, nor recruits. We do not need supplies, coin, or trade. If we wish to conquer, we simply do so."

"Then what do you need?" Lhaurent touched the grey star-metal band of Leith's ruby ring upon his index finger, a sign of severe distress. Khouren's hand tightened upon one slender fly-knife at his leather harness. He wasn't certain if he could throw it before the leather-clad man sitting at the table skewered his mind, but he'd certainly die trying.

"Control your cur, Scion of Alodwine," the mercenary suddenly growled, his flat grey eyes flicking to Khouren.

"He is a Scion of Alodwine also," Lhaurent spoke smoothly. "You owe both Khouren and I your allegiance, Khorel, for your debt to Leith's house. We negotiate because I am of a mind to reciprocate fairly with your Brethren. And not to create any undue rancor between us." His words were strong, but Lhaurent held out a hand in a pacifying gesture to Khouren. Khouren's fingers slipped from his blade, with effort.

"Tell me what you think of me, lad." The thick mercenary growled, his ancient dark eyes upon Khouren, utterly cold.

"I think my great-great-grandfather Leith made a mistake, treating with your kind." Khouren's voice was measured. Lhaurent allowed him to speak his mind at these negotiations, as it was Khouren who had introduced his Rennkavi to the Kreth-Hakir. And to their debt to Leith Alodwine, last King of Khehem. But since events involving the Kreth-Hakir had gone from bad to worse ten years ago with the Kingsmen, Khouren had come to regret his involvement in his Rennkavi's dealings with them.

"Leith Alodwine saw our vast promise," The big man sneered. "Though honey-tongued and fair of face, he was as cruel as we are. And could break minds just as fast as we do now. But he needed assistance, to bless his vast wonders upon our continent. So he made us. Thanks Be to Alodwine."

"You're nothing but slavers and thugs." Khouren growled, ice in his tone. "You carry no true blood of Alodwine."

The big man sat forward at last, the front legs of his chair settling to the dusty grey byrunstone of the floor. The hushed sound echoed through the vaulted hall, up through vast arches and gables, to flurry blue globes high above.

"Careful, blood of gods," Khorel warned. "The Kreth-Hakir carry a sliver of Leith's very *soul*. His *wyrric* fundament was split to give our line the gifts we now enjoy. Can you say the same?"

"I wouldn't want your bastard gifts." Khouren hissed.

"Wouldn't you, shadow?" The man growled, vicious. "If you'd had our gifts, you could have had her, you know. You could have charmed your tumble-haired beloved, seen those curling black locks strewn across your pillow by the light of a high, cold moon. Rather than that of a royal cuss who didn't appreciate her."

Khouren felt himself blanch. A shiver stiffened his posture. Frantically, he drove his awareness through the deepest reaches of his mind. The man had broken into his thoughts without Khouren knowing it, but where was he? At last, Khouren found it. A silvered line of thought, wormed into his consciousness, filtering through memories of Olea den'Alrahel. The bastard Kreth-Hakir had slipped his way in when Khouren had been unguarded, distracted by the tension of the conversation. He was now rifling through Khouren's deepest secrets with soaring ease.

Khouren's hand clenched upon his fly-blade.

"Easy, bastard of Alodwine," the mercenary crooned. "Or I'll speak unconscionable things to your blessed Rennkavi. Secrets from your mind directly to his."

Khouren shivered. He'd not told Lhaurent of his obsession with Olea. It was his secret, an enjoyed duty spying upon her these past ten years. He didn't know how Lhaurent would take it, his Rennkavi forever at odds with her.

Slowly, Khouren eased his fingers from this hilt of his blade.

"Smart." Khorel pinned Khouren with his scorpion's gaze. "The little cur can be trained. Too bad your grandfather Fentleith wasn't the same. In any case," he sat back, tipping his chair again, glancing to Lhaurent, "these are our terms. The Kreth-Hakir would like you to deliver the Twelve Tribes for our part in your upcoming war with Elsthemen."

Lhaurent tapped a finger upon the rim of his goblet. "You still haven't said what you want the Twelve Tribes for."

"Annihilation." It was said so plainly, that Khouren blinked.

Lhaurent sat back in his chair, regarding the mercenary with knitted brows, his version of a scowl. "You wish me to annihilate the Twelve Tribes. An entire *nation*, halfway around the world."

The man's amused twist of lips was triumphant. "Do this for us, Grey Eel, and we'll send as many Brethren into your little skirmishes against Elsthemen as you want. Not just this one, but the next, and the next. Until you have the dominance you need to control half the known world."

Lhaurent was silent a long moment. The pause stretched, breathless to the shadowed vaults. High above, blue globes had ceased to whirl, as if eager to hear his answer. "Why?"

The mercenary's thick lips screwed up in a vile snarl. "Because no one resists the Breaking of the Brethren. The Kreth-Hakir suffer no resistance." The man held Lhaurent's gaze, uncompromising. Those dark eyes shifted to Khouren, beyond Lhaurent's left shoulder. "Not even from the blood of our god."

Suddenly, Khouren was riveted where he stood. His limbs felt like lead, thick and useless. Nothing would move, not a finger, his muscles frozen. He tried to shiver, to jolt himself from the snare, but a vise gripped his body. It wasn't a suggestion wormed into his mind that he remain still. This was sheer dominance holding his mind and flesh.

He had been taken entirely by the iron grip of a High Priest of the Kreth-Hakir.

And he couldn't break free.

Khorel Jornath stared him down, dispassionate. Khouren saw the cold nature of the man. Those flat grey eyes sank into Khouren's soul as if there was nothing left in the world but despair. He couldn't blink, couldn't look away. He was nothing but prey, paralyzed by the Scorpion's sting.

"Do not molest my most loyal, Khorel." Lhaurent's tone was deceptively smooth.

Jornath's eyes flicked to Lhaurent, but Khouren was not released from his snare. "Or what? You are weak, Scion of both *Alrashem* and Khehem. You feint as if you have power, pulling the strings of lesser men, but we have been watching you these past ten years, Lhaurent. You machinate through poisons and treachery, sliding your way to power. You have not learned to take what you must. You have not learned strength. The deal we offer is more than fair in every way. Accept it, and be satisfied we do not gut you like the eel you are."

Slowly, Lhaurent eased to standing. Like a leviathan rising from black deeps, he stood tall. Khouren felt a rush of power flood over his skin. It bit like sharks, it strangled like tentacles beneath a terrible sea. Lhaurent's posture was fierce, angry, his face set in a hard scowl.

The Kreth-Hakir sat up, alert, his eyes narrowing upon Lhaurent. He rose from his chair to face Lhaurent, his posture ready, as if for a fight. "I feel power coming from you, grey eel. Power like I have not felt in eons. Not since the time of my god a thousand years ago…"

"Because I *carry* the power of your god, Khorel. Behold." Like a poisonous snake shedding old skin, Lhaurent shrugged out of his grey silk robe and let it whisper to the chair behind him. The braided knots of his doublet he released, then shrugged the doublet off, no shirt on beneath.

Before the Kreth-Hakir, Lhaurent stood bare to the waist in the eerie catacomb. His body was hard, tempered by time but without a trace of infirmity other than the silver streaking his temples. Not a scrap of easy living existed upon his impeccable leanness. And though Khouren knew he was at least seventy years old, Lhaurent had a touch of the Alodwine clan's longevity, looking hardly fifty.

All Lhaurent's affectations in the palace were a sham. His stoop, his slow walk, his servile demeanor. And the Kreth-Hakir had just made a grievous mistake, assuming Lhaurent was as submissive as he appeared.

Lhaurent took a breath. His body flared with curling light like the sun's rays shining into the chill deeps of the blackest ocean. Khouren felt his Rennkavi's power flood the room. A compelling urge took Khouren, to serve, to do anything, everything Lhaurent wanted. He saw the Kreth-Hakir fighting that same siren call, that eerie music, his eyes wide, his muscles shivering with tension. The light pooled and flowed, rippled and bent, sliding its way through Lhaurent's skin along a course of arcane tattooing that looked black in the dim light.

But Khouren knew those marks upon Lhaurent's body were not black. They were gold. And now, the Goldenmarks rippled with the force of Lhaurent's blessing. A power that recognized his unique nature, his single-minded determination, and his twinned lineages of Alrashemni and Khehemni.

The power of the Uniter. The power of the Rennkavi.

Khorel Jornath twitched. Lhaurent took a deep inhalation, and his Goldenmarks flared like the dazzle of sun on the ocean. Khorel made a strangled sound. Khouren could feel it, their battle of wills. The High Priest of the Scorpions, a man over a thousand years old, pitting his mind-warping against the convincing power of the Rennkavi.

Lhaurent did not stir. He did not so much as flicker an eyelash. Cold and calm, he was the essence of dominance, unmovable as oceanic deeps. Suddenly, Khorel roared in rage, flashing forward with a dagger in his fist. Lhaurent's hand shot out, smoothly slipping his arm past the dagger. His long fingers closed hard on the Kreth-Hakir's throat, gripping the priest like the dog he was.

Power flooded the room. Lhaurent's Goldenmarks lit the space, seething, swirling. Khouren could barely breathe. He was drowning in the luminous dark, drowning in a sea of cold purpose and utter conviction.

The conviction of the Rennkavi.

"You will serve me." Lhaurent's voice was sinuous in the rippling darkness. His gaze rested upon the Kreth-Hakir, pinning the man just as his white hand gripped him by the throat. Leith's ruby on Lhaurent's index finger glinted in the surging light from the Goldenmarks, responding with its own ancient magic. Blue globes floated down from above, swirling around Lhaurent as if recognizing the power of their creator flooding the ancient space.

"You and all your Brethren will do my bidding," Lhaurent continued, "because I am the only salvation for our world. *War is the burden of the powerful, and prosperity is their reward for sacrifice.* Your god, Leith Alodwine, uttered those words. I have sacrificed my entire life to bring a great prosperity to our world, just as Leith once did. His vision, in which he sequestered your assistance, nay, your *obeisance,* was the very foundation of your Order. I, *Lhaurent den'Alrahel,* born of both Khehemni and Alrashemni royal lines, have been chosen by Prophecy to complete Leith's vision. To bring a golden age where all will prosper under unified rule. Kneel to me. For I alone have been chosen to follow in the footsteps of your god."

Through this tirade, Khouren felt his Rennkavi's raw power pressing through the room. Thundering in the eaves and pummeling through his heart, Khouren felt that promise of salvation, the bliss of following a strong, unified rule. Just as he'd felt it decades before when he'd pledged his allegiance to his Rennkavi, he felt it again now. Surging determination. Uncompromising justice. Strength, pouring from Lhaurent, from the Goldenmarks upon his skin, curling like luminescence beneath the ocean.

Chosen. Lhaurent had been Chosen, to lead.

And bring them all to a golden age.

Khorel could have fought. He was bigger than Lhaurent, taller, his prowess in battle honed over centuries. But he was caught, trapped, broken just as thoroughly as any cur to his master's whip. A shudder took the Kreth-Hakir High Priest. With a hard choke, his knees buckled, and Lhaurent let him go. Khorel Jornath slammed to the stone before Lhaurent.

And in a final show of dominance, Lhaurent put one soft grey boot upon the man's chest and kicked him over to his back. Moving forward, Lhaurent set that foot over Khorel Jornath's throat, stepping down with weight. His cold gaze pressed the man down as much as his Goldenmarks pressed through the room like a flood, making it difficult for Khouren to breathe.

"Stay down until you know what you are." Lhaurent spoke.

All dominance left Khorel's eyes. On his back, he brought a shaking hand up. Setting the knuckle of his thumb to his brow, he closed his eyes, a Kreth-Hakir gesture of submission. Khouren was released suddenly from the priest's mind-grip in a wave of shivers. Stepping back, Lhaurent released Jornath in turn, a cruel twist of satisfaction to his lips. The priest stayed on his back a moment more, before pushing up to his knees. Placing a fist to the cold floor, he bowed his head. The man's shoulders trembled. His breathing was ragged.

"Forgive me," Khorel Jornath spoke. "Forgive me for doubting you. I had only heard of your power, given by the Prophecy... I had not seen, had not *felt* it for myself..."

"Forgiveness I shall grant you," Lhaurent murmured, "if you do my bidding. Do not fight me, Khorel. Follow me. Follow the blessed vision of your god Leith. Trust that all I do, I do because of him. Because I was chosen to. Because it is engraved in my blood and upon my flesh. I am the mouthpiece of your god."

Lhaurent's hand settled to Khorel's head like a benediction, long fingers slipping through his hair. Khouren heard a soft choke. He saw Khorel's head nod beneath Lhaurent's hand. "I will trust in my god. I will trust in his Prophecy, come to life at last. Blessed be the Uniter. Blessed Be to Alodwine."

Lhaurent's hand smoothed down Khorel's cheek, lifted his chin so he could gaze into the mercenary priest's eyes. "Rise, servant of

Alodwine. Rise with purpose, and do my bidding."

With unsteady movement, the big man trundled to his feet. His chest hitched. He blew out a hard breath through pursed lips.

Lhaurent's smile was subtle, pleased. "Now do you see?"

"Now I see." The man took an enormous in-breath, and his shoulders squared. "And through me, all my kin have felt your power. Thanks Be to Alodwine."

"For your allegiance, you will be rewarded." Lhaurent reached out to cup the man's cheek like a father might bless his son. "You and your Brethren will accompany Menderian forces to battle upon the Elsthemi border, ostensibly under the Khehemni Lothren's command, until Elsthemen is secured. Meanwhile, you will assist my rise in Lintesh, then throughout Alrou-Mendera. Once my nation is unified and Elsthemen annexed, I will take an army through the Stones and sequester the Twelve Tribes under my benevolence. A gesture of goodwill to your Brethren."

"You would not punish them?" The herringbone-clad mercenary's thick lips held a slight scowl.

"I will ensure they know that resistance to my Unity will not be tolerated." The sigils and script upon Lhaurent's torso flared, writhing with light, cutting through the gloom. "Go. Tell your Brethren of the Kreth-Hakir whom they now serve."

The Kreth-Hakir took a deep breath. "It will be done. They will hear the truth they have already felt."

Lhaurent lifted his goblet from the table. "To the Kreth-Hakir. Ever allies to House Alodwine."

The man turned and claimed his goblet, raised it in return. "To the blood of our god, Leith Alodwine. Without whose gifts we would never have come to be."

They drank in unison. Lhaurent's Goldenmarks began to dim as if settling back to the floor of the ocean. Khouren moved forward, claiming Lhaurent's robe from the chair, offering it with trembling hands. Lhaurent took it with a nod, slipping into it bare-chested as Khouren held it.

The two dangerous men faced each other at last, having come to accord. Khorel Jornath towered a full head higher than Castellan Lhaurent, though Khouren's Rennkavi was not a short man. The two did not clasp arms; they knew each other better than that.

Lhaurent beckoned with an effete gesture toward a section of wall that the mercenary could use to leave the Hinterhaft, back to the torchlit bowels of Roushenn. The big man nodded and stepped away from the table, avoiding eye contact. Lhaurent led and they moved off down shadowed stone halls. Khouren followed, though his presence as bodyguard was unneeded now after Lhaurent's show of power and Jornath's submission.

Lhaurent left them at the wall-access with an nod. "Khouren, see our guest out. Khorel Jornath, I look forward to your report from the Elsthemi front."

"My liege." The man gave a quiet nod.

Castellan Lhaurent den'Karthus turned, gliding back the way they'd come. Khouren was left alone in the shadowed blue corridor with a man he despised. Though he'd showed servility to Lhaurent's power, Khouren knew Jornath's kind. The Brethren of the Kreth-Hakir had never suffered dominance well from outsiders. In all their dubious and bloody history, the Scorpions had only ever been bested by one man, Leith Alodwine, the Last King of Khehem. Had Khorel truly been bested by Lhaurent's power? As the Kreth-Hakir High Priest prepared to leave, mistrust shifted through Khouren, setting his jaw, narrowing his eyes in the shadowed recesses of his hood.

But the Kreth-Hakir priest knew the flavor of Khouren's mind now. The man held Khouren's gaze, a smile lifting the edges of his thick lips. "You mistrust my promise to your god, young cur?"

"I mistrust everything about you." Khouren growled, unable to hide his true feelings.

"Careful, bastard of a Scion," Khorel Jornath stepped close, his breath scented of clove and cinnamon. "I have an accord with your master, but you are nothing. It is for respect of the strength he showed today that I do not set your own mind to flaying you alive. I can feel your thoughts, dog. Though the weft and weave of minds is an ever-changing thing, I need only make adjustments to maintain this silvery thread I have eased into your mind. I can keep it within you, as long as I wish. Perhaps I will."

Khouren could feel the man's mind-tether, a worm of gossamer silk still in his head. A slow poison that creeped along his thoughts like spilled ink. "Cross me and risk my Rennkavi's severe displeasure, priest."

The Kreth-Hakir High Priest chuckled in the dusky shadows, his cinnamon and clove-spiced breath blowing over Khouren's face. "Perhaps I'll leave you a gift, Khouren Alodwine," he murmured, intimate in the darkness. "Something to remember me by. When the time comes that you seek freedom from your master… I will be there. And you will remember that it was *my* power, my precious gift, that secured your freedom. Not your own will, weakling, but mine. Take care, young Scion of my god. Remember me."

Khorel Jornath dipped his head from his tremendous height, pressing a light kiss to Khouren's lips. Locked into stillness by the man's mind-bending, Khouren couldn't draw away, couldn't so much as take a step back. Khouren cursed himself again that he'd never learned mind-blocking from his grandfather. The only protest he was allowed, was breathing hard in fury as the man's kiss lingered, tasting of winter spices.

At last, Khorel Jornath pulled away. A low, dominant chuckle rolled through the Hinterhaft's silence. "Good. Hate me, lad. Hate everything that I am, and everything I represent. For in your hate, you'll be thinking of me." Khorel Jornath ran a calloused hand over Khouren's cheek. "And if you're thinking of me… then I own you, rather than your perfumed Rennkavi. And when it comes time, will his power win you? Or will mine? I leave you to a night full of unanswered questions. Farewell."

With that, the man stepped away. Pushing through the section of wall, he moved into the flare of torchlight from the cellar beyond. Then he was gone, leaving Khouren alone in the darkness. Cinnamon and bile lingered in Khouren's mouth. His body was free, but his mind was not. He could still feel that silver worm, deep in his mind. It was quiescent for now, but for how long?

A shiver of fear passed through Khouren, spiked with loathing. He should never have told Lhaurent about the Kreth-Hakir. But now it was far too late.

Ten years too late.

Khouren lifted a black sleeve, ran it across his lips, wiping away the taste of cinnamon. But nothing could banish the silver thread still wrapped through his mind. One thought repeated, tumbling over and over like an ocean pounding stark cliffs.

When it comes time, will his power win you? Or will mine?

The thought made Khouren want to slip through the nearest wall and keep going. Far away from the palace, away from everything. To leave it all behind and get as far from the dealings of the mercenary priest as possible and off into the night.

Khouren took a deep breath, squared his shoulders. He had taken an oath long ago, in blood. To serve and protect his Rennkavi. To do everything the Uniter needed lest Khouren's very body and soul be charred in flame and punished into ash. Fleeing was not an option. Seeking his freedom from his Rennkavi would never happen. Khorel Jornath had been mistaken, and whatever his gift was, it would never come to pass.

Khouren belonged to his Rennkavi, and no other.

Khouren turned and slipped silently through a wall, heading back the way Lhaurent had gone.

CHAPTER 6 – DHERRAN

Dherran den'Lhust glowered at his hand, cramped from writing. He heaved an irritated sigh. The past two weeks of keeping the Vicoute Arlen den'Selthir's notes had been arduous. He and Khenria had been scribing day after day as reports came and went from Arlen's manor near Vennet. Dherran was in a shit mood, his ire rising by the hour. He stretched his hand, then made a fist, wanting to hit something.

"I'm a fighter, Aeon-dammit, not a fucking scribe," he grumped under his breath.

Den'Selthir heard it, and held up one beringed hand to forestall the man now giving his report, his ice-blue gaze fixing upon Dherran like a hawk pins a rabbit. "Wearied, Dherran? I have chores if this bores you."

Dherran sighed, trapped. He looked up from his notes and met the Vicoute's iron blue gaze. Silence held court in the paneled drawing room, the high chandeliers unlit as midday sunlight streamed in through the tall windows. Dust-motes curled through the air between heavy green velvet drapes, stirred by a hot summer wind.

Dherran knew taking chores over scribing was a trap. He had jumped at this suggestion on the third day, and had spent the entire night mucking stalls, currying horses, and carrying buckets of water for animals upon the sprawling grounds of the Vicoute's country manse. And instead of breakfast the following morning, he'd received four hours of brutal training from den'Selthir himself.

And then it had been straight back to the scribing without food or sleep.

"Not at all, Vicoute," Dherran answered, with as much cheek as he could muster. Khenria glanced up from her own scribing at a small gilded table nearby, giving him a warning look from her big grey eyes. Dherran reached up, rifling his short blonde hair.

Vicoute Arlen held his gaze, unperturbed. The man sat back in his high-backed leather chair. His steel-hard frame seemed relaxed in his cream doublet and fawn breeches, but Dherran knew better. Arlen was a fucking blade, ruthless. And though you can trust steel, it will never hesitate to cut you.

"Dherran. Please recount to me the last minute of Whelan den'Yhenniman's report." Arlen said serenely, one hand rubbing his short blonde hair with its iron-grey streaks, then combing his trim beard.

Dherran narrowed his eyes and read from his tortured scrawl upon the white flax parchment. Arlen stopped him with one raised finger. "The goodwife of the King's Squire Inn had how many on staff who were listening to Whelan's words?"

Dherran glanced down to his parchment. "Seven."

"Eight." The Vicoute intoned. "And who was listening in from across the room?"

Dherran scanned his notes. "A woman in a red riding dress."

The Vicoute's pale blue eyes flashed, displeased. "A *noblewoman* in a red riding dress, slashed with gold sleeves. And red with gold around here is the color of House…?"

Dherran scanned his notes, not finding his answer.

"House den'Ennis, Dherran. Note it. And please note that she had two liveried retainers by the door."

Dherran grit his teeth and growled, scrawling it down in a terrible hand. Silence pressed upon his ears in the humid afternoon. He looked up. Arlen still held him with that hawkish gaze. Khenria had an *oh shit* look on her lovely face, and didn't even dare move when one of her short black curls fell over her forehead in front of her eyes. All of them, even the Kingsman giving his report in the chair across the desk from Arlen, were frozen like mice in a field.

"Dherran." Arlen's voice was deceptively mild. "Please tell me. What are we doing here?"

"Taking down field reports from Whelan." Dherran was churlish.

The Vicoute took a very long, slow breath. His blue eyes flashed in the suffering gloom of the drawing room. "We are *upholding the Queen's reign.* Sending our Kingsmen agents over the eastern reaches, spreading rumor to undermine the factions who have stolen her throne, Dherran. We are rabble-rousing, *subtly*, inciting unrest in the nation. Raising dissent against unlawful wars that kill off our people. That weaken our nation. So that when our Queen comes home, she has something to come home to. And because of our efforts, the countryside gradually wakens to our position."

Dherran's cheeks flushed hot. His untamable rage rose, simmering in his muscled fighter's frame. Everything in him wanted to hit the bastard, but he suppressed it. Striking out at Arlen den'Selthir was a good way to get unconscious. Or dead.

Dherran took a breath, squeezing his rage back inside like sticking a finger into a breaking dam.

Arlen stared at him a minute more, then glanced back to the man giving his report. "Continue, Whelan."

At length, the Kingsman finished giving his report. Den'Selthir nodded, then waved him out. He stood, drawing a hand through his graying blonde mane, the only sign Dherran had ever noted that indicated the Vicoute was wearied. Khenria sat tall, her young woman's frame leaning forward in her dove-grey doublet and breeches, ready for their regular quizzing. Her notes were invariably far better than Dherran's. And it seemed the Vicoute had a mind like a beartrap, forgetting no details though he never took a single note himself.

Arlen narrowed his eyes on Khenria, until she fidgeted with her goose-feather pen. "Khenria," he spoke at last, "please retire to the Underground. Sherina will spar with you tonight, and you can eat afterwards."

She nodded quickly, then bounced to her narrow boots, sneaking a look at Dherran before she padded out the doors. Den'Selthir swung his gaze to Dherran. "Dherran, walk with me."

Dherran rose from the desk, setting his pen and parchment aside. Straightening his hunter-green silk doublet and airing the high collar of his shirt from sweat trickling down his back, he followed the Vicoute from the room. Down the long corridor to the receiving gallery, they proceeded out the front doors of the manse. Pacing the flagstone path across the decorative gardens, they headed out towards the horse paddocks. Den'Selthir halted his long stride, waiting for Dherran to catch up, then lead on.

At last, their boots crunched over the last of the gravel, striding into the grass near the first paddock. The Vicoute put a boot up on the lowest pole of the fence and swung up to sit on top. Dherran did the same, staring out across leagues of pasture bordered by emerald woodland. Together they sat in silence, the mugginess of the afternoon a haze over the browning late-summer fields, towers of cumulus building in a thick summer sky. Horses cropped the grass before them in blissful serenity, unconcerned by the worries of men.

"Do you know why I'm putting you through all this, Dherran?" The Vicoute sighed at last.

"To torture me."

"To *educate* you. Pay attention! Why do I grill you on your notes five times more than I do Khenria?"

"I think my previous answer suffices."

Vicoute Arlen turned to look at him. "You've got a brain in there somewhere. I'll be damned if I give up trying to find it. Why do I remember everything my men tell me, Dherran?"

"To quiz me on it later."

Arlen's gaze was hard. "Don't be a callous cheek. To run a battlefield, Dherran. Details matter. How are you supposed to find nobles sympathetic to our cause? The finances and men to go with it? The influence? Remember the red and gold. That young woman of House den'Ennis stayed through the *entire* conversation at the inn, her teacup perched by her lips but not drinking. She's a sympathizer. She showed *interest* in the news. When Whelan returns to Pallisade Fhen, when we're ready to maneuver, he'll seek House den'Ennis, and ask for an audience with her directly. House den'Ennis controls nearly three hundred retainers. A small army. A *valuable* army."

"But why do we need her army when we have House den'Lhesh of the Gerson Hills?" Dherran rifled a hand through his sweaty blonde mane, airing it.

"You remembered something of value. Good." Arlen's pale blue eyes were appraising. "Yearlan den'Lhesh is moody at best. Some say the Battle of Phalanne addled his wits. He's an excellent commander and I've known him a long time, but his courage isn't what it used to be. Yearlan and his thousand may not come through for us. But Merikunne den'Ennis is a sleek tyrant of a woman, and rules her homestead with a bluestone fist. She listens most to her favored niece. And judging by our fair maid's escort of two liveried men at the inn, that was Melionne den'Ennis, out gallivanting as she's prone to. I'd send you out to negotiate with her if you weren't such a fool for Khenria's thighs."

Dherran bristled, but said nothing, knowing den'Selthir was right. He was a fool for Khenria den'Bhaelen and no other woman would do, not even for a casual, informative fuck. "Any more news from Lintesh?"

At this, the Vicoute actually growled, rubbing hand over his short beard. "None. And I've had no news from my Kingsmen contacts at the First Abbey, either. I assume hawks and ravens with messages are being shot down, the King's Chancellate desperately trying to halt the spread of any information that opposes them. I've sent a rider to assess the temperature of the capitol and make contact with Abbess Lenuria den'Brae. But such news is a week out, at best. If my man even makes it. We have no idea how closely the Khehemni are watching us right now. But that's beside the point. You need to pay attention, Dherran! Open your ears. Open your eyes. Notice people, notice their garb, the way they move. You've run from a mob enough times," the Vicoute snorted. "You should be excellent at these things."

"Then put me out there!" Dherran grumbled. "My talents are wasted behind a desk."

"You are not attending me for your note-taking." The Vicoute bit back. "You're there to listen, to learn *how* to listen. You're one of the best swordsmen I have, Dherran, and you've got the makings of a great commander."

"Then put me out there. Let me command."

"Tell me one thing about my men that I don't know." Den'Selthir eyed him.

"What?" Dherran's brows furrowed.

"If you want the respect of becoming a commander for the Kingsmen, for the Shemout Alrashemni, if you think you've earned it, then tell me one thing about my men that I don't know. On the battlefield, they will be your captains and lieutenants. You should know their strengths, weaknesses, and predispositions. What don't I know about my own men, Dherran?"

Dherran thought a moment, running through Arlen's retainers

in his mind. Over two hundred Kingsmen-in-hiding had come to Arlen's banner in the past few weeks, and the country manor was now strained to the gills housing and feeding them all. It was a growing army, a valuable one, rallied in the name of Queen Elyasin.

Aeon-hope she actually lived, though they had no real proof as yet.

"Den'Irliksen has a child with a woman in town."

"Obvious." The Vicoute snorted. "He rides out every third day and does not account for two hours of his time, but comes back smelling of talc with a smile upon his face. Tell me something else."

Dherran rifled a hand through his hair. "Den'Allouenne is sleeping with den'Orisset."

"And they think they're so sneaky. Fucking in the hay loft." The Vicoute chuckled. "Don't bore me, Dherran."

Dherran rifled his hair again. This next one was a gamble, and if he was right, it was bad news all around. "Den'Hout has found my friend Grump, and he's not telling you."

"What?" Den'Selthir's blue eyes snapped to Dherran, fierce. "Do not make idle accusations, Dherran! Are you certain?"

Dherran nodded, feeling far from certain. "He pulled a Dourienne's Cap mushroom from his pouch yesterday and nibbled it. Dourienne's is easily mistaken for Trundle-Bell, which sets men to paralysis. Only the most skilled woodsmen would be able to tell the difference between the two. And I've never seen den'Hout with the foragers. He knows Grump. And he's not telling you they've been meeting."

Den'Selthir stared a moment longer. "Come with me." He launched himself from the rails, striding off at a fast clip towards the stables. Marching into the barn, he stepped right up to Tristenne den'Hout, grooming a roan mare. Arlen snatched the big man's leather purse off his belt, dumping the contents all over the horseshit-laden ground. The other grooms ceased currying to stare, hands hovering near their blades in case of trouble.

"Here now, what?!" Tristenne protested, his ruddy face scowling as he tossed his curry-comb to a nearby hay-pile.

"Dammit to Halsos." Arlen snatched up a red-spotted mushroom from the dirty straw. "Explain this, Tristenne." Den'Selthir's gaze could have sliced bone.

Den'Hout lifted his double chin. "It's just a bit of mushroom, Vicoute. Dourienne's Cap. I got it from one of our foragers, Hannah. She finds them on the edge of the woods here. They're edible."

"He's lying," Dherran spoke up, hoping to Aeon he was right. "Dourienne's Cap likes swamps. There's no swamp near your land for at least a league, Vicoute. Only the poisonous Trundle-Bell likes the shaded verge at the edge of the woods bordering your land."

"Eat it." Den'Selthir held out the spotted cap to Tristenne. The jowly man took it without hesitation, popping it into his mouth, chewing. Den'Selthir glanced at Dherran. "How long until paralysis if it's Trundle-Bell?"

"Five minutes." Dherran shuffled a boot through the dirty straw.

Den'Selthir's eyes sharpened on Tristenne den'Hout, and time morphed into stone. Trained Kingsmen all, no one moved a muscle in the vast barn. Horses whiskered, kicked at their stalls. Den'Hout began to sweat under his lord and leader's scrutiny, though Dherran thought the brawny Kingsman kept his cool remarkably well.

At last, Vicoute Arlen snarled. His sword flashed from his scabbard faster than thought, the tip flicking right to the center of Tristenne's thick throat. "You should be paralyzed right now, Tristenne. Tell me who it was that gave you the mushroom. Or I will cut you down where you stand, so swear I by my Ink."

Tristenne's green eyes were wide, but he held his cool. "His name is Baruthane den'Mythen. He's a local woodsman, from town. Goes to the nearby swamps regularly."

Den'Selthir leaned in, searching his Kingsman's eyes. "Lies. Why are you lying to me, Tristenne? Do you remember what I do to men or women who lie to me?"

"Yes, Vicoute." The man swallowed hard.

"Do you want to spend a day in a hive? How about three days? And how about Jennaria? I'll have her fetch you from the hive. She avoids the bees like a plague, doesn't she?"

"Please!" Tristenne went pale. "She'll die if she's stung! Jennaria's all I have...!"

"She old enough. She's Shemout. And your daughter will carry out my orders if I ask her to deposit you into the hive. Or she'll join you there. Are you ready to tell me the truth?"

The man licked his lips. "Yes, Arlen."

"I'm waiting."

"I got it from a man named Grump." Tristenne hurried suddenly. "The same one you've been searching for. He's been foraging an herb for Jenni, something that keeps her throat from swelling around the horses. He mixes a tea for her. I met him in town, I swear, before I knew you were searching for him. Before I knew he was a Khehemni outlaw. I swear it, Arlen."

"Are you Khehemni, Tristenne?" The Vicoute's eyes were cold.

"No. I just can't lose Jenni." The man whispered, his green eyes pleading.

Arlen peered at him a long moment, searching. At last, he moved back. "Don't ever lie to me again. You've been warned." His sword flicked away, and he sheathed it in one long, smooth motion. "Fhellas! Enthin! Saddle five mounts. We ride."

Den'Selthir strode to the nearest tack, heaving a saddle and blanket into his arms and making for a broad bay gelding already in the curry-traces, settling the saddle over its back. "How far to the Khehemnas, Tristenne?"

"One hour on foot, off the Bitterwoods trail to the north. Near Thickhole Swamp."

Den'Selthir elbowed the horse in the ribs and cinched the girth tight. "Right under our bloody noses. Dherran! Grab a saddle! Fetch a sword from the tack room and let's go!"

"What about him?" Dherran glanced at Tristenne.

Den'Selthir looked up. "Tristenne knows I'll ride him down if he tries to run."

Dherran glanced behind at the groom, who had gone very pale. Within minutes their small party was mounted up, horses pacing with tension. The Vicoute took the lead and galloped out of the barn, past the paddocks towards a trail that broke the edge of the trees beyond the fields to the north.

But as they gained the trees, he paused, letting Tristenne lead upon his bay. They rode twenty minutes before the rolling forest became a small swamp, and here Tristenne dismounted and began to hunt for tracks. Muck-sucking divots made the horses shy and whinny, losing them any element of surprise. Dherran's black gelding paced nervously in the muck, and Dherran dismounted onto a mossy log, soothing the animal.

Vicoute Arlen had dismounted also. Tying his mount to a nearby tree, he was now picking through the swamp, his step nimble as he jumped between logs. Upon one he bent, scrutinizing the moss, touching it, then glanced at the black peat nearby.

"He was here," Vicoute Arlen pointed at a cluster of speckled caps rising from the duckweed-laced mud, and a boot print nearby.

Dherran jumped to the log and hunkered. "That's Grump's tread. He likes his boots wide for better purchase. See how the imprint of the ball is deeper. His soles are doeskin, and he paces on the balls of his feet. It makes him quiet."

"Impressive. Maybe you aren't worthless after all." Arlen stood, gesturing Dherran forward as he went to retrieve the horses. "Track him."

Dherran sighed, straightening. It twisted his gut to be tracking his friend Grump, but he had questions of his own that needed answering. Why had Grump disappeared that last day in Vennet? Why had he scuttled so fast from the inn when Arlen entered after Khenria's fights? Why did the Vicoute insist Grump was a Khehemni spy, and was any of it true? Dherran gazed around the low verge and saw hazelfern, newly trimmed, evidence of Grump's gathering. He stepped in that direction, and from there, his knowledge of the man made it easy. All he had to do was search for the next edible or medicinal plant, looking for disturbance.

Dherran kept moving, following a winterbloom harvested for its leaves here, a snakeroot plant dug out from its neighbors there. A laurel-urn was missing its lower flowers, and a section of miner's cabbage were missing their greenest tops. A whole bank of thimbleberry had been picked clean. At length, they came to a hill with a hollow of mherrl-bushes at the top, which showed evidence of a bedroll laid out, and a fire long cold.

"He's moved on." Dherran glanced back at Arlen. "Grump doesn't take his stuff when he's foraging. He probably knows your men have been after him."

"He's been meeting me every three days at this swamp," Tristenne spoke up, "with the herbs for Jenni's tea. He's due tomorrow."

The Vicoute eyed Tristenne like he was a lump of shit on his boot. "Enthin! Take a mount back to the manse and fetch us some water flasks and hard foods. Throw in a bedroll or two." The other groom put a palm to his Inkings and swiftly mounted up, riding back the way they had come.

Arlen turned, eyeing their small company. "Gentlemen. Make yourselves comfortable in the verge. We're going to wait him out."

Men dispersed in a wide ring, separating some distance from each other and circling the remains of the camp. Trained Kingsmen all, they melted into the gorse and underbrush as if they had never been. Dherran hunkered upon his heels, alone in the verge, his back against a stout alder. Late afternoon slid into evening, the forest silent around them but for the chorus of birds. Evening fell. Enthin returned, passing out bedrolls, water, and food. Dherran ate, drank, urinated.

Then waited again.

Dark fell, shadows deepening to a heavy red twilight under a thick blanket of storm-clouds. An owl hooted, with a swish of wings and a squeak of something caught. Dherran's knees ached viciously from crouching in his thicket. His horse, tethered a distance away with the other mounts, gave a soft whicker. The heavy mugginess that had sat in the air all day began to compress. A breeze rifled curling leaves overhead, and a rumble of summer thunder came from far up in the simmering dark. A flicker of lightning caught Dherran's attention through a gap in the trees. The wind picked up suddenly, the forest filled with the rushing of dry leaves and the creak of branches.

"Dherran."

Dherran's longknife was out in a flash, flush to the man's neck who'd surprised him in the dark. But the loamy smell and the small size of the man, not to mention his forest-worn garb gave him away. Dherran lowered his knife. "Grump!"

"What are you doing here?" Grump's sharp grey eyes glittered in the next flash of heat-lightning.

"Are you Khehemni, Grump?" It came tumbling out of his dumb mouth, but Dherran had to know.

The little man took a slow breath. "Yes. Can you get me protection from Arlen?"

"Why didn't you tell me?!" Dherran snarled, astounded. "And how do you know Arlen?"

Grump glanced around furtively, as if he was afraid someone was behind him. "I need protection. They're after me."

"They, who?"

Grump grasped Dherran's jerkin in both hands, giving him a shake. "Khehemni, Dherran! They're after me. Alert your Vicoute to my presence so I can ride with you! Whatever you think I am, whatever he's told you… please. Help a friend. I'm not the man you think I am, but I'm not as bad as Arlen would make me out to be."

Dherran gaped at Grump. The man's face was unreadable in the thick darkness, but he looked over his shoulder again as if he were in real trouble. Trouble worse than the Vicoute Arlen den'Selthir. Dherran stood from his hiding place, shouting out in the night. "Arlen!"

He saw men stand in their ring with the next flash of heat-lightning. But Dherran suddenly realized with a drop of his belly that there were too many men, far more than the five who had ridden out from the manor. With a shout, Dherran pulled his longknife in the close verge, spinning to protect Grump as an assailant closed from behind. Roaring and the ringing of steel accompanied the thunder and rising wind. Dherran could barely see in the storm-heavy darkness. He thought he slit a throat. He thought he felt Grump pull him around for a parry, protecting against another opponent. Small knives flashed in the dark with the next crack of lightning. Dherran whirled in time to take another man across the gut, and a third up under the armpit.

"To me! Alrashemni!" Arlen gave a mighty bellow nearby. "Mount up and ride!"

Dherran whirled, knowing his mount was in the direction of Arlen's call. He seized Grump by the scruff and hauled him around. By the next bolt of light he saw his mount, still tethered. They moved fast, feeling their way over logs and through verge. But Grump was faster, spry as a forest mouse, with keen eyes in the dark. He had the lead-line severed and himself mounted up before Dherran arrived. Grump held out a sinewed hand and Dherran clasped it, swinging up into the saddle.

"To me! Alrashemni!" Arlen's call came again, further away.

Dherran took the reins, wheeled his horse. They set off at a quick pace, twisting through black trees. He didn't dare risk galloping his horse. Any root or pit could mean a stumble, riders thrown, and death in the thick dark of the forest. Grump seized his hair suddenly, hauling his head to the side. Dherran heard an arrow whir past, thunking into a tree. He ducked to the neck of his horse, and another arrow came low, whirring near the horse's neck.

"Bloody fuck!" He growled, urging the horse to where he thought the Vicoute was. "Friends of yours, Grump?!"

"No!" The small man behind him growled over the surging wind. "Enemies!"

"Did you lead them here to fuck us?"

"No! I told you, they've been following me!"

Suddenly, a horse and rider joined them upon their path, shadows upon shadows. Dherran was ready to cut the man with his blade when Arlen's sharp shout stopped him. "Don't skewer me, Dherran! Angle left! Around the swamp! And shut up! They're shooting at our voices."

Dherran could just make out the Vicoute now, riding low against the neck of his mount. Two more arrows went whizzing by. Suddenly, another horse appeared between himself and the Vicoute. Dherran saw the rider lunge for den'Selthir, an enemy. Without thought, Dherran raked out with his longknife, slicing the enemy horse's neck. Rearing, the horse screamed and collapsed in a spasm, and a pained cry came as the man went down with it, crushed. Dherran's mount shied and whinnied as the next chorus of lightning came, thunder fast on its forks.

A driving rain began, pummeling the trees. A third mount and rider lunged up, but this man was as flat to his horse as Arlen.

"Vicoute! The others are dead!" Enthin shouted over the din of the storm.

"Ride!" Arlen shouted. "Ride now or die!"

They kicked their mounts, surging to more speed despite shying mounts and dark dangers. Riding in blackness with only the deep red of the sky far above, Dherran could make out nothing of the landscape. But the Vicoute knew the forest by heart, winding fast through the trees. The storm raged as they crossed the treeline, back to the manse's sprawling fields. Arlen kicked into a hard gallop once they broke cover, bellowing to wake the grounds as they flew over the downs. Torches flared in the red night. The manse lit from top to bottom as they rode hard towards it, lightning flashing and thunder rolling. Men and women flooded out, their garb rumpled from sleep, but weapons ready.

A bristling hive of hornets roused in the storm.

Dherran, Arlen, and Enthin skidded to a halt before the entry gable. Tree-thick Lhuder den'Mhens, Den'Selthir's top Captain, ran forward to grab their mounts. "Arlen! What happened?"

The Vicoute launched from his saddle, his sword whipping up as he whirled. Dherran would have thought Arlen's blade would go to Grump, but it whipped to Dherran instead, the razor-sharp tip right to Dherran's throat.

"Explain yourself! Explain this ambush you led us into!" Arlen roared, his blue eyes wild in the rain-spattered torchlight. Dherran was speechless. His mouth moved, but nothing came out. Rain poured down his curls, drenched his shoulders.

"It's not his fault, Arlen!" Grump's voice slit the night, bold, as if he could save himself and Dherran from the Vicoute's rage. Dherran glanced over, to see Grump standing peaceably in his worn forest garb, hands open at his sides as he was drenched by the rain. "I've come to talk. Don't hurt the boy. He had nothing to do with this debacle. Khehemni were following me. Dherran didn't know."

The Vicoute's vicious blue eyes flicked to Grump. A flash of lightning illuminated them ghastly white in the raging storm. "Seize them both! I will have the meaning of this escapade, or so help me, I'll gut every last man I see tonight!"

Arlen turned abruptly, striding away through the driving rain. Dherran was delivered a stout punch to the ear from Lhuder. He sagged, disoriented, and was seized under both arms, his hands bound roughly with a length of horse-rope. He did not resist when two of Arlen's best muscled him up the front stairs of the manse, down a hall, and then down to the lowest levels.

There, they tossed Dherran in a dank cell, so deep underground he couldn't hear the storm.

CHAPTER 7 – OLEA

It had taken nearly an hour to sort out who they were and why they had come through the Alranstone from Alrou-Mendera. Oasis Ghellen's wise-woman, the Maitrohounet, was nearly fluent in Menderian, and soon learned that Olea and her companions were not agents of Lhaurent den'Karthus. Once that was settled, she was far less hostile. At last, the woman rose gracefully to her feet in the center of the alabaster dome, her thin body carrying little infirmity. The sun's angle was only slightly deeper as she gestured for them all to rise with one elegant hand.

"Lourden," the Maitrohounet turned to address the spear-captain.

"Yes, Maitrohounet," Lourden clipped.

"The rotunda is not comfortable for long storytelling. We shall go to my home."

The Maitrohounet stepped forward, her dancing steps causing her crimson drape to sway. She crossed the circle of the golden sun set into the alabaster floor and Lourden rose to her side, beckoning the Menderian guests up also. They retreated from the rotunda, gathering up weapons and armor and proceeding back through the reed screen. Following the Maitrohounet, they turned right outside the rotunda. Lourden's *Rishaaleth* stepped into formation behind as the wise-woman took a path through the gardens. Palms shuffled high above in a mid-afternoon breeze that began to raise white dust, skirling it along the avenue and causing *shoufs* to be raised across noses and mouths.

At last, the party neared to a modest two-level abode decorated with mirrored tiles of glass in fanciful friezes. The Maitrohounet paid homage to Chiron at her doorway, an ancient, gnarled vine covering her lintel and posts. Lourden's spearmen took up sentry positions outside as the wise woman led them into a vaulted abode with a burbling white fountain at its center.

The Maitrohounet's home was bright and airy, with the feeling of an outdoor patio indoors. Slanting afternoon light filtered through lace-filigree stone walls. Afternoon wind skirled through holes in the stone, though reed screens kept out Ghellen's sand. Alabaster columns supported buttressed arches topped with water lilies, the vaulted ceilings sporting tile-art made from mirrors and minuscule squares of colorful glass. Stuccoed into every surface, the mirrors threw light and created rainbows in every alcove. Potted palms and blooming vines gave the space a garden atmosphere, lace-carven stone creating dividers to adjacent rooms. Pillows in garish silks were scattered in clusters upon ornate wool rugs, along with low reed-woven cushions for sitting.

A young woman brought them inside, then went to fetch refreshments. At last, all were seated among the silk cushions. A fizzy alcoholic beverage with the odor of plums was passed around in cobalt glass bowls, along with a silver tray of spiky crimson fruits. Known as *hesh-ti*, the fruit was a favorite of Lourden's children, tasting like a juicy pear. Refreshing in the heat, Olea took two of the fruits as water was brought in a ceramic urn and poured into clear glass bowls. The Maitrohounet lifted her alcoholic beverage to her lips and drank deeply, then took water, and ate liberally of the fruits, as if ravished.

At last, she set her libations aside. Pinning Olea with her grey eyes, she spoke in lightly-accented Menderian. "Now. Tell me why your heart simmered when I spoke the name of the Karthus earlier."

Olea stilled. "You could feel that? Do you have a *wyrric* gift?"

The Maitrohounet was elegant as she selected another fruit. "Such things are easy to see. Your hate of the Karthus is written in your body. To one who has perfected stillness, your anger churns like a storming ocean. But no, child, I have no *wyrria*. None in the Tribes have the old inborn magics anymore. Such blessings are gone from our lands. Which is why we weep."

"But aren't you Alrashemni? Your Inkings..." Olea glanced at Lourden, asking him as well.

"No, no." Lourden met her gaze, sad. "The *Alrashem* have been lost to us for a thousand years, along with their *wyrric* magics. But our tradition of Inking goes back to the dawn of our nation, nearly four thousand years ago. Twelve colors and twelve stars, for the

Twelve Oases. The mountain is for Chiron, our foundation. The lines of script are his teachings, wreathing our bodies like fruitful vines."

Lourden unbuckled his breastplate and set it aside, allowing Olea to gaze at the beauty writ upon his caramel skin in cascading color. Olea recognized the stylized shape of Chiron's heart-shaped vines with their white starburst flowers in the curling pattern. Arcane symbols flowed through it all, along with a slanted script Olea didn't recognize.

"What is that language?" She gestured to a line of script.

"High Vouniete. Language of Chiron. Forgotten, to all but the most learned." Lourden answered.

The Maitrohounet nodded, continuing. "The Language of the *Alrashem*, High Alrakhan, developed from High Vouniete, mixed with native tongues of the ancient nomads. From which Khourek has come these past thousand years." Her gaze shifted to Jherrick. "You bear an interesting name, child. Originating with the birth of Khourek, *Jherrick* means *Protector of Life*. Many honored guardians of our city have held this name over the past thousand years. The one who bore it first was a great fighter of the *berounhim*, who protected Ghellen during the Khehem Wars. It was said that nothing could kill him."

"Khourek is High Alrakhan combined with Ghrec, isn't it?" Jherrick spoke, leaning forward with interest in his grey eyes. "My mother once told me that she named me after a great Ghreccan hero."

The Maitrohounet smiled at the young scholar. "Just so. The name is also popular in Ghrec. And Khourek is our common tongue, a trade-language shared with the Southern Desert, and with the Ajnabiit of the eastern peninsula."

"A polyglot." Jherrick said. When the Maitrohounet raised her eyebrows, not understanding, he continued. "A language mixed from four others."

"Just so." She smiled. Her gaze flicked back to Olea. "But we lose our way in shifting sands. Why do you despise Lhaurent of the Karthus, child?"

"If he's been raising hate of Menderians in your nation, isn't that reason enough?" Aldris interjected sourly.

"Perhaps." The Maitrohounet's gaze returned to Olea.

Olea set her jaw, grim. "There are many reasons I mistrust that man. But you did not say how Lhaurent is connected to the Alranstone we came through. Why you thought we were his agents when we arrived." Olea turned to Lourden. "You said that Stone has been active ten years. Has Lhaurent been coming through it?"

Lourden narrowed his eyes in fierce anger. "For as long as can be remembered since the *Alrashem* left, that Stone was silent. And then, ten years ago, the tall eel came through, and we were amazed the Stone had awakened. The Karthus promised riches and trade, a great unity for our peoples, if our spearmen would come help fight his outlander war. But the Maitrohounet felt his lies, and she forbade us to join him. Then he tried bribes, emeralds. We did not want his useless gems, so he sent foreigners. They tried to take Ghellen, to break us with mind-bending magic. But the Tribes are bereft of *wyrria* now, and our minds could not be twisted. We battled with them, fierce and bloody. Some of them rode *diamantii*, great black scorpions of our sands, also found in Ghrec and the Unaligned Lands. Though the scorpion-riders fought well even without their mind-bending, they were few. And the Tribes are fierce in war, born to battle. Without their mind-breaking, the scorpion-riders failed."

Something in Olea went cold despite the heat. Memories from ten years ago flashed through her. The feel of crippling pain from the mind-touch of a man in herringbone leathers. Once in the forest outside Lintesh where he had ridden a massive black scorpion, and again when she was captured in Alrashesh. "These mind-breakers. Did they wear black leather armor in a herringbone weave?"

"You know them? You have felt their mind-snaring *wyrria*?" The Maitrohounet leaned forward.

"When I was a youth. Twice." Olea answered. "Men in herringbone leathers helped in a terrible purge of the Alrashemni in our nation. Those men assisted the atrocity." Olea gave a brief account of the King's Summons in Alrou-Mendera. Vargen and Aldris placed palms over their hearts as they listened. The Maitrohounet's gaze flicked to them, then to Jherrick, who was sober as the tale spilled out.

"We mourn the loss." The Maitrohounet sighed as Olea finished her tale. "We did not know our *wyrrics* still lived, and now to hear they are nearly gone…" She pressed a palm to her chest. "So heavy my heart. But you come back to us now. Yes. You come back to us."

"Does Lhaurent still bother your lands?" Aldris cut in, sipping his plum alcohol.

"Yes," Lourden answered, glancing to Aldris. "Though he does not come personally for many years, the tall eel sends curs from other nations, to raid our people through the Stones, to take slaves at night from all the Oases."

"Mercenaries."

"Just so. Paid dogs. So we watch the Stones, ready with many spears day and night. We send hawks to the other Oases when any Stone is active, so all Oases may marshal spears. We protect our people." Lourden turned his head and spat, his face a thundercloud.

Creeping unease rippled Olea's gut. "Lhaurent comes through all the Stones in the area? How many are there?"

"The Karthus came by himself first with his bribes, through all twelve Stones, to every Oasis. Now his dogs come for him, trying to steal slaves for his emerald mines and his Menderian war."

"*His* Menderian war." Olea thought she might be sick. Her world spun like a badly thrown top. Lhaurent den'Karthus had foreign mercenaries at his bidding, and he was culling foreign slaves through Alranstones. The Stones had their own agendas and seldom let people pass. But somehow, Lhaurent had convinced them to let him through. Aeon only knew how he had access to so many Stones, how he was getting them to send himself and his mercenaries through, and bring slaves back. And he was using those slaves to work in Menderian emerald mines and to fight in Alrou-Mendera's war.

Olea couldn't breathe. This treachery was so far beyond anything she and Alden had ever expected. Aldris, Jherrick, and Vargen rippled with a similar rage, bristling as if they were about to draw weapons upon their absent foe.

Aldris glanced at her, reached out and set a hand to her shoulder. "Are you ok, Olea?"

"I'm fine," she breathed. "I just… I had no idea how far Lhaurent's treachery extended. How deeply he was involved in all this." Olea glanced at Lourden. "The mind-breakers in herringbone leathers. Who are they?"

Lourden clucked his tongue, three sharp clicks of disapproval. "The Scorpions are Unaligned, from the wretched cold of the far north, past Ghrec. More than that, we know little. Only one was sent at first, then three. And when they could not break us, they sent nine, then thirty. But even thirty could not penetrate the minds of the *wyrria*-dead, a people bereft of magic, as we are here in the Tribes. In a way, we are thankful. We could not be broken. And though the thirty scorpion-riders and their foot-soldier brethren were tremendous fighters, my *Rishaaleth* drove them back through the Stone. They have not returned."

Olea exchanged a look with Aldris.

"This is bad, Olea." Aldris said, sober. "If this is true, then Lhaurent's marshaling armies of foreigners to do the Khehemni Lothren's bidding in Alrou-Mendera. *Armies.* The Shemout have long suspected him of unsavory treachery... but this?"

"Now you have proof." Lourden broke in. "Now you have the word of Ghellen's *Rishaaleth*. Our Maitrohounet sees the Karthus' heart. It is black."

Olea nodded, still reeling from the extent of Lhaurent's treachery. She'd never known he could have been amassing such power to aid the Khehemni Lothren. And she wondered, if Uhlas had found out about it, if that was why Lhaurent had poisoned him for the Lothren. In the light of recent events, the devastation of Queen Elyasin's coronation, the pieces suddenly fell into place for Olea.

"Whoever Lhaurent is, he operates alone," Olea murmured.

"Alone? Sounds like the bastard has plenty of allies," Aldris snarled, misunderstanding her. "Fucking eel does the Lothren's bidding, after all."

"Maybe he is allied with the Khehemni Lothren now, but he won't for long." Olea said, something deep inside her knowing that truth of it.

But the Maitrohounet nodded, understanding Olea's meaning. "Terrible men of great vision have no comrades. Only slaves. Dangerous slaves, uncertain alliances, cowed workers. When such men rise to power, they burn anything that arrests their way."

"They burn their bridges." Olea glanced to the Maitrohounet, who gave a subtle nod.

"He is a man… who believes." The Maitrohounet spoke.

"A zealot." Jherrick provided, leaning in with rapt interest.

"Indeed. And he is more than he seems, more than just an eel among sharks," the wise woman continued. "There is an ancient Prophecy in our lands, of the Uniter of the Tribes. One who will come upon the heels of the olive branch. The *Olea dihm Alrahel* is his herald, and opens the way for *wyrria*, the inborn magic of the Alrahel, to return to our lands. Uniting us all, righting ancient wrongs. The Uniter, the Rennkavi, will come in glory, Goldenmarked like the dawn to show his truth. This man, Lhaurent of the Karthus. He had Goldenmarks upon his flesh. And though we embraced him at first, thinking him to be our legend come alive, we came to see that he was black inside. Utterly black, like the darkest ocean. Like a night without stars, only desert demons. We would not follow him. We would not fight for his vision of so-called unity. It was a dark path. His own lust for power, not a true unity. But he believes in his task, and that makes the fire in him burn. So hot, it scorches all to char around him."

A deep silence fell about the bright room.

"Fucking hells." Aldris' murmur sliced the silence. He took an ample drink of his plum alcohol. "What is he doing in Alrou-Mendera? Is he trying to take the throne?"

Aldris' comment made the hair on the back of Olea's neck stand on end. "Not if I have anything to fucking say about it," Olea growled, vicious.

"Nor I," Vargen rumbled suddenly, his first exclamation this entire time.

The Maitrohounet straightened with a deep inhalation, spreading her palms in an encompassing gesture that included all her guests. "*Titha dihm titha semna hahni.* The enemy of my enemy is my friend. You are welcome in the Tribes, if you oppose this Karthus. He is our… how you say? Bane. Our bane."

"Fucking everyone's bane." Aldris snarled, downing his alcohol and holding it out for the young serving-girl to fill. He gestured for her to keep it coming, and she filled it to the brim.

"We feel your heaviness," The Maitrohounet sighed, "as terrible as the Shelf of Lost Hope. To find you, our *Alrashemnari* at last, and to hear such news. No *Alrashem* ever traveled with the eel."

"That's because Lhaurent is Khehemni-aligned," Aldris countered. "My organization, the Alrashemni Shemout, tracks their operations. But we had no idea Lhaurent's involvement was this extensive."

"Khehemni. You mention this word again." Lourden leaned forward, intense. "Are these people in your lands descendants of the Scions of Oasis Khehem?"

Olea had no answers. She glanced at the Maitrohounet. The wise woman's eyes flickered over them all. "A thousand years ago, the War of the Sun Tribes broke the hearts of the *Alrashemnari*, and they left us, taking their *wyrric* mysteries with them. They left when Oasis Khehem fell, devastated by a horrible war. It was rumored a Scion of Khehem's last King, Leith Alodwine, survived. That his daughter Alitha fled north through Ghrec with a few of Khehem's last warriors. They were hunted by the *Alrashem*, so that Leith Alodwine's atrocities could not spread through his last Scion, his only child."

"War of the Sun Tribes? What is that?" Olea asked.

A sad laugh came from the Maitrohounet's resonant throat. Fixing Olea in her clear grey eyes, she put a hand to her heart. "I shall tell you the story of the Sun Tribes. Of our fall, devastated by warring of Khehemni and *Alrashemnari*. You are our Lost Ones, after all, our *Alrashemnari*, and deserve to know your origins. But the name *Alrashemnari* did not originally mean Lost Ones. It meant Engraved Ones, their inborn magics honed via Chiron's teachings and engraved upon their hearts in beautiful Ink, just as it was engraved within their minds. But the Lost Ones have come home, and they have brought the Olive Branch of the Dawn. The Sun Tribes, who were once Thirteen yet now number Twelve, will be pardoned by the return of *wyrria* at last. But I am ahead of myself. We must go back. Back to the fall of Khehem, to the madness of Leith Alodwine, Khehem's last King."

Olea sat forward, rapt with attention, for this history she had never heard. From the way Vargen and Aldris leaned in, beverages forgotten, they had heard nothing of this either. All Olea had ever known was that the ancient Alrashemni had fled from a land far to the southeast, where war had torn their people apart. And now, as the Maitrohounet's resonant voice sighed around the airy room, palms rustling in the niches, Olea realized the story was deeper than she had known, and far sadder.

The Maitrohounet settled her hands in her lap and sat tall, surveying them with her clear grey eyes. "The history of the Sun Tribes, of this land," she began, "is a tale of beauty and heartbreak. Once, we were nomads. Our people formed tribes in the shifting deserts and wind-whipped mountains. War and raiding dominated our past, fighting over the oases that were our lifeblood. The most ancient *Alrashemnari* were wise men and women of the nomads, gifted with strange talents that ran in bloodlines, popping up here or there like desert Nightbloom. The *wyrria* were small at first, until our savior Chiron came to our shore. He taught the nomads how to develop their *wyrria* to enrich their lives.

"*Wyrric* magics can be strengthened by study?" Jherrick interrupted suddenly.

The Maitrohounet smiled at him, unperturbed by his question. "Indeed. Strengthened, changed, perfected. So the legends say. The nomads settled in the Thirteen Oases, adopting Chiron's ways of peace through the *Alrashemnari* he had trained. Warring and raiding turned into trade and cooperation, pacts and treaties and commonwealth laws. Each Oasis developed a special line of *wyrria*, became known as a center for the training of that line, for anyone in our vast continent with that gift."

"Others have such talents? In other nations? People unconnected with the Alrashemni or Khehemni?" It was Aldris who leaned forward now, interested.

"So it is said. Though I cannot confirm it," the Maitrohounet murmured sadly. "But from *wyrria,* the desert flourished, flooding with people from many nations for thousands of years. All came to learn from the *Alrashemnari,* our heart's pulse, who practiced the arts of Chiron. Eventually, their most accomplished formed the Order of Alrahel, the Order of the Dawn, priests and priestesses working toward a great harmony. Bringing us into a golden age lasting two thousand years, our Oases at last formed the Union of the Sun Tribes under the Order of Alrahel's leadership, a thousand years ago."

"Someone didn't like that, did they?" Aldris quaffed his drink, following the tale with hooded, dangerous eyes. "Someone resisted banding the nation together under centralized rule."

"One tribe," the Maitrohounet nodded, her tone dire, "Oasis Khehem, began to seed unrest. At the most prosperous oasis, the Thirteenth Tribe decided they did not wish to follow the Order of Alrahel. Their prince, Leith Alodwine, was descended from the *Werus et Khehem*, the Conflict of the Wolf and Dragon, a battle-*wyrria*. He was silver-tongued, fair-faced, fierce in war. Young Leith opposed the Order's yoke. The Order set a trap for him, and seeded their subsequent downfall. They imprisoned Leith for centuries, using him to train the Order's battle-*wyrrics*, until one came who set him free. Once Leith was freed, with the aid of his Queen-consort, the woman who had freed him, he slaughtered the Order in Khehem. He provoked war in the Sun Tribes, attacking his neighbors to roust out the Order in every oasis. The Alrahel tried every negotiation they knew. But he continued his campaign, overwhelming the smaller Tribes, interrupting trade to pressure the larger Oases into betraying the Order and giving up their names."

"The War of the Sun Tribes," Olea spoke. "It was started by Khehem. The Khehemni."

"Just so." The Maitrohounet nodded. "Chaos ensued. Ghellen was attacked, from which you see our broken walls, but we were not alone. King Leith Alodwine was too powerful with his battle-Queen by his side, and his army of *wyrrics*. But when all seemed lost, the Queen of Khehem took pity on the Alrahel. She betrayed her husband in a final battle that decimated Khehem utterly, that blackened its fair stone with char. She helped the Alrahel imprison Leith forever, it is said, in a sacred object at the heart of Khehem. An object from which he could see the outside world from his prison, but never touch it, ever again. So that he would always yearn like a hungry ghost."

"The ghost city." Olea said.

"The War of the Sun Tribes broke Khehem," the Maitrohounet continued sadly. "And it broke the hearts of the *Alrashemnari* to have been a part of so much bloodshed. Every child of the *Alrashemnari* had been trained to kill. Every member of the Order had used their *wyrria* for destruction. It brought the Sun Tribes to ruin to overcome Khehem, and caused the Thirteenth

Tribe's annihilation. And so, the Thirteen Tribes became Twelve. The spirit of the remaining *Alrashemnari* died with that war. Those few left gathered their sons and daughters and fled north over the mountains towards Ghrec, seeking a better life. It was rumored that some Khehemni also survived. Including the last Scion of Khehem, Alitha Alodwine, Leith's only daughter, who escaped the devastation and also went north."

"And all of them eventually wound up in our lands. Alrou-Mendera," Aldris interjected.

"How did the nation fare after such a terrible war?" Jherrick asked, riveted.

The Maitrohounet shrugged elegantly. "Without the peacekeeping of the Order, the Tribes learned to fear for their survival, for a time. They regressed into fractured parts, Twelve Tribes instead of Thirteen. But over the past thousand years, we have regained stability."

"But without *wyrria*." Jherrick interjected. "Without the magic that made your land flourish. That brought your golden age."

"Just so." The Maitrohounet sighed, taking a sip of water from her glass bowl. "The Twelve Tribes live with a deep misery, child. That we drove away our *wyrria* with such terrible kinslaying. That the hubris of our golden child Khehem caused the *Alrashemnari* of the Order of Alrahel to abandon us, making us fall from joy, hope, learning, and serenity. The Tribes remember what we have lost. And we carry with us a Prophecy that came out of Ghrec at that time. That a golden age would come again. That the last Scion of the Alrahel, a child of twinned blood from both Khehem and *Alrashem* would pardon the Thirteen Tribes and return *wyrria* to us. That their herald would carry an olive branch with the rising dawn, *Olea dihm Alrahel*. And that this would signify the coming of the *Rennkavi*, the Uniter of the Tribes, who would bring a lasting peace to every land."

Olea blinked, knowing that word, mentioned again. "Rennkavi? My brother Elohl said he'd had a dream atop an Alranstone, and the only word he remembered from it was Rennkavi. The night he had the dream, he was Inked by the Stone. All over his chest, shoulders, and back... engraved in gold."

The Maitrohounet startled, dropping the glass bowl of her

plum beverage. It bounced upon the carpet and rolled away, scooped up by her young attendant. The wise woman gaped at Olea, her grey eyes wide. "You know someone else who has been Goldenmarked? Someone other than Lhaurent den'Karthus?"

"Elohl den'Alrahel. My twin brother." Olea blinked. "Are you saying that Lhaurent has been marked in the same way as Elohl? Marked in gold by Alranstone also?"

"*Elohl dihm Alrahel.* The Rising of the Dawn. The dawn that will rise over the mountains." Both hands covered the Maitrohounet's mouth. Tears welled in her clear grey eyes and began to spill from her lids, tracking down her parchment-fine face. "Is a true Rennkavi come? Are we so blessed?"

"I *knew* the eel was no true Alrahel!" Lourden's baritone growled as he settled a steadying hand to the Maitrohounet's thin shoulder. "I told you he could not be the one! No matter that his name was Lhaurent den'Alrahel! No matter that he bore the Goldenmarks of the Rennkavi!"

Olea's world tilted sideways. "Lhaurent... but his last name is den'Karthus."

"No." Lourden's grey gaze swung to meet Olea's. "He named himself den'Karthus at first. But when he showed his Goldenmarks, when he revealed himself as the Rennkavi, the Uniter, he named himself true as den'Alrahel. Lhaurent den'Alrahel."

"*Den'Alrahel?* Lhaurent is *family* of yours, Olea?" Aldris interjected, gaping.

Olea's mind spiraled, thinking about the thin red leather tomes King Uhlas had once led her to find inside Roushenn's libraries. Two tomes that mentioned the Linea Alrahel, the original Line of Kings of Alrou-Mendera. Tomes that named Elohl and Olea's den'Alrahel line as closer by blood to the throne of their nation than Queen Elyasin den'Ildrian herself.

A bloodline that Lhaurent apparently shared.

Olea's gut dropped through her boots. She couldn't breathe. Her gaze swung to the Maitrohounet. Tears coursed down the old woman's face, and though her mouth worked, she could speak no more. She looked suddenly frail, old as her years, this great revelation shuddering her in small waves that made her body tremble. Lourden reached out, touching the wise woman's face in a kind, familiar Ghellani way. She closed her eyes, gathering herself with a slow breath, and at last nodded.

An unspoken agreement passed between them, and Lourden's hand fell away. Lourden reached over, touching fingers to Olea's elbow. "Come," he said. "The Maitrohounet must rest. Many things have been revealed today, and all need time to think. Stay again with my family tonight."

Stunned and wooden, Olea rose after Lourden, with Vargen and the rest following. She placed one hand on her Inkings before nodding and turning from the Maitrohounet, then ducked out beneath the woven reeds, hardly seeing the brightness of the late afternoon.

CHAPTER 8 – ELYASIN

Queen Elyasin den'Ildrian Alramir meandered a sprawling courtyard in Fhekran Palace, breathing in the cool summer air. She felt stronger today, almost like herself again. Luc's constant healings were more effective now that they were no longer on the road. Light and airy, a space for wandering and contemplation, the courtyard was in full bloom around her. No ornamentals sported their pretty little heads here. The beds interspersed with white stone paths held only edibles and medicinal herbs. Prickly telmen-vines climbed every wall, their white star-shaped flowers beginning to lose petals. It wouldn't be long before they had rich blue-black berries. The Elsthemi were a capable people, and Elyasin was learning that nothing went to waste in the Highlands. Not even a scrap of yard in the palace.

Movement stirred behind her. She turned to find her husband, King Therel Alramir, lounging against a stout pine roof-column. That high-gabled roof would shed heavy snows come winter, into deep melt-troughs that ran the circumference of the courtyard. Watching her in his lupine way, Therel leaned against the beam clad in what she was learning was his regular attire. No man for pomp, her King and husband wore a fine-spun wool shirt with a black leather jerkin and trousers, a shaggy grey wolf pelt around his shoulders. Even in the palace, he wore a sword at his hip, and his boots sported sheaths for knives upon the outside of his calves. The silver chain of a keshar-claw pendant worked in silver sigils dipped out of sight beneath his open shirt.

Therel's blue eyes pierced like daggers, wanting her. Flustered, Elyasin fidgeted with the wool of her trousers, clad as she was today in men's attire. Breeches and tan boots kept her warm in the chill air, a fawn jerkin and a soft white shirt with a white shrug of rabbit fur slung about her shoulders. She realized she had been staring for some time when he lifted one white-blonde eyebrow, questioning and daring.

"Therel." She kept her voice even, polite.

"Elyasin." His easy baritone was polite as hers.

She knew what he had done for her. All the Highswords were telling stories of it, each more preposterous than the last. Tales of Therel carrying her like a babe in arms as they raced to escape Roushenn. Lashing her to himself upon his saddle. Sleeping close at night, protecting her with weapons bared at the slightest movement in camp.

Therel had been dedicated, at her side night and day when he was not needed elsewhere, discussing the immense mess of their mutual political situation. Elyasin regarded him, and he stepped forward. His blue eyes were pale in the bright sun. His jaw had grown out with fair stubble, his white-blonde hair shaggy now from their week of hard travel. In all that time, he had done little in the way of advances, except touch her hair or cheek. Once they had arrived at Fhekran Palace, he had taken a separate room, giving Elyasin his own bedchamber.

Elyasin felt stalked as he came forward, though all he did was reach for her hand, lifting it to his lips. But his breath lingered, feral, and his thumb rubbed the back of her hand as he stared her down.

"How fares the sweetest of grapes today?" He spoke low.

Elyasin trembled, fidgeted with the knuckles of her free hand. Therel's presence drew her and unnerved her, as he had done ever since they had first locked eyes in Roushenn all those months ago. "The pain is better than yesterday. Your garden is lovely." She gestured to the vine. "Is this telmenberry?"

"Telmen is hardy. A survivor." He let her hand fall, fingers whispering past hers as he turned to regard the burgeoning vine. "Every winter, this vine is torn, mangled by heavy snows and falling icicles from the roof. And every spring, it grows back twice as strong. It never fails to enchant me with the most beautiful flowers. Their scent holds the essence of the berries to come. Here, smell."

Therel reached in, deftly maneuvering past quick-clinging thorns. Teasing out a floret, he brought it close to Elyasin's face. His hand brushed her neck to hold her hair away from the clutching vine. Elyasin shivered, inhaling deeply of the white blossom. A syrupy aroma rose to her nostrils, reminiscent of plums and thimbleberries. Elyasin lingered, drinking it in as Therel's touch whispered over her neck.

"They'll start with berries in a few days," Therel murmured. "At first they are hard and green, and then the darkening begins. Until they are black as death and sweet as midnight upon the tongue."

Elyasin straightened, eyes closed in rapture. Therel's touch was more seductive than anything they'd yet shared since the Elsthemi welcome feast at Roushenn. "With what does one enjoy telmen?"

"With whatever I like." Elyasin felt Therel release the vine, his touch caressing her neck to her collarbone. "Or with whatever you like."

"And would you eat telmen with whatever I like?"

"Anything." Therel stepped close to her back, murmuring in her ear. "You are my Queen, and for my Queen I would do anything. Anything except eating telmen with possum resin, or pickled keshar tongue. I hear those are quite atrocious."

Elyasin laughed, her eyes fluttering open at his sudden wit. She blinked, smiling, and turned towards Therel as he brushed her hair back over her shoulder. Gone was the sensation of a wolf in the darkness, replaced by a cocky raven, as he smiled at his own shiny humor.

"And would you eat telmen with pickled keshar tongue if I wanted to?" Elyasin intoned archly, lips quirking.

"Lady," his fingers stroked her neck again as he chuckled. "I would slaughter the cat and pickle it myself. Would you eat pickled keshar tongue for me?"

"I just might help you gut the cat and brine the vinegar." Elyasin countered. "We could try the first bite together. Then recommend it as a dish for your head cook."

"Ha!" It was Therel's turn to laugh, his pale eyes bright. "Well, cat-blood soup would help you recover your strength. But really, you only need blood-sausage to heal from such battle-wounds as you have taken, milady."

"So that's what it is!" Elyasin made a face. "Awful. I slip it to the wolfhounds, but Luc catches me and makes me eat it."

Therel grinned, scrubbing a hand through his white hair in a gesture that was at once rakish and shy. He offered his arm. Elyasin accepted and they began to meander. "Blood-sausage is awful. But there's nothing better to recover after being wounded."

"Have you ever been seriously wounded?" Elyasin asked. Therel didn't move like he'd ever been injured, but she had not yet seen him unclad. He had no obvious scars, except a few nicks upon his forearms and hands from training with blades. Scars that Elyasin herself had from her own training with Olea for so many years.

"I've been in my share of skirmishes," Therel nodded. "I was almost killed in an assassination attempt, like you. The woman got a knife in my back. It shivered across my rib and dug up under my shoulder blade. But I still had one arm free. Her mistake. I slit her throat and then lost my temper. I had a keshari polearm in my room and I hacked her limbs off and stuffed her in a trunk. I had nearly bled out by the time I was finished."

"So the rumors are true." Elyasin said, surprised but also unsurprised.

"Yes, the rumors are true!" Therel laughed, a bright, pleasant sound. "I stuffed a dead woman in a trunk. It's something of a joke, now. Father was on his deathbed, but he got out of it to walk down the hall and give me an earful as I lay in mine. I'd never heard him so brutal. He said if I died, I proved my *inanity*. Damned if I didn't drain every bowl of blood soup, determined to prove him wrong. Father got to die upon his deathbed with things, *as they damn well should be!* As he so delicately put it."

"And the other rumors? About your bed?" Elyasin had to ask. The innuendo she'd heard from Therel's Highswords was all too plain that Therel had been a cad in his youth.

Therel halted on the gravel path. Drawing her around to face him, his pale eyes were utterly honest. "Elyasin. Men and women take their pleasure in the Highlands. As a young man I allowed myself this freedom. Now that we are wed, I am prepared to be in your bed and yours alone, provided that we are well-met. But up here, what's done in a marriage is between husband and wife. If their needs are not well-met, they often agree to have open relations."

"And what if they disagree about such relations?"

Therel cocked his head, his pale brows furrowing. "Are you concerned we will not be compatible in lovemaking?"

Therel was far more plain in his speech here in the Highlands than he'd been in Alrou-Mendera. Elyasin's cheeks flamed, unused to men speaking so frankly. But it was the Highland way, to not mince words. Life was too hard in the northlands, too short.

"I've never... done this." Elyasin murmured, blushing furiously. "And you have."

Therel reached out, sober. He neither teased nor seduced as he grasped her hand. "I promise to be honest with you, Elyasin. To hear you out, to respect you. To be patient with whatever you need, however slow you wish to go."

"I don't want to go slow," Elyasin breathed.

Therel's smile was knowing, but strangely kind. "Here in the Highlands, men and women talk to each other, about everything. And talking it through, taking certain things slow and asking what one wants, figuring out what one needs, keeps relationships hale. Spouses respect each other's opinions, work as teams to survive the cold and the night, and the bedchamber. I need a woman who is a partner, not chattel. Not like other nations treat women. Queens can sit the throne in the Highlands without a King. And I will not abuse my position as either King or husband. I swear it."

"I didn't say that you would." Elyasin murmured, feeling shy, trumped. She fiddled with her knuckles violently, brushing them against the wool of her breeches.

Therel lifted a hand, touching her jaw, raising her chin so he could see her eyes. His demeanor had changed, something in him unsure. "Promise me something. As a wedding-gift?"

"And what is that?"

His pale eyes were earnest, and his words came out in a rush. "Promise that you will be honest with me. A man cannot read minds. Here in the Highlands, survival counts upon solving differences before they cause someone to be left out in the snow. Jealousies, anger, bitterness, remorse, all must be aired. If you need to work off any heat against me in the practice yard, I will let you. This *must* be a partnership. Please, Elyasin. If I do something, if I fuck this up——"

Something twisted Therel deep as he gazed into her eyes. Elyasin suddenly realized that he was worried he'd lose her. Her heart flooded with affection, bringing a smile to her face. Lacing her fingers through his, she clasped his hand.

"I will be honest with you, I swear it." Elyasin's lips quirked. "Besides, my temper is famous. If I'm tempted to boot you out in the snow, you'll know."

Therel laughed, a startled sound. He lowered his gaze, staring at their twined fingers. Moving his thumb, he caressed her palm gently. Elyasin shivered, ardor spiking through her. His eyes lifted, and the white in their blue ice burned. Lupine once more, he brushed a hand over her long golden braid, letting it linger at her collarbones.

"There's the hardy sweetgrape I was looking for," he spoke low. "I need a woman who's not afraid to fight for what she believes in, Elyasin. Or to fight me. I can be a hotheaded ass. I need a woman like a blade of steel to pierce my heart and pin me to the wall sometimes."

Their hands still clasped, Elyasin stepped closer. Therel took a short breath, eyebrows lifting in surprise. She lifted a hand to his jaw, stroking her fingers along his trim beard. "Do I pierce your heart, my King? Do I pin you to the wall?"

Seduction fell from his eyes. Therel actually swallowed, and for the first time, Elyasin saw his complete vulnerability, open and honest. "You pierce me like no one I've ever met."

Elyasin stretched up, kissing him lightly upon the mouth. She felt his breath stop. When she pulled away, his eyes were bright, fevered. "Were you serious about letting me work off heat in the practice yard, my King?"

A confused smile flitted across Therel's face. "I was, actually. You are welcome to wallop me with a stick anytime. If I misbehave."

"Would you bout your lady at swords today?" Elyasin's smile was cunning.

Therel's lips fell open in surprise. And then he grinned. "I was wondering about those blade-scars on your hands."

Elyasin smiled wider, pleased. "I trained with my Guard-Captain, Olea den'Alrahel, a Kingsman, since I was a small child. I am still weak, but I'm sure it will come back readily. Shall we adjourn to the practice yard?"

A smile spread across Therel's face. "This way," he offered his arm, "my hardy sweetgrape."

It was short walk to the outer doors that led to the wide swath of the practice grounds. Escorted upon Therel's arm, Elyasin found herself constantly distracted by the brush of his hip, the touch of his elbow at her waist. Therel did nothing untoward, and yet, she felt the tension between them hot like forge-sparks. When they arrived upon the practice grounds, stepping apart at the weapons racks near the wash-troughs, Elyasin shuddered in relief.

And disappointment. She wanted nothing like how badly she wanted to touch him. Elyasin rolled her shoulders and twisted into a stretch to distract herself from lustful urges, testing her wound. The scarred flesh in her side stretched, but held. Luc had done a spectacular job healing her, all things considered. The practice ground seethed with noise around them, groups of men and women fighting hard. The men were bare-chested in the mild mountain air, the women in short halters that bound their chests. No one seemed scandalized in the least. Men watched women spar, women watched the men. Men and women clashed in bouts together, all shuffling about the dusty yard, working hard to win the approval of their gods of war.

A roar of cheers went up from a nearby ring. Elyasin glanced over in time to see an ogre of a woman choking her sparring partner out beneath her armpit. Her triangle choke caused him to lose air while pinned to her ample bosoms. Though turning nearly purple now, he was choking out with a smile, and jeers went up around the ring.

"Ride him, Durstasya!"

"Lucky bastard!"

"Get a handful of those sweetmeats, Ghorin, before you're out!"

Whistles came from around the ring, as the choked man tried to get a hand up to fondle a boob. But then, he sagged to his knees and was released, sprawling unconscious onto his face in the dirt. The ample woman raised her arms to a chorus of rowdy cheers, then shook her shoulders to make her breasts jiggle. The cheering intensified dramatically.

Elyasin couldn't help but smile. Something in her ached to be as rowdy as the Highlanders. To be that raw with passion, all the time, fuck propriety. She began to shed clothes, readying for a fight.

Therel's gaze flicked to her as she slung off her rabbit-fur and unbuckled her tan leather jerkin, leaving only her shirt and binder beneath. Heat simmered in those fierce eyes, and Elyasin felt her body respond, alive with tingling tension.

Stripping away his wolf-pelt, jerkin and shirt, Therel gave a grin to see her watching him. Elyasin could not help but stare at how finely he was wrought, like a well-honed blade. Ornate Blackmarks decorated his chest, skirled through with script wrought in white, some ore in the pigment catching the sunlight like quartz. Therel left the silver keshar-claw pendant around his neck, as he went to select a blunted longsword from the wooden rack beneath the eaves. As he turned to lift swords from the rack, Elyasin saw the puckered white scar at his shoulder blade, from the assassin.

Wolf-whistles came from Therel's men, grinning to see their King and Queen upon the practice-grounds. Smiling with rakish delight, Therel took up his practice sword, then handed one to Elyasin, gesturing her to precede him to an unoccupied sand-ring. Elyasin took a moment to twist her golden hair back into a bun at her nape with a bit of leather, then strode forward confidently. She was weak, sore and stiff from so many days recovering, and it was time to limber up. Olea had taught her a limbering and strength routine, which she never failed to do in her chambers at Roushenn, but it had been weeks, and her body craved action.

Elyasin focused upon her opponent, studying him now with eyes that looked for weakness, not allure. Therel was taller, lean with muscle, but she could get in beneath his guard if she was fast enough. Elyasin readied her blunted longsword. Therel smirked, and then attacked. It was a lazy attack, bravado with no speed nor strength. He clearly didn't believe she could fight. Elyasin deflected it easily, her blade sliding over his to close upon his neck. Striding forward, she compacted a shoulder into his chest. Therel went off-balance in a huff of surprise, landing on his back in the dust with Elyasin's blade at his throat.

If they had been sharp, he'd have been missing half his neck. A huge uproar came from the yard, full of wolf-whistles, cheers, and laughter. Elyasin realized the sparring around them had ceased. Their bout was being watched with avid glee. Few of the Elsthemi had even seen their Queen yet, and a number of eyes were wide, smiles spreading across their faces.

Suddenly, Therel's boot swept Elyasin's feet out. She collapsed atop Therel, just as he wrested her blade away and flipped it, the edge at to her throat lightning fast.

Breathing hard in shock, Elyasin felt herself flush. Not from embarrassment, that she'd let herself get distracted by the crowd, but because she was now astride a man she had barely touched. And was now touching quite a lot of him. Therel rolled her to the dirt, atop her now, the edge of the dulled sword still at her neck. But he'd brought one knee up to roll her, and Elyasin had gotten her fingers on one of his boot-knives. Which was now planted, point firm and quite sharp, against his ribs. Therel's eyes flicked down as she pricked him, then back up with a fierce grin.

Roars of laughter progressed around the circle. Therel leaned in, sexual and close, his pale blue eyes burning. "My lady," he breathed, "I fear you have me at a disadvantage."

"Come now. Show me your Elsthemi fire, and I'll let you taste my Menderian grapes," Elyasin breathed back. Pulse pounding with fighting and heat, she lifted her head to brush her lips across his. Therel tried to kiss her, and she dug the knife in more, warning.

"Tease me, woman, and get more fire than your grapes can handle," Therel's eyes glittered with intrigue and lust. He chuckled, then pulled away, springing off her and offering her a hand up. Elyasin took it, and her King and husband hauled her out of the dirt. "Highlanders!!" Therel roared, spreading his arms wide. "Meet your new Queen! Elyasin den'Ildrian Alramir! Fiercest woman I've ever met!"

Another roar went up around the circle. Therel strode forward, pulling his other boot-knife from its sheath, pressing it into Elyasin's unarmed hand. "Keep them. They're yours. What better wedding present could I give you?"

"A sword." She held his gaze, firm. "I will not let myself be taken unarmed again. Not like Roushenn. Not ever again."

Therel bowed smoothly. He closed the distance between them, one hand sliding to her waist beneath her loose-fitting shirt. Elyasin pricked him again with one knife. "As my lady commands." He chuckled.

Therel turned to his Highlanders and beckoned, introducing

Elyasin to men and women all around. Most saluted with a hand to Inkings, but some only gave a traditional bow. Laughter went around, jokes about Therel's manhood and wedded bliss, speculation about whether they had been intimate. Elyasin blushed furiously, but held her head high. Meeting every eye, she laughed with the best of them, despite the pain lancing her side from her pulled wound. She strove to imitate how Alden had been with his men, clasping arms with the Elsthemi, loosening her Roushenn-bred formality. And found that the more she did, the more they liked her, a few women even slapping her on the back in camaraderie.

And then a stout man slapped her back, with a hearty, heavy hand. Pain lanced through Elyasin from her wound. She cried out under the blow, gritting her teeth. Her vision narrowed. Therel was there in a flash, a careful arm around her waist.

"My lord! My lady, forgive me!" A bear of a man with a wild black beard knelt in front of Elyasin, an anxious hand to his Inkings, worry in his eyes.

"It's all right, Darr." Therel said. "Elyasin, are you hurt?"

She shook her head, though one hand spasmed to her side, pressing the wound. Therel's eyes flashed to her hand, then to her eyes. Turning, he raised his voice, addressing the yard. "Elsthemi! The rumors you've heard are all true! I will be making a formal announcement later this week at the banquet, but you have the right to know, here and now. My Queen was stabbed most grievously on our wedding day, by my own First Sword! He was put down like a cur, no more than he deserved. Alrou-Mendera believes me at the center of this plot. They believe their Queen dead and are rallying against the Highlands. I'm afraid we will see war, my friends, and soon. Spread the word, start harvesting your summer fields and hone your weapons well. I do not wish for war, but the false rulers of Alrou-Mendera bring it to our doorstep, and we shall be ready! Until then, I must take my Queen to rest."

The yard fell silent, faces around Elyasin grim with fierce determination. In that Highlands way, every man and woman faced the certainty of war and death without blinking, standing tall and proud. A vicious wildness rippled through the throng around Elyasin, an untamable spirit. A voice shouted up suddenly from the back of the crowd.

"The sun rise on King Therel! The sun rise on Queen Elyasin! The sun rise on the Highlands!" As one, the entire yard echoed this sentiment with swords, knives, and polearms raised.

Elyasin saw it then, the loyalty of the Alrashemni. They were ready to die for Therel, their King, their leader, their kin. And now they were ready to die for her, their Queen. A great fierceness suddenly rose in Elyasin, echoing their chanted charge. Opening her hand, she pressed her palm to her chest in a traditional Alrashemni salute. And though she had no Inkings, they roared for her, saluting back, kneeling in a great wave.

"For my nation! And for yours!" Elyasin's heart spilled out with her words, in a ferocious battle-yell. "For all of you, and for my people! We will have truth! We will have justice! And when justice is done, we will have unity, and peace! This I swear to you upon my blood!"

Fervor had taken Elyasin. Lifting one of Therel's knives, she scored it across her chest. Not deep, but enough to cut true. Blood beaded. Elyasin lifted the blade to her lips, wild with the moment, tasting her blood's iron tang. Highlanders roared, coming to their feet. Therel stared at her, hard and ready. Elyasin reached out and gripped his hand. He gripped back. A snarl of a smile came to his lips.

He raised their clasped hands, roaring, "For justice! For truth! For unity! For peace!"

The Highlands roared. Together, the King and Queen turned as one, striding from the dusty practice yards, the roar of battle filling Elyasin's ears. Collecting their garb under the eaves but not bothering to dress, they walked hand in hand through the arched timbers of Fhekran Palace, back to Elyasin's rooms. But she stumbled suddenly from the pain gnawing her side. Elyasin glanced down. Red oozed out beneath her shirt.

"Come on. Back to Luc." Therel stepped close. In one smooth motion, he swept her into his arms. Elyasin grit her teeth as he carried her back to his rooms and kicked the door open. A door to an adjacent room was open nearly as fast, the healer Luc den'Lhorissian striding in, his golden-handsome visage lined with concern. Simmering at her weakness, Elyasin succumbed to Luc's ministrations. As his healing hands smoothed over her, Elyasin set her jaw, promising herself she would be stronger.

Day by day, she would be stronger for her people.

Luc's healing ceased at last, leaving Elyasin in a deep state of rest, eyes closed. She felt him withdraw from the chamber. A light rain began upon the roof, then drummed harder, windowpanes rumbling with a roll of late-summer thunder.

Elyasin knew she slept, and yet, she could see the room as if awake. Therel dozed in a chair by the fireplace, the logs burned down to coals. A flash of lightning lit the gloom suddenly. A naked woman stood beside the bed, revealed in the lightning's swath. Curvaceous and lovely, white waves of hair tumbled over her breasts to her navel. Luminous silver, white, and purple Inkings swirled over her skin in arcane glyphs and an unknown script. Arresting, penetrating, her eyes were the deepest cerulean Elyasin had ever seen. A white keshar-claw pendant dangled between her breasts, flaming with fire opal, amethyst, and onyx. Before the light of the bolt died, she reached forward, pressing a palm swiftly to Elyasin's heart.

Ice flooded Elyasin's veins, the cold ice of glaciers. Followed by fire, the fire of deserts aflame.

Elyasin startled awake, the name *Morvein* echoing off the beams from her shout. Therel came instantly awake, rising from his chair to come soothe her. The woman was gone from the bedside, if she had ever been there at all. But thunder still rattled the foundations of Lhen Fhekran, and the potency of that touch still raged through Elyasin's heart.

CHAPTER 9 – ELOHL

It was the third night in a row that Fenton had stumbled in well after dawn. Mumbling hello to Elohl, who was already up and breakfasted, he crossed through to his room without bothering to close the door. Elohl heard him flop down on his bed. Elohl smiled as he continued inspecting his sword. He glanced down the line of the blade looking for imperfections, watching the early summer sunlight flow along it in all its myriad colors through the windows.

"She's going to kill you, you know." Elohl raised his voice so he could be heard in the other room.

"Mmmph!" Came Fenton's muffled response from the blankets.

Elohl smiled wider. "No one can fuck like that every night and be ready to cross the Valenghian border in a few days."

A rustle of sheets came, and then a rumpled Fenton leaned in the doorframe, golden-chocolate eyes alight. "She can. I think she could fuck all night, every night, and be fresh for battle in the morning. Is there any breakfast left?"

Elohl nodded to the tray upon the table. "Help yourself."

Fenton glided to the table. He proceeded to take everything and bring it to his seat, beginning to eat before the dishes left the sleek red cendarie wood. Elohl had never seen anyone eat so much, but Fenton ate like this day after day, as if making up for starvation in his wire-taught frame.

"Mmph... she is..." Fenton said between bites. "Absolutely incredible...!" He picked through the meats, another piece of guinea-fowl disappearing. "If you know what I mean."

Elohl laughed, running clove oil along his blade with a thin cloth. He'd never seen the quiet Fenton so lighthearted. Granted, he didn't know the man well, but it seemed Olea had chosen a man who was sober and level-headed to be her good right hand.

"Don't eat it all, keshar!" Elohl chuckled.

Fenton slathered a piece of crusty bread with telmen chutney.

"Woman like that gives a man an appetite! Besides, we can raid the pantry anytime. I've already been with Merra. She loves raiding the kitchens in the middle of the night. To get more fuel for the furnace in her thighs."

Elohl eyed Fenton, smiling, enjoying their banter. "She'd probably enjoy riding her keshar down to the kitchens to raid the pantry for you. In between riding you."

"She'd probably do it buck-ass nude, too. Fully expecting a crowd of worshippers in the hall." Fenton chuckled, a knowing grin spreading across his face as he took another bite.

"Details." Elohl wiped his sword again, smiling.

"Uh, uh." Fenton shook his head, his brown eyes glinting merrily. "A gentleman does not brag."

Elohl lifted the tip of his blade, snugging it up under Fenton's jawbone. "Details."

Fenton grinned wider, merely putting another piece of bread in his mouth. "Slit my throat, Elohl, but I'll die with those secrets burned in right beside my Inkings unless you command me otherwise."

Elohl laughed, lowering the blade. Giving his sword one last rub with the cloth, he admired its long line, sliding it away into its scabbard. He set the scabbard aside upon the table. "Word's getting around about you and the High General."

Fenton chuckled smoothly. "Let it! I'll take my pleasure and say thank you when she's done with me. But a woman like that doesn't keep men for long." His words were cavalier, but his blithe demeanor faded around the edges. Fenton picked at his plate suddenly, moving items around upon it with his fingers.

"You think she'll give you up?" Elohl reached out for the water-pitcher, pouring for them both.

"She'll have to." Fenton's hand slid away from his plate. "We're crossing into Valenghia in a few days. The King and Queen are getting anxious to make their position known to my contacts in the bog. Merra already gave me their seals." Fenton patted his doublet. He sighed, a resolute sound, and looked up. "You ready? We've got cat-practice in ten minutes."

Elohl eyed him. "You sure? You didn't get any sleep."

"I got a little. In between." Fenton smiled, darkly pleased.

"In between her thighs?" Elohl grinned.

Fenton chuckled, giving no answer. He stood from his chair and took a long stretch. "Ready?"

"As I'll ever be."

Elohl buckled on his baldric. They were out the door in minutes. Making their way at a brisk pace, they navigated the palace, already bustling with dawn's activities. Exiting through a side-door, they marched down a short slope to the cat-paddocks. A group of keshari riders and Highswords were there already, and Elohl recognized tall orange-haired Jhonen waving them over.

"Lads!" Jhonen barked. "Elohl! Come meet yer cat-master! Jhennria Dhukrein, the palace's Keshar-Keeper and Master Trainer. Jhennria, Elohl den'Alrahel, First-Lieutenant Brigadier and Kingsman."

Elohl gripped wrists with the petite Master Trainer. Black-haired and full of spitfire, Jhennria couldn't have been eight stone soaking wet. A nasty set of scars raked across her face, though her eyes and full lips were undamaged. But there was a lithe bounce in her step and a hard glint in her piercing blue eyes as she regarded him.

With a grunt, she turned to Fenton and clasped wrists. "Fenton, good ta see you again."

"Jhennria." Fenton had met his cat Vhesh the day before and had earned her trust. But today was Elohl's first day, as Jhennria apparently insisted on doing only one cat-introduction per day.

"Right! Let's git to it!" Jhennria barked. "Slide through the poles, gents! Fenton, mount up on Vhesh, take her through her paces! Elohl, let's introduce ye to yer mount."

Jhennria gestured and Elohl and Fenton slid through the pine poles of the paddock behind the cat-cradles. Elohl was gestured to a massive tawny beast, Fenton to a buttercream cat with a black nose. As Elohl approached his cat, it lashed its long tail in warning. At the sides of the paddock's beams, Elsthemi warriors and keshari women crooned in amusement. Laughing softly, the Elsthemi in their leather and furs mounted the fences and sat watching Elohl and the keshar like they watched a bullfight. Fenton was already mounted up, doing circles around the paddock's far side. But today was Elohl's first meeting with his cat, and all the attention of the spectacle was on him.

"Right!" Jhennria's voice was clipped, though soft. "Approach yer beast, quiet like. Introducing a keshar to a new rider is a delicate affair, requiring quietude and *patience*. Respect. Men get their heads bit off if an introduction goes badly, ye ken? Or if bystanders are too loud." She shot a warning glance at the Elsthemi sitting on the paddock poles.

Irreverent chuckles followed her words, low whistles, though all were done softly.

Elohl focused on the beast before him, ignoring the Highlanders. Focusing upon the great cat, he projected peace, calm. Saddled by a harness that went around the chest and under the belly, a woven leather bridle about its ears already, the cat stood taller at its lithe shoulders than Elohl, nearly the size of a grown black bear. The color of wheat under a dappled forest sun, the formidable feline turned its flat, bulky head to regard him.

"Hand out." Jhennria prompted. "Let her sniff ye, hold very still. Goes on a while, so let it. Any shiver of fear puts 'em in a mood to hunt, so stand strong. Either ye get a rub or a growl. Men often get a growl from male cats, but rare from females. Thitsi here is a female. She generally likes men, but if ye get a growl, back off slow. An' git straight outta the paddock, ye ken?"

Not trusting his words, Elohl nodded. The tawny cat stared Elohl full in the face with suspicious golden eyes as he put a hand out for it to sniff. Arm-length black whiskers brushed his palm. Lifting its massive head, black fangs the size of Elohl's forearm protruded from beneath its upper lips as it stretched its muscled neck and began to sniff his face. The sniffing continued a while, roaming Elohl's face, then his body, sniffing at his groin down to his boots and back up. Whiskers at his face once more, ebony fangs brushed Elohl's jaw and neck. He held perfectly still, watching the cat's massive jaws, her enormous skull wider than his head.

At last, the she-cat gave a strangled yowl. She bumped her head against Elohl's with such shocking force that it knocked him backwards a step. Elohl breathed out in relief.

"Good," Jhennria crooned. "Step on close, cheek ta cheek. Let her mark ye."

Its approval won, it allowed Elohl to draw near. Putting his face to her whiskered cheek, Elohl did as he'd been instructed and rubbed his cheek against hers. The cheek rubbing went on a long time. First one side, then the other, the massive cat wiped saliva all over his face and hair. At length, a deep thrumming sounded in its throat. Elohl reached up, running his fingers through the sleek fur around the cat's neck, scratching behind its ears.

Which got him salivated on further. Drooled on, really. Gentle whistles sounded from around the paddock, low laughs.

"Good..." Jhennria crooned in a singsong. "Thitsi likes ye. Ye'll be a good match, like her last two riders."

"Who were her last two riders?" Elohl said in a soothing lilt like Jhennria's, chancing a glance at her as he continued scratching the cat.

"Strong men. Great warriors." Jhennria beamed with a classic Highlander smile of battle-readiness. "Ye should be thankful, Brigadier. Thitsi never suffers to bear the weak. She only carries men of prowess. General Merra had an inkling the two of ye would get along. So!" She gave Elohl a cheeky wink and a slap to the butt. "Mount up!"

Elohl set his hands to the high saddle-horn, gripping the reins. Setting his foot in the woven leather stirrup, he slung up, not unlike mounting a horse. Though this beast of the northern wilds was taller by a hand than any stallion he'd ever ridden. Thitsi shivered her tawny fur at his mounting, but was peaceable, turning her head for a bored lick at her shoulder. She then reached both front paws out in a massive stretch, extending claws longer than Elohl's hands, gripping the earth. Ripping rents, she scratched at the hard-packed ground like a house cat upon furniture, muscle rippling in her rolling shoulders. Elohl was flung forwards in the saddle, barely managing to stay upright. He'd finally readjusted to the rolling muscle in the cat's back, when she suddenly lay down on her belly.

Bored, her tail tip flicked in the dust of the paddock.

Jhennria burst into laughter. "Thitsi! Is that any way to treat yer new friend? Up, ye lazy beast! *Tsit, tsit!*"

The great cat gave her Master Trainer a suffering eye, then languidly rolled her shoulders and haunches and got back to her feet. Adjusting in the saddle, Elohl could feel the power of those muscles beneath him. The cat shifted its weight, and the sensation was liquid, like a boat upon the ocean.

Jhennria reached out, scratching the great beast under her whiskered chin. "There, now, don't look at me like that. Elohl is your rider now. Take care of him like ye did Ghoren and Rhugen."

Elohl cleared his throat. "What happened to Ghoren and Rhugen?"

"Not a cat-accident, if that's what yer thinking!"Jhennria laughed. "Thitsi is very protective of riders she likes. And she's fast. Flip those reins, let's take her for a stretch. And hold on!"

Elohl did as he was told, twitching the reins lightly. Which apparently wasn't lightly enough. The great cat leapt into the air from perfect idleness, a jump of nearly six feet that resulted in Elohl flying off backwards over her haunches and hitting the packed dirt, hard. Breath driven from him, he coughed, eyes stinging with pain and not a little embarrassment. The crowd around the paddock roared, able to be loud now that Thitsi and Elohl were acquainted. Elohl saw coin exchanging hands as Highlanders jostled and clapped each other upon the shoulders.

Jhennria shrilled laughter as she came to offer him a hand up, wiping away tears of mirth. "Brenner's Fire! Men are so daft with cats!"

Elohl took the proffered hand, a half-grin on his face, enjoying the joke though his ass and spine hurt like Halsos' Burnwater. He brushed himself off, then took a bow towards the rails. Cheering exploded, wolf-whistles. Elohl faced his cat, seeing that Thitsi had settled right back into her bored repose. Upon her belly in the dust, she watched him with mild interest in those great golden eyes.

"So what am I supposed to do with the reins?" Elohl lifted an eyebrow at Jhennria.

"Not flip them like she's some some fool-damned *horse!*" She clapped him upon the shoulder. "Lesson one, Lowlander: *release pressure* on the reins with your fingers, and on the cat's middle with your thighs when ye want a keshar to walk. Gather pressure *slightly* for a stop, or ye'll get a rearing attack. Left turn is a gathering of the fingers with the left hand and a slight twist of the torso left, right turn is the same to the right. The longer ye hold it, the more they'll turn fer a tight battle-spin. Keshar are *sensitive!* Flip or smack or gouge with heels, or Brenner forbid *spurs*, and ye'll have a very hateful cat. And a hateful cat means a bite, a mauling, or worse."

"Worse?" Elohl said. "How much worse?"

Jhennria sobered. The petite Master Trainer got right in his face. "Ever seen a house cat play with its food? Imagine that happening to you. And if that happens, ye'll get a blow-dart in the neck if we kin manage it. A relatively easy death. The cat will get six. We can't keep cats that go rogue. If ye cause a cat to become mean, yer responsible fer its death and fer yer own. And fer any other Highlanders a rogue cat kills before it kin be put down. Remember that."

Elohl placed a hand to his Inkings. Jhennria nodded, then grinned. "So, then. Ye gonna let Thitsi get the best of ye like that?"

Elohl turned to re-mount the great cat. But a shout from Jhennria stopped him. "Approach slow! *Always* approach slow, until ye've ridden her twenty times at least. Until yer scent is what she breathes day in and day out."

Elohl walked much slower, coming to stand before Thitsi. The keshar snuffled his face, then slammed him affectionately with her head. The saliva ritual began again. At last, Elohl mounted up, though it was easier with the great cat lying down. This time, he set his hands at the pommel and gently eased his hold on the traces with his fingertips. Thitsi immediately knew what he wanted. She rolled to her feet and prowled forward, slow and liquid.

Elohl had never felt anything move like this. She flowed beneath him like water over smooth river stones, her gait undulating and loose. It was a blissful sensation, smooth and liquid. He closed the fingers of his left hand on the traces, twisting slightly in the saddle, and Thitsi angled left. He tried the right, then took her in a tight circle. Thitsi was calm, used to riders, and her every movement spoke of boredom. At Jhennria's go-ahead, Elohl urged the great keshar into a liquid trot.

"Take her into a war-maneuver! Squeeze yer legs an' flip the reins! Forward pounce!" Jhennria called from the paddock's edge.

Elohl braced with his legs upon the ridged saddle, squeezed hard, flipped the reins. Thitsi responded immediately, leaping ten feet as Elohl flattened over her shoulders, high enough to have pounced upon a horse and rider. It was breathtaking. Elohl's stomach lurched in excitement. Her landing was as soft as her leap.

Elohl led her into a few tight turns, then made her do a fast twisting leap after Jhennria explained his cues.

"Ach, ye!" Jhennria called out from atop her own beast now, a dappled roan cat the color of autumnal leaves. "Take her out, Lowlander! Circle the side of the palace, then come back! I'll join ye shortly. We'll do the grooming-rituals to solidify yer bond this afternoon, but know that Thitsi's well and truly acquainted to ye now. She'll no buck nor bite, though she might swipe a warning if ye piss on her good sensibilities! So! Off ye go!"

The gate to the paddock was hauled open by a few brawny lads and women keshari riders. Elohl ambled his cat out to whistles, but the spectacle was over. Highlanders dispersed as he strolled the great tawny cat around the side of the vaulted timbers of Fhekran Palace. After a minute of ambling, he saw Fenton upon his grey-speckled beast stalking back to the cat-cradle.

"Ho, Elohl!" Fenton moved his reins to one hand, a grin splitting his placid face, his cat halting by Elohl's. "If I'd known how pleasant this was, I'd never have wasted time riding horses!"

The two she-cats were friendly, bumping heads and nuzzling faces, thrumming in their throats. Elohl laughed, gesturing at the beasts. "Horses don't rub spittle all over you before you ride them, though."

Fenton gave a secretive grin. "Keshar are like women. You need elaborate rituals to mount them."

Elohl raised an eyebrow, grinning wider. "Are we still talking about keshar, or a certain woman who's been keeping you up at night?"

A laugh bubbled out of Fenton, spontaneous and free. He was about to reply when Jhennria rode up at a stalking trot. "Ready to stretch their legs?"

Elohl blinked. "Haven't we already?"

Jhennria's smile was reckless. "Follow me, gents. There's a back gate down to the river-run, reserved just to exercise the cats. You think horses run fast? Think again."

With that, she spun her cat in a tight circle and dashed away. Fenton grinned, and he was after her in a flash.

"Alright you," Elohl leaned down, speaking low next to Thitsi's ear. "They say you're fast. Let's see what you're made of."

He'd hardly loosened his fingers when the great keshar leapt forward with fantastic speed, muscles bunching and rippling beneath her short tawny fur. Eager to join the chase they passed the palace and flashed out the back gate through a copse of pine and down to the river. Thitsi chased down Fenton's cat and passed it, then caught up to Jhennria's. Jhennria gave a triumphant laugh as Elohl passed her also, dashing to the river's edge. She flagged him down. Elohl made a small grip of his left fingertips, and Thitsi turned on a dime. He gripped the fingers of both hands in a short gesture, and she stopped flat, Elohl managing to keep his seat this time.

It was exhilarating. They took the cats through their paces for another half-hour, until Jhennria had led them through a multitude of battle-maneuvers and even broken out polearms, the main weapon they would use fighting from the saddle. Both men were in high spirits as practice ended and they returned to the paddock, and Thitsi rewarded Elohl by a copious session of cheek-rubbing, coating him in saliva.

They were just finishing up, corralling their cats back in the cradle, when Jhonen came walking briskly down from the palace, hailing them with a wave. "Kingsmen!" She shouted. "General Merra wants a word!"

"We're done here." Jhennria flashed Fenton and Elohl a smile as she secured the paddock poles. "Go. Be back tomorrow, same time. Today was short, lads. Tomorrow, we'll have all day. Rest up."

The wink Jhennria gave Fenton was not lost on Elohl.

Jhonen strode up with a whistle. "Lads! Let's go!"

They turned from the cat-paddocks, marching up the slope to the palace doors, with a brief wash of faces at the water-trough to get rid of cat saliva. With Jhonen in the lead, they soon arrived at General Merra's quarters. Jhonen took her leave, and Fenton and Elohl pushed in through the carven double-doors. Merra was lounging inside, wearing only a robe of sleek black ermine-fur, which left her cleavage artfully bared. She gestured to the pillows, then to the wine, a goblet to hand. Fenton settled beside her, but politely declined wine with a shake of his head. Elohl had the feeling he'd already quaffed plenty the previous three nights, when he had disappeared into Merra's rooms and not escaped until dawn.

Elohl settled to the cushions and accepted a goblet. General

Merra filled it and he nodded his thanks, then settled back into a cushion.

"So," Merra's ice-blue eyes were piercing, "you two louts believe you can ride with the keshari?"

Elohl nodded. "Cat practice went well this morning. So if it's the best way to get us across the mountains, we'll manage."

"Being out on the ride isn't like being here in Lhen Fhekran. Therel has domain over his nation. I have domain over my riders. Will you obey my commands as we travel?" Merra sipped her wine, gauging them.

"If your commands suit us," Fenton responded, level but non-apologetic.

Merra's eyes flashed at her lover. She gazed at him a long while, weighing him. Suddenly, her free hand flashed to her bosom, flicking a keen throwing knife hidden in her cleavage straight at Elohl. Elohl's sensate sphere flared and he moved on instinct, dodging her keshar's strike. The blade hit the far wall and clattered away.

"You invited us here to *test* me?" Elohl half-rose, incredulous and furious.

"Peace, Brigadier!" Merra made a calming gesture, inviting him to sit back down. "Therel told me about your talents, but I needed to see them for myself." Merra drew another fly-blade from her bosom, but this one she pressed into Fenton's palm. "Throw it. If he can sense your throw like he did mine, he'll be able to evade it."

Fenton's gaze flickered to Elohl, and they locked eyes. And in that moment of hesitation, Elohl knew to his very bones that Fenton was faster than he was. The man had some gift he wouldn't talk about, that allowed him to get past Elohl's senses, just as he'd done in the practice yards during the *jherra*-fight. Elohl's golden Inkings prickled like marching ants, up over his shoulders and down his spine.

Fenton's gaze hardened. "I've sworn to protect Elohl, Merra. Not skewer him."

She was up on her knees in her ermine robe, a thoughtful glimmer in her eyes. "You think you're faster than a man with premonitions of where his attacker will move. Show me."

"We don't need knives for that."

Faster than thought, Fenton's hand snapped out, cracking Elohl across the jaw in a stout slap. Elohl hadn't felt it in his sensate sphere. Not a tingle, not a whisper. He hadn't even seen Fenton's hand flash until it was too late. Yet again, Fenton had managed to avoid Elohl's natural protection.

And yet again, Elohl realized how little he knew about the man.

"How did you do that?" Fear raced through Elohl along with a shocked adrenaline as he rubbed his jaw.

"Practice." Fenton's golden-shot eyes held secrets. Something dangerous moved behind those eyes, and a trick of the light made them flash red. Elohl felt the man's presence intensify, though he couldn't have said how. Elohl opened his jaw and popped his ears, as if a storm had changed the pressure in the air. His golden Inkings surged, a quick throb that cascaded with prickles.

"What a pair of ronins!" Merra burst into laughter, nearly spilling her wine. She gestured to the goblets. "Please! Drink. Mounting up with my riders is no little thing. Therel has tested you, and now so have I. He trusts you, now I shall. My White Claws and Split Fangs will deliver you up over the Devil's Field. Be cautious: we must assume our ranks have been infiltrated with Khehemni, and they may be flushed out as we ride. But I tell you this. If you find evidence of traitors among my riders as we travel, they will be judged and executed by me and me alone. Not your Queen. Not Therel. And if I find that either of you is a traitor… then no amount of special talents will save you from my law."

Elohl inclined his head. "General. Your riders. Your justice."

"Indeed." General Merra's icy eyes pierced like claws. They moved from Elohl to Fenton, and settled upon the Guardsman a very long moment. At last, she drained her goblet and rose. "Gentlemen. We have much to do. In three days' time, we ride. So. Welcome to the keshari riders."

Fenton breathed a soft sigh as he and Elohl rose from the cushions. And Elohl wondered, suddenly, if this meeting hadn't been more a test to gauge Fenton's hidden abilities than Elohl's. He was still pondering that when Merra opened her robe and let it spill to the floor. Buck-nude, she reached for leather leggings and a chest-halter upon a chair as if no one else was in the room. Elohl turned his back in haste, heat rising to his cheeks.

Suddenly, a tingle lanced up Elohl's neck. He flinched sideways, just in time for a throwing knife to whir past his neck and bury itself in the woodwork of the door. He whirled, half-drawing his blade. But Merra was laughing as she buckled her leather jerkin and slid into a brace of knives, throwing her snowy pelt across her shoulders. She was still chuckling as she pulled on boots, then stood.

"Come! Idle cocks are not permitted among my riders!" Lithe as a keshar, General Merra Alramir strode to the door and hauled it open, disappearing into the hall.

CHAPTER 10 – TEMLIN

Temlin was good and drunk. Raising a mug to his lips as he shuffled through the First Abbey's halls, he tasted frothy summer ale like honey on his tongue. He couldn't recall how many days it had been since the coronation or the executions. One day of ale and vague memories had swigged itself right into another. Puking in a gutter as bells tolled. Falling asleep in a paddock to the bleat of goat. Laughing with a foreign man in black herringbone leathers, clinking mugs in a tavern.

Daytime was hateful as Temlin staggered through the First Abbey's vaulted bluestone halls toward Abbott Lhem's apartments in the Annex. Sunlight filtered in through colored glass windows of saints in their cupolas, searing his eyes, accusing him with their benevolent silence. He had been summoned today, he was certain, because of his unceasing bender. Temlin pushed brashly through the heavy ironbound doors of Lhem's apartments without knocking. A meal sat upon Lhem's stout desk, pointedly waiting for him with a tall glass of water. Temlin collapsed in the overstuffed chair across from Lhem and pushed the plate away.

"I'm not hungry."

"You've been drinking all week since the executions. Good gods, man, don't think I can't smell it on you! Eat." Lhem reached out and snagged Temlin's mug of ale, then dumped it out in a potted plant nearby. He pushed the food back. Temlin sighed and had a long draught of water, then took a hunk of bread, mopping it in roast chicken gravy.

"There. Happy?" Temlin spoke around his mouthful. "How is our seer girl?"

"Ghrenna's still unconscious. Eleshen is downstairs with her." Lhem eyed him critically.

"She's dying. Just like my niece. The last of my own blood." Temlin tossed the bread to the plate.

"Some battles we lose, Temlin." Lhem's ruddy face was set in hard lines. "I know the drink has you right now, but we need to discuss state matters. The King's Chancellate are asking the Abbey to be involved in the war on Elsthemen. And they want to search the Abbey for Elsthemi fugitives."

"Absolutely not." Temlin snapped.

"I agree." Brother Lhem spoke slowly. "But the Chancellate are putting pressure on us, threatening to cut off our grain shipments if we don't comply. We need to think out our next step. Fenton and Aldris are both vanished, but I heard from palace rumor that Fenton went with King Alramir and our dead Queen. Along with the Goldenmarked Elohl den'Alrahel."

"Elyasin's not dead!" Temlin slurred.

"Perhaps not, but we *must* plan our next move." A heavy hand settled upon Temlin's shoulder. Somehow Lhem had gotten up, walked around the desk, and stood beside Temlin now. "I summoned you today because I need you to travel through the Abbeystone, Temlin. I need to know what Molli's Seen in the past two years since Uhlas died. So we know how to maneuver all this."

"You want me to go through the Abbeystone." Temlin's gut fell through his feet, the ale in his belly curdling like sour milk. "Lhem. You know what that bastard Stone does to me. The last time you asked me to try and go through to Molli... it almost killed me. I was laid up in the infirmary for three weeks."

"Temlin." Lhem sat his ample bulk upon the edge of the desk. "We need to save Ghrenna, and we need prophesy. You must get through to Molli. We need to know what the right move is in all this chaos."

"No." Temlin's voice was a whisper now, remembering the horrible nightmare he had endured the last time he'd tried to travel through. Fear roiled through him, sensations of unimaginable pain. "I can't, Lhem. The Abbeystone could kill me this time. It doesn't care about my flesh, my body, or my sanity. Asking me to do this... could be a death sentence for me."

Lhem's stout hand settled upon his shoulder. "Temlin. I need you to do this for the Shemout. It's not a request. Even if you can't get through, I need you to try."

"Even trying could kill me."

"Still."

Temlin was far too sober now. The Stone hadn't worked for two years, and Lhem knew it as well as Temlin did. And the one time Temlin had tried to get through to Molli, it had almost been the end of him. But he was backed into a corner. Ghrenna was dying and Molli could save her. Prophesy from Molli could hold a key to blocking the Khehemni Lothren from this power play.

Prophesy from Molli could tell Temlin if Elyasin was alive.

Temlin spread his hands in a bitter mock-bow. "My liege. When do you want me to serve up my lifeblood upon this platter?"

"Cut the crap, Temlin!" Lhem barked. "You weren't accepted into the Shemout to be a bitter old bastard! Don't lapse back into being a surly drunk, skunked to the Crasos Canals! You know that Abbeystone only lets den'Ildrian blood travel through, other than Molli. Please. Do something useful for us, that only you can do, Scion of Kings."

"I didn't want this life, Lhem. I never wanted any of this..." Temlin sighed, running his hands through his greying red mane. He rubbed his eyes, then glanced at his plate. If he touched the Abbeystone again, it might just be his last meal. The last meal of a dead would-be King. He sopped the rest of the bread in gravy and slathered on a pat of butter.

"Fine. Let's go."

Lhem moved his bulk to the doorway to the Abbeystone, and Temlin followed. Pacing down a spiral stairwell, they came to a cavernous grotto far beneath the Abbey. Wan crimson light flooded from the granite byrunstone Plinth at the center of the room. The Abbeystone stood massive in the vaulted underground chamber, inert save for a bloody eye half-lidded near the bottom. Lamps had been lit, and a bed brought down so the unconscious Ghrenna den'Tanuk could be near the Stone in case it could somehow heal her.

It had done nothing for her yet.

Honey-blonde Eleshen den'Fenrir sat in a chair beside the bed, cradling Ghrenna's hand. Eleshen's heart-shaped face held a determined pout in the mingled light of the Stone and the lanterns. Temlin moved toward the bed, his heart heavy. Clad in a white shift, Ghrenna was soaked in sweat, shivering with a terrible fever. Her shift was dappled in blushed red droplets that wept out through her pores now along with her sweat. Blood dripped from her nose, her fingertips and toes were mottled purple with bruises. Her breath rasped, wetness filling her lungs.

Temlin watched blood seep from the corners of Ghrenna's closed eyelids, as if she wept in horrible nightmares. Reaching out, he touched one finger to those red tears. He already knew what he would see if he lifted Ghrenna's lids. Eyes obliterated by red, vessels burst. Even if she somehow recovered, her eyes would be forever milk-white with scars, her vision gone.

Just like Molli.

Ghrenna hadn't been unconscious at first. Awake and in horrible pain, she'd been brought by Shemout Brothers down to the Abbeystone two weeks ago, when Eleshen had notified Temlin of the seer's extreme illness. No salve had helped her, no herb could cure this. And no amount of pressing her bleeding hands to the Abbeystone had caused it to awaken from its slumberous stupor.

The malevolent Abbeystone stared at Temlin with its sleepy, half-lidded gaze. Blood seemed to pour through the room from that eye. Temlin stepped closer, through the Stone's ring of sight. He felt a shiver over his skin, like a thousand needles pricked his flesh. Pacing forward, Temlin approached his old adversary, gazing at its evil ruby eye. The bastard Stone exacted a terrible price for passing den'Ildrian blood through. So it had been for Uhlas, and so it was for Temlin. Each time he'd traveled through it to Molli, he'd paid that price, youth and vigor sucked from his body. With a hard sigh of defeat, Temlin stared woefully at that eye, grieving.

"How is she?" Abbott Lhem's subdued boom sliced Temlin's reverie.

"No change, still." Eleshen looked up, her pretty face bleak. "Ghrenna's not stirred for two days."

"I told you she's dying, Lhem. And this bastard only sits by and laughs at us!" Temlin seized a water-pitcher from the table and threw it at the Abbeystone in a sudden rage. The metal pitcher clanged off the half-lidded red eye. Temlin shivered, knowing he was losing it. The news of the past weeks, coupled with drinking, and now this, had run him ragged. His eyeballs felt glass-ground. Every joint ached. A baritone laugh cut through his memories, a man in herringbone black clapping him upon the shoulder.

Temlin blinked. The memory slipped away.

"Is she really dying?" Eleshen's voice cut through the tense silence. "Is there nothing we can do?"

"Only her King's Physician could help her now. And he's nowhere to be found." Temlin rasped, harsh in his anger.

Eleshen stilled. She was up from the bench fast, slapping Temlin across the face next, sending the spectacles atop his head flying. "Have some respect, you old drunk! A dying fellow Kingsman deserves that much from you!"

Temlin sighed, bending to collect his spectacles from the floor. "Fuck all this. Fine. You want me to travel through, Lhem? You want me to save her? Fine." Turning his attention to the bloody Abbeystone, he snarled at it. "I'll pay your price to save this girl's life, you bastard, if it's the last thing I do! Thank you and you're fucking welcome!"

"Temlin! You don't have to go right this minute, old man—" Lhem protested.

"Fuck you! Yes, I do! Ghrenna's got no time left."

Placing both palms upon the ruby iris, Temlin squared his shoulders, readying himself. Steadying himself beyond the terrible fear that trembled him suddenly. He would do this, had to do this. To save a life, to save a nation. To do something productive with his useless old blood.

Closing his eyes, Temlin sank into an empty space in his mind that was all-too-easy to access drunk. Suddenly, the demon in the Stone was there. It surged in his mind, rushing towards him. Temlin panicked, tried to wrest his hands from the Abbeystone, but it was too late. The Stone pulled him like scythes hooked around his body. It had him now, and it would not let his bones go until this dance ended in torture, or death, or worse.

Temlin felt his body spasm, his mind sucked into the Abbeystone's vortex. The creature within felt like a man but thought like a beast, carnal and devouring. It wanted a meal, a *feeding*, a mind warped from eons of isolation. Temlin screamed as scythes sliced his flesh, turning into iron-tipped flails that rained blows upon his back. Claws reached inside, tearing his guts, gripping his chest. A wail ripped from Temlin's throat as the claws of red pain clamped around his heart.

Silence, the Abbeystone grated into his ear. Temlin's screams were stolen, trapped in breathless agony. *You taste of mountains and hops and the blood of another. Give her to me. Give me both of you...*

That great claw wrapped around Temlin's heart, squeezing until it barely beat as the creature tore into Temlin's mind. Temlin's physical body only twitched, as he was savaged, eaten from the inside, tortured and used. Rent and ripped, Temlin shivered as flails came raining down. He shuddered as the malevolent Abbeystone took him, until he was broken and spent, his screams silent and despairing.

Give me the dying child, the Stone taunted, *and I will end this. Give me the girl I was promised...*

Temlin couldn't think. He had no reason. All he wanted was for the pain to stop. Reaching out, he clasped Ghrenna's hand upon the bed. He wasn't sane enough to care if she'd be tortured. It would probably kill her fast, end her misery.

The creature inside the Abbeystone surged, eager to torment her.

But as the demon reached for Ghrenna, the entire Stone convulsed. A sound like a struck gong concussed the grotto. An unholy wail rose from Ghrenna's dying throat. Her red eyes flew open and she vomited blood out upon the Abbeystone. Suddenly, Temlin was ripped away from the Stone's malevolence, Ghrenna's hand tight in his. Through the Stone they traveled, twisting and wrenched. Thrust through the eye of a needle and folded inside-out, bones crushed and re-made.

And then spat out, upon the other side.

Falling to his knees on a mossy knoll in a mountain valley, every inch of Temlin's body screamed with pain. Ghrenna convulsed at his side, her bloody eyes wide and weeping, gurgles of blood issuing from her throat and pouring from her mouth. Swift feet came running over the stones and moss. A slender, tiny woman with a wild mane of white curls ran up and knelt quickly beside Ghrenna.

Mollia den'Lhorissian. Beautiful as ever.

"Temlin? You brought the girl!" Molli's blind white eyes stared at Temlin, her fast hands whispering over Ghrenna's face. She looked so young still, but for fine wrinkles by her eyes.

"Help her, Molli! Quickly!" Temlin rasped through his pain.

Mollia bent to tend the girl, her fast hands more adept than any healer Temlin had ever met. She had been the bitter secret of the den'Lhorissian family. The first woman to ever bear the gift of the King's Physicians, she had borne it fifty times stronger than any son. Her miraculous hands whispered over Ghrenna, slowing blood, helping her breathe, mending her eyes. The dark blue of Ghrenna's irises returned as Molli worked, the girl blinking in pain. Her tears were no longer blood. Blood no longer dripped from her nose. Her skin was pale, but no longer mottled. She took a deep breath, then another. At last, her eyes settled closed, her forehead smooth.

"Rest, girl," Molli said, her hands stilling.

She turned those beautiful white-blind eyes to Temlin. And though his old body seared with pain, his heart sang to see her. Molli moved close upon the moss. Her hands began to flutter over him, and gradually his pains eased. Temlin's eyes slipped shut. He began to dream as she touched him. Each touch was bliss, each whisper of her fingers a holy rite. And when she was done, she kissed him gently upon the mouth.

Temlin's breath stopped at her kiss. An old fool's love.

"I'm sorry, Tem," she murmured at his lips. "I saw in a vision that I had to bait the creature in the Abbeystone to bring Ghrenna through to me, to save her. I had to halt passage through its Plinth, make it starved for den'Ildrian blood these past two years. Promise it a feast of both you and Ghrenna to make it allow her passage. Please forgive me. I know what you sacrificed to come here."

Temlin reached up, not caring about any of it. Only wanting to trap her and pull her back down into kissing him again. But she flitted away, slipping from his embrace like butterflies in summer sunshine.

"I couldn't heal it all, of course." Mollia's voice whispered nearby. Temlin looked over to see her crouching next to Ghrenna like a wild thing in her fine-spun wool shift, her healing hands fluttering over the girl once more. "Age causes its own infirmities that are quite difficult to undo. Believe me, I have tried extensively upon myself."

She tugged upon one white curl and laughed in her singsong voice. Temlin shifted and sat up. Gazing around, he saw he was in a wide glade of ferns and moss, ringed by cendarie evergreens, a small valley hemmed in by vicious glacial peaks. A seven-eye Stone commanded the center of the glade, thrumming restfully, eyes closed. Temlin took a moment to massage his shoulders and neck, feeling quite recovered, and actually more spry than he had in years. Moving over, he knelt next to Molli.

"Will Ghrenna live?"

"Oh." Mollia chuckled low, like she held a terrible secret. She had done that as long as Temlin had known her. "She'll live. But she's going to hate life for a while. Pick her up, Temlin, let's get her to the kitchens."

"I haven't carried anyone in *years*, Molli. Not with these old bones." Temlin balked.

"Try," Mollia admonished in a singsong chortle. "Just try."

Temlin sighed. Ghrenna was not exactly a little thing, though gaunt. He crouched, hearing both knees pop but strangely feeling no pain. Sliding his hands beneath Ghrenna, he straightened his back and pressed up with his legs. And like a feather in his hands, the young woman came away from the ground and into his arms.

He stared at Mollia.

She chuckled knowingly. "Some things are easy to heal. Strength, for one. Come."

Temlin followed as Molli slipped off into the forest. Just as she always had, Molli moved like she flowed to strains of music no one else could hear. At times she would twirl, or skip, or leap over a root or rock, barefoot upon the moss just as she had been all her life.

Past a stone bridge over a small stream, Molli's refuge in her secret valley at the top of the Kingsmount came into view. It had been a fortress, once. The upper turrets had tumbled, forgotten by time, but the bottom levels were still intact. It was to the cozy daylight kitchens that Molli now led Temlin and his charge. They descended a few steps, then went through an ancient cendarie door.

Four massive hearths graced the walls, rusted cook-ware hanging from irons. One hearth, lit with a cheery fire, held a simmering stew-pot upon a tripod. The rest of the kitchens were covered with woven rugs. Molli's loom sat in one corner, amongst a few cauldrons for dyeing. The rugs upon the walls and floors were atrocious, threads of every color woven in hodgepodge that turned the eye. Wool filled the entirety of the kitchen, overflowing in baskets. Stuffed into corners and hanging to dry from racks, it sat in various stages of carding, pulling, drying, and spinning.

"You still have sheep?" Temlin remarked as he laid Ghrenna down upon a woven pallet.

"Where do you think I get all this wool?" Mollia spread her arms and danced in a circle. "Those fluffy rats keep breeding! My next masterpiece will be the Alranstone in the Kingswood, I think."

"Are they all supposed to be Alranstones?" Temlin gazed around at the heinous tapestries.

"And *why* do you say *supposed to be*?" Molli lifted a haughty eyebrow and drew her thin frame up regally. Uhlas had learned that from her. He had been timid, before he'd learned to fake regality.

"Blind women can't weave color, Molli. You must know these are atrocious."

"Phah. My tapestries are the finest weave in all the land!" Molli drew her tiny frame taller.

"Their weave is very fine, Molli. Only the colors are Aeon-awful." Temlin brushed one hand over a tapestry of mottled oranges and purples. Noting curiously that his knuckles looked far less swollen than usual.

"You're just still pissed at me for bedding your older brother. Well, that's ancient news, Temlin! Let it go." She pouted.

Temlin coughed, feeling it like a punch in the gut. "We're not talking about Uhlas and me."

"We were. We were talking about *weaving*, my sweet love. And nothing is woven more complicated or so fine as love and hate and family. Why won't you forgive me? Look at us! We're old! And I haven't even seen you in two whole years!"

"You don't seem old." Temlin suddenly realized Molli didn't look old at all. Her hair had been a stunning white since she was born. The only way to tell Molli's age was the slight wrinkling around her eyes and mouth, and the thinness of her hands and body. Which, to Temlin, seemed like she was barely out of her forties though he knew she was almost sixty-five.

And at the moment, Temlin realized his body didn't feel so old, either. It was like time had turned back twenty years. He was as angry at Molli as he had been in his forties, a hot, untamable anger.

He looked at his hands again. They looked forty, the wrinkles and gnarled knuckles all reduced, with muscled bands of sinew like he was still practicing with his sword. His knees and back complained not at all, and he felt lean muscle bunch upon his bones as he moved, the muscle of a far younger man.

"You turned back the clock on me…" Temlin said, awed. "How…?"

"I only learned to do it recently. *Solitude* gives me ample time to work on my gifts." Molli gave a peeved pout, eyeballing Temlin with her sightless orbs.

"I didn't put you away here, woman!" Temlin snapped. "That was Uhlas. And these last two years after he died, it was your own meddling with that Abbeystone that kept me out. I didn't even know if you were dead or alive up here, pissing my life away in that damnable Abbey waiting for you!"

"It was your choice to join the Jenners, Temlin!" Molli snapped with scorn.

"Only because it was my last option!" Temlin snapped back.

"Well, I had no choice!" Molli yelled, red-cheeked and raving. "The King your brother put me here and he wouldn't suffer me to leave! Don't you put your monastic life on me, Temlin! You didn't have to join the Jenners to keep two eyes on a blind woman!"

"Your blindness is not my fault!"

"No. And your pig-headed temper and drunkenness is not mine."

Temlin sank to a cendarie bench at a table by the fire, tired of bickering. He didn't want to fight. But it was always this way with Molli. How he loved her, and how he hated her peevish, cryptic stubbornness. "Why am I here, Molli?"

"Why does the world spin? Why do ants draw grain? Because they must."

"Cock and Bull. Why did you rig the Abbeystone half-lidded so I could only get dragged through if I was touching Ghrenna?"

"Was it bad this time?" Molli's sightless eyes were sorrowful as she came to sit upon his bench.

"It's always bad." Temlin put his spectacles up on his head and rubbed his eyes. His sight was better, too, and the spectacles were giving him a headache. He scrubbed a hand through his red-blonde hair, finding it thick and lustrous. "You have no idea what *happens* to me in there, woman! You have no idea how *powerless* it makes me feel…"

"I know, sweet love, I know." A slender arm settled around his shoulders. "The madman in that Stone is cruel. I have never felt his like, no matter how many Stones I contact, and I have contacted quite a few, now. But the powerlessness is only a *feeling*. All feelings fade with time."

"Not this," Temlin rasped. "I drank to forget it. That first time, when Uhlas sent you here for safekeeping, when we all went through together… The *creature* in that fucking Stone snagged me. It *held* me. And every time I try to pass through, it happens again. It *fucks my mind*! And you used that, to bring the girl here. Aeon be merciful, I need a drink."

"It was the only way to bring her through… the Abbeystone only lets royal blood pass. Your blood, Temlin." Mollia rubbed Temlin's back with soothing hands. Her blind white eyes teared. "And now that Uhlas is dead…"

"How did you know of it?" Temlin asked, his fingers stealing out to clasp hers.

"I Saw his death, of course." Molli's face went rigid with anger. "Curse the Lhorissians! Curse my brother! He had no right to the title King's Physician. He was supposed to heal Uhlas, not be complicit to Lhaurent and Lhem in killing him with poison! Oh, their plots!" Molli frothed viciously. "Oh, that *horrible* Castellan, wanting to make me their puppet!! They wanted my hands, my gift used in their service! Together they came late at night when I was just a child, tormenting me by moving the mirrors until I wept, petrified! And then they dragged me *behind* the walls of Roushenn and bedded me in those horrid blue halls! All while my brother looked on, the cur! A girl of only twelve! Fucking me back where there was no one to hear me scream…!"

It was her regular tirade. Temlin sighed, enduring it. These fantasies had begun when they were young, and had only grown worse through her teens as her seeing talent emerged. Tales of rape, coercion, and torture levied at the King's Castellan, at Lhem, and at her brother. Until Uhlas at last sent her to the Abbey, unable to take her madness. Once she was there, even the Sisters could not tolerate her ravings. Uhlas had had no choice but to secret his then-blind and immensely gifted beloved away through the Abbeystone, at the tender age of sixteen. Keeping her a secret forevermore in the valley at the top of the Kingsmount, a place no one could access.

A place few knew.

Finally, Mollia calmed from her rage. Wiping froth from the sides of her mouth, she smoothed her flyaway hair. "Would you like some tea, Temlin?"

"Yes. Thank you." Temlin accepted, relieved her tirade was done. Molli poured from the pot over the hearth into chipped crockery, then threw in some herbs from a rack nearby. She sat opposite Temlin at her plain cendarie table, sipping.

"I saw her talent." Mollia's voice was smooth silk once more, caressing Temlin's skin. "The girl…"

"Ghrenna," Temlin chimed in.

"Ghrenna is quite unique. I have seen what she will be able to do, Temlin. Two years ago I saw it. She won't just contact Stones, as I do. She will be able to *unlock* their mysteries! A *true* Alran-keeper, like the Scrolls of Vheklan say. She needs the right herbs, the right coaching, but in time… Imagine! Every Stone, unlocked! Free passage and mysteries opened to those who need them."

"Why lock yourself away, Molli, when you saw the girl's fate two years ago? Why not just come get her like any normal person would have done when she arrived at the First Abbey?"

"Because of Lhem and Lhaurent and my brother! Plotting my subjugation! If I came through, they would have me! But the tides are turning, my sweet love. Lhem no longer rules the Khehemni game! Lhaurent turns the wheels, now, so he does."

Temlin scowled and ran a hand through his short beard, now thick and wiry again, dark russet. "Bull, Molli. Lhem's no Khehemnas! He never was, for Aeon's sake! He's always been Shemout Alrashemni, and he's no friend to Lhaurent! Besides, Lhaurent's position in the Lothren has never been confirmed. And your brother is dead now, by the way, so you can't accuse him of plotting anymore."

"Good riddance!" Molli snarled, vicious. "My brother was horrible, full of lies! They're *all* Khehemni! I have seen their secret rites of torture behind the walls of Roushenn!"

She trailed off, only a cursory nudge upon her madness. Temlin breathed in relief that this tirade had been short, sipping his tea to hide his unease. "Will I be able to go back through the Abbeystone, Molli?"

"But you just got here!" She glanced up at him, white eyes wide.

"I am needed out there, Molli. The den'Ildrian throne lies empty now that the Khehemni overthrew Elyasin's coronation. And if she is alive as I suspect... Then it's time I made myself known as her kin. Long past time."

"Elyasin's not dead." Molli reached out across the table, laying a slender hand over his. "I've Seen it. She's in Elsthemen, safe with the Elsthemi King."

"Elyasin's alive? Do you swear it?" Temlin put his cup aside, his heart hammering in hope.

"I swear it, Temlin. A rogue nephew of mine saved her life at the coronation, you know. He has the Gift. It seems the entire Lhorissian family wasn't a waste after all."

Temlin's fingers twined with Molli's, relief filling his heart. His niece was alive. "Thank Aeon and all the gods!"

"So you see? There is no reason to rush back and save the nation." Mollia blinked her pretty white lashes. "Besides, going back means touching *him* in the Abbeystone again. But he'll be angry. And I won't be on the other side to heal you."

"Aeon's balls!" Temlin cursed, rubbing a hand over his beard.

"Stay a while..." Molli repeated, twining her fingers in his. "Stay for me."

"Oh?" Temlin was acerbic. "You want me now that Uhlas is gone? One brother swapped for the other, is that it?"

"That's unfair." She whispered, that wing-feather voice caressing all along Temlin's spine. "I loved you both, you know that. But Uhlas was so very determined. He never gave me the chance to say no."

Temlin snorted, sipping his tea, wishing for something stronger. Something in Molli's manner was so angry, so longing, that Temlin suddenly stood, a heated vigor in his limbs. He felt like a man of forty again, with all the lusts and rages of one. Temlin rounded the table and scooped Molli from her seat. Pressing her close, he let her feel how young he had become. And how much he didn't give a damn anymore that she had bedded his brother first.

"I never said I didn't want you…" He murmured, drawing her slender little body close. "But you were fit for a King, and I was never going to be King. I was just a rash, belligerent drunk stripped of everything I might have been…"

"Kings and histories be damned." Mollia stood on tiptoe to brush his lips, though Temlin was not a tall man. "We're just two old people now, my love. And the one who came between us is gone to the grave."

"I'll take you away from here, Molli." Temlin whispered fiercely, gazing down at her luminous, sightless eyes. "Just like I once promised you. Uhlas is dead. There's nothing keeping you here anymore. There's no one to stop——"

"Shh." Molli's fluttering fingertips came to his lips. "We have someone to take care of, Temlin. I can't leave just now. But you're here with me, my love, and there's no one to tell us we can't be together. Not anymore."

Fire and heat surged in Temlin's veins. Her body was pressed to his, so close, so willing, despite all the ways they cut each other. It had always been like this with Molli. Tension, rage, love. Temlin lowered his head, pressing his lips to hers. And with that kiss, he felt a passion in his body and a sweetness come alive in his heart, a heart that had only been a bitter old wreck for years.

CHAPTER 11 – GHRENNA

Ghrenna woke to the sounds of bleating, and a soft swishing sound like someone working at a loom. Her eyes blinked open, her body purged but relaxed, laying on a thick wool pallet and tucked into soft wool blankets. Looking around, she saw she was in a vast kitchen, a lit hearth close to her bedside with a pot of stew simmering. Light streamed in half-round windows, the kitchen partly underground, with bluestone blocks solid as a fortress. Awful tapestries cluttered the walls beyond racks of cookware, spices, barrels of provisions, and countless baskets of wool. Everything had a haphazard look, as if the kitchen served as working and living space all in one. Smelling sharp rosemary and thyme in the stew, hunger rumbled in Ghrenna's belly, and she swallowed, her mouth parchment-dry. Moving her elbows beneath her, she pushed up to sitting in her thin wool shift. She still felt weak, but it was easy and light, like she had sweated out a fever.

"She wakes!" A tiny woman with wayward white curls and opalescent eyes danced to Ghrenna's bedside. Snatching up a water pitcher and filling a pottery cup, her fingers danced the cup to Ghrenna's hands. Ghrenna realized those white eyes were blind as she drank again.

"Where am I?" Ghrenna asked.

"Ah! Better to ask, who are you, and how did you get here?" The woman gave a tittering laugh like she enjoyed a private joke. "I am a healer, girl. Mollia den'Lhorissian, like your tall handsome friend with the golden hair. He got his mother's looks. I'm his aunt."

Ghrenna blinked, taking the strange woman in. She heard the bleating of sheep again somewhere outside. "Did Luc bring me here? Am I in his family home?"

"In a way. And I assume Luc is the name of my nephew?"

Ghrenna blinked. "You don't know him?"

The woman tittered again, more like a sigh. "I've been

161

secluded away from the world long before he was born, girl. Or your birth, for that matter." Her hands fluttered over Ghrenna's face like the moth wings, touching at the corners of Ghrenna's mouth and eyes.

Ghrenna shifted in her wool blankets, finding that though she was sore and stiff, everything was working properly. "So Luc didn't bring me here."

"No, no! My Temlin brought you to me. And a good thing he did. You were dying. Almost faster than I could get you healed. But once we stopped the bleeding from your throat, I knew you'd make it."

Ghrenna touched her nose, half-expecting her fingers to come away bloody. "All I remember was that Eleshen brought some Jenner Brothers to the inn with a litter. I was in so much pain, I hardly knew what was happening. They took me down to a dark room with a light like blood. I think I passed out. But a hand grabbed my wrist..."

Ghrenna stared, remembering the mind that had slid into hers. Remembering the pain of it, the awful triumph of its leer, of its claws. And how in a moment it had all been ripped away as she was flung somewhere else.

The woman's fingers fluttered over her back, comforting. "Be still, child. I will bring you some lamb stew." She bounded up, flying to the stew-pot as if she could see quite properly, and ladling a bowl. In a trice she was back, the warm pottery in Ghrenna's hands.

"Ah, child, we have so much to do!" The woman smiled as Ghrenna started to eat, ravenously.

Ghrenna set to her bowl quickly, sating the roaring hunger that cramped her belly. "What are you talking about? And where is Elohl? And Eleshen and Luc? Or Gherris and Shara? Where are we?"

"*You* are at the very top of the Kingsmount, my dear. In my secluded little valley." The woman gave her a regal sort of look, one white eyebrow arched. "As for your friends, I don't know them and I don't know where they are, other than my nephew. You are a *Dremor*, a True Seer like me, and an Alran-keeper, the first in hundreds of years! So. I will teach you, and you will do as I say, and we will get along splendidly! And if you get any headaches, tell me *immediately.*

We cannot let that interfere with your gift anymore. You will learn how to manage the pain, like I did. More stew?"

Ghrenna blinked, trying to take it all in. She set the bowl down beside her pallet. "I think I need to be alone for a while."

"Overwhelming her already, Molli?" A door shut in the back of the kitchens. A handsome forty-something man with wind-messed russet hair and witty green eyes strode in, dumping a load of chopped firewood beside the hearth. Dressed in a Jenner robe, he was barefoot, but seemed strangely strong and wiry for a Jenner, unloading the rest of the wood from a sack upon his back.

"I am not." The white-haired woman grumped.

The man strode over and knelt, placing a hand upon Ghrenna's brow. His green eyes had a fire to them, much like Eleshen, and his lips curled up in a good-natured smile. "You look far better. I watched you die for weeks, girl. There was nothing I could do. Molli here saved you. But we paid a price for traveling through to Molli didn't we?"

Looking into those knowing eyes, Ghrenna suddenly felt the twisting, writhing pain that had snared her from the Stone. And knew that for him, it had been far worse.

"What did it do to you, to bring me through?" She asked.

Long-suffering pain and rage surfaced in those humorous, hawk-sharp eyes. "Things I won't speak of. The sensations do fade. Eventually. But here we are, and here we'll stay, at least until you're better." He glanced up at the white-haired woman, his face wry. "Any chance you have beer, Molli?"

"No." Her scowl was sour. "Beer makes my visions *awful*. And you are not to go rifling through my herbs, either! There are things that would kill you in there, Temlin. If you want tea, ask me first. That goes for both of you," she fixed Ghrenna in her sightless white eyes to make her point. Gesturing at a far wall, she indicated shelving with canisters of every sort, glass and ceramic, fat and thin. Then, she gestured to a rack of pots and canisters by the fireplace. "The cooking herbs are over there. Play with those all you want. "

"We're not children, Molli." Temlin snorted, combing a hand through his trimmed russet beard.

She danced up to him, her tiny frame hardly coming up to his nose, her demeanor regal as a Queen. "*You* are a troublemaker! And an addict. Learn to harness your pain *without* the ale, Temlin!"

"Now see here, woman!" He huffed, eyes narrowing.

"No." She leveled a finger at him. "Just because we slept together doesn't give you any power here. You do as I say, *when* I say, and you just might break that addiction. She is going to be easier. She's got a threllis habit out of necessity."

Ghrenna's mouth opened in astonishment. The little woman nodded as if she had seen it, then danced over to the rack of medicinal herbs.

"Right, then." She muttered, hands fluttering over the canisters. Seizing one, she set it on the table, twisting it open. "Teller-wort. Clean out those humors! And…" She ran back to the shelf, near frenzy now, seizing three other canisters and depositing them upon the heavy table also. "Thorough-bottom, lanceola, and thuma." She glanced up and winked at Ghrenna with one blind eye. "No one knows about thuma anymore. But it opens the seeing-eye like nothing else! After that, you'll probably need heatherfern, or maybe deathstool, for focus and vision-travel."

She nodded decisively, putting pinches of everything into a mortar and pestle. Lean muscles bunched in her thin arms as she ground everything down. "It's so lovely to have someone to make tea for! It's going to taste like cow shit, but you'll start to awaken right after you've had some."

"But I am awake." Ghrenna mused. Rising from her pallet in her clean shift, she stepped over to have a seat at the table as she watched Molli with fascination.

"Ohhhh, you're not awake like *that* yet! I'd be able to sense you better if you were. Threllis does wonders for the headaches and seizures, but it dulls the inner sight. You've been trying to shut those visions out of your mind for decades with your addiction, though my Temlin's been trying to sober up as long as you've been alive. Ale is its own demon."

"Give me at least a little credit for trying to give it up all these years." Temlin grumped, arms crossed where he sat nearby upon a bench, extending his bare feet to the fire.

"Shush. I'll make a different tea for you. Something calming."

Temlin gave a beleaguered sigh. He spread his hands. "Why not? I could use it after that goddamn Abbeystone."

"You're not the only one it rapes, you know." Mollia fetched a cup, tipping Ghrenna's herbs into a set-in strainer, and pouring hot water from a kettle over the fire, letting it steep. Molli set about filling a second pot for Temlin. "Your horrible adversary sucks at my marrow every time I cross through, too, Tem. But I've had *years* more practice handling such pain."

Temlin snorted and looked away into the fire, disengaging from the conversation. Something horrible and tight lingered about his person, and Ghrenna thought again of the terrible pain and violation she'd glimpsed inside that Abbeystone. Whatever it was, it had attacked him, badly. Ghrenna shivered, thinking about that man in black herringbone leathers who had violently forced his way into her mind so long ago in Alrashesh. That feeling of helplessness, the utter brutality of it. The pain, cascading through her with no hint of ceasing, until she'd felt like she'd never be sane again. Gazing at Temlin, at the way he held himself so stiff, his visage burning with rage, Ghrenna felt that violation afresh.

And knew it had been the same with Temlin in that Abbeystone.

Mollia gazed off out the windows, now settling with evening's gloaming. Her head was cocked, as if listening to music Ghrenna couldn't hear. Leaving the teas to steep, she moved to Ghrenna, stroking her hair in a motherly way. Where her touch went, bliss followed, just as with Luc.

"You'd be proud of your nephew," Ghrenna spoke suddenly, breaking the tension in the room. "Luc is a good man. He'd protest it, but he is."

"Good… Not like his father, then," Mollia said. "His father was atrocious. But Jhulia was a caring woman. Too bad that palace ate her up, like it did so many… You're shivering! Shall we get you a cloak? Are you hungry again, dear? Tell me how you know my nephew."

Ghrenna told Molli of Luc den'Lhorissian as Molli fetched another bowl of stew along with a thick wool blanket to wrap about her shoulders. Mollia ate very little, perching upon a chair, birdlike, as she listened. She was very amused that Luc was a thief, and uttered proud words when she heard he had run away from his life at the palace.

"Good for him!" She crowed, laughing in a mad sort of way. She asked questions about how Luc used his gift, then grumped that he had a lot to learn and changed to conversation to Ghrenna's visions and headaches. How long she had had them, what made them worse or better, where they started and spread to. And when she asked what brought on the worst ones, Ghrenna told her about Elohl and his touch.

Molli gasped, dropping her stew bowl, which thumped to the table and rolled away. "This man Elohl, he is your lover? Tell me!"

"No, not anymore." Ghrenna shook her head. "We were lovers when we were young. But his touch never affected me like that before. But he has these markings, now, these golden Inkings he said came from an Alranstone in the mountains near the Elsee."

"No... no!" Molli's hands fluttered to her mouth and she moaned. "No wonder you were declining so badly, after enduring headaches for so long. He triggered you! A trigger! Marked with golden Inkings! I must ask Delman about this...!"

Molli suddenly became withdrawn, chewing her nails, blind eyes darting. She began to rock forward and back, fingers dancing upon her chin, and then she moaned in frustration, closing her eyes tight. Suddenly, she leapt from the table and raced out the back door, into the dwindling twilight.

Ghrenna sat alone at the table. She eyeballed the teas, still steeping, and wondered if Mollia had forgotten them, if the little woman was entirely sane. Reaching out, Ghrenna removed the strainer on her tea and Temlin's, then slid his across the table. He looked around from the fire, then rose and claimed the mug with a nod. Still distant, his green eyes roiled with pain. Ghrenna met his gaze, and for a second, she thought she could feel him. All his anguish, all his horror at what had happened in the Abbeystone.

Temlin gave a wry smile. With a salute of his mug, he turned towards the door. "I think I'll enjoy my tea outside. Catch a bit of the sunset."

He walked out, leaving Ghrenna alone in the cozy kitchen. Ghrenna had a doubtful look at her tea, so dark it was nearly tarry, the whiff of scent steaming off it no better. But if it helped her visions and headaches, she had to give it a try. Ghrenna sipped her brew, gagged. It tasted worse than anything she had ever put in her mouth, like a cross between horse piss and burning hair. Resolute, she set the cup to her lips and downed it entire.

Almost at once, Ghrenna felt warmth radiate from the center of her body. Reaching up through her chest, it caressed her heart, spreading through the pores of her lungs. Breathing was easier, and her body felt lighter. The warmth spread up to her throat, like a hand had wrapped around her neck, and it went down also, to the pit of her belly and deep into her groin.

Her face flushed, and she closed her eyes.

Mollia's tea was more arousing than any threllis Ghrenna had ever smoked. Ghrenna soon went to lie down, folding her hands over her chest. Flooded by warmth, she felt like hands reached inside her body, caressing parts she hadn't known were there. It flushed in her lungs and she sighed, and it surged in her heart, causing her to melt. Warming in her pelvis, an erotic sensation filled her. Ghrenna slid her hands along her skin, aching for Elohl's touch. And then it flared in her fingertips, and she felt like she could see *through* her hands. Ghrenna let her fingers flutter, touching everything.

Suddenly, it lanced up between her eyes and deep inside the center of her head. Her visions came upon that rush, for the first time without a single twinge of headache. Soft flickerings rather than a storm of pain, Ghrenna watched a storytelling behind her eyelids. The spot between her eyes thrummed, and she felt that it spun loosely, like an empty wine bottle across a tile floor. But she could make no sense of the visions, and as soon as they came, they fled.

Ghrenna sighed, the warmth of the tea fading, then sat up as it fled entirely. Stretching long and languid, Ghrenna opened every muscle that had been contorted in pain ever since she had touched Elohl. She found herself wanting to try the tea again, stronger, wanting to open to that blissful sensation further. She spied the water pitcher on the table and walked to it, pouring a cup, drinking slowly. It felt like a river going down, smooth and nourishing.

Suddenly, Mollia returned, bursting in through the doors like a ragged hurricane. Disheveled in the extreme, there were evergreen needles in her hair and moss on her shift. Smudges of mud graced her nose and chin, as if she had been rolling in it. Without pause, she ran for the herbs, hastily grinding up the same concoction she had made for Ghrenna already, but with copious amounts.

Ghrenna sat up in worry, tucking a lock of blonde hair behind her ear as she watched the disheveled little maelstrom. "Are you all right?"

"No time!" Mollia shook her head quickly, her face stricken, fluttering hands working fast as she tipped the crushed herbs into a new strainer and filled the cup with boiling water. "We don't have the time I thought we had. I must push you to open up quickly so you may speak with Delman! He needs to ask you about the Goldenmarks! What did you experience with the tea?"

Confused at Mollia's cryptic words, Ghrenna described everything she had felt, and Mollia nodded along. When she came to the part about the drunken spin between her eyes, Molli lifted her hand and pressed one finger to the center of Ghrenna's forehead.

"Good. It's working. We do it again. A stronger tea, this time. Five times stronger. But the rest will be five times stronger also. Here. Tea. Drink."

The new mug was thrust into Ghrenna's hands. She sniffed it, finding the brew much more pungent.

"Drink!" Mollia commanded, her voice sharp like a whip.

Ghrenna downed it in one gulp, gagging. But where she expected that soothing warmth, this dose hit her in a surge of ecstasy. Ghrenna stumbled to her pallet, her breath stolen. Her hands clasped her breasts, slid down her belly over her shift, but that wasn't enough. The heat was *inside* her, growing, bursting, thrusting in and sending her into spasms.

Ghrenna moaned, ripped her shift off over her head. The only thing she could think about was touching, to be touched. To light her fingers on fire with her skin and vice versa. And when she indulged it, her whole body trembled, back arched. Writhing like her body was not her own, surging and arching and gasping as her all-seeing fingers traced every part of her. Ghrenna's hands rose up the sides of her neck, combing through her hair in utter ecstasy.

She heard Mollia's voice, low and stern. "Prepare yourself. Focus. Here."

A touch came, one finger, to the throbbing ache between her eyes.

When Mollia touched it, the spin inside Ghrenna's mind

tightened into a spiral, twisting up through her crown and thrusting down through her whole body. Ghrenna moaned, her mind shooting like a star through the night sky, blazing a trail of white light behind it. She saw lakes and valleys, shimmering under summer moonlight. She saw unassailable mountains, riven with cracks. She saw a white tower thrusting up from a blue lake, ringed by glacial peaks. And she saw a tall seven-eye Alranstone in a broken amphitheater upon a mountainside.

And to it, she shot like a spear.

A man waited there, tall and slender, with red and white Inkings running down his spine and across his shoulders. Bare from the waist up but for fur-lined bracers at his wrists, he was wild like a lion with unruly russet hair. He turned as she catapulted to the Stone where he stood, his handsome face opening in shock.

"Morvein!" He whispered, reaching out to her. She reached for him, tried to grasp his fingers, but hers passed through his like smoke upon the wind.

"No…!" He whispered, trying to catch her. Ghrenna felt herself traveling backwards, drawn away from him as fast as she had come.

"No!" He screamed after her, lunging as if he might leap from the Stone, but prevented by an unseen hand. "Morvein!!! *Hahled Ferrian*!!" He screamed after her, his voice ephemeral now. "Remember me!"

Ghrenna sat up with a surge, crying out as orgasm washed over her. Clutching herself in a hot sweat, shivers cascaded through her body. Her limbs were not her own, twitching and writhing as she fell back to her pallet.

Mollia's strong little hand clutched her bare shoulder. "Tell me quickly! What did you see?"

"I was flung through the night, over the land," Ghrenna panted, trying desperately to recall everything in the flooding aftereffects of her pleasure. She described it in detail, and spoke of the man with red and white Inkings. "He reached out for me. He called me Morvein… And he said his name was Hahled Ferrian. And then I was tugged away."

"*Hahled* Ferrian?! Oh, my!" Mollia beamed, reaching out to stroke Ghrenna's pale waves.

"Do those names mean anything to you?"

"Perhaps. I do know that location. A very powerful mind lives in that Alranstone, but he shuts me out every time I visit."

"*Lives* there?" Ghrenna's eyes widened. "Are you saying that man was an Alranstone I just contacted?"

"What do you think Alranstones are, girl?" Mollia's white eyes seemed to twinkle, and she gave a chuckle. "Inert lumps of rock that someone waved a magic wand over like the fey-yarns? No. They are *bound souls* of gifted men and women. As far as I can tell, they were very powerful Alrashemni, teachers who bound themselves into Stones for the benefit of future generations. This Hahled fellow. Could you find him again?"

"I don't think I found him." Ghrenna shook her head. "I was... flung there. But the way seems clear. And he gave me his name."

"Ah! Yes." Mollia combed through her white curls, her deft fingers picking out cendarie needles and bits of moss. "The name helps. Something to focus on. Would you drink again this night? I don't think you should have more than three doses of tea in your condition, but one more won't hurt."

Ghrenna swallowed, tugging the blankets up around herself, conscious that she was unclothed, and how astounding that fit of passion had been. She shivered, a part of her wanting it again.

"Molli," she whispered. "Is mind-traveling to Alranstones always this..."

"Sexual? Intense?" The white-haired woman raised a clever eyebrow. "Why do you think I live all alone? Seeing is not for the prude, neither is contact with Alranstones. The heart behaves as it will during such things, propriety be damned. The mind loses all connection, and the body becomes an animal. But the mind goes where you send it, and gathers what you will, bringing it back for the heart to make sense of, if you're strong enough." She cupped Ghrenna's cheek. "And you are. Strong enough. More tea?"

Though some part of her balked at doing it again, Ghrenna nodded and downed a third cup of tea, which Mollia had already prepared. Falling back upon her pallet in the same wild ecstasy, she was flung straight to the seven-eye Stone in the amphitheater.

And this time, the man with the red and white tattoos was waiting for her. Disoriented by the speed of it, Ghrenna felt herself

170

reel, losing focus. But he was alert, and he grabbed for her hand, grasped it, held firm. Ghrenna *felt* their touch like lightning lancing through a summer sky, wild and passionate. She felt her mind-self pulled into the Stone with him, though her body was left behind in Mollia's kitchen, sweating and writhing.

He clasped her close, carnal heat in his umber eyes.

"Morvein! My love!" Those eyes pierced her, scalding and feral. Every bit as commanding as Elohl, his presence pressed through her, undeniable like a battle-lord. Ghrenna could see him better this time. Strong and tall with corded sinew, his golden-tanned skin was clad in leather breeches and kneeboots, his lion-red mane braided back from his face in thick Highlander cables. Script tattooed in red and white spread over his chest and shoulders, a mountain and five black stars in the center. A keshar-claw pendant inset with gold sigils dangled on a fine golden chain about his neck. Fur-lined leather bracers graced his forearms, and a ruby was pierced into the lobe of his right ear. Small streaks of white grazed the copper at his temples, a dapple of white in his stubble of beard.

"I'm not Morvein," she protested. "My name is Ghrenna."

"Ghrenna…" He blinked as if startled, then narrowed his eyes, searching hers. "What did you take? To come here? What did you take?!"

Ghrenna tried to struggle away from his intensity, but he held her firm. "A tea. With thuma."

"Thuma!" He made a disgusted sound in his throat. "You are far too strong for thuma! It will not hold us together long. You need fire-breathing, and the Thirteen Breaths of Focus!" He reached up, cupping her face, tender. "Morvein, do you not remember yourself? Everything we went through during the wars? Our life at Dhelvendale? When we tried to bring the Rennkavi, to Goldenmark him all those years ago?"

"What do you mean? What wars?"

"Dhelvendale, in the Highlands. Morvein! Do you not remember *us*?" His eyes burned now, intense as he smoothed a hand over her hair. Ghrenna shuddered in his hands, feeling her body far away begin to rise into her climax.

"You don't have time." He seemed to sense it, and gripped her close, urging her to pay attention. "Your newest Rennkavi has been

Oriented and Marked by me, but you have not. I cannot do it for you. You must meditate on Delman. Delman Ferrian! You *must* become Oriented and Marked in order to open the Paths for the Rennkavi! No one can travel through the Stones like you can. No one can rally them like you, my Nightwind! Remember yourself, Morvein! Find Delman...!"

Suddenly, Ghrenna felt herself ripped backwards as her body reached its climax. Hahled Ferrian shouted after her, his eyes as broken as she had ever seen upon a man. "Find Delman and come back to me! *Morvein!!*"

Her climax was ferocious, devastating. Ghrenna wept as she screamed and shuddered, her mind thrust back inside her body upon the bed. Lightning raced through everything. She clutched the blanket to her chest, weeping into it and rocking, wild, the ecstasy of her body and the confusion in her mind too much to bear. Her heart screamed in her chest, too open from the herbs and her encounter with the wild man, Hahled. As if the intensity of the meeting had ripped open something that could not be healed, some horrible grief and regret she had suffered for centuries, Ghrenna found herself swallowed by it. Her heart thudded hard in her chest, pounding with frantic need. She retched, her stomach cramping viciously from the herbs and from sorrow.

Mollia crouched behind her, running soothing hands across her back. "Shhh, child. There is no better way to open at first than thuma, but it taxes the body. Breathe. Tell me what happened..."

Ghrenna repeated everything through her choked sobs and bouts of dry-retching, the names and specifics firmly in her head. Everything, seemed more clear, from the marks and script upon Hahled Ferrian's chest to the set of his jaw as he stared into her heart. Ghrenna felt those hands upon her face, and it set her to weeping all over again.

Mollia looked stunned. Her white brows furrowed in confusion. "I have heard of the Uniter of the Tribes, marked in golden ink. Is this your Elohl? The man who was Inked by Alranstone? Was he Inked in gold?"

"He was. He is," Ghrenna whispered into the blankets. Eyes wide and staring, she saw again those golden Inkings spreading out over Elohl's collarbones and diving beneath his Kingsman greys, now juxtaposed with equally intricate Inkings in red and white.

"Ohhhhh…" Mollia half-moaned. "Child. I was right about you. The name whispers upon the minds of every Alran I have met. Morvein the Nightwind. They call her the Harness of the Plinths, and sigh as if besotted. I thought it was someone long dead. Or bound somewhere. But it's not, is it? The Nightwind is reborn… in a new vessel." Mollia eyed Ghrenna. "A new vessel, to do what she must."

Ghrenna swallowed hard, her mouth dust-dry. "And what must I do?"

"Harness the Plinths, child." She rubbed her tiny hands together, fingers fluttering with excitement. "Open the Paths for the Goldenmarked Rennkavi."

"What does that mean?"

Mollia chuckled mysteriously. "The Alranstones are known as Plinths, in the old tongues of the northlands. The ways that go between them are known as Paths. I have no idea how one goes about harnessing one of them, or opening a Path. But I know someone that does." Mollia eyed Ghrenna, sober. "And I have a feeling he will do anything for you."

"Who?" Ghrenna murmured.

Mollia gave a wry smile. "Why, Delman Ferrian, child. Brother to Hahled Ferrian, and one half of the Brother Kings of Elsthemen, who once lived in the palace at Dhelvendale. And who were both madly in love with Morvein Vishke, the Nightwind."

CHAPTER 12 – KHOUREN

Khouren had been watching when the dying Kingswoman Ghrenna had been torn out of her pretty little friend's fingers into the Abbeystone. Ghrenna and Brother Temlin den'Ildrian had disappeared in a flash of red light and a clap of thunder. And then there was only Eleshen and the Abbot, staring after them and blinking away the brightness.

But they weren't staring for long.

Abbot Lhem seized her by the wrist, crushing her bones in an iron fist. "Where did they go? What did your friend do to the Abbeystone? Were you in on this? *Tell me!*"

Khouren watched from within the wall, shrouded in shadows. Lhem roared into her face, showing his true self at last. He backhanded her across the mouth and Eleshen's head spun. The vicious Lhem backhanded her again, then pinned her wrist behind her back, wrenching her shoulder. Eleshen screamed, her shoulder ready to pop.

"I don't know anything!" She gasped, blood welling from a split lip. "I swear it!"

"I don't believe you." Lhem growled into her ear. "Up, girl!"

Khouren watched as Lhem hauled on her arm. Eleshen rose quickly from the bed with a shriek. He got his other meaty hand on her neck, and bullied her toward a far door in the chamber. Lhem was a vicious hippo of a man. The Abbot shoved the stone door upon the far wall with a fat shoulder, pushing the girl into a black oubliette beyond. Seizing a torch from a bracket, Lhem proceeded in after the woman, menacing forward with a sword now in his other hand from a rack near the door.

Khouren moved quickly through the wall, placing himself within the oubliette's stone, watching.

The torch revealed an ample space, a round room. Silent but for Eleshen's hard, scared breathing, time stretched as she and Lhem regarded one another. A low murmur rose in Khouren's ears from the depth of the silence, far below the Abbey and its grounds, deep in the earth. Khouren knew this room, and he knew what it was for.

He shifted in the wall, uneasy, watching their standoff.

Lhem flicked the blade up, pricking under her chin. "Back up, girl."

"Please, there must be some mistake…"

"I said back up." The Abbott's voice was impassive. The blade dug into her neck. Eleshen gasped and began sliding her feet back toward the dark center of the room.

"I thought Jenner Brothers didn't use swords." She chastised.

"Angle to your left, girl. You're missing the mark."

"And what is my mark?" Her voice was higher, scared. Her feet hesitated. Lhem pricked her again with the sword. She hissed, moving backwards again.

"The little bird can be trained, I see. But can she learn to sing for me?"

Khouren watched Eleshen tremble as she paced backwards. "You're not a Kingsman, are you? That's all a lie, isn't it?"

He chuckled, and it was utterly Lhem, vicious as he kept pace with her, sword still pricking her neck. "Your intuitions are keen, girl. What do you know that you don't think you know? And what can you tell me?"

Eleshen bumped black iron at the center of the room, stumbled backwards upon it. Reaching out to steady herself, Khouren saw her eyes widen as she touched the cold iron lattice, bolted into the stone floor. Khouren heard her squeak. Lhem held the torch out, setting it in a bracket upon the side of the lattice, illuminating the ancient torture-bed and an old grate beneath the girl's boots, rusted and stained.

Khouren knew that discoloration well.

Blood.

Eleshen's knees gave out. She sank down trembling with fear. Lhem's sword lashed down, slicing a rent upon her chest. Eleshen screamed, surging backwards against the lattice. The sword-tip flicked beneath her chin and her scream ceased in terror.

"Give me trouble, and you'll receive more. Are you going to give me trouble?" Lhem rumbled.

She shook her head, shrinking back against the iron. Lhem's sword-tip remained still as he stepped to one side, taking up an iron manacle, which he snapped around Eleshen's wrist and locked into place. The girl keened. The Abbott took up another manacle, securing her other wrist. Tears leaked from her eyes in the torchlight.

The Abbott hauled on the chains. They rattled upwards, wrenching Eleshen's shoulders, jerking her to her feet. She gasped, dangling upon the cuffs, wrists now wide over the spread of the iron lattice. The girl tried a kick at the Abbot as he went to chain her ankles. Quick as a wasp, the sword sliced a rent across her hip, shredding her breeches. Eleshen screamed. Her ankles were locked into place. Chains rattled again, hauling her legs apart. There was a shriek of rusted gears, and then the grate tipped backward, bringing her to level upon its bed of nightmares.

It locked into place. The torch remained upright in its stand, illuminating the scene. The Abbot walked around to where the girl could see him, cold dispassion in his eyes above those white mustachios.

"You are going to stay here," he said, "until you decide that telling me what you know of Ghrenna and of Elohl den'Alrahel is your wisest option. I will return, soon. If I do not like what I hear," he slid the sword down the line of her bodice, pulling it upwards with steady pressure. Her lacings popped as the sword bit through them, until the garment slipped from her torso, leaving only her thin shirt over her skin. "Then I shall continue. And if there is no more to continue with, then we will continue with the same to your pretty skin. Do I make myself clear?"

Khouren saw the girl nod hastily. "I don't know what you want, but I'll tell you everything, I swear it! Elohl is—"

The flat of the sword slid over her lips, and Eleshen trembled to silence, eyes wide.

"I don't want to hear your confessions now," Lhem rumbled. "I want to hear them later, after you've had a chance to think a while."

Lhem turned away, lifting the torch from the bracket and heading for the door. It boomed shut, and the only sound Khouren could hear in the darkness was weeping.

Khouren rushed away, running hard through the bowels of the Abbey. He couldn't let this happen. That woman was an innocent. It was plain from her fear, from her weeping, that she held no part in the Alrashemni's machinations, nor the Khehemni's. Khouren raced up the main staircase in the woman's dormitories. He didn't care if anyone saw him. Bounding up an auxiliary staircase to the fifth floor, and then into the tower, he barreled through Lenuria's door. His gaze raked her rooms, frantic. She wasn't here. Khouren bolted for the stairwell to the highest part of the tower, but when he entered, he found that empty, too.

Backtracking, Khouren dashed to her meeting-rotunda. Empty. He raced to the women's prayer chapel, then the cathedral, even scoured the ancient library, but all were empty of her stern presence. Khouren could spare no more time. Every minute he wasted searching for his half-sister was another minute the young woman might be horribly dispatched.

Lhem was not known for mercy.

Khouren raced back, slipping through shadows, darting through larders. His unease spiked as he returned to the oubliette's wall, peering through the stone into the torture-room. Khouren was too late. Lhem stood by the girl, a blade out. He had been busy while Khouren was gone. Injustice had been wrought upon the innocent. She was weeping now, her clothes sliced open, flayed, exposing her to the torchlight. The Abbott had cut her boots away, and small cuts welled on the soles of her feet, sending the fresh iron tang of blood wafting through the vault.

Lhem gazed down at his chained prize, his longknife to hand, his cowl thrown back. "Recite it again. Begin with Ghrenna. Once more."

Eleshen recited everything she knew about the woman Ghrenna whom Khouren had watched get yanked through the Abbeystone. Khouren listened intently, hearing information of import, about a strong seeing-*wyrria* the woman possessed. When Eleshen was finished, rasping, Lhem slid his knife away and reached for a water flask. He placed a meaty hand beneath Eleshen's neck, holding her head up as she gulped water. She mewled when he took it away, her thirst barely sated.

"I reward information," Lhem set the flask aside. "If you tell me something interesting, you can have more. Now, tell me about Ghrenna. Who is she, *really*?"

Khouren saw Eleshen blink. "I don't know what you mean... she's a thief. And a True Seer. And a Kingsman. I told you already, twice. I told you everything!"

Lhem reached out a hand, brushing wisps of honey-blonde hair from her face, stroking her cheek, his eyes fevered. Eleshen winced from his touch, but it followed her, implacable. His white mustachios quirked in a smile. The knife was out again, and it whispered over her skin. Taking a sharper angle over her chest, Lhem traced a circle around one breast. Eleshen shuddered. Khouren surged in the darkness, searing with rage. Lhem was a sick, sick fuck. And that smile on his musk-ox face said he was going to do awful things. Khouren twisted, watching. If he interrupted, if he fought Lhem to free the young woman, he would betray his Rennkavi. Lhaurent and Lhem were allies in the Khehemni Lothren, though it was a bloody and awful thing.

"You haven't told me what you *really* know." Lhem chewed his mustachios, his grey eyes shining with a vicious light. A slow malice, a calculating wrath. "You haven't dug deep. There is more in that mind of yours, pretty bird. Now. Tell me about Ghrenna."

"Go to Halsos! I've told you all I know." Eleshen spat. Khouren watched her harden her resolve, clenching her jaw. He knew that feeling. It was better to be defiant than afraid. Though no one's defiance lasted long beneath Lhem's blade, nor beneath Lhaurent's.

"Unfortunate." The Abbott leveled the tip of the knife upon her nipple, pressing in swiftly. The girl shrieked through gritted teeth as blood welled. The knife slid down to her belly, scoring a long line of pain and she screamed, writhing, though Khouren could see Lhem's cut had been shallow. The Abbott's blade flashed another fast line beneath one breast. "Tell me about Elohl den'Alrahel!"

Eleshen shrieked and imploded, sobs renting her frantic gasps. "He's a Kingsman! A Brigadier! He came to my inn! We traveled together! All he wanted was to get back to his sister Olea at the palace! We traveled through an Alranstone, and he got marked in gold by it, but I don't know anything else! *Please...!*"

Khouren's breath was stolen. His heart leapt to his throat. Inked in gold. This Elohl was brother to Olea, from the Linea Alrahel, the Line of Kings. And the girl had said under torture that he'd been Inked in gold by an Alranstone.

Khouren's mind spun. He had to get her out of here. But Lhem was still with her, and opposing him meant opposing Lhaurent. Khouren's teeth ground in the shadows, nostrils flaring as his breath heaved fast and silent.

The Abbott paused, considering Eleshen by the flickering torchlight. And then, like a painter creating diabolical art, Lhem sliced her in quick shallow strokes across her breasts, her belly, her inner thighs. And finally, across her cheeks, disfiguring that beautiful face. Her screams rose to madness. The Abbott turned, lifted a bucket, and sluiced water over her that reeked with the sour tang of vinegar. She shrieked like an animal, jerking in her bonds. The loathsome Lhem leaned over her, gripping one breast in his meaty hand, running his thumb deep into a cut. Eleshen shrieked, bucking, but he pressed her down with his weight, growling into her ear.

"Tell me what you know about Elohl, girl! Tell me soon, or I will do unthinkable things!"

"*Leave her alone*!" Khouren's hissed under his breath in the darkness.

"Tell me what you know!!!"

Khouren could feel the passage of the Abbott's keen blade as it slid down between the girl's thighs. Lhaurent and Lhem had always used well-honed blades, their passage intimate, brutal. Khouren knew the panic that rocked Eleshen, felt her annihilation as she began to gibber, trying to spasm away from the knife at her exposed nethers.

"Ghrenna has a hold upon Elohl! He loves her! But his touch sparks her! It sparks her and causes headaches! They love each other but they can't be together!! The Stone called him Rennkavi when he was Inked!!! Please! Please, *I don't know any more!!*"

Lhem flicked his wrist. Shrieks and sobs cascaded from Eleshen's mouth. Khouren surged inside the wall. He had to get her free before Lhem killed her. Eleshen's screams cut off suddenly as she lost consciousness from pain and panic. The Abbott stared down, chewing his mustachios. Khouren's breath was hard in his throat as he watched. Lhem didn't like to do them unconscious.

This might be Khouren's chance.

The Abbott turned, leaving the torch as he boomed out the door. Khouren was moving instantly. He ran to Eleshen's side.

Slapping her cheeks lightly, he got her to wake. Eleshen gasped, twitched, keened out. Khouren covered her mouth with one black-gloved hand.

"Be still!"

Her screams ceased. She stared at him, green eyes wide in the light of the torch. Slowly, Khouren took his hand away. Tears welled. "Please! Help me! I don't know who you are, but I'll do anything you say! Please!" She was on the verge of hysteria, breathless and frantic.

"Shh… keep your voice low." Khouren leaned out over the grate, lock picks in hand, sliding them into one of her ankle manacles. He didn't need them often, but once in a while, certain skills came in handy. "Be still while I get you out."

"Who are you? How did you get in?"

"I have my ways." Khouren's hands were fast, moving through the manacles. The girl winced as she sat up. She gave a mewl as Khouren tried to scoot her to the edge of the grate, tears leaking from pale green eyes as blood leaked from so many cuts. They were largely shallow, Lhem's preparatory art, but that didn't make them any better.

"Here." Khouren shrugged off his jerkin. He helped her into the soft leather, and she clutched it close as he unwound a new black *shouf* that covered his nose and mouth. "For your lower half."

She took it with a nod, winding his *shouf* about her hips. Setting one cut foot down upon the cold stone, she winced. "I don't think I can walk."

"I'll carry you." Khouren beckoned, and she slid into his arms, cuddling close.

"Why are you helping me? Are you a Kingsman? These aren't Kingsman greys…"

"No. I'm not a Kingsman. The Goldenmarks you described, Inked by Alranstone. Did this young man you traveled with, Elohl den'Alrahel, truly receive such a blessing?"

She cuddled close in his arms. "Truly. And he was changed afterwards…"

A shudder went through Khouren. If it was true, then everything Khouren had worked for, everything he had done in Lhaurent's service…"Come, girl, hold tight. Make sure your arms are touching my neck. Touching some of my skin."

"What?" She gazed up at him, broken, uncomprehending. But she did as he asked, and Khouren hefted her more securely in his arms, though she mewled in pain. But just as he turned to walk through the wall to the Abbey's larders upon the other side, there came the shirk of the latch thrown open, and the boom of the door.

"You, there! Hold!" The booming basso of Lhem's voice was unmistakable. Khouren's heart lurched, knowing he had nothing to cover his face with. But it didn't matter. Let the Lothren's puppet see him. If it was true what the girl said, then Khouren owed the fat Abbott nothing.

Khouren turned, letting Lhem see him.

"*You!*" Lhem hissed, though his eyes were wide with shock.

"You will leave her alone. She is innocent." Khouren stood tall, the young woman's weight as nothing in his arms. His voice held the hard command of his grandfather's line.

"You will leave her to me, or answer to your master, *cur!*" Lhem snarled back.

"You are a sick bastard," Khouren's voice was cold. "I will never forget that it was you who corrupted my master, taught him to wield such atrocities in the name of *vision.*" Khouren turned away.

"He was already corrupt, shadow! And your shade's tricks won't help you here!"

Khouren was nearly to the wall, Eleshen cradled in his arms. Suddenly, he heard a rush of movement behind him. Before he could turn, something heavy slammed him in the back, making him stumble. Fire flared through his left shoulder, a hot skewer of pain. Khouren fell forward, one knee driving to the stone. Lhem's fast breathing came from behind Khouren, thick and triumphant with a vile chuckle. That fat bastard had rammed his longknife right through Khouren's back, to the hilt. But Lhem had missed Khouren's spine, and his heart. He didn't know how to kill the Ghost of Roushenn. Khouren snarled in fury as he crouched to lunge through the wall.

But a sound from the girl made him look down.

In the flickering torchlight, he saw far too much blood between them, a dark stain spreading quickly over his blacks. The longknife had gone clean through Khouren's ribs, and the last many inches were buried in the girl's breast, clinging close as she had been. Her pale green eyes were startled. She gazed up at Khouren, not understanding. Her eyes rolled up. Her body went slack.

"No!" Khouren breathed. With a roar, Khouren grasped the blade that protruded through him, and thrust it backwards. He screamed at the pain of ejecting it, but he would heal faster without it. It clattered to the stone. He heard Lhem's grunt of surprise, that fat bastard, felt the man step back. Khouren felt a moment of lightheadedness, but then his body took over, already healing the bitter wound with a wretched searing like fire. Khouren picked the girl up again, hefting her body in his arms. He turned, glaring at the man behind him.

"You should be dead!" Lhem's plethoric face was wide-mouthed, gaping.

"*Ask me why my master keeps me close.*" Khouren growled.

The fat Abbott went pale. But even in his fear, he managed to squeak out a last question. "What binds you to Lhaurent? Tell me, Ghost."

"Nothing you will ever know about," Khouren snarled. "Yours is a small life in an ancient game. And you just killed one who might have been useful. Watch the shadows, Abbott. For when my master decides to be rid of you, my smile will be the last thing you see."

Khouren turned and surged through the wall. Heart pumping hard, his shoulder screaming with the blessed burden of quick healing, Khouren picked up his feet and ran like Halsos' hounds savaged his heels. In the lamplight of a larder, he could see Eleshen's white throat pulse. It was slow, but it was there. She wasn't dead yet.

"Stay with me…" Khouren raced against the seepage of blood from her chest. Gaping between ribs, the stab-wound was too high to have pierced her heart, but there were other vessels that could do nearly as much damage. Khouren's ejection of that blade had done him service but it was killing Eleshen, fast. Running up silent stairwells in the dead of night, he took back ways to Lenuria's tower. Khouren ran through dark cellars, through alehouses and storage rooms full of barrels. Swift and silent, it took him little time to gain the women's quadrangle and race up the back staircases to the abode of his Abbess.

The prayer tower in Abbess Lenuria's private rooms was lit with candles, flames flickering in the ancient cupolas. A sigh of relief slipped from Khouren's lips as he strode in, seeing that Lenuria was there, her tiny frame clad in a night-robe and wrap where she sat upon her knees on a tufted cushion.

"Khouren?" Lenuria lifted her head from her midnight meditations to spy him in the shadows, interrupting her view of the thirteen-spoked sun emblem upon the far wall. She shrugged her night-wrap closer, her silver-streaked ebony locks tumbling over her shoulders at the late hour. Her black brows rose as she spied what he carried. Khouren moved forward swiftly, and laid the girl before his Abbess upon the stone floor.

"Please, Lenuria, help her!" Khouren spoke in a desperate rush. "Lhem was torturing her. She knows about the Rennkavi! Not Lhaurent, another one! Save her... Shaper be holy, please save her...!"

"Oh, Khouren!" Lenuria's fast hands checked for a pulse at Eleshen's throat. Her fingers were hasty, opening Khouren's blood-soaked jerkin to inspect the girl's wound. She gave a soft cry, seeing the ruination Lhem had dealt upon Eleshen's pure skin, and the disfigurement of the girl's face. Lenuria's gaze fixed upon the chest-wound, leaking blood in a steady stream.

"Here. Hold her still."

Khouren moved to where Lenuria gestured, bracing his hands upon Eleshen's slender shoulders. Lenuria moved fast, placing her hands over the wound in the girl's chest.

Lenuria said a quick prayer, and then Khouren felt her incredible *wyrria* building.

"Forgive me, young woman," Lenuria murmured, "but you'll understand in time."

A pulse ripped the air, emanating from Lenuria's hands, straight through the girl's chest. Eleshen came awake with a gasp, and a wail that made Khouren thankful Lenuria's tower was solid byrunstone. She passed out again just as suddenly, which was for the best, as her skin began to split and writhe. Khouren watched Lenuria's gift unfold in the body of another, shifting her flesh, rearranging it, moving things that oughtn't have moved.

And suddenly, it ceased.

Blood and slicker fluids coated the floor beneath the girl. But she was whole, undamaged beneath Lenuria's hands. She bore not a single blade-mark upon her skin, pale as lily of the valley. But where her face had once been heart-shaped and smiling, it was now sharp and haunting, her eyes deep in shadow. And where she had once had locks like golden sunlight, they were now raven and straight, lustrous in the torchlight. Her lips were red, her cheeks holding a bare blossom of color, her curvaceous body now slender, waifish.

Her beauty would come back in time, Khouren knew. But never the same as before. From a sun maiden she had been transformed into a creature of moon-drenched snowfields. Lenuria's gift could not be controlled, and only it chose its final appearance.

Khouren's half-sister slumped, breathing hard. Khouren caught her by the shoulders. "Will she live?"

"Yes." Lenuria reached up a shaky hand to brush a cold sweat from her forehead. "She'll sleep for days, perhaps weeks, waking only in stupor to take broth. So it is when I change, especially if my change has healed such serious wounds. She'll be weak for a while, but her strength will return. I'll have the Sisters look after her. She'll be in good hands. Now. Let me look at your wound."

She turned to Khouren, moving her hands to his blood-slicked shirt, but he trapped her hands. "You're tired. I'm already healing. Just some salve, please."

His half-sister's gifts could heal Khouren without changing him. But it would exhaust her to do two healings in so short a time. It would take her months to recuperate. As it was, she wouldn't be able to shift herself again for weeks. Khouren pushed to standing, one hand cupping his wound. Lenuria stood also, her tiny frame barely reaching his chest, though Khouren was not a big man. Lenuria motioned him to take his shirt off. She stepped shakily to a hutch she kept for tending Khouren's injuries, and spoke not at all as she applied salve to the seeping hole, then bandages. He would heal fast, they both knew it. But he scarred less if a few measures were taken.

"I can't keep Lhem's position as Khehemni secret here any longer, Khouren." Lenuria's eyes held a red fire in the flickering candlelight, as she secured the bandage. "I know you feel a duty to that horror of a man Lhaurent... but I cannot have a torturer masquerading as an Abbott! I took vows. To not permit such atrocity under these gables!"

"And do your oaths to the Abbey stand stronger than the oaths you made to our Rennkavi?" Khouren trapped her tiny hand to his bandaged chest.

She looked up, grim. "Lhaurent den'Karthus is not our Rennkavi. I refuse to acknowledge his Goldenmarks! That bastard and the things he does behind those walls…! He is not the Uniter I swore to serve, all those hundreds of years ago. He has no conscience, Khouren! And if another Rennkavi has been marked…" Lenuria gripped Khouren's fingers. "I thought perhaps Temlin had just been drinking too hard. That he was making things up, when he spoke to me a few days past of a young man with golden Inkings, done by Alranstone. But this girl has seen another? She told you of another one Goldenmarked? A young man, a Brigadier?"

"So she spoke under Lhem's torture," Khouren breathed, his gaze straying to the unconscious woman. "She traveled with a man by the name of Elohl den'Alrahel. Who received the Goldenmarks during their time together. She swore they were done at an Alranstone. She said he's the brother of the palace Guard-Captain. She said they'd been here, to the Abbey…"

"So it is true." Lenuria breathed, her gaze astounded, as she turned to look at the girl. "Temlin asked me if I thought it could be the Prophecy."

"Did you tell Temlin our truth?"

Lenuria shook her head. "No. How can you tell a man that you are hundreds of years old, part of a lineage waiting for a mystical person to come Unify a nation so forgotten that even their symbols are no longer truly understood?" Lenuria's gaze drifted to the gold-worked Jenner Sun set into the stone of the far wall. Candles flickered below it, lighting the Sun in an uncertain glow.

Khouren's fingers touched her chin, turning her face back. "You'll burn, Lenuria. If you don't acknowledge Lhaurent as Rennkavi, your soul will burn forever. I can't let that happen to you, sister."

Tears shone in her eyes, bright and hard. "And I can't support a torturer, Khouren. Neither him nor his henchmen! If there is a chance, even the smallest chance, that this Elohl is our Rennkavi instead of Lhaurent, I will take it. And if I burn for eternity for being wrong, so be it! I will burn knowing I made the right choice."

"I wish I had your strength," Khouren's knuckles smoothed over her fine-lined cheek. "I wish I had seen this other Goldenmarked man for myself... then I would know for certain whom to follow."

"You do have strength," Lenuria rasped, fierce. "Leave Lhaurent, Khouren. Leave those Khehemni madmen now, before their atrocities get any worse. Take a chance! Have faith that someone else has come to save us."

Khouren shook his head, misery filling his heart. He twisted inside, burning with indecision. If only he had seen, had felt the power of this other man, this Elohl. But taking such a dire risk as breaking from his Rennkavi with no certain proof that another one existed was a gamble Khouren couldn't trust.

"I must go. Lhaurent will be wondering where I've been." Khouren murmured.

Lenuria reached up, touching his face. "Be careful, Khouren. Something is happening out there in the world. I can feel it quickening. Danger flows thick and fast now, for all of us."

"Take care, Lenuria." Khouren cupped his half-sister's cheek tenderly, then pressed a kiss to her brow. "Don't let Lhem trap you anywhere alone."

"I won't."

Her hand slipped away. Khouren stared down at her a moment more, pondering their line, seeing how even one so long-lived as Lenuria was finally coming to dust. He reached out, touching her hair. "So much silver..."

A smile quirked her lips. "Being able to reset my appearance every thirty years seems to dwindle. My *wyrria* runs out. And yet, grandfather looks as young as he ever did. But his blood thins in us."

"Grandfather still doesn't believe Lhaurent is our Rennkavi."

"After the atrocity at Roushenn... I do not believe it, either, Khouren. Only you do."

"You do not have to believe. Only accept."

"Accept." Lenuria's voice was bitter. "Accept such foul play on Lhaurent's behalf. Oh, pardon me, on the *Khehemni's* behalf. People *disposed* of, mercenary and foe alike. Wake up! See him for the devil he is, and beware."

"He bears the Goldenmarks, Lenuria. Even if another one has

186

been marked, Lhaurent was marked first."

Lenuria set her jaw. "Grandfather feels as I do. Lhaurent is atrocious, and you are mistaken to follow him, Khouren."

An unsteady silence stretched between them.

"He's left the palace. Grandfather." Khouren spoke at last.

"Has he? Is Fentleith off to ease his heart serving in battle somewhere new?" Lenuria's smile was wry with ancient pain.

"He followed the Queen's party north to the Highlands. She survived the assassination."

Lenuria took a deep breath, and her sigh was burdened. "Well. Maybe some good will come of that. But Khouren...You haven't told Lhaurent about us? About our clan?"

"I would never betray you, nor grandfather," Khouren declared fervently, "nor any of the others! To the House of Alodwine I hold fast, though Khehem and *Alrashem* united are first in my dreams. Lhaurent will never know he has a clan sworn to guide him, but that grandfather says it is so. And he doesn't. Despite how hard I've tried to convince him. So Lhaurent knows only about me, and that is how it will remain."

"Isn't that a betrayal of your Rennkavi?" Lenuria's smile was soft, sad.

Khouren shrugged. "I'm not burning yet."

"No, none of us are. And if there is another one Goldenmarked... then perhaps you won't."

Khouren cocked his head, pondering that. If there were two Rennkavis upon the playing field in this ancient, atrocious game, what did that signify? If none of Khouren's oath-bound clan were burning yet, did they truly have a choice in whom they might serve?

"Goodnight, Lenuria." Khouren stepped toward the candles upon the flickering wall. "Take care of the girl for me?"

"I'll see that she has good care. Keep well, Khouren." His iron-wrought sister said.

And then Khouren was back through the wall, gone like a ghost when the torches flicker.

CHAPTER 13 – THEROUN

A cold dawn filtered through the lower Lethian Valley on the Elsthemi border. Theroun waited upon his mount, wrapped in his cloak against the early morning chill. His horse shifted lazily, eyes slipping closed, barely awake. The spreading camp below his vantage upon the grassy hill was mostly silence, men who would be thrust into fighting now resting before they had to be up for the day. Organized in strict rows with wide avenues, tents now filled the entirety of the valley at the bend of the river. Twelve thousand men had trooped in over the past weeks, and their forces would be fifteen thousand strong by the time the last straggling companies arrived.

Theroun had supervised the setting of camp himself, and sometimes re-setting. Some idiot had dug privy-troughs too close to the river and men had been getting sick while washing, so Theroun had made them re-dig to the east near the foothills. Men with dawn duties moved through that well-laid grid now, smoke wafting up blue from mess-tents and smithies, lifting away upon the wind. Order, he saw, had been somewhat lost toward the western edge of the camp where the cavalry units were amassing, their picket lines crooked and tents bundled too close. Theroun could hear distant whinnies as the war-horses anticipated their morning grain. He set his jaw, making a mental note to ride through and reprimand the cavalry captains about the risk of late-summer fires.

His horse shifted again, flicking its ears back. Theroun heard the dry crunch of field grasses as someone ascended the hill at a trot. A man with red-blonde hair stepped up the deer-track, brisk. Early forties, clad in light leathers with the blue-and-white striped armbands of the Fleetrunners, his fox-like face collapsed into a scowl upon seeing that Theroun was alone atop the crest of the hill.

The fellow's gaze fixed on the General's chevron pinned to Theroun's jerkin as he approached, narrowing upon the top chevron done in gold. He halted with a crisp salute. "Sir! Runner-Captain

Vitreal den'Bhorus to report to General den'Ulthumen!" The man's clipped words held a severe north-border accent. "I was told he would be up here?"

"You have missed him by fifteen minutes, Runner-Captain." Theroun barked casually. "I am Counsel-General Theroun den'Vekir, General den'Ulthumen's advisory entity. You may make report to me. General den'Ulthumen is making inspection upon the cavalry units."

The man gave a clipped nod. "Yes, sir. Counsel-General, sir. I bring six Fleets from General den'Albehout. He was using us to run messages to the High Brigade, and coordinate attacks along the Valenghian border. My Fleetrunners and I are at your disposal, Counsel-General."

Theroun took the man's measure. Hardy and whip-thin, the Fleetrunner Captain had lines in his well-tanned face and the piercing blue eyes of north-blended stock. He did not wither under Theroun's gaze, only twisted the wire of his frame tighter, as if for a challenge.

"Good." Theroun barked at last. "And you've brought the High Brigade?"

The man flicked his head contemptuously. "No, sir. They'll be along tomorrow. They are a day behind us, traveling by foot. I have a man running between, giving me reports." Runner-Captain den'Bhorus give a sneer, like a fox. "Brigadiers can be lazy, sir."

"Thank you, Runner-Captain. The General has arranged command meetings every night at sixth bell. You will be present this evening. Inform Brigadier-Captain Arlus den'Pell via your runner that the Brigadiers are to double their pace. I want them here tonight."

The Runner-Captain saluted quickly, then paused.

"Speak."

"My pardons, sir, but I was under the impression that den'Ulthumen was leading this campaign."

Theroun gave a chilly stare down to the Fleetrunner Captain. "He is. And you will also note, Captain, that I am his advisory entity. An order from me is an order from him."

"I'd heard you'd come out of retirement, sir." The man's eyes glinted, still curious.

"You heard right, Captain. I am far more valuable at the front than rotting among the sweetmeats of Roushenn. You may pass along word of the rescinding of my retirement."

"The Black Viper returns." The Runner-Captain's eyes glinted.

Theroun looked the man over again. Den'Bhorus sneered, just a flicker, his eyes fierce. He did not sweat under Theroun's gaze. He held steady, unflinching, tough as a badger. Contempt poured from him, along with hate. Hate toward the Black Viper sitting tall in his saddle.

It was obvious what he was. Theroun couldn't see his Blackmarks, but he knew. Only Kingsmen looked at the Black Viper with that much bite in their eyes. Which meant Vitreal den'Bhorus was just the man Theroun needed.

"Walk with me, Captain. These eastern foothills are where your force and the Brigadiers shall be concentrated."

Theroun clucked his tongue and his horse paced forward. Vitreal den'Bhorus kept a brisk walk at his side. Theroun wheeled his horse toward the woods that creeped down the foothills in brush and oak. His horse was an easy beast, and Theroun found his side pained him little today as they rode up toward the tree line. In fact, his injuries had pained him less the further from Roushenn he had gotten. And in the past week of moving about camp, he found he had regained much of his former mobility.

It was a strange thing, returning to war this way. What made most men pained made Theroun hale. His lips almost smiled, but for the restless fox keeping pace at his side.

"Den'Bhorus!" Theroun barked suddenly, the camp out of sight now behind the hill. "Tell me what you see."

"Box-elder, sing-leaf, and Lhugard's Pine, sir. Scattered groupings of far-north strongoak and leatherleaf. Broken tree line at this elevation..." Den'Bhorus turned, making a quick survey of the hills bordering the spreading valley. "I'm betting there's rattle-viper up here, and itchwort. It looks dry enough. Risk of fires, sir. Terrain is stony like it is further north, with risk to stumble a horse or break an ankle from a badly-placed foot. Plenty of deer in these woods based on the tracks, lowlands bear, maybe a few wild keshar. Sir."

"You speak as if you know the northlands."

"Yes, sir. My grandmother was a Highlander. I'm from

Gerthoun. On the border. Sir."

"Gerthouni?" Theroun skirted his horse around a copse of box-elder. "So you grew up in hills like this. And how does a Gerthouni feel about being involved in a campaign against Elsthemen?"

Theroun saw the man set his jaw. "I go where the Crown sends me, sir."

"I see. And are you loyal to your Crown, Fleetrunner?"

"Yes, sir!"

"What I mean, Fleetrunner, is are you loyal to your Queen?"

The man's stride stumbled. "The Queen's dead, sir. I'm loyal to the Realm."

Theroun halted his horse. He gazed down at the simmering fox, then kicked his right foot out of the stirrup, managing his dismount with controlled movements. He turned towards the waiting man, ready to take a gamble on the fellow. "I am asking, if you are loyal to your *Queen*. Kingsman."

The man's ice-blue eyes narrowed. "I won't be tricked, Viper. I'm not a Kingsman, and our Queen is dead."

Theroun drew a long breath, willing himself to make this work. "Don't play fool with me. Your hatred of me speaks plainly, Kingsman. You and all your ilk hiding in the ranks are at risk in this war, and I am trying to stop a lot of unnecessary death, sir. So. Which of your men may I send north? I need to make contact with Lhen Fhekran, at once. Your Queen may be alive."

The fox blinked, astonishment opening his face. "You oppose this war. The Black Viper wants to save a few Kingsmen. Well, fuck me."

"Our Queen would have the same stance as I." Theroun crossed his arms.

"If she lives."

"If she lives." Theroun nodded. "So. Who among your men can I trust with this?"

Runner-Captain den'Bhorus flashed his sneer. "The question is, *sir*, can any of my men trust *you*?"

Theroun set his jaw. "I'm not a Kingsman, but once I was friend to King Uhlas. I do not agree with the forces now pushing at me. So. If you would like to save your men and serve your Queen,

Kingsman, I am giving you that opportunity. And the Brigadier-Captain also, if he is of your ilk."

The fox before him was startled into silence. At last, he sneered. "You lie. I won't be tricked into treason. And shouldn't you be calling me Blackmark? I heard that's what you called the ones you mutilated all along the Aphellian Way. The name's caught on, you know. Especially at Harvest-Fest. Are we going to have a Blackmark bonfire here, too, to rouse men into fighting fury?" He narrowed his eyes and spit.

"Dammit, man!" Theroun exploded, loud enough that a nearby ptarridge went whirring up from the grass. He seized the fox by his jerkin. "I'm asking you to be *smart*. I'm asking you to *honor your oaths, Kingsman!* Serve me or don't, turn me in or don't, but *we need a fucking runner to get to Lhen Fhekran and bring us news of our Queen!*"

"And what if I'm not a Kingsman?" The man stared Theroun down with his sneer.

Theroun released den'Bhorus with a grunt of disgust. "Then I'm wasting my time." He turned and set a hand to his pommel, his left foot in the stirrup, preparing to engage the arduous process of mounting up.

"You're vulnerable, you know." A dire murmur came from behind him. "I could stab you out here and no one would come looking until you were missed at sixth bell."

Theroun paused, his foot still in the stirrup. "Then do it, man. No one knows that we are speaking. But if you stab me and leave me here to die, you'll have to organize an army for Queen Elyasin all by yourself. We have a common enemy and a common allegiance, so make your choice. What we do not have is time to squabble."

Theroun paused, giving the man opportunity to knife him. Daring him. But there was silence. At last, Theroun put his weight upon the stirrup and clambered up. He gazed down, watching the Fleetrunner Captain, whose fox-bright eyes stared at the horse's withers.

At last, den'Bhorus looked up. "For my Queen. Not for you."

"For *our* Queen." Theroun weathered that sneer.

Den'Bhorus nodded. "I'll send a man named Herkhum den'Lhiss, with a small contingent. He's also from Gerthoun. Knows these hills like he knows his own breath. He looks Elsthemi, like me."

"He's trained in espionage? He can circumvent our scouts?"

The Fleetrunner-Captain's snort was derisive. "Our perimeter is paltry. Circumnavigating the outer scouts is beneath him."

"Good." Theroun held the man's gaze a moment longer. "Command tent tonight at sixth bell. Alert all of your men who are loyal to the Queen that they need to be ready to leave at a moment's notice. But hold your men for now, wait for my word. We are all under very close scrutiny. We'll speak more in a few days." Theroun wheeled his horse, heading back the way they had come.

"And if I expose you?" The Runner-Captain called after him.

"Do it!" Theroun did not look around, his horse ambling through the dry, knee-high grasses. "But you'll not find General den'Ulthumen as considerate to your plight, Kingsman. Nor Cavalry-Captains den'Bheck, den'Ferhn, or den'Lennos. Not to mention the Third, Sixth, and Eighth Foot. Want to fight back? Become a Viper and hold your stillness until the best moment comes to strike."

Theroun clucked his tongue and nudged his horse on.

* * *

The Fleetrunner Captain was at a low simmer when he whisked into the command tent at sixth bell. Theroun glanced over from where he stood in conversation with General Lharsus den'Ulthumen and motioned den'Bhorus over with a quick flick of his fingers. The man came to his shoulder and stood at attention stiffly, waiting to be recognized.

"... are positioned here, here, and here. We can have picket lines ready for the Ninth Cavalry when they arrive here." Den'Ulthumen tapped a spot on the hastily-drawn map of the camp.

Theroun crossed his arms and glowered, fully engaging his role as Counsel-General without backing down from the younger and less experienced den'Ulthumen. "Just as well. But the foraging is already trampled here. Move the Ninth to the eastern side of this area. They've come up from Lhennian and those rangy southlands stock tend to be hungry."

General den'Ulthumen rubbed his blonde beard, his green eyes flicking over the map. A commander in his own right, he nodded briskly at Theroun's counsel, impassivity upon his battle-scarred face. He handed the camp map off to a waiting guard, contemplating the much larger and more detailed map of the Elsthemi-Menderian border beneath it. Theroun knew their talk of arrangements was over and the real discussion was about to begin.

Theroun nodded to the waiting Fleetrunner Captain.

Who saluted smartly, no trace of sneer on his face. "General den'Ulthumen! Runner-Captain den'Bhorus reporting in, sir! My Fleets are settled, recovered, and at your service. We are in communication with Brigadier Captain Arlus den'Pell, who will arrive tomorrow. Sir."

Like flies to honey, the milling commanders gathered about the map table, sensing the discussion was about to begin. Den'Ulthumen hardly needed to raise his mellow baritone to call them to attend. A squire stepped forward with small silver pieces of horse and men and different badges to signify specialized regiments, and den'Ulthumen laid them out upon the map.

"Gentlemen," he began, lifting his head to peruse every eye. "Our muster is nearly complete. I have had report that our last outstanding regiments, the Ninth Cavalry and High Brigade, will arrive on the morrow. I know many of you come from the Valenghian front, and I thank you all for shifting your operations for the sake of our great nation. The assault and *insult* to Alrou-Mendera by the Elsthemi Highlanders will not go unanswered, for the sake of our belated Queen. Many of you have met Counsel-General Theroun den'Vekir," Den'Ulthumen nodded to Theroun, "and understand that an order from him is to be acted upon as an order from me. I will open this counsel with a report on our general strategy against the Elsthemi, from my Counsel-General. Theroun. Please proceed."

Den'Ulthumen motioned to him. Theroun crossed his arms with his customary glower. "Think Valenghia was hard fighting? Think again," he barked. "No man will leave this front un-mangled. We fight keshari legions now, and if you've never fought keshari, I suggest you spend ample time speaking with those who have. Men will lose their head from one bite. Men will have their beating hearts torn out of their chests. One rake of those claws to an unarmored back will pull out a man's spine. I have received word," he glanced at the Fleetrunner Captain, "That our outer camp guard is *paltry*. Triple it. I want the bronze weather-bells coming up from the coast tomorrow at every compass-point. If keshari break into camp, we're finished. Period. We maintain *vigilance and order*! Any turmoil is a sign we've been breached, and if that happens, you muster every man you have and grab the longest spear you can find and all your archers and send someone to those bells! Now. Pay attention!"

Theroun launched into a description of keshari-style fighting, and how the cavalry and archer-lines were going to engage the cats in the forest and the river-valley. Heads nodded around the map table, faces grim. Theroun found himself eyeing them all as the flicker of the lamps replaced the evening's gloaming, seeing if he could tell a Khehemni from an Alrashemni from a regular soldier.

He found that he couldn't tell any difference.

At last, his briefing came to a close. Den'Ulthumen dismissed the meeting, so all could see to their regiments and get settled for the night. Theroun departed with a nod to the General, and to his surprise, Runner-Captain den'Bhorus stepped out from the command tent at his side. They ambled off together, snaking through lantern lit avenues in a mutual silence, camp's evening bustle all around. At last, they came to the Fleetrunner command tent with its striped blue and white awning.

Vitreal turned, green eyes flashing in the light of a torch. "If we're going to do this, then I need assurances."

"Like what?" Theroun kept his growl low.

"Like my men survive this. Like you're not going to rat us out the moment things go bad."

"I can't promise that your men won't die, Captain," Theroun bit quietly under his breath as a soldier passed with a saddle over his shoulder. The man gave a salute and Theroun nodded as he moved on. "But I can assure you I mean every word of what I say. I gave my oaths once upon a time to King Uhlas. His nation, and his house, will always come first for me."

"Funny," Vitreal sneered in the darkness. "I wouldn't have pegged you for a Kingsman."

"I may not be a Kingsman, but I was the King's man," Theroun growled, stepping close. "Follow me or don't. But shovel the shit, Captain."

"Or what?"

"Or you don't want to know." Theroun snapped, losing his patience at last.

Vitreal eyed him. "You really are a fucking Viper, aren't you?"

"Ask yourself this, Fleetrunner: would you rather have my strike with you or against you? Which one do you think you'd survive?" Theroun snarled in the darkness.

The man sobered. He gave a soft snort, all sneer gone from his face. A considering look had taken Vitreal, and he reached up to rub his clean-shaven chin. "Arlus den'Pell is almost here. I've had a report the Brigadiers contingent will arrive tonight. I'll brief him on your plan as soon as they get settled."

"Do that." Theroun turned to go.

"Theroun." He turned back. Vitreal scuffed a boot in the dirt and put his hands on his hips, then sighed. "I'm not in if Arlus isn't. I don't know you. He does. And he fucking hates you. But I'll do what I can to convince him."

"Fair enough."

Theroun turned and strode away. There was nothing more to say. Either they would come to his banner or they wouldn't, he couldn't push the matter any further. Moving off through the settling darkness, he turned down avenue after alley, making his way to his own command-tent on the eastern rim. Lamps and torches had been lit at intersections to push back the oncoming night, brisk with a Highland chill. Men bustled by with gear, with tin bowls of supper, with water-buckets for oxen and horse-troughs.

Theroun was almost at his pavilion with its crimson and gold awning, when unease prickled him. As if he were being watched, the hairs on the back of his neck raised, causing gooseflesh to dapple his arms. He looked up, his eye catching upon a tall fellow threading past a group of carts. The fellow's black armor had a strange pattern in the torchlight. Woven of leather strips, metal studs glinted as the hooded man rounded an iron sconce by a mess tent and disappeared from view.

Unease gnawed Theroun to see a man in camp with such obviously foreign garb, and from a nation he didn't recognize. He left his pavilion, after his quarry. Striding around the mess-tent, his gaze raked the nearby tents, the avenue. All those around him wore the brown leather of the Menderian army. Officers with collars of cobalt to their jerkins tipped nods to their Counselor-General.

Leaving the mess-tent, Theroun scanned the alleys. Past a cart of water barrels, he noticed a flash of black with silver studs, slipping around a corner. Theroun crept forward, moving with surprising grace, adrenaline lending him poise on the hunt. His gaze raked groups of men huddling around braziers, warming their hands or dicing on upturned barrels.

It struck him suddenly, that this camp, the Seventeenth and Eighteenth Foot, were mostly men of swarthy complexion, chocolate-brown or ebony. With dark brown eyes that glittered in the night, they were mostly Southrons from past the Tourmaline Isles. Tall Jadounians slender as willows, broad-shouldered Perthians built like bulls, and the whip-lean, black-eyed men from the deserts of Desh-Kar. As Theroun passed, he heard slurring accents of many languages.

Suddenly, he saw his mark. Theroun stalked into the shadows of an empty fletcher's tent. The man was very tall, broad-shouldered, and honed like a war-axe. His hood was thrown back now, and white scars raked his face, like he'd been swiped by a keshar once. His hair was a sleek black, straight like mink, his cheekbones high and strong, slicing across his face like knives. Piercings dotted all the way up one ear.

Something about the man was familiar to Theroun, as if he had seen someone like this in his distant past. Theroun squinted at the fellow, frustrated, willing himself to remember. The man's stature, his dominant yet regal bearing. That look upon his face, stony and without compassion. But try as Theroun might, he could dredge up no memory of why the man rankled him.

The man in herringbone leathers spoke to a tall soldier with the ebony complexion of Jadoun. The Jadounian was animated, angry. Furious. His dicing-fellows began to rise from their barrel, bristling with knives as the argument deepened. The man in black herringbone leathers made a curt gesture with one hand. Suddenly, the Jadounian soldier's face went slack. His eyebrows knit in confusion. His fellows blinked, turned away, sank back to their seats. Knives were abandoned upon the dicing barrel. The man in herringbone leathers gazed over their now-quiescent company.

And then strode off to the darkness, a slight smile of satisfaction upon his lips.

Theroun emerged from the fletcher's tent with a deep scowl. His skin prickled with wrongness. Men that angry should have begun to brawl in the ranks. Someone should have ended up cut from such a tense interaction. But the man in woven leathers had diffused it with a flick of his fingers. Theroun noted the direction the man had gone, then approached the Jadounians. Two ten-sided Jadounian dice were hastily swept into a leather pouch as Theroun stepped into the brazier's light. The Jadounians stood as one, snapping a curt salute, towering over Theroun.

"You fellow, who was that man you were just talking to?" Theroun barked.

The Jadounian blinked. "Who?"

"That man." Theroun growled. "In the herringbone weave leathers. Who was he?"

"I do not know of what you speak, sir." The Jadounian's accent was very thick.

Theroun was about to raze him, but then he looked at the man's eyes. Pure confusion was in their ebony depths, apology. Theroun's old wound prickled. "You were just speaking to a tall man in herringbone weave armor, not one minute ago. Are you telling me you do not remember?"

The man shook his head. "Duthukan has been here, with fighter brothers, with the dice." He gestured to the table. "No man has approached Duthukan in the manner you speak. Sir."

"Did none of you see this man? You took up knives against him for Halsos' sake!" Theroun barked. Heads shook in apology. Shoulders shrugged. Confused glances were cast towards the knives still out upon the barrel-top. "Where are you from, Duthukan?" Theroun pressed, feeling something vastly wrong here.

The Jadounian's black eyes misted over. "I come from Quelsis."

"You were never born in Quelsis. Jadounian, aren't you?"

"Jadoun. I do not know such a place."

The man's face was open, honest. Utterly confused, as if he didn't recall where he came from. Theroun's gaze raked him. Everything about him was native Jadounian, from the scar-dot tattooing over his eyebrows, to the massive plugs of hathnou-tusk in his ears, to the lines of white scarring across his knuckles that told of his warrior's kills for his clan. His accent was classic, and his ebony skin was a giveaway.

"Where did you get those?" Theroun gestured to the man's knuckles.

Duthukan's eyebrows knit. He gazed long at his clan scars as if seeing them for the first time. "I... do not know, sir."

Theroun looked around Duthukan's kinsmen. All of them were looking at their knuckles now, confused, eyebrows knit as if trying to remember something.

"Who are you, soldier? What is your clan-name back home?" Theroun pressed, far more gently.

Duthukan flinched as if struck, and his gaze fell from Theroun's. "I... I am Duthukan. I... clan... I do not know."

Theroun stepped back. He blinked. It was like the man had been washed of all knowledge of his home. If this Jadounian had come to Alrou-Mendera looking for opportunity to feed his starving family by enlisting, he would have been crowing about his ability to fight and provide for them, lauding the strength of his clan and how he would prove it upon the battlefield. Jadounians were famous for bragging about bravery and prowess, about how they killed three lions with one spear after fucking their seven wives rotten. But this man wasn't. He was like a beaten cur, broken and spent.

His life and his country and his clan all unknown.

Theroun's gaze snapped to the others. One by one, every man at the dicing-table dropped their gaze. "And are you proud to serve Alrou-Mendera, soldiers?" Theroun asked.

"Yes, sir!" They'd said it as one, like good recruits. But not a one of them could meet Theroun's eyes. These men were broken, fodder for keshar-maws.

"Hear me now." Theroun barked suddenly, to Duthukan. "Your mind has been tampered with, your memories erased. A man spoke to you just now, in black herringbone leathers. If you ever see such a man around the camp again, you are to report immediately to me, Chancellor-General Theroun den'Vekir. Are we clear?"

"A man in woven leathers? Changing my mind? Erasing Duthukan?" The Jadounian scowled. Theroun saw a sharp mind working behind that language barrier. A sharp mind trying to come out from behind whatever had been done to him.

"Yes. You and your Jadounian brethren." Theroun gestured to the other men around the dicing barrel. "And I will find out why. You are dismissed."

"Evil!" Duthukan hissed suddenly, his face contorted in rage. A spark of ferocity lanced through his eyes, and Theroun saw the warrior within. Suddenly, Duthukan touched two fingers to his brow, a motion of Jadounian respect, and dipped his chin. "I honor you for caring what becomes of Duthukan. Of my warrior-brothers. For fighting such evil. I will report to you if I see this black *majiyenou. Verouni.*" The Jadounian made a proper Menderian military salute, then turned back to his fellows, a thoughtful frown upon his face.

Theroun blinked. The term Verouni, *Truth Warrior*, was generally reserved for the most respected Jadounian fighters or wise men. He nodded to the group and moved away, his gaze raking dark alleys for the man who was somehow at the heart of this mystery.

Theroun felt prickling lance across the back of his neck again. He snapped around fast, scouring the darkness between torch-sconces. And there, in a spot of black between two tents twenty paces away, stood the man. His manner held an imposing gravitas, even at this distance. Theroun could feel the pierce of the man's gaze, like a vulture. His leather armor was indeed woven, catching the light of the stars high above in a herringbone pattern, silver studs glimmering.

He stared Theroun down a moment longer. Then threw up his dark hood.

Suddenly, a wave of ferocious pain ripped through Theroun from nowhere. He stumbled to his knees in the trampled grass with a gasp, clutching his old wound. His gaze broke from the man in agony, his breath stolen by the pain like he'd been rolled under a merciless ocean.

By the time he could breathe again, could look up, the avenue between the tents was empty.

Forcing slower breaths, Theroun finally managed to get his pain under control. Cursing his old weakness, he struggled back to standing, eyes raking the nighttime camp. Stepping quickly to where the man had stood, Theroun turned in a circle, clutching his ribs, searching.

But the man in herringbone leathers was gone.

CHAPTER 14 – OLEA

A violet dusk swirled with evening winds as Olea and the others wound their way through Ghellen to Lourden's home. The group was silent from the dire revelations of the afternoon as they walked from the Maitrohounet's, thoughtful, *shoufs* pulled up over mouths and noses to keep out the blowing sands. At Lourden's home, a sprawling structure of colonnaded stone, he touched the vine upon the lintel and ducked beneath the reed-woven mat. Olea and the others did the same, entering the ample guesthouse of Lourden and his wife Thelliere.

Dark thoughts were soon banished by the warm smells of home and hearth, and the shrieks of children at play. Lourden's three youngsters tussled upon the saffron and ochre rug in the main room. Like the Maitrohounet's abode but cozier, Lourden's guesthouse was bright with silk pillows, ottomans to recline upon, and colored glass votives lit with candles brightening niches of alabaster stone. Bickering and biting like puppies upon the ample rug, the children were untroubled by strangers. They bounced up when their father entered, shrieking at his arrival and clustering around his legs.

Lourden changed instantly. He laughed as he removed his crested helmet, setting it and his long spear aside by the door. Kneeling so his children could pour all over him, he unbuckled his breastplate and shin guards, giving them to the children so they could run around the house with them like trophies. They paid little attention to the guests until Vargen ducked in. And then the middle one leapt into Vargen's arms, squishing his enormous biceps and giggling.

Lourden's wife Thelliere emerged from the kitchens, her grey eyes round at seeing her visitors home at an unexpected time. White bean-flour smudged her face, and she hastily tried to arrange her short plum garment, smoothing black curls as she beamed welcome.

Lapis and ochre jewelry adorned her neck and ears, and bracelets of lapis curled up her slender forearms and ankles like serpents.

Thelliere began speaking rapidly in Khourek, gesturing to her husband. Lourden spoke back, apparently summing up the conversation with the Maitrohounet. Lourden mentioned the words *Olea* and *Rennkavi* in his rapid speech. Thelliere suddenly clapped both hands over her mouth, eyes wide, and sank to her knees. Lourden was beside his wife in an instant, lifting her back to her feet, murmuring a few words in her ear. She shook her head, then nodded, then beamed through unshed tears.

She strode forward, embracing Olea like a sister, kissing her upon the lips. Ghellani women were familiar, often kissing in greeting. Thelliere proceeded on to Vargen, doing the same, then to Aldris. And last to Jherrick, who turned beet red just as he'd done the first time Thelliere had kissed him in welcome.

"*Welekhoum!*" She spoke Khourek, then continued in halting Menderian. "Welcome! Food ready soon. Sit, sit!"

She fussed about the living room, plumping silk pillows. Lourden grabbed her around the middle, forestalling her, and she squealed playfully. They kissed a long time. Ghellani were very frank in public, and had little stock in propriety, Olea had found. It went on long enough that Jherrick and Vargen started studying the glass-tiled walls, though Aldris leered with a wicked grin. At last, the Ghellani spear-captain and his wife broke apart.

"Thank you for your continued hospitality," Olea said.

"It is nothing!" Thelliere waved a brisk hand. "To oppose the Karthus, we serve. Dinner soon. So skinny!" She patted Olea's middle then bustled off, one child hot on her heels, pulling at her purple wrap.

Lourden laughed, a bright, carefree sound, and gestured to the cushions. "Sit! I will fetch *fürhen* for us to drink. Many celebrations we must have tonight!"

He strode to the kitchen from which good smells drifted, and Olea had a seat upon a thick pillow. Vargen had two little ones snuggled into his lap. The children tugged his beard and examined his scars, and Vargen made hard muscles so they could thump them and hang from them like little monkeys. Olea sighed as she leaned back upon her brightly-woven pillow, at ease at last after such a long day.

"Vargen's a natural with those kids." Aldris sat close, hands laced behind his head.

"Vargen had a son." Olea murmured. "They were estranged by the Summons."

"What happened to the boy?"

"He doesn't know."

Silence stretched as they watched. Jherrick scooted over to join the fun, posing and making muscles for the children, causing them to giggle and shriek. They loved Jherrick nearly as much as they loved Vargen, and soon the four were tussling about the rug, growling.

"What are we doing here, captain?" Aldris' voice was low. "Shouldn't we be working on a way to get home? With everything we heard today…" He shook his head. "I'm itching to get back and slit a certain throat, if you know what I mean."

"I won't refuse Lourden's hospitality, Aldris." Olea murmured. "The Ghellani think we're their lost *Alrashemnari*, and we are. We didn't plan to come here, but that Alranstone chose *for* us."

"Yeah… about that." Aldris scowled, crossed his arms over his chest.

"About what?" Olea prompted him.

"About the Alranstone. It's been bothering me for a whole damn week." Aldris took a breath, sighed, but it did not ease his tense posture. "And in light of today's revelations, it bothers me all the more. Why Jherrick? If you're this Olive Branch of the Dawn the Ghellani think you are, and me and Vargen carry Alrashemni blood, which comes from this very desert… then why did the Stone only respond when Jherrick set his hands upon it, Olea?"

"The Stones supposedly sense if you have a need to travel. The Alranstone must have sensed something in Jherrick, and it took us where his need was greatest."

"But Jherrick's not Alrashemni," Aldris continued. "He's not Shemout. Fenton and I were trying to keep men we trust on your watch, but Jherrick has a regular rotation. It was happpenstance that he was in the cells that day, that he came with us when we fled."

"What are you saying, Aldris?" Olea knew that mind. Aldris was chewing on some tangle, and he wouldn't rest until he had figured it out.

"Olea, what if..." Aldris trailed off. Olea saw him set his jaw, his eyes narrowing upon Jherrick. "What if Jherrick is one of *them*, Khehemni? What if he was on your guard that day because he was placed there by someone in the Khehemni Lothren? What if he came with us to watch you, keep eyes on you? What if his need was great at that Alranstone, because of what he is? Because he needed to stay on your ass like flies on shit."

Olea scoffed, dismissing the notion. "That's ludicrous. Jherrick has been my loyal right hand in the guardhouse for years. Of course he would defect with me."

"Would he?" Aldris' gaze was keen. "He's a coward, Olea. He's terrible in a fight. That kid drops his sword on the practice grounds and trips all over his boots like nothing I've ever seen."

"There. He couldn't be Khehemni. They wouldn't want him."

"Ahh, but they would." Aldris gestured to the lad, tussling with the children. "Keenest fucking mind I've seen outside of yours, Fenton's, and that lanky scribe of Chancellor Theroun's. No matter that Jherrick can't keep his glasses straight on his face. Which are gone, by the way. Have you noticed he's not squinting at anything?"

"But if his need was to follow me, why would the Alranstone respond to him?" Olea countered, thinking it through. "If I couldn't go through, he wouldn't have had a need to go through."

Aldris chewed his lip, curried a hand through his golden mane. "Maybe... his real need was deeper. Maybe deep inside, in a place the Alranstone could feel, Jherrick needed to come here. To learn about Khehem."

Olea sobered at that thought. Her gaze strayed to Jherrick, now sitting with one child in his lap on an ottoman, the boy showing Jherrick a puzzle-toy wrought of copper. "And only all of us together, traveling here, could address his need. Could bring out the story of Khehem."

"My thoughts exactly," Aldris watched Jherrick, her Second-Lieutenant cold as a snake.

"Now is not the time for fractiousness, Aldris." Olea's voice was low. "But we will address it. Give me some time. Let me speak to Jherrick. As much as I hate your reasoning... it has merit."

"Yes, Captain."

They were interrupted as Thelliere reemerged from the

kitchens, beckoning brightly. The group proceeded to the back terrace where they commonly dined, a lovely tiled space full of shade palms. The low glass table was already set for supper with colorful pottery and glass beverage bowls. The guests took seats, the routine familiar. Olea sipped her plum beverage, watching the children haul Vargen out into the garden beneath the lace-palms, to pick herbs for dinner in the evening's gloaming. Thelliere bustled around, lighting oil lamps in ornate glass sconces, illuminating the outdoor garden like a fae dream. A growling competition had commenced in the garden, of who could growl the loudest.

Vargen was winning.

Lourden laughed at the antics, settling his long legs out from a slingback chair next to Olea. Olea was about to say something, but he held up one hand suddenly. "Please. I must speak. I have been distant these past many days, but I want you to know it was of necessity. In my heart, I felt you were not one of the eel's dogs, *Olea-gishii*, but only the Maitrohounet could judge the truth. So I apologize for any…callousness, in my manner."

"I would have done the same in your position," Olea replied, taking a sip of plum beverage.

A knowing smile quirked Lourden's lips. "You are a woman of battle, *Olea-gishii*, like my spears. Long has there been peace in Ghellen, because our spears are fierce. But Lhaurent of the Karthus does not take no for an answer. Again and again he sends his dogs through the Stones. Our spears grow tired of such games."

"Is there a Stone at every oasis?"

"Yes, except Khehem. Legends say it was destroyed." Lourden sipped his plum beverage.

"Do you know how Lhaurent comes through the Stones? How he makes them open for him?" Olea leaned forward, curious.

Lourden shook his head. "No. We have tried to send spears after his retreating cowards, but the Stones allow no Tribesman to pass."

Olea fought a sinking sensation in her stomach. Castellan Lhaurent had more secrets than she'd ever dreamed. And knowing them now, was a nightmare. "You said there was once a Stone inside Khehem? It was destroyed?"

"When the Last King of Khehem, Leith Alodwine, was

206

imprisoned for his atrocities." Lourden nodded, then glanced around furtively. "Part of my duty also, is to protect Oasis Ghellen from Khehem. Another reason we patrol near the Stone."

Olea's eyebrows rose. "Why would Ghellen need protection from an abandoned city?"

Lourden's face was grim in the glowing light of the sconces as evening's shadows darkened the porch. "Khehem is cursed. The oasis is without people, but evil still lives there. Ghosts move the city. Men fall from bridges, they get trapped when walls shift. Stones drop out beneath your feet. On wicked nights, the whole city moves, sliding like snakes through the dunes. Very bad. Very, very bad."

Olea's glass nearly fell out of her hand, so violent was her shudder. Lourden sat up, his long fingers reaching out to touch her face in apology. "I have upset you! We must not speak of Khehem. Thelliere will cut my sack!"

"A place where ghosts move the walls... that's exactly what Vargen experienced in Roushenn." Olea nodded out to the fae-lit garden, now darkening beneath a swath of stars.

Lourden made a sound like a snake spitting. A rictus gripped his face. "He may say nothing of what he has seen in front of the children. Nothing! The older two, their first-father Gherlam died between the moving walls of Khehem. But we must discuss this once the children are abed. Two places where ghosts weave the walls! How can it be?"

Olea was wondering the same thing. But Thelliere interrupted, carrying reed-woven trays of supper out to the luminous porch. A delightful dinner began, Olea's appreciation sullied only by her preoccupation. Jherrick and Aldris were soon drunk on plum beverage, pink-cheeked, trying to twist their tongues around Khourek again as they dined on cucumbers in a spicy paste, and lamb in a cold red broth. Whip-smart, Jherrick's tongue slid around Khourek with ease, and Olea wondered about what Aldris had said. She pushed the thought away, watching Aldris play dumb for children, who corrected his Khourek mercilessly. Though Olea noticed Aldris was far less drunk than he seemed, snapping a wary eye to Jherrick now and then.

Conversation turned from languages to lines of trade, and Jherrick piped up with interest, rapt upon the conversation. "So your neighboring nations speak Khourek? To trade with one another?"

"Trade with Ghrec is very prosperous," Lourden gave a drunken smile. "With them, we speak Ghrec. But the other nations we border share Khourek, though they have their own tribal tongues."

"Ajnabiit blight-lands upon eastern peninsula, across mountains." Thelliere spoke up. She dumped a pail of small stones out upon the table, making a rough map. "Very hard travel there. Tribes Lukhaan, Niirm, and Drashaan fish the sea, gain medicines from squid and mollusk the Ajnabiit do not have. So we risk travel, trade. Make Tribes very wealthy. Lore says, black-eyed Ajnabiit once ruled our continent with machines and vast cities. But the Great Blight took all continent five thousand years ago. They died, became a small people. But much has recovered since the Age of Chiron." Thelliere smiled, clearly pleased that she had spoken so much in Menderian.

Vargen extended the line of stones north and west, outlining countries from Ghrec to Alrou-Mendera. He pointed to a location nearly off the table. "We come from here."

Lourden gave a drunken whistle. "So far. Did our *Alrashemnari* really travel that far?"

"Farther." Aldris moved his hands off the table, indicating the Highlands. "We have people up here, in Elsthemen. And over here," he moved his hands west. "The Tourmaline Isles. And here," he pointed very far southwest. "Perthe."

Lourden whistled again. Olea stared at Aldris.

"What?" Aldris looked peevish.

"Don't you think the extent of the Shemout Alrashemni's operations would have been good information to share *before* we left Alrou-Mendera?" Olea chastised. "We could have been smuggled out of Roushenn with the Tourmaline delegation."

"We couldn't have trusted that delegation." Aldris swirled his plum alcohol, scowling. "There were at least two Shemout among them, but I didn't know how many Khehemni might also have have been among King Arthe's retinue." Aldris' gaze flicked to Jherrick. But Jherrick missed it, studying the map upon the table.

"You were not to mention Khehem here!" Lourden had sat up straight, his face darkening. His gaze flicked to the children, asleep in

Vargen's lap, then to his wife. Thelliere was pale. She sat back on her cushion, drinking deeply of her beverage. Lourden bowed over his wife's hand. "Forgive me."

"No." Thelliere held up a hand. "The Khehem have only power you give them. Ghosts are ghosts. Tell me of these Khehemni. Alive? In your land?"

"Most captured Khehemni take their secrets to the grave," Aldris continued, staring at Jherrick, "even under severe torture. We know little about them. We have found out that they refer to themselves as the Broken Circle. One man I personally... questioned, said the Khehemni came out of a southeastern desert long ago, hunted by Alrashemni."

Jherrick looked up from the map, met Aldris' gaze. Something rippled over the lad's face before it was gone. Olea still did not believe Aldris' suppositions. She had worked with Jherrick for too long, scrutinized his every movement in the guardhouse. But Aldris' frank admission to having tortured Khehemni made her suddenly reconsider her Second-Lieutenant.

"I'd heard you'd tortured people." She said.

"I do what I have to, to protect Alrashemni." A hard killer gazed at Olea from behind Aldris' green eyes. "Fenton was the same, Olea. If you don't want to know, don't ask."

"What else haven't you told me, Aldris? About the Shemout, the Khehemni?" Olea wondered how many more surprises might come tumbling out of Aldris' mouth tonight.

"Some." Aldris held her gaze. "But I'd rather not expound it in present company. Even talking of the Shemout is new to me. Just before shit went down at the palace, Fenton insisted I make myself known, and I trust him, but..." His gaze flicked around the table, pinning Jherrick. "I don't trust *him*."

"Come off it." Olea growled, irate. "If you suspect Jherrick of something, just ask him, den'Farahan."

Aldris gave a dangerous look, his green eyes piercing. "He won't enjoy the way I ask questions."

Thelliere stood suddenly, waking the children, hustling them off Vargen's lap. She took them into the house, away from the tense conversation. Jherrick stared at Aldris as Thelliere left, a harder, colder gaze than Olea had ever seen from the lad. He reached out, adding spice-marinated dessert plums to his plate more carefully than Olea had ever seen him do anything. Those movements were smooth and controlled, a far different Jherrick than she was used to seeing.

"You don't have to put me to the rack and thumbscrews," Jherrick spoke once the children were gone. "I overheard you and Olea talking earlier. And you're right, Aldris. I am Khehemni."

It was an admission as smooth as his movements. The lad's manner was calm as the table suddenly erupted around him. Aldris was on his feet, one longknife to hand, lunging for the lad. Olea dove between them.

Aldris pulled up short, breathing hard, his green eyes on fire. "Move, Olea."

She pinned him with her gaze. "No."

Aldris snarled, feral, whipping his other longknife to Olea's throat. "I said move, Kingswoman!"

"And I said no, *Lieutenant*." Olea's voice was cold as she stared him down.

"Threaten your Captain, Shemout," Vargen's rumble sounded from behind Aldris, "and my steel goes right through your spine. I don't care how much you protected her over the years. Be smart. Think about whether the lad's life is worth yours right now, or if you should put the blade away."

Vargen shifted, and Olea could see he had a longknife between Aldris' shoulder blades, angled down towards his heart. One meaty hand was ready to bear down with all his mountainous weight behind its thrust. Lourden had moved also at Aldris' action, seizing a nearby spear from beside the door. He leveled it at Aldris with a curse now, joining Vargen's blade.

"And just like that, three Kingsmen fall." Jherrick murmured.

Olea's breath froze. That was not the voice she was used to hearing from Jherrick. It was deeper, robust. Far more assured. She turned her head from Aldris to look behind her at Jherrick. His grey eyes were empty of all emotion, empty like death as they flickered over the assembly, then settled upon Olea.

"I always liked you, Captain. You're decent, for Alrashemni. I could have killed you the day of the coronation, you know. The Lothren would have praised me for it." Jherrick's grey eyes were calm as lake water, his tone blank.

"Why didn't you?" Olea growled, turning to face him. Jherrick wore no weapons tonight, and Olea read no fight in his demeanor. He wanted this admission, for some reason.

And he was hoping it would go peaceably.

His eyes flickered over the others. "Put down the weapons and I'll tell you."

"Not fucking likely. *Khehemnas.*" Aldris snarled it in a bitter curse.

"Put down your knife, Aldris." Olea commanded.

"He's got some dirty Khehemni trick up his ass!"

"He's unarmed and he's not going to fight. Put down the knife. That's an order."

"I'll gut his throat first!"

"You will do nothing of the sort!" Olea roared, pivoting so she could face Aldris and Jherrick at once. "You will do as I command, or I will turn that blade and put it right through your Inkings, Lieutenant, *so I swear upon my blood!*"

Olea saw Aldris flinch, though it was just a flicker of his eyes. Lourden slid into a better position, his spear ready, his grey gaze raptor-keen. "All of you. No bloodshed here. I will not suffer violence in my home."

Crickets chirred in the darkness. The palms were still, no breeze to riffle them. With a wry twist of defeat upon his lips, Aldris slid his knife back into its sheath. Like a mountain melting, Vargen did the same. But Lourden stood ready with his long spear, for anyone to break his truce.

"Now," Olea rounded upon Jherrick. "You will tell us why you didn't kill me during the coronation."

"And you will tell us about the Khehemni," Vargen growled.

"And just who the fuck you actually are." Aldris snarled.

"Everything." Olea crossed her arms, fingertips near her longknives.

"Everything?" Jherrick's visage was empty. "Or what you *desire* to know?"

Olea hardened. She didn't know this young man before her. Nothing remained of his affable persona from the guardhouse. He was a stranger, cold calculation behind those grey eyes.

"And what is it I desire to know?" Olea murmured.

"The secrets of Roushenn. I know who controls it."

"Lhaurent." Olea breathed, knowing to her bones she was right.

Jherrick dipped his chin in a nod. A small movement, efficient. "But what the Khehemni don't know, is just how much power he truly has. Which is why I came with you when we escaped the palace. I want to see his power undone. And you can help me."

Olea took a deep breath, willing herself to be calm. She pointed at the table, to a chair far from Jherrick's, her gaze pinning Aldris. With a snarl, Aldris sat. Jherrick had a seat also, far from Aldris. Vargen settled his bulk beside Olea. Lourden's dark brows lowered in a scowl as he sat, his spear within easy reach. His long fingers drummed upon the table, a counterpoint to the desert night.

"Now. Tell me about Roushenn." Olea commanded Jherrick.

"Roushenn is set on a complicated series of gears." Jherrick began, stating the facts simply without embellishment. "It's like a Praoughian clockwork. The walls run upon a vast network of tracks. Mirrors and chandeliers and furniture are moved by threads on pulleys invisible to the eye. But the threads can be cut. And after they've been cut, they are visible. Some enchantment rides them, just like the stones and walls that fit seamlessly back together once they've moved."

Olea reeled, trying to take it all in. "What controls it?"

"Ancient *wyrria*." Jherrick lifted a blonde eyebrow. "Lhaurent controls it, somehow. He raises his hands, and the walls move." Jherrick told her of being one of Lhaurent's spies in the Hinterhaft, and Olea bristled as Jherrick continued. "I've seen things behind the walls, that I wasn't supposed to see. Not the *way* I saw them. Not with a critical eye."

Olea lifted a stern eyebrow. "Like what?"

Jherrick's grey eyes were chips of ice. "Like how a child who stumbled onto his affairs dies. Surrounded by a hall of mirrors, an oubliette of Lhaurent's making, left to starve to death. They gibber with madness before they go."

Olea fought to keep her face impassive. "And?"

"Do you need more?" Jherrick's eyes seethed hatred suddenly. "Women confused by the walls, raped at Lhaurent's command. Men hung by their feet, their manhood sliced off, left to bleed to death from chandeliers thirty feet up. Lhaurent has more power than the Khehemni Lothren ever intended, and keeps his own private network they know nothing about."

"So why tell us?" Aldris snarled.

Jherrick's grey eyes flicked to Aldris. "Because I believe rabid animals need taming, before they receive death's mercy. He needs to see his ambitions slip through his jaws." His gaze flicked back to Olea. "We need to see Oasis Khehem. If I'm right, it works the same way as Roushenn. It can tell us about Lhaurent's fortress, about how we might stop it, take it from him."

Olea narrowed her eyes. "Why now, Jherrick? Why betray your kind?"

"I was trained to hate Alrashemni from childhood," Jherrick didn't sugar his answer. "And Shemout Alrashemni are trained to hate us just the same. The simple fact is, no one knows in which direction true justice lies. But what I've seen behind those walls, Captain-General, is far from just."

Olea watched Jherrick, this man she did not know. No words came.

Lourden tapped his finger upon the table, then stood, breaking the silence. "Come. We will secure the Khehemnas for the night, and think upon all that has been said. I must take him to the Maitrohounet in the morning, so she can decide his fate." He fixed Jherrick in his formidable gaze. "You will submit to iron tonight. That, or you die where you sit."

"I submit to your will," Jherrick rose from the table with steady grace, quite unlike the gangly lad he had once appeared to be, placing his hands behind his head.

"Until he decides he'd rather slit our throats." Aldris snorted across the table.

Olea scowled at Aldris, and he shut his trap.

* * *

Olea sat upon her pallet's blue silk blanket, her head spinning from too many revelations and far too much drink. The tension of the night was gradually curdling her belly. Jherrick had been chained in manacles and secured in his rooms. Olea had said not a word as she'd relieved him of anything that might be used to pick his restraints. He'd had no words for her, only a piercing alertness upon her every movement that was entirely unlike the person she knew, as she'd taken his effects away.

A night breeze wafted through Olea's room now that the shades had been lifted. The house was quiet, all having gone to bed nearly an hour earlier. Incense drifted past Olea's nose, lit beneath the window to keep away sand-midges and moths. A shallow dish of oil burned upon the stone window-ledge, casting light about the room in flickers.

"*Olea-gishii*, are you well?" Lourden's low baritone came from her arched doorway. Olea blinked and looked up. The spear-captain ducked his long height beneath the raised door-screen, then leaned one shoulder against the wall, watching her from the shadows.

"Not particularly." Olea murmured.

"Would you like to take a walk?" Lourden asked. "I often find the night settling to heavy thoughts."

Olea sat up. She paused, unsure. Her gaze flicked over the spear-captain.

"You are conflicted. This is unseemly in your culture. I will go." He began to duck beneath the reeds, but Olea suddenly spoke.

"No. Yes. A walk would be welcome."

Lourden turned back. His grey eyes shone in the lamplight, so much like Alden's, questioning if she was all right. Lourden looked like Alden in almost every way. The two could have been brothers in another life. Olea rose, and he moved toward her from the shadows.

"Come. Let us take you out where one can breathe."

Lourden turned, leading out past the rolled-up screen. The guesthouse was silent as they stepped through the mirror-tiled darkness, only a single oil lamp lit in each room. They were soon out through the front, into a silent street. No night wind blew. No sand skirled about the avenue. All was peace and expansion around Olea in the drifting shadows of the palms. Olea looked up, seeing a night full of stars and a full moon above. Something within her eased, breathing for the first time all day. Taking a deep inhalation of the jasoune-scented night, she let it out slowly.

They began to walk. Winding beneath the stars, sometimes

they spied the round orb of the moon through the date-palms, but they never lost the wideness of the desert sky. On and on they moved through the midnight city, climbing staircases of stone, dipping through tight alleys, rising up to overlooks and then down to fountains.

Lourden stopped at last upon a high parapet, a section of Ghellen's ancient wall still standing. Far below, the desert spread before them, rippling like the ocean, dunes silvered with moonshadow. Their gaze was endless, over dark arroyos all the way to the northern mountains, their heights lost like a smudge of charcoal upon the horizon.

It was silent on the wall, a deep desert hush that brought Olea relief. She never realized how much her *wyrric* hearing intruded, jangling her nerves from every voice, every bootfall upon stone, every rustle of leaves. The sounds of a living city had crowded her for years in Lintesh.

But here it was silent. For the first time since she had lived in Alrashesh, Olea could feel silence like something velvet upon her skin, smooth and uninterrupted. Her eyes prickled, then burned. Drops of wet began to roll down her cheeks. Reaching out, Lourden touched her cheek. With a sigh, Olea gave in. She stepped close and Lourden wound his long arms about her, cradling her to his warm chest. He smelled good, like honey and mesquite. Olea pressed her forehead to his neck, breathing him in as her tears fell, silent and endless.

"Great misery rests upon you," Lourden spoke at last, his voice soft as sighing sand. "Like it did upon Thelliere when Gherlam was killed. She has had many years now, and a good man to warm her bed, to give her more children who cheer her."

"I don't want children," Olea half-laughed, half-sobbed.

"No, but your heart is longing." Lourden murmured, his lips soft near her temple.

"Alden." It came choking out of her throat, before Olea could stop it.

"Tell me of this Alden," Lourden said, stroking her back with a kind touch. "Tell me of the man you wish would come for you, while we stand here and drink the peace of the night."

Lourden tucked Olea close to his chest. And to his serene

permission and the silence of the desert, Olea suddenly broke. She wasn't a Guardsman here. She wasn't Captain-General anymore. She had no men to lead but Aldris, Jherrick, and Vargen. She might have had royal blood, but she wasn't a queen. It was safe here, to be a woman. Just a woman by the dead of night and the light of the moon and the curl of sand writhing across midnight dunes.

Tears rolled off Olea's nose. She sighed, leaning upon Lourden's smooth-muscled chest with all its colorful Inkings, muted in the desert hush. She began to speak of Alden with grateful surrender, and found she couldn't stop. One memory rolled into another. Olea was hoarse by the time she finally recounted Alden's death, when she had seen his body brought home, his head split from being dashed upon the rocks at the foot of the darkened lighthouse.

"All I could do was kiss him, Lourden, upon that stone bier in the catacombs of Roushenn. But he was dead, and so cold. He tasted like brine, and blood..." Olea stared at the retaining-wall, feeling Lourden's arms around her. "He died because he tried to come home, for me. The lighthouse should have been lit in the storm. My Dhenra had to pull me away, down in that catacomb. She was barely a woman, and she had to pull me off her dead brother's corpse. And now I've killed her, too."

"You caused none of these things." Lourden's voice was steady at her ear. "Someday you will realize it. Greater patterns weave our lives. Grieve, *Olea-gishii*, grieve and heal. Dream of your beloved and remember him as the desert moves, writhing with a power beyond our knowing."

Olea was silent a long time. "Lourden," she spoke at last. "I have to go to Khehem."

He stilled. "Khehem is cursed. Why must you do this thing?"

"I need to see the walls move. I *must* figure out how it works. I can never make Roushenn safe for my Queen, if she lives, if I don't know anything about it."

Louren's chest expanded as he heaved a sigh. "Khehem is for the dead. It is dangerous. We don't patrol inside it anymore. The walls of Khehem are not to be trusted."

"Neither are the walls of Roushenn. But I must see it. Please."

He paused, then sighed. "I need permission to take my

216

Rishaaleth to Khehem, from the Maitrohounet. She is not likely to give it. Are you certain you wish to do this thing?"

"I am."

Lourden pulled away a little, gazing at her by the high moonlight. Olea shivered, feeling a thrum in her body that hadn't been there since Alden's death, watching this man who was so like him. Olea could see heat in the Tribesman's frank stare. He was fascinated with her, and yet there was more. Desire. Hope, that she could save his people.

Lourden reached up, touching the bone pin at Olea's shoulder that held her wrapped tunic. A shivering tension hummed between them. He slid his fingers along the silk at her collarbones. A shudder passed through Olea. Tracing the edge of her wrap, Lourden slid his fingers down until Olea's Inking was bared to the night.

His eyes were faraway with need as he traced the mark with this fingertips. "So stark. Have our beautiful *Alrashemnari* become so dark now that they Ink only in black?"

"I don't wish to hold such darkness anymore." Olea murmured.

"Darkness is part of the light," Lourden sighed. "For only when it is blackest out, can we see the beauty of the moon."

Lourden leaned down. He brushed a kiss to Olea's Inkings, lingering. Olea ran her fingers through his curls, so much like Alden's. Lourden clasped her close, sighed her name like wind in the sand. And then he was kissing her chest, soft, working his way up the side of her neck. Cupping her nape, he breathed into her skin, drinking her in. And in the vast emptiness of the night, Olea's heart came to stillness. Pain eased from her as they touched, and Olea gave herself to it. She turned her lips to him, and they kissed long in the silent desert night.

At last, Lourden pulled away. Breathing hard, he clasped her close, pressed his lips to her forehead. "Forgive me," he sighed. "My wife is everything to me. But you draw me in a way I cannot deny, *Olea-gishii*. You are a legend. A tale from Prophecy come alive, here, in my arms. Around you, I feel the movements of ages. Ever since I first saw you, I have been denying this pull. But this, what I feel for you, is a wish as ancient as the sands themselves. A deep peace fills my warring heart, only to be near you."

217

Olea found herself upon a knife's edge of indecision. Something thrummed within her, wanting him. Wanting to give in to that stillness, that peace Lourden spoke of. To end her memories of Alden and her grief, to give herself over to this dark night and the silence of the stars.

"Perhaps we should go back," she breathed.

"Perhaps." Lourden nodded, brushing his lips over her brow.

Olea took the long breath of her Alrashemni training, steadying herself. Lourden wasn't Alden, and he never would be. And he loved his wife, with a beautiful passion Olea could never hope to match. And Olea had a duty to her Queen, Inked upon her skin so long ago.

She pulled away, leaving such dreams of peace to a dark desert night.

Without a word, Lourden followed.

CHAPTER 15 – ELYASIN

The past many days had all been keshar-practice. Elyasin had joined Elohl and Fenton out in the cat-paddocks, learning along with both Kingsmen how to move with the big cats. Her days consisted of practicing war maneuvers with her beast, learning how to fight from its back, keshari-style. A full day had been given to practice with the long pole-armed blades the keshari riders used. But after all three Menderians were exhausted and the cats beginning to flip their tails as the sun sank low on the horizon, they ceased.

Elyasin handed her pole-arm off to the cat-trainer Jhennria. The compact woman took it firmly in hand, setting the butt in her stirrup-hold. "Nice work today, my Queen. Ye'll have plenty of time to get used to the *avari*. These two," she nodded at Elohl and Fenton, dismounting nearby, "they'll need the polearm on their march over the mountains. Keshar do well with swords, but they're used to the *avari* during a fight."

"In case we run into something?" Fenton led his cat up next to them, Elohl at his side.

Jhennria nodded, turning towards the two Kingsmen. "Bhuirn are common in the Eleskis, and blackfoot stag. A blackfoot can take out a keshar and rider with their horns, and they don't back down. Believe me, you'll welcome having an *avari* handy when you meet a blackfoot bull, or a momma with a calf. Well. Tha's enough practice for today. We've got a feast ta get to!"

Jhennria dismounted with a lively grin, walking her cat back towards the cradle and taking the pole weapons to the rack at the side of the paddock. Elohl and Fenton followed. Elyasin dismounted, taking a moment to rub her mostly-healed side. At the cat-cradle, a great barn of a building with part of the cat-runs outside, they released the cinches on their saddles. After a wipe-down and a nuzzle with her snow-dappled beast, they turned the cats loose. Elyasin's white cat promptly leapt up a series of tree trunks outside to curl up in the last of the sun. Fenton's went to play, batting a massive haunch of something dead that was apparently still enjoyable. But Elohl's great tawny cat stayed close, nuzzling his face through the paddock's poles, until his shirt and hair were entirely slick with cat-spittle.

Turning towards the tack-barn, Jhennria nodded a curt farewell. "See you tomorrow, gents. Yer battalion rides for the mountains in the morning. I'll have yer cats ready to go at dawn. Milady Queen. Yer wanted for war-meetings all day tomorrow, yes?"

"Yes." Elyasin responded. "We'll have no time for riding."

"Then at least stop by an' give yer beast a nuzzle. Ye'll need ta bond daily, ye ken?"

"I shall."

Jhennria nodded, then gave a swift palm to her chest and turned away. Elyasin strode over to the paddock poles, watching Elohl still saying goodbye to his great beast Thitsi, Fenton at his side.

"She likes you." Elyasin extended a hand to touch Thitsi but got a low growl, and took her hand back. Thitsi glared at her with hostile golden eyes as Elohl nuzzled her one last time.

"She's protective." Elohl glanced over. "She doesn't understand that you offer me no danger."

"And yet, she is wise." Elyasin's smile was wry. "I do offer you danger, Kingsman den'Alrahel. Sending you over the Devil's Field to take our royal seals into a land that is now hostile to you. To us both."

"We would do no less for our Queen." Fenton broke in, his gaze level and mild.

Elyasin smiled. They had no reason to be loyal to her, and yet, there it was. True Kingsmen honor. Moved, Elyasin pressed a palm to her chest. Elohl and Fenton returned it at their Inkings, bowing low.

"My Queen." Elohl asked. "May we adjourn? Fenton and I need to clean up before the feast this evening."

"As do I," Elyasin gave a slight smile. "Although one might be able to attend a feast in Lhen Fhekran smelling of cat and dripping with spittle and sweat."

That got a bark of laughter from Fenton, and a decent smile from Elohl. Elohl had less levity than his sister, Elyasin had noticed over the past weeks, still waters that ran deep.

"My Queen," Fenton spoke. "Allow us to escort you back to the palace?"

"Please." Elyasin nodded and turned, and the two Kingsmen fell into step. Together, they made for the smells of roasting meats that now issued from the palace. The feast tonight was a dual celebration, both for Elyasin and Therel's marriage, and in honor of Elohl and Fenton's journey. Elyasin's stomach grumbled with a sudden violence at the thought of food.

"Hungry?" Fenton's steady gold-brown eyes glimmered with humor.

"Famished." Elyasin admitted.

"For food or something else?" Fenton's grin teased.

Elyasin blinked, realizing he was bantering with her. Over the past three days, she had spent a lot of time in the paddock with the two Kingsmen. And she realized suddenly that after their long hours of fighting atop the cats, she was quite suddenly being treated like a warrior.

"Famished for what satisfies," she smiled, sly. "I've heard you're getting some satisfaction these days, Guardsman." Elyasin knew how much time Fenton had been spending in General Merra's quarters. Indeed, the General was not shy about describing her sexual encounters in vast detail when she and Elyasin were alone, believing Elyasin needed some introduction to the bedchamber.

Fenton's cheeks colored as he grinned. Elohl finally laughed in a rich, rolling baritone. He had a fantastic laugh, and Elyasin smiled to hear it, to hear his lake of silence breached at last.

Elohl clapped Fenton upon the shoulder. "Elaborate rituals, my friend. Elaborate rituals."

Elyasin missed the joke, but she smiled as Fenton laughed. Together the three proceeded up the stone stairs of a side-entrance into the vaulted reaches of the palace. The two Kingsmen left her at the door of her suite with a bow. Elyasin retreated inside, finding her King and husband already in his dressing-parlor, washing in the wide copper tub by the lit fireplace. Moving to the open doorway, she watched him bathe. Therel was a magnificent creature. Long-limbed but roped with muscle, water cascaded down the hard planes of his shoulders and back as he sluiced soap from his pale mane.

Currying his wet mane back, he grinned, as he flicked water from his eyelids with his fingertips.

"I know you're there."

"And I know you're there." Elyasin teased, feeling ribald tonight.

"Come join me in the bath." Therel looked up, his pale blue eyes luminous in the sun's rays slanting in through the high arched windows.

"I think not." Elyasin leaned against the doorframe. "If I do, we'll never make it to the feast."

"Then let my eyes feast upon you," Therel's gaze simmered, hot and dark. "And I will need for nothing else tonight."

"Nothing else?" Elyasin's heart beat too fast, her cheeks hot.

"Not until later."

Elyasin's breath caught. She succumbed to that coil between them, taut with passion and tension. They still had not consummated their marriage, Therel respectful of Elyasin's healing. But riding cats these last few days had proven she was hale, and that look held all his desire, all his promise. Elyasin let herself feel it. And then she straightened, mastering herself once more. "I reek of cat. I'll be in my dressing-quarters. I'll see you in an hour for the banquet."

"My Queen." Therel nodded, his eyes daring and sexual, though he made no move to rise from his tub.

"My King." Elyasin turned, trying to get a grip on herself. Moving toward her own dressing-chamber, she shut the doors, heart pounding. She pulled the silk tassel for her chambermaids, and was soon attended. But her mind was elsewhere as they helped her bathe, then select a gown and adornments for the feast. All she could think of as she gazed upon ice-blue silk was the heat in her husband's eyes. As the gown whispered on, all she could feel were Therel's caresses. All she could smell as they spritzed her with perfume was Therel's pine musk as he held her close.

At last, she was ready. Issuing from her chambers, she found Therel had already gone to the Throne Hall to begin welcoming his clansmen. Lhesher Khoum was at her door to escort her, and when she arrived outside the hall, she was greeted by her Kingsmen.

Fenton and Elohl, immaculate in charcoal-grey Elsthemi

leathers, were the very picture of everything Elyasin had imagined the Kingsmen to be. Strong, lean, they both had a determined air about their persons. Their new garb was a gift from her King and husband, and had been made in leather the Kingsmen color, though it fit like Elsthemi war-gear. Tight breeches were tucked into boots with knives buckled on the outside. Their leather jerkins were short, well-fitted with numerous buckles for blades and blow-darts. And the high collars were tooled with the Kingsmount and Stars, a brooch of the same done in silver clasping charcoal wolf pelts about their shoulders.

Together, they bowed to her in Kingsmen fashion, palms upon their hearts.

"My Queen." Fenton spoke. "Will you allow your loyal Kingsmen to escort you into the hall?"

"My Kingsmen." The phrase gave Elyasin shivers. The two men stepped to her flanks, and Lhesher Khoum turned her over to them. Elyasin set her hands lightly upon their arms, and as one, they stepped forward into the throne hall.

Therel's gaze found her the moment she entered. Dressed as he'd been for their Roushenn wedding, he wore crimson and black, though tonight he wore the pelt of a shaggy black wolf around his shoulders. The ensemble highlighted his lupine paleness, and Elyasin saw small Elsthemi-style braids woven through his hair, a plain circlet of gold upon his brow. Therel went silent from his boisterous conversation with his clansmen, those arctic eyes fixed upon her as she moved forward through the hall.

Elsthemi retainers stepped aside, parting in a long column as she progressed. Men and women clad in battle-ready leathers went down to one knee as she passed, palms to hearts, hands on their weapons. Elyasin stepped up the three stairs before the thrones, and Therel reached out for her. There was no music, no fanfare of horns. Just this simple motion, of her Kingsmen bowing and relinquishing her, stepping backwards down the stairs. And then her fingers were in Therel's. Gazing at him, feeling his intensity, seeing his eyes light as a smile crept over her lips, she suddenly understood what this feeling was.

Love.

"My Queen." Therel murmured, hushed. "You are the most

beautiful thing in my life."

"My King." Elyasin moved close, feeling the strength of their uncanny bond. "You have my heart."

Therel choked. Astonishment opened his face. And then the widest smile she had ever seen made her beam in a tremendous smile also, filling her with joy. "By Aeon and the old gods, how I love you." Therel growled. Pulling her close, he crushed her to his chest, then pressed a kiss upon her that was anything but delicate. Full of passion and wild abandon, he kissed her until she sagged in his arms.

Kissing him back like it was her last breath to take.

"Long live the Queen!" The chant went up all along the hall, though it soon became fractured into roars of robust laughter as Elyasin and Therel's kiss went on and on.

"Get 'er, Therel!"

"Do yer wifey!"

"Yah, tha's how a man kisses his bride!"

At last, Therel broke the kiss, gazing down with light and laughter in his eyes. He snugged Elyasin close to his side with one arm, so they could both face the hall.

"Highlanders!" He roared. It got him a roar back, men and women lifting weapons in the air. "Tonight we feast! Tonight we celebrate my nuptials to this most amazing Alrashemni battle-Queen, and the unity of our nations! Though our nations are in dire times, we shall hold fast. For we have truth upon our side, the truth of a bond made where no man can put it asunder. A bond of the heart! Once our great nations were allies, built on trust, prosperity, and mutual benefit. And so we shall be again, when my Queen sits her throne at last! Who's with me?!"

Roars went up in the hall, weapons shaken, faces impassioned.

"But tonight! We drink! And I suppose we should also dine with our drink, eh?!" Roars came again, laughs. "We will dance and make merry, and take a cup for those who cannot be here tonight, already at the borderlands fighting for justice! Drink with me now, to justice and blood!"

"Justice and blood!" The shout went up. As one, Highlanders drank from their flasks and goblets and chalices. Therel had a short sip from a gilded goblet. Then passed it to Elyasin, and she drank deep of sweet, heady telmen wine.

"But before we get to the party," Therel continued, "there is a matter of state to attend. I call Brigadier-Lieutenant Kingsmen Elohl den'Alrahel and Guardsman-Lieutenant Kingsman Fenton den'Kharel to the front!"

Elyasin saw Elohl and Fenton share a glance. She smiled, eager for her and Therel's little surprise to be made plain tonight. As one, Fenton and Elohl approached, kneeling at the foot of the dais, palms to hearts, utterly confused.

Therel turned to Elyasin with a grin. "My Queen. Would you like to do the honors?"

"Indeed." Elyasin nodded. "Fenton den'Kharel. Approach."

Eyes locked upon his Queen, Fenton stepped up the dais. Elyasin reached out, accepting from Therel a longsword of impeccable workmanship with black obsidian laid into its silver-worked handle. Sigils of ancient Elsthemi origin covered the blade as she drew it from its leather scabbard, glinting in the light of the roaring fires all along the hall.

"For your service," she pronounced, dubbing him upon one shoulder and then the other, "you are hereby named Honorary Highsword of Elsthemen, and a Protectorate of the Realm. Take this token of your King's thanks, for all services rendered both past, present, and future, and know that in your hour of need, your King stands beside you." She slid the sword back into its scabbard and handed it over. Fenton was solemn as he unbuckled his Guardsman sword from his new leathers, and handed it off to Lhesher Khoum. Then received the sword from Elyasin with a dip of his chin, buckling it onto his baldric.

Therel reached out, handing Elyasin a white keshar-claw pendant inset with an ancient sigil of protection done in Elsthemi obsidian and silver, suspended upon a silver chain. Elyasin lifted the chain of the pendant up over Fenton's head, and settled the claw upon his chest.

"And take this token from your Queen," she continued, "a symbol of ancient righteousness, the keshsar-claw worked with the *lethouni*, the Highland glyph of protection. I hereby name you Kingsman Protectorate of Alrou-Mendera, to be the Queen's personal emissary in times of need. Thank you, Fenton. For everything you've done."

Elyasin moved forward, and placed a soft kiss upon Fenton's lips. He'd obviously not expected it, for he startled. Heat flushed in his face. Elyasin thought she saw red flash through his eyes, a trick of the firelight. Fenton knelt, bowing deeply, and Elyasin rested her hand upon his head, before letting it slip away. He stood and backed down the steps, one hand to his heart, one to his Highlander sword.

"Elohl den'Alrahel." Elyasin spoke next. "Approach."

The Brigadier did, understanding what was coming. Elyasin repeated the ritual, bestowing upon Elohl a Highlander sword inlaid with Elsthemi fire-opals and gold rather than obsidian and silver. He switched it for his plain Guardsman sword, and Elyasin moved forward to place a white keshar-claw pendant, this one worked with hahled opals and gold, upon his chest.

"Take this token from your Queen," she proclaimed, something about this moment with Elohl more pressing than it had been with Fenton. "A symbol of ancient peace, the keshar-claw worked with the *oleander*, the Highland glyph of ease in the heart. I hereby name you Kingsman Protectorate of Alrou-Mendera, to be your Queen's conscience in times of need, much as your sister once was for me, and I hope she can be again. Thank you Elohl, for being a light unlooked-for, for Therel and me."

She moved forward, to kiss Elohl upon the lips. He gazed down at her, tall and striking, something terribly sad in those storm-grey eyes. He did not close his eyes as their lips met, and neither did she. Something passed between them, a sigh like a breath, and Elyasin shivered as she pulled away.

"I hope you find the peace you're looking for." She murmured. She didn't know why she'd said it. But something flashed through his eyes, so dire, so tortured, that she knew she was right. Elohl pulled away, one hand to his heart, his gaze bleak as he stepped backwards down the dais.

Elyasin took a deep breath. The hall held a somber wistfulness. But it was time to end that. "Highlanders!" She raised her hands to the hall. "Let us eat, drink, and be merry! For tomorrow we may all die, but tonight, we live!"

Thunderous roars filled the hall. Boots stomped the white stone floor. Weapons clashed with ringing peals. And suddenly, the musicians began their cacophony of ribald dance-reels, and the feast began.

As the entertainment began and drinks went 'round, Elohl and Fenton approached the dais. They clasped arms with Luc den'Lhorissian, standing near Elyasin's throne in a place of honor. Elyasin saw Fenton exchange a hot glance with General Merra as he sipped a goblet of wine. War-horns sounded the coming of the feast, and all made their way to the long trestle-tables as lines of cooks paraded through the hall with meats and chutneys. Boar had been roasted, served with quail and ptarridge and a wild rice native to the Highlands. Telmen-chutney, apple-chutney, pear and quince and loganberry were served, with wild greens sautéed in a thick vinegar sauce. Highlanders were already eating and drinking heartily as Elyasin and Therel sat at the head table, none standing upon any ceremony.

Talk was boisterous as everyone ate. No one seemed in the least worried about the war. The late-summer was still high, and snows were not yet a worry. And as the talk grew louder, Elyasin saw the joyousness of a people who lived for merriment when they could. Musicians began again with Highland-style war drums and reedy instruments that cut through the night. Dancing began, the rough-and-ready Highlanders in no way fancy tonight. Men and women surged to their feet to the thundering drums. Challenging with bravado in a complex series of dances, they egged each other on with whistles and jeers shouted over drums and fiddles.

Elyasin laughed as a man tried a difficult leap in the men's dance, too drunk to hardly stand. He missed the landing of his flip and sprawled on the floor, laughing at his own drunkenness. A keshari rider clad in furs hauled him to his feet, pulling him in for a good, deep kiss. Roars of cheering went up. Elyasin smiled, feeling lighthearted among the boisterous Highlanders. She glanced down to her goblet, saw it was empty, and held it out for a serving-woman to fill.

"A toast!" She roared to the hall suddenly. "Fill every glass full, let's have a toast!!"

"Toast, toast, toast!" Began the chant. Serving-women and men went 'round quickly filling chalices. A woman named Harenya stepped in to fill Elyasin's goblet, then Therel's, Merra's, Elohl, Luc, and Fenton, everyone gathered at the head table.

Elyasin, quite drunk and reeling with merriment, lifted her chalice. "To the Highlands! To joy in every heart! To life and laughter, music and song!"

"And fucking!" Someone shouted. Laughter boomed around the hall.

"Just so!" Elyasin shouted back, though her cheeks colored.

"To life and lovemaking," Therel took up her toast now, his eyes burning all for her, "to bedding in lust and love and depravity whenever the animal in us calls!"

"Yar!" Someone shouted. Cheers went up.

"And to war!" General Merra shouted. "To bravery and sacrifice for justice! To the heat of our blood melting the snows!"

"To war!" They chorused.

"And to peace!" Elyasin finished. "May it find us all at last, safe in each other's arms at night, beloved in each other's hearts!"

"Peace!" The final chant rose.

Elyasin saluted with her goblet, and the Highlanders saluted back. She tipped it to her lips, the rest following. But nearby, Elohl spasmed as his goblet neared his lips. His chalice fell from his fingertips, slopping wine upon his hand and all over the white floor as it bounced and rolled away. Highlanders roared with laughter. Laughing also, Elyasin forgot to drink, but suddenly felt the goblet slapped from her fingertips by Elohl.

"NO!" He shouted, his grey eyes dire. "It's poisoned!"

Elyasin saw Therel pause with his goblet to his lips. His eyes widened, and he lowered it slowly down. Suddenly, a choking sound came from Elyasin's left. Luc den'Lhorissian staggered, clutching at his chest.

"Elohl's right!" Luc gasped, as he fell to his knees. "Poison!"

"Luc!" Chaos erupted in the hall as Elyasin rushed to Luc's side. Luc coughed, spat, as Highlanders roared, dumping their chalices out upon the stone floor. The white bonerock ran red with wine as someone ran up with a spittoon. Luc stuck a finger down his throat, gagged, and vomited. Head hanging, he waved Elyasin weakly away.

"I'm alright... at least I will be. Fucking hells. That's what I get for drinking before a toast is finished." Luc groaned, sitting up now, both hands to his belly. Elyasin saw him going into a healing trance, his head back as he wavered upon his knees, his face ashen.

Elyasin's gaze snapped around for the woman who had served them, Harenya. But in the uproar, Therel had gotten to her first. She lay in a sprawl upon the floor. Blood spilled from a deep gash in her neck, a spreading pool of crimson seeping out over the white stones to mingle with spilled wine. Therel breathed hard, his blade-tip wet with blood. Elyasin watched as he wiped the sword on the dead woman's body. Lupine and ferocious, his gaze snapped up, roving the hall.

"See the treachery of our enemies!" Therel snarled, quieting the ruckus. "And know that justice will be dealt, as swiftly as the wolf hunts! Take her body away. Throw it out for the ravens."

Roars went up, maddened, fierce. The body was hauled up by a dozen hands, and carried from the hall like trash. Elohl had stepped to the tables, taking it upon himself to lift every wine-pitcher to his lips, testing them for poison. Therel was tight with intent as he watched. Luc had recovered enough to rise, Fenton holding him up and getting him to a chair. Highlanders growled, watching Elohl. Elohl's hand had not spasmed testing the wine at the lower tables. But upon lifting the last pitcher to his lips, the one at the King's table, his body suddenly gave a shudder, dropping the pitcher to smash upon the stones. He raised his eyes to Elyasin and nodded, then gave a nod to Therel.

Therel raised his hands, commanding the hall to silence. "Drink, friends! And tell death to fuck off tonight!"

Cheers went up. Highlanders beat their weapons together in a deafening clatter. And the music resumed, pounding through the hall.

Not even death could stop Elsthemi revelry.

And so the night wore on. Clan-leaders from across the Highlands approached to swear fealty to Elyasin, and reaffirm ties to their King. Songs were sung of daring raids and Highland honor, of women and feisty gods and heroic love. Highland men danced their cock-of-the-yard dance for the women, and women danced their keshar-dance for the men. Therel danced for Elyasin personally, up on the dais. Cheered on by the entire hall, he squatted and lunged, leaped and tumbled, and performed complicated kicks, all of it danced with knives as if fighting for her against an unknown opponent.

Elyasin had not known the women's keshar-dance, but Merra came, dancing the lithe, sinuous dance cheekily, showing Elyasin how to copy it. And how Therel smoldered, drinking his telmen wine from a gilded goblet, his wolf-wild eyes all for Elyasin. Elyasin was flustered by the end, but Therel stood when she finished and swept her into his arms, smoothing her mess of curls falling out of their hair-pins. He'd given her a kiss, slow and deep, a thing of the wild just barely restrained. It was all Elyasin could do to not melt in his arms like spring snow.

Cheers went up through the hall from rowdy, drunk Highlanders. The musicians charged into another tune, and a couples' dance began. Elyasin's head spun. She rested back into Therel, watching the room whirl to the thundering of Highland drums. Therel pulled her close with a growl, his hands sliding up her silk to linger on her ribs. Elyasin leaned back on his shoulder, her face turned up into his. Therel ran his tongue under her earlobe, licking her neck. A low moan escaped her as her breath quickened.

"You'll wear yourself out breathing that fast, lady," Therel chuckled. "Didn't your physician tell you not to exhaust yourself tonight?"

"What if I want to be exhausted?" Elyasin lifted her chin up, lips upon his jaw.

"I could exhaust you, if we danced together."

"But I don't know the steps..."

"I can show you. I am a *very* careful teacher." Therel dipped his chin, kissing her neck, his hand sliding up to caress her breast through the silk. The dancing was at a frenzy in the hall, music and telmen-wine flushing Elyasin's veins. Therel bit her, just a little, and slid his thumb over her nipple.

"You tremble, my sweetgrape. Do we need to take you back to our rooms and allow your heady bouquet to... ferment?"

Elyasin could only nod. Therel chuckled with dark eagerness. He spoke quietly to Lhesher Khoum, and then they stepped down behind the dais to escape from the hall like thieves.

* * *

Elyasin sat upon the bed, her head reeling from wine and merriment. The great war-drums beat another dance for late revelry, reverberating through the palace. Elyasin pulled her hair-sticks out and tossed them away, letting her golden waves tumble free. Her breathing was fast, her gown's waist-cinch stifling. She began unhooking it, hastily, when a light touch fell upon her hands. Therel sat beside her upon the bed, gazing at her with a deep mystery in his blue eyes.

"Slowly," he murmured, guiding her hand languidly from one hook to the next.

"But I want you…!"

"I know. But still, slowly."

He bent, lowering his head to kiss her neck. Elyasin moaned. Her hand fell away from the hooks, and Therel took up the task. One hook to the next, the silk girdle sighed away at last. Therel's hand slid over her blue silk, pressing gently, lower. Elyasin moaned, arching. Therel bit her upon the neck. Her moan turned into a cry of pleasure as his hand gripped her ribs. Elyasin bucked in eagerness, and Therel leveled his body atop hers in one smooth motion.

"Gently, my sweetgrape," Therel's breathing was none too measured either, as he began to press his body down upon her. "Or you'll break me before we even begin."

"Break you?" Elyasin's whisper was harsh as his lips moved over her collarbones. His fingers rippled over her breast, teasing her nipple through the fabric. Her hips pressed up, and now it was he who moaned, deep and low in his throat.

"I don't want to hurt you, Elyasin."

"I don't care if you hurt me, just take me."

"Are you sure?" Therel paused, those lupine blue eyes boring into hers, ravenous with desire.

"I've never been more sure."

She lifted up to kiss him full on the mouth, hard. Therel groaned deep in his throat. And then he was unleashed. Her King pressed her to the bed with his kiss and his hips, his hand sliding down, fingers pressing at the fabric over her groin. Elyasin surged as he began stroking her through the thin cloth. She keened, breaking their kiss, struggling for breath. Therel grasped her carefully by the throat, stroking her harder. She cried out, heady, bucking beneath him as wetness flooded between her thighs. A slow smile spread over his face as he watched her, his blue eyes feral in the night.

His hand strayed, gathering the thin folds of her gown.

"Yes," Elyasin urged, arching.

"Submit to me, wife." Therel squeezed her throat harder, his wild eyes staring her down as he gathered her gown up over her hips. His eyebrows lifted and he gave a wicked grin as his fingers strayed to find no undergarment. "So eager."

"Therel, please…!" Elyasin cried out, needful.

But Therel merely chuckled, whispering his nose over hers, sliding his hand between her thighs. And suddenly, diving his fingers into her. Elyasin gasped with passion, both hands flying to the headboard. And then her husband dug deep, and Elyasin bucked as he rode her pleasure.

"Gods of the vine!" He rasped, a malicious tone to his heat, "how I punish the sweetest of grapes beneath my hand in the dark of night."

"Therel!" Elyasin cried out his name, breathless. He punished her hard until she was screaming, arching for the dawn and orgasming in a high, gripping rush. He released her throat as she climaxed. Cupping the back of her neck, he pressed her until she screamed again and contracted into a ball of pleasure, fingers dug into the carven wood of the bed. By the time Therel had stripped bare but for his silver pendant dangling over his black and white Inkings, she had stripped her gown off over her head. He lay out atop her, and she seized him with her legs, pulling him close. Therel pinned her arms above her head, and when he entered her, it was not kind.

But a kind man wasn't what Elyasin wanted. She wanted a rogue, a wolf in the darkness, a man who would punish his sweetgrape with his flesh. And so he took her. She danced for him, screaming with ecstasy. And when she spasmed her last and her Highland wolf roared his bliss to the night, he collapsed atop her. Utterly spent and smiling as she ran a hand through his sweat-slick hair.

Reveling in the feral man atop her, Elyasin felt blood trickle down her side. She didn't care. It was right, to be bathed in blood on a night like this. A night of Highlands pleasures, for a Highlands Queen. She closed her eyes with a smile as drums thundered on through the palace. Her hand fell motionless upon Therel's hair.

The fire burned low, the pop and hiss of resins spitting in the hearth. A wind moaned outside, shuddering the windows in their brackets. All had come to silence in the palace. The darkness of midnight held the room, the eaves shrouded in shadow. Elyasin drifted, Therel asleep and breathing slow at her side. Her gaze strayed from his lupine grace, drifting to the darkness.

And suddenly, she was there. The woman stood by the bedside, silent as a glacial night. Elyasin tried to move but couldn't, her body frozen. Like a wild thing, the woman with the white hair and terrible beauty moved close. Her eyes were pools of drowning midnight. Spirals of silver, white, and inky purple swirled upon her luminous skin. Swiftly she reached out, touching Elyasin at her heart, and whispered, *come to me.*

Elyasin woke with a yelp. Therel was awake instantly at her side, a knife brandished to the room from beneath the bed. But all was silence and shadows in the darkest hour of the night. Streaked in sweat, Elyasin shivered, pulling the blankets close. Therel scooted over, drawing her into his arms as he lay back against the headboard.

"Bad dreams?" He murmured, stroking her golden waves back from her face, nuzzling her cheek.

Elyasin's gaze strayed to the bedside where the apparition had appeared. "Therel. I've been dreaming. A few times since my coronation. They're tremendously vivid, like I'm awake, but I know I'm asleep. I can see the room, hear wind outside. And she's just suddenly there... standing at the bedside."

"A woman?" Therel's gaze darkened. "Does she threaten you?"

"No." Elyasin shook her head. "But I feel like she has something for me to do. She tries to press it into me, to make me understand. She's wild, like a creature of darkness, but beautiful..."

"Dreams often have meaning in the Highlands." Therel scowled. "We have men and women who train in such things, Dremors. I can find someone to interpret it, see what it means."

"Why? Do you think my dream is an ill omen?" Elyasin's brows knit, wondering at her husband's intensity.

"It's probably nothing." He gave a wry smile, kissed her temple. His hands cradled her, one stealing up to rub beneath her breast. Elyasin sighed, relaxing back into his warm nakedness. Therel kissed her neck, seductive. "Gods be merciful, but you are *quite* a woman, Elyasin. Was that really your first time, earlier?"

Elyasin blushed. But she found she was comfortable cuddling like this, naked with a man. "First, yes. But that doesn't mean I haven't dreamed about it."

"You've *dreamed* about me? Well, I hope I lived up to that." He chuckled and his fingers strayed, brushing from her hip down to her groin. Gripping her around the waist, he pulled her close. But Elyasin mewled as pain lanced her side. Therel lifted his hand away, a streak of blood upon his palm from Elyasin's wound.

"You need to see Luc. Dammit!" Therel cursed. "I've been too hard on you tonight."

"No. It's fine." Elyasin reached out, gripping his wrist. "A little blood doesn't stop me. Nor do war or bad dreams." Elyasin fell silent, thinking about the pale woman with the long white hair. The dream seemed alive by the flickering light of the fire, the shadows in the eaves haunting.

"My love? Where did you go?" Therel stroked her cheek.

"Something's happening, Therel. Something's changing." She spoke suddenly.

"Changing?" He chuckled. "We're married. We've had sex, an incredible first time. Change comes to the Highlands upon the wrath of the Nightwind, my love, but that doesn't mean it's a bad thing."

Elyasin could hear the moaning of the wind outside, a chill autumn drift down from the mountains. She shivered, and Therel clasped her closer. "My love? What is it?"

Elyasin turned in his arms, reached up behind his neck. She wanted to banish that dream, wanted to stay here with him, in heat and passion. Therel's gaze met hers and something sparked between them. His pale blue eyes lit with dark fire. And then he was shifting her from his lap, laying her down, moving over her. Pressing his lips upon hers, laying his long warmth out upon her to banish the chill of shadows and dreams. His fingers were expert as he stroked her, his lips exquisite as he kissed her, and Elyasin forgot the white woman. She forgot everything but her wolf-wild husband, and the feel of pleasure in the night.

CHAPTER 16 – ELOHL

Winding up into the eastern mountains out of Lhen Fhekran, General Merra's party took sparse trails through rocky valleys, ascending into snowpine and birch forests. They'd covered terrain fast upon cat-back in the past week. Winding up an elk-trail into the Highmountains proper now, snow was five feet thick upon the ground in patches of shadow that never saw sun. Skirting a river, the roar was fierce in Elohl's ears as they eased the cats up a tight ravine.

Near noontide, the ravine's course broadened into a flat area with a tumble of boulders at the base of a cascading waterfall. Merra's cats jumped up the massive boulders with ease, climbing to a flat lip of stone twenty feet above the waterfall's base and off to the south. Suddenly, Elohl saw one Highlander launch herself from her saddle with a whoop, stripping nude. Others followed, boisterous with yells and grins. Just as Elohl crested the boulders upon Thitsi, the first woman dove off the rocks. Elohl reined up and saw that the woman had plunged into a steaming pool large as a barn, near the waterfall's base but separate from the cascade. Other Highlanders joined her with yells, diving or cannonballing nude off the rocks.

Jhonen reined up beside Elohl and Fenton, already stripping off her pelt and jerkin. "Volcanic hot springs! They bubble up in this area near the river. Six of 'em, all in all. This one's called Just Right. Hop in, gents! Water's warm!" Jhonen launched from her cat with a grin, stripping buck-ass nude without a care in the world.

"Why's it called Just Right?" Fenton dismounted next to Elohl.

"Jump in an' find out!" Jhonen laughed, then dove off the rocks after her fellows.

"Might as well!" Fenton laughed. Not perturbed by Highlander frankness, Fenton was already shirtless, and hauled down his trousers. General Merra shot him a sexy glance, tending to her cat nearby. Fenton gave her a rash grin. In a running leap, he launched from the rocks into the water.

"It is just right!" He called to Elohl as he spluttered up, currying water back from his face and laughing.

Elohl couldn't help himself; he returned that lighthearted laugh. The Highlanders were a bawdy family, and Fenton had caught their bug. Suddenly, Elohl felt more lighthearted than he had in years. Stripping fast, he stepped to the edge and did an elegant dive. Warm water surged up around him, the temperature more perfect than any bath. He came up with a gasp.

"Damn, that's good," Elohl murmured, combing water from his hair.

"An' that's just the beginning." Sluicing nearby, her sexy warrior's frame half-out of the water, Jhonen grinned. "Minerals in the water will smooth yer skin like a baby. Jes be sure ta get out regular an' have a drink or a dip in the river. A man can overheat fast from the salts."

She moved off toward one edge of the pool, settling to a seat in the naturally smooth rock that formed the spring's bowl. Elohl moved over to her, finding a good depression where he could relax yet be mostly submerged. Fenton came to his side and the three settled back in an easy silence, floating in the water. All around, Highlanders had ceased cavorting, calming into a motionless peace. Elohl could already feel the heat easing aches of travel from his sinews like poison being drawn out by leeches. He breathed deep of the vaguely sulfurous air. The river's fall thundered around them, reverberating off the boulders, consuming Elohl's worries until nothing remained but peacefulness.

"A man could get used to this." Fenton sighed, echoing Elohl's thoughts.

"So it be." Jhonen opened her eyes. Gazing at Elohl, her attention roved his chest and shoulders. "Yer golden Inkings are far more intricate than I heard."

"What did you hear?" Elohl finally found his voice, lolling in the deliciousness of the pool.

"A rumor. That the swirls upon ye were given by the gods. They're lovely." Jhonen reached out, tracing one whorl of gold with a finger. "Never seen anythin' so ornate, rip me with four claws. Are they magical?"

"What?" Elohl said.

"Magic." Jhonen's head relaxed back upon the lip of the pool with a sigh. "I'll draw cards fer ye later. I was Dremor-trained, ye know. We'll find out if there's any magic to them. But right now…"

"Right now we don't really give fuck-all about anything, do we?" Fenton murmur was so relaxed, Elohl almost wondered if the man had spoken from sleep.

"Nah." Jhonen smiled. "Relax, Lowlanders. Take it while ye can…"

"… as they say." Elohl completed the famous mountain adage.

He relaxed back, letting worries slip from his mind. Elohl's eyelids fluttered shut, ease and heat taking him from head to heels. He began to drift. White light was soft around him in his daydream, a feeling of peace radiating from his center. All thoughts were stripped away, all worries. Until there was just the feeling of floating, and a presence, generous and benevolent, filling him.

Elohl breathed that sensation through his limbs, until there was nothing else. Peace and ease, rest and relief. Eternity filled him. A white spire appeared in his mind, far-off through clouds lit bright from a dawn sun. Elohl floated in that peace, that bliss, watching the dawn light the spire rose and gold in a sea of white. Warmth suffused him, deep, warmer. A searing sensation began to creep through his limbs. The vision clarified, and he was near the white spire, suddenly too hot in the reflection of the sun's rays off the spire's surface. White light blinded him. It burned into his body through his goldenmarks, limning the script in curling flames. Heat claimed him, licking at his body, every limb tingling.

His head was scorching. His eyes boiled in their sockets.

Elohl twitched. It startled him awake. He was hot, blisteringly hot. His tongue was dry, stuck to the roof of his mouth, the skin of his hands crenated from soaking too long. Struggling to lift his throbbing head, his vision blurred. His body felt weak from falling asleep in the pool.

"Fuck." Elohl struggled to grasp the edge of the rock. With shaking limbs, he pushed out of the sulfurous water and collapsed to his back. He lay on the cool stone by the pool, breathing fast, roaringly hot, his pulse pounding in his ears as steam boiled up from his flesh into the chill air. A wicked headache flared in his temples. Elohl coughed in a dry-retch. Fenton stood near, drinking deep from a water flask. He rushed over as he saw Elohl collapse, offering the flask.

"Whoa! Here, Elohl. Drink." Fenton helped Elohl gasp the water flask. "That heat really creeps up on you. I thought you might have fallen asleep! I've been in and out of the river three times already! Here, come on. Merra's riders have tents erected, with water buckets from the river. Let's get you doused."

Elohl did not protest as Fenton helped him stumble to a wide canvas tent at the tree line. He doused his head in the water bucket, the shock of it slapping his system, then sluiced his neck and shoulders with snowmelt. Afternoon sun was high above the pines, shining directly on their camp. Intolerable, it made Elohl's headache flare in fury. Fenton helped him inside a tent to a pallet, made him drink more water.

Elohl's vision finally started to clear. "Thanks. I owe you."

"Not a problem." Fenton smiled as he drank deep of a different flask. "Jhonen says people often get heat-exhaustion at these pools, from the high concentration of salts. Even I was surprised at how early I had to get out and take a cold plunge. Why don't you lay down and rest? They're roasting some elk that one of the riders brought down. I'll come wake you when it's ready."

"Thitsi?" Elohl asked. "How is she?"

Fenton grinned. "Apparently she likes me well enough. She let me strip her saddle and set her free to prowl. Don't worry about her. Get some rest."

Fenton moved off through the hide door-flap, and Elohl relaxed back upon the pallet. Closing his eyes, he rolled to his stomach, his headache still pounding. Somewhere in his overheated drifting, he heard the tent-flap open again. Someone came to the bedside, and Elohl felt no warning in his sensate sphere. A woman's touch slipped over his back. Elohl startled, eyelids fluttering open, but she pressed down gently.

"Easy, Kingsman..." An alto voice cooed. "Rest. The name's Erellia. Merra sent me in with a balm fer the heat."

Elohl glanced over his shoulder. White-blonde, her hair pulled back in a mess of braids, Elohl recognized Erellia as one of Merra's elite guard, the White Claws. Dressed only in the thin silk underwear and chest-binder the keshari riders wore beneath their leathers, muscles rippled in her arms and midriff as she twisted open a tin of salve.

Elohl closed his eyes as she massaged salve into his back and shoulders. It smelled of henroot and basalm, mint and chennery, and something else Elohl couldn't place. Where it soaked into his skin, a delicious cooling seeped into his muscles. Erellia set a small censer near him with a soft clink, and soon a wafting incense curled through the air, musky like sandalwood. It soothed Elohl's mind and eased him further, pushing back his headache.

He took a deep breath of incense-musk and basalm, letting it out in a sigh. "Thank you. That feels much better."

"Yer welcome. Yer one tough taut-wire. Stayin' in the pools so long."

"What's in that salve? I've never felt anything like it," he murmured.

"We call it wring-balm. Wrings the heat right outta the body."

"Where is Fenton? He said he would wake me for supper."

"Fuckin' the General, I'd wager," she chuckled, low and amused. "Anyhow, Merra's business ain't mine, an' dinner's not fer mebbe an hour. Well now, turn over. All of ye gets the wring-balm. *Tsit!*"

Elohl decided it was best not to irritate his healer. Ease filled him, so heavy that his limbs barely functioned enough for him to push to his hands and roll over. He re-straightened his shoulders, neck, and back upon the pallet, feeling far cooler. Erellia gazed down, admiration in her eyes as her fingers perused his golden Inkings. Elohl's eyes fell closed again. Her hands spread the balm, smoothing it over his collarbones and chest, then his abdomen, arms and legs, even massaging the tops and soles of his feet.

Ease and coolness seeped in. Heaviness filled Elohl, pulling everything down into the pallet. As if sucking tendrils writhed up from the earth and seeped into his flesh, every muscle cooled until Elohl felt like he swam in a bottomless mountain lake. A vast chill took Elohl suddenly. He was cold. Cold like freezing to death out in the snows. His mind was dull, slipping away beneath ice. His head was too heavy to move.

His breath struggled to rise, heavy like death.

Cerulean eyes drifted across his vision, behind his closed

eyelids.

Elohl's mind struggled to come awake. Danger flared in his skin, prickling like ants. Alarm raced through him. His body twitched as his golden Inkings flared, but it was distant. Fear and a vicious survival instinct twisted through him as his Inkings tried to heat his body. Elohl tried to thrash, attempting to roll away. But whatever she had done had been done well. All he managed to do was twitch.

Erellia held the incense near his mouth and nose, making him inhale its musk. Elohl coughed weakly, struggling for breath. His eyelids fluttered, fighting oblivion.

"There now," Erellia stroked his cheek. "You'll be dead in a little while, Kingsman. I've given you enough balm to kill a keshar, and the Regalia-musk works fast on the lungs. Don't fight it. It will be peaceful if you just let go." Erellia's lips pressed to his temple. Elohl tried to call out, but nothing happened. His tongue felt thick. Every inhalation barely moved air into his lungs.

"Just sleep," she whispered. "It's better this way."

She rose from the pallet. Elohl heard her whispering footsteps move toward the door-flap. Just then, a low yowl issued from the direction of the flap.

"*Tsit!*" Erellia hissed.

Elohl managed to flutter his eyelids, barely. His tawny keshar, Thitsi, shouldered her way inside with a low growl. She prowled to Elohl's pallet, curling around him as if protecting a kitten. Thitsi thumped him with her head. A black tongue snaked out, raking his face and neck, then his chest. With long strokes, Thitsi licked the chill balm from Elohl's skin. And where she licked, Elohl's strength surged back, his golden Inkings ripping and buzzing, screaming at him to fight, to live.

"Get away from him!" Erellia hissed. Able to turn his head a bit, Elohl saw Erellia with blades bared. She lunged, knives whipping out fast to cut his throat. But Thitsi's paw flashed out, lightning-fast, raking Erellia's front. She screamed, slashing at the great cat. Still at her repose, Thitsi lashed out, trapping Erellia between her paws. Claws flexed into Erellia's flesh. The woman screamed. Thitsi drug her close, baring forearm-long black fangs in snarl, whipping her tail. The tawny cat placed her jaws around the woman's neck and shoulder.

But did not crunch down. Pausing, her great golden eyes rolled to Elohl. She gave another growl, as if asking his permission. Elohl gasped air, his lungs working slightly now that Thitsi had cleaned him.

"Who are you?!" Elohl managed.

"No one!" Erellia cried. Thitsi's jaws flexed. She screamed as keshar-fangs pierced her shoulder.

"I know you're Khehemni!" Elohl gasped. His chest was so heavy. He fought to keep his eyes open. Thitsi had cleared some of the poison from his skin, but whatever had soaked in was still killing him. Cold to the bone, Elohl forced his lungs to work. Thitsi flexed her jaws and claws. The woman screamed again, blood coursing from her punctures.

"How many of you... among Merra's riders?" Elohl managed.

"You have no idea, Alrashemni," Erellia gasped in mortal pain, "how many of us walk in Therel's clans. By nightfall... less of you. *The reaping begins tonight!* Pray to whatever gods you like, because——"

Thitsi's jaws crunched down on her neck like a house cat crunches a vole. With a crack of her neck, Erellia hung limp, dead. Elohl was so cold. He struggled for breath in gasps. His eyelids fluttered closed. Summoning all his fading strength, Elohl screamed, but only produced a whisper.

Thitsi did it for him. Roaring loud, she shuddered the tent. And then roared again. And again.

Elohl heard the swish of the tent-flap.

"What in Halsos?" Jhonen's voice came. "Eri! Reghalia in the air!"

Elohl heard a battle-cry from Jhonen, fit to wake the dead. Suddenly, activity surrounded Elohl. Hands came, making him sit up. Hot water was sluiced over him. Something hard was used to briskly scrape his skin, scraping off the balm. The heat in the room increased. Able to crack his eyes now, Elohl could see five lit braziers. Hot stones ringed each brazier, seeping steam, his tent now a makeshift sweat-hut.

His eyelids fluttered closed.

A palm struck his face, hard. "*Stay awake, stay with me!*" Fenton growled. "*Breathe!*"

"Put that in his mouth, quickly!" Jhonen's low alto came, urgent. "Pinch his nose shut."

Fingers pinched his nose. Elohl twitched. Hot water poured into his open mouth as soon as his lips parted for breath. He gurgled, choking, then coughed, ejecting the small mouthful of water.

"Again! Choke him!"

Once more, water choking him, coughing. Dimly, Elohl realized his breathing was coming easier, his mind clearing with every cough. The process continued. They were trying to keep him alive. The poison stopped his breathing, but by choking him, they were forcing his body to struggle. Elohl redoubled his efforts to use his lungs. Inhaling the next mouthful of water deeper, his coughing went on a long time. At last, his lungs expanded on their own. But Jhonen didn't stop. Drowning, Elohl coughed again and again, until at last he could open his eyes and wheeze out, "For fuck's sake…!" He pushed at Jhonen, turning his chin away.

"Had enough, then?" Jhonen teased, but Elohl heard her concern.

A rough hand cradled the back of his head. Fenton's face swam into view. "You devil. I thought we'd lost you."

What Elohl thought was, *can't get rid of me that easily.* What he said was, "Cughe rimuh thisee." His eyes settled closed. A sharp slap stung his cheek. Elohl opened his eyes.

"Stay awake, Brigadier." Fenton's face was uncompromising, those gold-brown eyes piercing. "No sleeping on watch. I don't care how much drink you've had or how many women you've fucked or how many fingers are black. Stay awake."

Elohl smiled weakly. Those words were a ritual in the High Brigade. He'd said them countless times to his own men, always with the same dire tone. A tone that warned if you fall asleep in the Highmountains, it isn't just you that dies. If you fall asleep in the Highmountains on watch, you freeze to death, and your comrades do, too.

Elohl managed to twitch one hand towards his Inkings. "Commander."

His body still wracked with shivers. No fewer than six keshari riders were massaging his muscles, trying to keep the poison from staying. The tent was boiling, sweat trickling now from Elohl's skin. Jhonen forced him to drink flask after flask of water, and still tried to surprise him by pouring too much down his throat. At last, she dismissed the others, then began rubbing him with a new balm, one that smelled fiercely foul.

Fenton stayed, stripping down to abide the steam, hunkering next to Elohl's pallet. Suddenly, Elohl heard General Merra Alramir bellow outside the tent like the mountains spewed fire. Merra appeared, ducking beneath the hide flap, her sharp face a thundercloud as she hunkered next to Fenton.

"General." Elohl's voice held his resonant baritone at last. He was able to move his arms, flex his hands. Strength returned, though he was still wracked with shivers.

"Kingsman." Merra's fierce blue eyes roved over him. "You were born under a lucky sky."

Jhonen's laugh was an angry bark. "Erellia gave him enough put-down ta kill three healthy cats! Thitsi managed ta lick off enough to keep him from the grave. Right smart cat."

General Merra's gaze flashed back to Elohl. "You're lucky Thitsi was worried about you. She's been a handful at the lines, trying to get to you. Chewed through her tether. Thank your gods her instincts are keen. But now I have a problem. How many traitors do I have in my campaign, lowlander?"

"You've got a bigger problem than you know," Elohl managed. "Erellia bragged of numerous Khehemni among Therel's clans, among the keshari riders. She said, *the reaping begins tonight*. Does that mean anything to you?"

A snarl touched Merra's lips, but she shifted with tense uncertainty.

"Warn your riders not to let anyone stray tonight." Fenton's voice was low with warning. "If Erellia was working with others, someone might try to slip away and report."

"I've already posted sentries I trust. Discreetly." Merra snapped at Fenton.

"Whom are you certain you trust, General?" Elohl croaked. "I had attempts on my life in the High Brigade, men I thought were allies."

Merra's eyes flicked to Jhonen, and the two women shared a

long look. "Dhella's loyal, for certain." Jhonen said. "Rhone and Rhennon. Millea. Khrit. But I thought Erellia was trustworthy until today."

"Just like Therel trusted his First Sword." Fenton's voice was soft.

"I don't want a witch-hunt among my riders." Merra scowled. Outside the tent, cats suddenly started yowling, snarling. "What now?" General Merra launched to her feet, then ducked back out. Shouts rose among the tents in the early dusk. Angry voices, cat yowls.

And then Elohl heard the ring of steel clashing.

Fenton was up fast, pausing only to grab weapons. Elohl tried to follow, but Jhonen pushed him down. "You stay." She pointed at him as she hauled on her boots and buckled on weapons. "Thitsi, make him stay!"

The big cat growled protectively. She gave Elohl a mighty lick as Jhonen ducked out. Yells came, and cat-growls. Elohl heard a tirade of scathing shouts come from the General, though she was far enough away that her words were indistinct.

Suddenly, a clash of swords rang out in the thin mountain air. Elohl's golden Inkings blazed, rippling like fire ants. Listening to the skirmish outside, Elohl wasted no time. The flare of his Inkings had given him a burst of energy, and he used it to push up to sitting. Breath rasping from the effort, muscles still shaking and weak, he found his clothes near to hand. Still sitting upon the pallet, Elohl hauled on leather pants, shirt and jerkin, and secured his weapons. Thitsi eyed him as he flung a cat-pelt over his shoulders, then pulled on soft doeskin boots. She made no move to stop him, though his jerky movements spoke of the poison that still flowed in his veins. Elohl shook like he had a palsy just getting dressed.

The sounds of fighting outside grew more vicious. Ringing steel, shouts and screams of pain as men were damaged, battle-roars and cat snarls. Just then, a torn and bloody Merra careened into the tent, her visage vicious and blood-smirched. Merra wiped a crimson slick from her sword on Elohl's pallet swiftly. "Can you sit your mount?"

Elohl nodded as Thitsi uncoiled from her repose around him. "If I have to."

"Good. We have to ride. Fast." Merra gestured urgently to the door-flap, her blue eyes flinty. "Clan Khersus from the Elsee has come to greet us. Forty horse and thirty keshari have engaged the western side of our camp. Thirty of *my* keshari, stationed at the Elsee! There's not enough of us to hold them off. We have to move. Now."

Using Thitsi's bulk as a brace, Elohl pushed to standing. He gripped her tawny fur as they ducked out beneath the flap. She laid upon her belly for him with a soft growl, and Elohl swung up shakily by a handful of fur. "We're ready."

"Bareback?" Merra's eyes widened.

"She won't dump me." Elohl ran a hand through Thitsi's fur, certain of his words.

Merra nodded quickly, respect in her eyes. She raced to her own readied cat, the massive snowy beast only paces away, guarded by a tight ring of her White Claws. Clashes and growls came from the perimeter of the camp beyond the tents, horse whinnies. Merra leaped swiftly into the high-cantled saddle, seizing her polearm from its stirrup-sheath.

"Ride!!" She bellowed.

As one, the knot of defenders leaped away. Thitsi gave chase, scooping up two fully-packed saddlebags in her jaws as she ran. Elohl hunkered close, gripping her as best he could without a saddle, shaking with weakness. But her gait was liquid silver beneath him, and she put not a single paw wrong as she raced after Merra, who whistled for those battling on the edge of the camp.

Only a handful of cats whirled about, leaping to meet Merra and Elohl as they angled for the rocky slope up out of the ravine. Cats raced in a tight group around Elohl and their General. Merra ran without a backward glance at the dead. Their party had dwindled from thirty riders to fifteen. Fenton raced upon his black-faced cat at Elohl's side, unscathed, his calm eyes deep with rage. Jhonen raced upon Elohl's other side, red braids flying behind her.

Suddenly, Jhonen's beast gave an ear-shattering roar of pain and stumbled. Elohl glanced back. An enemy keshar had caught up to them and pounced, digging claws and fangs into the haunches of Jhonen's mount, trying to haul them to a stop. Elohl pulled up, just as he heard the crunch of cat jaws on the other cat's spine. With an ear-deafening shriek, Jhonen's mount lost its back legs. Fighting wantonly with its front paws, it raged in pain, wild.

"Give her up!" Elohl yelled.

Stricken, Jhonen gave a mighty leap from her beast onto Thitsi, clinging behind Elohl. Thitsi leapt away, just as another enemy cat pounced to subdue her. But Thitsi was fast. Despite her extra burden, she surged ahead with breathless speed. Rejoining the main group before the renegades could close, she hadn't even dropped the saddlebags she carried in her jaws.

Elohl chanced a look back. Twenty keshari riders with polearms were in pursuit upon out of the waterfall ravine. But horses from the traitorous clan were dropping back, unable to keep pace with the tawny cats. General Merra's party streaked up a rocky pass above the ravine, racing even higher into the frigid mountains, their enemies fast on their tail.

CHAPTER 17 – DHERRAN

The cold sluice of a pail of water in his face was the only way Dherran had known he'd slept. He spluttered awake, flicking water hastily from his eyes, cracking them open at the two Kingsmen standing before his cage.

"Up, Dherran." It was lean Fhennic who spoke, hard mistrust in his eyes, brawny Valdo standing quiet at his side. "The Vicoute wants a word."

Dherran nodded, rising from the crushed straw upon the floor. It was best to be silent in times like this. For three days he'd paced his cell, hardly sleeping, eating next to nothing, wondering what in Halsos was going on. Worry devoured him for Khenria and Grump. He'd not been roughed up, nor even visited except by Fhennic bringing meals and water to his cell and sliding them through the iron bars.

But he'd also not heard anything about his friends.

Brushing straw from his green silk doublet, Dherran scrubbed a hand through his hair, then wiped water from his face. Everything ached from sleeping on hard stone for three nights. He had done his exercises and stretching routines daily, but still, the comforts of a plush life began to be missed now at age thirty. These few nights of punishment, though, were nothing compared to what Arlen den'Selthir had put him through in recent weeks.

And nothing compared to what he would put Dherran through, if he thought Dherran was a Khehemni traitor.

Stepping peaceably out of his cell and following Fhennic, Dherran tried to not think about Arlen's retribution. He'd not seen Khenria or Grump flung into the cells, and that was a good sign. Walking along the underground hall before the two guards, he was prodded by a longknife at his back from Valdo. Dherran didn't cause a ruckus. They hadn't shackled him, and he wouldn't give them any reason to.

At last, they turned in through the doors of the manor's underground training-hall. The Vicoute stood bare-chested in the largest sand pit in the center of the vaulted catacomb. Oil lanterns glowed around the space, lighting it bright. Dummies of scarred practice-armor and racks of weapons lined the walls. Pikes and swords, longknives and short, quarterstaves and a display of fly-blades. And watching over it all, the enormous tableaux of the Wolf and Dragon. Inlaid upon the southern wall, the beasts snarled in the lantern light, wrought from polished silver and surrounded by a ring of golden flame.

An emblem that Dherran still didn't know the meaning of.

The ten sand-pits were empty, save for Arlen in the largest central one. A rack of swords stood to one side. He looked up as he finished wrapping one hand with a bit of muslin as Dherran was prodded into the ring. Arlen's eyes were sunken, hot with wrath. His angular features spoke of hard nights spent in interrogation rather than sleep.

He gestured to the empty space in the sand pit before him. "Put him here. Then leave us. Close and bolt the doors." Fhennic and Valdo bowed their way out, and Dherran heard the sharp clack of the doors bolted. Finishing wrapping his hands, the Vicoute gestured to the rack of swords. "Choose one."

Dherran's eyes flicked to the various weapons in the rack. There were no staves here, no practice weapons. All were cold steel, and all showed the play of lantern-light upon sharp, honed edges. Dherran locked eyes with the Vicoute, his decision already made to not fight Arlen while the man was angry.

"No."

"Fool boy." Arlen gazed at him a moment, and then his hand whipped forward faster than a snake. Snatching up a sword with good balance and a needle-fine point, he wasted no energy with his thrust. It was all Dherran could do to avoid it, whipping his hip back and pivoting out from the path of that strike. The Vicoute came again, slicing the sword up to cut Dherran beneath the armpit. Again, Dherran dodged away, but the attack was unrelenting. The Vicoute slashed and Dherran backed up to the rack, feeling for anything to protect himself, emerging with a honed broadsword that barely kept Arlen's fast cut from beheading him.

Dherran slid his blade past the Vicoute's, stepping in to shove the leaner Arlen back a pace. Arlen stepped back and they regarded each other, both men bristling like wolves in a contest of dominance. Arlen's eyes were appraising, fierce and hot rather than their usual self-possessed iron. "Good. Now come at me, Dherran."

"No." Dherran refused again, though he kept his blade ready.

"Use my father's sword and come slaughter a Kingsman, traitor!" Arlen barked.

Dherran did not glance down at the blade in his hands, even though surprise lanced him to know what weapon he held. "I'll not slaughter a fellow Kingsman in cold blood. But if you press me, I will defend myself, Arlen. That ambush three nights ago was no doing of mine. Nor Grump's."

Arlen stood very still. Dherran felt that wrathful gaze slide over his face, the set of his shoulders and hips, like a python coiling up him. Judgment was in Arlen's eyes, and a bitter grimace twisted his mouth.

"You have refused to kill a Kingsman three times just now." He spoke at last. "You also protected my life three nights ago. Don't think that went unnoticed." Arlen walked to the rack and put his sword away. He turned, eyeing Dherran. Confused, Dherran lowered the point of his blade to the ground, and was preparing to place it back in the rack when Arlen's hand stopped him.

"No. Let me see how you move with it."

Dherran lifted an eyebrow. The Vicoute nodded, stepping back out of the sand ring. Once Arlen was a safe distance away, Dherran began to move. The two-handed broadsword was of good balance, its pommel long enough to make the blade nearly effortless. It was lighter than he expected, with a keen edge all the way to the hilt. The leather-wrapped handle was plain, but offered an excellent grip, and Dherran took it through center-line and cut-defend maneuvers with ease, the blade long enough to protect him shoulder to hip.

The Vicoute let him sweat a long time, watching. Dherran controlled his breath, moving how he'd been taught and how the Vicoute had been instructing him, though he was soon sweating in his green silk doublet. It was already ruined from fighting three days before, and from Dherran's rank sweat of worry in the dungeon. But the Vicoute offered him a chance to prove himself, and so Dherran flowed unceasing through his forms with more control over his rage than he'd ever shown before. Cool and precise, he was one with the sword, sliding peacefully through his forms as he breathed steady and slow.

"That's enough." The Vicoute spoke at last. "Put it away and come with me."

Dherran did, glancing to the Vicoute as he massaged out his hands, wondering where all this was going. Arlen turned abruptly, striding to the door and banging upon it with one fist, raising his voice to exit. A heavy beam was slid back from the opposite side, then the clatter of the iron bolt, and the doors pushed inwards. Fhennic and Valdo lifted eyebrows as the Vicoute exited, clearly surprised to see Dherran in one piece. Arlen strode down the hall and Dherran followed, the two Kingsmen on his heels but with no knife in his back this time. They angled up the stairs, and soon turned in to the Vicoute's study.

Arlen closed the heavy ironwood doors and bolted them, then strode to his ironwood desk carven with hunting scenes, to sit in his high-backed leather chair. Extending his legs and crossing his boots, Arlen steepled his fingers beneath his chin. "I don't waste talent, Dherran."

"Yes, Vicoute."

"And you have very good talent. Better than I've seen in a score of years."

"Yes, Vicoute." The Vicoute's level appraisal, devoid of wrath now, squeezed the air out of Dherran's lungs. Never had he felt so shamed for having done nothing amiss.

"But you're a liability. You're hotheaded, you give your heart too easily, and you're readily swayed on emotional matters. I've interrogated the man you call Grump, and he is indeed the man I knew him to be. A Khehemni traitor and a spy. He professed it easily and honestly, and begged for asylum. Tell me, Dherran. Why do you trust him? And moreover, why should I?"

"Who's after Grump?"

"*Answer my question.*" The Vicoute's blue eyes were hard.

Dherran stuffed down a ripple of unease. A man's life was in his hands, and the strength and honesty of his answer might determine the outcome. "Grump had every possible chance to kill both myself and Khenria these past few years. He knew what we were. I was Blackmarked, and Khenria looks Alrashemni through and through. But he never lifted a finger to harm either of us. He fed us, foraged for us, hunted for us, cared for us when we were sick. Helped us survive in a world with a hatred of Kingsmen. I owe him my life, Arlen, countless times over."

"Why would you defend a Khehemnas, when they destroyed everything you loved?" Arlen's gaze was petrifying.

"Because I believe Grump's a good man. No matter what he is or once was."

"And do you believe I am a good man, Dherran?"

"I believe you're trying to do a good thing, Vicoute."

"You don't like me at all, do you?" Arlen's mouth twisted into a wry smile.

"No. Vicoute. I don't."

"Good." Arlen's lips turned up, vicious. "I don't need men around me who like me. Emotions get men killed on the battlefield, and I need my men to keep a level head. My father would have said *Kill the bastard and be done with the risk.* You are lucky I am not my father, Dherran. I'm willing to take a risk, and have taken many to gather a force here and keep it hidden. Grump exposes all that. Halsos, *you* nearly exposed it, all on your own. Now that the Khehemni Lothren have our position and know my involvement, we are at *terrible risk.* I cannot embrace *any* new face, Dherran. Will I not be second-guessing every man who comes to me wearing Inkings from here out? Do I even risk remaining here at our stronghold? Answer me."

"So it's Grump's people who hunt him? Khehemni?"

"Answer my question, Dherran." Arlen's eyes were icy.

"You'll have to move your operation. You dare not remain here, exposed."

"Yes. And?" The Vicoute nodded.

"You'll go where your support is strongest."

"And where's that?"

"Where your best contacts are. Lintesh. The First Abbey."

"Good. And what will happen if two hundred-some men and women suddenly come seeking refuge at the First Abbey?"

"Any look-and-listen men for the Khehemni will become

suspicious."

"And? Who else?"

Dherran blinked, feeling like an idiot. "Us. Other Alrashemni in hiding."

"Gooooood." Arlen's tone dripped with sarcasm. "So?"

"So we win and we lose, making a journey like that. Any who wear Inkings and see us travel in force will join our group. And the same in Lintesh."

Arlen chuckled, wry. "Good, Dherran. Very good. So what have we gained?"

"Support. But aren't most of the Kingsmen dead?"

Arlen slid his boots back underneath him and stood. "You've seen how many have come silently to my banner these past weeks just here in the eastern reaches, Dherran. Men and women who were not home but abroad when the King's Summons went out ten years ago, who were not able to go to Lintesh in time. Who returned after the atrocity was finished, and have been hiding ever since as farmers, tradesmen, and lesser nobility. It's time we showed Alrou-Mendera a force of Kingsmen, Dherran, to bring the rest out of hiding from the military, the navy, and elsewhere. We're sending out ambassadors. Groups of four, to travel abroad and *mistakenly* show their Inkings, and tell the others to make their way back to Lintesh. But what must I do before we make such a dangerous journey?"

"Fortify your position here."

"Good. And what allies will I use?"

"The ones we have been courting. House den'Lhesh. House den'Ennis. House den'Mithea. House den'Phulo."

"And are they enough?"

Dherran blinked. "You mean enough numbers-wise or fighting-wise?"

"Both."

Dherran paused, then shook his head. "No. The support of those baronies gives you only three thousand at the most. Almost none of them Kingsman-trained."

"So what am I left with here if I take my entire Kingsmen force to Lintesh?"

"Holes. Weakness. You need more men to back up your forces here, or else leave a contingent of Kingsmen behind."

"Which I am loathe to do, as we need a strong force to march on Lintesh when the time comes ripe." The Vicoute ran a hand through his sand-iron hair. "Not to mention that I can't trust anyone who comes wandering in now because of your *friend* Grump. So who do I need?"

Dherran racked his brains, lacking an answer. When suddenly, it hit him. "Allies. Old allies."

The Vicoute gave a hard, rewarding smile. "Old allies. Which I have. In two places other than Lintesh. There is a contingent in the bog north of the Thalanout Plain who I believe I can call to my banner in times of need. Mixed Kingsmen and Khehemni traitors, they live in the trees like monkeys and come out to the wider world for little these days. Their leader, a man by the name of Purloch den'Crassis, owes me much. He will come to my call, though he will most likely hate it."

"Mixed Kingsmen and Khehemni traitors?" Dherran had picked up on this interesting note, leaning forward in his chair.

"You think your friend Grump is the only one to ever break from his breeding, Dherran?" Arlen gave a small chuckle. "There are those who hate the slaughter, the in-fighting between our groups. Once, not so many years ago, there was a great push made for unity among our kind. It failed, miserably. But the remnants of those idealists live in the Heathren Bog, under Purloch's peacekeeping. Isolationists they are now, but once they were honed fighters. And the dangers of living where they do have kept them fierce, Dherran. I need them. Moreover, I need you to go and get them for me. And when you've accomplished that, you'll travel on to Valenghia, to Velkennish. There is a contingent in hiding there that I also need you to woo. And only your... particular tempers and talents, will do."

Arlen gave another chuckle, though his eyes were hard iron. The hairs on the back of Dherran's neck prickled to hear Arlen laugh when he was not playing the idle lord. "You want me to go to Valenghia? To recruit fighters back to your banner?"

"You'll not be going alone. Khenria is adept, she will go with you. And Grump, of course, as your guide to the politics of both the Bog and the aristocracy in Velkennish."

Dherran sat back. His hands upon the armrests of his chair, he brushed the velvet nap beneath his fingers, thinking. Wondering if this was a trap. "You're letting Grump go?"

"No. I'm letting you take charge of him. He is now in your service, and through you, in mine. Spies are valuable, no matter where their loyalties lie. Turn one, and receive the benefit. But be sure he is turned, or reap your downfall."

"Is Grump turned? Does he wish to serve the Kingsmen?"

"You'll have to determine that as you travel, now won't you?" Arlen gave a hard smile. "I'm giving you a chance to command, Dherran. This is how it begins. Take your force of three into the wilds. Win me a force of thousands. Bring them back and hold this manor, these grounds. You have two months, until the end of autumn. I will remain here with my contingent until then. But once the first frosts come, I expect your return. With my reinforcements, both from the Bog and from Valenghia. So. Can I trust you?"

Dherran eyed him. "You know I dislike you."

"Generals are not likable men," Arlen dismissed, eyeing Dherran like hawks do mice. "I will ask you no further times. Can I trust you, Captain, yes or no?"

Dherran took a deep breath, steadying himself. This was his chance. To step into something larger than his rage, his brawling. The Vicoute was giving him opportunity, and Dherran knew it would not come again. But still, Arlen was a dick, and Dherran didn't mind saying so. Dherran rose from his chair. He didn't go to one knee and he didn't bow his head. But he did set a palm to his chest.

"I accept your mission. And I will follow it to the letter. But if you want me to do this, you need to show me that Grump and Khenria are safe and undamaged. If you've hurt them, then this is off. I leave, and I take them with me, and you'll never see us again."

"Or?" Arlen gave a chilling smile, as if he knew Dherran's answer.

"Or I fucking gut you."

And to this, the Vicoute actually laughed. It was a ripping, wrenching laugh, yet had natural levity to it. Arlen's blue eyes shore with a hard battlefield mirth as he rose from his leather chair, then beckoned. "Come, Dherran! Come see your companions."

Arlen strode to the door, hauled it open, and moved off down the marble hall. Dherran stepped quickly to his heels, ascending the grand front staircase of the manor, wondering what he had just agreed to. His heart was in his throat as they strode the short way to Dherran and Khenria's rooms, guarded by four Kingsmen with steely eyes and bristling weapons. They set palms to hearts as Arlen approached, then stepped aside. Arlen pushed in through the carven door, into Dherran's apartment.

Khenria and Grump were inside the room. When Dherran entered behind the Vicoute, he found Grump sitting upon the bed, soothing a very flustered Khenria. Upon seeing Dherran, she flew out of Grump's skinny arms in her green and brown forest leathers, running to Dherran and flinging herself into his embrace.

"Dherran! They said they were going to get you out of the cells! Are you...? Did he...?"

"No," Dherran kissed her narrow face, her high cheeks, her pretty lips. "I'm fine. I just needed a few nights to cool off. No one hurt me. Grump?" He gazed past Khenria to Grump, seeing even from here that Grump was reasonably unharmed, other than scratches and bruises he had gotten in their flight from the forest three nights ago. The skinny forest mouse of a man actually looked hale, dressed in green and brown forest leathers and homespun like Khenria, everything clean as if recently washed. Not a spot of dirt besmirched Grump's narrow hands or face, and his wild grey hair was smoothed back from his forehead, giving him a debonair appearance.

"Likewise, fine, my boy." Grump's lips quirked, his eyes twinkling with high humor. "Your friend the Vicoute did not need to beat any information out of me. I gladly gave all I know. Being hunted by your own kin does that to a man. I've been hunted for years, Dherran, by the Khehemni. Years upon years. Even before I took in Khenria. How else did I learn the woods so well?"

Dherran heard the door to the room close behind him. "Sadly, most of Grump's information is fifteen years old," Arlen den'Selthir commented, dispassionate. "It is, however, substantial. As he has agreed to be my agent in a complex mission devised these past days, which uses his *particular* talents, then his life is of value and therefore spared. As long as he is of use to us."

"And when he is no longer of use?" Dherran eyed the Vicoute, but it was Grumps' harsh titter that caught his attention.

"Then you kill me, boy! Either way, I'm dead eventually. But this way, I'm dead a little later than I'd otherwise be."

Dherran blinked, rage rising in a hot slice within him. He turned his simmering gaze upon the Vicoute. "I'm supposed to kill Grump if he disobeys this mission?"

"Command, Dherran." Arlen's face was stony. "Or leave."

Dherran took a deep breath, cooling off. Gradually, his mindless passion dropped to a manageable thrum. His gaze swung to Grump. The man was already outfitted with his knives, and his bow and quiver sat nearby upon the bed. Khenria was likewise dressed for travel in her dark green leather jerkin with tan leather trousers and a fresh white shirt. She had a weapons harness newly minted nearby upon the bed, complete with a longsword, two longknives, and a brace of eight fly-blades. Similar forest garb awaited Dherran upon the bed, plus all his weapons. Dherran's gaze strayed to the breakfasting table, where a meal sat ready, three rucksacks packed and leaning up against the chairs.

Dherran gave a bitter chuckle. They had discussed this and come to a decision, without him. Setting his hands on his hips, he glanced to Grump. "You agree to this, Grump? To be Arlen's spy, his negotiator? Why?"

Grump gave a long sigh, his eyes drifting out the open window in its arched gable. "Because, Dherran, a man can only take so much bloodshed, before he begins to question what it's all for. Two groups with such an ancient hatred that no one really knows what it's all about anymore. Believe me, Dherran, I've asked among my own kin. I've asked Khehemni high-ups. And you know what they all gave me? Dogma. Siege this group of Alrashemni because they killed your ancestors. Slaughter that group because they killed your parents. Why did they kill our parents? Because our parents killed theirs. And on it goes…"

Grump's gaze rested upon Arlen. Dherran saw something pass between the two men, like an understanding, an accord. And suddenly, something else fell into place. "You two have been allies before."

Arlen's gaze swung to Dherran. For the first time, Dherran saw complicated emotions roiling in those icy blue eyes, the weight of a history the Vicoute did not wish to share. "Grump knows my contacts. It's enough to lead you safely where you need to go."

"He spied on you once. Infiltrated your ranks." Dherran glanced from one man to the other. The lack of response from both was all he needed as confirmation. Grump was the one to break it, moving to the table and wrapping up bread, meat and cheese, and some fruits for travel. "Come, Dherran my boy. Death waits for no man."

It was a strangely chilling statement, as if Grump had relinquished his life entirely to Dherran's hands. To the Vicoute's hands. The room settled into an icy silence, Dherran and Arlen staring each other down. Pulling away from Dherran's arms, Khenria glanced over to Arlen, her nervousness betrayed by a fidgeting of her hands at her weapons.

At last, the Vicoute spoke in a low whisper as if reading Dherran's mind. "You'll do what you have to, when you have to. That is what commanders do, Dherran. They sacrifice. Sometimes it's men, sometimes it's idealism. Sometimes it's love, and sometimes it's giving up their own life for the greater good. And sometimes they relinquish the hardest thing to give up - their rage at all that's been stolen from them."

Suchinne's beautiful face surfaced in Dherran's mind. The reason for his rage, the core of it. Her heinous death upon the battlefield all those years ago, which Dherran could never forgive. A cold shiver took Dherran from head to heels. As if the Vicoute had seen into his very soul, Dherran felt flayed open, more vulnerable than he'd ever been in any fight. There were no weapons against this, no way to block it. Emotions came, piercing deep into his heart, and Dherran felt himself choke on the monstrosity of the Vicoute's attack.

Because it was real, and there was no hiding from it.

"What do I not waste, Dherran?" Arlen queried.

"Talent." Dherran shivered, understanding the answer but not the riddle.

Vicoute Arlen den'Selthir held his gaze quietly, and his next utterance was softer than Dherran had ever heard him speak. "*Life*, Dherran. I don't waste life. Not mine, not yours, not Grump's. Not anyone who wants peace deep down in their heart. Have you noticed my family crest on the shield over the great fireplace in the dining hall?"

"*Liberatmes Aetma Pretienne.*" It was Khenria who answered, her voice subdued.

"Life is precious." Grump's whisper saturated the room.

"Life is precious. *All life* is precious." Arlen stared Dherran down. "And you three are in the unique position of encouraging such a thing. Grump will take you and Khenria, my emissaries, to the Bog and then on to Valenghia. You will find for me the allies I need. And then you will come back, with no life wasted. Anyone who welcomes unity is honored under my banner."

"Why me?" Dherran asked, confusion rippling him. "I know you want me to command... but why send me for this particular mission?"

"Because, Dherran," Arlen sighed, running a hand through his iron-blonde mane, "you don't carry hatred in your heart against the Khehemni. You've such a beast of passion within you that I feared you hated Khehemni like my father did, but you don't. Your hatred runs a different variety, a flavor of love lost, and believe me when I say I know its bitter taste well. But you don't hate Khehemni, not really, just like I don't. Don't mistake me. I *will* slaughter any Khehemni who attack my people, just like those in the woods who tracked Grump. And I cannot yet announce my personal feelings among my Kingsmen. Many of them remain bitter at the Summons, and would not welcome merging forces with Khehemni. But like Grump, I've seen too much bloodshed, much of it at my father's hands. Some things make an impression on the young. I was taught to kill, and I learned well, but I put my skills to use in a different way. I want peace, Dherran, like I built here for so many years. Find me Alrashemni and Khehemni traitors hiding in the Heathren Bog, hiding in Valenghia. *Find me* those men and women who want peace as much as Grump and I do. That, Captain, is your mission. Find them and bring them here, and we will all move upon Lintesh when the time is right."

Suddenly, everything that Vicoute Arlen den'Selthir was, everything he represented shifted for Dherran. Dherran felt his heart open to the man, truly open, like Khenria's had so many weeks ago. A lump rose in his throat. Slowly, Dherran sank to one knee. Placing a palm to his Inkings and still gripping Arlen's father's sword, he spoke, "My liege."

"Your General." A wry smile twisted Arlen's face, but it was pleased. "And *do* use my father's sword in a better way than he ever chose to."

Arlen looked the company over as Dherran came back to standing. The weight of his piercing gaze rested upon Grump. The forest mouse of a man nodded, and Arlen gave a terse nod also. Arlen's gaze came to Dherran, and Dherran straightened under that burden, knowing everything he had yet to prove, all the rage and hate he had yet to master.

Last of all, Arlen's gaze pinned Khenria. She fidgeted under his scrutiny, one hand sliding to the hilt of a longknife, her long fingers rippling upon the weapon. She stood tall, flicked one of her short curls from her eyes with a haughty toss of her head. Moving forward, Arlen came to her, until her fidgeting became vicious. Reaching out, he lifted her hands from her weapons, and held them in his.

"I would have given you everything." Arlen said, his visage pained. "Everything I have. Rest, comfort, a home here. And yet, I must use you for the warrior you are. For what you have become, honed steel, fierce as a hawk and thrice as cunning. Letting you stay would undermine what you are becoming. A blade. A blade, to pierce the heart of that throne in the White Palace, like you were meant to."

Tears filled Khenria's grey eyes. Her words entirely stolen, all she could do was take one hand from Arlen's and place it upon her chest. "How did you know?"

Arlen gave a sad smile. Reaching up, he moved a loose curl out of her eyes. "The Shemout keep track of those who turn the tides of history, though you escaped us for so many long years. Grump has filled me in on your missing years. Love the Alrashemni, Khenria. And love where you came from at birth. Bring us together."

She swallowed hard. And then suddenly moved forward, wrapping her skinny arms around the Vicoute in a firm embrace. "I will. I won't disappoint you."

Arlen gripped her shoulders gently, pulled her away. His blue eyes shone with unshed tears. "Good girl." With a deep breath, he stepped back, letting her go. Those blue eyes flicked to Dherran, fierce. "It is up to you to keep your party safe, Dherran. Know that you will answer to me if Khenria or Grump come to harm unnecessarily."

Dherran nodded, wondering at Arlen's manner with Khenria. It hadn't been a heat of passion between them, and it was nothing he found he could feel jealous of, as if the Vicoute held immense tenderness for the young woman but no sexuality. Their interaction triggered something in Dherran, something that simmered with jealousy not over his lover embracing another man, but because he had no one to care for him with that kind of familial tenderness.

"I will keep them safe, Arlen," Dherran spoke, setting a hand to his Inkings. "I promise."

"Good. Then make ready to ride. You leave today." Arlen clasped his hands behind his back, an iron-cold commander once more. "I will put it out that you three escaped, and I will lead a nominal hunt in the wrong direction. You will not find it easy to rejoin us, but I expect that you will have enough men to make my Kingsmen evaluate their hate when you return. By then, my men will be ready to bring our forces together, I'll make certain of it. Good hunting, Dherran, Grump, Khenria. Bring me back something I can use."

Turning, the Vicoute strode from the room, shutting the door behind him.

"You planned this, didn't you?" Dherran glanced at Grump. "You planned all this. Was that why we came to Vennet, Grump? To rendezvous with Arlen? Join forces with him?"

Grump winked at him, grinning with a devious glee. "Believe what you will, my boy. I knew coming to Vennet was risky for all of us, but no man can know where fate will turn him. I merely pushed the waterwheel and hoped for the best. You and Khenria needed training, training I couldn't give you. And perspective and direction for your rage that I could never supply."

Though he simmered, piss-mad at having been used, Dherran also found himself grinning. "You cunning, sneaky fucker."

"Spies keep their ears open for the turnings of the world, Dherran," Grump's gaze was hard now, level, as if he was a different man entirely from the one Dherran knew. "And something is happening out there that leaves me chill inside. I felt it coming even before news of the Queen's supposed demise. So! We'd better get a move on, Dherran my boy, and I'll explain it better when we're on the road. Rucksacks are filled. Change of clothes and weapons are there for you on the bed. Horses are ready for us in the eastern woods, near a pond I know. We have an hour until dark, so if you want a last hot bath and a stout meal, take it now!"

With that, Grump turned, flitting over to the table, his skinny fingers walking all over the delicacies as he popped them into his mouth with a clever smile.

CHAPTER 18 – OLEA

Vargen had given Olea a concerned look when she finally arrived upon the terrace for breakfast, but he was mired in children, two in his lap as he sorted food out. Olea had not come home this morning until dawn glimmered over the eastern mountains. For the past ten nights since she had taken her walk with Lourden, she had gone out walking to clear her mind. Walking Oasis Ghellen alone all night, taking naps in the heat of the afternoon while they waited until they could travel to Khehem.

But today was the day. The Maitrohounet had finally acquiesced to let them venture to Khehem, under the protection of Lourden's spears. All had dressed for running the desert this morning, wearing their light Ghellani garb with weapons in harnesses, *shoufs*, loa-skin bracers, and silver shinguards over their boots. Thelliere moved by with a basket of fruits, encouraging Olea to get food with a kiss to the lips. Olea glanced through the kitchen at the high shelf where Lourden's spear and helmet were normally set by the door, and found them gone.

"Where is Lourden?" Olea helped herself to fruits and cold meat from a platter.

Aldris lounged in a chair on the terrace, dark smudges under his eyes but the laziness of a man well-fucked about his person. Olea knew he'd been spending his nights with a very compatible friend of Thelliere's. He and Olea had come home at nearly the same time this morning. Olea didn't blame him for wanting distraction.

"Lourden went out," Aldris responded. "Said something about needing to see the Maitrohounet and his First-Spear, about today's arrangements. Said he'd be back soon."

"And Jherrick?" Olea asked. "Is he up?"

Aldris' gaze soured. "He's up. *Chained* up, good and tight in his room. I checked him at dawn. I told Thelliere not to feed him, but she brought him breakfast anyway."

Lourden arrived upon the terrace, dressed in his full guard-attire, red-crested helmet under one arm. He beckoned to Olea and she stood, moving aside so they were out of earshot. Aldris watched them with a slight frown, but kept his seat.

Lourden looked Olea over critically. She was dressed for journeying today, her white silk with its colorful border pinned into a short tunic, longknives ready at her harness but her sword left in her room, too heavy for a run. Her white *shouf* was slung about her shoulders, ready to be raised into a deep hood to keep off the sun. Loa-boots, bracers, and shinguards were already cinched to her person. A water flask was ready at the table, to be slung from her belt next to her leather belt pouch.

Lourden made an approving sound, then handed Olea a small stone jar. "All must smear this liberally over any exposed skin today. To protect from the sun. Keep it in your pouch. We will run much this day, and you must weather the scorch. Keep your hood up. When you begin to feel faint, soak your hair and put your hood back up. There is good water in Khehem. We will not be without. Make your men ready to travel. We go."

Lourden turned, making for the house, but Olea stopped him with a hand to the arm. "Lourden. Forgive me for bringing trouble to your home. I know how much I'm asking of you. I appreciate the risk you are taking... because of me."

His brows furrowed, then he sighed. "It was childish of me to think the coming of the Olive Branch would be an easy thing. And now that you are here... I find myself torn with disturbing thoughts." He searched her eyes, and suddenly his visage was tender like it had been the night they walked the city.

"Do you know what you wish to find in Khehem?"

"Answers." Olea replied, fingering her belt pouch. "Roushenn Palace has far too many secrets. I need to unravel them. Jherrick does, too."

His brows knit, his eyes worried. "Do you trust the Khehemnas?"

"No." Olea responded, thinking of how completely Jherrick's mannerisms had changed since his revelation five nights ago. "I don't trust him. And I won't underestimate him, either."

"I will fetch him and make him ready to travel." Lourden gave a brusque nod, then turned, ducking into the guesthouse.

It was time. Olea beckoned to Aldris and Vargen. They rose without comment, Vargen giving the children quick bear-hugs before he joined Olea by the door. Soon, all was in a flurry as they prepared to leave. In the foyer, Thelliere went around, giving them packets of food to tuck into belt pouches. Everyone checked weapons, gave them a last cleaning with cloths, checked gear. Jherrick was brought to the main room in manacles, ready in his desert garb but sans weapons. When they had seen her yesterday, the Maitrohounet had insisted Jherrick go to Khehem with them, after much meditation and casting of bones and swirling of incense.

At last, all were ready.

They set out through the maze of Oasis Ghellen at a brisk walk, heading toward the western wall. The sun was searing in the early morning, though dawn had come and gone just an hour ago. Passing through the break in Ghellen's massive wall, they acquired a party of twenty Ghellani spearmen and women, members of Lourden's *Rishaaleth* attending them upon the venture of the day.

And then, they were past the city, moving out along the broken promenade towards Khehem.

It was a longer trek than Olea had thought. Distances were tricky in the desert of white sand and stone. What looked like a close walk to a low hillock of dune took twenty minutes, the broken pillars of the causeway spaced further apart than they seemed. Mirages licked the horizons, obscuring the purple mountains to the north and south. They proceeded along the half-arches and tumbled pillars of the ancient road for nearly an hour, past the Alranstone plaza before the causeway opened up near the walls of Khehem.

High as sixty men, maybe more, the gargantuan ring-wall of Oasis Khehem was as badly damaged as Ghellen's, riven and blasted, the alabaster granite burned black. Olea's gaze scoured the breached wall and the city beyond. She saw now that the dark hue of Khehem, which appeared so sinister from afar, was scorch so thick upon the white stone that one could have cut it like butter from the walls. Even the press sandstorms and time had not dislodged that thick char, and Olea shivered at the thought of magic so powerful as to have ruined such a stalwart city for so long.

Proceeding toward the breach in the wall, they moved into a

wide plaza ringed by statues of broken beasts that once might have been Khehem's eastern gate. Enormous lintels of stone rose before them, cracked and burned, many of their blocks scattered like children's playthings. Sand piled against the outer wall from the desert, the morning wind fierce as it shrieked across the hardpack. Olea pulled her *shouf* over her mouth and nose, imitating Lourden's spearmen. Some had even pulled the hoods of their wrap down over their eyes. Olea tried it, noting that the gauzy fabric was readily see-through. Not good enough for a battle, but good enough for moving like ghosts through a dead city.

A few more steps and they entered the breach in the towering, broken wall. Thirty feet thick, sections of the wall still stood intact above them, an ancient portal-gate. Olea gazed upwards as they passed under an arch into shadow, feeling the enormity of the once-flourishing oasis. Grander than Ghellen, this city had been built to defy time. As Olea passed beneath its mighty wall, she saw evidence of a high culture gone to ruin. Wolf's heads protruded from the stone, waterspouts of their mouths dry and full of sand. Dragons curled up staircases that wound to upper levels unseen. Iron gates long rusted showed evidence of red and saffron paint. Blue waterlilies carven up beneath the main gate's arch in the shadows still shone with color, untouched by sand and wind.

Their group passed quickly beneath the wall at a trot, spears leveled, eyes darting. But Oasis Khehem was silent as death. Lourden flicked his fingers at his *Rishaaleth*, gathering them into a group once they emerged into a wide stone fountain-plaza just inside the wall. Olea joined them at a trot, Aldris and Vargen falling into step behind her. Jherrick's irons clinked as he followed, at the end of Vargen's lead-chain. Vargen was a steady man, and Olea knew he would not lift a hand against Jherrick unless the lad did something to merit it.

Aldris, however, had not stopped fingering his belt knife since they'd set out from Ghellen. Olea put a hand on his arm and he ceased with a startle, unaware he had been doing it.

Lourden gathered the group with a motion of his spear. He raised his voice, addressing his *Rishaaleth* in Khourek, a fast, lilting speech. He then turned towards Olea's men and began his address again in Menderian.

"We will hunt for whatever you seek until sundown. Once the sun touches the mountains, there," he nodded to one particularly tall mountain at the southwestern rim of the desert, "all will head back here, and meet in this plaza. We depart Oasis Khehem once the suns' rays are gone. Any who remain once the sun is behind that peak will be left here. Truly, I say to you. We will leave. The walls are restless after dark." He pierced Olea with his storm-grey eyes. "We will come back at dawn, for any who did not make it out by nightfall."

"And how many have you found in the morning?" A slow fear churned in Olea's gut.

Lourden's grey eyes were hard. "Alive? None." He paused a long moment. "Do you know what it is you seek, *Olea-gishii?*"

"Something that can tell me about these." Olea slid her fingers into her belt purse, fishing out her white silk pouch embroidered with an olive branch. She opened it, dumping all the tiny pieces of the clockwork Elohl had found ten years ago into her palm. The precious ores glittered in the sunlight, as she stretched her hand out to Lourden. His eyes widened, snapped to hers. In all these weeks, Olea had not shared this secret with him, and she saw it arrest him now.

Lourden flicked his fingers to his group, saying something rapid in Khourek. The *Rishaaleth* leaned in one at a time, gazing intently at the items in Olea's palm before stepping back. Lourden was the last, cupping Olea's palm with his hands as he bent to scrutinize the pieces. He stepped back with a nod, his touch slipping away. Olea's chest gripped, losing that moment with him, feeling like a chasm opened up between them because of this secret she'd not shared.

A secret that his life, and every other life here, depended upon today.

Aldris stepped forward, eyeing the clockworks with a grunt. When he stepped back, Jherrick at last had his turn. He frowned a long time at the pieces, then looked up.

"You found them in Roushenn?" Jherrick asked, a hint of concern gracing his voice, almost like the lad she once knew.

"They're involved in Roushenn's mystery," Olea nodded, "but I don't know how. Have you ever seen anything like them?"

Jherrick scowled. "Not exactly. But I saw a broken section of wall, once, in Roushenn's Hinterhaft. It had metal gears at the bottom where it joined the floor, like those. Those look too small to be wall-gears, though. Only…there is a room at the heart of Roushenn. A massive room Lhaurent never lets anyone enter. Perhaps those belong to something in that room…"

Olea blinked. "You think it's a control room of some kind?"

"All Praoughian clockworks have a wind-core," Vargen interrupted, "to power the mechanism. A room like that might be where the palace's function is wound, so to speak. Where it's powered."

"If so," Jherrick continued, "then we're looking for a vast room, perhaps underground, in the heart of the city. Maybe in the center of a palace."

"I know where we must go." Lourden's black brows furrowed as he turned, speaking quickly to his group. They all nodded, looking nervous. Lourden removed his crested helmet, then handed it off to one of his *Rishaaleth*. Rifling a hand through his sweat-slick curls, he regarded Olea with a look of such intensity that it could only mean they needed to talk, privately. Olea returned the clockworks to her pouch, stepping to Lourden. With a gesture of his spear, he led off a few paces, over to the shade of Khehem's wall, near a lion's head fount clogged with sand.

"Lourden," Olea spoke quietly. "What is it? Your men look fearful."

He ground his jaw. "We must go inside the palace, at the heart of Khehem. If this room is anywhere in the city, it would be there, underground. But the last time we ventured inside the palace, we lost ten spears. Gherlam was one of the ten. He was pinned between two walls right in front of me." Lourden stared out at nothing for a moment. His hand tightened upon his spear, his knuckles white.

"Gherlam was more than just your wife's first husband, wasn't he?"

Lourden blinked, roused from his nightmare, and gazed down at her. "Gherlam was my brother. Like you and your brother, we were… dual. Two. Ah…" He wiped a hand over his face, frustrated.

"Twins?"

Lourden nodded, his gaze empty and sad. "Twins. Yes. I feel his essence… ripped from me. Every day." He reached out, gripping her wrist. "If we venture inside the palace walls, *Olea-gishii*, men are sure to die this day."

Olea fingered her belt pouch, the clockworks in the silken bag safely within. "I know. But I must find out how it works, Lourden. If you want to help me, then help me. If not, I'll do it on my own. You and your men can wait here in the plaza. You've done more than enough. I'll meet you here by sunset."

Lourden shook his head, a sad smile lifting the corners of his mouth. His fingers slipped from her wrist to grasp her hand, a small movement, but it was enough. Olea's tongue caught. Her cheeks burned. She could feel the flare of passion rise between them. She'd turned from it, and Lourden had stuffed it away that night upon Ghellen's wall, but it wasn't gone. They'd been dancing around each other ever since, Lourden careful to not touch her, Olea careful to not watch him when Thelliere was around.

But here it was. On a day that any of them might die, a day Olea had asked for, a day Lourden had given her. He twined his fingers in hers. Olea swallowed, gazing down at their hands because she couldn't meet his eyes. He ran his thumb over her palm, and Olea could feel everything unspoken pouring between them.

She looked up. His grey gaze roiled, speaking eons in a moment.

Olea knew hers did the same.

Lourden nodded, drew a breath. He straightened his shoulders. "I will join in your search, *Olea-gishii*, and invite my spears to also. Any may join us, or refuse, without punishment. Today will be a dangerous journey, and I would not suffer that risk upon the unwilling. But I am willing. I will come, for you."

Olea's eyes prickled, hot. She blinked, swallowing hard. "Thank you."

Lourden gave a sad smile. His fingers slipped from Olea's and her heart twisted to let him go. Turning decisively, he strode back to the group. Olea heard a fast flurry of Khourek, then a short dialogue between Lourden and his First-Spear, Jhennah. Olea rubbed her throat, trying to stifle her flooding emotions. She turned, to see the *Rishaaleth* separated into two groups. Lourden spoke a few words to those on the left. They saluted with spears across their chests in a quick movement, then strode back to the shade of the wall, settling in and opening water flasks.

Lourden addressed Olea as she approached. "My Second-Spear Ghistan will remain here with a small contingent. Some have families they wish to return to this day. It is no dishonor. They will wait for us until sundown."

Olea nodded, gazing out over the spires and sprawling domes of Khehem. It was a veritable warren. Charred alabaster stone turrets and arches tumbled in every direction, not just a maze, but a ruined maze that would be treacherous. Khehem had the look of a hive, Olea realized suddenly, and without Lourden's intimate knowledge of the city, they would have been lost.

"Then let's get to it," she sighed, fingers checking both longknives out of habit.

Lourden nodded. Taking up his helm, he spoke a quick phrase to the remaining group of eight warriors that would travel into the city with them. They hefted spears, saluted, and dark-eyed Jhennah stepped forward, saying a quick phrase back.

"We are ready," Lourden commented to Olea with a gesture of his spear. "We move toward the palace. Come. We must travel fast, for we have a long way to go."

He turned, leading the spearmen toward a broad avenue upon the right. Olea nodded to Vargen and Aldris. Vargen rattled Jherrick's chain, and a few choice curses came from Aldris' lips as he checked his weapons. But they were Kingsmen, and readied themselves for the unknown. Even young Jherrick showed fire and steel in his countenance, though he had nothing but his hands to fight with.

Olea trotted to catch up to Lourden's loping grace, her stride easy and long. "Lourden? How far is the palace?"

"Many leagues. In the heart of the city." Lourden's response was smooth, his breathing easy as he ran. "Most of the outskirts are little more than domiciles and marketplaces and gardens. They don't tend to move, so I do not believe your control room is there. There are three Circles of Oasis Khehem. Once we reach the Inner Circle, everything tends to move at a moment's notice. That is where the palace resides, in the heart of this circle. Keep your steps quick and light. Stones of the plazas shift as well, opening up holes in the earth. I've lost men down them before. Only fountains do not move. If everything is moving, run to a fountain and jump in it. The moving areas are built around Khehem's springs."

Olea nodded as she jogged, keeping easy pace. "And the palace in the Inner Circle? How far into it have you ventured?"

Lourden's brows furrowed as he jogged, spear tight in one fist. He nodded at a side avenue, and his group made for it, rounding a domed structure undamaged by time. They leaped a section of rubble, then dodged a fallen colonnade. "I have not been inside the... bulk of it. I lost my twin venturing in through a side-door. Everything shifted the moment we entered."

Olea frowned. "Have you ever seen anyone in Khehem's ruins? Anyone living here?"

"No." Lourden shook his head. "Not other than people we came in here to find, unwary caravans who hadn't heard the stories of Khehem's danger."

Suddenly, the avenue began to open up before them, sand over the flagstones shifting like snakes underwater. Lourden's company dodged fast, splitting to avoid the hole now gaping in the causeway. Olea angled to the side Lourden had gone, but he outpaced her in a burst of speed.

And she saw why. The side they had chosen was opening in a second rift, shedding white sand to unseen depths. Lourden gauged the distance, bolted, and jumped. It was easy, only four feet, but widening fast. Olea sprinted, jumped, and landed upon the other side with a foot to spare. But it yawned, cavernous, as Vargen and Jherrick got to it, Aldris having chosen the other side. Lourden's shout brought them up short.

"Stop! To the fountain!" Lourden gestured with his spear to a spreading fountain at an intersection fifty paces left. Vargen and Jherrick hastily backtracked, the rift widening massively before them. They sprinted to the side, avoiding the gap.

Suddenly, Olea felt the stone under her feet shift. Sliding, the paving stones began to tilt out from beneath her. Olea bolted, leapt from the unstable surface, rolled forward to steady ground. Launching to her feet, she sprinted with everything she had for the fountain. Lourden and his spearmen were nearly there, Aldris hard on their heels. Vargen and Jherrick were taking the long way around, though their ground had stopped shifting.

But Olea's hadn't. She felt stones sliding out beneath every step, as if some ravenous beast pulled them down to a dark oblivion. She put on a burst of speed, her gaze riveted to the fountain. Men and women beckoned there, shouting with urgent fear. Aldris had made it to the fountain's basin, doubled over coughing. Lourden was pale, his gaze riveted to Olea, his knuckles white on his spear.

Stones slipped beneath her boots, falling.

"*Jump!*" Lourden and Aldris reached to her from the fountain's basin, roaring. Olea compacted and leapt for the rim, just as the world dropped out beneath her. Her hands hit the rim. Her chest slammed into stone, knocking the breath from her body. Her lower body and feet hit nothing. Strong hands seized her, Lourden and Aldris hauling her up over the fountain's rim. They collapsed backwards into a handspan of brackish water. It was a long moment before Olea could move, terror still thrumming through her veins as she caught her breath. Lourden rose to his feet, but Aldris sat in the water, gasping.

And then laughing. A near-maniacal laugh of terror, his green eyes on the edge of reason. "Aeon's fuck, Olea! What did you let that fucking Khehemnas get us into?"

Vargen strode over through the water, giving Aldris a stout slap that rang his bell. Aldris glared up, sane once more in his anger. But the mountain of a man wasn't finished, seizing Aldris by his weapons harness and hauling him up out of the water.

"Stow that!" Vargen growled, shaking the smaller man. "You're a Kingsman! Act like one. Keep your cool or die here. We won't mourn the passing of a man too rash to think properly under pressure!"

Aldris' mouth worked in silent surprise. He shut it, then snarled, "Unhand me."

Vargen did.

Aldris' eyes flashed to Olea. "I didn't come here to die for a filthy Khehemnas."

Olea sloshed through the water, putting her nose in Aldris' face. "You came here because your Inkings signify a duty, Lieutenant. I suggest you figure out what that duty is."

Aldris stared at her. It was the most authentic Olea had ever seen him, rage and suffering in his visage, the real man buried beneath the good looks and witty charm. "Khehemni slaughtered my entire family, Olea," he choked, anger surging through him in a hard shiver. "They weren't even Kingsmen, they were horse-breeders! So when the Shemout Alrashemni came to recruit me, I made my choice." His eyes flicked to Jherrick. "*Him*, and all his kind, have to pay."

"How many have to die in this ageless war before we put up our blades?" Olea growled at him. "Did Jherrick kill your family? Look at him! He's not a day over twenty-three, for Aeon's sake! He's got a story of pain to match yours. Halsos, I do, too. Vargen saw his wife murdered before his eyes. When are the deaths enough?"

"He's got to die." Aldris rasped, his red-shot eyes pleading for her to understand.

"And are you going to be the one to make that call?" Olea pulled a longknife from its sheath, pressing it into his hand hilt-first. "Go ahead, Lieutenant. Kill him. Look into that boy's eyes, judge him, and kill him. Do it."

Aldris' hand spasmed upon the knife. Olea felt the point dig into her, and she backed away. Aldris' green eyes were hooded, dangerous as he turned, pinning Jherrick. Jherrick didn't move as Aldris approached. Coming close enough that their breath mingled, Aldris set the tip of his blade between Jherrick's ribs beneath his heart, angled up for a deep killing thrust.

"Aldris!" Olea called out. "Just ask yourself one thing. Is this *Kingsman* justice?"

Aldris froze. Olea watched the blade tremble, the point digging in. Jherrick's breathing quickened, though he held immaculately still. Aldris put weight behind the knife, and it began to slit silk, gouge flesh. Blood trickled from the knifepoint. Jherrick winced. He stood firm, but his eyes were wide, frightened.

The wild revelation of the young, who always think death will come for them later.

But then, Olea heard the rough sob of a man breaking. Aldris' shoulders shook. His knife shivered away, scratching a red line and falling out of his grip to splash in the water. Relief filled Jherrick's eyes. He backed away to the rim of the fountain in his manacles.

Tears welled in Aldris' red-rimmed eyes. He looked away rather than face Olea. Lifting her hand, she set her palm to the center of his chest. Aldris' tortured eyes flicked up, away. He lifted his arm, wiping away tears. A heavy hand settled to his shoulder, and Aldris glanced up. Vargen's rumble was so low it was almost a purr.

"You've earned those Inkings today, Kingsman. More than you'll ever know."

Aldris nodded, rubbing his face on his arm again. He fiddled at his belt for his water-flask. Olea's hand slid away. She bent to retrieve her longknife from the water, wiped it, and slid it away in its sheath.

"Everyone drink deep and fill your flasks," Lourden's smooth voice cut in, breaking the tension. "We've got a lot more of this ahead of us."

The sun was scorching as they departed from the opposite side of the fountain. Olea gazed at the hole in the avenue as they ventured forth, and saw that it was not truly bottomless. Thirty feet down, there were passages beneath the city, the stone still alabaster, painted with bright friezes in the gloom. Sand spilled over ancient furnishings and rotting, sun-bleached tapestries.

A city beneath the city, just like Lintesh.

Lourden was silent as they moved on, deeper into the warren of arches and buildings. His *Rishaaleth* were tense, eyes darting to every shadow. Olea scanned for movement as they took up a swift jog. The party tracked carefully through the avenues now that they had experienced the first opening of the bowels of Khehem, staying in a tight knot. Rumbles of stones moving sounded in the distance.

Olea sidled close to Vargen as they rounded the curve of a tumbled amphitheater. He stepped up, tugging Jherrick. Olea narrowed her eyes upon the young man. "Jherrick. You said Roushenn moves by invisible strings and clockwork tracks?"

"Yes. And the way the pavingstones rolled under near the fountain here, I'd assume Khehem is the same. I've seen that at Roushenn." Jherrick added.

They turned another corner, passing a blasted-out pile of rubble. "Blades can slice strings, but to see how it all works, we'd need something to jam the gears." Olea said.

"Bitterwood is stout. We can use it." Lourden hefted his spear. "Five men can balance on each end of a spear over a pivot, and it won't shatter."

"Now we just have to catch Halsos' walls in action."

Surprisingly, Aldris chimed in.

They didn't have long to wait. A building next to them suddenly began to involute, walls rolling outward and collapsing in, the roofline moving to reshape and accommodate the walls. Foundation-stones slid away from each other in a wide gap. Olea yanked Jherrick's chain from Vargen and tossed it to Jherrick. She unsheathed a longknife and pressed it to Jherrick's palm.

"Show me how it works! Quickly!"

Jherrick didn't waste time. He darted forward, Olea just behind, her other longknife out as she ran. Wrapping his chain up around his neck out of the way, Jherrick made a straight line for the center of the chaos. He froze upon the stilling point in the middle of the churning walls, glancing around quickly at the melee. Like a heron, he darted to one wall, snicked the longknife out as a mirror appeared. The mirror fell askew, a blue cord fine as spider's silk dangling over the surface, one recoiling above. Olea whipped her blade at the other side of the mirror, guessing where the other cord would be. The mirror fell, shattering, silvered glass spilling over the stones as the wall ground away.

"Spear!" Jherrick yelled.

Already in the melee with them, Lourden heaved his spear to Jherrick. The young man caught it and snaked forward, almost getting flattened by a moving wall. With a swift thrust like he skewered boar, he sent the spear into a shivering mound of sand near the still spot. There was a grinding squeal, a sound to shatter eardrums. But though the spear shuddered, it did not break. With a groan, the nearest wall ground to a halt. Another one backed up into the first, and groaned to a halt also. Then another. Everything shuddered into stillness.

Catching her breath, Olea eyeballed Jherrick. "Never seen you move like that on the practice grounds, den'Tharn."

Jherrick heaved, breathing hard. When he glanced over, a cocky twinkle shone in his grey eyes. He gave a soft chuckle, the sound a man makes when he knows he's impressed a woman. A sound she'd never heard from him before. "Shall we investigate, Captain?"

Olea nodded, and together they stepped to the spear. Olea bent, clearing away the pile of sand. A long groove became apparent in the floor. As Olea swept sand out with her fingers, tooth-edged metal gears began to show.

"Just like in Roushenn." Jherrick nodded decisively. "There's a locus like this, I've discovered, in every hundred feet of flooring. It controls all the nearby elements. There must be walls that don't shift between the loci, but it's difficult to discern when everything is moving." He nodded at the clear space. "But there's a spot like that near every locus. About three feet square where nothing moves."

Lourden crouched by Olea, fingertips touching the gears. "All this time I thought it was magic."

Vargen came through the maze, gave a low whistle. He knelt, using his *shouf* to brush gears clean, feeling them with his fingers. He pointed to one. "This is the primary crankshaft Jherrick jammed. See here, how it extends beneath this bit of flooring. There's an eddle-spindle. And a hammer-latch. No...*eight* hammer-latches. Eight walls moved, eight stopped moving. One for each latch." His fingers slid in, feeling beneath the floor. "There's a gurney-track under here. I can feel flagstones beneath the floor. They must slip up into place as the wall slides, making it seem like the whole thing moves naturally." He pulled his fingers out. "Very sophisticated. That must be how the avenues open up."

"What are you thinking, Vargen?"

"What I can't figure out," he continued, gazing around thoughtfully, "is how it's all so *seamless*. These stones should be chipped after so much grinding and movement, no matter how well-joined they are."

Lourden's mouth quirked. "Ghosts. Magic."

"*Wyrria*, not ghosts." Jherrick said. "I'm certain of it."

Olea tousled her hair. "*Wyrria* comes from a person, doesn't it? Not objects?"

Jherrick shrugged. "Alranstones are imbued with *wyrria*. What's to say these stones aren't, also?"

"Alrashemni gifts are often complex," Vargen rumbled. "It would stand to reason some of those gifts might be able to shape the elements. To give stone or metal certain properties, like movement."

Olea brushed off her hands, glancing at Jherrick. "What happens if we pull out Lourden's spear?"

He shrugged. "I've never jammed active walls before. I wasn't even sure it could be done."

Olea gazed at Jherrick a long moment. "You ran into those spinning walls on a whim? Betting your life against that spear? That it would hold when you thrust it in, not flattening you when you tried to get out of that chaos?"

Jherrick held her gaze. He gave a wry smile, something like his old self. "Maybe I'll prove myself to you someday, Captain. Maybe you'll find I don't want to be your enemy."

Olea's gaze drifted to Jherrick's hands. He offered her longknife back, hilt-first, his wrists still manacled. He'd run into certain death, chained, just to prove his dedication. Just to show her he meant everything he said.

Speaking his truth, perhaps, for the first time in his life.

Olea held one hand out to Lourden. "Keys."

"What? No! Olea!" Aldris protested, shocked.

Lourden hesitated, one hand near his belt-pouch.

"Keys, Lourden." Olea ordered again. "I take full responsibility for Jherrick's actions, from here forward. Keys. Now."

A small key was fished out of Lourden's pouch and pressed to her palm. Olea unlocked Jherrick's manacles, letting them fall to the sandy flagstones. He rubbed one wrist, then offered her knife again.

"Keep it."

"Why?"

"Because you're a better man than I gave you credit for," Olea held Jherrick's gaze, stern. "Show me, Jherrick. Show me how we can stay alive in Khehem, in Roushenn. Show me how to find the stillpoint, where to look for the locus, where to cut the blue cords. Show me who you really are. And where your loyalties lie."

His young grey eyes searched hers a long moment, before he nodded. "Captain."

CHAPTER 19 – GHRENNA

Ghrenna reclined in the yard in a soft patch of grass, her hands folded upon her belly. Sheep grazed on the other side of the stone berm, their bleating a chorus to the whisper of the wind. Cool mountain air tickled her hands and face, her bare feet pricked by grasses. Warm and comfortable in the fine-spun wool shift Mollia had given her, Ghrenna lounged, drifting. The sun was gentle through the evergreens, the silence soothing. She had been free of pain since yesterday, and had not needed Molli's healing touch nor threllis today. For six days, she had taken restorative teas, focusing on regenerating her body and healing her mind.

Ghrenna had not touched Hahled Ferrian's Plinth again. Molli would not let her take the mind-opening tea, saying that Ghrenna had to learn to journey to the Alranstones organically. The opening-tea was toxic and using it too often apparently ruined a person's liver and urinary system. Molli had been teaching Ghrenna different breathing exercises to achieve the same erotic trance state, in place of the tea. Ghrenna used the breathing now, smoothing her body and mind into a wandering-space that she'd not known existed until she'd come to Molli's valley.

Breathing steadily, Ghrenna's limbs felt loose and calm, her skin buzzing and pleasant. Her eyes slipped closed as she began to do fire-breathing, a rapid series of fifty breaths repeated three times and held between each set. The buzzing in her skin increased, a ripple passing over her as if she had stepped through an Alran-ring. Her mind strayed with the heightening of her senses, as her body went deep into stupor.

Focusing on that buzzing, feeling it smooth over her, then recede, then surge again, Ghrenna went deep into trance. Her limbs began to heat, a slow flush that evened all temperatures outdoors. Her breathing became deep and slow, her body heavy like it weighed thirty stone. As if Molli's tea had given her a map to follow, the heat began to shift, enfolding her chest, warming in a subtle eroticism.

Loosing heat into her solar plexus and deep into her groin, the tingling touched her deep, exploring places Ghrenna had only begun to understand. Touching her inner wrists, smoothing over them like fingers. Activating energy channels that thrummed through her body like live lightning, charging her, yet pulling her deeper into trance. Those insubstantial fingers touched her ribcage, slid up to dive behind her collarbones. They lifted her hair, touching the sides of her neck, then every knob of her spine. Ghrenna's lips parted, her breathing deep and slow, feeling energy shift and move inside her body, lighting her up from the inside.

Those fingers slid up the rear of her skull, finally touching the crown of her head. Expansion blossomed within Ghrenna; her mind opened like a bird's wings, breathing in every direction. She saw stars in the mind-space. An eternity of stars in a black void, all around her, shining with so much light. Ghrenna gazed around in wonder, feeling her body there, even though it still reclined upon the grass.

A chuckle rolled through the starry void.

A hand of white fingers slid over her shoulder from behind.

Ghrenna sat up from the grass with a gasp. Drenched in the musky sweat of arousal, her breath was hard and fast from the sudden surprise. The strangest sensation tapped at her, like a moth fluttered against a pane of glass inside her body. She gazed to the pasture before the ruined fortress, out over the stone bridge towards the Alranstone's meadow, feeling something calling her. Rising, she skirted the pasture and crossed the stone bridge to the forest. Her gaze fixed in the direction of the Alranstone, instinct pulling her onward. She could feel the Stone's presence even from this distance, as if it was drawing her.

Trees arched over the old road, moss and stone cool beneath her feet. Ghrenna's vision was sharper, her body clear and invigorated now as she approached the meadow. The Stone's pull quickened, and Ghrenna's heart began to race. She could feel its ephemeral touch, smoothing at her inner wrists, activating her inner ankles. Touching inside her hips, pulling her with invisible fingers upon every knob of her spine.

Bringing her, here.

Ghrenna broke through the trees and the meadow opened up before her. Humming filled the clearing, buzzing in the reaches of her mind. Her body was alight with that ethereal touch. Fingers danced over her skin, pulling her closer to the seven-eye Stone that rose from the meadow's buttercup-dotted swath. Ghrenna stepped into the grass and flowers, and the humming rose, fingers wisping over every inch of her body. With each footfall, the humming rose and intensified, until Ghrenna's skull rang and every sinew vibrated like loosed bowstring, vivid and alive.

The Stone sang as Ghrenna stepped to it, a chorus that rose and fell in pitch, the vibration making her tremble. Setting one palm to the Stone, a flare of sensation ripped through her, making her knees collapse as she cried out. Touches filled her, stroking everything, calling everything higher and higher. Her mind spiraled up through her crown, even as her body spiraled into a deep sensation of pleasure.

And then, she exploded out into expansion once more.

A void of stars filled Ghrenna's mind. Pleasure sang from every inch of her body. And the man's hand came again, smoothing over her shoulder. She could feel him, lean and tall, stepping to her back. Long-fingered hands settled to her shoulders, caressing. Gathering her backwards into his body. She could feel muscles, lithe and solid, behind her. Taller than she by a head, his lips pressed to her hair. She felt his in-breath like a bellows, pressing his chest into her shoulder-blades. His hands smoothed down her arms, clasping her at the waist. Those smooth lips touched her ear and Ghrenna rang like a bell, filled with pleasure.

And he chuckled. *Welcome, my love. It's been a long time.*

"Delman." The name fell from Ghrenna's lips like dew beneath the moon.

His arms snugged her closer. *You remember me. I've been calling to you.*

"The vibrations when I meditate. The humming. The touches. It was you." On her knees in the grass, one hand resting upon his Plinth, Ghrenna could feel his touches lipping over her skin. Amusement sang with his pleasure, though his presence still stood at her back, cradling her close.

It was me, he murmured. *I've been calling you ever since Molli told me that you were flung to Hahled in your trance. I thought it was you, my Morvein, when you first traveled through my Stone. Your resonance was so familiar, even though it was black with death at the time... I've been on edge, breathless to touch you again. I've been unhinged. I couldn't stop myself from hounding you like a man besotted.*

"Unhinged?" Ghrenna breathed it, feeling a subtle humor flowing between them. Something long known, something familiar, though they'd never met before. Her lips curled up in a smile. "If this calm I feel from you is unhinged... I'd hate to see what abandonment looks like."

His chuckle was scandalous. She felt him smile in the mind-space of stars, just behind her ear. *Abandonment I can do. And I will. Long have I missed feeling your beautiful flesh in my hands, Morvein. So very long...*

His hands smoothed over her ribs, gripped her. Ghrenna flared, heat rising to her cheeks, a deep need taking her. Whatever he was, whoever he was, passion was in his every movement, and it struck Ghrenna deep. She gasped, loving it, hating it. Loving how easily he aroused her, and hating that she had no control over it.

"Stop." She breathed, shivering before the Plinth.

Why? His hands slid down her waist, fingers at her low belly, sliding towards her groin.

His fingers slipped down, between her legs. Ghrenna shuddered and cried out. One hand moved back to lift her buttock, spreading her. And then his fingers slipped in from the front, sliding deep. Ghrenna gasped, his pleasure taking her in a vast wave as his fingers dove in slow, deep. Sagging against the Plinth, she set her back to it, head thrown back in the rush. Fingers slipping out, he gave a dark, teasing chuckle by her ear.

So much pleasure. He sighed, kissing her earlobe. *So much between us, my love. And this is just the beginning.*

Ghrenna gasped, trying to catch her breath. His fingers smoothed up to her shoulders and then he began kissing her neck, lifting her hair aside to kiss her nape. Ghrenna cried out, then pulled away from the Stone. Breathing hard, she tried to gather herself. She could still feel him like a dark ocean, surging around her, pulling her in.

"Stop," Ghrenna gasped. "I'm not yours."

But you are, my love. My Morvein. His tingles came, rushing through her skin.

"No!" Pulling away from the Plinth, Ghrenna reached out and slapped one palm to the blue-grey byrunstone. "My name is Ghrenna, Ghrenna den'Tanuk! And I am not yours!"

She felt him struggle beneath her palm, fighting her, flooding his pleasure towards her. *You are Morvein Vishke, my love, my Nightwind, and I am your beloved Delman Ferrian. You loved me once, and you will love me again, just as you also love Hahled my brother. Through the valleys of time you have thrown your winds, Morvein, commanding even death itself to do your bidding. Binding yourself into a new body, a new life, a new chance for our Rennkavi to be found, and do as should have been done eight hundred years ago. Bring the great Unity, the golden age we longed for so badly when our continent was riven into war, and when it all fell apart… Remember. Remember who you are, my beloved!*

His tirade was all-encompassing. Ghrenna felt Delman in the mind-space, his presence enormous, surging through the void of stars, filling it. Pressing in upon her, shoving his energy through her body, lancing her like a thousand knives. Ghrenna screamed, her back arched against the Plinth, her body alive with pleasure and pain. She shrieked, on the edge of spasm, when Delman bound his hands about her, crushing her close.

Thrusting every bit of his energy into her.

Through her.

Her skin was alive with a river of ecstasy. Arched against the Plinth, Ghrenna couldn't move. She was bound into shudders, held fast, even as she felt the energy breathe through her skin. Like water now, and now like smoke, and now like a surging wind that swallowed her into its maelstrom, that energy engulfed her. Rent her, ate her through with passion and pain and bliss.

And where it passed, Inkings blazed upon her skin. White light seared from Ghrenna's flesh, writing markings from the inside out. Limning script, flaring sigils that faded to a luminous white. They etched upon her chest, curling through her Kingsmount and Stars. They scrawled over her shoulders, lancing down her arms to her palms. They seared down her spine and up her nape, calling to that energy that rode her deep within, making it surge outward with a searing bliss. They wrote themselves down her breasts and belly, lancing to her groin and etching a dire sigil there, too.

Ghrenna arched. She screamed in passion like a hurricane come alive. Memories flooded her. Shuffling like a deck of cards, she could make out none of them. And yet, they swallowed her, erupting from deep inside. She saw herself, with white, silver, and purple Inkings like telmen-wine, naked by an enormous fireplace in a vaulted palace. Fire-opals dripped from her ears and cascaded in an ornate necklace down her bare breasts. Her white locks tumbled down her back as she arched, her nipples sucked by not one lover, but two. One fierce and wild like a lion, the other deep and slow like moonlit midnight.

She saw them, her Brother Kings. Hahled and Delman Ferrian.

And she loved them.

Ghrenna shuddered to stillness in the wake of her vision. Breathing hard against the Plinth, the meadow expanded around her with the bliss of the summer sun. Robins chirped in the pines; a sweet cool breeze licked her sweat away. She opened her eyes and was smitten by the beauty of it all.

And then shivered as fear surfaced, of how it would all be destroyed.

A sob hitched her. And then another. Memories shuffled through fast, searing flashes of a vast and terrible war. A bloody battlefield, fifty thousand men and women ripped to pieces. Bowels rent and seeping out upon filth-soaked ground. Gullets sliced, putrid grins of death. Horses torn to pieces, keshar-cats maimed by terrible arts. War came flooding back, and Ghrenna shuddered with sob after hitching sob.

Delman cradled her through her agony. His touch smoothed over Ghrenna, touching specific points, a seeping kindness easing into her body. *I'm sorry it had to be that way,* he murmured by her ear. *When we planned this, so long ago... none of us knew how the magics would turn when you were born into a new body. How they would affect you...*

Ghrenna swallowed, wiped a sleeve across her face. She gathered a hard breath, then another. "I trapped you here, didn't I? Morvein. She placed you here. To keep an eye out..."

Delman's chuckle was sad, his hands kind as they smoothed down her hair. *Khenthar Rhegalatoria, we called this valley in my time.*

Respite of the Rulers. A place to escape. A place to gather, to plan, to meet in secret. When times are bad for the Alrashemni. And as it happened once before, so it is happening again. War is taking the continent. The signs have come, just as they did eight hundred years ago. Either we rise or we fall. Morvein refused to let us fall last time. And though I did not understand why she bound me here then, eight hundred years gives a man plenty of time to consider history. And plenty of time to allow his rage to calm.

"What are you?" Ghrenna asked. "If you were once a man, what are you now?"

Expansion, he laughed suddenly, *I am ultimate expansion! Morv... Ghrenna. I was chosen to hold this Stone because I have wyrric gifts of immense ability. The ability to do as you do, as Molli can do just a little. To be a Gerunthane, a Toucher of Minds, not just a seer. To reach out from the Void and send myself to others, talking to them. Keeping them sane. Holding us all against time's ravaging. I may be bound to a Stone, but that doesn't mean I'm any less of a man. Nor are any of the others. And all of them need the human sensation of touch and interaction, now and then.*

"The other Alranstones," Ghrenna pushed, "you can talk to them?"

Yes. Delman sighed, a harsh sound, tingles rippling over her skin. *But they wane, now. Most do not have my gifts. They cannot travel from their Plinths, and are truly trapped within the stone. Isolated within their own minds. Some feel they have nothing left to live for and have fallen silent. Some are sorrowful, a woe so torpid and deep they cannot surface from it. Some talk to themselves, gibbering with madness.* He sighed again, bitterly, his touch rising to stroke Ghrenna's cheek. *Eternity is a very long time. And I fear... I fear we will all end up that way. Mad. Eventually...*

Ghrenna felt sadness seep into her, a sinking sensation, and it gripped her heart like she might cry. She couldn't tell if it was Delman's or her own. A ripple passed, suddenly, dispelling the melancholy moment as Delman rolled the wave of melancholy back from Ghrenna's mind. *Forgive me. You are more sensitive than Molli. I must watch my emotions around you. Let us speak of other things.*

"You say I am a Gerunthane? One who can touch minds?" Ghrenna picked up the thread of their conversation, shaking off the sadness. "But all my life, I've been a seer."

Seers and Gerunthanes are often confused, Delman continued with a wry smile. *Ask yourself this: were most of your seeing-events common-thread?*

Did you witness them as they were happening?

"Most, yes," Ghrenna responded, intrigued. "Like I'm inside the person's body, I feel the event they experience. All their pain, their suffering. I see it, through their eyes, but also from outside their body, like I'm floating above the event."

Delman gave a subtle chuckle. *Then you are predominantly Gerunthane. Gerunthanes actually send their mind-essence into others. For you, it has been happening by accident, mixed in with a smaller wyrric gift for True Seeing. Molli has True Seeing dominant to her gift, with only a hint of Gerunthane. You are the opposite. When your gift matures, you will be able to bend minds if you wish. Break them. Enter them at will.*

Ghrenna shivered, thinking of the man in black herringbone leathers all those years ago. "And Mollia's herbs? They ease my headaches and visions. Will they open up my mind-touching gift?"

She felt Delman shake his head. *Mollia knows her herbs, which work for her. But she is a much different talent than you. Herbs will not take you where you need to go.*

"And where must I go?" Ghrenna asked.

You must go deep inside yourself, and remember being Morvein.

Delman's touch slid down her arms until his hands cupped hers, his thumbs settled into the center of her palms. Ghrenna looked down. Opalescent Inkings caught the sun and flared in her skin like white quartz. The script that had Inked itself upon her from her experience in the void showed vivid. Curling in a script she didn't recognize down into spirals upon her palms, they ended in a central dot.

"What are these?" Ghrenna pulled up one sleeve, gazing at the Inkings now flowing down her inner arm.

Ancient bindings. Delman stroked her white marks with loving fingers. *Bindings Morvein once wore, which she entrusted me with to mark her when she came again in a new body. They are yours now.*

"Where did she learn such magic?" Ghrenna spoke, marveling at the complexity of the sigils, wondering what they meant.

In her time, Morvein traveled far, Delman continued, *when war began to ruin our lands. Searching for strong magic to bring the Rennkavi legend to fruition in our time, to save us, she went to the wilds. There she met an ancient, a giant somewhere in the mountains. He taught her sigil-binding, arcane arts lost to all, save him. These scripts, these markings, they are his design. Binding-magic to* create in Morvein a focus of dire proportions. So that when the time comes, she can act as the eye of the needle, through which all the Alranstones are bound, in support of the Rennkavi. So she can bring them all and command them to do the Rennkavi's bidding. The sigils I wear are the same. When the time comes, I act as one-third of the focus, harnessing Alranstones and channeling them into Morvein. Or at least, that was how it was supposed to happen. We never got that chance. Everything fell apart during the Rennkavi's Goldenmarking ceremony eight hundred years ago… He was not strong enough to hold such ecstasy as the Great Unity demands. And when he died, the magic went horribly awry.

Ghrenna turned to look back at Delman. Her brows furrowed, tension filling her as she tried to focus upon him within her mind. The image she thought she had seen of a tall man with white hair vanished, replaced by nothingness.

No, no. That will never do. He chuckled. *You'll never be able to see me that way. No, take a deep breath. Allow your body to melt as the breath sighs away, as Molli has been teaching you. Melt into the grass, into the sun… disperse every pore…*

Ghrenna felt herself doing as he said. Settling down upon the grass, her body sank into the ground. Her muscles and spine melted as her breath and chest eased upwards into the rays of the sun and the tickle of the wind.

Good… Delman soothed, just behind her ear. *Now turn and see me. See what I am… breathe and see Delman Ferrian at last…*

Now as she turned in her mind's eye, Ghrenna could see a wisp of substance. And suddenly the wisp turned to two stunning grey eyes in a handsome face. Long white hair framed that face, luminous like he stood beneath the stars, though most of it was braided back with barred owl feathers. Utterly naked like a creature of the wild, his body was fit and lean, a tall grace. Whorls of silver, white, and purple Inkings curled over his chest and shoulders, dipping down his abdomen, lancing down his arms and legs. Beauty was his in abundance, though the planes of his face were masculine. A scruff of beard graced his angular jaw, his eyes set beneath straight brows, his face intense, lips smooth.

Ghrenna remembered how it felt to kiss those smooth lips. How it felt to suckle them, drawing such pleasure into her mouth and making him sigh. A laugh rippled over her skin, and in her mind's eye she saw him throw his head back a little as he did it, levity suffusing his dark intensity.

Yes… Delman chuckled, grey eyes bright. *You do that to me, Morvein. Flood me with a pleasure so high I drown in it. Once we were that way.* He reached out, a knuckle sliding over Ghrenna's cheek. *Perhaps we may be that way again.*

Ghrenna shuddered with pleasure. That one touch sent energy licking through her body, deep. "Stop." She demanded. His touch slipped away, though his eyes tensed in suffering and the smile fell from his lips. "Tell me about Hahled, Delman. Tell me why I was flung to him first, when I took that tea Molli made for me."

Delman paused, and all thrumming in Ghrenna's body ceased. His image faded and disappeared, as if he had shut himself away from her. Thinking he was gone, Ghrenna was about to stretch and rise when she felt a firm palm set upon her chest, pushing her down to the earth.

Stay. It was a command, not a suggestion. *Tell me what has passed between you and Hahled.*

Ghrenna blinked, unnerved by his sudden change in demeanor. She felt anger flaring from him, thick and viscous like something she could drink upon her tongue. Jealousy coiled through it, ridden with sharp barbs, his visage still hidden from her.

"If you can travel to Plinths, don't you know about it? Don't the two of you speak?" Ghrenna struggled up to sitting upon the grass, warning flaring within her. Some memory surfaced. The Brother Kings, quarreling. Fighting. All of it falling to ruin, because they were fighting over her. About some decision she had made. She blinked. "Why did you and Hahled quarrel, Delman, so long ago?"

Rage flared in him. Cool and liquid, it wasn't a hot spear, but a bitter flood. *Tell me of your encounter with Hahled.*

"That's private." Ghrenna bristled suddenly, wary of his vast tension.

Tell me!

Ghrenna was suddenly gripped in a head-to-heel bind. It held her fast, and though she tried to struggle, breath rising in panic, she could hardly twitch. Her heart raced, her body taken over. A thrumming darkness raced through her, diving into her body, seeking every niche of her mind. Ghrenna's eyelids fluttered uncontrollably, her chest spasming and unable to breathe. Eyes rolling up in her head, all of her muscles tensed, shuddering but unable to flail. Racing thoughts filled her, a shuffle of quick images, emotions, sensations, memories. Her encounter with Hahled upon his Stone was grasped, shuffled through. She felt Delman searching her for any trace of a sexual encounter, jealous with a writhing, dark envy. As if he didn't believe that her meetings with Hahled had been chaste, he flowed back through other memories, shuffling them, faster.

Dredging up her dreams of Elohl, Delman ransacked Ghrenna's mind. Flooding her with misery at not knowing where Elohl was. Prickling her eyes with tears as he pulled up their last encounter, when Elohl's kiss had given her such horrible pain. Flaring in her mind's eye the dual images of Elohl's golden inkings, flaring like sunlight underwater, and the white spire, rising like a fang to a clear mountain sky.

"*Enough!*" Ghrenna's scream roared out, whipping through the glade. She felt it slap Delman back, something within her vastly strong, able to counter his ransacking.

The Rennkavi! This Elohl wears the Goldenmarks! Hahled has touched him, has given the Rennkavi his Marking! Thrust back a pace, Delman moaned. His energy was darkly reckless now, a deep contrast to the teasing, immutable wisdom of before. *Gods of the Nightwind! The Rennkavi is your lover in this lifetime…. no…!*

Ghrenna felt a rush of energy pressed to her lips, surging into her mouth and flowing past her tongue. Pulling her deep into his everlasting self, Delman Ferrian released a jealous passion down her throat. His energy raced to her heart, a torrent of love and devotion, a surging river that filled her chest. Inundated, Ghrenna drowned in his energy as Delman drew upon her, needful, insatiable. His tongue slid into her mouth, coaxing her deeper. And as his bliss reverberated back, Ghrenna's own surge came, unstoppable. Thrust into fulfillment upon the grass, she arched and writhed as he attained his own climax, dire pleasure surging through them both.

A torpid cry sounded in her ears. Ghrenna didn't know if had come from her throat or his. She shuddered upon the grass, felt him shuddering inside of her. His energy still driven deep through her, his lips made of nothing kissed her gently, reveling in languid, post-coital delight.

Ghrenna pulled back, away from his kiss, furious. "Release me."

Gods, how long it's been...! Delman pulled her close, tongue licking into her mouth.

"You. Will. Obey me." Ghrenna was firm, forcing her eyes open, resisting his pleasure. She felt him shudder, felt him try to keep kissing her, but it was sporadic, struggling. As her will and rage strengthened her focus, Ghrenna felt something drain out of her. Like black smoke boiling off a burned pot, his energy was ejected from hers.

Struggling to her hands, Ghrenna pushed up to sitting.

Stay! Morvein... Delman's kisses struggled for deeper purchase. But Ghrenna shook him off with ruthless anger, pushing finally to standing. Breathing hard, her hand flew to her chest, and above her Inkings, she formed a fist.

"Go now, or I will pull you out of me, Delman Ferrian, I swear to Halsos I will." Ghrenna tightened her fist upon her chest.

Morvein! He gasped, fervent, shuddering her skull. *Do not be so cruel! What harm have I done?*

"You have disrespected me," Ghrenna seethed, something hard and cold rising up inside her. "You did not have permission to take what you did. Not the kiss, nor the rest. And certainly not my memories of Elohl."

But Morvein! The Rennkavi is not your beloved, no matter how much you believe it. You are a chalice for him, nothing more. A vessel to be filled when the time is right, for him to take and use. But us... we are beloved. Please remember!

She could feel Delman's desperate woe. It was awful inside Ghrenna's mind, in her body. Tears that were not hers pricked her eyes, as her chest hitched with his sobs.

"Control yourself!" She snarled. "My name is Ghrenna den'Tanuk. I am not your beloved. I am not Morvein. Whoever she was, though she lives in me, her life is not mine. Learn to respect me, Delman, or I will cut you from me. Whatever I am, I can feel the edges of this power. If you will not obey me, I will drag you out."

No! Delman's shout was awful. His hands rushed to her, corralling her, pulling her close.

Ghrenna tightened her fist upon her chest, digging her nails into her palm. She pulled with all her strength, with all her might of will, mind, and heart. Pulling threads of smoke and darkness from her body, trembling from the strain. Slowly, it came away, all his torrent of energy with it. Ghrenna snapped her elbow fast, jerking Delman Ferrian out of her body.

She felt his presence surge back, trying to get in. Ghrenna hardened herself, throwing up a barrier of still calm that she had learned to keep visions at bay. She felt Delman dash himself upon it, shudder like a broken moth. And then release his pursuit as a sorrowful cry reached her ears.

Ghrenna could still feel him, his jealousy, his anger and need as she reached out to touch the Alranstone. Muted, he rushed at her like a snowmelt river, pummeling her unassailable cliffs. Slowly, she took a breath. On instinct, she slipped a small knife from the pocket of her shift. Somehow she knew what she had to do. Sliding one fingertip across the knife, she drew blood, then set that finger to the Stone. Closing her eyes, she pressed her blood to the Stone, pushing her will, her mind and heart in with it. The Stone shivered, a tense hum spreading out from it. Slowly, Ghrenna traced an unfamiliar sigil. Her blood stood out fierce upon the blue-grey Alranstone, marking it.

Commanding it.

Wind shivered through the glade, rushing through the trees and bending the buttercups.

"Come to me!" Ghrenna demanded in a stern voice that resounded through the glade. "By the call of the Nightwind I command you, Thellas Alran! Be bound to me, to my will, to the pull of the Nightwind! *Alran aenti vhesserin! Ahora! Ahora! Ahora!*"

The jangled humming from the Stone suddenly tuned in a fell note that sound sliced through her mind. Ghrenna opened her eyes, gazing up at the Plinth. All seven eyes stared wide from the ground up, rippling with light. All but Delman's lodestone, still stubbornly half-lidded, his everycolor iris at the very top fighting her call by his own strength of will, iron as it had ever been. Delman had never been a fool, nor a weakling. He would not give in to her. Not until he was entirely satisfied that she had the power to take him.

The power of the Nightwind.

The power of Morvein.

"Delman Ferrian," Ghrenna commanded gently. "Come to

me."

She let her barrier slip away. Delman strode forward, catching her so angrily by the throat in the mind-space that it forced her physical head up at the base of the Plinth. He sent waves of cold rage to her, his grey eyes fierce. *You need not command me like a mongrel, Morvein. You know what I am. You know I love you. You know I would die for you.*

"I know," Ghrenna whispered, memories of a lost life flooding her at his fierce touch. "But as it was before, so it is now. You will not bind me in the chains of your love, Delman Ferrian. Your kisses were ever deep, and my time wrapped around you more passionate than anything I have ever had. Hahled never seared as brightly as you do beneath the moon. But I cannot chase false dreams, Delman, not now."

She spoke of things only barely remembered. Delman's eyes were ravaged, listening to her. But as memories surged between them, torpid with emotion, terrible with longing and passion, tears gathered at the corners of Ghrenna's eyes.

Delman's touch was tender now upon her throat, with everything that raced between them. He moved closer, gazing down, his grey eyes still angry, but less so. *You loved me first, before Hahled. Before this Elohl. Before any of them.*

"Yes." Ghrenna spoke, tears slipping down her face, feeling that love resound within her, also. "I know it. No matter how many come to my bed, there will always be you. But yours was a love I couldn't sustain, Delman. I would have drowned in it, and done nothing of what I needed to. But you had a choice then, as you do now. To join me, help me. I need you bound to me so I can call the Alranstones, the Thellas Alri, for the Rennkavi. So *we* can call them, you, me, and Hahled, like we began to do before. For Elohl."

A great sigh rippled through her mind, and Delman began to stroke her skin. Ghrenna vibrated from it, shivers cascading over her flesh. *You still thrum to my touch. Our harmony will always ring through your bones, as it does mine. My Nightwind... I have waited so long to feel you again. I allowed myself to be bound here at your desire. I didn't want it. I wanted to die when you chose the path of your Rennkavi. You should have let me die...*

"You were too valuable to let go," Ghrenna murmured, leaning close to the Plinth, her lips whispering over it. "We needed a

Gerunthane to hold the lodestones through the ages. The strongest. You. You and Hahled. My Brother Kings."

He moaned as her lips whispered over the Stone. In her mind, Ghrenna was at his Inkings, her lips moving over every vein of black, silver, and purple that decorated his chest. Darkness and a simmering passion beneath the moon had always been Delman's power, and he had been Inked to reflect that.

Ghrenna felt his arms wrap around her, solid as flesh. *You bitch,* he sighed in her ear as he took her body down to the moss at the base of his Plinth. *Why can't I hate you?*

Because the Wind of Night flows through you, also, Delman. You and I are far too alike… which is why I need you now. Come to me. Be bound to me now.

You need me? Delman's smile was alluring, wicked as he touched her, clever fingers trailing over her skin.

I do. Ghrenna began to writhe upon the moss to his touch, cool like a rushing river.

How much? The sensations intensified, a hand gripping her throat, touching her, everywhere.

More than you know. Ghrenna's body arched, thrumming.

Say it again. Say… 'I need you, Delman, more than you could ever know.'

"I need you, Delman," Ghrenna whispered, "more than you could ever know."

Then I will bind myself to you… yet again. My Nightwind. My Morvein.

Delman's passion surged and he thrust forward, his lips upon hers, his energy pouring into her mouth and throat. Drowning her heart, flooding her belly and loins. And then he thrust into her deep. Ghrenna arched in pleasure as he took her, needful and generous and wild, just as he had always been.

CHAPTER 20 – ELOHL

The cats raced into the heights. Thitsi was breathing hard carrying
two riders, but she did not slow her pace behind General Merra's
riders. At the back of the pack, Elohl and Jhonen fought with those
upon their heels. Elohl urged Thitsi right, and Jhonen stabbed
backwards with her polearm, causing the keshar behind them to
snarl and slow. They dodged left, stabbing at another cat. This one
swiped a paw at Jhonen as it ran, and she sliced that paw with a
quick flick of her polearm. The cat yowled, threw its rider in pain,
and leaped to a boulder, abandoning the chase.

Still weak, Elohl clung to Thitsi while Jhonen did the fighting.
Riding Thitsi backwards, Jhonen batted away a thrown knife, to
clatter off a group of boulders. Jhonen and Elohl held on as Thitsi
leapt up eight feet to a rock shelf where Merra's group now
gathered, cats halted and panting. The shelf had a cave behind it,
and snow-dotted scree flanking it where rockslides had come down
the mountain. Elohl and Jhonen jumped from Thitsi just as the
keshar collapsed, run-out. General Merra and her group had
dismounted upon the shelf. Backs to the cave, they brandished
polearms, protecting the weary cats.

But though the cats took their rest, they watched their rider's
every movement, lifting whiskers to snuff the air. Elohl drew his
sword, stepping up next to a grim-eyed Fenton. Twenty keshar and
their riders prowled below.

One of the riders below, a woman with short-cropped blonde
hair, raised her voice in demand. "Give up, Merra! We'll have forty
horse up here by nightfall, with bowmen!"

Jhonen stepped up beside Elohl, planting her polearm.
"Traitors!" Her voice dripped with scorn. "We'll string you by your
sinews, Belumia! Kordesh, Fella, Thormun! The rest of ye! Your
days number less and your nights are filled with shadows!"

Belumia laughed, and it crawled across Elohl's skin. "It doesn't have to be this way! Give up the Menderian Kingsmen, and we'll see what can be seen."

"*Faithless!*" Merra stepped up beside Fenton, hurling the curse down. "I will cut your Inkings from your chest myself!"

Belumia's laugh below was amused. "Don't you think I cut away my ties to these markings years ago? Give up the lowlanders, and our realm may yet find peace."

"Is that what they said? Is that what they told you?" Fenton called down. "That if Elohl and I die, if Elyasin is stolen away and murdered quietly, then the Menderians will leave Elsthemen alone? And you believe that?"

Elohl saw doubt enter Belumia's eyes. She reined her keshar in a tight circle. "Lowlanders don't belong here! You Scunners bring trouble to the Highlands!"

Merra stepped up to the edge of the drop-off, menacing. "I don't see any trouble up here, Belumia! But I see a shitheap of it down there. I commend yer keshar fer balancing such a magnificent pile of shite on its saddle, wiyout spilling over."

Belly laughs went around the line of women and men upon the ledge. Belumia flushed scarlet.

"Laugh until nightfall!" She called out, circling her nervous cat again. She signaled her contingent to hunker down and wait.

General Merra spat off the ledge, then flicked her fingers at two men brandishing polearms beside her. "Rhone. Rhennon. Take first watch. They twitch so much as a *whisker*, I want to know about it."

The brothers nodded, then hunkered to their heels to keep watch. Their cats remained with them upon the ledge, but the rest followed Merra and her snowy beast further into the cave. A dead-end in the mountainside, the cave didn't go very far back. Clearly used as a scouting stop-over, the cave was stocked with dry wood and lamp-oil, and barrels of dry provisions and replacement gear. Merra's riders began to rifle through saddlebags and open barrels, pulling out edibles, drinking water, and getting a fire started. Thitsi nosed at the saddlebags she'd picked up, and Elohl rummaged through them, finding thick pelts for warmth and sundry foodstuffs. He hauled out a haunch of something and threw it to Thitsi. She growled, then hauled off her kill to the far end of the cave.

But Elohl noticed she kept one eye on him as she gnawed her meat. His skin seemed to tingle with Thitsi's watchfulness as Fenton hunkered, handing Elohl a water flask. "You're looking better."

"Thanks," Elohl murmured. His muscles still ached from being poisoned, but he was alive.

"Ye were lucky ta survive the put-down, Lowlander." Jhonen hunkered nearby, taking water.

"Why's it called put-down?" Elohl tore into a bit of dried meat, suddenly ravenous.

"Puts down the cats that get too torn-up in battle. You massage it into their ears and face. It soaks in, they fall asleep, stop breathing. Normally, it's a merciful way to go." She grinned at Elohl. "Unless you're a fighting bastard Inked by the gods. You should be dead twice over, Menderian. And I'm guessing by all the old scars on you, more times over than that. Maybe you've got nine lives like they say the keshar do." She nodded over at Elohl's cat, happily crunching the bones of her haunch. "Thitsi's something of a legend, you know. She should be dead thrice over. Pulled through every time, though. She may be old, but she's not feeble."

General Merra stood behind them suddenly, her blue eyes piercing and feline by the light of the kindled fire. She planted the butt of her polearm, commanding attention of the group. "Listen up, riders! We're in a right bind. Our mission, given by the King of Elsthemen my brother and the Queen of Alrou-Mendera his wife, is to deliver these two Lowlanders across Bitterrift Pass to the Devil's Field into Valenghia. Anyone *else* who has a problem with that, can get the fuck out. Now."

She waited. No one stirred so much as a whisker, not even the cats.

"Good." Merra's icy eyes roved over her party. "Now they've got horsemen on the way, archers. And even though that bitch outside boasts they'll assault us by nightfall, we know they won't. The terrain is too steep. Horses will be too blown by the time they get here for a mounted assault, and they won't risk broken hocks and stumbles on all this scree in the dark. That's not our concern. What is, is that Belumia is going to try pouncing down from above to take us in the dark before the horses get here. We've got a tidy nook, but I don't want fighting with our cats exhausted and our backs to the wall. Thoughts?"

Elohl and Fenton exchanged a look. Merra's open discussion of their next move was something of a military novelty. But like the High Brigade, Merra gave every one of her soldiers a say before they tackled a tricky situation that could mean lives lost.

Jhonen was the first to speak. "I've got wild-tinder in my saddlebags. We could light a few pots and toss 'em. Flash out the cats down below. Make a run for it."

Merra considered it, then shook her head. "We need that wild-tinder to keep warm up on the glacier. Save it. It would provide a good spook, but then we'd have to abandon the mission. What else?"

A man by the name of Kronos spoke up in a rumbling baritone. "Khelji has a good vertical leap. We could get to the top of the cave, circle around in the dark, kill as many as we can."

Merra gave Kronos a wry smile. From the way she did it, Elohl was almost certain they'd been lovers at some time. "No sacrifices, Kronos. We all get out of here alive. What else?"

A massively muscled woman to Elohl's left sniggered. "Thitsi's got the nine lives. Send her out and see what happens."

This time Merra paused, her gaze shifting to Elohl. "Thitsi's unpredictable, it's true, but Elohl's too weak to fight atop her, and Thitsi's given him the pride-bond. She won't let anyone else ride her until he dies."

Elohl lifted his eyebrows at Merra. "What am I missing, here?"

"You ride a hellcat, lowlander." The general chuckled with a slight smile. "She'll maul the living piss out of anything to protect her kittens. And you, my friend, are now Thitsi's adopted kitten. Trust me." Merra turned back to her riders. "Other options?"

The conversation continued, but Elohl was no longer listening. His gaze strayed to Thitsi, mauling her haunch of meat in the gloom. Fangs flashing, her tawny hide lit by the evening's fire, she gnawed in a bored manner. But when Elohl shifted, Thitsi paused her crunching. Ears flashing forward, she watched him intently. Something called Elohl through her gaze, something that spoke of pack and pride. Elohl heard a rushing of blood in his ears. A taste filled him, a flavor of musky beast and iron-sour meat. A sensation of unity with his cat rolled off his skin in a wave.

His skin tingled as Thitsi's gaze intensified, her golden eyes reflecting the flickering fire. And Elohl knew, suddenly, that Thitsi would die for him. Her devotion was so pure, so absolute, that it created one mind between them, a unity of purpose that could never be undone. Elohl's golden Inkings prickled, racing with a burn. The aura of unity overwhelmed him. The feel of fur against his skin was her skin growing that fur. The smell of blood in his nose was her nose inhaling. His muscles rippled with Thitsi's as she gnawed her kill in the darkness.

The feeling of oneness blossomed within Elohl like night-lotus, reaching out.

There is only one way we all get out of this alive. Attack. Now.

Engulfed in the sensation of oneness, Elohl rose like a dreamer. He wasn't sure if the thought had been his or Thitsi's. A low growl issued from Thitsi, her gaze pinned to him. Poisoned muscles steady as if drawling upon Thitsi's strength, Elohl strode slowly to the entrance of the cave, then out to the lip of stone. Evening's gloaming purpled the sky, a soft grey shroud settling down the mountain. That sense of oneness sighed out around Elohl, curling upon the chill night wind as it blew down off the glaciers.

Thitsi had risen from her haunch and padded to the mouth of the cave. She came to Elohl, butted his chest with her blocky head. He reached up, rubbing her ears, smoothing his hands through that tawny fur, soft as silk.

"You're with me, aren't you?" He realized. "To the end."

She gave a thrumming purr, head pressed to the center of his chest. Like a Kingsman might press a palm to their Inkings to swear fealty.

Attack. Now. The thought came again, her mind mingled with his. Elohl's chest seared with heat, his back aflame down his spine. Purpose flowed from him, a sense of rightness and belonging he had never felt before. The feline sensation of being one with Thitsi catapulted his mind outward. Energy rolled from his body in a tirade.

Elohl turned and stepped to the edge.

"Elohl!" Fenton called out from the mouth of the cave. "What are you doing?"

"Fucking hells!" General Merra cursed, running up behind. "*Stop him!*"

Elohl slung over the ledge before he could be stopped. Climbing down by touch, his gift was lance-sharp, more attuned than it had ever been. The party waiting at the bottom surged to their feet with growls and the rasp of drawn steel in the dusk.

A streak of tawny fur launched off the ledge after Elohl with a furious roar. A unity of thought and action radiated from Elohl as he stepped forward into danger, Thitsi racing into battle before him. Thitsi roared, bolstered by their twinned energy as the rogue keshari beneath the ledge surged forward, muscles of the great cats rippling, fangs bared. Elohl's chest and back burned as Thitsi faced off with the closest pair. His muscles thrummed with life as she became a blur of dusk-tawny speed, massive paws ripping, fangs ruthless.

With a powerful thrust, Thitsi sank fangs into the leg of a rider. Elohl tore open his jerkin with a growl to bare his burning skin, feeling her satisfaction as she ripped the man from his mount. A crunch and his screams were cut, his neck bitten through. Elohl roared, feeling Thitsi's triumph, his torso on fire. He ripped his jerkin and shirt off over his head, standing bare-chested in the frigid dusk.

A golden glow like underwater sunlight gave light to the battle, streaming from Elohl's Inking. Illuminating riders and cats in their vicious onslaught, the light rippled over Thitsi as she fought for him with unprecedented fleetness even for a keshar. Tail lashing, she held a tight line to protect her human, speared on by their connection, blistered to ferocity by the Goldenmarks. Elohl lifted his arms. A searing heat rushed from his shoulders to flame his palms. Thitsi roared, defending Elohl, hackles raised and spitting mad. Elohl's energy surged, boiling out in every direction.

Touching all of Merra's riders far above upon the ledge, touching all the cats.

Inciting them to come join them. To be one, in battle. In fury.

Fenton landed swift and silent at Elohl's side, sword to hand. With a unified roar, the rest of Merra's riders launched from the overhang. Incensed by the unity channeled through Elohl, Merra's cats and their riders fought like dervishes. Battle surged upon all sides. In the haunting illumination issuing from Elohl's Inkings, the cats fought like tawny streaks of death to protect their pride, Merra's riders no less vicious with polearms and swords.

Elohl burned. Heat speared his body deep inside. Heat flared down his arms to the tips of his fingers. Heat flamed down the backs of his legs to the soles of his feet. He stepped forward, arms wide, words from nowhere suddenly upon his lips.

"Come to me. Come to your Rennkavi. Be One in the Light."

Elohl felt the battle turn. The renegades broke like snapped kindling, fear flooding the rogue keshari and riders. They cowered with it, they shuddered from the force of the bond, the singular mind that Elohl and Thitsi had wrought. Polearms were dropped with stricken shouts. Ferocious cats slunk back with confused hisses.

"ENOUGH!"

Elohl's voice rolled out with a power so great, that the rocky scree skittered underfoot. Keshari and riders upon both sides halted like some great hand had suddenly pulled marionette-strings. The battle came to a sudden, shuddering silence that breathed with the whisper of the night wind.

"We were not meant to kill each other."

Elohl had hardly murmured it, but some strange sense told him every ear had heard him in the deepening dark. Ethereal light from Elohl's Inkings painted the darkened slope in the shifting tones of underwater sunlight. With a sudden need to be all-together in unity, Elohl set his hand upon Fenton's shoulder.

Fenton shuddered, his eyes flying wide upon a swift intake of breath. And then Fenton placed his hand upon the shoulder of his opponent. Who shuddered in turn, breathless, and placed her hand upon the man next to her. Who placed his hand upon the haunch of a cat. Who nosed her face into another beast. One by one, every cat and rider upon the slope came into the connection, as the fey light glimmered over every silent visage.

"We are One," Elohl spoke, his intention spreading out in a wave, spiraling into the great union he had wrought. "We are kin. We have always been kin. We will always be kin. Be still now."

The burning upon his body deepened until he thought his very bones were afire, then slowly died away. And with it went the strange light, leaving friend and foe alike breathing hard in a true aurora-lit twilight, silent and stunned. As if summoned to the silence, Ghrenna's cerulean eyes suddenly flooded Elohl's vision, perfect and oceanic.

Elohl shuddered, and his hand slipped from Fenton's shoulder.

It was over. Those upon opposite sides of the battle now stepped past each other in chagrin, tending to their beasts and their wounded, checking pulses of those who lay motionless in pools of dusky crimson. Cats yowled in mourning for riders they had lost, a chilling dirge in the hushed night. Men and women knelt by fallen comrades, palms to Inkings.

Merra crouched before Belumia's corpse, silent. At last, she stood. Her eyes met Elohl's. A silent reckoning passed between them. A hard question with no answers. Elohl broke her gaze, reaching down to don his shirt and jerkin. His body no longer burned, but the Inkings of gold upon him had spread from what he'd done, whatever magic he'd wielded tonight. Lines of script now flowed down his arms to his inner wrists, decorated with sigils. Surrounded by sigils, a spiral of gold graced each palm. Elohl was certain his legs looked the same, a burning tingle dying away from his calves and feet.

Thitsi padded back to Elohl with a low yowl, mushing him in the chest with her head, rubbing her bloody jowls all over his face, his hair. Elohl reached up and scratched her under her gore-slick chin.

"You great beast... what have we done?" He murmured.

Thitsi thrummed with a pleased purr. Elohl felt that surge of heat in his Inkings again, though it was just an echo of what had come before. He knew what they had done. They had created a pack tonight, a pride made from the renewed bonds of kinship. They had come together in one mind and yoked every living thing to their unified purpose.

It was both exhilarating and terrifying. The power still shivered through Elohl as he buckled his jerkin, checked his weapons. He saw Merra on the edge of the group, speaking low words to one of the enemy riders. The man nodded, then sank to one knee before her, a fist to his heart. With a sharp whistle, he summoned the renegades, only seven of them left. They wheeled about on their cats and dashed off down the rocky slope.

With a shout, Merra summoned her faithful back up into the cave, leaving their dead where they had fallen. Back inside, provisions were handed around. Weary men and women hunkered by the fire, lost to silence, eating, drinking, tending weapons and cats.

Glances settled upon Elohl; flicked away. Merra came to the fire and sat with a hard sigh next to Elohl and Fenton. She drank deep from a flask of whiskey; handed it around. A few riderless keshar stole off to the night. Curled around Elohl, Thitsi raised her head, watching them slip away.

"Where are they going?" Elohl spoke, watching the big cats melt into the darkness.

Merra glanced back over her shoulder, just as the last tail disappeared beyond the fire's light. "Out to hunt. All our cats will have full bellies by morning, and you and I will have meat as well. The ronins, the ones whose riders have been killed, will hunt to feed us all. They're part of the pride. Some may suffer a rider again. But most don't."

"You sent the traitors back down the trail." Fenton spoke, watching Merra.

Merra eyed him, her ice-blue gaze hard. "They will redeem themselves by killing the horsemen of Clan Khersus. They will fight until they fall, or until our back-trail is clear, whichever comes first."

Merra's hard gaze turned to Elohl, weighing him in the fire's light. "Man pulls a stunt like that, sacrificing himself among my riders, he gets the whip."

Elohl lifted an eyebrow. "Good thing I'm not one of your riders."

"Aye. Good thing." A thoughtful gaze had taken Merra's wind-chiseled face. She settled back upon her elbows, extending her boots to the fire. "You're touched, Lowlander. Touched by the hand of some god we humans canna ken. You remind me of Therel, you know. Therel's touched by something, too. He'd deny it to Halsos' chasm, but I know it's true."

Merra regarded Elohl soberly, wariness mixed with respect. Her eyes flicked to the golden Inkings now visible upon his wrists and palms. "I would have slaughtered them, you know. My own kin. For their treason. But when those Inkings of yours lit..." she shook her head, a mysterious smile lifting the corners of her lips. "I felt it. A *call*. To embrace them. Pardon them. I never would have forgiven those traitors, not in a thousand winters. But you called me to. And so I have. They will go to their graves honored to fight for their King and for the Highlands. Their deaths will mean much, because of you."

Silence stretched between them. Fenton gazed over to Elohl, his dark eyes sober by the fire's light. "What was that today, Elohl? What did you do to us all?"

"If I knew, I would tell you." Elohl shook his head, feeling the echo of that burning light in his skin. "It was like a great wave took me. A sense of kinship. And I felt, that slaughter of our own people, kin annihilating kin, wasn't right. That all of us should be unified. Together, in peace. Somehow."

"Us?" Fenton gave a slight smile, though his attention was keen. "Last I checked, you are not Elsthemi."

"I don't know." Elohl settled a branch of highland pine on the fire. "All of us? All people everywhere? I don't have any answers."

Fenton nodded, but from his gaze Elohl could tell he had been affected deeply. Whatever had passed between them during the battle was stronger than Alrashemni loyalty, stronger even than their dedication to their Queen. Fenton and Elohl had a new understanding of each other, a bond. Like a rope spun out of ether, Elohl could almost feel it, gathering from Fenton's core and bound to Elohl's.

Fenton's regard was wary, excited, careful. Secretive. But fierce with a dedication Elohl didn't understand, yet could feel. Elohl's gaze slipped to Merra, and she held a fierce snarl. Their eyes locked, and he could feel the bond there, too, ethereal yet strong. His gaze went round the fire, and whomever they touched upon glanced up, meeting his eyes, just for a moment.

All of them. He felt that same bond with all of them. A subtle surge spilled through his Inkings, an echo of flame. Elohl shivered, exhilarated. Terrified.

"Can ye control it? What ye did today?" Merra asked at last.

Elohl shook his head. "I control nothing these Inkings do. I don't even know what they're for, or why they were limned upon me. It was Thitsi's bond to me that sparked them today."

"Thitsi is loyal to her riders, to a fault. She protects you like her own flesh. Rhugen used to remark on it. She would guard him at night, like she does you." Merra nodded her chin at Thitsi, curled around Elohl, who rested upon her breathing flank.

"Was Rhugen Thitsi's last rider?" Elohl reached out, stroking her sleek tawny fur.

Merra's mouth twitched, wistful. "Rhugen was my husband. And her last rider, yes."

"Tell us of him." It was Fenton who spoke, something ancient in his voice, sad.

"Well, he had dreams like Therel, and he looked somethin' like you. Fucked like you, too." Merra glanced over at Fenton, a teasing smile playing about her lips. In a gesture of affection, she placed a hand on his thigh. Fenton moved closer, settled an arm about her waist. Merra sighed. "Rhugen was my First-Captain, my good right arm. We kept it quiet. Most didn't have any right to know, but Therel knew. I wanted a highmountain husband, a man who rode a keshar like the world died in fire, and I had one. For a time. He died savin' me on patrol up this same pass, in a skirmish against a pack of dwelven, two years ago. Thitsi had her flank torn open trying' ta protect him, a mortal wound. We left her behind. But come spring, guess who showed back at Lhen Fhekran, nothing to her but bones? Wasn't the first time she'd come back from the dead, either."

"I'm sorry for your loss." Fenton murmured.

The General shrugged in that fatalistic highmountain way, then leaned in to give Fenton a deep kiss. Fenton pulled Merra close, uncaring that others looked on. It was the highmountain way, to take it where you could get it. And when.

Just then, Jhonen settled down next to Elohl, giving him a stout punch in the shoulder, breaking the tender moment. "Renegade! Gonna glow fer us any more, light-bug? Ha!"

A grin flickered over Elohl's face. "Not unless we have ten more riders on our asses."

"Not ten, but ye could have one! Ye looked damn fine without yer shirt earlier!" Jhonen winked.

Elohl chuckled, shook his head. "I'm spoken for."

"By whom?!" Jhonen whipped her head, pretending to scowl at the other women. "Sephoni? I'll tan her skinny little hide! She hasn't got the thighs to ride you properly!"

"Dreams?" Elohl cocked his head, intrigued. "Do you know dreams, Jhonen?"

"I was trained by Vhensa herself! I'm Second-Drem, ye great daft Lowlander! Do I know dreams!" Jhonen looked personally affronted.

"Forgive me, did I offend?"

"Vhensa was our High Dremorande, our nation's dream-interpreter." Merra clarified. "Jhonen is an elite pupil of hers. Only one other in the nation is stronger than Jhonen, a woman by the name of Adelaine Visek, who lives up on the tundras. I follow the old ways. I keep a Dremor in the ranks, to catch dreams of portent for battle. Rhugen was my Dremor for a long while."

"And a damn fine one! After Vhensa passed, Rhugen taught me much," Jhonen interrupted.

"Jhonen. Have you heard of a real woman appearing in a man's... waking vision?" Elohl felt strange airing the visions he'd been having of Ghrenna. But he needed answers, and it seemed Jhonen might be the person to ask.

Jhonen sobered, gazing at Elohl intently. "Waking visions? Were you hit hard with a stave?"

Elohl shook his head. "An old friend of mine, Ghrenna. She and I have always had a strange connection, but she's... shown up more often since these marks were given to me." Elohl gestured to the gold at this wrist. "She's a seer. But I have visions of her while I'm awake, not just in dreams. As if she's... calling to me."

"Did she speak to you? Are you sure she's alive?" Jhonen leaned forward, rapt.

Elohl paused. "I don't have confirmation that she's alive, but I feel it."

Jhonen steepled battle-hardened fingers beneath her chin. "Vhensa once told me, that there exist people who can enter minds. They enter dreams, too, and can cause waking visions. Some are very strong, and can control minds, cause people to do what they wish. We have legends about them, the Scorpion-Priests of the Unaligned Lands, though no one's seen one in centuries. Our Dremor-in-exile Adelaine is the only one I know who can enter minds, but even her talents are weak compared to the old stories. There is a very old legend..."

Merra chuckled, settling back against Fenton. "The Nightwind. You're going to tell that old fey-yarn?"

Jhonen shot her General a look. "Vhensa swore it was true!" She turned back to Elohl. "There is a *very* old legend, that speaks of a woman named Morvein. She came from the ice tundras, and she had the whitest hair and the bluest eyes of any woman ever known. Morvein lived many centuries ago, at a time when the Highlands were in terrible turmoil, a civil war that coincided with vicious wars in Alrou-Mendera, Valenghia, Praough, and far further. She was a witch. Wherever she went, men sighed to their knees as if the Nightwind had stolen their very souls, and so she was named. She could read a man's soul through those blue eyes. And once she had, she would come to his dreams, to take him and ruin him. The Brother Kings fell to her charms, Hahled and Delman Ferrian. They ruled in the ancient seat of the Highlands at Dhelvendale, up north. They forged a great peace with the Menderian King at the time, to stop the madness spreading through the continent. And then they disappeared. Most believe Morvein was to blame. She disappeared too, like the winter Nightwind does, never to be seen again."

Merra chuckled. "Fey-yarns for children."

But Elohl leaned forward, rapt. "Did Morvein have any special talents other than entering minds?"

Jhonen nodded, serious. "Many. It is said she was the most talented Dremor to ever live. In her youth she was plagued with vicious headaches, almost unto death before her gifts blossomed forth. It is said she came to her full talent at the hands of the Brother Kings. She was their lover... both of them! And also their High Dremorande."

"And does the word *rennkavi* mean anything to you?" Elohl pressed.

Jhonen blinked, brought out of her storytelling reverie. "Rennkavi? No. What's that?"

Elohl shook his head. "Just a word I heard once. It's nothing."

Brought near by thinking of her, Ghrenna's lake-blue eyes hovered about Elohl's vision, framed by white-blonde waves. A shiver passed through Elohl. He took a draught from the whiskey flask. But as he did so, he caught Fenton's gaze.

Fenton was watching him closely, intense. That etheric bond between them surged, and Elohl's golden Inkings prickled.

"I think I'll turn in." Elohl said, unnerved and exhausted. He rose and stepped away from the fire. Thitsi was instantly alert, coming to her feet at his side. Fenton was about to rise and follow, when General Merra tugged at Fenton's jerkin, holding him back.

"You. Stay. Keep me warm tonight."

Fenton settled back beside Merra, but his dark eyes were all for Elohl, fierce. And troubled.

CHAPTER 21 – THEROUN

Six nights later, Theroun saw the man in black herringbone leathers again.

He'd not been able to track his quarry since that first time, his nights filled with testing cat-raids from the keshari, swiping their camp over and over to find a weakness as the war finally began. But tonight, the dark was still early, and Theroun was out walking the Southron companies. He had found over the past many days that nearly all the foreign soldiers could not recall personal details about themselves. Sometimes it was as little as forgetting the origin of a tattoo, sometimes as much as not even recalling sailing out from their homeland. But the more Theroun investigated, quietly, the more certain he became that most of the Southron soldiers were not here of their own volition.

And tonight, as he left a blacksmith's tent after speaking with a man who couldn't recall his own wife's name, the glimmer of black studded armor caught his eye again by the flickering torchlight. Theroun followed, keeping to deep shadows. He saw the man in herringbone leathers approach General den'Ulthumen's weapons-tent, get barred by two guards who crossed spears. But with a slight motion of the foreigner's chin, like a bull lowering horns to fight, the guards suddenly broke and stepped away, bowing.

Theroun's eyebrows rose. The man entered den'Ulthumen's weapons-tent and the flaps slipped closed. But just as he did, Theroun caught a glimpse of his other cheek in the torchlight. This man had no keshar-claw scars on his face. He was a different man than before. Theroun stepped up fast to the guards. They blinked at him, dazed, like someone had just socked them in the face.

"Who was that man you just gave entry?!" Theroun demanded, his growl low.

"What man?" The guards exchanged worried looks, knowing they were about to have their asses handed to them, but not knowing why.

Theroun snarled and ripped past them, into the weapons tent. Scouring the gloom, lit only by two torches in iron brackets by the door, he searched for the foreigner. Dashing down a row of horse-armor, he rounded a rack of spears, heart fast in his chest, one longknife drawn. But just as the one before, this man had eluded him. Theroun snarled. His neck prickled like something watched from the shadows, but scour as he might, he saw nothing.

"Damn you!" He cursed, his knuckles white on the hilt of his longknife. Breathing softly, he listened for any sound; a footfall, a crunch of grit in the trampled grass, an exhalation. Gradually, the prickling of his neck ceased. Theroun growled in the darkness, sliding his knife away.

Whoever that man was, he had escaped just like his comrade.

Theroun was just about to leave when something caught his eye. Upon a shelf to his left, buried in with sheathed swords and knives, was a rack of small clay pots, each sealed with a top of red wax. Theroun frowned. Clay ampules like that were used for only two things in war. One was explosive salt-peter from Ghrec, but that was worth its weight in diamonds, something the Menderian army could never afford except in the smallest quantities.

The other was something that made his blood run cold.

Theroun stepped to the rack, his gut churning bile, hoping it wasn't what he thought it was. He knelt, pulling his knife and curling sealing wax carefully from the rim of the ampule until the lid cracked open. Setting it cautiously upon the ground, he lifted the lid with the edge of his blade. A slick oil greeted him, filling the pot. Silver-dark with a green and blue sheen, the oil caught the torch flickers, bouncing light back like the filth it was.

"Fucking hells…!"

Theroun growled, his gut churning bile. Pain birthed from rage lanced his old wound. Slowly, Theroun re-capped the earthen pot and set it back upon the shelf. Standing briskly, he strode from the weapons-tent. He debated busting into den'Ulthumen's personal tent and whipping the bastard awake with the flat of his sword. But the more he thought about it, the more such a vile act as bringing that oil to the war-front made sense.

Whatever all this was, it was connected. The man in

herringbone leathers, the killing-oil in clay pots, ready for war in den'Ulthumen's weapons-tent. It all stank of the Khehemni Lothren. A nasty trick, to rob men of their thoughts of home, their identities, sending foreign recruits to the battlefield like mindless slaves to play their little game bearing weapons of such foul nature they would surely perish. It was slippery, sneaky, and the stench of it smelled all too familiar. With a snarl of raw rage, Theroun turned, massaging his ribs as he marched toward the blue and white striping of the Fleetrunner's command tent the next avenue over.

Theroun threw aside the flap, striding in to find Runner-Captain Vitreal den'Bhorus in consultation with Brigadier-Captain Arlus den'Pell. Vitreal looked up with a scowl on his fox-narrow face and rifled his red hair, his blue eyes piercing. Arlus was casual, leaning his massive frame against the stout map-table. Brigadiers were always slouching, as if they'd expended so much energy upon a climb they had none left to stand up straight.

Den'Pell's grey Alrashemni eyes, however, were alert. A bear of a man with a grizzled beard, Arlus had a wayward shock of salted black hair. Thick-shouldered, the man's massive hands showed his climbing prowess with countless scars. With twenty-five years of command under his belt in the High Brigade, Arlus been a personal friend of King Uhlas. He and Theroun had spoken once since he'd arrived, forming a tenuous alliance primarily because Vitreal had ensured it. But Arlus was old-guard Kingsman.

And he hated Theroun.

"Viper." Arlus' booming basso was soft, deadly.

"Arlus." Theroun was equally hostile.

"Is there something we can do for you, Counselor-General?" Vitreal den'Bhorus sneered.

"Actually, yes." Theroun strode into the keshar's maw. "You can send a cadre of guards to sweep the camp and have them arrest any men you see in black herringbone-weave armor on sight."

"What are you talking about, Theroun?" Vitreal blinked, his face a picture of astonishment as he settled his fingers to the tabletop.

"I'm talking about mind-manipulation, dammit!" Theroun snarled, slamming his fist into the desk. "Two whole companies of Southrons! Those men are being brainwashed, somehow, and I've seen two different men in black herringbone armor that have something to do with it!" Theroun briefly explained his encounter with Duthukan and the Jadounians, then the event at the weapons-tent. Vitreal's face opened up further, shocked.

Arlus had moved close. "This stinks of Lothren's tricks."

"You don't say?" Theroun barked, vicious.

"Maybe a poison in the water?" Vitreal offered.

Theroun shook his head. "They're brainwashed, not sick." Theroun's ribs suddenly decided to cramp. An inopportune moment, Theroun dug his fingers in, massaging as he breathed into his side.

Vitreal's shrewd blue eyes fixed upon Theroun. "You think those companies are being targeted. Singled out for this... mind-manipulation."

"Since when has Alrou-Mendera recruited abroad to fight our wars?" Theroun continued, breathing into his side.

The two captains shared a look. Arlus spoke. "A lot has changed at the Valenghian front since you left it, Theroun. More and more, one sees black-skinned Southrons fighting, in the ranks on both sides. You think they're indentured? Pressed into service?"

"That's *exactly* what I think." Theroun bit. "Both here and there. *Someone* has been recruiting most viciously in the southern nations. These men might be getting paid a wage on the books, but I'll bet my life that's not why they signed up."

"Bastard Aeon sonofawhore!" Runner-Captain den'Bhorus hissed.

"You think the Khehemni Lothren are behind this." Arlus' booming voice was soft. His grey eyes were accusatory. Both captains knew what Theroun was.

"Yes." Theroun nodded. "I've already given you names of the Khehemni agents I know are here in our ranks, but I don't know them all. Anyone could have orchestrated this. These men have the look of the Unaligned Lands, but I don't recognize the armor. I would, however, bet my cock they're working for the Lothren. Be vigilant, gentlemen. If they're using such tricks on foreign soldiers, they will have no compunction against using those tactics upon Kingsmen. Watch your men for any sign of forgetfulness. Also, I trailed that Unaligned fellow tonight, and found a stash of Pythian-resin in den'Ulthumen's weapons-tent."

Brigadier-Captain den'Pell's thick eyebrows raised in shock. He held Theroun's gaze, arms crossed over his hoary chest and ancient leathers. Old military veterans, they both knew Pythian-resin. As Theroun watched, Arlus' face drained of color. The man looked sick. He opened his mouth, hesitated, then spoke quietly.

"Theroun. You should know we intercepted a wagon on its way to den'Ulthumen's weapons-tent yesterday. It broke down in our camp, and we repaired it. We had a look at the wares while we sent the drivers off to inform den'Ulthumen his wagon would be late."

"And?" Theroun barked.

"And it was full of Devil's Breath."

"You can't be serious. Fucking shit in a wound." Theroun blinked at Arlus, horrified. His rib spasmed viciously. Theroun gripped his side and pressed, feeling nauseous. He may have been the Black Viper, but he had some scruples. Protecting his men meant he would never use such evil means as Pythian-resin and Devil's Breath. "Combined with what I saw, it makes sense. We have to assume den'Ulthumen means to use them against the Elsthemi."

Arlus gave a sober nod.

But Vitreal was a younger commander, and did not know his war-history quite as well as the two veterans. He glanced from one to the other, utterly confused. "What are you talking about?"

Theroun glanced at him. "Pythian-resin is a sticky oil that eats flesh to the bone. You put it on arrows, catapult-stones, spear-tips. The problem is, the resin is thin and has a tendency to splatter, maiming as many of your own men as your enemy's. Devil's Breath is a powder you loose into the air, by tiny pouches on the tips of arrows. They burst on impact and spread a fine dust. Chokes enemies on the spot. They die gasping, clutching at their throats. But when the wind blows…"

"It comes back at you." Vitreal looked horrified. "Did you use these awful things, Viper, on the Aphellian Way?"

"No." Theroun shook his head. "They were experimental creations of herb-chemists in Perthe. Uhlas bought some nine years back, thinking they might give us an advantage in Valenghia. The Thirty-Fourth Company tried them out during battle. They died. To a man. Took their enemies with them, but it was complete chaos, a massive loss."

"Not to mention a vicious way to die," Arlus rumbled. Theroun and Arlus shared a look. They were at odds on many counts, but on this, they were in agreement.

"I counted at least twenty pots of resin. Do we know how many carts of Devil's Breath have been sent through?" Theroun asked.

Arlus shook his shaggy black head. "Not for certain. But my men have noted five suspicious carts passing through that didn't look like weapons, gear, or foodstuffs."

"Sweet Aeon and all the gods. The Lothren are orchestrating a massacre. On both sides. And the companies den'Ulthumen will send will be docile enough from brainwashing to simply walk right in and carry it out, dying in droves... and we are supposed to carry this out with our own hands." Theroun couldn't stand any longer. He turned to the nearest chair and sat, massaging his viciously-gripping side.

Both captains eyed him, sober.

"I'll keep scouts around den'Ulthumen's camp," Vitreal said. "See if we can figure out how much poison he's got. And monitor their comings and goings."

"I'll take hand of the brainwashing situation," Arlus responded. "Send some of my men to hunt for these fellows in herringbone leathers."

Theroun gazed at them, realizing what formidable allies both men could be, when they were motivated. Kingsmen had been accused of high treason in the realm ten years ago, but for the first time, Theroun had begun to realize his hatred of them was largely founded upon lies.

By men who were manipulating them all.

Suddenly, the hollow striking of bronze weather-bells rang out in the night. Theroun straightened, alert. Keshari, another goddamn raid. The camp around the tent erupted in noise, men waking, shouting, throwing on gear and taking up weapons.

Theroun strode from the tent, his Captains on his heels. Both had proven assets these past many nights, and tonight would test them again. Roaring orders, Theroun mustered the Fleetrunners and sent Arlen for his Brigadiers one camp over. He was up on someone's horse without a twinge. Riding out from the eastern perimeter with two companies fast on his heels, he found the eastern hill swarming already with battle.

Shouts rose in the night, snarls, whinnies of frightened horses. Torches raced up the hillside as men headed off the keshari attack with spears, cavalry and archers close behind. But even from this distance, Theroun could see it was another test. The keshari numbered only fifty, if that. A clashing of weapons began. Theroun was up the hill fast on his horse, bellowing orders, gaining control. Slashing with his sword, turning his horse in tight battle-maneuvers while raging commands, he soon had the keshari hemmed in on three sides with four hundred or more of his own men.

The cats fought like dervishes, leaping, swiping, roaring, biting, their riders no less fierce with their long swiping polearms. Throats were speared, heads crunched, brain matter and entrails splattering the moonlit ground. Theroun's forces were falling, swiped and bitten, bile and feces leaking out from their torn bodies, stinking the night with fetid filth.

Theroun got Fleetrunner archers lined up behind the spearmen, now being bolstered by Brigadiers, and loosed volley after volley. Cats yowled in pain, keshari riders screamed. Theroun's horse was swiped by a cat across the chest and went down. He vaulted from it and rolled, coming up with sword ready. The cat pounced, fangs wide to bite his head and Theroun lunged with a furious roar, ramming his sword down its gullet. Massive fangs grazed his shoulders. Blood poured out over Theroun's arm and chest. The great cat choked and fell, rolling on its rider and crushing her to the grass.

At last, Theroun's forces gained control. Overwhelming the keshari, the last cats and their riders turned to the forest and fled, streaks of tawny shadow in the moonlight. Wiping blood and filth from his blade upon a dead Highlander, Theroun straightened. Screams and moans issued from all around, cries of the dying. Choking in their own vomit, feces spilling out upon the dark grass. The round moon was high in a chill autumn sky. It was the only thing that had been in their favor. Most keshar were tawny or white, and the moon had lit the Highlander raid bright. The alarm had gone up the moment those fucking beasts had ripped from the tree line.

It hadn't been much of a warning, but it had been enough.

Theroun gazed around, counting corpses by the stark light of the moon. Only thirty keshari dead. It had been a small raid, in traditional Highlander style. Fast, dirty, efficient. A compact party of elite warriors. Someone finally put down the last cat, a yowl splitting the night, but from the swath of bodies upon the bloody hillside, Theroun knew they'd paid for it.

Perhaps two hundred Menderian soldiers, and at least fifty horse. Decimated. Vitreal had proven a worthy ally again, keeping his Fleetrunners closely marshaled around Theroun, loosing volley after volley of arrows. Arlus had done no less, holding the line of pikes to the last man, though most of his own Brigadiers had survived behind their fast longknives, ferocious.

Theroun growled and spit blood. Fucking bastard of a keshar had gotten a claw across his lower lip. He kicked the dead beast with disgust, then turned back towards the torchlight.

And stopped as he heard a groan.

He turned. The keshar that had tried to eat him was shuddering. Theroun's hackles rose as his sword flashed out, old pains forgotten in a resurgence of battle-fever. But the keshar was moving only in one section of its broad ribs. Like it was being shoved from beneath. Theroun circled, sword leveled. The Highlander woman trapped beneath the dead beast was alive, her eyes glinting viciously in the light of passing torches. She growled at Theroun, and he leveled his blade at her throat.

"Kill me, then," She snarled, in a flowing Highlander accent. "Do it. Be a big man."

"What's your name?" Theroun snapped.

"Wha's it matter to ye?" She rasped, coughed with a wince.

Theroun considered her. If she was hale enough beneath that mass of cat-muscle, she'd do to lead den'Bhorus' runners through to Elsthemen. If he could keep it quiet enough. Theroun slid his sword away, hunkered by her head. "It matters that I know the name of the woman who will escort my emissary to King Therel and Queen Elyasin." He said sternly.

The woman's eyes widened, then narrowed, thoughtful. Suddenly, a fit of coughing took her. Wet, ominous, her face screwed up in pain as she hacked up a frothy bubble. She spat, her breath a hard rattle now. Blood trickled from the corner of her mouth. "They call me Levva, ye right bastard. But I'm no yer lass fer emissary to our King and Queen. Ah'm done fer, so I am."

Theroun growled, his hopes dashed. "You've seen Queen Elyasin? She survived the assassination at Roushenn? Tell me quickly - is she alive?!"

The woman lifted her chin, eyes flashing defiantly. "Aye. Ah've seen her at the palace. Alive and right pissed at her countrymen who usurp her and battle her King and husband's nation."

The woman spit at Theroun. He evaded it. "You're certain?"

"Ye no knew yer own Queen lives?" Her keen eyes flickered over him. "Ye've got Menderian general's pattern on yer pin. Are the Menderian Generals split about the war?"

Theroun's mouth quirked. Highlanders only looked like barbarians in all their furs and leather, riding their massive battle-cats to war. Theroun stood, ignoring the lancing pain in his ribs.

"Hold fast, keshari. Just a moment longer."

Her eyes narrowed, but she gave a nod, her breathing rattling more by the moment. She had pierced lungs, probably from broken ribs, and wasn't long for this world. Theroun strode briskly towards a knot of flickering torches. Vitreal was rinsing blood from his hands and face from a water-flask when Theroun marched up.

"Come with me. Now." Theroun growled.

Vitreal looked up, drying his hands and face on a clean bit of cloth. "Sir, my men need a rest after that skirmish."

"Not them, just you." Theroun overlooked the Runner-Captain's casual address. "Meet me over there. At that dead keshar. Quickly." Theroun turned back towards the darkness.

"What the bedevilment…?!" Den'Bhorus was whip-fast despite his exhaustion, circling Theroun and placing a hand to his chest before Theroun could limp out of the torchlight. "What do you mean?"

"We've got a live keshari rider, says she's seen Queen Elyasin. Safe at Lhen Fhekran."

"Well, shit on toast." Den'Bhorus grinned wide.

Theroun pushed past the younger man, into the darkness. Only Brigadiers and Fleetrunners now paced the quiet hillside, swiping torches as they searched for any soldiers still alive. Theroun flicked his fingers quickly at Arlus, who stepped to his side. Vitreal trotted up fast. Theroun walked them to the dead keshar, and the Elsthemi woman beneath it.

Her eyes glittered in the darkness, watching them. Her breath was laborious and slow, wet, her coughs weak. She gave dire grimace. "My luck. Three Menderian bastards ta send me on my way."

Theroun crouched, and his Captains did the same. "Tell them what you told me. The truth."

She gave a condescending smile, thick with black blood. "The truth? That yer all daft. Yer Queen Elyasin lives, safe in our land, with her husband King Therel. An' she's been betrayed. By her own countrymen, no better than dogs." She summoned a great rattling breath, and used what strength she had left to spit blood at their faces.

Her breath rattled once more, and she was gone.

"My command tent." Theroun hissed at his Captains. "Now."

But suddenly, alarm-gongs sounded again, clanging with raucous peals down in the main camp. The clanging of the watchtower gongs were urgent, far down near the river. Theroun's head whipped up and he cursed a blue streak. "A secondary raid! Dammit!"

But before he could get so much as twenty paces, a runner-lad of den'Ulthumen's ran up, blocking their path. The lad snapped a smart salute, breathless. "Counsel-General den'Vekir! You're needed in the General's command tent at once! You and the Runner-Captain, and the Brigadier-Captain! Sir!"

"Dammit, boy!" Theroun snarled. "Can't you hear there's another cat-raid?! We're needed at the river!"

"It's being dealt with, sir! Please. Follow me."

Even now, Theroun heard keshar screaming down near the river. And men and women. Screams of agony, of fear and pain. A twisting, vicious kind of pain far worse than death. This was no ordinary skirmish. Those were not the sounds of men being bitten or raked or impaled upon steel. Theroun grimaced. His injured side gripped him in a torpid ache. He shared a look with his two Captains, and all knew what was occurring.

"He's using the poisons, testing them on the raid! Fucking

den'Ulthumen!" Theroun cursed a blue streak. The runner-lad shrank back. Theroun was readying to mount up on a new horse, when den'Bhorus stepped swiftly to his side, confidential. "My runners? Our emissary to the Queen?"

"Send them. Now." Theroun spoke close so no others could hear. "They may be taken prisoner, but we *must* get a message through to Queen Elyasin. Tonight."

Den'Bhorus nodded. "I will join you shortly," he breathed. And then he was gone.

Theroun rode down in fury, listening to the sounds of screaming near the river. This was as bad as anything he had ever heard. Almost. It brought flooding back the sounds of men and women upon the Aphellian Way, strung up by their necks or nailed up to monoliths by the wrists, babbling and pleading for mercy. It brought back madness for Theroun, a kind of madness he never wanted to revisit. Dismounting at den'Ulthumen's command-tent, he whipped back the flap and strode in, furious as a thunderbolt.

And stopped dead.

"Good evening, Counsel-General." Castellan Lhaurent den'Karthus' oily voice slid over Theroun's skin like a basketful of eels.

Theroun gaped at the man in his spotless grey silk.

"*YOU!*" Theroun's hand whipped to his sword. Suddenly, spearmen surrounded him. Their keen-honed tips glistened with oilslick, a shifting peacock green in the brazier's light. Pythian-resin. It was enough to stop Theroun cold. One drop of that upon his skin would burn a hole right through all sinew, deep into bone, like the venomous bite of a spinner-hole spider.

The tent-flap was thrown back. Theroun heard den'Bhorus' hiss at the tense situation inside. Theroun gave a growl and eased his hands away from his weapons. At Lhaurent's nod, the spearmen backed down also, stepping to the margins of the tent. Lhaurent gave an oily smirk. General Den'Ulthumen stepped around the map-table and stood beside Lhaurent, facing Theroun and the two Captains.

"We've received orders, Theroun." Lharsus boomed.

"What orders?!" Theroun barked.

"Orders from the Chancellate. Castellan Lhaurent was sent

personally from Lintesh to convey them on behalf of the High Seat." Den'Ulthumen's green eyes were hard. "The Chancellate has ordered a push up the valley. To take Lhen Fhekran posthaste."

Theroun pinned den'Ulthumen with his formidable gaze. "Lharsus. As your Counselor-General, I *strongly* oppose these orders. You will be condemning *thousands* of men to slaughter! We haven't even begun to rout the keshari yet! Even if we manage a push, we won't get as far as Lhen Fhekran. That's a hard three-day ride. This is madness. Stay the course and wear their armies down from this fortified position. Skirmishes will win this battle, slowly. An all-out push is certain death."

"They are *our orders*, Theroun." And from the way he said it, Theroun understood exactly what General Lharsus den'Ulthumen had received. Khehemni Lothren orders.

"And I suppose you have companies picked out for this push?" Theroun ground his jaw.

General den'Ulthumen nodded, his green eyes frank. "Brigadiers, Fleetrunners, the Twenty-Third through Twenty-Sixth Cavalry, and the Seventeenth and Eighteenth Foot. Headed by you. You have the experience we need. You will have certain… amenities… at your disposal, Theroun. It won't be a rout."

"Define *amenities*."

"I think you know the ones I mean." Den'Ulthumen's green eyes shied away.

"You fucking bastard." Theroun's gaze snapped to Lhaurent. "You're the reason the river is howling with atrocity, right now!"

"*Careful*, Theroun." Lhaurent's smile had gone glacial. "Those tools are necessary to secure our victory, and General den'Ulthumen understands that. As emissary of the Chancellate, I could give you a court-martial and have you executed right now for disobedience. But I'm giving you a chance. You have a stunning record of service. And you, more than most, know how to effectively deploy weapons of such devastation. This is your task. Step right, or step wrong."

Theroun set his jaw, snarling internally. Spearmen with Pythian-resin still ringed the tent. If he made a move, he was dead, a very slow, horrible death. As could still be evinced from the faint screaming yet issuing from the river.

"Gentlemen," Lhaurent gave an oily nod. "I take my leave.

Your push through the forest and up the valley begins in three days' time." With a final glittering gaze, the eel slithered out of the tent.

"I'm afraid I have to keep you under guard, Theroun. Until the push. Castellan Lhaurent was most explicit. You understand." Lharsus den'Ulthumen's green eyes were apologetic, and he rubbed at his blonde beard.

Theroun drew in a deep breath. "So that's it, then? I'm under arrest?"

"I would rather you fight for us Theroun, not against us." Den'Ulthumen's eyes were sad. "If this push goes well, it could end the war. We could capture Elsthemen. But the Castellan warned me that you wouldn't like this assignment. That you might defect."

And just like that, Theroun realized that General den'Ulthumen was not Khehemni Lothren. He wasn't trusted enough to be in the inner circle. Den'Ulthumen didn't know why Lhaurent was sending Brigadiers and Fleetrunners into a slaughter. He didn't know that the entire purpose of the war was to kill off Kingsmen.

"So you're not high-up enough in the Lothren to know what in Aeon's fuck they're up to, are you?" Theroun's voice was scathing.

"We all have our orders, Theroun," den'Ulthumen muttered.

Theroun gave a soft chuckle. He was not a man who chuckled. It worked. Den'Ulthumen blanched. "I'll be your Black Viper," Theroun murmured, rather than his usual bark. "I'll give you an Aphellian Way you'll never forget. My oaths are strong, and to them I will hold until death takes me."

Den'Ulthumen nodded, misunderstanding his Counselor-General's words, as Theroun had meant him to. For Theroun held to oaths far stronger than the ones to the Khehemni that he'd made after his family had been killed. Oaths he had taken in the beginning. When he had been a young man full of idealism, who won the hearts of men on the battlefield with care for their welfare and cunning tactics. When he had knelt in the throne hall of a King, and been promoted to the position of First-General of the Realm, kneeling with a hale body as Uhlas had touched the ceremonial sword to his shoulders.

Theroun had looked up, to see the shining eyes of a little sun-haired girl standing by her brother and father, green eyes that had already carried the shrewd nature of the King himself. Eyes that already held all the piss and vinegar one needed to be a good Queen.

Theroun went very still. His was a deadly stillness as he planned the battle ahead. He had the men, he had the regiments. And he had the weaponry for an overwhelming and decisive attack.

Though it wasn't going to be an attack upon the Highlanders.

"I will lead your battle in three days' time. If that is everything, then I need some sleep." Theroun turned and strode disrespectfully from the command tent. As he'd anticipated, a group of four spearmen followed him out, tailing him to his own tent. Theroun ducked inside, hearing the guardsmen take up positions outside, jailing him in. That was the last of camp Theroun would be allowed to see for the next three days. Going to the meditation cushion he always kept upon campaign, he took a cross-legged seat before the brazier, staring into its flames.

How he'd like to see the Eel of Roushenn roasting over its glowing coals.

Theroun settled in, to meditate on the strategy of his strike with all the stillness of a viper.

CHAPTER 22 – TEMLIN

Temlin breathed in the quiet of the ancient armory, stepping back to maneuver his blade. It all came back readily, the skills of his youth. Moving with the blade, time seemed to fade as early afternoon sunlight trickled in cracked panes of glass, lighting dust motes that swirled around racks of rusting armor and forgotten weapons. Slice and pivot, parry and cut. He had cast his Jenner robe aside sometime in the first hour of practice, long sleeves tangling his movement. Free now, he moved only in his black trousers, a cool mountain breeze licking sweat from his youthful skin.

Temlin's spectacles lay upon the dusty stones by his black Jenner-robe.

His sight was fine now. Better than fine.

Aligning with the sword, Temlin raised it to an unseen opponent, beginning again. His vigor was restored, muscles bunching and twisting, supporting his every move. The sword felt like it had been in his hands for years. At last, he put the blade up, sweating in rivulets. And was startled to see Molli sitting on a dusty bench near the open armory door, her blind eyes wide.

"Do it again," she murmured, enrapt.

Temlin wiped his brow with one slick arm. "I'm sweating like a horse full-blown, Molli." But it felt good to move with a blade again, as if a part of him that had been lost was now found. Temlin began again, slicing and pivoting.

"Such patterns!" Molli's fingers twitched, fluttering like moths as her whisper filled the gallery. "Uhlas was never so fine a dancer as you, my love!"

At last, she rose. Temlin ceased his cuts, resting the sword-tip upon the stones as she stepped close. Fluttering hands wrapped around his middle, and Molli snugged her chin between his jaw and shoulder. Temlin nuzzled his lips into her wild white hair, inhaling her scent. Molli smelled of good wool with a hint of cinnamon birch tea, and it pulled him to a sweet ache.

"Temlin, my love," she said, "it's time to come back."

"What if I want to stay in here forever?" Temlin nodded around the armory at caches of shields and dummies sporting full sets of ancient armor. All of it was covered in dust, most of it rusted beyond repair.

"You need to eat, my love. You've been in here since sunup." A fluttering hand combed through his russet hair, now thicker and less grey than it had any right to be.

"I have water." He gestured at a water flask nearby. "Why are you here, Molli? You're not worried about me losing a bit of paunch."

"Am I that transparent?" A wry smile replaced her usual haughtiness as she kissed his shoulder.

He brushed back a strand of her wayward curls. "Always. And never."

"I've had a vision. About Lhem."

"Bad or good?" Temlin gazed at her intently, his brows furrowing.

Her face was enough to tell him the answer. Molli had that faraway look, the prelude to her madness. But the rage, strangely, didn't come. "He's damaged a girl. She was an innocent, like I was. But she's not anymore." Molli shuddered, shrugging her wool shawl closer in the brisk air.

"Was she a Khehemni spy?"

"No, not at all. But Lhem is."

"Now, Molli—"

"He is!" Molli snapped decisively. "No Alrashemni would do that to an innocent! That poor girl! Her long honey braid, it was splattered with blood. Such a pretty chirping bird...!"

Temlin's heart sank through his toes. "Eleshen den'Fenrir! Aeon's fuck. Is she hurt badly?"

"Hurt beyond all care. Tortured." Molli's face was woeful, vicious as she gazed up at him. "That bastard Lhem! He pollutes everything! Him and my brother and that awful Lhaurent!!"

Temlin felt her tirade coming. He snugged Molli close with one arm, held her until her trembling ceased. She sighed heavily. "I have other news, Temlin. Ghrenna has made a breakthrough. She has opened the Alranstone here in the valley. She's made a connection to Delman."

"Who is Delman?"

"Delman Ferrian. My friend in the Stone here." Molli's smile was cryptic. "The important thing is, with her newfound strength in taming Alranstones, then I believe you have a way back to the Abbey, perhaps even today. But if you go, you must guard against Lhem. It is good that you are remembering a blade in your hands, my love. Lhem is old now. He will be slow."

"You want me to use this body you gifted me with to kill Lhem." Temlin blinked at her. "My Abbott and my superior in the Shemout, not to mention my closest *friend*. He's not the demon you think he is, Molli. There's nothing I don't know about the man."

Molli set her jaw imperiously. "There is *much* you don't know about him. And though you might hesitate to kill him, know that he will not when the time comes."

"Good gods, woman!" Temlin's brows furrowed. "What have you seen?"

"The Abbey needs you to take command." Molli's grimace was feral.

With those cryptic words, Molli turned and fluttered out of his arms. Temlin sighed, taking his sword to the rack and sliding it away without a single pain in his joints. His body was more fit than it had been even in his forties. Temlin reveled in the feel of haleness as the breeze cooled him, running a hand through his russet hair to dispel sweat, feeling how thick it was.

He had seen his face in the stream yesterday, and almost hadn't recognized himself.

Mollia moved around the cluttered room with ease, as if she could see all the suits of armor on their moth-eaten dummies, the pegs of bridles and saddles, the racks of pikes. Moving toward a set of sturdy wooden doors covered in cobwebs, she shoved a tiny shoulder against the wood. It didn't budge, and Temlin stepped in. Temlin hit it hard with his shoulder, and the ancient door jounced inwards, nearly spilling him over dusty flagstones. A small chamber was revealed, but this held the most precious weapons. One rack held a suit of lightweight armor that shone a silvered white, as if made of a metal not from this earth. Next to it was a table with three glass cases. One held a longsword with a ruby set in a pommel of the same metal, on a bed of crimson velvet. The other two held longknives of a sickled variety to match.

Temlin moved inside, drawn to the priceless weapons, still pristine though the armor needed a wipe-down from the dust. Opening the longsword's case, he found the blade balanced perfectly with the ruby hilt. Etching ran up the blade, in a script Temlin could barely recognize.

"Gods, Molli. These are ancient." Temlin squinted at the script. "This is some form of High Alrakhan... I think it says, *Test me not, lest you be tested*." He ran the back of one fingernail against the blade, a flake of his nail peeling off readily. "Fucking sharp."

She nodded. "Delman told me of a few secrets that live here."

"Who is this Delman again?" Temlin turned the blade over in his hands.

Molli glanced away, fidgeting with her fingers. "A friend. Trapped in an Alranstone."

Temlin lifted an eyebrow. "You're blushing."

"I'm not!" Molli snapped, white eyes fierce. "In any case, he told me these were here, and that they were worked by some man who could imbue steel with everlasting properties. Take one, try it out."

Temlin needed no urging. He moved back to the main room, trying a few pivots and lunges. It was heavenly. The blade sang in his hand. He could barely feel its weight, and it slipped through the air like cutting silk. Temlin flowed through his forms, feeling fighting settle into his sinews. He remembered how to manage his breath, how to dance through forms that fended off not just one opponent, but two, three, and four. Temlin whirled and brought the blade up in a fast slice through a dummy. The wooden dummy parted on the diagonal, the rusting armor upon it clanking to the stones, neatly cut through.

Impressed, Temlin inspected the blade. "Not a damn nick. Cut solid wood, and steel to boot."

"You should have the set, Temlin." Molli's hands fluttered over the blade. "Take the armor as well. Wear it under your robe."

"I don't need armor. No one's going to take a swipe at me, Molli." Temlin protested.

"Please. For me. You don't look like an old Jenner any longer."

Her white eyes were luminous and it raised heat in Temlin's veins. He had forgotten how much he loved such things. Passion. Fire. Fucking. Making war. Flexing his hands, Temlin could feel blisters upon them. He hadn't cared to wrap his palms, and now they bore the marks of his obsession. It was always like that with him. A sword or booze or books, it didn't matter. His mind had always burned hot.

Mollia wrapped her hands over his. Temlin felt the blisters fade, skin hardening into callouses as if he'd been practicing for years. Molli knew strange things sometimes, and if she said he needed armor, he wasn't going to gainsay her. Stepping to the small room, Temlin retrieved the luminous breastplate, gauntlets and the rest, plus the longknives and a harness for the weapons. His brows lifted, finding the strange white metal surprisingly light, thin and flexible.

Molli came forward, settling her hands to his arms. "Put them on, Temlin, my love. Destinies turn. You need to go, today."

"Now?" Temlin's heart clenched, unnerved by this sudden direction. He didn't want to go back. He didn't want to face that creature in the Abbeystone again, didn't want to leave Molli now that he had just found her again. His throat gripped, and he pulled her close, breathing in her tea-spice scent. "I don't want to lose you again."

"You won't," she pulled away with a kiss to his neck. "But time waits for none of us. What I have seen… Ghrenna is ready. You must go. You and I will have time, my love. Later. We will have all the time in the world…" Lifting up to her toes, she placed a kiss upon his lips.

Temlin took a deep breath, nodded. Molli handed him a smooth undershirt from a bundle she had brought, and he slung it on. Taking up the strange white armor, Temlin buckled it on. It was flexible and moved when he did, more like flowing links of mail than plate, molding to his body like silk. Once he was fully clad, he could hardly tell it was on.

"Think it's strong?" Temlin gazed at his gauntlets doubtfully.

Molli gave a clever smile. She spun, ripping a longknife from a nearby block and slamming it to Temlin's breastplate. Bending, the knife sprung from her hand and skittered away across the floor.

Temlin's eyebrows rose. "Good enough."

He reached for his Jenner-robe, but Molli's hand stopped him. Producing another garment from her bundle, she held it out. "Wear this instead, my love."

Sleek and trim, the garment fit close like a longjacket rather than a robe, Temlin found as he donned it. Buckling at the front, it had a high collar and deep hood. The drape was split into panels for fighting and cropped to the knee. Molli produced boots from her bundle, soft black boots of lamb's leather, tooled with the Kingsmount and Stars. She gave Temlin black leather gloves and a belt to match, and Temlin found himself once again astounded by the depth of her inner sight.

Settling the weapons-harness over his robe, he positioned the longsword over his left shoulder for a fast draw, the knives at his hips. And then, it was complete. Fully clad, Temlin gazed down at himself. He was transformed. Gone was a Jenner monk, replaced by a trim, honed fighter in black garb that seemed more like a lord of assassins than monk. Though made of wool rather than leather, it was not unlike the Alrashemni greys, Temlin mused, and smiled that Molli would have crafted him such a garment.

Molli stepped back, smiling in a pleased way as if she could see it. Her hands reached out, fingers fluttering over the fit like moths. "Perfect. Such a transformation, Temlin, my love…"

He pulled her close, breathing her in, tears pricking his eyes suddenly. "Why does it feel like you're saying goodbye?"

"It's not goodbye, my love," she kissed his jaw. "Just so-long for now." Stepping back, she patted his cheek. Without lingering in solemnity, Mollia turned, moving out through the open doors. Temlin's heart hitched. He took a breath, then followed into the bright sunshine. But rather than return to the kitchens, they took the path up the hill through the forest. Stepping out into the glade, Temlin was hit with a sudden shock.

Ghrenna stood before the Plinth, and as they approached, she did not look around. She stared at the Stone as if entranced, ignoring them utterly, one hand upon the grey-blue granite. Molli had been industrious these the past few days, and Ghrenna wore stout black wool breeches today, kneeboots, a light black shirt and black leather jerkin. She was armored to the nines, with a hardy yew longbow slung across her back and a quiver full of arrows, a brace of throwing-knives across her chest, and two needle-vicious longknives at her hips. She didn't have a sword, but Temlin was fairly sure she was just as deadly without one.

Temlin suddenly realized they looked like Kingsmen. He gave a soft laugh at Mollia's brilliance. They would come back through the Abbeystone, and the world would see the truth. He couldn't run from it, couldn't hide. Molli had turned back time for him, and returned everything else along with it.

Molli moved close, touching Ghrenna's pale blonde hair with kind hands. "You can still hear him, can't you? Delman?"

"Yes." Ghrenna said, startling. She fiddled with her weapons, adjusting the leather straps of her harness. "And I can hear others out there. After Delman and I... talked."

"And Delman?"

"He's still here." Ghrenna's lips twisted wryly. "He'll never be gone. Not from me."

"Do you think you can reach the Abbeystone in Lintesh? My Temlin needs to go back. Today."

Ghrenna's somber blue eyes focused upon Temlin, then she cocked her head as if listening to something. "You'll die. The man in the Abbeystone wants you. But Delman is mentioning another way to get through Lamak den'Thun's Plinth."

Temlin chilled to his bones despite the pleasant afternoon. "Lamak den'Thun? That *thing* in the Abbeystone was a man?"

"Many of them are going mad." Ghrenna's blue eyes were hard. "Lamak was one of the first to warp from time. He had a cruel nature. Has. Had... Has." She shook her head, frowning. "His Plinth only connects to the Abbeystone, intended to be a safe haven for royalty. They selected Lamak as guardian at the Abbeystone for his ferocity. They didn't count on him going insane..."

"Are you all right, child?" Molli reached out a hand, settling it over Ghrenna's.

"No." Ghrenna's deep blue eyes roiled suddenly. "It's like there are two women within me, Molli. One who remembers being Ghrenna, and one who remembers other things. Dark things, horrible times. Desperation, war."

"Who is this other woman, child?" Molli whispered, stroking the girl's hand.

Suddenly, a voice came out of Ghrenna's mouth that was not hers. Deeper, resonant, this voice carried the heft of time and sent prickles rushing over Temlin's skin. "I am Morvein Vishke. I am the Nightwind. Lamak den'Thun will bow to me or be sundered from his Plinth."

Ghrenna's lake-blue eyes stared at nothing, and Temlin felt the afternoon crawl. Molli met his gaze as if reading his thoughts and reached out to squeeze his hand. Temlin's attention returned to the Plinth. Ghrenna was doing something with it. Rigid and staring, she shuddered in the dappled sunlight. At last, she heaved a sigh, eyelids fluttering. Her staring blue eyes came back into focus, empty of emotion.

"We can go now. Delman will put you through to Lamak's Plinth in the Abbey." Ghrenna shuddered, but not, Temlin thought, from the brisk breeze.

"Me?" Temlin turned, eyeing Ghrenna. "Not you?"

"I stay here." She murmured, her eyes faraway. "Delman and I have much to discuss. But I will travel to Lamak's Plinth with you and do what must be done, before I return. To do what I must do."

"And what is that?" Temlin asked.

"Find Queen Elyasin den'Ildrian. And King Therel Alramir."

Temlin's body was electric. If Elyasin was truly alive and Ghrenna could get through to her, it would change everything. Suddenly, Temlin made a decision. "Tell Elyasin, if you find her, that the First Abbey is with her. I don't know how I can manage it, but I *will* convince them to stand with our rightful Queen my niece in this conflict. Tell her she will have allies in Lintesh. I promise it."

"I will."

Ghrenna's gaze fixed upon him. Those midnight-blue eyes were hard and strong, a far cry from the dying girl that had been brought to the Abbey. As if something within her had suddenly come to the forefront, she regarded Temlin without mercy or compromise. He thought of the name she had uttered, Morvein Vishke the Nightwind. Temlin had never read the name Morvein in the Annals. But he'd heard of the Nightwind, in whispers of legend. And wherever the Nightwind went, it was written, upheaval followed. *The mountains tremor in the wake of the Nightwind,* Temlin remembered from one ancient journal. *When the Nightwind calls, all the Inked follow.*

Temlin shuddered, though the afternoon was calm and bright. Beneath those lake-blue eyes, he felt his knees turn to water, so potent were their call.

"It's time." Ghrenna said. "Temlin, Mollia, put your hands upon Delman's Plinth."

Ghrenna set her hands to the Stone. Temlin had hardly done so, when a rush of wind and a clap of thunder gripped him. Faster than thought, his mind was sucked into the Plinth to an in-between space. And the creature, Lamak den'Thun, focused upon him. Like a trough of corpses, Lamak's vibration surged vibrant and full of horrors. Claws reached out, trapping Temlin's body before Delman's Plinth, hands spread over the blue byrunstone. Pain came, a riot of pain. Temlin screamed, sagging but still fixed to the Stone. Claws scored his back, fangs savaged his neck. Lamak's laughter pealed in his ears, gleeful.

You come again, my dear prince. The beast grinned. *To embrace your annihilation at last. Just as Lhaurent said I could have you, one day.*

Temlin tried to focus through his pain. *Lhaurent den'Karthus?*

Lhaurent feeds me, so I permit his travel from the palace. He talks with the Abbot. Did you not know, my prince? So many things you do not know… Snarled lips curled over bloody fangs. *I feel how you love her, Temlin, your damaged little moth-ling. Such a broken woman, Mollia. I've tasted her blood. Sweet. Just like Lhaurent and the Abbott tasted it so many times… I have heard Lhem speak about her, you know, speak of all the dark things he did, when he fucked her. Over and over and over and over…*

Rage surged in Temlin. A blinding heat that shook him to his bones, as he suddenly realized that every bit of Molli's ravings were true. Confirmed by this hateful creature, Temlin felt fury rush through him, as he thought of Lhem and Lhaurent, and what they had done to his beloved. Done for so many years, torturing her. While everyone, including him, thought she merely raved with madness.

Temlin's heart screamed.

Suddenly, he heard a vibration, like music upon a nighttime breeze. Lush and hallowed, the music blew through the mind-space, thrumming and caressing him, pushing back the beast's pain-giving. All Temlin could see were Ghrenna's lake-blue eyes, vast as the ocean. Like a cocoon, they gathered him, wrapping him in their protection. Those eyes fixed upon Lamak. The beast that had once been a man quailed. He salivated, he surged, he began to rake claws down his own flesh. Temlin felt the force of her music drowning Lamak.

Come to me, pretty Being! Lamak screamed, desperate. *Your wind is purification in my soul!*

Your loathsome pleasures are not for me. Wind shrieked around Temlin now, protecting him, carrying the voice of the woman inside Ghrenna. The voice of Morvein Vishke, the Nightwind. *Kill yourself,* she whispered to Lamak. *Now is the time to be released from your misery. There is only one man here who can end your torment, Lamak. And that is you. Kill yourself.*

The beast began to howl. As it roared, it dug at its own eyes, it ripped out its own fangs. Temlin could feel the wind around him pushing the man's madness, driving it to the brink of annihilation. It shuddered and tore at itself and wailed and began to thrum discordantly, coming unraveled.

Lake-blue eyes fixed upon Temlin. *Do you seek revenge? I could give him endless pain… make him inflict it upon himself forever.*

Temlin swallowed hard. A part of him wanted nothing more. A part of him wanted to tear Lamak apart. But he saw the man's torment now. Felt for how many hundreds of years Lamak had been trapped, going insane, learning to love only pain. And seeing that horror, the man now writhing, gouging out his own throat and belly in the mind-space, Temlin felt only sadness.

His hate was reserved for other men.

Just kill him, he whispered to the Nightwind. *Make it fast.*

He felt her nod. Her cerulean eyes fixed upon Lamak den'Thun. There was a great flash and a howl, and suddenly, Lamak's tune was silent, his visage in the great in-between utterly gone. Temlin breathed in relief, his mind flooding with peace. A sigh rippled through the space, a blessed silence.

Who will take his place? Ghrenna spoke suddenly.

I will. A chirrup came from Temlin's shoulder. He gazed down to see Molli smiling up at him in the mind-space. Her eyes were a sparking green, her body young and strong, her face unlined with the ravages of time. She lifted up on her toes, and gave Temlin a kiss that thrummed through his soul.

Temlin, my first love. Be strong for me. I am in a better place here, where the scourges of the world can no longer touch me. I have seen my path, and it lies within the Plinth.

Temlin felt himself ripped out of her arms. One last touch of her moth-fluttering fingers, and then he was spat out upon the other side of the Abbeystone back in Lintesh, the underground grotto no longer blood-red but flooded with the brightness of a summer's day. He stumbled to his knees upon stone. Molli had not come through. The Stone behind him surged, Molli's bright music rippling over him as it flooded from every open eye.

And then, surging in warning.

Prickles lanced Temlin's spine and he unsheathed his sword fast, bringing it up sharply to block the downward slice of a swordsman. They contested a moment, the younger man clearly surprised by what had come through the Abbeystone. Shouts went up around the underground grotto. Temlin shoved forward, lunging to his feet in a smooth pivot. His Jenner vows split asunder as he slit the young man up under his arm and across his throat. Gurgling to his knees before the bright Abbeystone, every eye of Molli's Plinth witnessed the lad die.

But Temlin was den'Ildrian, a Dhenir of the Realm and a Kingsman before he was a Jenner. With a roar, Temlin engaged his foes, and saw them blanch, at such viciousness.

"For the Kingsmen!" Temlin bellowed. "For den'Ildrian! For my niece the Queen!!"

The fight didn't last long. Temlin's soul rejoiced to do battle, spurred on by Mollia's bright love. One by one, the false Jenners fell, leaving him panting in the grotto, six corpses bleeding out around him. Temlin turned to gaze upon Molli. The Abbeystone glowed from top to bottom, the eye at the top blindingly everycolor. Temlin felt a touch like moths brush his face as the Stone's awareness passed over him, and the joy in his heart turned to rage.

"I'll kill Lhem for you, Molli," Temlin snarled. "And then I'll kill Lhaurent. Forgive me, for never believing you. Let Lhem see my sword bloody as I come for him!"

The top eye flared. Temlin roared through the passage away from Mollia's Abbeystone, sword unsheathed. He burst through the hidden door into Lhem's apartments, death in his eyes and a snarl upon his lips. Temlin's gaze whipped over Lhem's quarters, finding them empty. Barreling through the doors, he seized the first Brother he saw by the throat, pinning him to the wall. Brother Bauer's rheumy old eyes widened at the manhandling as he took Temlin in from head to toe.

"Temlin?!" Brother Bauer reached up a gnarled hand to touch Temlin's hair in astonishment. "Sweet Arrow of the Way! How—?"

"I haven't got time to explain." Temlin released him. "Where is the Abbot?"

"Lhem told us you were dead!"

"*What?!*" Temlin drew up in a seething rage.

"He said you died in a horrible accident with the Abbeystone! We mourned you! We had a funeral and everything, though there was no body to inter!"

"As you can see, I am *quite* well!" Temlin snapped. "Where is Lhem?"

"The Abbot was inspecting the brewery, just an hour ago—"

Temlin was already sprinting down the hall. Lhem's treachery had to be answered. Rushing down the stairwell, he burst through the doors to the outside. Rounding the edge of the Annex at a run, sword out, Brothers stepped hastily back from his fevered flight. As Temlin careened around the edge of the ornate masonry of the brewery, he finally saw the man he was searching for.

Temlin doubled his pace, coming for Lhem like an avalanche.

Lhem spied him, started to twist. Temlin charged, blade up at his shoulder. Steel flashed as Lhem pulled a sword from a slit in his black robes, raising it just in time to deflect Temlin's charge. Lhem flicked his sword up and around, stumbling Temlin with more force in that fat frame than he had any right to. He'd hardly lost any of his old strength. Many was the time Lhem and Temlin had dueled, before Temlin had come to the Abbey. Nearly ten years older, Temlin's father's Third-General was not a man to be lightly put aside.

Temlin danced in, Lhem stepped back. Temlin's fight was brutal and heated, rash with passion, but Lhem had gone to a place of cool calculation. Lhem was a mountain of solidarity to Temlin's quick speed, deflecting thrusts with the barest movement. Suddenly, they locked. Lhem gave a mighty shove, and his sword-point went ripping across Temlin's ribs. Temlin staggered back with a cry, but though his blacks were rent, the white armor shone through undamaged in the light of the sun.

"Give it up, Temlin!" A vicious smile lifted Lhem's jowly face. "You never were able to best me. Too skinny and reckless by far…"

"*You sick fucking bastard! I'll kill you for what you did to Mollia!*" The voice that ripped from Temlin's throat was one he hadn't heard for ages. A young man, pained and tortured, broken by love.

"What you know isn't even the half of it." Lhem spoke coolly, a sneer on his face. "I did things to Mollia you can't ever imagine. And the *witch* deserved every last *inch* of it."

Red rage stole Temlin's vision. Fury unmanned his sanity. The blade consumed him as he clashed. Lhem parried desperately, shock in his eyes. Temlin suddenly realized that he was fighting a slow, fat old man. Lhem had been living slack for years, his body let go to hops and delicacies. He was still strong, brutishly so, but as he shoved Temlin out of a clinch, his strike was slow.

Temlin's blade flashed out. Lhem missed his parry, and Temlin's blade slid up, biting deep into the Abbott's armpit. Lhem's eyes flicked wide, and he sagged with a gasp, his blade dropping to the dust. It would have been fatal had Temlin been in top fighting-form, cleaving into the ribcage and into the great vessels of the heart. But Temlin's angle had been shallow from years without practice.

Their eyes met over the blade.

"What you gonna do, Temlin?" Lhem growled. "Let them all see the beast you've become? Just because I fucked your little sorceress bitch and laughed while I did it. And you never believed her…"

A roar built in Temlin's throat, spilled out. Stepping back, he pulled his sword from the wound, making Lhem's agony last. Lhem was on his knees now, his sword-arm dangling as blood poured out, grimacing in pain. A crowd had gathered. Shocked faces, Brothers and Sisters flooding in from every compound to watch the battle in the dry summer dust. Silence suffocated the wide brewery plaza. But

Temlin saw a few who wore grim smiles of satisfaction, and he noted each face well. Far back in the throng, Temlin picked out Abbess Lenuria, her cowl up and hands folded in her sleeves.

Watching what he would do.

Letting him do it.

"Brothers! Sisters!" Temlin bellowed through the dry air. "I place this man, Lhem den'Ulio under arrest for High Treason to the Realm. He has been complicit to the murder of a King, a Dhenir, and plotting the assassination of a Dhenra, and is allies with a faction who seek to usurp the Crown! I make this arrest not as Temlin, Second Brother Historian of the Annals, but as my original name and station, Dhenir Temlin den'Ildrian, brother to King Uhlas den'Ildrian, uncle to Queen Elyasin!"

Murmurs passed through the crowd, shock opening faces. Few had known him, as surnames were not used in the Abbey. Temlin was going to speak on, when something hard hit him below the ribs. He staggered. A shortknife thudded to the dirt beside him. Temlin was already turning, rage searing him. Lhem's thrown knife had been deflected by the white armor. But not to be undone, Lhem was already rising, taking up his sword in his left hand, an old codger with too many tricks in his Ghenje.

But Lhem's fat bulk was too slow getting up from his knees.

Temlin was already there, slicing his sword across the bastard's throat. Blood washed crimson from the gash. Lhem goggled at Temlin, his mouth working soundlessly. The Abbott fell forward onto his jowly face in the dust.

"You deserved *every last inch* of that." Temlin kicked Lhem's sword away with a sneer of disgust.

Silence held court in the Abbey, a hushed breathlessness that rang in Temlin's ears.

"Jenners!" Temlin turned, his body buzzing with fury. "I do not claim Regency, but I hold the throne for my niece, your Queen! I have received word that she lives! Exiled in Elsthemen, she does not wish for this false war! I urge you, Brothers and Sisters of the Way - stand up for the peace of this land! The First Abbey has power, and it's time we used that power as we must!"

Temlin threw down his blooded sword. He unbound his weapons harness, then stripped it and unbuckled his longjacket.

Standing in his boots and breeches and white armor, he unbuckled the breastplate and bared his chest. Then picked up one longknife, and drew it across his sternum. Crimson blossomed forth, baring his Bloodmarked Inkings for all to see, the Inkings of a Shemout Alrashemni.

Silence settled over the courtyard.

Watchful, interested silence.

"Kingsmen!" Temlin's voice rolled out over the plaza. "Alrashemni! Know that your time in the shadows is finished! Stand with me now! Stand with Dhenir Temlin of House den'Ildrian, one of your own royal line marked the same as you! One who will never betray you, never hunt you. Who lives only for the rightful rule of this land, under my niece our Queen. Stand, and fight for the throne you were sworn to protect, fight for peace in our nation! *Alrashemnesh ars veitriya rhovagnetari! Toura Corunenne!*"

"*Toura Corunenne.*" A rumbling basso boomed from Temlin's left. Temlin looked over, noting stern Brother Sebasos from the brewery, bare to the waist also, his body of middling years still hard as stone. Black Inkings stood out upon his strong chest. "For those who don't know, it means *Long Live the Queen!* Our throne has been under siege for as long as can be remembered, Brothers and Sisters! Temlin's father, slain before his time! Our Dhenir's untimely *accident*! Our King's strange sickness! The Queen, nearly assassinated! The Way is the Path and the Path is the Virtue, and every last soul has virtue! Will we stand by and watch our country come to slaughter, engaged in a war with both Valenghia and Elsthemen, crushing us until there are no souls left to save? I say no! I say, *Toura Corunenne*, Brothers and Sisters! *Toura Corunenne!!*"

Abbess Lenuria had moved up through the crowd. Standing at Temlin's side now, the petite Abbess threw back her cowl, her iron-shot black braids stunning beside the wrath in her eyes. Lifting her chin defiantly, she spoke soft words, but they resounded through the dry air like a gong.

"*Toura Corunenne.*"

And like a tidal crest breaking, the men and women before Temlin began to surge, throwing back cowls, *Toura Corunenne* hammering Temlin's eardrums like mountain thunder. He felt the turn of the tide. Jenner-cords unknotted and slipped to the dust, robes rustled as they went up over heads from dozens of those gathered before the brewery. They stood before Temlin with the Blackmark, heads held high and fire in their eyes. Alrashemni men and women bare-chested, proclaiming themselves after so many years.

Proclaiming the strength of the Kingsmen at last.

Suddenly, a redheaded Sister in the front who had not disrobed took her belt knife and slit her robe's collar to the middle of her chest. There, she gouged a vertical slash in her flesh like a falling star, her eyes fierce. A bloom of crimson Ink spread through her skin, limning the Mountain and Stars. A Bloodmarked Shemout Alrashemni, like Temlin. Someone Temlin had never known, due to secrecy in their cells. Suddenly, others began to slice their robes, cut their chests. Less than ten total, their number was still surprising. Temlin surveyed these unknown allies with steel in his eyes, nodding his thanks to each and every one of them.

His gaze flicked to Lenuria. Her robe's collar sliced, the Bloodmark stood out defiantly upon her chest. Her iron gaze locked to Temlin's, and she nodded.

CHAPTER 23 – ELYASIN

Sweat rolled down Elyasin's face in the warm late-summer sunshine, tracking through the dust that grimed her face. Her fingers were numb where they gripped her quarterstaff. Six times now, Lhesher Khoum had flipped her face-down in the dirt. Bruises peppered her body from the staves of flexible yether-wood. Her only saving grace today had been nimble feet, and rolls taught to her by Olea.

Lhesher was a big man. All muscle and little fat, the grey streaks in his wild red hair belied his strength. Four white scars ripped across his chest, his Inkings disfigured by their raking spread. The same ripped down his left arm, with chew-marks. Elyasin had heard the story. He'd given a wild keshar his left arm to chew while he gouged its eyes with his right.

All to protect his young King, Therel, only fourteen at the time.

Lhesher's stave whirled at her head again. Elyasin ducked, bringing her stave close to her belly and rolling. She flicked it as she rose, catching the Highsword's heel, but he whisked out of the way. She rolled to standing and he engaged, leveling his stave at her gut. She pivoted, hips twisting, but her balance was bad from exhaustion. He whipped the other end, catching her in the back. Elyasin grunted and fell, managing a forward roll, whipping her stave at the back of his knee from her crouch. He defended, planting one end of his stave in the dirt, but she slid up it and thrust, catching him in the groin from her knees.

Lhesher huffed and doubled, the dirt-end of his stave flicking up. It smacked Elyasin smartly beneath the chin, sending her sprawling backwards. Her skull rang; her teeth ached despite the soft leather between them. Lhesher's stave flicked to her throat. But he was doubled over it, and pain filled his eyes.

It was the third blow she had landed upon the man today.

Three more than yesterday.

"Right in the stones! Well done!" Clapping sounded from the

edge of the ring. Elyasin looked over to see her King striding onto the dirt. Curious eyes settled upon them from other fighting-pits, watching. Therel reached down, Elyasin clasped his arm. He hauled her up, grinning at the bruises on her bared skin. She had on the tight-wrap of the keshari riders today, and Therel's hand stole around her middle. He brushed briefly at her assassination scar as if he was proud of it. Elyasin spit her leather mouth-guard into her hand and gave Therel a kiss, which lingered despite the gawkers and her bruised chin.

"My king! Queen Elyasin gave me three hits today." Lhesher's voice boomed merry. He was nothing but serious ferocity when they trained, but afterwards, he was the uncle anyone would have loved. He strode to her, clasping her arm and giving it a firm shake, then Therel's, then a clap to the shoulder for each of them.

"Ah! Young love! What I wouldn't give to have some again!" He turned to face Elyasin. "You! Study the forms of Khenthar I taught you today. Lowlanders have forgotten their Khenthar. We have to catch you up. Though she has many hidden talents, my King."

Therel stroked her dusty braid. "And here I thought your hidden talent was stubbornness! Or maybe fucking."

Elyasin was getting used to Elsthemi frankness, but she blushed anyway. Lhesher laughed and slapped his thigh, planting his stave in the earth with gusto. "Fucking and stubbornness! A good combination in a wife. The gods have favored you, Therel!"

"They surely have." Therel stroked her neck, gazing at her with admiration. But he quickly turned back to Lhesher, his blonde brows frowning. "Lhesher, whom do we have to interpret dreams now that Vhensa has passed on?"

Lhesher frowned. "Adelaine was Vhensa's first pupil. Jhonen was a quick study, but she's ridden out with Merra. I wouldn't trust any of the others to read dreams with any accuracy."

"Adelaine." Therel took a slow breath. He sucked his lip, a rare tic. "Is there anyone else?"

Lhesher shook his head. "You know as well as I that Vhensa trained only two pupils to follow her as High Dremorande. Martin and Adelaine. Anyone else is only Second or Third-Drem."

"Martin deserved what he got." Therel said flatly.

"Aye, that's so, my King." Lhesher nodded.

At last, Therel sighed. "Adelaine it is. I had hoped she wouldn't be necessary, though I sent to Hokhar up on the Ice Plateau some weeks back for her to be present for Elohl's return, to answer questions about his Goldenmarks. I've received word by raven that she's on her way. She'll need to take up residence in the palace. Will you arrange everything?"

Lhesher nodded curtly, all smiles gone. "That bitch is going to create a stir."

"Don't I know it." Therel scowled.

Lhesher stroked his stave, as if he wanted to hit this woman, whoever she was. "I'll select a detail to keep her in line."

"Nothing can keep her in line. Short of a beheading." Therel gave a bitter grimace.

"If only you could. But the gift comes to whom it comes."

Therel ground his jaw. Elyasin reached up to stroke his blonde scruff. "Whoever she is, if she interferes with me, I will beat her to a bloody pulp."

"You would, wouldn't you?" Therel grinned wide. "My sweetgrape has a nasty bite."

"Just give me a reason." Elyasin hefted her stave with a grin.

"Oh, she'll give you ten." Therel's face fell.

They walked towards their garments, Therel dismissing Lhesher with a flick of his fingers. The Highsword bowed away, collecting Elyasin's quarterstaff. As they arrived at the wash-area, Therel caught her around the waist, dipping his chin, kissing her upon her breastbone. "My warrior-Queen. What a fantastic woman you are! Inkings or no."

Elyasin laughed and wrangled him by the hair. They kissed, deep and long. A number of jeers and whistles wafted their way, though the Highlanders kept a respectful distance. Elyasin pushed Therel off teasingly, dipping a rag in the water-bucket.

"How old were you when you received your Inkings?" Elyasin began to sluice away sweat and dirt.

"I was fully Inked by the time I was nineteen." Therel stepped to her back and kissed her neck as she washed. "Merra had hers at seventeen. In the Highlands, we train hard, young, and Ink as soon as we're advanced."

Elyasin turned her head, so that they could kiss, then stepped away to wash her neck without Therel's intrusion. "That's not much of a childhood."

"Children don't stay children long here. Even ones who won't be Inked." His eyes remained pinned to her as she sluiced sweat away.

"How do you know which are which?"

"Aptitude tests. Fighting, intelligence, peacemaking ability, dreaming. Most children fail because of the dreaming. They have common dreams. Those who become Alrashemni have dreams of great battles, flying, life under the ocean, or dreams that twist and turn with magic."

"Magic?"

Therel lounged with arms crossed at the wall, though he was sober now, his pale eyebrows drawn in a line. "Magic-dreams. Like the one you're having about the white-haired woman. Dreams that repeat, or feel lifelike, or are tremendously vivid."

Elyasin straightened, sensing a dire mood had taken her husband. "Therel? Are you all right?"

His brows knit in a dark scowl. And then his gaze flicked to her, his smile twisting up in a cover of humor. "Didn't you know I used to have magic-dreams? Of painting sigils in blood upon the floor while wearing the pelt of a silver wolf, its teeth and claws dangling about my neck right next to my keshar-pendant. Of candles ringing my masterpiece, and laying you down in the middle of it all, fucking you rotten until all the braziers light from our heat and the crystals explode."

Elyasin blinked in astonishment, her wash-rag forgotten. "What?"

Humor faded from Therel's arctic eyes. He shuddered, then reached out for her. Brushing her tousled braid over her shoulder, his gaze was intense. He fished in his leather belt-pouch, then pulled out an object wrapped in white silk. Therel unwrapped the item with reverence, revealing a keshar-claw pendant upon a fine gold chain. Bone-white with a gilded tip, the claw was worked in sigils inlaid with gold, a twin of the one he wore in silver.

"I was going to give this to you later, but... now is the time, I think. It's a family heirloom. It's been sitting in a box for years. It passed from my grandmother to my mother, then to Merra, but she never wears it." Therel's brows furrowed. "You're supposed to have it. May I?"

"It's beautiful." Elyasin stroked the claw with one finger.

Therel lifted the chain up and placed the pendant around her neck, tucking the long claw gently beneath her sweaty halter. "In the circle, you were wearing it..."

Lifting it out of her halter to examine the ornate sigils, Elyasin blinked, comprehending. "In the circle? Your magic-dream with the sigils in blood? You actually dreamed that? Of us?"

Therel nodded, tried to grin, failed. "We were... somewhere under the earth. Fires raged around us. Towering crystals exploded." Therel swallowed, his next words a harsh rasp. "All of it inside a ring of Alranstones. Seven times seven crystal Alranstones. All their eyes were open, my love, and these," he touched his own pendant, "were burning with a heat I can't even begin to describe."

Elyasin stepped close, wrapping her arms about him, frowning. "When did you have this dream? Recently? Like my dreams of that woman?"

"No." Therel gave a bitter chuckle. "I have it every year. At Highsummer, and again at Darkwinter. Since I was seven."

"You've dreamed of me since you were *seven years old*?" Elyasin blinked. So much about Therel was suddenly clear. How he had looked at her from the moment they'd met. The electricity she felt between them, the intensity. The fierce heat, possessiveness, and vulnerability.

He'd been dreaming of her since he was seven years old.

"Every time, you're wearing that pendant, and nothing but that." Therel nodded, his voice rasping. But his brows furrowed again, and Elyasin knew he was holding back. She lifted up, kissing him upon the mouth. Therel returned her kiss, but his ardor was gone. Elyasin was about to ask him more, when Lhesher Khoum, fully clad and arrayed with his usual weapons, came barreling out of the palace doors.

"My King! My Queen!" Lhesher placed a swift palm to his chest. "A messenger has arrived from Alrou-Mendera!"

"Finally!" Therel pulled away. "What news?"

Lhesher cleared his throat. "My lieges, a young man has been sent to us from one of the Chancellors. He has a message for Queen

Elyasin personally. I was just informed that he was caught at the border and brought in by the Third Claws. They roughed him up, but he's a stubborn lad and threatened to set fire to his document with phosphor matches if they tried to take it. He's in the Gable Room, under guard."

Elyasin nodded curtly, reaching for her clothes. "Feed him something hearty. Give him water and telmen-wine. Show him courtesy. We will be there momentarily."

Lhesher nodded, then marched back through the doors. Therel turned to look at Elyasin, eyebrows raised, the storm of his dreams clearing. "What do you think your Chancellors want?"

Elyasin quickly donned her breeches, shirt, jerkin, and the rabbit-pelt she was becoming used to in the Highlands. She pulled on her tall leather boots with their knife-sheaths, doing up the last buckles. "Hopefully, they're suing for peace. But somehow, I don't think that's likely."

"Indeed." Therel extended his arm and Elyasin took it, and together they marched into the palace. It was a short way through the vaulted halls to the green silk-draped comfort of the Gable Room, a space of tall windows, bookshelves, and comfortable chaises used as a reading retreat. Elyasin knew the lad as Chancellor Theroun's scribe as soon as she stepped in the door. Sitting at a modest table with a meal spread upon it, the blonde bespectacled creature was her own age, but seemed far younger. Thaddeus jumped up the moment she and Therel entered, relief flooding his face.

"You're alive! Thank Aeon and all the gods!" Thad sank to his knees.

"Thaddeus!" Elyasin strode forward and laid her fingers upon his shoulder, urging him to rise. "Did someone feed you, Thad?"

"Most generously Dhen... I mean, my Queen." He gestured to a bowl of stew, wine carafe, and sweetmeats upon the table, cheeks flushed beneath his spectacles. He fished in his jerkin, dirtied and tattered from travel. Bruises sat upon one cheekbone, and he moved with hesitance, as if he'd been roughed up. Elyasin scowled, making a mental note to tell Therel's retainers that emissaries from Alrou-Mendera were not to be harmed. At last, Thaddeus produced a parchment, stained from sweat. He looked at it sheepishly as he handed it over.

"Forgive me, my Queen. We did not plan ahead as far as an oilcloth."

Elyasin waved her hand dismissively, scanning the document. Her eyes widened, and she drew a long breath. "Evshein and Lhaurent! Rudaric!" Her eyes flicked up to Thaddeus. "And Theroun himself? All Khehemni agents, in secret? Working together to take my throne?"

"So he said." Thaddeus nodded. "He is in grave danger, my Queen. He believes his alliance with the Khehemni is betraying him, and his life already at risk."

"Did you know of this? Did he ever speak of it?" Elyasin narrowed her eyes.

"No, my Queen." Thaddeus shook his head hastily, wide-eyed with fear. "The Chancellors were having a meeting of strategy. They nominated Chancellor Theroun as Counselor-General to the Elsthemi war front. But during that meeting, something in Theroun snapped. He took me out to the Kingswood that same night, wrote this, and then sent me to you."

Elyasin fiddled with her knuckles. She knew about Thad's talents. The lad had a memory of steel. He forgot nothing he looked at, nothing he read, nothing he heard. Theroun had sent her names of those Khehemni responsible for ousting her from her throne, but he had also sent her something vastly more valuable.

Thaddeus himself.

"Thad," Elyasin began. "Do you know why Theroun sent you to me?"

Thad must have seen something in her eyes, for he blushed, looked down, then up. "Because I've been present at the Chancellate meetings. Because I have information on what they're planning."

"You are far more than a parchment of names could ever be. The parchment was intended to get you here safely, with courage through any danger. You will tell us *everything* you have heard, at once. If you are well enough to do so."

"Yes, my Queen. My King." Thad nodded quickly, a spark of determination in his gaze.

Elyasin flicked her fingers at Lhesher. "See that this man is given every hospitality. He needs a room, proper garments and a hot bath once we are finished here. Any who threaten his safety make personal threat upon me. He is an honored guest of this house. Do I make myself clear?"

"My Queen." Lhesher set one hand to his heart, then left with a smart nod, two of Therel's other Highswords remaining in the room. Just as he left, a tray of foodstuffs was brought, elk stew and bread with butter and telmen-jam. Elyasin motioned it towards Thaddeus. The lad ate hastily, nodding his thanks, clearly having been ill-fed for weeks. At last, he slowed, and Elyasin cleared her throat.

"Are you well enough to stay some hours in council with my King and me, Thad?"

"Yes, my Queen." He gave a half-bow where he sat.

"Good. Then tell us everything you have heard in the Chancellate sessions since my attempted assassination. Leave nothing out."

It took some time. Thaddeus was detailed, recounting the hanging of the Elsthemi retainers, the declaration of war upon Elsthemen, session after session of planning movements at the front. And the fact that the Chancellate made only paltry efforts to find an heir to the throne. Elyasin gave him paper, and he wrote detailed lists of supply lines, and names of Captains, Battalions, Companies, and Generals involved.

"They have foreign men flocking to our banner," Thad spoke, writing out numbers of troops in various battalions. "I don't know how they've had such successful recruiting efforts abroad, but Jadounians, Perthians, and even men from Desh-Kar swell the ranks. Theroun estimated that the initial muster at your border will be fifteen thousand, but another fifteen thousand are currently training at the coast. Twenty thousand foreign troops were recently delivered to the Valenghian front, bringing the total numbers there up to sixty thousand, my Queen. But the Vhinesse has matched it, somehow. So the war upon the Aphellian Way and through the Long Valley are at the same stalemate as ever. But Alrou-Mendera has resources to send here to the Elsthemi border, should they need to."

Elyasin paled at such enormous movements of troops. She and Therel shared a long look. "Foreign recruits? The Chancellate have been recruiting among the Southrons for our wars?"

"Heavily, my Queen. Though Theroun wasn't certain the reports were accurate. Even before he was given his post as Counsel-General, he was eager to make a trip to the war-camp, and see for himself."

Elyasin paced before the roaring fireplace, furious, the wine goblet in her hand forgotten. "And you say that Chancellor Evshein leads *all* state proceedings?"

Thad nodded briskly from his seat. "Yes, my Queen. Since they declared an emergency State of Civil Right due to the war."

Elyasin glowered, her blood boiling with wrath. "When the royal line breaks, they are *supposed* to operate as a panel of equals, until such time as a suitable blood-heir is found! Are they even *looking* for an heir?"

Scarlet crept across Thad's cheeks. "It hasn't been mentioned. To be fair, my Queen, they're not entirely sure you are dead, though that's what they've told the nation. Some think you may be a captive."

Elyasin issued a very un-Queenlike curse, one of Alden's old favorites. She set her wine goblet down upon the table so hard it slopped. "Well, I'm clearly *not* a hostage. I am here because my Chancellors have been plotting behind my back!"

She heard an uncomfortable shuffling from Thaddeus, and it made her come back to herself. "Thaddeus. Forgive me. I am tired. Perhaps we should adjourn—"

"Forgive me, my Queen, but there is something else you, and milord the King, should hear," Thad interrupted before she could dismiss him. "It involves your keshari outriders, the hunting parties that secure game and forage herbs for the war-front." Taking his spectacles off and lipping them like a nervous horse, Thad's gaze darted to Therel. Though Thad's complexion was drawn, his visage was level and carried weight as his eyes returned to Elyasin.

His manner made Elyasin's hackles rise. "Continue, Thaddeus."

"I saw something up in the mountains, as I was crossing the border." Thad took a deep breath as a shiver rippled him. His gaze strayed long, his eyes haunted. "Something unexplainable. I had been riding five days up over the Kingsmount. I was dropping down, perhaps ten leagues from where the forest breaks to the northern part of the Lethian Valley, when I saw smoke through the trees. I knew I was in Elsthemi territory, and from my view upon a slight ridge, I saw it was a keshari camp below me, spread out in a clearing. They had game trussed up, draining, far more than their band of forty needed. I assumed they were supplemental hunters for the main army. I was making my way down a ridge to rendezvous, as Theroun had instructed, when something suddenly broke through the trees into the field. It... stunned me. I pulled my horses back, and hid behind a copse of aspens, watching."

Thad took a deep breath. Elyasin refilled his wine goblet, and he took a tremendous swallow. "My Queen. I don't even know how to describe what happened next. What broke into that clearing among the keshari and their cats was a horror I've never seen the like of. A massive man, dressed all in black woven leather armor, rode a battle-scorpion right into the keshari's midst."

"A what?" Therel stepped closer, his eyebrows lifting in incredulous alarm.

Thad met his gaze. "You may believe me addled from travel, but I know what I saw. That man rode a scorpion, thrice the size of any keshar and black as death, right into camp. The keshari erupted into battle, vaulting to their cats, but they were too slow. This man, he... he drew a massive two-handed longsword from his back. He guided his scorpion by no noticeable means, but it was as if they shared one mind, darting in, slicing, stinging. Cats were seized by the neck with those terrible pincers and crushed, tossed away like dead vermin. Men were stung, so fast it was a blur. And when an Elsthemi warrior would get too near, he... stalled them with a look or a gesture. Or sometimes he looked at them and their next blade-cut was across their own throat. One time he laughed, and pointed his sword at a knot of advancing warriors. They turned on each other, my Queen. Killed their arms-brothers and sisters to the last man. And when the carnage was done, not a single cat nor rider was left alive. He walked calmly through the dead, finding the injured and letting his scorpion savage them to finish them off. And then he let it... feast."

Thaddeus shuddered. Taking up his wine goblet, he drained it. "He didn't see me. I thank Aeon that my horses were stolid beasts. Neither of them bolted nor so much as whinnied to give my position away. I spent the night on that ridge, shivering in the cold, terrified he would come back. But when dawn came, there was no trace of him, though wolves and ravens had come to make a fair meal of everything left behind."

"Aeon and all the gods…" Therel's utterance was stunned. He moved close, staring at Thaddeus. "He decimated one of Merra's hunting parties? They're some of the most ferocious warriors we have."

"I have no doubt he was culling other outrider parties as well," Thad spoke low. "When he rode in to battle he had… hair. Scalped hair in reds and coppers and Highlander blonde… braided together as decorative fringe along his scorpion's claws and stinger. As I watched him finish off the dead, he took more. Not all of them, just certain colors from warriors who had given him the most resistance in the fight. He took the time to braid it in among the rest, before he departed."

"Halsos' hells." Therel set a clenched fist upon the table.

Elyasin was stunned. Her mind raced, examining every angle of this terror. "Has this man been seen in the Elsthemi camp?"

"No, my Queen." Thad shook his head. "When I described him to the riders of Clan Keth Malek that finally found me, they had not seen him upon the plain, nor in any of the skirmishes your forces have been sending to harry the Menderian camp and test their defenses."

"Do you know for certain whether he was aligned with the Menderian forces?" Therel asked.

"No, my King." Thad shook his head. "He wore no discernible Menderian armor nor pins of military rank. But from his actions, the man either has a severe grudge against your nation, or he's been called in by someone to aid the Menderian military, killing off your Elsthemi support system quietly. Eliminating your extra food and herbal medical supplies. Trimming your army. And he enjoyed doing it, my King. His smile had a dominant twist to it, and his visage shone with pleasure to have killed, and taken those trophies. He knelt by some of the dead, traced a sigil upon their foreheads and spoke words, almost like a benediction. Some part of me thought him a monk that he made such adulations, but what man of the cloth would enjoy such carnage?"

Thaddeus lipped his spectacles, then rubbed a tired hand across his face. He blinked hard, as if he'd not gotten much sleep since that event. Elyasin stood, rounding the table and setting a kind hand upon the lad's shoulder.

"Thad. Thank you for this information. You have done well, protecting your country. Please go and rest. Therel and I have much to discuss. Attend us for breakfast tomorrow. I have more I wish to ask you, but rest first, and recover your strength."

"My Queen." Theroun's scribe stood with a tired heaviness, giving a low bow. He departed the chamber, followed by a Highsword.

Elyasin glanced to Therel. His fists were pressed to the table, and he stared at the wood with vicious eyes, his jaw set and a vein pulsing in his temple. He gave a soft snarl, then looked up. "Some of Merra's outriders have seen men of that description in the mountains these past few years. Always in bands of two or three, but riding horses, not some beast of legend. They vanish when they're looked upon, leaving no trail. Many Elsthemi don't even remember they saw a man in black herringbone weave armor until much later. I've had parties of outriders slain by them before, but never in such number or by just one man. Merra and I never knew their purpose in the mountains. But now it seems likely they've been working for the Khehemni."

"Perhaps," Elyasin mused, "or perhaps it's something recent that brings them into alignment with the Menderian forces. Gods, Therel, what kind of man could cause keshari riders to slit their own throats?"

"Someone with a powerful mind-bending *wyrria.*" Therel fingered the silver claw pendant around his neck. "And if someone is harrying our border with that ability, then I must impress upon you, Elyasin. *Do not* take your pendant off, waking or sleeping. They protect against such thought-invasion. I would not see my wife bleeding red from having slit her own throat."

Therel stepped to Elyasin, clasping her about the waist. His eyes were haunted as he gave her a chaste kiss, then wrapped her in his arms, pulling her close to his chest. He made no move to step from their embrace, only let it linger. Elyasin relaxed into his warmth, nuzzling her face into his neck. "Will such a man cause havoc on the battlefield?"

"No." Therel smoothed her hair back from her neck, kissing her below her earlobe. "I'll send word to the front to be on the lookout. Have Merra bring this man down by archers from a safe distance. Almost all mind-benders need to be close to their victims for their *wyrria* to take effect."

"You sound like you've had personal dealings with such."

"I have." Therel gave a hard sigh. Then spoke again, seductive, his breath at her ear. "I need a break. Perhaps a bath. We have facilities for bathing below the palace, and you've not seen them yet with your healing wound. Would you like to come get naked with me? In public?"

Elyasin's eyebrows rose, her brooding interrupted. Despite the heaviness of the afternoon's revelations, a laugh escaped her. "You are quite the wild wolf, aren't you?"

"Always. That's why you love me." He pulled back and grinned, part of him a cocky raven.

"I do love you." Elyasin reached up, stroking his blonde stubble, watching those wolf-wild eyes. Her fingers found the silver chain around his neck, pulling out his keshar claw. "What does it mean, Therel? Your dream? This connection I feel, ever since we first locked eyes? This terrible situation we find ourselves in with our nations, despite all this passion between us?"

Therel lifted her fingers from the talisman. "If you come with me to the Heat Pools, I'll tell you a story that may shed illumination. A tale of wild northern magic to distract us from warfare for a little while. Come. You know you want to..."

Elyasin laughed. She nodded, and Therel kissed her, then escorted her out of the room and through the hall, then down a set of spiral stone stairs. Deep in the bowels of the palace, they came to a set of white stone doors, through which steam leaked. Pushing through, Elyasin found herself in a massive underground hall, filled with red cendarie tubs set into the white bedrock with cendarie walkways between. Bare Highlanders lounged everywhere, soaking away stress and worry. Steam curled through the air, moving with currents in the humid space. Ivy and hanging mosses twined the walls, illuminated by skylights in the walls that let in the last of the day's light.

349

Elyasin gaped. It was paradise beneath Lhen Fhekran. And at the center of it all, a massive Alranstone of pure crystal stood wreathed in steam, standing like a silent watcher in the mist. On the far southern wall, just visible through the humidity, Elyasin could see an enormous vaulted alcove of bedrock. Inside the alcove sat a door that towered as high as the Alranstone, made of a rosy quartz blushed through with veins of white smoke. Onyx and gold and white star-metal sigils decorated the entirety of its surface, swirled in vast, unintelligible patterns that surrounded arcane runes. And though lichens and mosses creeped over every other surface of the massive underground hall, that door was pristine, untouched by time.

With a chuckle, Therel took Elyasin's hand, leading her to a set of benches where men and women were disrobing. "Fhekran palace is built upon natural hot springs. It's open to all travelers. Though you won't get told about it unless you're a friend of the Highlands. How about that Alranstone, huh?"

"It's enormous," Elyasin spoke. "And crystal? Does it work? Does the door work? Where does it lead?"

Therel gave a rolling laugh. He shook his head. "That Stone and the door have never worked. No one knows what they're for, or where that door leads. No one's ever been able to travel out of Fhekran Palace, though Aeon knows people have tried. The Stone is inert. No one ever feels any tingle around it. Though old wives will tell you that these springs have special healing properties, an old magic about them that the Stone influences. Who can say? For me, it's just a relaxing place to work out difficult thoughts."

Therel kissed her, then pulled her toward a wooden rack filled with clothing, weapons, and boots. Soon, they were disrobed, just as naked as everyone else, relaxing in three feet of searing water in a cedrunne tub that smelled of sulphur and winterbloom. Elyasin's gaze roved the hall, seeing every age of person from the very young to the very old. But the Highland elderly had eyes sharp as hawks and twice as deadly, their skin tired but their muscles still roped beneath. Elyasin's eyes tracked one old woman with black Inkings and straight white hair to her waist. As she swished that hair over one shoulder to get in a tub, keshar-claw marks were plain in stripes down her back.

"That's Zhenaya Khehim." Therel followed her gaze. "She's older than dirt, but don't try arm-wrestling her. She once held Merra's position, High General of the Keshari, under my grandfather, Bhorn. She still rides a keshar named Yirghi. Near-toothless but still devoted to his rider." Therel grinned, his eyes sparkling. "You think Merra loves her men? There are rumors about General Khehim. That she would take five men at a time to her rooms and all would leave exhausted in the morning. But she'll clap your ears if you even so much as hint at it."

Elyasin smiled, bruises and tension of the day seeping out of her. "Sounds like you know from experience."

"I tried to woo her when I was fifteen." Therel sniggered. "On a dare from Merra. General Khehim beat me bloody at the end of a stave, in front of my father. I deserved every bruise. He called me disgraceful, to attempt to demean such a decorated Highlander. He was absolutely right."

Zhenaya Khehim turned, saw them looking, and saluted with a gnarled but still strong-looking hand to her Inkings. Therel nodded, his own hand to his Inkings. She settled into the tub across from theirs and leaned her head back upon the rim, eyes closing.

"Therel…"

"Mmmm?" He glanced over, wolf-eyes serene.

"You knew we would marry, didn't you? Because of your dream."

"No." He smiled, almost shy. "I never knew what those dreams meant. Not until I finally saw you a few weeks ago. All these years our kingdoms have been allies, and yet you and I never actually met." He chuckled, blushing. "It was all I could do to not run to you. To bury myself in your kiss the first time I stepped into your presence."

Elyasin ran her finger lazily through a puddle of water at the rim of the pool, smiling. "When you spoke to me of grapevines that first time we conversed, were you thinking of that dream? Of me, naked…beneath you?"

"Vixen." Therel gathered her into his arms, kissing her neck. "In that dream, I feel every inch of you. Every rumble of your power, every searing brand of your fire, milady. And when we met, I felt it all anew. That dream came alive for me the moment I saw your eyes, your face. And I knew, I *knew*... we were supposed to be together."

But he gave a sigh then, sad. "My First Sword Devresh Khir served my father before me, and he was a good man. I learned woodcraft and tracking from him. I can't imagine what made Devresh do what he did. But when Elohl slit him open, I wanted it to be me behind that blade. I wanted to have Devresh's guts in my fist for even *attempting* to hurt you."

His eyes flicked up, viciously blue. "You mean more to me than a man I've known my *entire* life, Elyasin. I've loved you since I was seven. I've lusted after you. I took my dreams to Vhensa when she was still alive, and Vhensa said they were portents, strong ones. She said it *will* come to pass. Somehow." Therel stroked a finger down her cheek, and Elyasin shivered. "Somehow you and I will wind up in a ring of seven stones, each with seven eyes. And when we do... the world will light with our fires, and explode with our power."

Elyasin took a deep breath. "And what about the blood?"

His eyes took on a deeper cast, dangerous. "In the wild, there is always blood. In the Highlands, blood is the way and the sacrifice." Therel stroked her scar, below the water.

"Therel, who is Adelaine?"

He flinched, their deep moment broken. "Adelaine Visek was a mistake."

"A conquest of yours?"

"A lover, yes." Therel sighed. "In my youth I was not... entirely up-front about not wishing to make her my Queen. It was ugly. I asked her to leave the palace."

"And Martin?"

"Martin was her brother." He grimaced. "I ran him through. And I would do it again. He sent that assassin after me. A *gift*, he said. A pretty young thing to take my mind off the trouble with his sister. I believe he did it by Adelaine's command, but I couldn't prove it. Martin used to bow to Adelaine, in everything."

"Therel." Elyasin murmured. "Might Martin and Adelaine have been Khehemni?"

He blinked at her, then furrowed his brow. "Their family has been loyal for generations."

"So was your First Sword."

Therel's mouth shut. He stared off at nothing for a long moment. "I will consider it. But until we have proof, I can do little. Adelaine is a bitch, but she's the most talented Dremor we have. And you, my love, need to have your dream evaluated by the best. But I won't leave you alone with her."

Therel pulled Elyasin close, kissing her sweat-streaked waves. "No one should ever be left alone with Adelaine."

CHAPTER 24 – OLEA

It was a long, terrifying race to the center of Oasis Khehem. Holes opened again and again in the avenues, and Olea and Lourden's group skirted them, running hard for fountains sometimes blocks away. Even so, four of Lourden's *Rishaaleth* were lost. One was crushed when she slipped into a hole that opened and just as suddenly closed, pinning her through the middle. Another tried to vault a rift and missed his mark as it widened, cracking his head as he fell thirty feet into an ancient cistern flowing with black, viscous water. And two fell into a hole that opened right beneath them, a bottomless black pit that swallowed all light. Olea had bit her hand to keep from crying as their screams faded out to nothing.

An endless fall that terminated nowhere.

Lourden was terse in their fourth hour of running, his face drawn, pushing their party faster toward the center of Khehem. Sweat-streaked and tiring, Vargen, Jherrick, and Aldris were grim. Lost to grief, conversation among the party had died. At last, they rounded a corner and the sand-strewn Khehemni palace causeway opened up before them. At the other end of the war-plaza encircled by colonnaded arches, the palace rose, unblemished by time, unmarred by scorch. As if this part of Khehem was still protected by long-lost magic, the turrets and domes and latticed stone were white and pristine, throwing the sun's rays in a dazzling display the rest of the ruined city could not match.

Racing across the plaza, they made for a grand fountain in the center of the promenade. Vaulting the fountain's rim, they splashed into calf-high water. The fountain was five times the size of any they'd yet sheltered in, a writhing statue of an alabaster dragon curling around a fighting wolf filling the center of the structure. Around the fighting duo, sylvan women and men watched, beckoning to the pair as if the battle filled them with ecstasy.

One spout still issued water, from a maiden's teats as she

writhed upon her back, laid out in an erotic pose back over the dragon's muscled hind-thigh. Aldris cast back his hood, dousing his head and filling his mouth from the maid's abundance. The rest moved in also, filling flasks, dousing heads, scrubbing faces to cast off sweat. Some of the *Rishaaleth* laid down in the chalk-thick water in the bowl, soaking their garb while they held knives and spears out above their heads.

Olea wet her *shouf* and hair, filled her flask, then allowed others in. Taking deep drinks, she let down her wet curls so the afternoon wind could air them. Gazing around at the plaza during the respite, she saw buttressed columns and soaring arches, all carven to resemble snarling beasts and fighting men.

It was a place of war. A place of strength, even though the beauty of crafting sated the eye at every turn. Unlike the Ghellani's lovely city that sported images of abundance and restfulness, Khehem was a place of brutal artistry. Olea glanced over to see Jherrick standing alone at the rim of the fountain, his gaze faraway as he took in the center of the city. Since people had begun to die, Jherrick had been silent, brooding more than the rest today.

This place weighed on him most of all. This horrible city was the legacy of his people. Olea moved over to him, settled to a seat upon the fountain's rim. "How are you?"

Jherrick looked over. His smile was pained. "How am I supposed to be, seeing the origin of my people? Seeing how… bloodthirsty… they were. Everything in this place speaks of death. Of conflict. War." His gaze strayed, and his chest rose and fell in a heavy breath.

Olea took Jherrick in, the square of his shoulders, the way he stood tall, facing it like a warrior. "It bothers you, doesn't it?"

He glanced over. "Death doesn't sit lightly upon me, Captain."

"I don't think it sits lightly on anyone." Olea saw Aldris nearby. He was watching them, leaning against the haunches of the wolf. He didn't have a hand to his weapons, only his arms crossed, a thoughtful frown on his face. Olea could see Aldris' mind churning, trying to make sense of Jherrick.

Jherrick followed her gaze and gave a soft laugh, though it had sad notes to it. "I think the Second-Lieutenant hates me."

Olea shook her head, locking eyes with Aldris a long moment.

"No." Olea spoke at last. "He's just thinking. Aldris is hot-headed, not stupid. He sees you, trying to be a better man. I believe you can be. So Aldris is trying to figure out why you give a damn, and why I'm giving you a chance."

"Are you sure you want to give me a chance?" Jherrick asked, turning from Aldris to lean upon his elbows at the rim of the fountain.

"I already have." Olea crossed her arms, gazed out at the terrible, beautiful plaza. "I know who you were in the guardhouse, Corporal. I believe that generous person is in there, that he's a part of you just as much as this version I'm seeing now. Maybe you've been living two lives this whole time. Two lives, unreconciled."

"I have been." Jherrick's voice was soft. He gazed down at his hands, watching them in the play of sunlight off the water. "I feel like I've never really known who I am."

"Maybe it's time to give yourself a chance," Olea reached out to set a hand upon Jherrick's shoulder. "Maybe it's time to let that duality die, Jherrick. Time for you to be resurrected, as the man you want to become, rather than the shadows you've been."

Jherrick glanced up. His eyes were tight, red-rimmed. "How do I do that? How do I unmake all that I've become?"

Something broke inside Olea. Jherrick was too young to carry such terrible misery. In a wash of fierce care, she gripped him by his shoulder and swung him around into an embrace. He gripped her, desperation in his posture. Jherrick gulped a breath, and Olea knew he was trying not to break.

Gripping the back of his head, she pressed their foreheads together. "You don't unmake where you've been. You remake it, into where you're going. Choose your best self, Jherrick, every hour of every day. Be that, and the destiny of who you are will find you. It comes out, from within. You have a good heart, Jherrick. Follow it."

He hitched a hard breath, nodded. Olea released her grip, steadied him by the shoulders. Jherrick wiped his face with his thumb and forefinger, until at last he could meet her gaze. Bright pain shone in that young face. Anguish.

But there was hope, too.

"Thank you." He rasped.

"Anytime." Olea smiled. "Let's just get through today, ok? I need you on point, Guardsman. Can you do that for me?"

Jherrick heaved a breath through pursed lips, then nodded.

"Good." Olea clapped him on the shoulders, then turned away. Her gaze met Aldris, still watching from the fountain. She didn't know if he was in earshot, but it seemed likely. Aldris' blonde eyebrows had drawn into a line, but it was his thinking face, not his pissed face. Olea left Jherrick at the fountain's rim and stepped over to her Second-Lieutenant.

"How's the kid?" Aldris asked, as if he truly did want to know the answer.

"Not good." Olea was frank. "He's seeing the truth of a bitter legacy, Aldris."

"He's got battle-shock," Aldris commented, turning his head to watch Jherrick moving back to refill his flask.

"He's seen too much behind the walls of Roushenn," Olea murmured. "And now he's seeing even more here. The cruelty of Lhaurent plus the terrible history of his people... watch him for me, ok? I'm worried about him."

Aldris held her gaze. Olea expected some nasty quip, but yet again, her Second-Lieutenant surprised her with his frank calm. "You really believe in him, don't you, Olea?"

Olea watched Jherrick filling his flask, watched him splash his tears away under the maid's founts. "He's hurting, Aldris. He's trying to be a man, but he doesn't know what kind of man he is. But the very fact that he's hurting, that he's twisting trying to figure it out... means he has a heart. A good one. He's been used as a spy, manipulated, but I don't believe that's what he aspires to be. So watch him for me, will you? Do your Aeon-damned job for once and stop being a righteous prick. Protect the innocent."

Aldris' lips were turning up in a smile, a humorous light in his green eyes at last. "Kid's no fucking innocent, Olea."

"No. Because someone used him hard far too young."

The smile was wiped from Aldris' face. His gaze strayed to Jherrick, watching the kid with sympathy now. "We all got used far too fucking young, didn't we? Fuck this bullshit. Fuck the Khehemni and the Alrashemni, ruining all our fucking lives..."

And from the way he said it, Olea knew Aldris was once again her good left hand. She clapped him on a shoulder, then turned away. Approaching Lourden, who rested against the dragon's neck by Vargen, she gave him a nod. He nodded back, taking up his spear where it leaned in a fork between the dragon's talons.

"Ready?" Lourden asked, his gaze flicking to Jherrick, then Aldris.

"They're ready to go." Olea confirmed. "Are you?"

Lourden gave a bitter smile. "No. But a man goes whether he is ready or not. *Fhekktir!*" He barked, summoning his *Rishaaleth* with a wave of his spear. "*Andiiste!*"

But his First-Spear, Jhennah, moved forward suddenly and planted her spear in the water. "*Ih tannaa. Gheme hehlia ahwei.*" She came to one knee, setting a palm to her heart. Olea knew that look of pleading in Jhennah's eyes. As one, the remaining *Rishaaleth* took a knee behind her, bowing their heads with a hand to their hearts.

Olea's gut twisted. She didn't need to know what Lourden spoke as he held a short conversation in Khourek with Jhennah. The hearts of their guides were broken from losing so many today, and the *Rishaaleth* would go no further.

Lourden turned to her with apology in his eyes. "I will not force them to their deaths. Jhennah and the others wish to remain here, to stand as sentry for us until we return."

Olea gave a soft nod. She placed a palm to her heart, honoring them for doing as much as they had. The *Rishaaleth* saluted with spears across their chests as they rose, but only Jhennah could look Olea in the eyes. Before their party could leave, Jhennah handed her spear to Lourden, to replace the one he'd lost. Lourden received it with a sad wisp of smile. He beckoned with Jhennah's spear, vaulting from the fountain. Olea whistled for her men, and they did the same.

The jog to the palace was not a great distance, though all were wary as they ran the short minute through the rest of the grand plaza. But the silence held as the party finally approached a filigreed stone sun-shield at the great palace ingress. Carven to resemble a waterfall with a curtain of tumbling mist, the sun-shield was a wonder of artistry. In the center of the waterfall blazed a tremendous sun, surrounding the stylized wolf and dragon fighting in an ever-balance. The alabaster stone was carven to the perfection of frosted lace, every detail of the two snarling beasts unmarred by weather or time.

Behind that, the doors of the palace lay. And though the sun-shield had not been disturbed, the true palace entrance had been blasted into oblivion. Timbers rotted by time and flaked with ancient paint lay scattered, humped runnels of sand behind them. Towering lintel-stones were cracked and broken, leaning upon each other and restricting the entrance. Olea ducked beneath one after Lourden, stepping into a murky, dusty darkness silent as tombs.

Nothing moved. Olea held her breath, letting her eyes adjust in the gloom. A thin beam of noontide sunlight from an oculus dome far above was the only light, shining down upon them and choked with swirling dust. Lourden stepped toward a complicated series of pulleys set in one wall, moving a few. A horrid groan came from up above, then shrieks like metal grinding.

Suddenly, the beam of sunlight from the oculus was reflected into the murky darkness. Bouncing off a series of elevated mirrors, it illuminated a vast royal entry hall bright as day. Olea glanced up to see a wide, shallow mirror-disc suspended twenty feet up, reflecting light to the other mirrors.

"They used mirrors?" Olea stepped forward, awed.

"All the palaces of the Tribes have these," Lourden nodded, joining her, "for halls without windows or glass domes. For the rest, I have flint, steel, and oil. We may find torches as we go. Last time we came, there were some, and they burned well."

Olea stepped forward into vast opulence. Magnified twenty-fold in the grand entrance hall, the light illuminated arches and columns, dry fountains and blasted-out doorways. An alabaster floor spread before them, inlaid with curls of gold that made sigils and script. Friezes of glass tiles decorated every wall and column, with blues so vibrant they seemed to run like water, and yellows so bright they shone like the sun. Every surface was tiled, where it had not been marred by damage. Godly creatures stared down from buttressed domes. Lions with wings, serpents with claws and powerful appendages. Women and men fair of face and dark of hair, spearing ferocious beasts of legend. Angelic realms, where all was paradise and feasting and wine.

"Aeon and all the gods..." Vargen's slow sigh echoed through the magnificent space.

"I think all the gods are here. And Aeon, too." Aldris

commented with a chuckle.

Olea stepped to one column, brushing her fingers over the tiles, feeling how tight and impeccable their joins were. "The Khehemni must have been incredible craftsmen."

"From all the stories, they were," Lourden commented. "Oasis Khehem was the jewel of the Thirteen Tribes, with a wealth of water, spices, crops, arts, creativity, and prosperity. Until King Ordeith Alodwine, grandfather of Leith the Red."

They walked forward through the magnificent entry hall, gazing at every niche and corner. Despite the magnificence, evidence of the war was plain here. Stone benches had been exploded into ruin, scorch blasted a number of the columns, their tiles exploded away. And bleached bones decorated every crevice where wind gathered the sand.

They followed the grand entry hall, until it narrowed through a blasted-out arch into a smaller corridor. The tiled friezes continued high above and upon the walls, Olea saw, as Lourden adjusted another pulley with a screech to capture the light. The spectacular tableaux were at odds with the ruin of statuary and benches, urns and bones. Corridors branched off the main hall at intervals and led off into darkness. Now and then, Lourden would stop and adjust a mirror, lighting the hall once more as the beam bounced away.

"King Ordeith?" Olea prompted, after a long silence from Lourden.

"He was a tyrant. A warlord." Lourden continued, scanning the shadows, his spear ready. "He forced trade with five of his neighbors, invading them, breaking a longstanding balance between the Tribes. He sent heads of Alrahel negotiators over walls during sieges, kidnapped women and sent them home with Khehemni babes in their bellies. He enslaved those he invaded. Part of why Khehem became so mighty, why you see the works you do here."

"King Ordeith used slave labor." Vargen growled.

"Yes." Lourden peered around a corner. But still, nothing around them moved, and he walked on after a breath. "Slaves built this palace. The Maitrohounet once said messages are found in the tiles. Prayers to overthrow King Ordeith. Images of gods the slaves prayed to, and their animals of power."

"Did it help?"

Lourden shook his head. "Not for over a hundred years. King Ordeith's reign eventually fell to his son, a weak man. But when he took the throne, before young Leith could take power, who was the very image of his grandfather, the *Alrashemnari* banded together and trapped the boy, forcing his father to surrender."

"What happened then?" Olea asked.

"The Order of Alrahel took over rule of Khehem. There was peace for hundreds of years as the Order ruled the Oases, and created the Union of the Sun Tribes. But long-lived Leith eventually escaped his prison, rallied Khehem. He made war upon the Oases, trying to rid them of the Order. You have heard the rest from our Maitrohounet, of how badly that all went wrong. Of how Leith's Queen betrayed him, and how Khehem became ruined like you see it now." Lourden gestured at another pile of bones in an alcove, scattered in a drift of white sand.

The corridor they were walking suddenly opened up into a grand hall of stone and tiling, lit by tall windows and domed skylights. Vaulted ceilings arched above, columns in four rows marching down the cavernous space, once a grand receiving-hall. Colored glass windows down both sides of the hall depicted bloody scenes of battle, of prowess in the dunes. Alcoves along the front held bone-dry fountains snarling with dragon heads and fighting wolves. Statues of men in crested helms and full battle-regalia pointed spears at the ingress, as if to warn any guest. The paint upon the statues was still vivid, with crimson helm-crests, white and crimson geometric borders upon their loa-armor and saffron-bordered white tunics underneath. Lapis decoration coiled the boots and gauntlets of the spearmen, and as Olea stepped closer, she saw they were dragons.

"Over here." Jherrick's voice echoed in the hall. Olea glanced over, to see him pointing at an unobtrusive alabaster arch. "Servant's passages."

Olea stepped over, the rest of the group gathering in the alcove as well. "Like Roushenn. You think they'll access a behind-the-palace?"

"If there is one, yes." Jherrick nodded. "From what we've seen already, I'm betting so."

Jherrick slid his hands over the smooth stone. His hands

stopped, and he pressed a small catch in a divot carven with a tiny sigil. The door sighed back, opening to plain passages. Jherrick filed in, then Olea, Lourden and Vargen, with Aldris bringing up the rear.

It was dark in the passage, bereft of light from the mirrors. A chill breath of air moved around them from caverns unknown, causing Olea to shiver in her thin desert garb. Jherrick moved off down the passage, instructing them to trail their fingers upon the left wall. They walked on for a minute, single-file, Olea feeling emptiness occasionally as branches came off the passage, burrowing further into darkness.

Jherrick suddenly made a pleased sound, and halted. "Torches. Here."

Jherrick pressed an object toward Olea. She reached out, feeling a smooth glass rod. But the downy material wrapped at the end was dry, despite its crumbling. She passed the torch back to Lourden, who soon had it lit. Three more were in the bracket, and Jherrick collected them all, handing them back.

"Just one, for now." Lourden cautioned, before Aldris could light another from the first. "We do not know how long we travel, or how many such as this are left."

Nodding, Jherrick accepted the lit torch back, then continued on. They walked in silence down a few turns, into dead-ends, ancient storehouses for the palace with desiccated shelves and barrels. One held rotted sacks gone to mold, another ornate furnishings piled atop each other and weathered with dust, yet another was packed with shelves of rotting scrolls, heaped in a haphazard fashion. But Jherrick continued on, from room to room, thoughtfully silent.

"What are you looking for?" Olea ventured at last.

He glanced back. "I'll know it when I see it. Whoever built Roushenn had a similar style to this place, a similar knowledge. But we're still in servant's areas, not a true Hinterhaft." Suddenly, Jherrick halted, peering down a side passage. He stepped in, raising his torch, gazing at the gables, the vaulting. He peered at the sparse ribbons of tiny tiles, colors inlaid just like at Roushenn, indicating in which directions storerooms and kitchens and quarters lay.

Jherrick stepped up to one ribbon of inlay, pulling the torch close. And then Olea saw it. Next to the ribbon of gold, indicating the direction of the throne room, there was another ribbon of inlay embedded, thin and white like the alabaster stone. It was so well-joined in the original stone, and so close of color, that Olea would have missed it had she not been squinting at it from inches away.

Jherrick liberated his borrowed longknife, and ran it over his thumb. He pressed the welling blood to the line. Blood seeped into the line and began to flow along it, like ink wicking through water painted upon paper. Red tendrils curling through the thin white line, it drank Jherrick's blood until the line glowed crimson, stretching away down a corridor to their left.

As the line blossomed, sigils suddenly began to appear along it. Some of which, Olea recognized from the Alranstones.

"Here. This." Jherrick tapped the sigil-encrusted line, his finger indicating one sigil in particular, a crimson pyramid beneath a crown of red stars, underscored by a bloody river. "These sigils indicate access to the Hinterhaft, and various rooms within. And this one, the pyramid, may lead to the control room. I always saw this around the area I couldn't access. That massive space walled off at the heart of Roushenn. It was marked by a pyramid between a river and stars."

"So how do we get in?" Vargen rumbled.

"If it's like Roushenn, there should be a pivot-wall." Jherrick flicked a look at Vargen. "Spies like myself always entered by pre-set entrances where the walls would pivot or slide back. Lhaurent set them so he wouldn't have to monitor everyone's coming and goings. But there were only five access-points in the entire palace."

"Great." Aldris sagged against the passage, arms crossed, glowering. "Just fabulous. Shall we go make a feast of those moldy sacks, then? Might have been wheat once. We could bake some bread while we search this whole fucking place for one damn pivot-wall."

Olea glanced at Aldris and he shut his trap. She looked down the bloody line, then gestured to Jherrick. "After you."

He nodded, somehow understanding that because his blood had illuminated the sigils, he was now officially their lead. Jherrick moved off down the corridor, following the crimson line. After thirty paces, the blood faded, and Jherrick pressed his cut thumb to the line again. It flared, drinking his blood like wine, and the line raced off down a black stairwell.

They continued down, Jherrick refreshing the line at intervals. And when Olea was convinced she was utterly lost in the twisting labyrinth, the crimson line suddenly came to a halt in an arched alcove of an ancient catacomb. The wall before them was blank. There was no door, no sigils. Jherrick moved forward, pressing his bloody thumb to the bare wall, but nothing happened, no crimson adornment appeared.

Olea's heart sank. She was about to tell the group to take a rest, when she suddenly felt a tug upon her belt, coming from her leather purse. She blinked, hauling the white pouch with the clockworks out from her belt-purse, then stood close to the wall again, wide-eyed.

The pouch twitched, tugging towards the wall.

"Take them out." Vargen moved up next to her, his eyebrows lifting.

Olea opened her silk pouch, dumping the clockwork contents into her palm. Which immediately flew toward the wall, assembling as they went. With a clack and a clatter, they created a perfect rectangular piece just as Elohl had described in Vargen's workshop, with a sun of gold in the center and spokes radiating outward. It flipped before it hit the wall, and Olea heard it latch into place, right in the center of the alcove, where a piece had recessed to form a receptacle for it.

And there it sat, waiting.

"Damn me to Aeon's halls!" Vargen breathed. "I knew those clockworks had magic."

"Should I touch it?" Olea glanced at him.

"It might be dangerous. Allow me." Vargen reached out, covering the rectangle of assembled pieces in his meaty hand. Sliding his fingers over it, he tried to turn it, then to pull it from the wall. But despite his efforts, the piece did not move.

He shrugged, stepping back. "Elohl found it, did he not? If it fell apart for him, and went back together for you…"

"Then perhaps I should try."

Olea stepped forward, her fingers sliding over the assembly. It shivered beneath her touch, and then promptly turned without her assistance. A click sounded, somewhere deep in the wall. The wall slid back with an aching groan. The clockwork flew off the door and flashed ahead into a cavernous darkness. Olea stepped forward, feeling the expansive pressure of an enormous space as she crossed the threshold. A black wind sighed around the space, chilling Olea's skin and raising goosebumps. Jherrick slid in, raising his torch high. The light touched nothing, neither ceiling nor walls nor adornment of any kind. Only an endless alabaster stone floor, and a wall behind them that seemed to disappear into infinity. Jherrick beckoned with his torch, and everyone stepped forward, lighting their own.

Even then, the light could not penetrate the darkness.

Aldris' whistle was unmistakable as it died on the air. "Where in seven fucks are we?"

"The center of what lies beneath." Jherrick's murmur was nearly lost to the cavernous black. "This is where all my knowledge ends."

The five of them hesitated at the threshold. The darkness seemed thick, like something watched them, like a presence occupied the entirety of that tremendous space. Something vast and old, something that slumbered but was not dead, something that lived and ate lives.

Something that breathed with *wyrria* so vast, it made the hairs on Olea's neck stand up straight.

"Be on your guard," she warned, "there's something in here with us."

"Yeah, no shit." Aldris' words were tense. "This place makes me want to turn tail and piss myself."

"Whatever answers we're looking for," Jherrick murmured, "they'll be here."

"Better hope you're right, kid." Aldris shot him a glance, squared his shoulders. "Better hope you are so fucking right..."

Aldris stepped forward. Olea summoned her courage and stepped after him, raising her torch high, drawing one longknife. The rest of the party set into motion at their backs, moving into the cavernous space away from the arched doorway.

They had hardly taken five steps before the darkness suddenly convulsed around them. Like a massive roll of thunder, a boom echoed through the chamber, ricocheting off the walls and floor, shattering the thick silence. It rippled across Olea's skin, it beat her eardrums. It lifted her wrap and tugged it like a roaring wind.

"Down!" Jherrick's bellow was nearly lost to the roar, but Olea heard it. Dropping her torch, she dragged Aldris to his knees next to her. Something massive sliced the air where their heads had been. A shriek of grinding metal, of gears long unused. And then it was gone, like a beast of legend taken wing.

The floor began to heave.

Like the tumbling of an earthquake, pillars of stone thrust to the sky. Rising at random from the floor, pillars shot up like stomping boulders. Olea's party rolled and jumped to avoid being crushed with shouts of alarm. Rumbling split the air, but Olea was lost in a labyrinth of heaving columns slamming to the blackness above. Trying to find a pattern, she darted forward rather than turn back. Stone beneath her soft boots heaved, and she was already rolling, off the thrusting plinth. Landing upon her feet, she dodged another upthrust, swerved around yet another.

Suddenly, Jherrick was at her side, then Aldris.

"Run! There!" Jherrick beckoned toward a motionless space far ahead. Olea and Aldris dashed for it, keeping eyes on that spot through the thrusting columns. Aldris was suddenly thrown into the air. He twisted like a cat, landing upon his feet, running on. Olea's left foot upheaved. She rolled right, regaining her feet. A column crashed up, knocking Jherrick in the shoulder. He cried out, blood pouring from a wound, but he clutched it and ran, eyes fixed upon the unmoving section.

Olea took the lead, not knowing who followed. Her lungs split at her mad dash. The area ahead held a soft glow of light, a beacon for her intent. She pressed speed, lungs burning. Lourden was at her left, dashing for the light, Aldris on his heels. But the light ahead was fractured, bouncing off humped dark piles that obscured a massive glimmer of crystal. Olea thought she could make out the glint of metal, of swords and buckles in those piles. Dark armor. And the parts which were not armor were flesh. Twisted, parchment-dry...

Olea skidded to a halt, realizing what she was seeing.

Bodies. Thousands of desiccated bodies, heaped in a wall like cordwood.

"Go!" A shove moved her, Jherrick. Olea's trance was broken. She was fast on his heels, running toward the horror she now realized was an army slaughtered upon the dais ahead.

And then, they were in the light.

A ripple passed over Olea's skin, like stepping through the ring of an Alranstone. The tingle set her senses aflame. A million ants burned her skin. Molten ore flowed through her, searing her from the inside out. Pain like she'd never before known flooded her, pain that promised torment if she went any further into that light.

Olea screamed, and her screams were echoed by others who had reached the light.

But though Jherrick screamed, he did not slack his pace. Through tear-blurred eyes, Olea saw him stumble to his feet and lurch for the massive crystalline object at the center, through a gap in the piles of mummified bodies. Near-blind by tears of pain, Olea ran after him.

Olea and Jherrick reached the center of the corpse-ring nearly in unison. A plinth stood there, and it was from this that the light emanated. Tall as a cedar tree, it towered over the carnage, not stone but crystal so pure Olea could see veins of gold tracking deep through it, like dragonflies trapped in amber. Luminous, the crystal flared as they approached, twisting with a *wyrric* light that pierced like talons, that dug into Olea's brain, that made her pain sear, tearing her apart.

And in the center of that twisting light was the clockwork, adhered to the surface of the Plinth.

Jherrick sagged to his knees with a cry, eyes rolling up in his head as he passed out just feet shy of the Plinth. Olea collapsed forward in wrenching agony, reaching out to the Alranstone as she stumbled her last step. Blind with pain, she fell against the crystal, and it blistered her with heat. Her fingers alighted upon the clockwork. As she touched it, the light emanating from the Alranstone suddenly flared to a cool blue brilliance.

Olea's pain ceased.

Everywhere, the massive chamber flooded with smooth blue light. Illumination rolled out from the Alranstone like a living thing, lancing into the darkness. The floor ceased to heave, settling into a placid sea of white, the enormous cavern come to breathing silence. The floor beyond the dais began to roll back, displaying an ocean of clockwork gears, passages of white stone leading down into a labyrinth of gold and silver, copper and steel.

The light brightened. Olea saw they stood beneath a dome vast enough to encompass ten throne halls. The ceiling of white stone turned clear like glass. And then, above and all around, Olea could see the sky, violet with desert twilight and new stars. The mountains that surrounded the Thirteen Tribes purpled the distance. Craggy and austere, they swallowed the evening's light, constellations of bright stars arching above.

The image flashed, and Olea was standing atop the tallest peak. Craggy mountains surrounded her, her world swallowed by stars. She had a moment of wonder, staring up at such beauty. But then her eyes were drawn down to the horror all around, lit by the Alranstone. Corpses lay beneath those benevolent stars, ringing the Stone. So many corpses. Olea choked, taking in the horror of such slaughter. Ruthless, cruel, bodies stacked here for eternity to rot.

And that charcoal grey leather. Olea took a step toward the mounds, away from the crystal Alranstone. Narrowing her eyes, she saw. The design of the buckles, the tooled patterns on sword-hilts. Wrinkled, dry Inkings upon desiccated flesh.

The Kingsmount and Stars. All around her.

The Kingsmen.

Olea swooned, falling back against the crystal Plinth. Her heart died, her eyes filled with tears. Bile rose to her throat and she choked it down, a hard sob rushing up to fill its place. Lifting her hands to her lips, she stared, tears falling, and what she saw she could not un-see. Olea bit her hand, and when she felt no pain in her shock, she bit it harder, willing herself to understand.

To make sense of such a horrible thing.

"Den'Alrahel." A soft voice slid into her torture. Someone stood at her shoulder. She hadn't heard him approach. Olea stiffened, feeling that voice slide over her like a barrel full of eels. "Such a pity to find you here."

Olea was already turning. Her blade was in her hand, a scream of rage was in her throat.

But the bite of a knife ripped across her neck, and took her scream away.

She staggered. Blood surged out over her chest, soaking her wrap, spattering the Alranstone. Olea gasped, but only a gurgle came. Her windpipe was severed. Blood poured down her, warming her chilled skin, freezing her from the inside out. The world slid sideways, and Olea collapsed to her knees. Her mind dulled to white as she sprawled upon blood-soaked stone. Her eyelids flickered, her lifeblood pooling out around her cheek.

Through collapsing white, she saw Aldris and Lourden, running toward her from beyond the corpse-piles, faces contorted. Mouths open. Shouting her name? Blades out…

But she couldn't hear them anymore. A thin white buzz filled her ears.

The last thing Olea saw was one soft grey boot, that nudged her face, and then departed.

CHAPTER 25 – ELOHL

Ice scoured Elohl's cheeks. A ferocious wind ripped at his facewrap, threatening to tear back his hood. His gloved hands upon his iceaxes were numb, but still, they picked his way up the ice wall in the yawning crevasse with a steady rhythm. Elohl's hands moved right, deftly avoiding a hairline fissure that could have led to a vicious splitting of the glacial wall.

And a drop into a black chasm through skirling snows to who-knew-where.

Vaguely, Elohl heard Fenton's call through the cut of the ice-edged wind. Three tugs came upon the rope. Elohl set an ice-iron and clipped in by his leather harness, peering down through the blizzard. Resting, he set one iceaxe in the wall so he could flex his numb hands. He watched Fenton fifteen feet below, managing a tangle in the gear-lines from the merciless wind. It was bad and Fenton was tired, his gloved hands moving sluggishly, fingers unable to pull the knots.

They were both exhausted from battling the fierce wind that whipped thirty knots faster through these cuts than up on the surface of the glacier. It had been thus for more than a week. Elohl gazed around the sheer sheet of ice they traversed. The top of the crevasse was too far, more than three hundred spans up. He couldn't see it through the blizzard, but he knew from counting his movements descending the side they had come down, before crossing the snowy chasm at the bottom.

Glancing to the side, Elohl searched for someplace to rest. And found it. He tugged the rope four times. Fenton set another iron to stabilize the load and looked up. Elohl gestured to the dark hole in the ice he could barely make out through the skirling snow, fifteen paces right. Fenton narrowed iced eyelashes against the wind, glancing right. He nodded, relief plain upon his swathed face. Setting irons laterally, Fenton began to take the load of their packs over towards their destination.

Elohl did the same. They crab-set the load to the right for a fifteen-span, and then Elohl was at the lip of the dark ice bubble. Ice bubbles were tricky, but they could save a man's life. This one was sturdy, with a strong lip. Elohl could see the hole burrowed nearly twenty feet back into darkness and had a solid floor. Setting two irons inside the lip, he hoisted up, then clipped in the line. Sitting just inside the stout edge, he gasped deeply to catch his breath, monitoring the edge for Fenton. Presently, Fenton came up and over, clipping in and turning to haul on the pulleys to bring up the gear. His face swaddled in furs and a thick wrap, all Elohl could see was the relief in Fenton's eyes as Elohl gave him a hand. In moments, they had the gear up and in.

Moving further back into the ice cave, Elohl set irons so they could move about freely. Each man tugged the lines, making sure they were clipped in, and then they humped the packs at the lip of the ice-hole to block out the wind and clipped those in, too. Their gear and persons secured against any fissuring of the hole, Fenton and Elohl reclined against the walls of the dim blue space, digging a cold meal of salted venison and hard bread out of their packs. Elohl chipped ice into his flask, then bound it close beneath his fur-lined jacket to melt. He did the same for Fenton. Soon the two men were relaxing, working out their muscles with massage and stretching in the long-learned manner of the High Brigade.

"Aeon's balls," Fenton cursed mildly, massaging his rear thigh, his head cocked as he listened to the wind outside. "When's this storm going to let up? A full fucking week, ever since Merra's cats had to turn back from the thin air."

Elohl snuck a peek through a crack in the humped gear at the mouth of the hole. He saw only white, shards of ice shearing the air as the relentless wind whirled. "The cats were spent, traveling days without a break, especially up here where they can't breathe." Elohl commented, massaging out his cramping hands. "Better that Merra turned her keshari back, to get down to the war-front where they're needed. You and I can manage on our own, Merra knew that. It was her suggestion from the first."

"That's what we get, being Brigadiers, I suppose." Fenton grinned, a mischievous glint in his gold-dark eyes. "Fuck these

371

mountains."

"Fuck these mountains." Elohl echoed the famous High Brigade sentiment. He grinned back, some part of him feeling ruthlessly alive in the climb-or-die environs of the Highpasses. Palming his pipe out of its pouch in his thick-padded furs, Elohl packed the ironwood bowl. Carved hastily in the past week, this pipe wasn't as nice as the one he'd gifted Fenton, but it would do. Elohl struck a phosphor match and puffed, encouraging his blend of dry herbs to light.

Ready with his own pipe, the one of the Beast that Elohl had gifted him, Fenton held out a hand for the herb blend, and Elohl handed it over with a match. His facewrap finally undone, Fenton's cheeks and brows were hopelessly raw where the wind had scoured. Elohl knew his own face was just as bad, his lips cracking. Their body heat warmed the cave now, and Elohl pulled back his hood, scrubbing a hand through his sweat-laden ruff of hair. Pipe-stem between his teeth, Elohl closed his eyes, letting his head slip back to the wall. He heard Fenton rummage in his pack, saw the flickering glow of a candle through his closed eyelids, lit from Fenton's pipe.

Fenton gave a deep sigh in the echoing silence. "What I wouldn't give for a woman right now."

Elohl opened his eyes, seeing the blue of their cavern shifting now with the flame of a single fat candle. He massaged his aching hands and forearms. "Do you miss her?"

"Merra?" Fenton's grin was wistful as he puffed. "Any man would miss a woman like that. That last fucking she gave me when we dodged behind that cluster of boulders as the cat-team took a rest… magnificent. It was her way of saying goodbye. Even with rocks and snow biting my ass, I wouldn't have missed a moment of it."

"And yet, you let her go." Elohl murmured, massaging his fingers.

"Merra has a duty. So have I." Fenton eyed Elohl as he tapped out the finished pipe upon the blue ice. "We're not star-held lovers, Elohl. Merra is a fierce woman, and I'm a career soldier. We never placed any idle dreams between the two of us. She knows the highmountain code as well as I do. Take it while it's hot…"

"… as they say." Elohl finished, reflecting upon Fenton and

Merra's leave-taking. When the time had come, Fenton and Merra had been dry-eyed. A final kiss they'd shared, tender, as the keshari had made ready to depart at the edge of the Devil's Field glacier. And then Merra had mounted up and given her call. The band had turned, loping back down the snowy ridge and disappearing around a cluster of boulders.

Fenton's goodbyes with Merra had been both brusque and tender for a reason. Merra's riders were headed straight for the war-front. Their next weeks would be filled with slaughter, the kind of vicious fighting few came home from. Elohl could see the marks of heartache upon Fenton's every movement. The man didn't complain; he didn't mope. There was nothing one could outwardly observe about him that indicated sorrow, but it was there all the same. A tightness around his gold-russet eyes. The way his lips twisted in a wryer way than usual when he smiled.

"You still good climbing lead?" Fenton asked, changing the topic, massaging one shoulder.

Elohl nodded. "How are you doing with the gear? Those pulleys and ice-irons are getting tricky in this wind."

"Passable." Fenton stated. "I can manage a bit longer. Though truth be told, I'm nearly ready to stop for the day."

"I can climb second for a while." Elohl watched Fenton closely. The man was a steady climber, but all the same, when men tired, they made mistakes. And mistakes got people killed.

Fenton gave a wry smile, eyeing Elohl frankly. "You're as tired as I am, Elohl. I saw you massaging your hands. Fucking numb, aren't they? We've got a good rhythm, you as lead-hand, me as second, and you set a route just as easily as I do. But neither of us is a god, my friend."

Elohl nodded, still sweating mercilessly beneath his gear from their grueling climb, though he removed none of his clothes. Catching a chill was deadly in the highmountains. "Up and down for a week, crossing this glacier without long-poles or ladders to bridge the gaps. Fucking exhausting."

"You're telling me." Fenton chuckled. "We can continue tacking around the small crevasses, Elohl, but with these that are too wide, where we have to descend and ascended through these wind-rifts... I don't know how much more of this I can do, honestly."

Elohl took a long breath, let it out. Exhaustion swamped him. He could have closed his eyes and fallen asleep where he sat. "Normally, I would make a good show for my men, but you and I are beyond that, aren't we?"

"I suppose so," Fenton chuckled. "The Elsthemi don't call this the Devil's Field for nothing. Toughest section to cross in all of the border-mountains. You either ascend Mount Ghirlaj to the south, fucking obsidian climbing for twenty leagues, or clip in to the Cannus Rift to the north and sleep in hammocks with your ass out in this wind. And between is this bitch. Thirty leagues of down and up, down and up, down and up. There's a reason no one patrols this section of the passes."

Elohl cocked his head, thoughtful. Fenton was a man of many secrets, and Elohl had just heard the edge of one slip from Fenton in his current exhaustion. "You've climbed through this way before. You've crossed the Devil's Field before."

Fenton blinked. His hand paused where he rubbed his shoulder. A slow smile lifted his lips, though his eyes were hard flint. "It's not something I relish reliving."

Elohl took a draw on his pipe, watching the man he'd come to call friend, though he still knew so very little about Fenton. "What aren't you telling me?"

The man looked down, smiling slightly as he massaged his hands. "You're smart enough to know that there's a lot I don't share with you, Elohl. And I'm smart enough to know there's a lot you don't share with me. Like what your golden Inkings *really* did during that skirmish." Fenton pulled off one glove, inspecting his fingertips for ice-rot. They were healthy and pink, Fenton's wiry body with its voracious appetite effortlessly suited to the far north.

Elohl picked up a chip of ice and tossed it idly. Fenton had avoided his question, and posed one Elohl didn't want to answer. Elohl lapsed into silence, listening to the shrieking of the wind. "I tell you what. I'll answer a query of yours, and then you answer one of mine. Fair?"

Fenton began inspecting his other hand. "Fair enough."

"What would you ask of me, Fenton?" Elohl said. "What do you want to ask that you hold back?"

"Well," Fenton made eye contact again, his dark gold-brown

gaze frank. "You can tell me what happened during that skirmish, Elohl. Why in Aeon's name your golden Inkings *glowed* and what the fuck you did to all of us. How you made us feel... bonded. Bound to you."

Elohl sighed, not having any answers. "Is that how you feel? Bound to me?"

"I'm committed to you, you know that," Fenton's voice was more gentle, "but this is something different, Elohl. I feel... *compelled* to help you. I asked Merra about it and she said the same damn thing. That she felt compelled to follow you when your Inkings flared. To give you whatever you asked for, whatever you wanted." Fenton eyed him, almost angrily.

Elohl blinked. "I wouldn't ask Merra to fuck me, Fenton."

"No. Not *that*." Fenton rolled his eyes. "We still have free choice. But it's an *urge*. Like you have exceptional charisma."

Elohl smiled wryly around his pipe. "No one has ever said of me that I have exceptional charisma." He rubbed his hands over his face and short beard, trying to remove the lingering sting of ice and wind.

Fenton leaned forward, his gold-brown eyes intense. "But that's just it. You *do*. Some strange, animal charisma. The cats felt it. Thitsi felt it. She protected you with her life. And when your Inkings lit..." Fenton's eyes lingered upon Elohl's jacket, "*Everyone* felt it. I would have followed you into anything at that moment. I would have stood by you and fought an icebear, Elohl. To my death. Technically, those men and women have sworn allegiance to the King and Queen of Elsthemen. But make no mistake," Fenton's brown eyes were piercing, "We are *bonded* to you. By whatever fucking magic is in those Inkings of yours."

Elohl's head fell back against the ice. He could feel the truth of Fenton's words, that etheric cord still stretching between them, strong, commanding. "I didn't ask for any of this." Elohl sighed.

"I'm serious, Elohl." Fenton did not grin. "Those men and women you bound with your Inkings will follow you into battle. Without hesitation. They'll follow you, wherever you go, whatever you want. So what I want to know is," Fenton leaned forward, intense, "what *do* you want? What might you use this hold over me, over us, for?"

Elohl filled his pipe, lit it, puffed. It was a question he'd never considered before. Always, he'd been the soldier, the blade for someone else, for a King or a Queen. Never had anyone asked what he wanted out of life, nor what he might use other men for, if he truly held them in thrall.

"Peace," Elohl spoke at last, his heart aching and raw. "I'm sick of all this war, Fenton. Ten years of climbing and skirmishes with the Red Valor. Ten years of assassination attempts because of my Inkings. My people ruined. And now this. More war, where I'm just a pawn. Never in control of my destiny or the destiny of my loved ones..." He sighed. "I just want some peace, Fenton. Is that too much to ask?"

Fenton regarded him a moment, his gaze piercing in the gloom. Elohl had a moment of strange sensation, like oceanic fingers seeped into his mind. He blinked, lightheaded, a press like thunderstorms in his ears. He opened his jaw and flexed, popping the pressure. The strangeness passed, and Elohl took a puff on his pipe, putting it off to fatigue as he listened to the shrieking of the wind outside.

"Men buy peace with their lives, Elohl. With their blood." Pulling his gloves on, Fenton had eased, his demeanor less tense.

"But what if we didn't have to? What if peace didn't have to be bought with blood?" Elohl mused, resting his head back against the ice. "It struck me when Merra's riders turned upon her, Fenton. Kin against kin, split down the middle like so much rotten wood. A bitter battle between those who were supposed to protect each other, because of Khehemni and Alrashemni feuding. That isn't a war, Fenton. It's madness. Ancient madness that poisons us all. But what if there was a way to heal that rift?"

As Elohl spoke, he could see a vision of peace in his mind. Of brother embracing brother, of men upon a battlefield throwing down arms, of light lancing from heart to heart. As he dreamed it, he felt a surge go smoothing through his skin, like warm water being poured through his Inkings. It flowed down his spine, into his belly, easing him, bringing a wistful smile to his face and letting his eyelids slip closed as he smoked. Until his body thrummed with a pleasure more satisfying than sex, and more calming than sleep.

"There..." Fenton's voice was soft in the cavernous silence.

Elohl opened his eyes to see Fenton's attention upon him. "That's it. I felt it again. What you did during the skirmish. Elohl, unbind your jacket."

Elohl blinked. Tapping his pipe out upon the ice, he pulled the flaps of his padded jacket back, unlacing and unbuckling until he could see his undershirt. Then he pulled the laces on that, too, opening it wide. Fenton's intake of breath was confirmation that Elohl's eyes were not playing tricks. Softly, like sunlight underwater, the fine script of his golden Inkings glowed in the dim blue light of the cave. Rippling along the golden filigree, the Inkings undulated with a rhythm like ocean waves.

Fenton whistled low. He closed his eyes, eyebrows knit as if in pain. "Put those away, Elohl."

"What would you do for me right now?" Elohl asked, testing the magic.

"Anything." Fenton muttered, eyes still closed, face turned away. But his voice was fervent.

"Kill for me?" Elohl pressed, uneasiness prickling his spine.

"Yes." Fenton shuddered, his breath hard in his throat.

"Die for me?"

"Absolutely." The man hesitated not at all.

Alarm surged through Elohl. A dire feeling like evil fingers gripped the nape of his neck. But he had to test the magic, what it was doing to the man sitting before him. "Would you kill Merra for me, Fenton? If she were here, right now? Would you do that for me?" Elohl murmured, his heart bleak.

Fenton's eyes popped open, pained. He hesitated, indecision upon his lips.

"Look at the Inkings, Fenton." Elohl pressed, making his heart hard despite his trepidation. "Would you kill General Merra for me? Would you kill a woman you love?"

Fenton's dark gaze flicked to the Inkings. His brows pinched in a line. His jaw set, and a snarl came to his lips. Suddenly, it struck Elohl that Fenton looked dangerous, fierce, like a lone wolf with nothing to lose. A massive shudder took Fenton. His body trembled like a leaf in a gale, and he made a strangled sound. The wind outside the cavern screamed suddenly in fury. Elohl thought he saw a flash of lightning outside. Tension simmered in the cavern, a thin, electric sensation. The hairs upon Elohl's body lifted. Elohl surged with alarm as the sharp sound of ice cracking exploded to his left, deep inside the glacier. Another crack sounded, deafening like exploding flash-powder.

And just when Elohl was about to tell Fenton to move his ass to get out of the cavern, thinking the glacier was going to bust up around them from the strength of his Inking's magic, everything suddenly ceased. The wind dropped outside, the sensation of an electric storm dissipated. The ice was silent again. Elohl's gaze tracked to his comrade. Fenton sat utterly still, breathing softly as if all his fight against the Inking's magic had gone out of him.

"If you wish it. Yes. I'll kill Merra." Fenton turned his face away in suffering. A shiver of fear went through Elohl, knowing that whenever his golden Inkings had done in this cavern today, it had just broken a man.

A good man.

"Listen to me closely," Elohl leaned forward in the blue gloom. "I do *not* want you to kill General Merra, Fenton. Do you hear me? I will never give that order to you, I promise it. I swear it, Brigadier to Brigadier. Brother to brother."

The lines smoothed out from Fenton's face. He let out a long breath, shaky. But he did not open his eyes. Elohl laced his shirt, then buckled his jacket back into place, nestling his wrap around his neck so that nothing of his Inked skin showed. Trepidation slid through his gut. A deep fear at what his Inkings could do. How they could command a good man to do a bad thing, perhaps as much as they could command a bad man to do a good thing, like getting Merra's renegades to throw down their weapons.

It was fell magic. Double-sided *wyrria*. Powerful.

Fenton opened his eyes at last, stricken. "Aeon, Elohl. When you told me to kill her... I actually *wanted to*." Fenton's eyes flicked away. "I wanted to..."

"Powerful magic," Elohl murmured.

Fenton's honest eyes flicked back. "*Frighteningly* powerful magic."

"Did you feel it?" Elohl asked. "What happened just now? The electricity?"

"I felt it. Do you think that was your Inkings?" Fenton's eyes narrowed.

Elohl took a deep breath. "I think maybe it was because you fought it, Fenton. When you fought the power in the Goldenmarks, it caused a reaction, like a storm. I thought I saw lightning outside. A moving energy..."

"Our glacier cracked." Fenton gazed into the deep darkness of the hole, then rose to inspect the ice. "Whatever happened might have destabilized our position."

"Fenton." Elohl's murmur was soft.

The man looked back, stopped. "Yes?"

"I answered your query, about my Inkings. You owe me. Tell me how you move faster than I do."

Fenton's demeanor went very still, as if he had just blended into the ice of the cavern. For a moment, Elohl felt the man disappear from his sensate sphere entirely. Elohl thought he saw the man's eyes flash red in the dim space, though it was just a trick of the guttering candlelight. "Is that an order?"

The feel of claws skittered over Elohl's skin. Prickles, lancing over his golden Inkings, as if Fenton had just given him a warning. Elohl crossed his arms, a deep uneasiness creeping in his gut. "Do I need to make it one?"

Fenton took a deep breath. He crouched, settling to his heels, his manner intense. "What do you want to know about me, Elohl?"

"Do you have inborn Alrashemni magic? Like my intuitive gift?"

Fenton's smile was hard, and it did not touch his eyes. "Something like that. Though I wouldn't call it Alrashemni magic."

"Sometimes I don't feel you at all," Elohl said. "As if you can make yourself disappear from my senses altogether. And I know you're aware of it. You're confident. You know you have an ability that trumps my reflexes... and you know how to wield it."

"I know how to use what I am, Elohl." Fenton held Elohl's gaze, frank, intense. "But it doesn't mean I choose to. Not often."

"What are you?" Elohl asked, intrigued.

Fenton's eyes seemed to die suddenly. As if a man had been there one minute, and was replaced by a beast the next. A beast that cared nothing for the sanctity of life, of honor, of camaraderie. A cold thing replaced Fenton den'Kharel suddenly, and Elohl saw it.

Saw its eyes glow red and remain.

"I am something Kings would kill to wield." Fenton's eyes burned with a slow fire, gold and red illuminating the brown in shifting hues, like a writhing pyre. "And I am in *your* service. To the death."

Elohl's Goldenmarks seared. Every limned line, every florid filigree. They lit with fire all along their length, a simmering light that responded to whatever Fenton was, whatever he was doing. To the burn in his eyes.

"Tell me what you are." Elohl growled, alarmed.

"I am your servant, Rennkavi, until the day we both perish. That is all that I am."

That one word told Elohl much, and yet, nothing at all. "How do you know that word, Rennkavi?"

Fenton glared with fire-red eyes beneath dark brows, a frightening visage. "Do not order the devil to disclose himself, Elohl. Not until you wish to see the fullness of his power."

Elohl's Goldenmarks flared in warning. "You're not really Alrashemni, are you? Even though you bear an Alrashemni Shemout Bloodmark. You're something else."

"Originally, yes." Red fire seethed in Fenton's eyes, like smelting gold. But strangely enough, the red died suddenly, back to honey-brown, leaving Fenton calm, somber. The two men regarded one another, but there was no shiver in the air now, no electricity, no magic. It was as if Fenton had simply put away whatever he was, back into a cage, an impenetrable lockbox.

Silence filled the cavern.

Suddenly, the glacier around them gave a tremendous shudder. Ice split beneath them in a deafening concussion, the floor of the hole buckling. Fenton gave a roar, springing toward his gear in a powerful leap. Elohl rolled, his hands on his iceaxes with the speed of instinct as the floor fell away altogether.

Elohl was falling. Ice crumbled in massive sheets, dizzying. He jerked as his line was arrested by a clamp, then tumbled as it broke, then jerked again, tumbled. Elohl managed to catch an unmoving ice spar before him with an ax, wrenching his shoulder, stopping his plummet. His heart beat like galloping hooves. His breath came hard, puffing in wraiths as ice sheets smashed somewhere far below.

"*Elohl!*" Fenton's bellow came up from below, echoing out of a massive cavern. Elohl struggled to get the other iceaxe chipped into the unmoving ice. Above him, ice continued to slough and crumble from the edge of the crevasse. Below, all was darkness, a depth of gloom terrifying to behold.

"*Elohl!!*" Fenton's cry came again from somewhere below. "Hold that position! I'm coming for you! Whatever you do, Aeon in blazes, don't drop!!"

Elohl glanced over his shoulder. A flame had lit down below in the massive, yawning darkness of a tremendous ice-cave. Elohl blinked, his vision unclear. What he was seeing was impossible. The flame came from nothing. The fire burning placidly at Fenton's side was lit from the blue sheet of ice he stood upon. It was impossible. Elohl must have hit his head in his fall. But as he watched, he saw Fenton move his hands, molding that fire, shaping, sending it snaking over to a cruel patch of ice stalagmites fifty feet below where Elohl dangled.

Elohl could see now that Fenton had slid down a massive slab of ice that angled down to the floor of the cavern. But that chute was ten feet to Elohl's right, past an impossible gap. The ledge Elohl clung to with his axes was riddled with cracks. Nothing but a slender spar held his weight. And as he watched, cracks lanced outward from his axes in that delicate lace, with the tinkling sound of little bells.

A sound that meant only one thing to a Brigadier.
Death.

With a last pop, the spar gave way, bursting into a million glittering fragments. Elohl plummeted with a shout. Some part of his shocked mind heard Fenton roar. Elohl twisted in midair, seeing the cavern below, the enormous quagmire of ice-stalagmites that would skewer him.

A flurry of lightning lanced the cavern, blinding, reflected a million times in the ice.

And then Elohl hit water, a vast black lake, where only glittering ice had been before.

Elohl came up spluttering, coughing. He surfaced with one iceaxe between his teeth by its handle, the other still in his hand. Every muscle screamed from his impact upon the black water. He crawled along the rope toward the shore and the glimmer of the fire, the packs having mercilessly landed just out of the water. Fenton waded in and hauled him out when he got close, quickly helping Elohl strip his wet clothing. Elohl was naked in short order, rubbing his chest with frozen hands.

Stripping off his clothing, Fenton wasted no time. In the brusque, impersonal manner of every Brigadier, he soon had Elohl bundled into his arms. He wrapped an Elsthemi wool blanket from the packs around them both, laying his dry clothing beneath upon the ice. Together they huddled by the *wyrric* fire, Fenton's wiry arms wrapped around Elohl, Elohl rubbing his chest. He started a heating breath long-learned from his time in the Brigade, and behind him, he felt Fenton do the same.

Fenton's body warmed faster. The man was soon a furnace, his skin hot. Elohl watched the *wyrric* fire brighten as Fenton did his breathing. Elohl soon forgot his breaths as he watched the fire's writhing gold glow. The blaze twisted before them without sound, burning from nothing upon the blue ice, though it gave heat aplenty.

Fenton's breathing died out to stillness, and they sat a long moment, watching the flames writhe.

"You saved my life." Elohl murmured at last.

"I will always save your life. I am your servant and protector, Rennkavi. It is all I am." Fenton's words were soft, genuine. They were said with such sincerity that Elohl suddenly believed. This man was in his service to the end, no matter what he was, no matter how many secrets he hid. Secrets Elohl could unravel gradually rather than push, making of the man an ally rather than a chained foe. An ally, as Fenton had tirelessly proven himself, ever since the fighting at Roushenn.

"Why?" Elohl almost didn't want to know.

"Because you wear marks that are important to me," Fenton said. "The Goldenmarks of the Uniter, as told by prophecy. Long ago." Elohl felt Fenton's light touch trace the circle that spanned his spine and shoulder-blades, felt him tracing the wolf and dragon locked in battle within the ring of flame.

"Who are you, Fenton?" Elohl breathed.

"Fentleith."

Elohl glanced over his shoulder. "What?"

"Fentleith." The man heaved a sigh. "My name is Fentleith Alodwine. Not Fenton den'Kharel."

Somehow, it wasn't surprising to Elohl. "And you can wield flame." Elohl's lips twisted in a wry smile. "And I thought I saw a tirade of lightning vaporize those ice stalagmites into the lake I landed in."

"*Wyrric* parlor tricks." From the side of his eye, Elohl could see Fenton's dark grin.

"Bullshit." Elohl turned a bit more, to look at the man fully. "You just vaporized thirty-foot columns of ice into water with a lightning strike."

"Sheet-lightning. More effective than a single strike." Fenton slid out of the blanket's confines now that Elohl was no longer shivering. The man liberated his clothing, pulling on his trousers. But as he turned his back to don his shirt, Elohl's eyes suddenly widened.

"Hang the fuck on...!" Elohl stammered.

Fenton glanced over his shoulder, paused with his elbows in his shirt, not yet dragging it on over his head. "They're glowing, aren't they?"

Wordlessly, Elohl nodded. Cascading over Fenton's back was a magnificent marking, made entirely of the twisting smelted light like the fire. But it was inside Fenton's skin, snaking through his veins like his body breathed flame, shifting through arcane sigils and glyphs. And spanning his spine and shoulder blades was an exact replica of Elohl's own Goldenmark, a wolf and dragon caught in an endless encounter, tearing each other to pieces within a ring of flame.

Except that flame was made of living fire upon Fenton's back.

"What in Aeon's hells is it?" Elohl murmured, entranced.

Fenton dragged his shirt on. He came to sit next to Elohl, not bothering to don his jacket. Staring at the flames, he heaved a deep sigh. "This was made by the touch of my people's magic, *wyrria*, long ago."

"Your people?" Elohl felt his Goldenmarks surge, as if they listened to Fenton's words.

"Khehemni, Elohl." Fenton's gaze was apologetic. "I'm Khehemni. And even though I wasn't born in Khehem... my heart remembers Khehem. The city that is my home. The city that is my birthright."

Elohl's Inkings flamed. Astonishment rippled through him, uncertainty. "What do you mean, birthright? And you're Khehemni? How?"

Fenton's gaze strayed to the sorcerous fire, tired. "I'm the last King of Khehem, Elohl. The last one crowned, anyway, even though the city was destroyed before I was born. Technically I'm the last Scion of Khehem, the last one to hold the burden of the Wolf and Dragon firemarked within my skin. I ceased the tradition with my own children. The bloodline of Khehem lives on, but I wouldn't punish any of my sons or daughters with the *Mehrkordiat Desik*, the tableaux you see upon my back. That you also carry. I wouldn't give them such a burden. So I carry it alone. And now you do, too."

Fenton's words were strange. Elohl felt buzzing within his skin, like thousands of bees, swarming to Fenton's words. Giving them credence, lending them power. Slowly, Fenton sat up. Settling into a meditative seat, he rested his wrists upon his knees, palms up. Breathing steadily, he closed his eyes, sinking into a slight rocking. Suddenly, his brows knit with a dire anger. His nostrils flared, his jaw set. A snarl lifted his lips and a low rumble like a wolf growling issued from his throat.

Power surged in the space around them, thick with electricity. And suddenly, all that power concussed inwards, like the air had been sucked out of the cavern. Elohl's eardrums thumped in a whomp. And as he watched, two whorls of balled lightning cracked alight in Fenton's palms.

"Holy fuckstone!" Elohl breathed.

Fenton shot to his feet. His eyes snapped open, his face contorted. Power flooded from his body, scalding, blistering. With a scream like a tortured beast, he set a powerful fighting stance and hurled those balls out, one and two, into the black lake. Water erupted, cascading with electrified plumes. Ice all around the perimeter vaporized, widening the lake substantially. Elohl felt Fenton slam some barrier up, and the rippling lightning curved around them, leaving them untouched upon the icy shore.

With a huff of exhaustion, Fenton collapsed to his knees. Palms to the ice, head hanging, he breathed hard in deep gasps. At last, he stumbled back to a seat beside Elohl. The fire had dimmed dramatically, just a writhing splutter now upon the ice.

"Halsos' Burnwater." Elohl breathed.

Fenton could only nod. "That's only part of what lives inside me, Elohl. That's only a part of the curse I bear. Something that's getting stronger, day by day. Harder to control now, because of an... accident. Recently."

"Accident?" Elohl glanced over.

"I'd rather not talk about it." Fenton's jaw was set. He stared at the fire, grim.

"What can I do to help?" Elohl offered.

Fenton startled. He blinked, looking around, his dire mood interrupted. "You would try to help me?"

"You saved my life, Fenton. A few times now," Elohl murmured. "Don't think I don't realize now how you got us out of Roushenn all those weeks ago. You fought that creature. You used this... whatever this is, this terrible magic, to get us all out. To save Elyasin, Therel, Luc, me. And now you used it again, to save me here. I owe you. If you say this *wyrria* of yours is a dire burden, then I believe that it is... and I'd like to help you find peace."

Some unnamable expression settled in Fenton's visage. At first it was distant, then woeful, then ancient. And at last, his face settled into a steady silence. As Elohl watched, a tear slipped down from those haunting gold-brown eyes, and then another. Fenton shed his misery in a soft silence, neither looking away nor wiping his tears from his face. A small smile lifted his lips, secret, sad. "My Rennkavi wants to help the Last Scion shed the curse of Khehem, his destiny. Will the Shaper never cease her wonder..."

"Curse?" Elohl asked.

"Conflict." Fenton's murmur was dire. "The ancient magic of Khehem, the *wyrria* of the Wolf and Dragon, is the essence of conflict. And it's a damned curse. The kind of conflict that burns a soul to ashes. The kind of conflict that eats a good man alive until there is nothing left of him."

Fenton's words were heartbreaking. They tore at Elohl, making something writhe deep within him. Elohl reached out, gripping Fenton's hand. "I don't know what you are, Fenton, but you need keep no secrets from me. And I will try to be honest and truthful with you. We were thrust together in a deadly game, and I don't know why, nor what fate has in store for us, but I tell you this. Fuck the magic. Fuck the markings. All I want to do at the end of the day is die in peace, and bring that peace to all of us. Will you help me?"

Fenton's face softened. His fingers tightened upon Elohl's. "Peace. I could use a bit of that."

He opened his lips as if to say more, but suddenly, something went knifing through Elohl. Like a spear of light was thrust through his body, it made his spasm, arching in a taught wave. A scream erupted from his throat. And was cut off as he felt his own windpipe severed by the cold steel of a blade.

Elohl gasped. Shock ripped through him, setting his golden Inkings alight. His throat wasn't cut, but it was. His windpipe was severed, but it wasn't. He couldn't scream, couldn't breathe, but he could. He felt blood gush down his chest in a wave, hot and sticky, and it wasn't his.

But it was.

"*Olea!!!*"

His scream was the roar of a thousand beasts. The sound ripped from him like a howl on the wind. His soul flooded out upon his breath, flying to her. Elohl felt it rush long leagues, over forest and sea, desert and mountain, searching for his twin. His soul went with his breath, traveling far, his eyes no longer seeing the ice cavern around him but seeing leagues upon leagues of desert, cracked hardpanne, dune-mountains, vast canyons and arroyos. Then a black city. A dead palace. Spiraling in with the force of his horror, he came through to a cavernous room with a crystalline Alranstone right in the very middle of an enormous dais littered with desiccated bodies.

And in the middle of it all, surrounded by a pool of dark blood, Olea. Dumped on her side, her cheek in the spreading crimson. Elohl watched as the light dimmed from her eyes.

"*Olea!*" Elohl screamed again, dimly aware that he was thrashing, held in Fenton's strong arms.

His vision snapped out, and he was lost to darkness.

CHAPTER 26 – JHERRICK

Jherrick sat upon the dais of stone at the center of the corpse-piles, cradling Olea's cold body. The Castellan was long gone. Jherrick had revived from unconsciousness too late, his eyes fluttering open just as Olea's throat was sliced. All of it happened too fast for his pain-riddled body to do more than twitch as she fell. Lhaurent had placed his hands upon the stone to return from whence he came. There had been a rush of air, and seven eyes upon the crystal Stone had suddenly flared open in a brilliant flash. And he'd disappeared from the center of Khehem without a backwards glance.

Jherrick brushed Olea's curls, thick with clotting blood, away from her face. It felt right to touch her, a closeness they'd never shared in life, though they had poured through ledgers together by candlelight enough times. Aldris and Lourden had seen Olea's murder, but had been too late to save her. At the edge of the dais, they had been trying to save Vargen, crushed between the upheaving stones before everything had settled underneath the dome of stars. Together, Lourden, Aldris, and Jherrick had pounded upon the Stone. They had said all the ritual words they could summon, hurled all the curses they knew at it, but it had been futile. Whatever magic that allowed Lhaurent through was gone, the Stone's seven eyes not just closed but disappeared entirely, dead to their plight. Soon, ritual words had turned to roars of pain and rage.

And finally, to a cavernous, echoing silence.

No one had spoken for a long while. Aldris and Lourden sat a few paces away, eyes red-rimmed but dry, their postures broken by failure. Vargen's mangled form lay in a tacky pool at the edge of the dais, broken, his soul fled to wherever Olea's had also gone. Jherrick's gaze strayed to Vargen's humped body, then beyond, to the humming clockwork in the pits around the dais. Vivid images of Oasis Khehem flickered upon the dome high above. Jherrick didn't look up. They didn't interest him. His fingers smoothed Olea's hair back again, tracing her beautiful bloodstained jaw.

A heavy sigh came from the dais. The soft scrape of boots razed Jherrick's ears as someone walked over and settled a hand upon his shoulder. "Leave her, kid. C'mon." Aldris' voice was broken, no trace of malice left to it.

"I can't." Jherrick stroked Olea's tacky curls again.

Aldris squeezed his shoulder. He knelt, drawing a knife from his belt. He slid it along her black curls, trimming one off, pressing it into Jherrick's hand. "One for you." His blade slid out again, trimming off another curl. "One for me." And a third time, the blade slid out, biting into her beautiful locks. "Lourden?"

Lourden's gaze rested upon the piles of corpses that ringed them. The Ghellani spearman rose in a fluid motion and came forward, kneeling beside Aldris. Aldris pressed the final curl into Lourden's palm, and the tall Ghellani nodded. Aldris' knife slid out once more, snicking off another curl. He reached out, fingers opening Olea's belt-purse reverently, retrieving her white olive-embroidered pouch. Tucking the curl inside he placed the white pouch in his own belt satchel.

"Who is that one for?" Jherrick asked.

"Her twin. Elohl deserves to know how she died." Aldris reached out, lifting Olea's longknife from her dead fingers. He pressed the longknife into Jherrick's palm. "Here. You should have the set. She would have wanted it." He carefully unbuckled her weapons harness with its twin knife-scabbards. Lifting her body to slide it out from beneath her hips, he handed that to Jherrick, also.

Tears pricked Jherrick's eyes as he took up Olea's weapons. "I don't deserve them."

"Nonsense." Aldris rose, gazing down on him. "Olea knew quality when she saw it. She rewarded those who were faithful."

Jherrick dashed a tear away with his thumb. "Faithful."

"Yeah. Faithful." Aldris kicked his boot against the inert Alranstone. "Give us each a moment with her, huh?"

Jherrick startled, realizing the truth behind Aldris' words. Three men had watched her die, and each had loved her, in his own way. Loved her, and never gotten a chance to tell her. Jherrick took a deep breath, then leaned over, kissing Olea upon the lips. "For everything you taught me," he whispered. "For the blessing of being by your side as long as you would have me. I will remake myself, Olea, I promise. I will become the man you saw in me. Every hour, every day. Until I see you again."

He slid her body gently off his bloodstained thighs, then stood with her weapons to hand. Aldris clapped him on the shoulder. Jherrick turned away, walking to the edge of the desiccated corpses.

He couldn't help but look back, watching Aldris say his goodbyes. The Kingsman knelt a long time, his lips by Olea's ear, murmuring as if telling her a story. As fresh tears fell from his eyes, he kissed her upon the lips, the same as Jherrick. Then rose, and walked away.

Lourden knelt. But unlike the other two, Lourden pulled her into his lap, rocking her slowly, as if their leave-taking could comfort her, or perhaps him. He rocked her a long while, singing a slow, sad tune beneath his breath. When it was finished, he set her back down without kissing her. But he did cup her head in his hand, pressing their foreheads together, as he set one blooded palm to her Inkings.

"If only they had not been so stark…" Jherrick heard him murmur. At last, Lourden rose, wiping blood from his hands upon his stained *shouf*, then raising his voice. "We must return. Blood has been spilled and night has fallen. It is a bad combination. This place is cursed."

Tearing his gaze from Olea, Jherrick's gaze flicked up at mountains gone to deep dusk, pictured upon the dome all around. Staring at the Plinth, he saw it was silent, inert, as dead as the woman who lay at its roots. Jherrick pulled his eyes away, and they fell upon the corpses. He walked towards them, entranced, coming to stand by Aldris. Aldris reached out, his fingers brushing a pattern woven into a charcoal-grey leather belt, and then the tarnished silver buckle, done in a florid but functional design.

"Kingsmen…" Aldris' sigh was soft like a midnight wind. "All the Kingsmen… every last fucking one of them stupid enough to go to that cursed fucking palace…"

Jherrick blinked. His head swam as he realized what he was seeing. Before him, upon all sides, piled so high they formed a barrier-wall taller than Lourden, were the Kingsmen. All of them. Two thousand Alrashemni Kingsmen, all disappeared in one fateful night, and disposed of here.

"Aeon in his bright heaven..." Jherrick sank to his knees. Tears stung his eyes and fell. Never, in all his bitter years, had he imagined something so very evil.

A grating chuckle came from Aldris. "Still want to serve Lhaurent? I do. I want to serve him his guts on a fucking *plate*." Aldris gave a wretched growl of such pure fury that Jherrick's eyes filled with tears all over again.

"He had them piled here like cordwood..." Jherrick whispered.

Aldris made a strangled sound. He walked away. Jherrick was left upon his knees by the dead. He reached out, his fingers sliding across a face, the skin stretched and parchment-dry. Fine bones showed through the hollowed cheeks of what had once been a woman. A warrior, like Olea. His fingers came to rest at her earlobe, shriveled like an apricot. A ruby pin was set in her ear, still luminous in its gold setting like a drop of blood.

She'd worn jewels to battle. Jewels like blood to war.

Jherrick's fingers slid over it. Unhooked the backing. Slipped it out of her dry sinew. Watching her hollow eye sockets, he raised the earring to his own ear, set his jaw against pain, and thrust it through. Setting the backing, Jherrick felt the warmth of fresh blood drip down the angle of his jaw.

"For you." He whispered. His eyes strayed up, seeing slack-jawed faces. "For all of you. For what Lhaurent's done. I promise you... I will do whatever it takes to bring him to justice."

Jherrick rose to his feet, power flooding his sinews. Something within him steeled, ready, something that coiled and snarled with a strength that was at once hot and so very cold. It shivered his limbs with energy, tightened his sinews for war. In one smooth motion, he lifted Olea's weapons harness and donned it, re-buckling it across his body for a better fit across his taller frame, his broader chest.

Her weapons hung heavy at his side.

Heavy, like a promise.

"Ready to go, kid?" Aldris' voice grated in the silence, hollow with exhaustion.

"Yeah. I'm ready."

Gazing down the avenue between the corpse-piles, Jherrick scouted for the entrance they'd come through. He saw it, far off, a hole of darkness in the shifting images upon the high dome.

Stepping to a break in the corpses, his gaze fell again on Vargen's ruin at the edge of the dais. A lump rose in his throat. Jherrick found himself putting a palm to his chest in the Alrashemni fashion, honoring the fallen Kingsman.

Jherrick let his hand fall, but not before Aldris saw it. Aldris eyed him, then walked on, taking the lead away from the Alranstone through the corpse-piles. Lourden followed without glancing back, his spear in hand, his footsteps tired. Jherrick was about to follow, when something pulled him back. A tug on his mind, a sensation of something unfinished. He turned, his gaze alighting upon the assembled clockwork still fixed to the Stone's smooth surface. The feeling in his mind sharpened, as if he needed to take this item, as if it called him in a language made of wisps, easing into his thoughts like ink through water. Mesmerized, he walked forward, until he stood right before the Stone.

His fingers brushed the clockwork, nestled into the crystal.

They broke apart. The pieces clicked away from the crystal, and then flew from it as if repelled by a blast. Careening down the aisles of alabaster stone, they dispersed into the clockwork pits. The most horrible shrieks came from every direction, of metalworks jamming and gears grinding to a halt. The humming and clunking died out to nothing. Until only the starry night upon the dome was left in the echoing silence, and a smooth blue light issuing from the Alranstone softly illuminated the mounds of the dead.

One piece of metal remained beneath Jherrick's fingers upon the Plinth. He stroked it, and it came away in his hand, a round disc of gold. Feeling like he was meant to have it, Jherrick pocketed it in his belt-purse.

"What did you do?" Aldris approached, his face incredulous, but he had missed the movement.

"I touched the clockwork, and they all flew down into the machine." Jherrick didn't mention the disc of gold he'd pocketed.

Jherrick moved back through the break in the corpse-piles, Aldris at this side. They walked toward Lourden, who stood at one raised walkway of alabaster stone, gazing into the silent machinery pits. Jherrick stepped to Lourden's side, looking down. All was silent below. Complicated gears, pistons, hammers in precious and semi-precious metals, all were pristinely still, the blue light of the

Alranstone gleaming eerily off their polished surfaces.

"I think it's jammed," Lourden's voice was tight with mourning, though it carried a note of awe. "If this place controls the city, perhaps we will survive this night. Come. We must leave."

The white walkway dipped into the clockwork pits and then rose at the edge of the dome, leading them to the open doorway. Lourden moved off down it, Jherrick and Aldris upon his heels. The pits were a marvel of clockwork precision. Jherrick had seen an expensive timepiece of Praoughian make once, but even in miniature, that had been nowhere near as complex as this. Ferocious metal teeth gleamed upon every side. Hammers and tracks, gurneys and sliding parts now still, the wind-core at the heart of Khehem was a brutal beast. Like a snarling wolf, it seemed to menace Jherrick from all sides, gnashing for his blood.

He shivered as he passed through, and was grateful when they ascended the other side.

At last, they passed from the dome. Like a terrible weight was released from him, Jherrick felt a lift return to his steps as they passed the boundary of the catacomb arch. Even though they stepped into utter darkness, their torches long gone in the upheaval, Jherrick found his mind eased. His heart still weighed heavy with loss as he navigated the stone passage, turning along a path he'd memorized coming in, but he no longer felt the press of that terrible, alert *wyrria* he'd felt entering the dome.

Something still lived in the center of Khehem. Something that waited and watched. But they were leaving it behind now, still trapped in the center of the palace, as Jherrick was suddenly certain it was. He shivered off the sensation of ruin as he navigated the passages, Aldris and Lourden behind, trailing his fingertips along the white blood-line to find his way out.

Soon, they emerged in the gloom of the vaulted receiving hall, the stone warriors with their spears casting fierce shadows in the starlit darkness. Faded out now, the light mirrors reflected only cerulean tones of night. Lourden's brows knit as he gazed around. He finally spied what he wanted, a few of the moldy, moth-eaten torches in a bracket. Lourden lit all three from flint in his gear, then tossed one to Jherrick and Aldris without a word.

They continued on, backtracking through the glass-tiled tomb of the Khehemni palace. Jherrick peered up at stories told in friezes between gables as they passed, brought to haunted life by the light of the torches. All was silence in the palace, but for their footsteps. They'd have no more movement, Jherrick was certain of it. Whatever those clockworks had done, they'd frozen the city and the palace, and no sound of shifting stones came drifting through the dark-domed gables. They arrived at the colonnaded entry hall without incident, and were soon back out through the tumbled door, rounding the latticed sun-shield.

Lourden angled left, making for the war-plaza's fountain in the cool starlight. They gained the rim, and all three men vaulted inside. Lourden propped what was left of his torch in the hands of a full-figured woman giving blessing to the wolf and dragon, who was missing her head. Filling flasks once again, the three men shared a cold silence.

Jhennah and the *Rishaaleth* had left. Jherrick didn't blame them. Lourden's instructions had been explicit, that no one remain inside Khehem past sundown. And now, Lourden settled to a seat at the edge of the bowl, out of the brackish water. Staring out over the silent domes and minarets of the city, he watched the sickled moon cast an eerie light over blackened rubble and white towers.

Jherrick settled in the fountain, gazing up at the beheaded priestess in the moonlight. Exhaustion swamped him. His fingers slid into his belt-pouch, fingering the little disc of gold as he rested. The priestess shifted, replaced by Olea in his mind as his eyes slipped closed. Her bluebottle curls catching the sun. Her white throat flashing when she laughed. Her hands, fast and deadly with knives, whipping out to block during practice.

I would have called you Queen. Jherrick mused, sliding towards sleep.

A soft sound woke him. A clinking, like a handful of tiny metal pieces had been dropped into the basin. Jherrick's eyes fluttered open. He glanced down. In the white dark, he saw metal glimmering in the brackish water near his hand, gold and silver, and pale star-metal.

Jherrick blinked. He glanced around. Aldris and Lourden were still dozing, leaning against the fountain's rim, eyes closed. Without a sound, Jherrick dipped his fingers in the water, taking up all the pieces of the clockwork and slipping them into his belt pouch. As he put in the last piece, he suddenly felt them shift and jangle beneath his fingertips. Jherrick's breath halted. The clockwork pieces shuffled themselves together, into a single ornament once more.

Something concussed suddenly in the night. An implosion that sucked air, right beneath Jherrick's fingertips.

And the clockwork was complete.

Aldris snorted awake, a fast knife brandished to the night. He blinked, his gaze fixing upon Jherrick. "What the fuck was that?!"

"What was what?" Jherrick played dumb. He slid his hand out of his pouch, fastening it while gazing around the silent city, pretending to look for danger. Aldris slid his knife away. He stood, staring long out over Khehem. Lourden had wakened and was standing also, eyes narrowed upon the city.

"Something has changed." Lourden murmured. "The city wakes. We must go."

Jherrick launched from the fountain-bowl with the other men, his secret making his heart pound hard. If any more people died tonight, it would be his fault. Six deaths were already on him today, including Olea's. His stomach twisted. He didn't know how he could bear it if Aldris or Lourden got swallowed by an avenue or crushed between moving stones.

But their trek back through the city was strangely uneventful. Avenues remained inert, walls remained silent, bridges and staircases shifted not at all. They gained the edge of the outer circle an hour after dawn, and were greeted by the shrill whistle of a scout. Whoops and shouts went up as they entered the plaza they had set out from the day before. But died out upon the morning breeze as Lourden's spearmen and women saw how few had returned.

Jhennah strode forward with sorrow in her eyes. Shedding her reed-woven breastplate, she went straight to her spear-captain, crushing Lourden in a fierce embrace. Jherrick watched as Lourden's shoulders began to shake, as his sobs finally came raking forth. The other *Rishaaleth* were walking forward, shedding their gear. They surrounded Lourden and his First-Spear, wrapping them in loving arms. A knot of humanity formed, a knot of love and support in a harsh land.

And Aldris and Jherrick were on the outside, alone with their sorrow.

Keening began in the knot of Lourden's spears. Begun by the women, it was taken up in low tones by the men. A few spearmen peeled away from the group, picking up shed spears and breastplates. The keening group began to move in procession, hands upon one another, toward the breach. Jherrick followed, Aldris at his side, their footsteps heavy as they passed beneath the shadow of Khehem's wall. Emerging into the sunshine upon the other side, Jherrick felt pressure ease back further from him, to be leaving the city of Khehem behind.

A city he never wanted to see again.

Out on the white stone highway, the procession moved toward Ghellen in the far morning mirage. *Rishaaleth* at the periphery began to beat the breastplates they held with their spears, like a warring army. But the woven breastplates made only a dry, rattling sound when hit, and it was this death-rattle that the funereal march proceeded home to. Beneath the rising sun, now baking the cracked plain, a song began. Lourden's low baritone rose at the center of it, his deep, broken voice hitching with sobs, but strong, the song tearing from his heart with every rattle of spears.

It was the same song Jherrick had heard him sing to Olea, before he'd let her go. Jherrick understood suddenly, that this was no ordinary death-song. It was a war-march, and a mourning, and something older. Something that spoke of a people bereft losing all hope, yet struggling on. The song was picked up by every throat, guttural and aching, its dirge droning forward with every shuffled boot through sand, with every rattle of spears on red-dyed reeds.

Jherrick's throat opened, swallowing the aching song. Swallowing bitterness of hope lost and desired. He swallowed that song, digested it, and then it came pouring from his own throat. Everything that had made him, shaped him, dropped away in that moment. Every teaching of his Khehemni elders, every bitterness of his lineage. Every hate against the Alrashemni, every perception of a people wronged, every atrocity he had committed for Lhaurent den'Karthus.

And what he was, in that moment, was a man in mourning. All he was, was endless mourning, for a woman lost, for innocence lost, for his youth lost. Tears poured from his eyes. Jherrick didn't stop them. He raised his throat to the baking sun and sang out his misery along with the rest of them, remaking himself with the power of that song. Remaking his legacy from the duality of two men who had no place in life, to one man who had the power of the now.

Remaking himself, as the man he wanted to be.

A man in mourning for the hope he had lost.

A hand snugged his waist. Jhennah drew him close to the group, folding him into a sweet embrace. Jherrick closed his eyes, walking on, feeling the sorrow of his ancient kin cocooning him. A presence shuffled the dirt to his right. He opened his eyes to see Aldris, head proud, green eyes dry and grim, walking alone. Jherrick ached for Aldris suddenly. He held out his hand, palm open. Aldris glanced at it and hesitated, his stride breaking.

And then the Kingsman moved in. Jherrick snugged his arm up over Aldris' shoulders, and Aldris' arm gripped around his waist. Head high, eyes grim, Aldris resisted the power of the dirge for a while. But Jherrick felt it when Aldris began to shake, those fierce green eyes too bright.

And then the song came pouring from Aldris, too.

Renting from him, on the broken heels of every sob.

CHAPTER 27 – DHERRAN

Dherran eyed Grump across their low-burning campfire. They were five days out of Vennet and still Grump had yet to say a word about being Khehemni or where they were going. Clearly, Vicoute Arlen den'Selthir had told Grump specific instructions, but Grump had given Dherran and Khenria only his usual idle chatter as they crossed the valley towards the eastern mountains. And now Grump prattled on about fall mushrooms as they roasted supper in a clearing of lowland alder and spruce, stars rising in a violet sky.

Dherran lost his patience at last. Tossing a hunk of moss into the campfire, he snarled, "Grump! Enough about the mushrooms! We need to speak about the bog. How are we to find Purloch's folk, and once we get to Valenghia, the Khehemni traitors you know? Are there even any who wish to rebel?"

Her back against a downed log, Khenria whittled upon a piece of oak, but looked up as the real conversation began. Brushing back her short loose curls, blue-black in the fire's flickering, her grey eyes sharpened like a hawk. Her training at Arlen's hands had been formidable, and Dherran was sure she would memorize every word of their conversation tonight.

"Well, Dherran, my boy, it's not really that simple." Grump poked at one of his bunny crunch-wraps in the coals. Wrapped in wide, waxy chellis-leaves, the large packets with their mixture of rabbit and field roots inside had yet to drip grease.

"Who are you really, Grump? And how much about all this do you know?"

Dherran eyed Grump across the flames, so much as yet unspoken between them. It was as if another man stared back at Dherran suddenly, the idle prattle of his forest-mouse friend rolling back to reveal a battle-hardened veteran. Grump aged years in moments, the lines in his face too severe, the grey in his rangy hair more pronounced in the harshness of the fire's tones.

"Dherran," he spoke softly, "I know more than I will ever speak. I have lived more lives than any man should, and seen more of death than any man needs to. I have killed my score of Alrashemni and Khehemni both, and now I belong nowhere, lad. Now I belong to the forest, and the forest belongs to me. But for Arlen den'Selthir and a few men I used to know who hunt me... I would be of the forest yet."

"You choose exile, rather than be with your people?" Dherran eyed him across the fire.

"They are not my people!" Grump's voice was sharp like a whip-crack in the dusk. "The only people I have are you and Khenria."

"But they were, once." Khenria interrupted, her whittling forgotten.

"Once." Grump poked at their wraps with his stick. "But now, like Arlen, I have no people. I know you think Arlen is Shemout Alrashemni. But though he wears the Bloodmark and leads the Shemout, he is not of their heraldry. He marches to his own piper, and pulls others to his will. Like Arlen den'Selthir, I am tired of bloodshed. I was once high-up in the secrets of the Khehemni, though I haven't been for some time. Too many massacres slaughtered my heart. I took to the woods not long after I ended up killing a few of my own."

"Kingsmen? Or Khehemni?" Dherran eyed him.

"Khehemni, mostly." Grump held his gaze. "I am wanted among them. But now we seek others whom I trusted once, who engaged this rebellion with me, and with Arlen. They have fled into the bog, and beyond the borders of Valenghia. Where we go now."

"And go through a war to find them." Khenria scoffed, sliding her knife over her stick. "How easy will that be?"

"Do you doubt me so much, Khenria?" Grump chuckled across the flames. "Is there no forest I can't traverse? No terrain I can't navigate?"

"We should be nearing the Heathren Bog." Dherran narrowed his eyes. "We've been heading northeast for two days. We're just south of the Long Valley. Either we start ascending and run into soldiers watching the border, or we breach the Bog."

A mischievous twinkle lit Grump's brown eyes. "The Heathren

Bog is a bane of a place. And past the bog we hit Velkennish. We shouldn't have trouble with any part of the war. No one really lives in the Bog, technically, and it's a bitch to get through, so why protect it at all?"

"You bastard." A grin stole across Dherran's face. "So we lance like a spear, right to the heart of Valenghia. Right to the capitol, without any interference. And what are we supposed to do there once we arrive?"

"We?" Grump gave Dherran a teasing grin. "You, boy. Once we hit Velkennish, your fight starts. Discreetly. In rings that I know of, rings where you often see the Kingsmount and Stars. Each of us has a part to play in this endeavor. Mine is getting us safely through to Velkennish and finding some contacts when we arrive. Your job, will be to show your spirit and win them to our cause."

"Outlawed fight-rings where Kingsmen compete openly," Khenria growled eagerly. "I heard such things existed in Velkennish."

Grump smiled, poking his creations. "Outlawed professions for outlawed men and women. Who may join us with the proper motivation."

"You said all of us would have a part to play," Dherran glanced at Khenria, "what's Khenria's part in this endeavor?"

Khenria went silent. The smile dropped from her face like a stone. Her eyes flicked to Grump. The two held each other's gaze for a dark moment. At last, Khenria looked away, staring at the fire.

Grump gave a wistful sigh. "I'm sure she'll know her part when it arises."

Dherran looked between them both. "What are you two not telling me?"

"It's not my story to tell, Dherran." Grump waved a hand. "Khenria has a past in Valenghia, and being the leader of the Shemout, Arlen knows some of it. He's hoping to use it to our advantage, that's all."

Dherran blinked, turning toward Khenria. "But, how can you have traveled to Valenghia? Before you met Grump—"

"I don't want to talk about it." Khenria stonewalled him, turning away and wrapping her arms around her skinny knees, gazing deep into the fire's light.

Dherran was used to her temper, but this was more of what plagued her. Deep down, in a place she didn't trust anyone to breach. He wondered how much Grump even knew of her past before he found her in the forest. Dherran reflected upon Arlen's tenderness the day they had left the manor. Rolling it over in his mind, he knew this was a part of Khenria's mystery. Who was she to the Alrashemni, that the Rakhan of Shemout would have kept tabs on her or her family, until he lost word of her when she took to the forest with Grump?

But Dherran could see that now was not the time to press. Khenria gripped her shoulders so hard over her crossed knees that her fingers were white. A shiver took her in the cooling night. Dherran scooted close, gathering her into his arms and pulling her to his chest as he leaned back against the mossy log. She gave a growl of protest, but he insisted, and at last she sat back, pulling his arms tighter around her.

"Are you okay?" He asked, tucking a lock of her black curls behind one ear.

"Leave it, Dherran." She snapped, though she cuddled back into him.

He left it. Khenria was not a woman to push. She would tell him about her past when the time was right, or she wouldn't. Dherran snugged his arms around her skinny waist and kissed her temple, then looked over to Grump.

"So you have a past with Arlen."

Grump gave a lopsided smile, poking at the wraps, now dripping grease with a sizzle onto the red coals. "I have many pasts with Arlen. The first past, I infiltrated his men and slaughtered a good number of them. The second past, he caught me and tortured me for information on the Khehemni Lothren, and I escaped. The third past, I infiltrated Purloch's people, who were aligned with Arlen at the time and only used the bog as a convenient retreat. I was caught again by Arlen, and tortured. But one of Purloch's people vouched for me, that I was changing and believed in unity between our peoples rather than wanting to continue as a spy for the Khehemni. That man helped me escape Arlen a second time. Then I went back to Purloch's, living in secret among them, a secret kept from Arlen. But Arlen's lover found out on a trip through the Bog.

She betrayed me, and Arlen nearly declared war on the Bog, his own allies, to roust me out. They wouldn't give me up, you see. I was valuable, spying against the Khehemni by this time. Through some very tense negotiations, Arlen nearly came to see reason."

"How did that happen?" Dherran asked.

"I helped Arlen and his lover mount a military offensive along with Purloch's people," Grump continued, utterly frank. "A united Khehemni and Alrashemni force, deep into Valenghia, to the capitol of Velkennish. We were going to take the Vhinesse's throne, stop her bastard machinations with the Valenghian Lothren and the Menderian Lothren. This was some seven years before the war, before the Kingsman Summons. Valenghia was having their own Purge of Alrashemni at the time, and it was a horrorshow. We lanced all the way to the Palace of the Vine. We were in the throne hall, we had taken the Vhinesse prisoner. When it all went wrong suddenly. The day was lost. Our forces were surrounded. We fought for our lives in that hall, and escaped Velkennish by the skin of our teeth, those who escaped at all. We scattered. Those from Valenghia went deep underground. Those from the Bog raced back to their trees. And Arlen and his remaining company fled to Vennet to hide and lick their wounds for years."

"Holy Aeon, Grump," Dherran spoke. "Why didn't you ever tell us any of this?"

The old man shrugged, lifting tongs to turn the roasting meat wraps. Well-charred now, the waxy pocket-leaves dripped fat from the rabbit and roasted roots within. "You didn't need to know, Dherran my boy. Telling you and Khenria such things would have only gotten you killed."

"So why now?" Khenria spoke up, pulling away from Dherran to sit cross-legged. "Why push us towards meeting Arlen in Vennet? Why get us involved in a decades-old conflict?"

"What gossip do I hear in the taverns when we travel?" Grump eyed them both. "Talk of war, of troops moving not just to the Valenghian front, but away from it as if for other conflicts. What do I see in the markets? Supplies being bought up by mercenaries for purpose of battle. Someone pulls deep strings in Alrou-Mendera, but to my tastebuds it has only a slight flavor of the Khehemni Lothren this time. Something is happening in Alrou-Mendera. Arlen and I have discussed it at length. A great evil stirs, and is gathering forces, building munitions for an immense conflict. And it warrants an attempt to unite our forces once more. The two of you are excellent fighters, motivated, each with a history that may speak to the people we are trying to rouse from hiding. So I urged us to Vennet on a hope, even if it is just an old fool's hope."

Dherran gazed at the old man as he fetched the rabbit-wraps from the rack over the coals, settling one in each of their bowls and two in Dherran's. "So you still believe in Alrou-Mendera united, Grump? Khehemni and Alrashemni working together?"

"I believe in all of us united, not just Alrou-Mendera, my boy," Grump nodded. "I detest this kin-on-kin slaughter. For we are all one people, Dherran, though some believe there is an ancient hatred that divides us. But if you didn't see an Inking, would you know friend from foe? Khehemni are often as dark-haired as Alrashemni, and all are mixed with Elsthemi blood these days, not to mention the blonde of the native Menderians. Do you have a reason to hate Khehemni? Personally?"

"They almost killed you." Dherran gave a smart-ass smile.

A slow grin blossomed over Grump's face, until he beamed with delight, looking almost his normal self again. "Wraps are done. We—" But suddenly, Grump perked, his brows drawing into a fierce line. His hand flinched from the rabbit-wraps to a large water bladder, which he used to hastily douse the coals.

"Grump! Our supper! What—?" Dherran's ire was silenced instantly by a slice of Grump's thin hand. Grump set two fingers to his lips, his eyes wide. Rising, he crouched and slid with perfect silence out of the clearing. With a glance to Khenria, Dherran followed. He and Khenria tracked Grump for a short minute to a rocky promontory that overlooked the road to Quelis some distance below, where they hunkered in the bushes, watching.

And there, swallowing the road, was a Menderian battalion marching in force. Led by heavy cavalry lancers and archers, Dherran counted at least five hundred men kicking up the evening dust before the rest of the army was lost to view in the trees. At the front of the column, near the standard of the Long Valley Brigade, were two men in strange woven leathers that shocked Dherran into a sudden cold sweat. Both men sat astride an atrocity, a massive black scorpion larger than a bear. The scorpion's chitin glimmered in the evening light like stars far above, a horrible beauty. The men that rode them sent chills deep into Dherran's gut, their kind remembered from when he and Suchinne and the others had been caught all those years ago in Alrashesh.

A soft hiss issued out from Khenria beside Dherran.

Grump swiped his hand in a fierce gesture, commanding her to silence.

Far below, one of the men riding a scorpion pulled it aside to the grass, letting the column pass by. His gaze flicked up to the ridge, searching. Fear swamped Dherran. And suddenly, the image below wavered like a heat-mirage. Where there had been an army passing, there was now nothing but road greying out in the evening shadows.

He was about to say something, when Grump's light hand upon his arm forestalled him. "They're still there," Grump breathed. "Quiet."

They waited in the brush, cramped and tense, for over an hour. At last, Grump shivered, then blinked, settling back into a crouch upon his heels. He gestured them to return, and they slid slowly through the trees to their clearing. Grump went to the dregs of their fire, picking out their sodden wraps and handing them around, lost in a brooding silence.

"What the devil was all that, Grump?" Dherran asked at last.

"*That* was something I was afraid of." Grump bit into his wrap and chewed, his visage still fierce, wrathful. "Arlen's Kingsmen have not been discreet enough with their recruiting. They're about to be answered in force."

Khenria gave a low moan beside Dherran. "That was a regiment of the Long Valley Brigade, being led by those scorpion-riders. I know those riders. They're not Menderian."

Dherran glanced to her, wondering where Khenria had seen the herringbone men before.

"They serve the Khehemni Lothren," Grump's words were very soft. "Or some specific person very high-up in the Lothren. They're known as Kreth-Hakir, and they're specialty is breaking minds, breaking resistance. We were lucky today, *very* lucky, that they were in a hurry and merely blocked our minds rather than sifting through our thoughts to find out who was watching them. And I fear their presence marching on the road to Vennet can mean only one thing. Arlen is about to be sieged. Badly."

"We need to go back!" Dherran turned to grab his gear. "We need to warn Arlen!"

Grump seized his arm in an iron grip, forestalling him. "No, Dherran! If we go back, we get broken, too! Our best hope now is to get to Purloch's House in the Bog, fast. We need support for Arlen, and Purloch and Delennia Oblitenne can give us that. Eat up, and then we ride! Sleep will have to wait. Tomorrow morning we'll reach the bog, and it'll be tough going from there to Purloch's House."

Grump's manner left no room for dissent. He was scared. Dherran could feel it, vibrating from the man like tight bowstring. And that alone, made Dherran's stomach grip in an answering fear. Dherran ate, silent, Khenria snuggling close. In a swift dance, they packed up all their gear, loading the horses once more. And as the moon rose, they set out, eating distance through the forest at a swift pace.

* * *

That long night led to a miserable next morning as they crossed through a section of lowland pines and entered the Heathren Bog. Never had Dherran been so dispirited in his life. Over and over, he went into a tirade, slapping mosquitos and tisk-midges that struck every bit of his uncovered flesh. Grump made them dismount from their horses early in the day to forage for a skunky broad-leaved plant to wipe all over their exposed skin, as well as the horses. The mosquitos and midges were less pressing after that, but a few still managed to worm into Dherran's ears, their whining utterly maddening.

Muck coated Dherran to his knees. They led their horses now, to save the poor animals from sinking too deep in the peaty black morass. Everything smelled of ferment and the sour tang of minerals. His horse snorted, and Dherran reached back to brush midges from its nostrils and eyes.

The slick sound of someone slipping came. A lively, high-pitched curse from Khenria again.

"Slower!" Grump called back. "Pick your way along my route,

and keep to the center! And for Aeon's sake, don't step on any stones or tree roots. Step *between* them. The muck may look deep, but it's better than slipping wrong and breaking an ankle!"

Khenria cursed lividly, and Dherran heard a snort from her mare as she jerked the traces.

"Don't scare the horse, girl!" Grump called back. "She's already as irritated as you are!"

"Is there any end to this, Grump?" Dherran called ahead, swatting at a colony of midges as he passed through and they tried to keep pace with him.

"End? Not until we get to Velkennish, lad! But soon we'll come to the waterways, and then you'll see something interesting!"

Dherran grumbled, but held his tongue. Squelching into the next peaty ooze, he felt it fill his boots yet again. The forest loomed around them, the trees ancient and undisturbed by axemen. A hushed breeze lifted trailing moss from the gnarled limbs. Bird-calls came, haunting whistles and low hoots like reed pipes in a moorish wind.

Slogging along, the morning wore away in the slapping of midges and snorts from the horses. Dherran had thought the endless mud and grass-tufted paths were the best they could hope for, when at midday, a wide, twisted watercourse suddenly opened up before them. The rangy trees lifted their woe-hardened branches over the broad, slow-moving water. Dripping from every branch, moss formed willowy curtains of living grey-green around them. Strange birds Dherran had never heard trilled in the thick air, flitting near the waterline. The entire watercourse seemed alive, and yet was motionless, in a placid yet dangerous way.

A massive shape roiled beneath the water to Dherran's left. The horses spooked, shying, and tugged at their lead-lines.

"Easy," Dherran reached up to soothe his beast. "What was that, Grump?"

"*That*," Grump peered intently at the murky water, "was an aelakir. Keep the horses away from the water, and maintain a sharp eye if they wish to drink. Aelakir can take down a horse. Not to mention a man."

Grump allowed his horse to drink, briefly, watching the water. He motioned Khenria and Dherran forward to water their mounts, keeping his gaze intently on the murk. After a minute, he waved them all back, and backed up his own mount. "That's enough. The aelakir are growing too interested."

As they backed away, Grump fished in his leather forest-jerkin, producing a slender reed pipe. He blew it, and a thin, rangy note lifted into the air and took wing far out over the watercourse. Cocking his head, Grump listened, then sighed. "We're too far out of range. We have to push on. Follow me. Keep the horses as least seven feet from the water's edge. Better muck than blood."

Dherran glanced at Khenria. She lifted her dark eyebrows.

Following the edge of the sluggish, murky water and slapping midges, they continued on, Grump blowing his reed pipe at intervals. Weary and agitated, the horses' tails whipped, though Dherran and Grump had refreshed their musk-leaf countless times. Khenria's mount took her head again, jerking Khenria and sending the poor girl flying into the muck. Splattered in mud, her pretty face was grim, her jaw set as she slogged up from the peat, her green and tan forest leathers entirely soiled. Dherran might have laughed had he not been as miserable as she. He had nimble feet, but his bulk weighed him down far more than Grump and Khenria. He was filthy up to his hips, and exhausted to boot, his heavy stride needing twice the energy to pull himself from the peat than they.

It was nearly four hours later that Grump blew the reed pipe and a whistle sounded back from the northeast. Grump perked, then gestured emphatically. "This way! We're nearly there."

Dherran put his head down and squared his shoulders. He tugged his unwilling mount forward, and it complied with a snort. Minutes seemed like hours, seconds like eons as his tired muscles struggled through sucking squelch.

But then, he heard the resounding clop of horse hooves on wood planking. Dherran looked up, just in time to gain a walkway of wooden planks without stumbling over them. His horse scrambled up onto even footing, and Dherran's tension eased. He heard Khenria sigh behind him as her horse struggled up also. Following Grump's lead, irritation smoothed from beast and man alike. The planking arched out over the sludgy river into a low-spanning bridge supported by a clever cable suspension of woven vines. Climbing up and over, they followed the bridge until they were far out over the river.

Before them, the bridge split. Grump sounded his whistle, listened. An answering whistle came. Grump grunted, then chose the right-hand way and continued on. The bridge eventually gained land, but did not angle down. Instead, the walkway split into broad avenues and platforms, all suspended from cables of vines hanging from the moss-covered trees. Movement hushed through those trees suddenly. Dherran narrowed his eyes, spying shadowy figures clad in grey-green the same color as the mosses, flitting from one platform to another. Suddenly, a sharp three-tone blast came from up ahead. Grump halted their group with an upraised hand, then raised his voice to the green shadows.

"I am Grunnach den'Lhis! I seek urgent audience with Purloch den'Crassis, Master of the House!"

Dherran blinked at the name, having never heard Grump address himself thusly. But before he could comment, a stern voice drifted down, stout like the foundations of ancient trees. "Grump! You old bastard! You owe me ten crown!"

Dherran heard a sigh of bows eased. Like a green mist, over fifty camouflaged men and women slid out of the shadows upon the platforms all around. In their path ahead emerged a tree-trunk of a fellow, dark of hair and eye, every bit Alrashemni. Enormous of stature, his greying dark curls and beard were rangy like a mountain man. A jerkin of scaled leather with a pale moss-woven shirt and breeches clad his thick, muscular frame, his boots the same grey-brown as his jerkin. Armed with a bow, quiver, and countless knives upon his weapons harness, he swept down the wooden plank-way, then swooped Grump up in a bear-hug so tight, Dherran thought he heard the old forest-mouse's bones creak.

The massive man growled and laughed, squeezing Grump. Grump chuckled, embracing the man back before pulling away. They clapped hands upon each other's shoulders, grinning like idiots, though tiny Grump barely came up to the man's collarbones.

"My friend!" The big man chortled, a sigh heavy with time and memories. "So goddamn grey you've gotten." He reached a bear paw up, tousling Grump's mane with a chuckle.

"Aeon-dammit, Purloch, stop it! You're as fucking grey as I am." Grump whisked his head away, but he grinned even as irritation flashed through his eyes. Grump turned, motioning to Dherran and Khenria. "You two! I'd like to introduce my old friend, Purloch den'Crassis. Purloch, meet my children, Khenria den'Bhaelen, and Dherran den'Lhust."

"Children?" Purloch looked them over with dark humorous eyes every bit as shrewd as Grump's. "If you've had children, I'll eat my beard! These are *Kingskinder*, and welcome they are! I've had rumors from my Dremor, Grump, that you were coming. You look terrible, by the way! All sinew and bones! Have you not eaten?"

"Ah, friend!" Grump laughed in a sad manner. "It's been decades since we last supped together, and you think I should still be a lad! No. I've been living in the forest. Take us back to the House, for I have news for your ears only, my friend. Dire news, that needs addressing at once."

"Aye." Purloch gazed over them all with steely eyes. "You all have an air of trouble about you. So my Dremor has seen. Come, come. Give your horses to Finna, she's a good hand with beasts. This way, to the House."

Purloch gestured and Grump stepped to his side. Dherran and Khenria handed off their horses to a woman who swung in on a vine. They pushed through a clever camouflage barrier of vines and moss, and suddenly, Dherran saw Purloch's House.

A veritable maze of tree-ways and shelters opened up before them, cobbled a hundred feet above the water. Purloch's House was an aerial compound, large enough for hundreds of men, if not thousands. A rangy city that sprouted from the ancient trees, it was connected by bridges and walkways, send-lines with carts and baskets, and swing-rope platforms. Bowmen and women in garb of woven grey-green moss came and went, fleet along the ways like lizards. Vine-pulleys transported goods and foodstuffs in woven baskets up and all through the canopy. Dherran watched two men haul at a pulley, sending a basket of mushrooms to a platform buried in the trees. Here was a cluster of yurts where cooking busied twenty folk, there a lounging-space of hammocks woven into a massive net where men smoked. Abodes sprouted out of the mossy trees like odd mushrooms, each constructed in a ring around a host-tree, with walls of woven vines and thatch of thick, curling bark. Live vines supported the structures, dotted with stunning orchids and set with small lanterns that glittered in the oncoming dusk like fireflies.

Grump whisked along the swinging walkways, his gait rolling like a sailor's. The walkways made Dherran nauseous, and he glanced back at Khenria, who also looked green. Her gaze flicked to the sides, and Dherran noticed their party was being flanked. Ten men and women in grey-moss hooded jerkins with leather buckles followed on adjacent paths accessible by rope-swings. All of them wore knives, in addition to bow and quiver, gazing at Grump's party with steely-eyed glances.

Purloch bellowed as they went, he and Grump chatting of idle things, though Dherran got the feeling both were stalling. Whatever was to be discussed was to be done in private. All that discoursed between the two men were jibes about wagers won and lost, and the changes in the compound since Grump had been there. At last, Purloch ushered them into a large rotunda that surrounded a tree with thick, leathery bark, an adjacent longhouse extending over to another rotunda around a nearby tree. Vines thick as Dherran's thigh kept the structure aloft, the entire thing resembling an enormous Cennetian finger-trap toy.

Dherran ducked under the woven door-flap after Grump, and found himself inside a basket, with woven vines from floor to arching roof. Thickly-laid mosses had been tramped into floor with a springy cushion to it. Lounge-areas had been sculpted out of the moss, divans and seats, with woven moss curtains creating privacy in the longhouse area. Fat-lamps burned in small bowls nestled in wall-niches, giving the interior a cozy feel.

Moss was draped over windows, and as they entered, Purloch went around, lowering all the window-covers to cast the interior into the fae hush of the fat-lamps. Purloch settled in one of the mossy divans, and Grump took a seat in a cozy nook something like a chair. Dherran settled into a wider seat like a couch, and Khenria snuggled in next to him. The moss was silken to the touch, not at all as scraggly as it looked. Dherran realized what fine fabric it must make, remembering the archers with their grey-green jerkins. Unrolling a scaly leather square over the moss, Purloch created a table. Which he loaded with fruits and pods from baskets upon one wall, mushrooms, and a few hunks of jerked meat. Water was dippered from a wooden bowl with a rain-collecting spout outside, into carven bowls for drinking, then offered around.

"Drink, friends!" Purloch boomed.

Grump drank, obviously unconcerned about poison, and so did Dherran and Khenria. Purloch offered the foodstuffs, and Grump immediately set to breaking open pods and popping fruits with his belt-knife, then sharing the contents around on wooden platters.

"Here, lad, try the pink one. Looks disgusting, but tastes like wintermellon! Khenria, you'll like the yellow-orange, the sticky one. It resembles a passionberry. Try!"

Dherran and Khenria exchanged a glance, then set to. The fruits were every bit as good as Grump said, and the jerked meat delicious with a heady, sweet spice. But Dherran noticed Grump left a few items behind upon the table. Most notably, a handful of purple-capped mushrooms with orange gills.

"Testing me, Purloch?" Grump chuckled darkly as they ate.

"Just seeing if you remember." Purloch gave a subtle, tense smile.

"Hagsgill. I remember." Grump kept eating, munching a bit of jerky.

"Mmm…" Purloch sipped his water. "That was a fine day."

"There are five hundred dead souls who would disagree with you, you know…" Grump snorted, acid in his tone.

"They deserved it." Purloch shrugged, though his manner was still tense. Dherran realized the true parlay Arlen had sent them here for had begun. He kept silent, he and Khenria watching, listening.

Grump looked up, his forest-grey eyes steely. "Deserved it or not. It was an awful thing to do."

Purloch went viciously calm, his dark grey eyes every bit the war-general. "Them or us, Grunnach. You did right to report their movements to me. No lance that size should ever have penetrated the Bog so deeply from Valenghia. They had a few someones on the inside among us, and they were here to wipe us out. You did well, and hagsgill was the only way."

"It was sneaky and dishonest," Grump bit back, "adding that to their water-barrels. You didn't listen to them shitting their asses out and puking and moaning until they died. I did. I stayed, to make sure it was done to the last man. You got to remain here, snug, the tip of the Vhinesse's sword never even *touching* your precious House."

It was a scathing tirade. Purloch and Grump stared at each other like a pair of fighting mongooses, bristling.

"In any case," Purloch stated, "I didn't tell anyone you'd run out on us after that, Grunnach. When folk asked, I said I sent you on a long scouting mission. Maybe years. I've done a lot of thinking about your desertion. Maybe I was wrong to ask you to do what I did, but maybe it was also necessary. Maybe I should have considered what you've seen of warmongering, and taken that into account."

"Maybe you should have." Grump bit tersely, his eyes flashing with a bitter passion.

"I've missed you, old friend." Purloch sat back with a sigh, gazing at Grump with deep wistfulness. "Nothing's been the same since you left us."

A long silence stretched between them. It pulled like taffy, with slow, deep emotions Dherran didn't understand, and had never seen from Grump. Grump scowled, ran a hand through his wayward grey hair, then finally sighed.

"I did what I had to." Grump crossed his arms, staring Purloch down, though something in it was vulnerable. "But war rises around us again with the Queen's deposition, despite my best efforts to stay out of it. I need your men to rally, Purloch. To take up arms in the greater world once more. And I also need you to put Dherran, Khenria, and I through to Velkennish immediately."

"Why?" A flash of anger flitted through Purloch's eyes.

"Since you'll never leave your cozy tree-fort, what do you care?" Grump sniffed.

"I do care. About you, my friend. But why do you join the plotting of nations again, when it only caused us so much suffering? So much rancor..." Purloch's eyes narrowed, and there was deep rage there.

Grump gave a huff. "There was a time, *friend*, when we fought to oppose injustice wherever we saw it. Or have you forgotten?"

Purloch crossed his strong arms over his chest, scowling. His jerkin of scale-leather creaked, the only sound in the room. His eyes flicked to Dherran, then Khenria. "Never thought you'd take on a couple of green Kingskinder."

"They're hardly green." Grump reached out for some more

jerked meat.

"Are they Inked?" Purloch raised an eyebrow with a glimmer of interest.

"He is." Grump nodded at Dherran.

"Fucking the lad, are you, then?"

"No." Grump fixed the man in his gaze like an eagle, vicious. "Besides, that's none of your business anymore. But I need your men, Purloch. And Delennia Oblitenne's. Arlen is rallying his forces again against the machinations of the Lothren, but I saw a Khehemni answer upon the road last night. A battalion some two thousand men strong, headed to Vennet. With Kreth-Hakir. They're involved again, Purloch. Which is why we need you, and Delennia. Arlen is facing far more than he knows, and he needs us."

"Kreth-Hakir..." Purloch pursed his lips, his dark brows furrowed. Dherran recognized the single long breath of Alrashemni training. "Careful, Greyhawk. You don't want to get mixed up with Arlen again, especially if mind-benders are involved."

"Arlen led us to victory last time."

"Arlen led us to *slaughter* when he betrayed us so suddenly in the Vhinesse's palace, *precisely* because of mind-bending!" Purloch's gaze was hard. "We escaped, yes, but at a cost too high for you. And for me. And for Delennia."

"We knew the risk." Grump said it as if trying to convince himself, his eyes sad. "And Arlen is about to be in serious trouble, Purloch. Are you saying you could abandon him in his hour of need?"

Surprisingly, Purloch slipped a massive paw out and set it upon Grump's thin shoulder. "People are matchsticks to Arlen den'Selthir. Strike, burn, and toss the char away. We were no different. And Arlen broke to mind-bending last time, and because of what happened, Delennia is full of hatred, stewing in that fucking fortress of hers. You couldn't court her for all the gold in Praough."

"But Arlen didn't break to the Kreth-Hakir," Grump countered, "only to the Vhinesse herself. I *can* convince Delennia to join us once more, Purloch, lend us that mind of steel she has, along with all her militia. Because I have something she wants." Grump gave a sly smile, and its utter deviousness lifted the hairs on Dherran's neck.

"What do you mean, you old goat?" Purloch lifted an eyebrow.

"We have a means of persuading Delennia to our cause this time. Wake the Bitterlance again."

Dherran felt a rush of cold water run through him at Grump's cryptic words. "What is the Bitterlance?"

Grump chuckled softly, ominous. "Delennia Oblitenne is nicknamed *Die Berkzat*. It means *the bitter one* in Old Valenghian. She used to have a consort. His nickname was *Der Skerrzen, the lance*. I'll give you one guess as to whom the lance is."

An electric certainty passed through Dherran. "Arlen den'Selthir."

"Have you ever met a better swordsman, boy?" Grump's voice was soft.

"But Arlen said he had a wife, that she was killed."

"Delennia was not killed. And she wasn't his wife, she was his long-time lover. But the unity of the Bitterlance was destroyed in our push to the Palace of the Vine, so long ago. It broke, right there in that throne hall when Arlen suddenly betrayed us because of the Vhinesse's mind-bending, and Halsos' Hell was the price we all paid. Most deeply, Delennia and Arlen."

Dherran frowned. "What do I possibly have that can win this woman to our banner?"

"Wait and see, Dherran." Grump gazed at him, a long thoughtfulness. "You and Khenria will both have your roles to play once we reach Velkennish."

"Why don't I like the sound of that?" Dherran narrowed his brows.

"Are you certain these two have something that can persuade the Bitch of Velkennish to join Arlen again, Grunnach?" Purloch gazed at them thoughtfully.

"Indeed they do." Grump selected another fruit. "Two somethings, that she won't be able to walk away from. Not this time."

Purloch's shaggy eyebrows rose, as he took Dherran and Khenria in. "Indeed."

CHAPTER 28 – THEROUN

Men with spears ringed Theroun den'Vekir. But that was fine.

Theroun had sat silent for three days, planning his strategy. And this dawn, he'd been hustled out of his tent by guards with Pythian-resin upon their spears, and shuttled to General den'Ulthumen's command tent. They'd been waiting a half-hour. The guards were slouching now, shifting from foot to foot. Theroun's two Captains were also present, though not under arrest. Arlus den'Pell sat upon a bench by the tent-wall with his thick climber's arms crossed, glowering under his black brows. Vitreal den'Bhorus was similarly nonplussed, his foxlike face pinched, re-crossing his boots in irritation as he sat back against the stiff canvas.

Standing in the center of the tent, Theroun was perfectly content. Outside, sounds came of the camp waking. The clop of horses being walked through. The slosh and roar of someone who'd been drunk splashed awake with a bucket of water. The continuous *tink-tink,* of a hammer shaping a horseshoe. Smells of cooking rose from the nearest mess-tent, full of peppercorn to fortify men in battle today, thick with thyme and rosemary to stave off infection from the wounds they would take.

But if Theroun was careful, the wounds would be few.

Few, at least, for his regiments.

"Attention!" A call came from beyond the closed tent-flaps, and the guards inside straightened. General Lharsus den'Ulthumen strode in, wiping his thick hands off on his breeches as if he'd just eaten.

"Theroun! It's time. Approach the table. You too, Captains."

Theroun's hard glower was no more nor less than usual as he stepped to the vellum spread upon the table. Den'Ulthumen eased, his jaw relaxing beneath that well-trimmed mane of gold as he realized Theroun was going to give him no trouble this morning. At least, not overtly. Theroun leaned over the map, settling his hands upon the table. His eyes flicked over the schema, memorizing the markers that indicated Menderian companies and their movements. He'd seen it all before, but this was his last chance to see it before battle.

"Your assigned regiments are assembling at the picket-lines in the north field," Lharsus leaned over the map at Theroun's side. "Your companies will form a wedge up this hill, breaking from the river and riding through the forest, effectively securing passage for the armies after you. Fleetrunners will march first, armed with dual-blades…"

Theroun kept his usual glower as Lharsus outlined the plan. Theroun paid attention, wanting to know what Lharsus expected him to do, so he could anticipate the moves of the main force.

"You have one week, Theroun," Lharsus concluded. "But we expect you to secure the near valley by the river as soon as you can. Send riders back to confirm your rout of the Elsthemi camp, and we will ready the main force to march upon Lhen Fhekran."

Theroun was quiet at den'Ulthumen's side, arms crossed over his jerkin. "And the special supplies? The resin and asphyxiating-powder?"

Lharsus looked up, a frown upon his golden features. "We have enough Devil's Breath arrows for ten apiece per archers, so make sure they're used effectively. The Pythian-resin will be lashed to draft stock. Split the wax seal on the crocks and have men dip their blades before you engage the keshari. Don't spill them. If anything tracks through it…"

"We'll lose hooves off horses and feet off men. I know. How many crocks do we get?"

Lharsus was silent a long moment. "Ten. That should be more than enough."

Theroun eyed Lharsus severely. The man was holding out on him. "You're sending my men in to wipe out the Elsthemi on the plains before your main drive can even get there, Lharsus. We're talking about maybe ten thousand fighters versus one-fifth of that in my force. If you want me to implement your plan, I need all of the poisons. Every arrow, every crock."

"I'm only authorized by the Chancellate through Lhaurent to give you half, Theroun. The rest is to be saved for breaching Lhen

Fhekran." Den'Ulthumen rubbed his beard, frowning.

"If I fail, Lharsus, you won't have that chance." Theroun stared the younger General down. "This plan will fail if you only give me half of what I need. But when I finish, you can use the remaining poisons for your initial strike upon the city."

"Dammit, man! You put me in a bind." Lharsus drummed his fingers on the map table, stroking his short golden beard with the other hand. Finally, he hitched a sigh. "As you will. But if you waste every damn arrow and barrel on this push, the Chancellate will have both our heads."

"And if I fail, Lharsus, they'll have your cock. My head will grace the cat-pommel of the Elsthemi High-General, so I have the brighter future. But it is upon you and I to ensure our own victory with the supplies we have available."

At that, the younger General's lips quirked. "You'll survive this, I'm sure. Back when I was just a green recruit, they always said General Theroun den'Vekir had more lives than a keshar."

"I've had more lives than any man should." Theroun barked severely. "But I live for King and country. And that's all I've ever done."

Lharsus smiled a bit more. "Shall I show you to the supplies outside in my weapons-tent?"

"Don't bother. I'll find them." Theroun's bark was short. There was no reason to pretend patience, nor camaraderie. "Den'Bhorus! Den'Pell! With me!"

Theroun left with his Captains in tow, and the guards let them walk out. But Theroun noted Lharsus' guards trailed behind as they crossed the bustling avenue toward the General's green-and-black weaponry tent.

Den'Bhorus stepped close. "We're being watched, General."

"Obviously." Theroun growled. "Wait until we have a moment. Stay close."

His Captains nodded. They stepped to the weapons-tent and Theroun pushed inside the canvas to find the tent already in action. Heavy-hooved carthorses were being lashed with clay pots the size of a small melon. Smaller beasts were laden with baskets of arrows, points tied with sachets. The sachets were no bigger than a man's thumb, but even that much Devil's Breath could easily asphyxiate men and beasts in a twenty-foot radius.

Theroun barked orders to hurry it up and get the special supplies to the north field. Men loading the horses saluted crisply and jumped to. Theroun and his Captains moved through to the other side of the tent, where a press of soldiers geared up.

For a moment Theroun lost sight of their watchdogs.

"You two. Listen." He growled quickly to his Captains. "I'm certain den'Ulthumen or the Lothren have spies in our regiments. As we get to the field, proceed as the General outlined. He must believe we'll carry out the plan. You'll receive my true orders when we're a fair way into the trees. Set your ten best men upon horseback, to ride at the rear of the column and keep eyes open for informants. If any break away, kill them. *None* of your men are to dip their blades in that resin, nor take up devil-arrows before we leave the field. Follow my lead, and we'll all survive this day."

"Yes, sir." "Aye, sir." Den'Bhorus and den'Pell scowled, their veteran faces betraying nothing.

Neither man argued Theroun's lead.

They gained the farthest rim of tents, then the northern picket-lines, seeing two thousand strong assembling upon the sloping field. It was a small contingent, with two hundred mounted cavalry. Only a spare sliver of the fifteen thousand assembled at the border. It was a suicide mission, Theroun saw at a glance. Too few horses, too many foot soldiers. An entire battalion of press-ganged men from Jadoun, brainwashed, with little loyalty. Theroun's gaze surveyed the horses being untethered as the cavalry mounted up. Scrawny mounts from the south, not a single war-horse among them.

But that was all fine. They weren't going to execute den'Ulthumen's plan, not while Theroun had breath left with which to bellow orders.

Theroun's squire found him with a horse and his light leather armor. Neither den'Bhorus nor den'Pell had a horse, so Theroun handed his beast to a nearby soldier and motioned him to follow through the assembled masses. All eyes were upon Theroun as he waded through soldiers and horse lines with his Captains flanking him.

The field fell silent, enough to hear ravens squabbling at the tree line. Men parted like grain before the scythe. Theroun was a vile legend, but a legend all the same. More than once came murmurs of *Black Viper*, a hushed sea of wary respect. Theroun strode to the front, watching men hold firm or shy away before his scowl.

Suddenly, one tall black-skinned man shouted out, "*Verouni!*"

Theroun halted. Squinting against the morning sun cutting his eyes from the flanks of the Kingsmount, his gaze picked out the tall fellow who had spoken. Duthukan. Dark-skinned Jadounians were nodding, affirmation in their eyes. Murmurs of *Verouni* spread in a ripple.

"They're calling you Truth-Warrior," Vitreal den'Bhorus spoke. "It's a vast compliment in Jadounian."

"I know what it means." Theroun looked around, watching dark-skinned men knuckle their brows in respect. In the center of his army now, it was a good time to do his speech. Signaling for his horse, he set a foot in the stirrup and mounted up, surprisingly smooth. As if his body remembered battle, it gave him youth again as he settled into his saddle. He took up the reins and led his well-trained warhorse in a tight circle to see his army.

"Take a look around!" Theroun bellowed. "For many of us will die today!"

Men shifted uneasily, falling silent. This was not a typical beginning to a rallying speech. But it caught their attention, and their attention was what mattered.

"Some of you know my reputation!" Theroun continued in his dawn-slicing roar. "I am a feared commander, gentlemen! But I am also ruthless in protection of my men! We carry dangerous weapons this day. The mishandling of any item will be your painful demise by acid that burns through to bone, and powder that chokes you to death! Follow my orders *explicitly*, and we will all live to see dawn tomorrow!"

He had their attention. Every face was turned to him, rapt. Many scowled, but some were wide-eyed in fear. Theroun's guess had been right. None but himself and his two Captains had been told the horrors they wielded today.

"As such," he continued, "I demand that you follow my orders, and the orders of the two Captains beside me, for your safety and the safety of your fellows. Beware the clay pots and the arrows with sachets – they are not to be touched unless you are instructed to do so! My orders will secure minimal losses, but only when followed *to the letter*! Give me an *aye, sir* if you understand!"

"Aye, sir!" It was a weak call, from frightened men.

"Damn it to Aeon, give me an aye, sir if you understand!!" Theroun roared, his voice carrying far over the north field. This time, the roar that came back was deafening. Men looked haler, angry rather than scared. Roaring before battle was good for fears.

"Now!!" Theroun led his horse in a tight circle again. "We march! I will lead the column. Stick to the river, stay tight! We will distribute the resin-barrels and special arrows after we gain the tree line. Fleetrunners, first wedge! Brigadiers, second wedge! Foot after Brigadiers! Horse at the end of the column!"

With that, Theroun jabbed his horse in its flanks, and it trotted up the slope to the front of the crowd near the tree line. Den'Pell peeled off to his High Brigade, and den'Bhorus to his Fleetrunners, giving special orders. Theroun saw ten men each shoulder through to the cavalry lines and get mounted up on extra horses. Theroun's squire handed up his battle-leathers. Buckling on his breastplate, greaves and gauntlets, Theroun kept an eye on his men as they made final preparations. A cinching of a loose saddle-girth here. Adjustment of a breastplate buckle there. A scabbard lashed over a horse's withers for a better mounted draw.

And then, the great spread of readiness came over the field. Theroun knew that feeling to his bones. There came a time in every battle, when men have made themselves ready for whatever comes next. And in that moment, Theroun could taste their expectancy upon the early-autumn breeze. A hawk shrilled above, and ravens screamed after it, harrying the raptor. Theroun looked up, watching the ill omen, putting little stock in it.

His eyes fell upon his army. Their eyes watched him back.

"Move out!!" He bellowed.

The war-horn blew. Theroun wheeled his horse and set pace at a walk, heading toward the bank of the river. A standard-bearer was mounted at his side, Alrou-Mendera's cobalt mountain-and-stars banner snapping in the early air. As his horse gained the incline near the river and plodded to the forest's edge, Theroun allowed his gaze to settle upon the blue banner, the Kingsmount and five crowning stars sewn in gold upon it. If any doubted that Alrashemni had founded this nation, it was there, all too plain upon the standard. Below that emblem was the roaring lion of House den'Ildrian done in gold, wreathed in olive branches of peace.

Such a sham.

Den'Bhorus and Den'Pell had found horses and migrated up to Theroun's flanks now. Theroun focused on the trees as they entered the dappled shade, hardy oaks and copperpine and red cedar. Scouring the forest, he saw no sign of keshari riders. Oh, they had spies watching the Menderian camp. Theroun could feel his skin crawling with feline attentiveness in a least two directions. But there was a good six hours of marching through these hills before they got to the Valley of Doors, where the Highlanders were camped.

Ambush would not come for a while yet.

Further into the dappled shade they went, up a forested hill-crest and then into a broad gully. Theroun made mental notes upon the topography as they went. The river churned fifty feet below to their left, beginning to cut a canyon through the hills. An ancient road followed the river. The old road had been carved into the canyon long ago, but was too narrow for an army, pocked and broken from time. Horse couldn't hold a slope as steep as what led down to the canyon, but keshar could. Theroun scoured it for any sight of cat, knowing that the keshari's first plan would be to chase Menderian horses down that slope into the gorge.

He wasn't going to let that happen.

Theroun rose in his stirrups, twisted his damaged body to see the column stretching back into the forest behind him. Tingling upon Theroun's neck grew more vicious as they proceeded onward, the rushing river hundreds of feet below in the gorge. He could almost feel the keshari noose cinching tighter in the shadows.

The cool morning turned hot, summer's last gasp. Men wiped sweat from their brows. Steel plate clanked, leather gear creaked, branches cracked underfoot as boots and hooves stomped through loam and over rocks. A small buzz of talking began in Theroun's army. Dice-cups came out, and soon rattling could be heard as Jadounians wagered with laughs of bravado.

"So." Den'Bhorus broke the silence at the front of the column, riding to Theroun's right. "Orders, sir? We've been in the trees three hours now."

"Not just yet." Theroun kept his voice low for only Vitreal and Arlus.

"What are we waiting for?" Den'Pell rumbled, eyeing Theroun.

"For a good spot to cache our weapons."

"*What*?!" Vitreal turned in the saddle to face Theroun, and even Arlus showed a tremor of shock in his mountainous frame. "*Cache* our weapons?"

"You heard me. The poisonous ones, at least." Theroun barked softly, keeping his eyes on the verge. It was too soon for an attack. They had hours left to march and the keshari would want to catch them nearer their own camp where reinforcements would be handy.

But one never quite knew in battle.

Vitreal snorted, his sneer firmly in place. "So we go into Elsthemen weaponless?"

"And naked."

"*Naked?*" Arlus rumbled. Vitreal was too shocked to comment, his mouth hanging open and his eyes huge.

"What happens if we take an army into enemy territory fully armed, gentlemen?" Theroun continued. "When we're facing an adversary known to attack first and take stock of the situation later?"

"We engage." Arlus' low rumble was thoughtful.

"Yes. They engage us, and we must engage back." Theroun nodded. "As the Chancellate meant us to. And if we engage, we have to use what weapons were given us to survive keshari, the resin and the asphyxiation powder."

"Which decimates our own forces." Arlus rumbled back. "Securing Kingsmen deaths."

"Which is counter to our objective, gentlemen. Vitreal, did your men get through three nights ago?"

Den'Bhorus blinked, coming back from his surprise. "Yes, captain. I had a runner back this morning that they made it to the Elsthemi camp. Though General Merra Alramir is apparently holding the rest as hostages."

"We'll get them back safely if all goes to plan."

"So... naked?" Den'Bhorus was unnaturally subdued.

"Problem, Captain?" Theroun glanced over. "Afraid the keshari women will see what you've not got?"

Den'Bhorus colored, then sneered with ire. The barb worked,

returning the man to his usual cunning self, which was what Theroun needed. "Far from it, General. Surrendering unarmed is one thing, naked is another!"

"Naked will buy us what we need from the keshari."

"Which is what? Jeers?" Vitreal sneered.

"Precisely."

The fox-like man blinked. "Excuse me?"

"Jeers and jests will keep our men alive. Laughter in the keshari ranks will ease their tension enough to ask themselves *why* men are marching naked before they strike. And since they have spies watching us right now, they'll be doubly confused about why we disrobed mid-march. Disarmed. Which is what I need if we're to live through today."

Vitreal's face opened up in awe. He blinked, a slow smile lifting one side of his lips. The man was almost handsome when he wasn't peevish. "Fucking Viper." He half-laughed. "Who knew it would come to this? You were famous for your viciousness upon the Aphellian Way, but men will call you mad for another reason entirely after today."

"If all goes well, Captain, my madness will save the lives of each and every man behind us now. And save the throne of our Queen. This is a good spot. Halt the column here."

Theroun reined his horse, scanning the verge. Halfway through the hills now, the trees had opened up into a wide swath of meadow, sun lighting the clearing gold before they ascended back into the forest. It was wide enough for the two thousand to amass, and Theroun's riders would see any spies who peeled off into the trees. He wheeled his horse to face the front of the column as the rear came to a shambling halt. Soon all were stopped and facing him expectantly. He raised his voice to a roar, to be heard throughout the clearing.

"Soldiers of Alrou-Mendera! Your Queen lives, and this war in her honor is a sham!"

Theroun watched two thousand men absorb this sudden revelation. Men shouted, they called out, they cursed. Their faces opened in shock or closed in anger. Men shuffled, glanced at each other, until they finally began to quiet, attending back to Theroun.

Waiting. He lifted his voice again.

"This day will go down in history, and I will tell you why! Today is the day we lift no weapon against our foe, because our foe is already behind us! Your nation of Alrou-Mendera has been usurped, gentlemen, by its own King's Chancellate! I have news that Queen Elyasin is alive, hale, and safe in Elsthemen! So I am leading a revolt against that tyranny, right here, right now. All who wish to return and serve your Queen's enemy may do so. Now."

Theroun's hard eyes pierced his men. Indecision filled faces, darkened brows. Muttering began, surreptitious glances. All were looking to see if any would call Theroun a liar and rejoin the main force. Theroun's gaze scanned the rear of his army near the tree line. Fleetrunners and Brigadiers sat their mounts, hard eyes scanning the crowd. Grim faces. Theroun didn't think any of the Lothren's spies would be so obvious as to leave now, but they certainly would during what was coming next.

"Many of you think me insane." Theroun barked, catching all attention again. "The Black Viper sits before you and speaks treason. But I tell you, gentlemen, that my one and only duty is to the true throne of this nation, and that that throne is yet occupied by Queen Elyasin den'Ildrian Alramir! Dispossessed she may be, but I honor my oaths. Will you honor yours? Will you come with me, trust me, in what we next must do to return our nation to its rightful ruler?"

Many shifted, some muttered. One plucky younger Brigadier shouted. "What is it we're going to do, General?"

Theroun allowed himself to smile. A hard, bloodthirsty smile. "What we do now will save your life, and the lives of the men next to you, so pay attention! We're going to get naked, gentlemen! And then we're going to join the only force that can help Elyasin win her country back! The Highlanders!"

Startled guffaws broke out among battle-ready men. Jeers, whistles, laughs.

"The men thought they just heard you say we're going to get naked and then defect!" One Fleetrunner Lieutenant bellowed, grinning.

"They heard right!" Theroun shouted back. He let his face harden, showed them how serious he was. "We're going to drop our weapons, right here, right now. You will then drop trow and bundle all clothing and weaponry with your belt and cinch it to the nearest horse, even your boots! All riders will dismount and lead their steeds in rows between every tenth row of foot soldiers."

Men had gone quiet. They gaped at him.

"We're going to walk to the enemy buck-ass naked?!" Someone shouted out.

Theroun's gaze went very hard, the cold gaze of the Black Viper. He reached down, unbuckling his sword and longknives, letting them fall to the grass beside his horse. Then went his gauntlets and gloves. Then he unfastened his chest plate and greaves, shucking them off. His black jerkin was next, then his shirt, belt, everything he could get to without dismounting. A number of low whistles came when his men saw the massive ropes of scarring that ruined his right side. And then he did dismount. Theroun faced his men and knelt to unbuckle his boots then kick them off.

Then he stood, unbuttoned the fly of his breeches, and dropped them.

No one laughed. No one jeered. No one made a sound.

"He's fucking serious." Someone near the front muttered.

"Yes, gentlemen!" Theroun barked, bundling his clothes and boots and weapons together with his belt and cinching it tight, affixing that to his saddle. "The only way to disarm our enemy is to be fully disarmed! When they come for us, some may yet attack first! And that is why you will now sort yourselves into groups of ten by the nearest cavalry horse! Tie your bundle to the horse, and if an attack comes, you will run to that horse and get behind it. *Do not, under any circumstance, pull weapons!* Cavalry, your horses are to be blinded. If keshar attack, you will push the horses into the path of the cats! Are we clear?"

"And get fucking eaten! No weapons against keshar?!" Someone yelled.

Theroun glowered, then mounted up buck-ass nude so everyone could see him. "It's either this, or we use the poisons provided us! Who would like to be the first to try Pythian-resin upon their skin? How about Devil's Breath in their lungs?"

Men shifted uneasily. "Better that than being naked against keshari legions!"

Theroun finally singled out the troublemaker. He sat on horseback, one of the cavalry. Theroun flicked his fingers to Vitreal, and the Runner Captain reined his horse close. "Take his horse. Bind its eyes and hobble it, tie it to that tree." Theroun gestured to the furthest edge of the clearing, to an oak sixty feet away. The wind was in the correct direction to not blow anything back towards them. "Have the man use a blade dipped in resin to give the horse a shallow cut. Then have him come back to the edge of the group and shoot it with a powder-arrow."

Vitreal gave a grim nod. His green eyes were hard as he went to the dissenter, got the man to dismount. All was carried out to Theroun's specifications as a curious army looked on. The horse was tied to the tree and hobbled. The dissenter approached with a spear dipped in resin. With a twist of contempt on his features for Theroun, the man flicked the spear to give the horse a shallow cut upon the shoulder, believing all this merely a strange punishment for his bellyaching.

The horse immediately broke into screaming.

It lashed out, tried to rear and buck like hornets stung it from all directions. But the hobbles held and it ended up crashing to its side, writhing violently. Screaming an unholy sound that horses were not meant to make, its shrill squealing pierced every ear. Worse than a beast that had taken a spear or a flaying by keshar-claws, men put hands to their ears at the unholy torrent that issued from the creature.

All could see the hole being eaten in the horse's shoulder, fast. Longer than a man's forearm now, the cut was deepening to bare bloody bone as the beast writhed. The man began to sprint back to the group, eyes wide with horror.

Theroun nodded to Vitreal. The Fleetrunner Captain stepped to the dissenter's shoulder and proffered a warbow, carefully holding a single arrow with its small sachet. Men made way for him, shrinking back from whatever horror was next.

With ginger fingers, the man took his weapons.

He looked to Theroun, terror in his eyes. Apology. Anguish.

"Loose that arrow, soldier. See what General den'Ulthumen and the King's Chancellate intended for your hide today." Theroun's voice was hard, his face even harder. All his men had to see the terrors they carried. The terrors Lhaurent had wanted used today.

The horseless man squared his shoulders. His steed was still screaming, writhing at the edge of the clearing. A taut silence settled over the men as the fellow lined up his stance, took a breath, then swiftly nocked, drew, and fired in one smooth shot. The arrow sped toward the horse, pierced its flank. A cloud of white dust enveloped the beast, like someone had burst a bag of flour upon the saddle.

And suddenly, the screaming was cut off. Rasps came from the beast, gurgles. The horse struggled, then lay still. Silence filled the clearing as the white dust dissipated upon the wind, blowing east into the trees.

"Fuck that." Someone muttered from the throng.

And then it began.

Baldrics were shed, swords and knives clattering to the earth. Warbows and quivers were loosed from saddles. Cavalry dismounted and foot soldiers began to shuck armor, then clothing. Jadounians grinned, a fire lighting their eyes, their southern war-humor visible at last as they jested and congratulated each other in their native tongue for having various phallic attributes. And waggled their parts with buoyant laughter. Menderians soon joined in, laughing and boasting as they stripped, some of the younger men with blushes, some of the veterans merely stoic.

And Theroun saw also, a curious camaraderie happening among the Brigadiers and Fleetrunners. Shucking baldrics and gear, leather jerkins and sweat-stained shirts, these men were realizing who wore the black Kingsmount-and-Stars upon their chests. They grinned at each other. Arms were clasped with startled laughs, as Kingsmen long in hiding finally recognized friend among friend. They were mostly old veterans, but a few were surprisingly young. And as Theroun watched, he realized that fully half of both companies wore Alrashemni ink, nearly all of the veterans and commanders.

Theroun glanced at Runner-Captain den'Bhorus, and Brigadier-Captain den'Pell. Both were naked, re-mounted atop their horses. But the both of them had nicked their chests with their belt-knives, and now red Inkings blossomed over their chests like bloodstains in the high autumn sun, displaying their markings proudly to their men.

A wry smile touched Theroun's lips. He should have known they were Shemout, the secret Bloodmarked spy faction of the

Alrashemni. The two Captains were regarding him back, cautiously. They'd followed him, but they didn't really trust the Black Viper. He wasn't Alrashemni. Theroun wore no marking upon his body except for his twisted scars.

No marking he was going to show anyone, at least.

At last, the boisterousness was dying down. Theroun straightened in the saddle. "We will cache our dangerous weapons anon. But the first keshar we see - all hands laced at your heads! Fall to rank and march on!"

Theroun dropped off his horse to the grass. He passed his beast off to a stout Brigadier, then strode from the clearing. Arlus and Vitreal were close on his heels, and soon all three men marched side-by-side on foot, leading the column.

Buck-ass nude.

Vitreal glanced over with a smirk. "None of us is ever going to live this down, will we?"

Theroun had half his attention upon the ground, avoiding stones, and half his attention upon the trees, scanning for keshari. He glanced behind, to feast his eyes upon a sight he'd not soon forget and might never again see.

Two thousand cocks swinging in the early autumn breeze.

A number of the nearest men grinned, especially the Jadounians. Theroun faced forward again, picking his steps with care. It wouldn't do to pierce his foot on a stick and die from infection.

"Gentlemen. I commend you for staying true today. I am not an easy man to follow."

"You know, they said the Black Viper was a madman. Now I believe it."

Theroun glanced over, to see Vitreal smiling to his right. Arlus gave a basso chuckle from his left. It had been a long time since Theroun had been teased by a comrade. And for the first time in a long while, it made Theroun smile.

It was good to be back in war.

CHAPTER 29 – ELYASIN

Elyasin was exhausted. Her eyes blurred, staring at the map on the table in her quarters as she lounged in her cobalt night-robes by a roaring fire. She had already dismissed herself from the late revelry Therel was having with the leaders of Clan Burrskin, her drinking no match for hardy Highlanders. The past days had been one war-council after another with clan leaders on their way through Lhen Fhekran to the border. Elyasin and Therel's meals had been hasty, their nights hastier. All their hours were spent pouring over maps, and looking over supply lists and reports of skirmishes against Alrou-Mendera. Worrying over whether their smaller Elsthemi forces would hold if the Menderians marched in force. Villages near the border had been evacuated. Herds were being moved from the Lethian Valley up into the Highlands proper, everything except what was needed to support the war.

Taking another sip of telmen-wine, Elyasin glanced over a report from Clan Six-Tooth. General Merra had arrived at the front, they reported. She had stopped for a night on her way back from the mountains to affirm that her delivery of Elohl and Fenton had been successful despite a clan-clash. And then moved on at once, to where she was needed.

A knock came at the door. Elyasin blinked and set her goblet down upon the table. "Enter!" She glanced at the door just as a blonde mane popped around the door.

"Thaddeus! Come in." Elyasin motioned him in. Lanky Thaddeus moved forward to stand before her, shuffling his feet. Elyasin reached to the wine carafe upon the table and poured the scribe a glass. He stepped forward and took it, still standing awkwardly.

"Sit, Thad."

He edged into the proffered seat. "My Queen is too kind."

Elyasin laughed, enjoying his bookish manner, such a contrast from the bawdy Highlanders. "I don't bite, Thad."

"No, my Queen." He shook his head briskly, then blushed and looked down, his hands laced tight.

"What troubles you, Thaddeus?"

"Have you... have you had any news of General Theroun?" He spoke at last.

"No." She shook her head. "Although, he is most likely at the Elsthemi-Menderian front by now. His description is being passed to the clan leaders. If he's spied during battle, they are to send a keshari rider posthaste. But why are you here, Thad? Not to discuss Theroun, I suppose?"

"No, milady." He shook his head hastily, then hesitated. "I was thinking, that if you are ever to retake Lintesh, there might be an easier way... than the Lethian Valley."

"Excuse me?" Elyasin blinked.

Thaddeus cleared his throat, had another sip of wine to fortify himself. "I enjoy maps, you see, and... I was pouring over a few in the weeks before Theroun sent me out, looking at the terrain the war would be fought upon. And I came upon a very old map in the Annals. It had passages... under the mountains marked upon it. And there was one," Thaddeus stepped out of his chair. Setting his wine aside upon the floor and eagerly whisking up Elyasin's map, he refolded it so he could peruse a certain area. "Yes. Here. Right here. See where that crag juts out behind Lhen Fhekran? There's a tunnel there, that comes out in the Kingswood on the southern side of the mountains. A passage that goes all the way from somewhere very near Lhen Fhekran to Lintesh."

Elyasin rose from her chair, her wine forgotten in her hand. "Are you certain, Thad? Absolutely certain?"

"Well... yes." He fumbled the map, flustered. "I remember what was inked upon the map. But the vellum was terribly delicate, and marred. The map may have been nearly a thousand years old..."

Carefully, Elyasin set her goblet down upon the side-table, then took the map from Thaddeus' fingers and walked to Therel's desk. She spread the map of the Elsthemi-Menderian border out fully, then fetched an ink pot and feather nib. "Here, Thad. Draw these tunnels."

And with a hasty nod, Thaddeus sat at the desk, his scribe's clever hand setting to the map precise lines and turnings. Elyasin tracked his progress, wondering at his finesse. "Where are you from, Thad, that you learned to ink so precisely, and memorize as you do?"

He looked up, his green eyes faraway, then gave a sad smile. "I was Alrashemni, milady. I learned my letters young, at the Court of Dhemman, my home. I never told anyone at the palace. When the Summons came, I was captured. I was hit on the head, knocked out by soldiers. My memory for my childhood has been vague ever since. But for everything else, my memory is impeccable." He shrugged ruefully, his cheeks coloring. "I don't even remember my true name, milady, nor those of my parents. I was named Thaddeus by the family of mapmakers who adopted me. The Lhor family were good to me. I learned to love them."

Elyasin reached out, shifting a lock of Thad's tawny hair out of his face. "You're Alrashemni. But you're so..."

"Blonde?" His mouth quirked, his hand sketching on. "I remember my mother was blonde. She had the greenest eyes. Just like yours."

"And your father?" Elyasin queried.

Thad's brows narrowed, and his hand stopped. "My father was a silversmith, I think. Or maybe a blacksmith. He was like a mountain, so it seemed when I was young, with iron-black hair and kind grey eyes." Thaddeus pressed one palm to his chest. "My Queen. I know I'm not a Kingsman, and I can't fight. But... know that I am your man, through and through. And like Theroun...I would give my life for you."

Elyasin placed her hand upon the crown of his head. Thad closed his eyes and sighed as if a mighty burden had been lifted from him.

"Thaddeus den'Lhor. I accept your service. I cannot give you back what you have lost, but know that your actions on my behalf have secured you a place at my side. Though I cannot call you Kingsman, I can call you friend."

And it seemed to Elyasin that another man entirely looked up at her, his eyes fierce and ready behind his spectacles, all traces of meekness bleeding away. "My Queen." He glanced down, then began sketching again, faster, determined. Elyasin gazed over the tunnel-lines and strange markings Thad had writ down, in no language like she had ever seen. Just then, a right drunk Therel came stumbling in the doors, two retainers of Clan Burrskin upon either side.

"My Queen! Clan Burrskin would like to make their farewells—What is it? What's happened?" Therel's demeanor changed, noting her. He glanced at Thaddeus, then back to Elyasin. His words were only lightly slurred now, Therel pretending to be far more drunk than he actually was when in conference with the Clans.

"Therel. Thaddeus has information for us."

Therel was at once all business, turning to his retainers. "My Clansmen. My Queen and I will give you our farewells upon the morrow. Enjoy our hospitality for as long as you like tonight. Excuse me."

The clansmen bowed their way out, and the doors were shut. Therel strode to the wine carafe, filled a goblet, then came to the desk. Sober and frank, his gaze perused the map. "What is it?"

"Passages, Therel." Elyasin spoke. "Beneath the mountains, from somewhere near Lhen Fhekran to the Kingswood at Lintesh. Thad has inked them for us. He saw them upon a map in Roushenn. In the Annals."

"Passages under the Eleski mountains? Are you certain?" Therel studied the map, noting all the places dark with fresh ink. "Why have I never heard of this?"

Elyasin shook her head. "I have never heard of it either, but Thaddeus found an old map in Roushenn that had them inked upon it."

Thad cleared his throat. "A thousand-year-old map, my liege. I don't know if they're any good anymore… they could all be tumbled in. Even if we can find them. But if they're there, they might help the war effort."

"Aeon be damned." Therel clapped Thad upon the shoulder, grinning. "If there are any that are viable we may be able to take Lintesh quickly without all this fuss at the border. Where did you find this?"

Thad cleared his throat. "I had access to the King's Maproom in the Annals. Because of Theroun. He had me researching all the military maps of the border-wars in some of the older annals. I came across that one, bundled in an old sheaf of rotting parchments. There were more symbols upon it. If I may?"

Therel nodded, and Thad dipped his pen. Adding a few sigils to the map, he marked some at entrances of passages, some at intervals beneath the mountains. "I didn't find reference as to what the symbols mean, sire. But there was a folio bundled in with the map written in Old Elsthemi runes that spoke of two someones called the Brother Kings. Apparently, they used these passages to make secret pacts with King Belarin den'Yesh to cease some ancient civil war in Elsthemen."

"The Brother Kings?" Therel's eyebrows shoot to the roof. "Hahled and Delman Ferrian? I thought they were a myth! Hedge-legend says they had a palace at Dhelvendale, a massive fortress that was destroyed during Elsthemen's Dark Times about eight hundred years ago. There is a whole complex of foundation-stones around Dhelvendale like there was once a keep, but the local legends of the Brother Kings are passed off as fae-yarns more often than not. And all of Elsthemen's history tomes begin just after the Dark Times. Legend says there was a great library at Dhelvendale that held all our ancient lore, and that it was destroyed. The Ferrian Kings! Well fuck me on an Alranstone..." His gaze flicked up to Thad, intent. "Did they build these passages, Thad? Did the folio say?"

Thaddeus pulled his spectacles off to polish them. "There was mention in the folio that the passages were old even when the Ferrian Kings used them. That they were built by an ancient race long lost. Sire. May I request permission to go through your library here at Lhen Fhekran, and look for any mention of these tunnels or the Brother Kings?"

Therel straightened with a chuckle. "Look no further than the nearest nursery for a book on the Brother Kings. Although... our most accomplished Dremor is due to arrive on the morrow. The Dremors are educated on the arcane knowledge of our people, lost in all but Dremor oral traditions. Adelaine may know something of the Brother Kings, or these tunnels."

"May I speak with her, sire?" Thad asked.

Therel's eyes went hard. "You have our permission to investigate the library. But you do *not* have permission to converse with the Adelaine when she arrives. My Queen and I will do that. Leave us."

Thaddeus nodded, eyebrows knit in confusion, then said his goodnights. He stole out of the room as quietly as he had come in. Elyasin's gaze was locked upon her King, surprised by his vehemence. Therel walked around the table, and gathered her into his arms.

"You're protecting Thad from Adelaine. Why?" Elyasin asked. Therel kissed her neck but said nothing. A strange feeling of foreboding grew within Elyasin the longer Therel was silent. She tried to struggle out of his arms, but he held her fast. "Tell me why you're protecting Thaddeus, Therel."

"Because Adelaine's dangerous." He spoke. "Thaddeus is an asset with the things he knows. But if Adelaine worms her way into his mind, he becomes a liability. She twists minds, Elyasin. She would twist him, make him talk about what plans he's been privy to. Adelaine used to adore that tactic for her spying games. Wrapping sexually tortured young men around her littlest finger and making them spill everything they know."

"Therel." Elyasin looked up, catching his gaze sternly. "You still haven't told me hardly anything about Adelaine. And she arrives tomorrow? When were you going to mention—"

Just then, the double-doors to the room pushed inwards. A woman barged in, flanked by two guards and followed by a distraught Lhesher Khoum. About Therel's age, she moved like royalty. Her hair was so white it looked like snow, braided back so its long wisps didn't get in her face. Her chin was sharp, her pale blue eyes fevered, and she was so thin she was swaddled in a cascading robe of white snowrabbit furs. A bitter smile graced her pale lips. Her blue eyes were two shades lighter even than Therel's, nearly white. The overall effect was like a snowbank swaddled in frozen dead animals.

"My liege!" Lhesher Khoum rushed forward, taking the skinny snowbank by one arm. "She just barged right in the moment she arrived...!"

"A royal summons." The woman's voice was chill as glaciers, her eyes scathing as they raked Therel. "To what do I owe this *pleasure*?"

"Adelaine." Therel gave a tremendous sigh. He set his hands upon his hips, then motioned Lhesher Khoum and the others out. "It's all right, Lhesher. Leave us." The big Highsword stalked out, eyeing the skinny woman like she was a rabid weasel as he shut the doors.

Therel sighed again. "Elyasin. May I present Adelaine Visek."

Adelaine sniffed, lifting an eyebrow as she gave Elyasin a chilly once-over. "*High Dremorande* Adelaine Visek. And this is the Queen, I suppose?"

"And you are the infamous Adelaine." Elyasin narrowed her eyes, instantly disliking the bony bitch.

"Indeed." The Dremor gave a haughty nod of her pointed chin. "Therel? What's this all about? Why summon me from my *blessed* tundra estate?"

It was then that Elyasin felt worming fingers easing into her brain. Up and in through the base of her skull, they seeped towards the center of her head behind her eyes. Elyasin shivered, her eyes snapping wide. Adelaine gave a teasing laugh, like the tinkling of bells. "Just testing, dear. But you're wearing a royal pendant. You're safe from me."

"Cut the shit, Adelaine." Therel gave her his most wrathful gaze. "I didn't call you here to be a pain in my ass."

"Indeed?" Her eyes opened wide, mocking. "Perhaps I'll be a thorn in your side, then. Why did you call me here, Therel? And don't be coy. It's so *unbecoming* on you."

"I called you here because I need—" Therel began.

"Because you need my help!" Adelaine interrupted, her pale eyes shining with mirthful wrath. "Oh, isn't this a treat? You. Needing me. I suppose I should be flattered. Let me guess..." Her gaze shifted to Elyasin, raking her. "Your Queen of dreams. I should have known. How scandalous, that you would lust for her all these years, and finally have her come to your very bed!"

"You knew about Therel's dream?" Elyasin's lips had fallen open, and she knew she blushed.

"Oh my dear girl." Adelaine's smile was chilly. "I broke into his mind, didn't you know? When he was young and stupid, he took off that pendant he now wears religiously. And I took full advantage of it. But even then, even with my... *suggestions* that I be his Queen, he was already besotted with you."

"You raped my mind, you bitch! While we had sex." Therel growled it. Elyasin looked over, to see him gripping his goblet so hard he was shaking. "That wasn't yours for the taking."

"No. It wasn't." Adelaine straightened up tall. "But you were conveniently distracted, and like I said, dumb to fuck anything that moved back then. And now you need my help to interpret your Queen's dreams, is that it?"

"Fuck this." Therel growled suddenly. "I never should have brought you here!"

"Your mistake," Adelaine hissed at him. "And I never should have—hold." Her gaze had fallen upon the map spread out upon the desk. And then her pale eyes widened. "*Tehlim shouloufki ah Remniak da Ferrian!* The Ways of the Brother Kings! You've found them?"

"What are you talking about?" Therel had narrowed his eyes.

"There! Those!" Adelaine gestured to the map, then leaned over it. "I thought they were myth! Where did you get this map?"

Therel snorted, drinking deep of his wine, but he moved closer to the desk. "Everything about the Brother Kings is a myth."

"Hardly." Adelaine's tone was scathing, though her eyes still perused the map. "It's just that only my people, the Moruhaine of the far northern tundra, remember the oldest legends."

"Myth and cocksgobble." Therel snorted.

"Obviously not!" Adelaine gestured to the map. "And here, someone has found proof for you, Therel, don't be daft and stubborn! Wild magic calls to wild magic, and the Brother Kings were as wild as they came! Their line came half from the Moruhaine of the tundras! It was said that Delman the Younger even had our coloring, along with our fey gifts!"

Therel wiped an exasperated hand down his short, wolf-ragged beard. Elyasin moved over to stand with her King before the fire, and he pulled her close. His gaze was dire, like the rictus of a dead man as he stared deep into the flames and then reached out, stroking the fine chain of Elyasin's pendant. "I'm sorry, my love, that I didn't prepare you for this. Don't take your pendant off while she's here."

Elyasin pulled the keshar-claw from beneath her robe, gazing at the golden sigils in the fire's light. "It's a talisman? Against her mind-invasion?"

Therel chuckled. "Yes. It won't protect you from her ingress, exactly, but it does prevent her from messing with anything in your mind while she's in there."

Elyasin admired the pendant, running her fingers over the smooth-worn bone. "You were going to tell me that story, Therel. About these pendants."

"*I* can tell you that story." Adelaine was watching them, having helped herself to a cup of wine from the carafe on the desk. She swirled it haughtily. "It is said that Hahled the Elder Ferrian wore the gold claw, for he was firstborn. The Sun of the realm, the leader of battle and the clever tongue for politics. And Delman the Younger Ferrian was the second from his mother's twin-laden womb, and he was the night sky of his people. His eyes held ancient stars, his dreams and wisdom were the heart of the Highlands. He wore the silver. And so were the pendants passed down the King's line. Always gold to the firstborn, silver to the secondborn. None outside the native Elsthemi Kings and Queens have ever worn those pendants. Until now." Adelaine's eyes flicked to Elyasin, scathing.

Elyasin fingered her pendant. "You told me that Merra didn't take this one. Why not, Therel?"

"Merra cried when mother put the silver one around her neck at Darkwinter Fest," he sighed heavily. "She wouldn't have it no matter how my parents tried, saying that it burned her. Father gifted me with mine, and I felt nothing. But later that same night, I dreamt of you for the first time."

"What happened to the Brother Kings?" Elyasin asked.

"It is said in legend," Adelaine interrupted, "that they tried to save their kingdom from ruination, approximately eight hundred years past, when a terrible war began to crumble all the kingdoms upon our continent before the founding of Lhen Fhekran. But it is also said that they killed each other in the most bitter duel ever fought. A duel in the deep midnight of a glacier beneath the mountains somewhere, a place torn to pieces by the force of their hatred and their magics. And when they perished in a flash of lightning and thunder, there suddenly rose a ring of seven Alranstones to mark the site of their great battle, and all wept blood from seven times seven eyes, never to forget the evil of such hatred of brother upon brother."

Elyasin blinked at the vicious story. "Why would they kill one another?"

"Much is told of a woman named Morvein Vishke," Adelaine continued archly, "Queen-Consort to the Brother Kings. Some say she was at the heart of a great movement for unity and peace in those times. But something happened. The stories do not remember Morvein well. She is often depicted as a witch, a temptress, a cruel mind-bender. She was the reason the Brother Kings killed each other. Jealousy."

"Honestly, do you really believe all that?" Therel scoffed.

Adeline glowered at him with her frighteningly pale eyes. "Who was it that inked those tunnels and sigils on your map just now, Therel? This record proves the Brother Kings existed! And that they used those tunnels. The ring of seven-and-seven Stones fabled in those stories, and featured so *prominently* in your dream with your little Queen, I might add, has never been found. And yet... half of your dream has come true now, has it not?"

Therel growled at the Dremor, but Elyasin's hands upon his chest stopped him. He gazed down, his lupine eyes frightful, intense. "I hate to admit it, but Adelaine's right. When I saw you for the first time in Roushenn, Elyasin, I nearly lost myself not only because I suddenly saw you existed, but that I *knew* my dream was real."

"What if the other part of your dream lies in these tunnels?" Adelaine intoned with import.

Elyasin shivered, feeling foreboding creep over her like a rising dark tide. "Must we find this place, Therel?"

"Legend speaks of a great power in that ring, Therel," Adelaine broke in, "a power that can unite nations at war. Something that can be called. Something that can change the face of our entire world, that the Brother Kings were about to call when they fractured and killed each other. And it all slipped away."

"Ancient magic." Therel's gaze rested upon the flames in the fireplace. His pale blue eyes snapped to Elyasin, intensified upon her, haunted and wild. "Ancient magic we could use right now. We can't hope to take on thirty thousand men, Elyasin. Barely fifteen thousand clansmen have gathered from the Highlands, and some of those are still en route. If the auxiliary trainees Thad mentioned move up to the border to join those already at the front, we're done for, keshari or no."

"You need to go there, Therel." Adelaine's voice was hushed now, like tundra ghosts. "Your dream is a portent. For you and your Queen. And this map now in your possession is proof. To win this war, you need the ancient magic of the Brother Kings."

Elyasin tried to banish the ice that had settled in her by snuggling close to Therel. "And you say we must go to these tunnels to find it."

"Be careful, my love." Therel nuzzled her jaw, his words breathed low, for her ears only. "Adelaine knows more than she tells. Even if she can't twist your mind, she can still bend what you believe. Sometimes her honest words are worse than her mind-manipulations."

"Do you think she's right?"

"I don't know yet."

"I'm standing right here." Adelaine's icy voice cut in. "Don't speak in hushed tones and think I don't know what you're discussing."

"Go. Now." Therel addressed Adelaine, though he did not release Elyasin from his arms. "You've done enough damage tonight. We'll summon you again when we're damn good and ready."

"How *dare* you!" Adelaine hissed, her pale eyes flashing. "After all the information I've given you? You—"

"Lhesher!" Therel shouted.

The doors boomed open at once, as if the big redheaded Highsword had simply been waiting for his moment. He strode to Adelaine without being told and gripped her roughly by her skinny, fur-swaddled arm. "Throw her out?"

"Fast as you can." Therel's grin was mean.

Lhesher Khoum manhandled Adelaine out of the room, as she shot a furious glance back towards Therel. "You can't silence me, Therel! I—" The doors boomed shut. She was gone, and the room came to silence.

"Fucking bitch." Therel gave a hard sigh, running a hand through his pale mane.

"Easy, my love." Elyasin lifted her lips and kissed Therel. "She can't ruin anything unless you let her."

438

Therel gazed down at Elyasin, trouble in his pale blue eyes. "I wouldn't count on that. Adelaine can ruin more than you know."

But as Elyasin moved away and prepared for bed, it wasn't Adelaine's pale visage that troubled her. As shadows licked through the room from the fireplace and candles, a second pale woman drifted into her thoughts, a dire beauty of tundra snows. And as Elyasin and Therel settled into bed, she wondered if the woman in her dreams would come again this night.

Morvein Vishke.

The name haunted her mind like a rung bell struck in a cold night wind.

CHAPTER 30 – KHOUREN

She was in one of the deepest catacombs of the Unterhaft. Khouren had taken her body after Lhaurent came through with it by the Kingstone. In his arms Khouren had carried her, down and further down, through wall after wall, passage after passage. Lhaurent had told him to dispose of it, discreetly.

But in this, Khouren had disobeyed.

One of the first disobediences he'd ever made.

Khouren gazed down at her now, his beloved Olea den'Alrahel, laid out upon a berm of stone in the catacomb. This was where the ancient Kings had been laid, once, before collapse of a passage had rendered the place forgotten. Khouren had brought candles for the sconces, and the chamber of dusty bones with their fine crowns and jewels was lit once more. A low moaning draft from the underground river flickered the candles, casting shadows across Olea's pale skin.

Khouren stood by her bier. He brushed a hand over Olea's fingers, clasped upon the hilt of a sword at her chest, and then the armor mail he'd dressed her in. He'd always imagined her like this, dressed as a fighter-Queen, with all the proper trappings of state. The mail wasn't hers, of course, nor the armor or the sword. Khouren had atrociously dragged the set from some long-crumbling bones of an Alrashemni Queen laid to rest, but he didn't care. He'd polished everything for hours, until it shone like spun silver. He'd washed Olea carefully and carefully sewn her throat shut with white thread and painstaking, minuscule stitches. Then he'd dressed her like the queen she should have been, and lain her out in state, with a red velvet pillow beneath her fine black curls and a diadem of rubies for her passionate life.

None remembered the Linea den'Alrahel, the Line of the Dawn, save for Khouren, and the others of his clan. The original kings of Alrou-Mendera had fled the Thirteen Tribes and their misery.

He reached out, tracing Olea's cheek with the backs of his fingers. She was still lovely. The cold in the catacombs had preserved her, even though her skin was sinking now as her fluids dried out. Khouren clasped Olea's still fingers close around the hilt of the sword. A fine thing it was, encrusted with jewels, but it looked cheap compared to her. Many nights, Khouren had watched her. Many days, lingering in the shadows and slipping into a wall when her head turned. Olea den'Alrahel had been a bastion of fierce pride and sweet mercy and undoubtable justice. Always, Khouren had counseled his Rennkavi to patience with Olea den'Alrahel, citing their family, the importance of their mutual bloodlines.

And now she was dead.

"Killed by your own kin." Khouren murmured to the silence, his hand resting atop hers. "He shouldn't have killed you, even though you feuded. You would have seen reason eventually, had he told you the truth. I know you would have come to believe in the Unification..." Khouren paused, then bent over and kissed her dead lips. "Sleep well, my beloved... be at peace."

Khouren's words echoed from the low arches of the catacomb. He stroked Olea's cold fingers, then turned, sliding into a wall and leaving the candles to burn out to her immortal night. Making his way steadily up from the catacombs, Khouren threaded through larders and cellars, ghastly blue halls and black oubliettes.

Until finally, he slid into a well-known room.

Gears churned and hummed in the massive space at the heart of Roushenn Palace. The Clockworks Room thrummed with Leith Alodwine's ancient magic, a part of his excised power causing the gears and machines that controlled the palace walls to spin on in endless monotony. Khouren moved forward along one arched path of blue byrunstone, machinery chugging in the pits below. This oblong room held two items of power, one of which Khouren's Rennkavi used daily, the enormous Plinth of Metrene al'Lhask at the front of the hall.

The other hidden deep in the clockworks, a small pyramid containing Leith's true power, which was known only to Khouren.

Khouren made his way to the byrunstone Plinth upon its slate-grey dais. His dark hood was up, a new faceweave in place leaving only his eyes visible. Everything was swaddled in a charcoal so flat it fit his brooding mood. His steps held the silence of centuries as he approached the dais. Metrene's Plinth had seven eyes, the Kingstone an item wrought by Leith long ago to connect this fortress with his others. Every eye upon the Stone was open, Metrene's soul within alert and awake, seven irises of various colors flooding the dais with multihued light.

The dome far above the dais shifted with images of Lintesh beneath the stars tonight, and sometimes from further in Alrou-Mendera. There was the Kingsmount, and then the Elsee, then the Abbey of the Jenners, then a small cabin in some mountain valley Khouren didn't recognize. Peace filled the humming space as Khouren gazed up, though the fact that he could see the city now in the dome's vast eye made him wary. This was new. The reaches above Metrene's Plinth used to be swaddled in shadows, not even a single blue globe here to light those ancient vaults. But ever since Khouren had set his grandfather's hand to Leith's pyramid all those weeks ago, the true power of Leith's stronghold had awoken.

And the images in the dome were proof of that. The magic crawled over the land, bringing the Rennkavi vistas of whatever he focused on, via the power in Leith's ruby ring. Lhaurent was still barely able to use the dome, still learning how it worked, and mostly the images were still random. But Khouren knew his skill with it was growing day by day. As it had been when Lhaurent first learned how to vibrate his being into harmony with the walls of Roushenn in order to move them, Khouren's Rennkavi was a fast study.

The Rennkavi stood with his back facing Khouren, speaking to a woman standing before the Plinth. As they conversed, the dome suddenly fixed upon the white spires of the Palace of the Vine in Valenghia before drifting back to the cabin in the mountains. Khouren narrowed his eyes upon Lhaurent. He was getting stronger. Khouren had not yet seen the dome reflect any location outside of Alrou-Mendera before.

The regal woman dressed in a draping white and silver dressing-robe shifted, stroking the fingers of one hand through the long unbound tresses over her shoulder. Silver as moonlight upon midnight lakes, the Valenghian Vhinesse's hair was as compelling as the rest of her. Beauty was not lacking in the ethereal Valenghian people, and the Vhinesse was the epitome of her kind. Tall and slender, her pale skin shone luminous in the light streaming from the Kingstone. She wore no crown tonight, and her robe was the quilted comfort of the bedchamber rather than finery meant for her royal hall, as if she'd come to speak with Lhaurent right before retiring to sleep.

Khouren waited patiently at the edge of the dais, lingering in the shadows. The Vhinesse did not like anyone to listen in upon her conversations with Lhaurent. She was a dominant personality, and Lhaurent showed her grace, allowing her to be headstrong in certain ways. Allowing her to believe she had the upper hand in their dealings.

For now.

Khouren watched, unblinking, unfeeling. Just stood with his natural emptiness. At last, the Vhinesse nodded to Lhaurent. He gave a genteel bow. She turned, and setting her hands to the Kingstone, disappeared in a flash of light and an imploding sensation that sucked air from the room.

Khouren's ears popped. The vast hall settled to silence. The dome above flashed to the vaults of the palace, then to the long swath of the Elsee. Lhaurent den'Karthus turned, a ripple of light upon his grey robes betraying his motion.

He lifted one cool eyebrow. "Khouren."

"Rennkavi," Khouren's murmur was a soft sigh, as it always was in the palace. He stepped into the ring of light.

"Is everything arranged for our next maneuver?" Lhaurent asked, impeccably still.

"Everything is…" Khouren suddenly fell silent.

"Khouren?" Lhaurent's voice was cool with patience.

Khouren roused himself. "Are you certain you wish to proceed with your plans, Rennkavi?"

Lhaurent arranged the folds of his open robe over his grey silk trousers. "Our timing to take the nation is right, Khouren. The Valenghian Vhinesse is pleased at the Dhenra's deposition, and will, at my insinuation, double her forces at the Menderian border. She will be ready to make a feint toward Lintesh in less than a month. The Valenghian army will drive straight to Roushenn, as she and I have arranged, until the wisdom of my negotiations can turn them back."

"And the Lothren? The Menderian Chancellate?" Khouren asked, his throat dry.

Lhaurent's smile was subtle, and it did not touch his eyes. "Khouren. We've discussed this at length. My comrades in the Khehemni Lothren must fall, as must the entire Menderian Chancellate. It is the only way to unite our nation. Evshein and his antiquated hatred will keep the Khehemni forever divisive and war-mongering. I seek to bring those wars to a close, Khouren. You know this. Is everything in arrangement for you to take action?"

Khouren swallowed. "I need no arrangements, Rennkavi. Just a knife. And darkness."

Lhaurent's small smile was pleased. "As ever, the darkness lives in you, Khouren. Cherish it. For only from such darkness can we raise the true light. The true dawn of Unity."

"Rennkavi." Khouren nodded and kept his chin bowed.

"If everything is in order, then I wish you to make your move tonight. The news will spark Valenghia's push, and I am eager for the Vhinesse to proceed with her arrangements. My succession as Alrou-Mendera's regent must be in place prior to our move at the Elsthemi border, so I may have the situation in Elsthemen well in hand before I respond to the Vhinesse's machinations."

"Will you be comfortable stepping into the gaze of the nation when the Chancellate falls?" Khouren moved not a single muscle. Nothing would betray his discomfort, his churning thoughts that grated like the chugging of the machinery below.

Lhaurent den'Karthus watched his dark guest. "It is where I must be eventually, Khouren. I only do what I must. To bring our blessed Unity. A new dawn of prosperity for all."

"You will annihilate your opposition in Alrou-Mendera, but then what? What about the other Lothrenni in Cennetia, Praough, Crasos, Ghrec?"

Lhaurent drew a steady breath. His brows made a line in a rare show of irritation. "Only Crasos promises to come to us when I take the Menderian throne. Ghrec is considering their position. Cennetia and Praough will not join us. They still fight their annexation by the Valenghian Vhinesse."

"The foreign Lothrenni do not believe in what you do."

Khouren murmured.

Lhaurent's gaze sharpened. "I am sending parties of Kreth-Hakir to bring them in line. Long have the Khehemni Lothren been a stubborn lot. They cannot comprehend Unification. Their squabble with the Alrashemni has caused them overlook the blessing a true Unity would bring. All the Lothren need to be eliminated as much as the Alrashemni, to bring a true Unity to our continent."

"Yes, my Rennkavi." Khouren's reply was automatic.

Lhaurent's gaze narrowed upon Khouren. Silence stretched between them, until at last Lhaurent prompted him. "Khouren? Why this dissent tonight? Something vexes you, I can feel it. Speak."

Khouren came to a studied stillness. He had always spoken plainly with his Rennkavi on political matters, and he needed to do so now, despite the uneasiness burning in his gut. "I see killing the Chancellate and the Menderian Lothren as unnecessary," Khouren stated. "Your influence casts wide, through Valenghia, the Unaligned Lands, and even Elsthemen. Pull strings. Bargain with the Chancellate, the Lothrenni. Use the Kreth-Hakir to strong-arm them, even. But please do not ask me to do this thing. To have more... blood, on my hands."

Lhaurent stepped forward from the Kingstone a pace. His shrewd eyes were considering by the Plinth's light. The dome far above flickered to an image of stone Kings and Queens in tombs of eternal rest, deep beneath Roushenn.

"You were hours late attending me tonight, Khouren," Lhaurent spoke softly, dangerously. "Tell me, why are you going to the Alrahel Catacomb so often of late?"

A shiver passed through Khouren. His eyes flickered, all of it betraying him. The dome high above shone with the image of Olea's resting place. Though her body could not be seen in the view, Khouren's gut dropped in dread. He opened his mouth to speak, shut it.

"I know where you go now when you have time alone, Khouren," Lhaurent's voice was steady. His grey gaze rested upon Khouren, almost sympathetic. "Ever since you woke the entirety of the Unterhaft and the city to the yoke of Leith's ring many weeks ago. I feel Roushenn like my own flesh these days, and your vibration moving through the walls leaves a trail like wind upon my skin. Khouren. You have been haunting the Kings and Queens of Alrahel again."

Khouren's lips closed upon any apology. A rigid defiance suddenly rose in him, something he'd never felt before. A flash of silver lanced across his vision as he stared his Rennkavi down.

"Is it any man's business that I spend my quiet hours among the bones of the dead?" Khouren spoke.

Lhaurent's eyes glittered by the Plinth's light, dangerous. "It's *my* business," he said softly. "You didn't get rid of Olea den'Alrahel's body like I asked you to, did you?"

Though the dome far above did not show Olea's body, Khouren didn't need to lie. "She sleeps where she was intended to sleep, Rennkavi, as she should have ruled. Olea den'Alrahel could have been a powerful ally for Unification. Yet you made of her a corpse instead."

"Olea never would have seen reason." Lhaurent's voice was cold. "She was a thorn of the Alrahel line, and that branch needed pruning. Your unconsummated obsession with her is disgusting, Khouren."

Khouren bristled. A temper rose in him that had long slumbered. The temper of Leith Alodwine's line, the heat and fire of conflict. He stepped from the shadows and fully into the light, menacing. And was pleased to see Lhaurent eyelids flicker in astonishment. "Rescind your order. Take back this thing you have ordered me to do, slaughtering the Menderian Chancellate."

Lhaurent stilled. He stood tall, quietly domineering. "Need I remind you of your Oath? Of what happens should you turn from serving your Rennkavi?"

As if on cue, the dome flashed high above, the tremendous reach of it filling with the image of a farmer's field, of an enormous bonfire lit from scrub-trees and brush cleared from the land. A twisted tree on the pyre suddenly broke. Tumbling to either side of the roaring blaze, it sent up a plume of ash high into the starry summer night, and a shower of sparks.

It was a better reminder than anything Lhaurent could have said of the ancient Oath Khouren had sworn upon his grandfather's blood. Khouren's cheeks flamed in chagrin. He stepped back to the shadows at the edge of the dais.

"Show mercy, Rennkavi," he pleaded. "Please."

Lhaurent smiled bloodlessly. "I think not. Tonight the Chancellate shall die. Valenghia will have a clean line of attack and I will be able to dictate movements upon the Elsthemi border. No amount of your hovering over Olea den'Alrahel's dead body is going to change that. Tell me, Khouren. Are you yet loyal to your Rennkavi?"

Khouren clenched his jaw. In his place among the shadows, he did not kneel. Silver flared in his vision, but subsided in a wash of fear. He would burn over Halsos' flames if he disobeyed his Rennkavi. Not just his body, but his very soul. Bound by his grandfather Fentleith's ancient Oath all those years ago, Khouren had but one choice.

He knelt.

"It is my honor to serve the Unification. All shall be United in prosperity, a golden age in our time. You are the only True Way. Rennkavi Lhaurent den'Alrahel."

Lhaurent squared his tall frame warningly. "Careful, Khouren. Until I step forward with my given name and assume the throne, I am to be addressed as Lhaurent *den'Karthus*. Not Lhaurent den'Alrahel. No one is to know I come from the ancient Line of Kings until the proper time."

"Yes, Rennkavi."

"But do not forget." And here Lhaurent unfastened the high collar of his silk doublet. Holding his collar open, he displayed his gold Inkings in the Plinth's light. Letting Khouren see their fine script upon his neck, tracing down to his collarbones. "Do not forget whom you serve."

At the sight of the Goldenmarks, Khouren bowed his head. Warring emotions surged within him, but he held them in check. Silver flared in his vision, a small shiver passed in its wake. At last, Khouren felt the intensity of Lhaurent's demeanor dismiss him. Without another word, Khouren rose, turning to the darkness beyond the dais.

Conflict surged through him as he traversed the arching path over the machinery and slipped through the wall of the Clockworks Room. His destination was set, to the darkest halls that would put him out near the bedchambers of the Chancellate members in the

Third Tier of Roushenn.

His Rennkavi's will would happen, and it would happen tonight.

Khouren's dark brows narrowed as he slipped through a wine-cellar, then a dungeon, then into the fey blue lights of the Hinterhaft. A black mood had taken him. And as he churned his conflict over and over, examining it, he found its source. He'd slit throats for his Rennkavi before. It wasn't that, in and of itself that bothered him. What really festered, as Khouren strolled through a section of Hinterhaft cluttered with ornately rotting furniture, was that Lhaurent was the Rennkavi. He was supposed to Unify the hearts of men. To win them to his cause.

Not mow down dissenters like grain before the scythe.

Khouren took a pilfered apple from a larder and began to crunch it as he walked, brooding. Khouren tossed his apple core into a chamber-pot as he passed through someone's boudoir. He heard a woman shriek, and then he was through, back to the Hinterhaft. Khouren made his way up a forgotten staircase, coiling up and up like the writhing of some serpent in torment, lipid blue globes lighting his path.

Lost in bleak thoughts, Khouren's focus upon his feet suddenly strayed, and his foot sank through the next stair. Stumbling, Khouren whisked his leg up, back to solid stone. He stopped and gazed down at the stair, breathing hard in shock. His churning emotions had almost caused him a broken leg.

Careful, Khouren. It's not your duty to question the Rennkavi. Only to serve him. That was the trade of your blood-Oath, to enjoy your grandfather's longevity. Swear to serve the Rennkavi, and live to see the day Unity comes at last.

"But I was just a boy when I swore Fentleith's damn Oath," Khouren argued with himself. "I didn't know the Rennkavi would be so cruel."

Khouren's voice died in the abandoned stairwell. The plainness of his words shocked him. The depth of his doubt. Silver flashed through his vision, then faded away. Khouren found he was still staring at the stone that had nearly broken him. A blue globe waifed down, curious about his torment.

Khouren shivered, and his feet found their way once more.

It was the deepest hour of night when Khouren made his way to his final mark. Moving through a thick stone wall from the Hinterhaft, he slid through a tapestry, into a bedroom lit by the uneasy flickers of a single candle upon a bedstand. Khouren slid forward, into the headboard of a massive teak bed. Carven with dragons and bees, the palatial spread of the bed dwarfed the aged man within.

Khouren gazed down upon his mark, the man's face serene in sleep where the candlelight touched his aged skin. It was easier that way, to think of them as marks. Just a task, just an item to be ticked off a list, like shopping at a merchant's stall. Not to think of them as men, as people with loved ones and honor and a beating heart.

Viewed by the light of the candle, Chancellor Evshein den'Lhamann looked frail, curled up on his side in the midst of that gargantuan mattress. The elderly leader of the Menderian Lothren wore a thin silk tunic to bed, and had sprawled from beneath the quilted blue coverlet, one lanky leg dangling off the bed. Thin blue veins reflected the candlelight, writhing like worms of death in spotted, parchment-thin skin. Evshein's flyaway hair was mussed terribly, like dandelion fluff tangled in spider's webs. His eyes were sunken, shadows lingering in his hollows. His breath came in slow rattles that spoke of the ill-health of advanced age.

So serene the Lothren's leader looked in sleep. Innocent. Weak. Khouren could remember a time when Evshein had been robust, a barrel-chested man with sinew for strength. A skilled negotiator who didn't skimp practicing in the yards, though he'd never been a soldier. But now, Evshein had the look of a man being eaten by time. Lines were carven in his face, his neck. Skin hung in loose folds from his thinning chest and arms. His ribs rose in an uncertain rhythm with every rattling breath.

Khouren moved forward through the headboard, his knife ready. His black garb was clean from the previous killings, not a drop of blood or filth upon him. He was impeccable in the darkness as he repeated a filthy task. Evshein lay in an awkward sprawl, his head to the side. Khouren took a knee to adjust for the angle as he moved silently forward, his body half-in the tufting of the thick mattress. Khouren's knife was clean of blood from the others; Evshein was the last, of both the Menderian Lothren and the King's Chancellate, and his death was as necessary as the rest.

Khouren maneuvered his arms silently around the elderly man, hovering near his neck. Ready to embrace, Khouren imagined he was an angel of mercy, delivering a suffering man from the ruthlessness of time. With the silence of shadows, his blade reached around the front of the old man's neck, poised above Evshein's jugular.

"Forgive me," Khouren murmured.

Evshein's eyes popped open. His inhalation died in a gurgle as Khouren ripped his knife into the old man's throat, shoving Evshein's head forward into the blade's passage with his free hand. Blood spilled in a black wash by the light of the candle as Khouren released Evshein's head back to the pillows. Rolling his eyes up to see the face of his death, Evshein made a small o with his thin lips as blood pulsed from his throat. Khouren had slit his artery, and his windpipe. Evshein had only a moment to see the shadow who dealt his destruction, before the light dimmed from his eyes.

The death had been silent, just like all the rest. No alarm had been raised. No Guardsmen barreled in through the Chancellor's bedroom doors. Khouren stood a moment, gazing down at his work. Blood seeped odious as warm tar by the light of the lone candle, slipping over that frail chest, soaking into the old man's nightshirt and sheets.

It was done. The King's Chancellate were dead. The Menderian Lothren were dead. Lhaurent would come to absolute power in Alrou-Mendera.

"Aeon help us all." Khouren spoke to the dead man. Glassy now, Evshein's eyes stared up at Khouren, accusing. Accusing Khouren of everything he was, everything he had done in the name of his Rennkavi.

"I had to." Khouren whispered to the dead man. "Forgive me... I had to."

Glassy eyes stared back, as shunning as his grandfather's. Khouren wiped the knife clean upon the sheets, sheathed it. Silver washed through his mind, a tremble of unrest that flooded out from his mind, coiling through his body.

And in that moment, Khouren saw it, the curse of his work. Blood. Darkness. Death. Khouren shuddered. The silver rippled through his body, and with a sudden shock, Khouren recognized the touch of the Kreth-Hakir High Priest. Like it had been called by Khouren's conflict, the silver thread of Khorel Jornath's curse spread with tendrils fine as spider's silk, seeping deep into Khouren's heart.

When the time comes that you seek freedom from your master… I will be there.

The Kreth-Hakir's words slit through Khouren, like a knife across his throat. With a soft choke like the night mourning, Khouren slipped back into the wall, lost to darkness.

CHAPTER 31 – ELOHL

Elohl woke, screaming. A hand pressed him down to thick furs. Confused, his eyes tracked up to a deep gloom that gathered dark like snow clouds. End-of-autumn fithris-snow. Hard flurries that signified bad times. Bad climbing.

But that wasn't right.

He wasn't climbing, he was in a tent. Slowly, his confusion passed and Elohl remembered falling from the ice-pocket, and what that came after. Every limb ached. The ground was hard beneath Elohl's bedroll, ice barely padded. His body seemed to weigh thrice what it should, his insides hollow. Within the tent, one of Fenton's *wyrric* fires burned without charring the hides. The writhing red and gold firelight played tricks on Elohl's mind as he stared up at the tent ceiling.

Elohl reached up, touching blue-black curls swirling in the shadows.

He knew Olea was gone. He could feel it. Every inch of him screamed in torment, like half of his soul had been ripped away. And it had, hadn't it? As long as he had served in the High Brigade, as long as they'd been separated, Elohl had always known Olea lived. But now she was gone, and the hole in his heart burned. His twin had been ripped from him, dying in a place far away that Elohl could not reach.

Dark blue eyes shifted through his vision. Elohl pushed them away.

"You're awake." Fenton sat beside the pallet, concern etched upon his brow. "Thought I'd lost you."

"You didn't lose me." Elohl's voice sounded hollow. Like a soldier who had nothing left to fight for, it was dull and tuneless. Elohl stared at the tent ceiling, watching the shifting shadows.

"Want to tell me what happened? You screamed Olea's name, before you collapsed into a seizure." Fenton watched him, patient, careful. Worried.

"Where are we?" Elohl asked.

"Still in the ice cavern, at the edge of the lake. I didn't want to move you during such a nasty fever. It's been four days. I've barely been able to get water into you. The last number of times you woke, you were delirious."

Elohl nodded, gaze fixed upon the tent's ceiling. But some urge gnawed at him, to move, to get up, to do anything rather than lay here and suffer this chasm inside. He managed to sit up, then instantly regretted it. A famished emptiness seized him and he dry-retched, his stomach rebelling.

Fenton offered a flask. Elohl seized it with shaking hands, pulled the stopper and drank deep of ice-cold water. He began to sweat almost at once, beading out upon his chest and brow. Elohl lifted a hand to his forehead, feeling his feverish state. Some part of him knew he was disoriented, sick. He gulped water, then put the flask aside, taking deep breaths to keep the water down.

"Want to tell me what happened?" Fenton's voice was low, probing.

"Olea is dead." Elohl grated it, his voice hardly his.

A palsy rippled Fenton. His color drained, his jaw clenched. Pain suffused his eyes and they flashed red. "Where? *How?!*"

"I don't know. I saw her... felt her throat get cut. I felt her die."

Fenton's eyes were too bright, burning with red in the writhing firelight. "I should have stayed with her," he growled, strangled. "I should have gone to the cells...! I should *never* have let Aldris go in my place!"

"It's too late." Elohl looked away, not wanting to see Fenton's pain. His own emptiness was enough.

With a roaring growl, Fenton surged to his feet, prowling the small tent. He seized Elohl's boots and threw them at one hide wall. He whirled, looking for more things to throw; clenched his fists when nothing was nearby. With a roar of rage, Fenton seized his rope-knife and raked it across his chest, cutting through his shirt, spilling blood. Sagging to his knees upon the ice, he cried out, keening as the knife dropped from his fingers. Cradling one hand to his chest, blood cascaded out beneath his palm.

Some part of Elohl sparked in alarm. Fenton had cut himself

453

deep, done himself harm. And now, Fenton's prickling electricity rose inside the tent, dangerous to them both. Shivering air rippled between Fenton's fingertips, crackling with charge. Scooting naked from his hides, Elohl seized a shirt and quickly tore it into strips, knotting a bandage. He knelt beside Fenton, dry-eyed as the man roared again, then began to weep. Hoisting Fenton's rent and bloody shirt, Elohl wrapped the bandage tight over Fenton's wound.

"Stop crying," Elohl intoned. "I can't get a good fit."

Fenton choked, incredulous. "Did you not love her? Your own sister?"

Tears stung Elohl's eyes, responding to Fenton's agony. But now was not the time. Elohl banished his pain to that endless well of suffering that held all his ascents, every night he'd lain near death with cold, crawled into an ice cave with a gale howling outside. That held the face of every man who'd tried to knife him in the snow and received a knife in return. That held every person he'd loved and lost, loved and lost again.

Eleshen. Ghrenna. Olea.

He sat upon his pallet-bed, numb, staring at the twisting golden fire. It was a long while before Fenton's hitching sobs died out. Silence etched its way into their hearts. Elohl checked Fenton's bandage. Then he rose to dress, pulling on pants, wool socks, kneeboots, shirt. But Elohl sank to his haunches suddenly, dizzy. A chill gripped his bones. He tried to rise, but the world spun viciously and he put a hand down to steady himself.

"Where are you going?" Fenton's voice was tight.

"Anywhere. Anywhere but here." Stubborn, Elohl stumbled up, staggered to the wall of the tent. The world spun madly. Elohl fell to his knees, retching water and bile. Collapsing to the tent floor, he rolled to his back, staring up at a ceiling spinning with shadows.

He wanted to get up, get out, but he found he couldn't move. His face and head burned. His limbs were weak, his fingers and toes so cold he could barely feel them. Shivering began, so deep he could feel his bones rattle. Aching pain exploded behind his eyes and seized his neck. The hide beside him shifted with Fenton's light steps. Fenton swam into view, his strong, calloused hands sliding beneath Elohl.

"You're not fit." Fenton hauled Elohl up as if he weighed

nothing. He settled Elohl back upon the furs. "You're raging with fever. We can't travel."

Dimly, Elohl realized Fenton was helping him drink more water. After a number of gulps, Fenton helped Elohl shuck his garb. Sliding into the furs naked was agony, a hard shiver gripping Elohl from head to heels. Elohl clutched the furs, visions of Olea's death crowding him. Fenton packed furs around his head, but still Elohl felt chilled. Numb and trembling, he could no longer feel his feet, and the room spun. His teeth chattered. He twisted his neck, restless, temples pounding. A shiver of spasms gripped him into a ball. Breath ragged, he flinched as Fenton's hand stroked sweat from his brow. He was vaguely aware of Fenton slipping into bed fully dressed, doing his breathing until he was fiery as a burning forest at Elohl's back.

Gradually, the warmth of Fenton's body eased Elohl's rigors. His jaw came unlocked, his spasmed eased. His limbs released, settling back into the cradle of Fenton's frame. Elohl's breathing settled out, and his mind strayed.

He was in a highmountain valley deep in the grips of winter, surrounded by lofty white glaciers between cruel peaks. A lake was cradled by those peaks, its waters still like glass, though unfrozen. In the center of the valley it shone blue and clear against all that white, cold and fathomlessly deep. As Elohl looked, he saw a spire of white rise from the depths like a leviathan, surging up into a cloud-heavy sky. Drawn upward with the spire's rise, Elohl traveled to those heights, soft white obliterating the world. At the spire's cruel pinnacle, a platform sat, supported by graceful white arches.

And upon the platform, surrounded by the nothingness of white, lay a woman.

Eyes as drowning as the mountain lake, white-blonde waves cascaded over her shoulder as she lay back upon her hands. Ghrenna was entirely naked, luminous in her pale beauty against the white stone. Her eyes widened, as if she hadn't expected him. Silver laced her Inkings, ornate with sigils, patterns she'd never had. Rippling in ornate whorls over her chest, silver and white and a purple so deep it looked like telmen-wine decorated her breasts, poured down her belly to her groin.

Elohl held out a hand to her.

Her fingers lifted, reaching for him.

In her lake-dark eyes, there was need as he drew near. Obliterating, crushing need. Like the whisper of the night wind, her voice sighed across his heart as he sank to his knees upon the stone, as he crawled over her, as she lay back beneath him. Deep in the grips of fever, some part of Elohl knew he hallucinated. But it was also real. He was touching Ghrenna, caressing her, drawing his fingers down her body to her navel. Ghrenna sighed, her arms above her head, white waves spread out upon opalescent stone. A smile curled her full lips. Elohl lifted his fingers, tracing that smile, the smile he longed to see with every inch of his soul.

"Is this a dream?" He whispered at last.

"Yes." Hardly a murmur, her voice pulled at him, twining around his heart like wind through vines. His fingers played over her neck and collarbones, tracing those marvelous silver and purple Inkings. She sighed. "We're in a dream together."

"Olea's dead, Ghrenna. I felt her die." The words choked in Elohl's throat like a spike of ice.

"Shh…" She reached up to stroke his face, her pale brows knit in sorrow. "I know. I felt her light pass from this world. But now is not a time for pain. Now it is your turn, to hold the light. To take everything your twin held within her. Every beautiful moment. Everything she cherished, that held her stalwart. Take it, Rennkavi. Take her memory, her love, her surety. Her light. Take it…"

Ghrenna's eyes drowned him. Her words were a rush in his ears, a full wind sighing through high mountain pines. Elohl's fingers traced her sternum, over those Inkings glimmering in the sylvan light like a sky full of cold stars. Elohl felt her pull, her silent passion, deep like his own need. Leaning down, he drew his lips over hers.

Elohl could not look away, riveted by the dark splendor in her eyes.

"Sigh for me…" He murmured. "Sigh for me across every field, over every glacier, and through every Stone. Sigh for me, Nightwind. Gather the world… for me."

It was not a name he had ever called Ghrenna. But somehow, it was right. Elohl leaned in, kissing her. Her obliterating eyes released him as they closed. He was above her, his hands twining in hers. He was between her, her legs wrapping around him, pulling him close.

And then he was inside her, and a voice whispered through the night.

Rennkavi...

Elohl sat bolt-upright, his body slick with sweat. He *felt* Ghrenna in the dim light, wrapped around him. Her blue eyes swallowed his mind, her scent in his throat drowned him, her nightwind whisper roared in his ears. Shivers wracked him as he ran both hands through his short hair. The shivers grew into spasms, his muscles jerking in a palsy he could not control.

Seizing from the force of a gale that ripped through his body.

Elohl screamed. Fenton came awake in a rush beside him. Soothing arms wrapped around Elohl, cradling him. Elohl's Inkings were on fire. They burned with unimaginable heat, searing, blistering as that wind tore through his body. Elohl flailed, scratching at his Inkings, trying to rip out the burn. Fenton seized his wrists, restraining him, grappling. Elohl fought, bucked, screamed, burning. Fenton wrestled him to the pallet, muscles straining, cordage standing out upon his neck and forearms as he yelled words Elohl couldn't hear from the roaring of wind in Elohl's ears.

And suddenly, with a clap of thunder like an imploding firestorm, it was gone. Elohl lay beneath Fenton, panting, blinking at the suddenness with which Ghrenna and the dire magic between them had left. Sitting upon Elohl's naked hips, Fenton had Elohl's wrists pinned down by sheer determination.

"Are you done?" Fenton's breath was hard, whistling fast through his nostrils, his face inches from Elohl's.

Elohl blinked. Slowly, Fenton withdrew his hands, then pushed off Elohl, coming to a seat by Elohl's bedside. He breathed fast, as if it had taken all his strength to keep Elohl pinned to the bedroll so he didn't damage himself. Elohl shivered, suddenly aware of his nakedness. But as he reached down to claim the furs, his golden Inkings slid through a wash of sunlight ripples. Where his muscles bunched at the shoulder to lift his arm, an everycolor light went pouring through the whorls and script of the Goldenmarks like a rip tide.

"Chasms's grace!" Fenton startled, staring at the Inkings.

Elohl touched his chest, tracing a line of script. Where he touched, the script blazed, then faded away like ink in a glass of water. His movement caused more ripples of fey sunlight to ease over his collarbone, curling down his sternum.

"What happened just now, Elohl?" Fenton asked with a frown, his gaze riveted to Elohl's Goldenmarks.

"I was dreaming. Ghrenna… she came to me in a dream. We touched. We…" Elohl fell to silence. He couldn't recall the entire fever-dream, only the sensation of her, all around him. Rushing over his skin and through his body, like wind.

"The Nightwind." Elohl murmured.

Fenton sat up like a bolt of lightning. His eyes flashed red by the light of his fire. The flames within the tent leapt high with a vicious twist. "*What* did you just say?"

"Nothing. Nightwind." Elohl shook his head. "I don't know why I said it. I was just dreaming about Ghrenna. And then something overwhelmed me, like a wind. When I woke, the golden Inkings were burning. Like someone poured molten sunlight through my skin."

Fenton's body was tight, his eyes intense. A subtle fire writhed within his eyes a moment more, then snuffed out. "Would you like some water?"

"Please." Elohl nodded. Fenton handed over a water skin. Elohl drank deep, grateful for the fresh meltwater from the cavern. Strangely enough, he felt better, his body no longer cold, his belly famished but not churning. The water went down and stayed down, and he drank it off.

Fenton received the flask back. "You seem better after that seizing episode, though Shaper knows how you would be." He held a wrist to Elohl's sweat-slick forehead. "Fever's broken. We'll be able to travel soon. Food?"

Elohl nodded. Fenton rose, then slipped out of the tent. Elohl heard the clank of the ladle in their travel-pot. Fenton was soon back with two hot bowls of broth, thickened with venison jerky and lentils. He handed one over and Elohl began to eat with a ravenous appetite as Fenton reclaimed his seat. They ate in mutual silence, in the determined fashion of veteran Brigadiers. Putting their bowls aside at almost the same moment, they were left staring at each other by the fire's sorcerous light.

"So." Fenton's dark eyes were mysterious. "Do your Inkings

always light when you dream of old lovers?"

A smile touched Elohl's lips. "They say love has magic in the old fae-lore, don't they?"

"So they do. And so it does. Some of the strongest magic there is." Fenton lapsed into silence.

"So you're Khehemni." Elohl said. "When were you going to tell me that?"

Fenton gave a subtle shrug. "When it was relevant."

"And you have *wyrria*. Powerful *wyrria*."

Fenton looked up, met Elohl's steady gaze. "I won't pretend to be chagrined for not telling you, Elohl. My secrets are mine for a reason."

"Because you're afraid someone will use you." Elohl murmured, intrigued, his strength returning from food now sitting calmly in his stomach.

"Because I know *exactly* who would use me. If he knew about me." Fenton's gaze was ancient, direct. "A man who would use me to kill you, if he could manage it."

"Who?"

A snarling smile lifted Fenton's lips. "Who is the slimiest person you've ever met?"

Elohl's brows furrowed. "I don't know who you're talking about."

"Yes, you do." Fenton liberated a slender throwing-knife from his jerkin, began walking it between his fingers. "You've met. Not officially, but you've seen him. At Roushenn Palace during the coronation ceremony."

Suddenly, Elohl knew whom Fenton meant. He'd only seen the man once, but the King's Castellan had left an imprint of dangerous duplicity flowing in his wake. His stature had been tall, his hair a sleek black with elegant runnels of silver at the temples and in his immaculately-trimmed beard. With an impeccable demeanor, he'd been the perfect servant, directing his army of maids and butlers like a general of the pleasure-house. His silks had been the most unassuming grey, and his grey eyes had missed nothing, attending to every detail of the coronation.

And yet, he'd been a cold motherfucker.

Elohl had seen all he'd needed to of Castellan Lhaurent

den'Karthus the moment their eyes had met during the melee after the Queen's stabbing. The man was ruthless, an eel hiding in deep waters, ready to strangle anyone who let their guard down.

"Lhaurent den'Karthus." Elohl said.

"Lhaurent *den'Alrahel*." Fenton's gaze was bitter. "He's of your house, Elohl. A Kingsman house, though he's changed his name to hide his origin. The man has mixed Alrashemni and Khehemni blood, just as you yourself do."

Elohl's brows knit, unease stirring in his gut. "How did you know my mother was Khehemni? She never told anyone that, excepting my father and me, and..." Elohl trailed off. Saying her name was still too painful.

"You think I've lived as long as I have without learning to have a network of my own?" Fenton gave a chiding glance, though it was sympathetic. "I had people watching your family for generations. You, and a few others with the Old Blood. When the Summons came, we had little time to act. But we set people in strategic positions to protect you, as much as we could. I knew your mother was Khehemni, just as I knew Lhaurent's ancient bloodline of den'Alrahel had gotten mixed, also. And I knew that the herald of the Rennkavi was supposed to be a child born of Twin Blood. I once thought that part of my mother's prophecy meant simply blood of Alrahel and Khehem twined together... but now I know it also had another meaning. Lhaurent had a twin, a womb-sister. His twin died during their birth. Lhaurent's birthing-cord was wrapped around her neck three times. She didn't have a chance. So he was born alone. But like you and Olea, he was a twin of the twined lines of Alrahel, the original Line of the Dawn, and of Alodwine, the line of Khehem's ancient kings."

"Alodwine." Elohl looked up. "You're Alodwine. That's what you said. Fentleith Alodwine."

Fenton's mouth quirked. "I don't know how many greats- down the line you are descended from me, Elohl. My ancient blood has been diminished over the years. But you are as I am. A Scion of Khehem. As Olea... was."

It was a dagger to Elohl's gut. He felt the empty space of his twin suddenly, felt her absence. But as the emptiness swallowed him, a new sensation poured through him. A soft glow of love, remembering her. How beautiful she was, how kind, how stalwart.

Elohl wondered suddenly, if Lhaurent felt this hole inside himself each and every day from his dead twin. But where Elohl's hollowness was matched, twinned by this sensation of fullness now, this bliss of remembrance and light, Elohl suddenly knew that Lhaurent experienced no such thing. That hollowness in Lhaurent den'Alrahel had been left somewhere deep inside. An ache that would never be filled. A loneliness that would never heal, only fester.

Elohl reached up, rubbed his sternum. His heart beat on with a steady drum that his life didn't feel. Even his love for Olea still hurt, raw. Elohl's golden Inkings rippled with sunlight in the dim tent, where his fingers touched his skin.

"Fuck, this hurts," he whispered.

"Your Inkings?" Fenton asked.

"No. Olea." Elohl took a deep, shuddering breath.

It was matched by Fenton, who blew out through pursed lips. "You should know Elohl, that I loved her. Every day as I watched Olea grow and prosper, into the capable fighter she was, beloved of kings... I grew more and more proud of her. She was everything she should have been, a daughter of two ancient royal lines, Khehemni and Alrashemni. She was a Queen, Elohl. She wasn't the one who sat the throne, but she was a Queen in her own way."

Elohl swallowed past the lump of agony in his throat. His Goldenmarks rippled with a subtle light, as he felt the pain of his love for his sister, and the fierceness of Fenton's love for her, too.

"I never knew," Elohl said, "that my mother came from Khehem's kings. That Olea and I were descended of two royal lines."

"Because your mother never told you. Or your father. I told Ennalea not to tell anyone that, when she left her secret Khehemni life, the life of my clan, to become Alrashemni for your father. For his love." Fenton's voice was sad. "She wanted to live as Alrashemni, to wear the Blackmarks, and that was the price she had to pay. Keeping our clan's secret, even from her most beloved."

A hard lump rose to Elohl's throat, thinking about his vivacious mother. About Olea, so much like her that they'd fought like dervishes. "Where does this leave us?" He asked, trying to take it all in though his mind whirled.

"With more questions than we have answers." Fenton replied.

"What do you mean?" Elohl looked up.

Fenton walked the slender blade over his knuckles. "My mother was a prophetess, Elohl. She saw the coming of the Rennkavi. But I was not yet born when she foretold of your coming, about the Rennkavi and the Goldenmarks and the Unification. She died when I was just two years old, caught in a battle. Some of her battle-maids survived, raised me. Told me tales of my courageous mother, of my evil grandfather Leith, and my grandmother Maya, who was a hero. Khehem was destroyed, and we were all that was left, nomads on the run, a people without a home. I was the Last True Scion of Khehem. But my mother's battle-maids only knew pieces of the prophecy."

"What do you mean?" Elohl asked, curious.

"My mother wasn't in her right mind in the last days of Khehem," Fenton continued. "When she fled from her father Leith, she saw the Prophecy in a fit of madness. She told pieces to certain people, and pieces to others. Some survived the battles during the Fall of Khehem, some died. Some were scattered to the winds, and spread the Prophecy as they traveled. Different pieces of it flourished in different lands, grew into legends mixed with local lore. By the time I heard them third-hand or worse, I had no idea what was original. So as her son, I knew little of the man or woman I was supposed to dedicate myself to. But I knew, that I was born for one thing. To birth the Rennkavi from my line, as long as it might take. And to protect him or her, to the death. And so I swear my sword to you, Elohl. My magic, my very blood, is yours to command. Not Lhaurent's."

Fenton's gaze was dire by the light of the twisting flames. Softly, he slid his dagger back into its sheath upon his jerkin. The movement was somehow more dangerous than anything Elohl had ever seen. "I'll serve you to the end, Elohl. And beyond, if I have to."

"Why?" Elohl breathed.

"Because my blood destroyed peace in Khehem, and this entire continent. And my blood will restore it."

Elohl watched Fenton by the light of the fire. His posture was regal, his manner direct. He believed every word he was saying.

Elohl had seen the man do wonders. He'd seen things he thought impossible, *wyrria* known only in fae-lore. All from a man with calm brown eyes and a placid nature. Who some overlooked at first, but who drew the eye back again and again.

Because he was neither placid, nor calm.

"You're the Dragon," Elohl murmured, "and the Wolf."

"*Werus et Khehem.*" Smelting-fire sparked in Fenton's eyes. "I am a Scion of the Wolf and Dragon, Elohl. And so are you. And *our hearts remember Khehem.*" Fenton lifted his palm, set it to Elohl's sternum, the center of Elohl's golden Inkings, over his Blackmarks. With a writhing fire, Elohl's Goldenmarks came alive to Fenton's touch, smoothing like sunlight upon water, rippling with breath like wind. Opalescent runnels of light shifted beneath Elohl's skin, flowed, merged, flowed again.

Fenton's eyes were tight with woe, bright with ancient fervor. A tear slipped down his face. "I love nothing like I love you, Elohl." Fenton breathed. "The love of a thousand suns. The love of a million people, all gone to dust and sand. The love only a grandfather can bear his grandson, though my own grandfather had no love to give me. And now that Olea is gone, I give it all to you. Everything I can. That I promise, my Scion. That, I swear."

Fenton's palm slipped from Elohl's skin.

Another tear eased down Fenton's cheek. At last, he rose. Moving through the tent flap, he was lost to the echoing silence of the cavern.

CHAPTER 32 – THEROUN

Plodding along in the hands of a nearby Brigadier, Theroun's horse snorted suddenly. It shied to the side, and Theroun knew the keshari noose around his army was almost in place. They'd been marching for five hours now, two of those in the nude. The Pythian-resin and Devil's Breath had been stashed far off the march-line in a fall of hollow logs an hour ago. And without dice to occupy their time, cock-banter had gradually died, the men becoming tense the closer they approached Elsthemi territory. Now, even the most careless soldiers narrowed eyes against the slanting afternoon shadows, watching the trees. Arlus rode up to Theroun's left, naked upon his black warhorse, then vaulted down, handing his reins off to one of his men.

"General." Arlus gave a lazy Brigadier salute. It was an improvement. The man had never actually saluted Theroun before. "Four informants have been slain so far. My men made sure to follow at a distance and kill them far enough away that it wasn't heard at the rear of the column."

Theroun stepped over a sprawling root, his bare foot squelching into mud. "Keep your men and den'Bhorus' on horseback, hidden at the rear. A few spies are likely to bolt when the keshari show, steal horses in the confusion. Don't let them get far."

"Sir." Arlus gave a lazy two-fingered salute again. He vaulted his thick, hardy frame back into the saddle and rode back to the rear of the column, just as Vitreal arrived upon Theroun's right. The man sprang from his saddle like a whip, light on his feet as he landed, all sinew and nothing else.

"General." Vitreal didn't salute. But he was consistently using Theroun's title now, and he wasn't sneering anymore. "My men have identified three more to watch. They keep looking back, making eye contact with one another."

"I've sent Arlus back to tighten the watch during the melee."

"Do you think we'll still have one, sir?" Vitreal asked. "Marching naked, no weapons... The keshari spies must have seen us practicing our surrender by now."

"It still could be perceived as a trap," Theroun muttered, watching a cluster of dark-shaded cendarie trees. "Disarm a man utterly and the enemy wonders what else you have up your sleeve."

"We haven't got any sleeves, sir," Vitreal grinned. "And if they think we're hiding knives up our—"

Suddenly, Theroun felt the forest change. He lifted two fingers and Vitreal instantly fell silent, snarling in high alert. A tiny thing, a visceral instinct, the sensation filled Theroun from head to heels and lifted the hairs upon his neck. He'd felt it so many times upon a battlefield, just before a charge. And it warned him now, tensing everything in his body. His eyes sharpened upon the forest ahead. And then, Theroun saw a tawny keshar with a rider slide out of the thick shade beneath the cendarie evergreens he'd been watching.

Hastily, Theroun raised his hands, fingers laced behind his head. "Hands up! To knees!" He bellowed for the two thousand naked men behind him. The drill had been practiced no less than six times in the past few hours. Theroun sank to his knees in the thick loam, his army coming to its knees behind him. But his eyes were fixed upon that solitary keshar and the stony face of the cat's rider.

"We surrender!" Theroun bellowed to the electrified forest. "My name is General Theroun den'Vekir of Alrou-Mendera, and we surrender!"

The forest paused upon a knife-edge of suspense. Silence echoed in the vaulted cathedral of old growth. The woman on the cat ambled forward through the thick shade. Her blue eyes narrowed. She tossed fiery orange braids back from heavily pierced ears, one lobe pierced through with an eagles' talon. A twist of amusement and deadly ferocity rode her full lips. Regal in the saddle, a massively built woman holding her tall polearm like it was a part of her, she was either a sentry or a captain, but Theroun was betting a captain. Prowling forward on her great beast, a black keshar-pelt riffled around her shoulders in the breeze, tight-buckled leathers beneath that had seen much of war.

Her eyes roved him, evaluating. Curious. Amused. It was what Theroun wanted, and he breathed in internal relief. He had no doubt the forest was seething with cats around them. Tense watchfulness prickled from every shadow. But she'd not signaled for ambush.

Suddenly, eight tawny beasts rushed in with battle-snarls from behind a copse of box-elder. Like battering-rams they hit the horses at the perimeter, swiping and roaring. Men scrambled and screamed. Blinded horses reared. And suddenly, everything was going wrong. Theroun did the only thing he could think of. He vaulted to his feet and ran forward, falling to his knees before the sentry-captain's tawny cat. As the cat opened its massive jaw to snarl, he stuck his head in its mouth, right between the saber-fangs. It choked, hissed, pulled back, spitting. The rider's attention came to him, wide-eyed in amazement.

"We surrender, Aeon-dammit to fuckhells!!" Theroun bellowed up at the sentry-captain, hands behind his head. "*In the name of Elyasin den'Ildrian Alramir, we surrender!!! Quit killing all her men for fuck's sake!!*"

It worked.

The rider produced a horn from her high cat-saddle, and gave three sharp blows. But the melee wasn't stopping. The sentry-captain scowled viciously, cursed. She set her lips to her horn again and blew six sharp notes. The forest around Theroun and his army erupted in cats. Out they came from the dense foliage, ghosts in sunlight or shade. Lithe as leviathans they leapt, struck into their own fellows. The eight who had been harrying Theroun's men were fallen upon by their brethren. Theroun's army split, pulling to the rear and front of the column in helpless, naked knots, as the cats did battle in the center.

Roars came, shrieks, screams of riders maimed. Blood sprayed, painting the foliage. And just as suddenly as it had begun, it was over. Seven cats and ten riders lay on the ground. Riderless cats slunk away, licking wounds. More than thirty horses groaned upon the ground, dying. But of Theroun's men, only twenty lay bleeding out in the loam.

Victory flooded Theroun. Keshari had slaughtered their own to protect his men. He looked up at the sentry-captain. Their eyes locked beyond the blocky head of her dappled beast.

"Having as much trouble with spies and traitors as we are?"

Theroun growled, his smile dire.

He'd thought he might have gotten a snarl, but the woman threw back her head and laughed. "Daft Menderian!" She grinned, her clear blue eyes roving him with appreciation. "Ye've got bollocks to address me thus while on yer knees and in the buck!"

"As you can see." A fierce war-snarl lifted Theroun's lips.

She took it the way he meant it, sexually. The bold-framed woman threw back her head and laughed. "Fuck me ta blackest night! The Black Viper of the Aphellian Way! As I breathe! Legend said ye had bollocks, but I didna expect this! Cocks all swingin'! Fuck me...!"

The woman had been joined by thirty others, stalking to her flanks from the blood-soaked battle. Suddenly, the forest around Theroun erupted into taunts, jeers, and whistles.

"His Viper doesn'a look black, now does it, Jhonen?"

"Thought all they needed were their *extra* swords, didn'a they?"

"Wha? Were ye gonna wallop us with yer big, hangin' sacks, then?"

"Two thousand naked men, marchin' straight for my tent? The gods have heard my prayers!"

Keshari and riders ringed them now, women and a few men completely given over to laughter. They slapped leather-clad thighs, they made lewd gestures. A few had dismounted and were now meandering about the naked men, stroking a back here, grabbing a crotch there, pulling someone they fancied in for a downright scandalous kiss. One stout woman had grabbed Arlus, vaulting into his tree-thick arms and wrapping her legs around him like a monkey. He had no choice but to hold her up as she slapped his cheeks and grinned in his face, then kissed him. Another was raking her fingernails down Vitreal's lean sinew appreciatively.

The man was grinning. In fact, most of Theroun's army was. It was better than Theroun had hoped. If all went well today, Theroun supposed his men would be well-satisfied come the dawn.

But there was still negotiation to be had.

"I demand parley with your General, Merra Alramir." He barked up at the rider-captain, Jhonen.

All humor left the woman's face. Leveling her spear at Theroun, she put the tip right to his throat. Her cat came alert, putting its blocky head in Theroun's face and snuffling him with lips lifted. A low growl issued from its massive throat.

"Ye come to parlay with our General with two thousand soldiers? I think not."

"I come thus because I could not come any other way," Theroun barked. He rose to his feet, hands unlaced, standing his ground. "And I think Queen Elyasin and King Therel will be pleased to have my host at their command. Loyal Menderian retainers are valuable to my Queen just now."

"Bold words." The sentry-captain arched an eyebrow. "But ye must be tellin' me *why* I'm to spare yer worthless hides, Black Viper?"

"I am the Black Viper of the Aphellian Way, yes." Theroun growled. "But I speak true when I say I serve my Queen, and her nation is in grave danger from forces that would bring Alrou-Mendera to its knees. I need to get a message to Elyasin, that she has allies on the front. Myself," Theroun nodded to Vitreal, and then Arlus on their knees near the column, "the Fleetrunners and High Brigade and all the rest here. We stand loyal to our Queen, and her King."

The woman Jhonen raised her red-gold eyebrows in her battle-hardened visage. "Then be delivered to my General, Viper. Riders! Circle up but do not engage! Form a perimeter and herd!"

Suddenly, cats melted out of the shadows upon all sides. Hundreds of them, they came rippling like water over rocks, padding swift over loam and fern. Their massive shoulders hunched and rolled as they moved, their giant, blocky heads hung low, mouths open to catch the scent of men and horses and blood. Whiskers shivered the air as riders reined in, forming a tight perimeter around Theroun's entire host. Strangled yowls came from cats denied feasting upon dead flesh.

Theroun stood his ground, trusting the rider-captain Jhonen to have her cats firmly in hand.

Gradually, the rear of the column began pushing forward, cats startling the blindfolded cavalry-horses and making them move. Keshari at the front opened the circle, allowing Theroun to rejoin the main host. He received the reins of his warhorse from a Brigadier. Theroun mounted up. Arlus and Vitreal took his lead, mounting up also. Cavalrymen removed blinds from what mounts were left, their horses firmly in hand. A few shied with nervous whinnies around the cats, but all had been trained for war and were quickly settled.

Gradually, they made their way in this tense, controlled standoff, over the remaining hills. Though Theroun rode his war-charger, he made no move to dress. The terrain at last began to descend. Theroun's men were eyed by riders upon all sides, though taunts and jests still flitted back and forth. The Jadounians were especially avid to tease the keshari women and waggle cocks at them, which the riders enjoyed, sometimes flashing breasts back. But even so, spears were leveled, lethal from their mounts. The Elsthemi Highlanders had steel in their eyes no matter how much they grinned and jested.

Theroun's army had been taken prisoner, and that was plain.

At last, the head of the column broke through the trees. And down the grassy, shrub-dotted slope where the forest petered out to the endless golden plains of the northern Lethian Valley, Theroun saw what he'd hoped for. The standard of Elsthemen's High General Merra Alramir, the White Keshar, snapped high above a white command pavilion near the river. The near part of the plains was a sprawling war-camp. Perhaps ten thousand strong, Theroun picked out no fewer than fifty different banners of Highland clans. There seemed to be no organization to the cat-corrals, horse-pickets, and general hodgepodge, except for a long line of latrines dug to the far north, well away from the river.

Surrounding the river to the west, Theroun could just make out the colossal mystery that was the Valley of Doors. The hill they were on dropped away in sheer cliffs to the left, into a cul-de-sac studded with thousands of doors carven into the rock. Spanning both sides of the river, shale-flats continued on the far bank, doors rising upon byrunstone cliffs at the other side also. Forming a massive amphitheater with the river cutting through it, the Valley of Doors was the outlet of the ancient road. Which split in those shale-flats, one spar going to a bridge long tumbled that had once spanned the river to the doors upon the other side.

An ancient place, an unknown mystery. Thousands upon thousands of doors, carved from the byrunstone cliffs Aeon-knew how many hundreds or thousands of years ago. All of them closed, impenetrable. A bad place for fighting. The near bank was effectively a blind pocket surrounded by cliffs, the shale an unsteady, treacherous surface, if it came to getting boxed in there.

"Circle tight!" The sentry-captain Jhonen halted, commanding Theroun's attention once more. The cats paced in, hounding Menderian soldiers and horses into a compact ball on the grassy hillside, with spear-jabs from the stony maidens atop them.

"You, with me." Jhonen flicked two fingers at Theroun.

"I want assurances." Theroun barked at her. "These men are not to be harmed. They are a gift for my Queen."

Jhonen sneered, flint in her blue eyes. "I make no such promises, lowlander. Some may get scratched or bitten if they piss off a cat. But I can tell ye, I have more honor than any Menderian dog. Ye've asked to parley with the General. And parley ye shall." She flicked her fingers again, beckoning.

"Halfway." Theroun insisted, stilling his horse from sidestepping. "There are codes in war. I will come halfway with my guard, and your General will come halfway with hers. We'll meet there," Theroun jerked his chin towards the valley, "by the river where the hills drop away."

Jhonen scowled, but at last, nodded. Flicking her spear at a smaller woman to her right, she barked, "Go, Shaina! Tell Merra." The other woman rode off, streaking fast down the verge-dotted hill. The keshari commander glanced back to Theroun. "Which'll ye bring? Code of parley allows twenty."

Theroun nodded to Arlus mounted at his left, then to Vitreal on his right. The men angled their horses through the Brigadiers and Fleetrunners, reaching down to touch shoulders. These men stepped forward, close upon the heels of Theroun's mount, his guard of twenty for the parlay.

"Fine." Jhonen snapped. "But leave yer horses. I'll not have ye sprinting 'em across the river."

Theroun set his jaw and went through the painful process of dismounting. One of the Brigadiers stepped forward to take his horse, then moved back as den'Bhorus and den'Pell dismounted also. Far below upon the plain, Theroun watched the Elsthemi camp break into furor as they noted the arrival of Theroun's army. War-horns sounded, bronze bells were rung with clangs from massive hammer-blows.

The clans turned out, leaping to cats and horses in the slanting sunlight of the dying afternoon. It was impressively fast. Elsthemi lived and breathed survival in the Highlands. Theroun saw a keshar-contingent break from the rest, forming up around a fierce woman with red-blonde braids upon a massive snowy battle-cat. She took the lead, heading toward the river.

Theroun's escort clicked her tongue, heading her cat the same direction. Theroun motioned to his twenty, and they started down the grassy slope behind Jhonen. Walking was miserable after having come so far barefoot. And now that his battle-fever had left him, Theroun's side lanced violently. But it was all worth it as he approached General Merra's party; as he saw the amazed grins upon their faces. Sniggers and guffaws came, wolf-whistles, as polearms were leveled with mirth rather than ferocity.

"I call for parley with Elsthemen's High General, Merra Alramir!" Theroun barked, cutting through the ruckus.

The handsome woman upon the white keshar ambled her lithe-muscled creature forward. She looked Theroun up and down, dispassionate, her icewater eyes hard as she assessed him. The slanting sun turned the white keshar-pelt around her shoulders blinding against her thick red-blonde braids. But the sun did not touch her ferocious blue eyes, which were currently warm as glaciers.

"And who's asking?" Her purring alto was as chill as her eyes. A killer's voice, as idly menacing as her snowy cat, who now stalked a tight circle around Theroun.

"He's the Black Viper of the Aphellian Way, Merra, like them Menderian lads said, what came through two days past. He speaks true, he comes to talk. Fer Queen Elyasin." Jhonen ambled her cat to her General's side.

The Highlander General cocked her head as her snowy cat continued to circle Theroun. A slight amusement lifted her lips as her gaze flicked to Theroun's groin. "Brave in war, I see. And brave your men, to follow you in such a risky gambit."

"We did so to prove our loyalty to Queen Elyasin and as a gesture of good faith, General." Theroun barked. "I have brought you two thousand swords. Two thousand less men to attack your

471

forces. Two thousand more to swell your ranks."

"So I see. And well-honed swords they are." Her lips lifted in higher amusement. Her chill eyes thawed to a sexual sparkle as she gazed from one Menderian body to the next, then flicked back to Theroun, chilling. "But there is one among you who is far more than a bared blade. One among you who is a Viper. A cunning Viper, to bring me two thousand men naked so we wouldn't attack."

"Had we come dressed," Theroun growled, "there would have been a battle. And then we would have needed to use the weapons given us by the traitors who now hold Alrou-Mendera. Poisons they insisted be used."

"Poisons?" Her red-blonde eyebrows arched.

"Pythian-resin. Devil's Breath." They dropped like stones from Theroun's lips, and he couldn't help the snarl in his voice at his disgust.

General Merra Alramir reined in her cat. It paused mid-stride, a liquid stillness. Her pale blue eyes were vicious with shock, and a nasty snarl lifted her lips. "You have these things? Where?"

"Stashed in a cache two hours back in the woods."

The General's gaze roved Theroun, then the naked men. He followed her gaze, seeing it rest upon the black or crimson Alrashemni Inkings on many of those who stood at Theroun's back.

"Black Viper." General Merra's voice was soft but utterly commanding. "Your men have my amnesty for the moment, do they keep civil. If they try my patience... well. These twenty cats before you are hungry. They have not had a battle to feed from today."

Theroun drew tall. Vitreal and Arlus were solid at his sides, grim, following Theroun's example. They watched him for orders, facing General Alramir but angled towards Theroun. And Theroun was suddenly grateful to have Brigadiers and Fleetrunners behind him. Both divisions had reputations for being fierce, dedicated, and utterly loyal. Theroun chuckled, appreciating the irony of the situation, that as a Khehemnas he led an army of Kingsmen.

General Merra arched a red-blonde eyebrow. "Something funny, Viper?"

Theroun placed his hands on his hips, as comfortable now buck-naked as he was in full battle-gear. "My men are utterly loyal to their Queen, Highlander-General. I don't think you could find any other Menderians so ready to die for Elyasin."

General Merra's eyebrows rose. Her gaze roved over his twenty Menderians, then flicked up to the tree line where the rest of his host waited.

"Elsthemen is Alrashemni-controlled!" She barked suddenly. "In your lands, you are known as Kingsmen, sworn to the Crown. Here, we are simply men and women who live by a code of honor, who fight hard and die well."

As she spoke, the General was unbuckling her sword-harness, slinging it across the pommel of her saddle. She laid her white pelt down, then unbuckled her leather jerkin and a waist-cincher. Shucking those, she followed it with her undershirt. At last she sat proud and bare-breasted upon her vicious white animal, displaying the most glorious set of black Inkings Theroun had ever seen. Not to mention a very fine, battle-scarred body, as lithe and fit as the cat between her thighs. A ripple of impressed murmurs spread among the Menderian men.

"You've shown me yours, and now I've shown you mine!" She shouted, proud and defiant. "If you be loyal to your Queen, who lives quite well with our King her husband and beloved, then there is but one more task to be done!"

A shifting of confusion came from the naked men behind Theroun. A breeze of evening promised the chill of Highland autumn as the sun suddenly winked out behind a stand of cendarie by the river. The Highlander-General's pale eyes flicked to Theroun.

"Show me yours, Viper."

General Merra's soft words were barely audible, but Theroun knew what she meant. It was even more plain when she pulled a bone-hilted knife from a sheath upon her saddle and flicked it, sending it point-down into a tussock of grass by Theroun's feet. With a tight snarl for what she was making him do, backing him into a corner, Theroun knelt to retrieve the blade. Moving with slow fluidity, he stood once more, the bone-handled knife to hand.

He locked eyes with General Merra. She nodded. Theroun drew the blade over his left shoulder, just enough to bleed, then flicked the blade back to pierce the grass near her keshar's paws. Gasps came from his men. Outraged cries from those who knew what they were looking at as the stinging of blood mingling with red dyes limned Theroun's skin. But before the potency of his action could be drowned in anger or fear, he took command, raising his voice with a hard rasp.

"For those that don't know," Theroun barked, eyes locked upon General Merra, "This is the mark of the Khehemni, ancient enemies of the Alrashemni! Some of you know them. Some don't. Some have heard of Khehemni only in evil bedtime stories. But know that they exist, and they are strong! Khehemni have usurped the Menderian throne, and plot the extermination of Alrashemni from Alrou-Mendera, Elsthemen, and Valenghia! War is the vehicle, gentlemen. And I am the bitter hand of that war, the Black Viper of the Aphellian Way himself!"

Theroun stared Merra down, righteous fury in his eyes. "You can believe that, if you want," he growled, "or you can believe that I am sworn to my Queen, Elyasin den'Ildrian Alramir. That her life is worth more to me than my own! That I would gladly kneel, here and now by this river, and let every one of you slit my throat and bleed me upon this autumn grass, did it mean that Elyasin lives and ascends her rightful throne. Believe what you will, Alrashemni. Kill me now or do not. But know that I fight for Elyasin, not the Khehemni. I fight to unman those who stole her throne and demanded I use fearsome poisons against Elyasin's allies and her own men. For nothing else, do I fight."

Theroun did not kneel before the pressing fury emanating from every Kingsman behind him. He did not cower from their loathing and rage. His eyes did not flinch from Merra's gaze. He knew his moment of judgement had come.

And General Merra was giving it to the men behind him.

"I'll not take his life, though Aeon knows he deserves it!" Vitreal's cutting voice from beside Theroun was loud enough for everyone to hear over the river's churning. "My father, First-Lieutenant Vikktor den'Bhorus of the Stone Valley Guard, was slain by the Black Viper when Theroun went mad upon the Aphellian Way, though I'm sure Theroun remembers it not. But one thing I know, is that Theroun is *capable*. No General has ever had as much success in war-making in Menderia's recent history! I do not like him, my Alrashemni brethren, I do not trust him. But I trust what he can do for our Queen. So decide, lads! But I'll not be putting any

474

blade to his throat before we see what he can do. Not even as much as I want to."

The clearing came to silence. The silence stretched.

At last, General Merra nodded, satisfaction in her eyes. Theroun realized his judgement had come and gone. He wasn't going to die this day, not by her hand, nor by the hands of those who stood behind him.

"See to yer men," General Merra said, her gaze complex upon Theroun. "Jhonen will help get everyone settled in. All may retrieve their gear and dress warmly, as night falls hard in the Highlands. Your men will be split in fives, to bunk in with my clans. Tether the horses where there's room. Any who run will be fed to the cats. Your poison-cache we'll see about tomorrow. You an' I will parlay tomorrow evening, but ye'll sleep in my tent, under guard. Those are my terms, Black Viper."

Theroun nodded. She was civil, this Highlander General. And fair. "Just so. And my name is Theroun."

With a lift of amusement to her lips, General Merra turned her great white cat, ambling it off towards the pavilion by the river as she slung on her clothing. Theroun glanced to Vitreal and Arlus, who nodded. They'd heard the Highlander-General's orders, and would see everything carried out. Theroun held Vitreal's gaze a moment longer as Arlus turned away to his Brigadiers. Vitreal's lips quirked in a sad smile, but there was no sneer there now.

That moment said everything both men needed to say. Vitreal nodded at last, and placed a palm to his chest, then turned away to address his Fleetrunners. Theroun turned back to the hill, a rippling wind of evening rustling the golden stalks, surveying his small army still hale upon the ridge. A rider had been sent up the hill fast, and the entire force was now being corralled down towards the Elsthemi army with little fuss.

Theroun took a deep breath, allowing himself a pleased smile. This day had been won.

CHAPTER 33 – DHERRAN

Two days later, Dherran returned from walking the far reaches of the House, exploring the walkways. Purloch and Grump were in private counsel yet again within Purloch's personal quarters, discussing whether or not the Bog would come to Arlen's defense, especially against Kreth-Hakir mind-benders. Dherran and Khenria had been given rooms in the longhouse to wait out the tense negotiations, and Dherran strode into the rotunda to find Khenria curled up in divan of moss, reading from an ancient parchment out of Purloch's library. She looked up, smiled, and Dherran came to sit next to her.

He'd thought Purloch's guesthouse empty but for them, when a ghost of a woman moved to the edge of the heavy curtain from the backrooms. Tall and lean, she was dressed in a scaled hunter's corset, a moss-shirt of the finest weave under her leather, draping down her arms and shoulders like silk, with a hood down her back. Her breeches were cinched above her calves, her high-arched feet bare as she moved forward without a sound. A luxurious white mane was braided back at her temples, her eyes a white so pure they shone like glaciers, ringed with a pale icy blue.

Standing before Dherran, her gaze fixed upon him, then flicked to Khenria. Cocking her head as if listening to ethereal music, her gaze traveled the reaches of the room a moment, the motion so wild and unusual that it gave Dherran shivers. And just as suddenly as she came, she left, ghosting out the door of the guesthouse and disappearing from view.

"What the fuck was that?" Dherran spoke, watching where the woman had gone.

"That's Elyria Kenthar," Khenria said, pushing up out of her moss divan. "She comes and goes. She's a Dremor, apparently, from the Highlands. I met her yesterday. Well, not really met. She ghosted by just like that, staring at me. I was with that fighter Yenlia and she laughed, telling me Elyria's strange but harmless. Apparently, that's how Purloch knew we were coming. Elyria saw it in a dream. Purloch keeps her close just for that reason."

"Fucking spooky." Dherran was still watching where the woman had gone.

Khenria laced her arm through his. "Want a shower? They're free right now."

That broke Dherran's trance. Any reason to get naked with Khenria was good enough for him. He followed as she tugged him by the hand, around a moss divider to the divided-off rooms, the far commons around the second tree distantly visible. Upon the left was a foyer with thick moss towels hanging on wooden racks, and an open door-flap that led to the plank platform of the guesthouse showers. Khenria tugged, and Dherran stepped out into the dappled sunshine, the both of them shedding clothes. They both wore new garb of Bog-make, soft shirts and leggings of pale moss, with scaled aelakir leather belts and boots, and hooded jerkins of dark moss with leather buckles.

That first day, all their belongings had been carefully cleaned of peat, but the Bog-gear was comfortable in the humid climate, breathable as soft silk, and Dherran preferred it. He and Khenria had also discovered the sun-heated showers that first night, and had been reveling in them ever since. Sweat sluiced off them now as they held each other in a private cocoon of moss, warm water from a high wooden cistern sluicing over them from a spout at the pull of a braided vine. Both were quiet, enjoying the moment alone, kissing and touching with easy solace. And when at last Khenria began scrubbing her black curls with a cube of soap, Dherran kissed her and took his leave.

Gathering up his belongings, he headed back to the door, then down the short hall. Pushing back the flap of his room, he opened it to a cozy interior like a spongy nest, lit up the sides with oil-lamps. Woven baskets lined the front wall, containing his belongings, pack, and saddlebags. After settling his weapons in a long basket, Dherran flopped to the pallet of moss. Soft and spongy, the moss yielded with a firmness far superior to the best feather bed. Dherran dozed, and soon felt Khenria snuggle in beside him in his fugue, drawing a blanket up over them. He slung an arm about her as she peeped and adjusted for comfort, and then both were asleep.

Purloch's guesthouse had the silence of deep night when Dherran's body grumbled for food. He tried to ignore it, but the more he tried, the more his insistent belly prodded him to wakefulness. With a sigh, he rose, kissing Khenria lightly, then donning his shirt and breeches to step out. Padding barefoot toward the common area, the spongy texture of the floor swallowed his footsteps, his passage silent as a ghost. Oil-lamps burned low in the empty common rotunda. Dherran stepped to a basket with bowls of a thick, burnable paste and a wooden spoon. Grabbing a bowl, he spooned out paste into the low-burning lamps, and they fluttered to life as the paste melted.

As the room brightened Dherran saw he was not actually alone. A woman blinked at him with very white eyes from where she sat at a low moss-table, plying a deck of colorful fortune cards. Elyria's face was blank, and Dherran had the feeling again that she wasn't completely *there* in her body. But then she blinked and smiled, pleasant, motioning him over. Intrigued, Dherran sat at the table across from her. She scooped up the cards and mixed them in her deck, shuffling, gazing at him.

"The Boar comes…" She whispered, her hollow-reed voice sending chills racing up Dherran's spine, her rolling northern accent making words sound like exotic spice. Her gaze searched his eyes, not blind, but not entirely *there*, either.

Dherran prickled, unnerved, then cleared his throat. "Can I help you?"

"The Great Boar and the Undoer's Child will wake the Bitterlance," the woman spoke softly, her gaze faraway. "They will drive through the Vine, to liberate the Unifier who comes to yoke us all. The Vine shall yield fruit and the Hidden become known, and the Land of Grain become ripe. And the Great Boar will lead men. Oh, how he will lead. For the Glory and Reaping of the Unifier."

She blinked, then raised a hand to her nose, from which a small drop of blood now came. Her pale fingers came away slick in the flickering light. She gazed at them, and then with this blood she marked Dherran's brow.

"Great Boar," she spoke, raising all the hairs on Dherran's body. "*Charge.*"

She took her hand away, but the damage was done. Every nerve in Dherran's body felt jangled. He shifted in his seat, suddenly aching for something to hit. She seemed to see it, and placed her non-blooded hand upon his wrist. "Not yet. Know when it is time. Until then, listen. Night is when dreams walk. Night is when the world wakes. The night will soothe you, until it is time."

She gestured around them, as if indicating the night outside. Dherran opened his ears, focusing on sounds beyond himself, as Suchinne had once taught him to become calm against his rage. But he heard only the cozy silence of the nest, and the sizzling of oil-lamps. Elyria smiled, then reached out to lift a window-flap. A night breeze wafted in, guttering the lamps. Dherran saw it was full dark outside, long past midnight. As he held his silence, he heard thousands of growlings and peepings in the night, a chorus all through the deep forest. Elyria's white eyes shone with pleasure as she listened. She pressed the window-cover open upon a wooden hook.

"They always sing thus, at night." Elyria began to shuffle once more, and Dherran's attention returned to the cards, his rage soothed.

"What is that you're doing?"

"Some call it reading destinies." She shrugged. "I don't. But it soothes me to look at the pictures, and sometimes they spark the right reading. Though I don't need cards to do a reading."

She pulled one from the top and flipped it over upon the leather table. "The Great Boar. That's you." She smiled at him, then flipped three more. "Hmm. The Witch, Aeon, and Lady Justice." She paused, her blue-white eyes faraway. And then flipped one more, gazing down. "Death."

Elyria's white eyes flicked up, sad. "She died. The woman I see twined with you. You never had a chance to be together the way you should have been." Elyria drew one more card. "Ah. Restraint. She was as the vines around the boar's hooves. She restrained you from your rage."

"How do you know of Suchinne?" Dherran rasped, tears burning in his eyes, his throat tight.

"I don't." She shrugged. "I just see the weave of energy. Hers is still with you. Woven into your breast. She will never leave you,

Great Boar. Draw your strength and certainty from her love. She always believed in you. She believes in you still. Remember her love. You will need it."

His chest hurt, his throat was tight. "How can she believe in me? She's dead."

"Not all that passes on is lost." Elyria smiled secretively.

"What do you mean? Can you contact her?"

"No." Elyria reached out to smooth his beard. "The dead have their secrets, Great Boar. Best leave them to it. But they leave imprints twined in us. Their love, hopes, joys. Her love lives, for you."

But here her blonde brows furrowed. She paused, then pulled another card. "The Lovers, inverted. Your love is everlasting. Your path will take you to your beloved, Great Boar. And only your rage will save those you love from destruction."

She turned another card. "Binding. You will bind yourself, to set someone else free." Dherran peered at the card, seeing chains woven through each other in a complex pattern, forming an obscure sigil. Elyria turned another card, and let out a long, slow breath. Dherran glanced at this one, seeing nothing on it but a sky full of stars.

"Oblivion. You will come to know the Great Mystery." Elyria's white eyes were distant, so haunted that Dherran actually shivered from the crawling sensation that wafted over his skin. Something cold stalked him, a touch like chill fingers upon his wrist. He shook himself, feeling like cobwebs clung to every pore, his breath snatched from his lips.

Suddenly he knew all too well, what she spoke of.

"My death. You've seen it. How I die. When."

Elyria's pale eyes turned upon him. Her gaze seemed to bore into his flesh. She blinked, then shuddered, then took up all the cards and shuffled them back in the deck. The sound of her shuffling was the only noise in the night as Dherran sat, barely breathing. His body hummed in the wake of her reading, his nerves jangled. Ready to run, to fight, to do anything but sit and wait here for his own death. She seemed to sense it and reached a hand out, settling it upon his.

"Wait. It does not come yet, your Oblivion. Gather your storm,

Great Boar. Gather your rage. He will need it."

"He, who?"

"You will know when the moment comes."

Dherran breathed out the single breath of his training. Ice speared his gut. Elyria nodded, going back to her shuffling. Trying to still his shaking limbs, Dherran listened to the endless susurration of the night, trying to focus on it. The call of creatures that never saw day, that only knew the hiddenness of the dark. A soft shuffling of feet behind him made him nearly jump out of his skin. But it was only Khenria, padding into the light.

Elyria looked up, beckoned to the girl, and Khenria moved forward to sit by Dherran. "What's going on?"

"Fortunes and fates in the deep of the dark." Elyria spoke with a kind smile. "Would you like to know yours, Undoer's Child?"

Khenria cocked her head at the strange name, then glanced to Dherran. "Did she read yours?"

Dherran found he couldn't say anything, and Khenria reached out to take his hand. "Are you all right, Dherran? What did she see?"

He shook his head, then breathed out, long and slow. "Not anything I care to repeat just now."

"His fate is dire, and difficult. He will need time. Do not prod him, child. Let a man make of his fate what he will."

Khenria glanced to Dherran, worry still knitting her pretty black brows, before turning back to Elyria. "What do you see in my fate?"

"Do you really want to know?" Elyria's smile was dire, otherworldly. Her hands had already begun shuffling her cards.

"Yes." Khenria was decisive, her chin raised defiantly. "Tell me."

The Dremor nodded, and then her hands moved out, drawing cards from the deck and laying them out in a complex pattern, different than Dherran's impromptu reading. When she had them where she wanted them, she reached out and flipped the one in the center.

"Your mother loves you."

"*What*?!" Khenria's hiss was vicious. Dherran looked over, to see she had gone deathly pale.

Elyria nodded, serene. "Empress, inverted. It rules the house of love. I see the love of a mother, strong, vicious, furious like dragons of ice, bitter in its estrangement. Do you hate your mother, child?"

"She gave me up at birth." Khenria's voice was stony. Her eyes were chips of flint. "She never loved me."

"She did. She does. She regrets what she had to do." Elyria's white eyes were frank, challenging. "The cards never lie."

Khenria swallowed. A shine of tears came to her eyes, but weren't shed. "Show me the rest."

Slowly, Elyria turned the next card. A small sound issued from her lips.

"Wound." Her eyes flicked to Khenria's. Khenria blinked, and a tear rolled down her face. Elyria nodded sagely. "Yes. You know your wound. You know why you were targeted, so young. They found out about you. And rather than killing you, they tried to break you, didn't they? Though the marks have healed from your skin, you were never whole again." Elyria reached out, cupping Khenria's face. "Women know such wounds, child. Do not let it tear you apart any longer. From this wound you have gained tremendous strength. For your blood can only strengthen by conflict. That is its ancient nature."

She flipped the next cards all without looking. "The Sundering. Wanderer. Knight. Your journey is just beginning. A bond will break, and it will catapult you out of everything you know, and into the unknown. It will lead you to the full power of your nature."

Turning the last four cards, Elyria stared into Khenria's eyes with her etheric presence, not looking at a single card. "Wolf. Dragon. Lovers. Choice. You will be called to choose between your natures, child of two righteous bloodlines. And the choice of your lover will make all the difference. Or the world will break all over again. But that time is yet to come."

Tears coursed down Khenria's face. Dherran had never seen her so ravaged. He pressed her hand tenderly, but her eyes were riveted to Elyria. "I don't want to be Khehemni." She whispered, so low it was only a breath in the night.

"You cannot deny what you are, child." Elyria's murmur was gentle as she came back to herself, relaxed once more. She brushed away one of Khenria's tears with her thumb. "Very soon now, you will begin to feel it rise, the Wolf and Dragon within you. You've already felt it, haven't you? That storm?"

"Like my very blood boils." Khenria swallowed. "Like there's a fire inside me. Like… lightning… thrusting through my veins."

"It awoke when they took you, child." Elyria smiled gently. "For the ancient line of Khehem is always thus. Conflict spurs its uprising. Conflict is its power."

"I don't want it." Tears fell from Khenria's eyes, thick and fast as she shook her head.

Elyria cupped her face in both hands, giving her a stern shake. "You have it whether you like it or not. Embrace the conflict. Not even your Great Boar will ever know what burns inside you, though his fight is strong. But where his power comes from righteousness, your true power comes from your bloodlines. From the vastness of an internal war waged upon the battlefield of unceasing conflict. The endless battle of Wolf and Dragon."

"Do you know who they are?" Khenria choked out. "Can you tell me their names? My Khehemni birth parents?"

Sadly, Elyria shook her head. "That information is veiled. Your journey will uncover the truth. I only see the two energies twined within you, battling for dominance, Undoer's Child." Elyria's hands slipped from Khenria's face, and she shuffled the cards back into the deck. With a sigh she stood, gazing down at Dherran and Khenria.

"Comfort each other. Push back the darkness. There will be enough of that in days to come."

And with that, the strange Elyria stood and walked toward the guest rooms. Khenria snuggled close to Dherran and he wrapped her in his arms, nestling them back into the curved wall of moss. Khenria's breaths were silent in the chirruping night. Dherran could feel she was at some precipice, someplace she needed the support of strong arms around her to breach. He held her close, wondering what was coming, until at last, she heaved a sigh.

"I suppose I have to tell you what that was all about, don't I?"

"Not if you don't want to." Dherran murmured at her temple.

"I have to." Khenria paused. "I have to release some of this… fire I feel inside. And you've gone long enough not knowing a damn thing about me. Loving me anyway. If I can't tell you, Dherran…"

Frogs chorused in the night. When Khenria's voice came again, it was resonant, strong. "When I was a child, I lived in Dhemman, one of the Courts of the Kingsmen. But I wasn't born there. My Kingsman parents were loving people, but they weren't my birth parents. I was given to them as a baby, to keep me safe from those who would have harmed me."

"Why would someone wish a baby harm?" Dherran asked, a thrill passing through him, astonished to hear of Khenria's early life at last.

"Because I'm Khehemni royalty."

Dherran went utterly still. *"What?"*

Khenria took a deep breath. "I was born in Valenghia, so my Kingsmen parents told me. To a royal house in Velkennish. I don't know which one. My adopted parents wouldn't tell me, for my safety. There are seven royal houses in Valenghia, all fractiously related to the throne, and some come to power in certain decades and others at other times. The line of succession is not straight. The heir who is selected Vhinesse is chosen by an aptitude for the bloodline of the Wolf and Dragon, the ancient line of the Kings of Khehem. *Khehemni*, Dherran. Those who express talent for the ancient Khehemni magic are chosen as leaders in Valenghia."

"You're Valenghian royalty?" Dherran couldn't quite wrap his mind around it. "Khehemni?"

"Lethir and Hemria den'Bhaelen, my Kingsmen parents, told me my birth parents were in trouble when my mother was pregnant," Khenria continued. "They were involved in a vicious battle close to the Valenghian throne, and my mother kept her pregnancy a secret, even from her mate. She gave me up to a man she trusted when I was born, to pass me through Shemout Kingsmen channels into a safe home, far from the conflict. That's how Arlen knew about me, though he professed to not know my true name. His Shemout watched me, for the eight years I was safe in Dhemman. And then the Summons happened. I was caught by the men in herringbone weave armor..."

Khenria trailed off. Dherran smoothed her black curls. "So that's how you knew them when we saw the battalion on the road. We were all caught by them, Khenria, and their mercenaries masquerading as Palace Guardsmen."

She shook her head, fierce as she pulled away. Turning to look at him, her eyes seemed to flash red by a trick of the flickering lamplight. "No, Dherran. The herringbone-weave men, when they broke my mind they found out what I knew of my past. They separated me from the rest of the Kingskinder. I was hooded and bound, drugged, taken I know not where. Somewhere lights burned blue in dark halls, where fey globes swirled above my head in vaulted reaches like some demonic underground cathedral."

Khenria took a deep, ragged breath, closing her eyes. "I was raped there, Dherran. Countless times, over many weeks. A girl of nine, I was raped by grown men. Some were seductive, trying to make me enjoy it. Some were brutal, hitting me, forcing. Sometimes it was just a man in herringbone leathers breaking my mind, trying to ferret out what I knew of my origins. They didn't know what I was, Dherran, but they knew I was important to someone high up in Valenghia who had been part of the resistance to the Vhinesse's rule. Things I didn't know until Arlen spoke to me the first night we were at his manor, and which Grump has confirmed since. My parents were involved in Arlen and Grump's rebellion, somehow. Enough to put them in severe danger. But at the time, I had no information beyond the vaguest things I had been told of my origins. And one night…" She took a deep breath. "One night, when I was being brutalized, something within me snapped. I was letting it happen so it would be over, but then… this great beast rose inside me, Dherran. This presence, this… power."

Khenria shuddered. "One moment, I was being raped. And the next, lightning was lancing from me and the man who had been raping me was blasted to the far wall. My shackles were melted away. I ran through that blue darkness. Someone picked me up as I ran. I screamed and fought like an animal, but he slung me over his shoulder like a sack of grain. And I swear to you, Dherran, he ran me right through the walls of wherever I was. Again and again, we disappeared through walls like hot smoke, and then we were outside in the woods. He shoved a rucksack into my hands with food, clothes, and a knife. All he said was, *run, little girl. Run far from the beasts who reside here.*"

"So I did." Khenria shuddered. "I ran. I slept in hollow logs during the day, and ran all night, through the forest towards the rising sun. I eventually learned I was in the mountains east of Lintesh, so I made it my journey to get back to Dhemman. I did, but there was no one left there. So I made my way further east, starving and wild, toward Valenghia. It was then that Grump found me, nearly frozen to death in the depths of winter. You know the rest."

Dherran was stunned. He could barely breathe. And suddenly, Khenria made so much sense. Her viciousness, her temper, her desire to be loved. Her wound. Dherran blinked, thinking back over Elyria's reading. "So when you said you were placed in a tradesman family after the Summons—"

"Was a lie." Khenria was stony.

"And you go to brothels…"

"Because I have a demon inside me that never quiets." In the gentle darkness, Khenria's eyes flashed red again. Dherran sat up, his hackles ripping up straight, knowing it had been no trick of the light this time.

"What the fuck was that?!" He stammered, alarmed. "Your eyes!"

"Sometimes they flash red." Khenria's voice was a dire breath. "When I feel it… when these beasts fight within me."

"Wolf. Dragon." Dherran recalled from the reading.

Khenria's laugh was terrible. "Yes. The ever-battling Beasts of Khehem. Ancient Khehemni *wyrria*. I'm cursed, Dherran. You shouldn't be with me." She stood suddenly, pushing away, turning her back.

Dherran rose fast, netting her in his arms. "I don't care what fury runs in your veins," he murmured in her ear. "To me you're a hawk. Not a dragon. Not a wolf."

"What if that's not true?" Her sob was wrenching, miserable.

"Our lives are what we make of them, Khenria. Right here, right now." Dherran growled fiercely in her ear, protective. "I love you, no matter what you are. And to me, you are Alrashemni because you choose to be. You fight the good fight, not because you're warring inside, but because you have goodness in you. Whatever you got from your adopted parents, it's not just a war of torment. It's a flame of righteousness. Love. Be that. Be more than the storm."

She turned in his arms, staring up at Dherran with a glowing passion in her lovely grey eyes. "Like you. Be love… like you."

Dherran choked. He dipped his chin, pressing her with a hard, passionate kiss. "I once thought my love was dead," he whispered roughly. "But you resurrected it, Khenria. How could you do that if we are not the same? Fierce. Loving. Righteous. I'm a fool for you. I would do anything for you. Any way I can protect you from whatever threatens you, I will. I promise."

"Even if it's inside me?" Khenria choked, her grey eyes bleak.

Dherran kissed her upon the lips, gently. "We'll find a way, Hawk Talon. We'll find an answer, some way to tame those beasts. I swear it. Together."

"Together." She nuzzled into his chest, kissing his stark Blackmarks. "My Kingsman. My Dherran."

Dherran bound her close in his arms, as if his strength could hold them together forever in the chorused silence. But the strangeness of the night and the bitterness of all that had been revealed pressed upon his heart. The Oblivion card with its cold emptiness rose in his mind, its night full of pale stars that whispered of his own mortality. Gripping Khenria closer, Dherran held her in defiance of the night, of their fates.

Of whatever was coming.

CHAPTER 34 – GHRENNA

Sigh for me... Sigh for me across every field, over every glacier, and through every Stone. Sigh for me, Nightwind. Gather the world... for me.

Ghrenna sat bolt upright from her dream, gasping in the early dawn. Elohl's voice rang through her ears. His storm-grey eyes roiled in her soul. Every inch of her skin flared, feeling his touch flowing over her like living fire. A need like Ghrenna had never known tore through her. Visions flashed. Memories roiled in an unholy tirade. Her breath came fast and wild in hitching sobs as her mind sundered. Everything tore, the visions now a tirade, a deluge, a maelstrom. Sobs turned to shrieks as the shifting visions pierced like daggers through her skull, in a lustful dance far worse than she had ever endured. Ghrenna's body erupted into spasms so rigid her teeth clamped tight and her back bent like a bow, heels of her feet and crown of her head pressing to the bed, thrusting everything high in a rigor of pain.

Ghrenna screamed desperately inside her mind. And from nowhere, strong hands clamped upon her shoulders, holding her steady.

Breathe, Morvein, breathe...

Delman's voice was her lodestone as Ghrenna struggled to draw breath. Her mind stormed, obliterated, her body searing with Elohl's touch. Thrashing in the pallet bed, she kicked the blankets to the stone floor of Mollia's kitchen. Delman's hands solidified on her shoulders as if made of true flesh. His presence drew close, standing strong behind her. She could feel the owl feathers in his braids catch the night wind and flutter like moths. One palm moved to her forehead, the other palm now cradling the back of her skull. Delman's hands poured a soothing balm into her mind as his presence became her focus, his repeated word *breathe*, her mantra. Gradually, his touch pushed back the madness of her careening visions, flicker by terrifying flicker.

Ghrenna gulped a breath, then two. Collapsing to the mattress, her tension suddenly broke. Sweat slicked her chest and dampened the bed. Her eyelids fluttered, eyes still rolled up in their sockets. Gradually her breathing slowed. The deluge of sensations and images dwindled, and then suddenly stabilized into a wide-open space of immense calm.

Ghrenna heaved a sigh, and felt Delman release her head at last.

There... Delman's voice whispered through her. *That was a bad storm, my love. You need to bind Hahled, soon.*

With a deep breath, Ghrenna struggled up to sitting. Clutching the wool blankets to her chest, she shivered in the wide kitchen of Mollia's fortress. Coal still glowed red in the hearth, the night just beginning to show the slow creep of dawn. Ghrenna's head pounded with a three-day ache, though it dwindled as soon as she began the breathing regimens Molli had taught her. Palming sweat-damp locks from her face, headache waning, Ghrenna asked, "Hahled?"

My energy was never very good at controlling your gifts. Delman sighed. *Only helping you expand and let go, to let your mind range the Great Void. But without control you storm. You need both openness and control. When we are bound together, Hahled lends you control. Because he is rash, it is what he must perfect, and thus what he has to give. Because I am too secretive in my nature, I must perfect openness, and so that is what I have to give.*

"But I thought you hate Hahled." Ghrenna reached to a pitcher of water upon a table at her bedside. Lifting it to her lips, she drank deep and her headache rolled back more.

I don't hate my brother. Sorrow came from Delman, the touch of fingers sliding over her bare shoulders. In her current stillness, Ghrenna could just see a glimpse of his wry smile. *Jealousy and hate are two very different things. I don't hate Hahled, I just hate sharing you. Like I hate it that I have to share you with the Rennkavi...*

Curiosity lifted in Ghrenna, pushing back her exhaustion. *You said Hahled had not told you he'd marked Elohl as the Rennkavi. Do the two of you speak, you and Hahled?*

She felt Delman shake his head. *Hahled wants nothing to do with me. Anytime I approach his Plinth with my mind, he turns his back. He never reached out, never told me about Elohl.* A wry smile again. *Our ancient quarrel still burns in him. Hahled is proud, and has always been far more stubborn than I.*

Ghrenna stroked fingers through the air just behind her shoulder. She felt them brush Delman, felt him freeze in surprise. Some part of her that was Morvein remembered she had always been able to touch his insubstantial form. Reaching out for Delman, she turned in her bed, following the thread of connection between them. A thread silvered like the moon, and white like tundra ice, and purple like bruised blood. Her fingers sighed over his chest, tracing the purple, silver, and white Inkings at his heart. She felt Delman's answering fingers touch her wrist, thrilling her before he pulled her fingertips carefully away from his heart.

No more, Delman sighed. *Your touch pains me far too much. I cannot have your love in this lifetime, and it sunders me beyond anything you can understand.*

"You have a place in my heart, both you and Hahled," Ghrenna murmured. "You know that. Even though I love Elohl, the part of me that was Morvein will always love you and Hahled, though both of you were stubborn as stones."

And now we're both trapped in Stones. Delman laughed, wry.

"What's done is done." Ghrenna's hand fell to her sweat-slicked ribs. A long silence stretched between them.

What triggered your Raging? Your spasm? Delman spoke again at last. Ghrenna felt his curiosity easing around her like spectral fingers. But he held his mind out of hers with a careful respect, after how she had banished him nearly a week ago from taking her without permission.

"I dreamt of Elohl." Elohl's storming grey eyes still pulled Ghrenna, far too present from her dream. Laying down upon her pallet, she snuggled the wool blankets around her shivering body, trying to banish the feel of Elohl's touch upon her skin. "I can still feel him. Like he... commands something inside of me."

What kind of man is our Rennkavi, that he makes my Nightwind shiver so? Delman sighed. *That he can command she who binds all others?*

Wrapping her in his arms, Delman pressed a protective kiss to her temple. His lips whispered over her hair the way pine boughs whisper past each other in the dusk. Ghrenna saw it suddenly. Morvein and Delman twined in each others' arms by moonlight, safe in a forest bower. Listening to the sigh of boughs and the trickle of a stream in the silvered darkness. Delman was warm where he lay naked against her, drowsing. A keshar-claw pendant slipped from his chest, to fall between Morvein's breasts. Chilling her with its cold silver tip.

Reminding her of an Oath she wanted to forget.

Ghrenna shivered. A white pendant formed in her thoughts, upon her own breast in that forest bower. Chased with grey-red fire opal through the white of the keshar-claw, the pendant held inlay of amethyst like telmen-wine, and terrible sigils of pure black onyx. The pendant filled her thoughts until it was like a white spire in the night, towering up to a wreath of stars in an endless sky.

Ghrenna startled awake. The sensation of Delman's arms gone. She slid from her narrow bed, the hearth's coals burned down to grey ash as dawn peeped in the vaulted windows. Stepping to the hearth, she poured a kettle of water into a wide wash-basin, then curried water over her nakedness, sluicing off sweat. Donning her black wool and leathers worked in Kingsmen fashion, her last gifts from Mollia, Ghrenna braided her long white waves back into a bun, then ate a hasty meal of cold bread and sheep-cheese. Buckling on her weapons, she checked the sword over her shoulder, her dual longknives at her hips. Everything had been replaced from the fortress' armory, her new blades of fine make, even ancient as they were.

Pushing through the ironbound doors of the kitchens, Ghrenna set out towards Delman's Plinth. Striding up the road toward the glade, she reached out for Delman. Fixing his countenance in her mind, she searched for that strand of silver moonlight. And suddenly, he flooded in faster than she thought possible, his mind pouring into hers like a waterfall.

I am here, my love. A light touch brushed Ghrenna's cheek. *You feel far better this morning.*

"Whatever you did earlier helped me, thank you."

For now. Delman warned. *I cannot say when another Raging may come. It may be never, or only a matter of seconds. We must get you to Hahled soon. If they get too strong, they could kill you.*

"I don't have time to go to Hahled just now. I need to find my pendant." Ghrenna thought again of the fire-opal and amethyst keshar-claw from her dreams, knowing somehow that it was important.

Ah. Delman's chuckle was sad. *Yes. The white pendant. Your focus for our mind-scrying. To control the gold pendant that you made for Hahled and the silver one you worked for me.*

"What do they do, Delman?" Ghrenna asked as she walked the forest path.

Your memories of Morvein are scattered, indeed, that you do not remember. Delman's visage frowned in her mind's eye, his pale brows drawing together in a line. *You fashioned the gold and silver pendants to protect Hahled and I from mind-scrying, from anyone except you. And to protect us from each other, in those awful days. We would have torn each other apart had we not worn them. And the white claw bound in pale star-metal was your focus, for the Rennkavi's ritual.*

"I hardly remember them." Ghrenna shook her head. "Much of Morvein's memories are not yet open to me, Delman. How do I reclaim them? There are things I must remember…"

He paused for a very long time. *You need to get through to Dhelvendale. To reclaim your pendant where it is buried. But you need to see Hahled, first. You need control over your mind, my love.*

Ghrenna shook her head. "I need my pendant first. And the gold and silver ones." Ghrenna stood tall, closing her eyes, feeling out with her mind though the Void as she walked. It was misty still, her control not complete, but she felt the gold and silver pendants like a tug upon her energy, somewhere to the northeast. "I feel them. Someone, two someones, are wearing them."

Yes, Delman spoke. *They are worn by the King and Queen of Elsthemen. I can sense them, in Lhen Fhekran.*

"How far is Dhelvendale from Lhen Fhekran? Is there a Plinth I can travel by?" Ghrenna arrived at Delman's clearing, bright with buttercups. Stepping to the Stone, she reached out, letting her fingers play over its surface.

She heard Delman sigh at her touch. *There is no useful Plinth near Lhen Fhekran. I will not be able to put you through there. I can put you through to Dhelvendale, but from there you have to go by foot. Seven days by keshar. A fortnight's walk.*

A memory nibbled at Ghrenna's mind, something about traveling under the mountains. "Can I take the… tunnels? To Lhen Fhekran?"

They are blocked. Do you truly not remember? Delman chuckled, his voice bitter like ice over pines. *You blocked them yourself, after you sealed Hahled and I away. I watched you do it from the privacy of my very own Plinth. If you do not remember how to open them, then I cannot help you.*

Some part of Ghrenna's mind twitched in sorrow, though she couldn't exactly recall what Morvein had done so many centuries ago. *You agreed to be in this Plinth, Delman, if things went badly. To be a touchstone for the ages until our true Rennkavi came, and I was reborn.*

Because you gave me no choice.

Ghrenna set her jaw. She felt Delman brush her cheek again, angry, sad, apologetic. *For what it's worth,* he said, *I'm sorry. For my part in this mess. My fight with Hahled, over your decision.*

I'm sorry, too. More than you'll ever know. Ghrenna's fingers skated over the Stone. *But I must know how I can get to Dhelvendale. I need to collect the pendants. To… open them, once more.*

I can put you through to Dhelvendale. Delman brushed her shoulder with a woeful touch. *But Kenthos has been silent for many years. He is asleep, riddled with dreams of dusk and battle. His Plinth at Dhelvendale was broken during the wars. It grievously wounded him, and his sleep is deep and torpid. But if you can recall but a little of your gift, Morvein, you should be able to summon Kenthos to wakefulness through my Plinth. Come in, my love. If you can wake Kenthos, I can put you through to Dhelvendale.*

Ghrenna took a breath. Setting her palms to the Stone, she leaned in, closing her eyes. She felt Delman behind her, stepping to her back. A light touch came, his palms upon her head, one over her brow, one at the base of her skull.

Breathe, my love, he urged. *Let go. Feel my touch and let yourself expand. Let your awareness flow into mine, into my Plinth, into my body…*

Like a sweet wind, Ghrenna felt herself flowing backwards into Delman's touch, and forward into his Stone at the same time. A vast nothingness embraced her, a black Void studded with a million stars. She had no body any longer, and yet there was a sense of being herself, free and unfettered. She could see her abandoned body, fallen at the base of Delman's Plinth. Her lungs still breathed and her heart still beat, but everything else was inert, frightfully delicate and temporary.

Yes, very delicate our bodies are. But not so, our consciousness. Delman was at her back for real, his laugh moon-bright, his arms trapping her about her middle. They seemed to intertwine, an embrace of breezes and gauze, his breath whispering at her ear, his lips upon her neck. Ghrenna both felt and heard his wicked and sensual laughter rolling around her.

Ah! To feel you again! So solid! So real! Delman celebrated, his musical baritone sending shivers through Ghrenna. But she saw Delman glance back through the confines of the Plinth to the solid world, felt his sudden ripple of concern. *Alas! There is no time for us. Your body weakens.*

Ghrenna knew a sudden pang of alarm, almost enough to send her racing back to her body, but she felt Delman grip her firmly. *Calm yourself. Time passes differently here in the Void. Only a few hours have passed in the solid world. But still, we must hurry. Come, my love. This way.*

Surging forward, Delman blazed through the mind-scape, high over the Kingsmountains to the north. Ghrenna felt herself whisked along with his essence, their energies intertwined, like a leaf flowing along a rushing stream. The Void opened up before her, but it was not empty at all. Paths of glimmering starlight led from Delman's Plinth in every direction, the entirety of the continent spread out far below. Surging forward, they leaped glacial peaks, strode high over forests and plains. Ghrenna turned in her mind's eye to look back, and saw a shimmer settle out in their wake like dust from a kicked-up road. Delman's trail was moonlight and the deep bruise of plums. But Ghrenna's was a white so pure and flat it looked like sun-bleached bones, with a river of amethyst and a black glitter of onyx running through it.

Yes. You leave a trail the same as Morvein's, she felt Delman smile.

But the pendant I made was shot through with fire opal also, Ghrenna noted, curious.

The fire-opal in your pendant binds Hahled. Delman's answering chuckle was wry. *The amethyst binds me. The onyx hones your own abilities, but there is a fourth color to the pendant. The white star-metal of the chain and the setting. The star-metal is for your Rennkavi. To bind you to him.*

They strode onward, over berms of coastal mountains so ancient they had crumbled to little more than bluffs of scattered stone. Ghrenna could see Elsthemi towns below, tiny ephemeral lights, as if the domiciles were too transient to make a solid impression upon this mind-world. The Void was neither day nor night as they traveled, but a perpetual twilight that writhed like the Fithri-Ile, the fey-lights of the aurora far out over the northern tundra.

At last, they came to a high berm of mountains. And in the cleft of one sheltering crag Ghrenna suddenly saw her beloved home. Dhelvendale lay in ruin. Broken colonnades and grassy mounds of tumbled stone were all that was left of the pride of the Highlands, ruins choked with brambles and telmen-vines. Here was the fountain where she had so loved to sit, trailing her fingers in the water as Delman read his books. There were the hot-baths where she had laughed and drunk with Hahled until they were both hot-cheeked and sweaty, tumbling from the baths for a passionate fuck in the snow. There was her garden, burgeoning with herbs from across the continent, and here it was covered in straw for the icy winter. But all of it was ruined. A ghastly scene of rock and boulder and bramble, the music and lights of her city dead beneath lichen and moss.

A mournful wisp of thought caught her mind, like a touch of shroud.

Ghrenna turned, dread settling in her belly. There was her grave. Carefully laid by the scribe Metholas, marked by a plain white stone at the base of Kenthos' Plinth. A circle of moon-cap grew around it, and in the fey light of the mind-realm they seemed to glow. She could feel her body down there, her bones. Ghrenna surged forward with a cry like a wild thing. Delman's hands were fast upon her, holding her, rocking her as she keened over her grave. Smoothing back her hair in the mind-realm, he pressed his cheek to hers. Her hands lunged forward to the grave, and he pulled them back. She struggled against him in the Void, yearning for her body long dead and gone.

Easy, my love. Delman's voice was kind in her ear. *Our Oaths sealed us to this, you know that. These bones you feel buried here are no longer yours. I've seen my own bones, back at the Circle. They're naught but withered chalk, my love. Nothing of me remains there. I am Delman Ferrian. I am in my new body, my Plinth. You are in yours, my love, as you so chose. You chose this. Gods of the tundra, my love, please remember...! You will go mad if you don't remember what you are...*

I don't remember anything! Ghrenna screamed it to the dusk of the

Void as she fought free of Delman's grip. But instead of tearing at the earth, she suddenly had fists, and she pounded them upon Kenthos' Plinth. *Wake, Kenthos! Wake, damn you!*

As if her fists had rung a great war-bell, a vibration thundered through the valley. Determined, Ghrenna dug fingers of pure will into the broken Stone. A shivering assaulted her fingertips, like steel over chalk, as she touched Kenthos' dreams. Drugged, horrible dreams of bloodshed and battle, war-chariots and surging devil-flame. She felt his mind stir to her touch. The images of battle flickered, fading. Ghrenna growled, a torrent of wind in her mind, a demanding maelstrom, calling him to wake. She felt Kenthos panic, felt him try to rip away from the pain of lucidity. But Morvein's energy was relentless. She dug in her claws like a keshar, and when she had him by the heart, she *pulled.*

Kenthos came to wakefulness in a long, bitter howl. Morvein's triumph filled Ghrenna. Kenthos struggled in her grip, a bear of a man with rangy black hair, piercing blue eyes, a fighter's resistance. And a riven heart from the pain of living far too long.

No! Kenthos screamed in the mind-space, raging with despair. *Is it not enough that I bled for you, Morvein?! That I fought for you, protected you? When all your promises of my liberation proved false? I have cried eons of tears for your treachery! How cruel can you be, playing with the hearts and souls of others like pieces upon a game-board! Gods... how cruel...*

Morvein's energy held him firmly in her grip, suffering his tirade. Ghrenna's words were cold and heartless, memories flickering awake inside her. *I need you once more, Kenthos. And if all goes well this time, you shall have your release from this Stone. I promise it.*

Make me no promises, woman. The once-mighty warrior shuddered in her grip, his words bitter. *For promises in your mouth are naught but ice and ash. I feel Delman bound to you again. Ask him how all your promises worked out. Heartless witch.*

Ghrenna felt Delman shudder. Though he said nothing, he also did not reach out to comfort her. Ghrenna twisted to hear that word again from her childhood, *witch*. The word that sundered her, her legacy and her curse. Her essence, once Morvein and now Ghrenna, still called witch by all who knew her. But Morvein's energy waking inside her was a cold thing, determined. Morvein had never let the opinions of others stop her, and one more who hated her was only another drop in the ocean. As she had done with Delman, she now did with Kenthos. Ripping a knife across the pad of her thumb, she traced the binding sigil in blood upon the broken Plinth, calling out the old words.

Come to me! Ghrenna demanded. *By the call of the Nightwind I command you, Thellas Alran! Be bound to me, to my will, to pull of the Nightwind! Alran aenti vhesserin! Ahora! Ahora! Ahora!*

Like some terrible storm, Morvein's energy surged through Ghrenna, rampaging out in a maelstrom around Kenthos. She could see it in the mind-space, wrapping him in a dark, howling wind, blistering his skin. And though he screamed and resisted, the wind formed coils of black smoke around his neck, his wrists, his ankles. And where they passed, they limned sigils of onyx upon him, binding him. Ghrenna could feel Morvein's knowledge controlling it, placing each sigil, knowing what they meant, though Ghrenna did not. Delman had come willingly, and had not needed such a cruel binding, but Kenthos received bitter treatment, the black carving into his body like brands.

When it was done, Kenthos fell to his knees in the mind-space, mastered. Bound. Weeping, his big warrior's shoulders shaking.

Pass me through, Kenthos. Ghrenna spoke, sad. *You have no other choice.*

He looked up, his blue eyes burning with hate. *I will pass you through, you bitch. Into autumnal snows in a dead city. But I will not pass you back.*

And then, he thrust Ghrenna through. With a cruel wrenching, her body was suddenly pulled through from Delman's Stone and smashed back into oneness with her consciousness, then spat out through Kenthos' broken remains. Stumbling to her knees in a drift of snow at the base of the broken Plinth, Ghrenna sprawled right on top of her ancient grave. She gasped at the pain still twisting her body from such a cruel traveling, her mind disoriented at what she was seeing.

Two cities lay ghosted upon each other as she looked around. The Dhelvendale of Morvein's memories was a bastion of the north, a center of trade, lights, and song. Arches and columns of white stone, carven with fanciful beasts of legend. Sprawling fountains and rotundas with clever melt-ways for the snow, a citadel to last the ages. Teeming with brawny Highlanders, with the white-haired Fithrii of the ice tundras and their elk-drawn sledges, and with bronze-skinned foreigners from Mherkhet, far to the southwest by sea.

But the real Dhelvendale was nothing but barren stones and brambles humped with a dusting of Highland snow. Destroyed, grand arches and buildings were tumbled, overgrown, the land taking back its mighty stone. Nothing yet stood, all of it being swallowed by moss and verge. Ghrenna shivered in her black leathers, a whipping autumnal wind skimming dry snow across the stones. Gazing out over the ruins, she realized time arced strangely in the mind-space. She had left Delman's valley just after dawn, but had arrived just before nightfall, long shadows swallowing the tumbled ruins as the sun lingered low over the western peaks.

Though she itched to unearth Morvein's bones, survival came first. Shrugging her black hood up, Ghrenna ran her fingers up her jerkin's buckles, raising the collar to her chin. She pulled on black gloves at her belt, checking her belt-pouch. There was flint and a packet of phosphor matches, needle and sinew, and her threllis-pipe with a pouch of fresh herb. That and a pitiful bunch of ancient coins she had found in the armory, as she had not expected to leave Molli's valley this day.

The sun kissed the mountains by the time she found a place for overnighting. Sheltered by a tumbled wall that prevented the worst of the winds, it was overgrown with telmen-vines with a clearing in the center. A lee of flagstones crouched before the wall, with enough tumbled rocks to prevent the wind's fingers from digging through. Ghrenna tunneled into the wintering telmen brambles, until she had a cozy nook with her back to the wall and a thick bower above to keep off snow.

Her breath icy, Ghrenna bundled dry vines for a fire, upon the bare flagstones. Hands numbing, she made a nest of dried telmen-leaves, then napped a spark onto the tinder. The spark chewed into the leaves, ravenous with a wisp of smoke to tease her. Lifting the tinder to her lips, she breathed out, fanning the coal until the tinder burst into life-giving flame. Tucking the flame into her kindling, Ghrenna knelt low, blowing. Fire licked up, and she arranged wrist-thick vines upon the smaller fuel. She soon had her blaze, the wall's stones warming at her back.

Shelter first, fire next, water third. Ghrenna rose, her lips parched and throat smoky. Wind had piled dry snow into drifts against toppled turrets and ruined domes, plenty enough to melt. Bits of bric-a-brac peppered the rubble, and Ghrenna soon found a broken pottery bowl. Back at camp, she nestled the pottery in the coals, humping snow upon it to melt.

The strangled yowl of a keshar went up out in the city's ruins as she drank. And then an answering yowl, standing the hairs on Ghrenna's neck straight. Memories long buried flickered in this place of ghosts, voices long forgotten calling in her ears. Morvein and Hahled, fighting side-by-side upon their great white keshari, Hahled's roaring battle-cry in her ears. Morvein and Delman, heads craned over ancient scrolls by the fire's light. Hahled and Delman in the Hall of Kings at Dhelvendale, standing at ceremony to receive their Highguard. Radiant, the sun and the moon standing before their thrones of twin snarling keshari, Delman's wrought of pure crystal, Hahled's wrought of a single massive grey opal with veins of crimson flame.

Ghrenna sat bolt upright. Blinking at the coals, she suddenly remembered a fell dawn. Hahled screaming her name, digging her out of the snow of an avalanche near the Elsee. Cradling her inside his furs as he rushed her to a hide tent of their war-party. Delman, his clever fingers administering his medicines and warming balms as they heated the tent to an inferno. Both brothers, twined around her for warmth as she shivered with a fever she thought would never break.

Fever-dreams had plagued her for three nights. Morvein had stepped from the tent that final dawn, clear at last, knowing what was about to happen. A ronin keshar, a white male twice the size of the largest beast she had ever seen, came running down from the tree line, making straight for her in the center of camp. It had leaped for her, snarling in a mad attack. As one, the Brother Kings had speared it clean through its heart. Its heartblood had seeped out over the snow. Morvein had looked down, and seen her own blood also, her chest raked open by four all-white claws. Sinking to her knees, she had clasped that ancient paw with her blood upon it. She had taken those four claws, as her fever-dream had told her to, and made four rune-scripted pendants.

And suddenly, the pendants and what they meant came rushing back to Ghrenna.

One for the Sun, who fires the people so ardently.
One for the Moon, who silvers the people with mystery.
One for the Nightwind, who binds the ancients in misery.
One for the Dawnspire, who frees all who come from ancestry.

Morvein's desperate purpose came flooding back upon that memory, howling through Ghrenna like a horrible wind. Ghrenna keened, an ancient cry echoing into the darkness from her brambles by the fire. All of Morvein's sins and futile machinations came roaring back. The name *witch* stormed in Ghrenna's ears, just as Morvein had been called by all those who had hated her, who hadn't understood. Morvein's drive. Her vision.

Her terror, at what would come to pass for the world if she failed to find the Rennkavi.

And just as men had hated her then, they would hate her now. For Morvein had promised so much to so many, and had delivered only ashes. She had failed, utterly, when the Rennkavi's Marking ritual had gone wrong. But this memory was veiled. Sorrow flooded Ghrenna, Morvein's anguish at what had happened at that ceremony, but Ghrenna could see nothing. As if Morvein had banished those memories of the Rennkavi's rituals from her own mind, Ghrenna found a gaping wound, a hole. She couldn't recall where the ritual had taken place, nor how they'd arrived there. Nor anything that had happened, except for a feeling of disaster.

And the smell of char and blood.

Shivering with foreboding, Ghrenna stood, rolling out her shoulders, stretching her aching muscles. She knew her destiny now. She knew the preparation for everything that had to be done, the first steps to take, just as Morvein once had. Breathing in, she sighed out the single long breath of her training. Despite it all, she was still a Kingswoman. So she had sworn, both then and now, though then her oaths had been made to the Highlands, to the Brother Kings.

And some Oaths are not able to be broken.

Stepping from her shelter, Ghrenna retraced her steps to the Plinth. Daggers from Kenthos prickled across her skin as she stepped within the ring of his sight. But she was not here for him. Ghrenna stepped to the edge of the ring of fae-caps at the base of the broken Plinth. Within that circle, Morvein's bones lay. Within that ring it was always Highsummer, and no snow brushed that ancient grave. Ghrenna pushed bitter thoughts from her mind, shouldering her responsibility as she sank to her knees, crushing the fae-caps.

Removing her gloves, she spread her hands over earth kept warm by Morvein's ancient *wyrria*. Hands forming claws, she began to dig, pushing the dirt aside. It came away readily, eager to be unearthed. And yet, Ghrenna knew that had she been any other creature or person, it would have lain immutable. Deeper she dug, tossing earth aside and ripping her hood back with besmirched fingers to get air. At last, her fingers smoothed over ancient bones. Clearing dirt away, Ghrenna found the contours of dead eye sockets.

Morvein's skull stared at her, beseeching, pleading.

"What do you want of me?" Ghrenna asked the filthy bones, sitting back upon her heels by the shallow grave.

Finish our work. Morvein's voice was in her, of her.

"What are we?" Ghrenna smoothed dirt away, uncovering cheekbones and jaw, teeth.

We are the Wind of Night. The one who binds every Alranstone to the Rennkavi. So we swore, when the fever-dream came upon us. So we swore upon our own blood in a terrible Oath, and made the Brother Kings swear also, to do what was needed to bring the Rennkavi at last. And now one has come, and our work begins again.

"We weren't always the Wind of Night," Ghrenna spoke, clearing soil from Morvein's collarbones. "We weren't always called witch."

No, we were beloved once. Ghrenna's own mind sighed in the rich alto of Morvein. *When we first came to Dhelvendale it was as the Highsummer Tithe of the Fithrii to the Brother Kings. They were well-pleased with such a gift from our people. We had seen a mighty vision, that a great golden age could be forged for the continent should we travel forth from Fithri-Lhis upon on the tundra. But the corruption that marred the continent had already speared Dhelvendale. We came as the tolling of the bell after death, the body already in decay. And where we toiled to undo that death, people began to hate, even though Delman and Hahled believed us and kept us close.*

"But we demanded too much of them," Ghrenna murmured as she uncovered a rib, then another. "When the wars finally swept us, when we began to feel the rotten treachery consuming every nation, we made tools of the Brother Kings, didn't we? Men to be used like funnels when the time was right, channeling the weave of Alranstones into us, demanding that they come to heel for the Rennkavi. And promising release…"

Ghrenna's hands brushed an object, clasped between the finger-bones upon Morvein's chest. She worked the edges, smoothing cold dirt away. "We promised to release them all from their torment. No more Alri. No more souls bound in eternity to those vile Plinths. Such a cruel fate, one we did not want to cause us any more nights of sobbing when we touched their madness."

Her fingers dug in, prying under the keshar-claw and pulling it from the earth. Smoothing dirt away, she revealed curling script in grey fire-opal, black onyx, and purple amethyst set into its white cruelty. Capped with white star-metal, it weighed like a dead thing in her hands, austere and forbidding. She traced the sigils, so carefully wrought over three days of fasting and trance.

"But we learned to not care. We forced the Alri into bondage, to gain power so we could do what had to be done to prepare for the Rennkavi. To fill the White Circle and provide his Way. *For the Way is the Life, and the Life is the Peace, and the Release shall be great when he finds his Way at last.*"

Ghrenna let the pendant fall from her hands until she held it by the fine star-metal chain, pale like bones and death. Unbuckling her jerkin, she lifted the chain over her head and let the pendant slip down between her breasts. It was a cold weight, a millstone, and the pale star-metal tip chilled her very core. Taking the single breath of her training, she let it out slow. Morvein's burden was hers now. She was the only one who could wield it.

And wield it she would.

Sharpening her mind like a lance, Ghrenna raised a storm in her mind. A howling of wind, of power. Vibrating through her body until all her bones and flesh sang with it, the enormous power raised the Nightwind around her, whipping her white hair about her face as she stood and turned southeast.

Queen Elyasin den'Ildrian. King Therel Alramir, Ghrenna roared in the mind-space. *Hearken to me.*

Like the tolling of a great bell, her command sliced the Void, rolling out like a peal of thunder in the dusk and spearing straight to Lhen Fhekran.

CHAPTER 35 – ELYASIN

Elyasin dropped the wineglass she had been holding, and it shattered upon the stone floor of the octagonal war conference room. Therel spasmed at the same moment, sending his pewter wine goblet cascading from the map-table to dash wine across the white stones. Crimson in the sinking light of the sun that streamed in through the western windows, the spilled wine from Therel's goblet and hers shone upon the floor like blood cascading across fresh snow.

Elyasin shuddered as she caught Therel's gaze. The lofted room fell utterly silent as the gathered clan-leaders and Highswords stared at their lieges, confused. From the fury and fear in Therel's lupine eyes, Elyasin knew that he had heard it, too. That sound like a struck bell inside her mind. That rush of wind after it, furious and consuming like a twisting storm. And upon that frightening power, their names, clear as a command shouted to an army at war.

Someone had Summoned them.

Inside their minds.

"*Adelaine*!!!" Therel's face was suddenly a thundercloud. "Bring me that bitch!! *NOW*!!!"

Three Highswords rushed from the chamber, the door banging behind them. A wave of disorientation suddenly swept Elyasin, as if she were flying above mountains. She stumbled, putting both hands to the map-table to keep from falling over. Thaddeus stepped to Elyasin's elbow, but she waved him off. Passing a hand over her eyes, she sank to a nearby chair, blinking rapidly as her head spun.

"It has been a long morning, gentlemen," Elyasin spoke, trying to control her vertigo. "Your King and I must speak about the matters here presented. We shall adjourn until tomorrow. Dismissed."

Heads of clans and Highlander battle-captains nodded all around the room, uneasy glances darting to their King and Queen. But they filed from the room until only Thaddeus was left, his eyebrows raised behind his spectacles. Elyasin nodded at him to go also, and he moved swiftly from the room. Now alone, Elyasin's gaze darted to Therel. He leaned heavily over the map-table, shaking his head as if to clear it.

"You too?" Elyasin asked. "Like you're flying? Seeing mountains?"

"Ah…" He pinched his eyes. "Something like that. I'm… seeing the old ruins at Dhelvendale. There's a woman sitting in dirt at the base of the Plinth. She's filthy, like she's been digging. You heard the call? That summons? Inside your mind?"

"I heard it. What was it?"

"I have no idea. Let's hope that bitch Adelaine does." Therel gave a bitter grimace as he touched his pendant. "These things are supposed to be impervious to mind-attacks. They've always worked in the past. But someone's fucking with us now."

"Perhaps their magic is wearing off?" Elyasin's fingers slipped to her gilded pendant.

"Perhaps." Therel picked up his goblet and moved unsteadily to a carafe upon a side-table. Pouring a generous amount of wine, he drank it back quickly. Then gave a sour grimace. "Don't do that. What I just did. Wine *really* doesn't help."

Elyasin almost laughed, but then had a diving sensation so strong she had to lean her head over her knees. "Oh, gods! I'm going to vomit."

Breathing slowly, she choked down the bile as Therel moved over to stroke her back. Just then, Adelaine boomed in through the doors. Swaddled in her white furs, her face was pinched, her demeanor arctic. She halted, gazing at Therel and Elyasin imperiously as Highswords backed away and shut the doors.

"Well?" She sneered, then lifted an arch white eyebrow. "Neither of you look healthy. Did someone poison you?"

"Cut the shit." Therel snarled. "I know you've done something to the us. To our minds."

Adelaine startled, which she covered quickly with a sharp smile. "Done? Other than grace you with my presence, so rudely summoned as I was straight from the bath?"

"Not amusing." Therel growled. "I know you've gotten past our talismans. And you will either tell me how you've done it, or I will have the living piss pounded out of you."

"*Therel.*" Adelaine's tone was admonishing. "No need for such threats. I did come to your palace when I was called, did I not? I have not left by the dead of night. So. You need to tell me what's happened."

Therel was silent, his hackles as high as Elyasin had ever seen them. Adelaine smirked. "Come, now. You have to *tell* me for me to have any opinion on whatever you summoned me about, you know. That how being a Dremor works."

"Therel and I heard our names called, just now, in our minds." Elyasin spoke, interrupting any argument. "Forcefully enough for physical effects. And now we're both having severe vertigo."

Adelaine's white eyebrows rose, her pale lips fell open. She covered her surprise with a small adjustment of her posture, but Elyasin had seen it.

"You don't know what happened." Therel had seen it, too.

"I never said I did, or that I didn't." Adelaine snapped like a beaten dog.

"You've figured out a way past our pendants." Therel pressed again.

"And don't you think that if I had, I would be *deigning* to wait upon you?!" Adelaine rounded on him, hate in her eyes, her voice as frosty as her face. "I would have *commanded* you to have given me what's mine and been done with it, Therel! I'm tired of all this! Vhensa trusted me, why can't you?!"

"You tried to have me killed, Adelaine. I can't forgive that." Therel turned his face away.

Adelaine's mouth fell open, then shut. Her eyes flicked to Elyasin, scathing. "You two deserve each other. The bitch-Queen of Alrou-Mendera who brings her wars to our soil, and a bastard of a King. Blessings upon your *happiness*." She turned and spit upon the floor, then strode to the door. The Highswords to either side shifted nervously, their eyes flicking to Therel. "Let me pass! You can't hold me here against my will! I am High Dremorande! Cast me in irons or let me go!"

"You're not High Dremorande, Adelaine." Therel's words were stern.

"I am." She turned back, battle in her eyes. "And a far better one than Vhensa ever was. If you would give me the position, you would see that. Coward."

Therel shook his head, his pale eyes vicious and cold. Adelaine bit her lip, trembling, drawing up in a haughty tension. And suddenly, Elyasin saw what their old quarrel was all about. Adelaine wasn't in love with Therel, and perhaps never had been. It was about acknowledgement, the position of esteem. She was furious, but Elyasin could still see she was holding back tears of wounded pride.

"Let her go. Open the doors." Elyasin motioned to the Highswords. Therel blinked at her incredulously. "Let her *go*, Therel. We solve nothing here."

Therel ground his jaw, but at last the fury of the wolf eased. He nodded at his Highswords. They opened the doors and Adelaine whisked out, head high and slender features too proud.

Elyasin turned to Therel. "Let me talk to her."

"What good will that do?"

"Let me try. She's wounded, Therel. She'll never say it, but not having the position of High Dremorande kills her pride."

"Tough leather!" Therel bit. "She tried to have me assassinated. If she can't help with this mind-invasion, then she's of no use."

"You didn't even get to that part, Therel," Elyasin admonished. "Please. You two are steam and lava. Let me try."

Therel shook his head, but his eyes were finally clearing of their wrath. He moved to Elyasin, sliding his hands over her shoulders. "If you want to try, fine. But don't say I didn't warn you."

"Fair enough." Elyasin gave him a quick kiss, then moved through the double-doors, making her way down the hall. She stopped by the kitchens to fetch a serving-girl with a tray of edibles and some wine, then arrived at Adelaine's guarded room and knocked at the ironbound door.

"Just a bit, just a bit..." She heard from inside. The door was hauled open, and a pale, sharp face framed in furs appeared. "Oh. It's you." Adelaine's frosty eyes looked Elyasin over, then glanced at the tray. The rolling-tray was artfully arranged, a few late-summer blossoms in a blue pottery vase in the center, with ample telmen wine to act as libation. Three bowls of savory stews there were, and a selection of cured meats and cheese, with a dish of tiny fruit pies for dessert.

Adelaine's gaze lingered upon the fruit pies, then she let out a put-upon sigh. "Oh, I suppose."

She opened the door wider, and the girl pushed in the tray, then went about setting everything up on a breakfasting table within. After tasting it, the girl retreated with a solemn bow. Elyasin turned, standing in Adelaine's presence, waiting. A very long moment passed, the sun down now beyond the high windows and the evening settling into purple shadows. A roaring fire crackled in the massive hearth, with far more logs than it needed, blistering the room with heat.

A flicker of a smile graced Adelaine's lips at last. Reaching up, she lifted down her furred hood and combed a hand through her fine white hair. "Oh, you're as stubborn as I am, aren't you? I suppose you should sit. Let us have something to eat."

She motioned regally to the table, and they sat. Elyasin poured wine, sipped from the goblet, then offered it to Adelaine. Adelaine accepted it with one thin white hand. The edge of her lip twitched up at the classic offer of a Highland truce. Elyasin poured another goblet for herself and sipped, letting the weight of her offer sink in.

"Am I going to have to like you?" Adelaine sighed, setting her goblet down.

"No." Elyasin sipped her wine. "But if you give me a chance, you might find I'm not so awful."

"They told me you were a firebrand." Adelaine's mouth quirked.

"They were right."

Adelaine raised an eyebrow. "Tell me, lowlander Queen, what is your gain in the Highlands?"

"Allies. Strength. Trade. Therel."

"So you do love him." Adelaine gazed down at her goblet.

"You already know that I do. You already know that he loves me. You already know exactly who I am to him."

Adelaine looked up, swirling her wine wistfully. Her wry smile was the saddest thing Elyasin had ever seen. "Yes. The most powerful portent-dream I've ever heard. I was jealous of that dream. Vhensa dithered over it, the old crone, but I knew it was a true dreaming. He's a fool for love, you know. Therel. He'll do anything for it. For you."

"Did you do it? Send the assassin after him?" Elyasin shelved the sympathy Adelaine's words had provoked. Blunt frankness was the best way to find out if one was dealing with an enemy. Or so Chancellor Theroun had always said.

"And even if I didn't?!" Adelaine actually laughed, desperate and futile. "Would there be anyone left in this *barn* of a palace who might believe me? No. Therel and his father made sure of that with their slander. How convenient to force me to leave court, in shame. But the last laugh is mine. Vhensa died. And now they need me."

"Did you do it?" Elyasin took a sip of her wine.

"What do you care?" Adelaine's pale eyes flashed.

"Did you do it?"

Her lips pressed together, but there was no lie in her eyes. "No."

"So why the misunderstanding?"

Tears pricked Adelaine's mist-pale eyes despite her rage. "Because Therel's father was a horrible man. He thought I was *lowborn*. He had it out for me."

"But you used mind-tricks on Therel."

Two spots of color bloomed in Adelaine's pale cheeks. She looked away. "I did what was necessary to secure my position at court."

"You tried to bend his mind. To bend him into loving you."

"Is that such a crime?" Adelaine shot back.

Elyasin settled back into her chair, swirling her wine. It was a nasty thorn in the Elsthemi court, this business about the Dremor. Adelaine's presence had sparked gossip flowing through the court. Elyasin had heard more stories than she cared to ever hear again about Adelaine and Therel's rather indiscreet relationship not so very many years ago.

"Speculation is being passed around. On whether you'll try to kill him again. Or me."

"I only want what's mine." Adelaine shot her an angry glower. "And I'm not going to get it from a dead King with no heirs. What use have I for Therel's death?"

"What use *do* you have for Therel's death?"

"None." Adelaine's pale eyes were proud. "I wanted him alive. In *my* bed. And myself as High Dremorande and Queen at his side. But *that's* all ruined, now. If Therel ever decides to rescind my exile from the tundra, I'll eat all my furs."

"One might have evaded a summons from the King, up where I hear you're living." Elyasin mused, swirling her wine.

Adelaine set her lips. "One might. But I want what's rightfully mine."

"And that is?"

"My title." Adelaine set her goblet down with finality. "I *am* High Dremorande of this nation. Vhensa had *no one* of my ilk. I was *surpassing her*, even when I was a girl. If I could get my title, I could take apprentices. I would have a royal stipend. I would have a place at court." She blinked, a little rapidly. "I'm not built for the far north. The tundra may be in my blood, but…" She gazed ruefully at her thin white hands, then shook her head. "It matters not. Here I will stay until Therel dismisses me, and then back to my exile I will go. Rotting away. Dreaming…" She sighed bitterly. "And not able to use even the least of it."

Elyasin regarded her a long moment. "I may be able to speak on your behalf."

"What? Why?" Adelaine's gaze whipped up, her frost-pale eyes narrowing suspiciously.

Suddenly, the wild sensation of flying passed through Elyasin, and she swallowed down bile. "Because someone's in my head. And if that someone is part of what caused my own exile, I want to get to the bottom of it. And you're going to show me how."

"Your exile?" Adelaine was regarding her now. Carefully. Respectfully.

"Do you think I enjoy wasting away here when my presence is desperately needed back in my own country?" Elyasin's mouth quirked.

Adelaine blinked. "Perhaps… we may reach an understanding."

"Perhaps."

They sat silent, appraising each other. And though Adelaine was not royalty, her pride was as strong as any royal Elyasin had ever met. Elyasin was counting on that pride. But trusting a woman everyone said was a treacherous bitch was going to require finesse.

As long as I have the pendant, I can trust her.

As if Adelaine had read her mind, those frosty eyes flicked to the gilded keshar-claw. "Tell me what you are experiencing. And any recent dreams. We will start there." She reached out, selecting a cut of meat and some cheese with one slender white hand. Nibbling, she sat with rapt attention.

"That's it? No crystals? No beads or lengths of yarn to read?" Elyasin's mouth quirked.

Adelaine pursed her lips around a bite of meat. Her tundra-blue eyes sparkled with a clever wit. "And do I wear lengths of fringed shawl about my hair? Or do you see any rattling bones for a necklace?"

"Indeed." Elyasin smiled. She moved on, recounting the call, then the visions and sensations of flying. When she told of her dream of the woman with the lake-blue eyes, and that she had wakened with the name Morvein upon her lips, Adelaine sat bolt-upright, her pale eyes wide. But when Elyasin mentioned Therel's vision of the Plinth at Dhelvendale, Adelaine clutched her chest.

"What did this woman look like? Was she near the Plinth? And she was doing what?"

"He didn't say what she looked like." Elyasin reached for a fruit pie. "And she was at the base of the Plinth. Dirty, like she'd been digging."

Adelaine shot to her feet with a cry. "Take me to Therel! Now! This cannot wait!"

"What do you mean?" Elyasin rose to her feet warily.

"It is said that she will come again." Adelaine's pale eyes were frightened.

"Who?"

"Who do you *think*?" Adelaine snapped. "Morvein Vishke! And when she does it *'Will be as the tolling of a great bell for those who are Needed'.*" She threw up her hands in exasperation. "Has no one learned the Lay of Metholas?! Come, we must speak with Therel! I don't care if he has me whipped or set in irons! This is *important*!"

Adelaine stormed from the room, more purpose and power in that slight, fur-clad body than Elyasin would have thought possible. Elyasin followed in haste, and together they strode to the royal chambers. Pushing in through the doors, they saw Therel reclining shirtless by the fire upon a snowbear pelt, drinking and staring at the flames.

He turned to look but did not rise, simmering in his inebriation. His jaw flexed, his eyes icy. "So. You've tamed the prodigal she-beast."

"Be civil, Therel." Elyasin did not take his bait. "She has information we need."

"Information she may have, but at what cost, my love? You don't know the half of what she did to me."

Elyasin softened and moved to the pelt. Sinking to her knees, she reached for his hand. "No. You're right. I don't. But I see a clever, motivated woman who might be an ally if we only give her that chance."

"I won't forgive what she did to me." He set his jaw.

"You needn't forgive her, Therel. Just hear her out." Elyasin sighed.

Therel eyed her, then swigged his wine. "You surround yourself with too many double-bladed weapons, my love. Luc. Fenton and Elohl. Thaddeus. Now her. Too many risks, with people whom you know hardly at all."

"I took far too few risks with people I knew all my life. And look where it got me. I have little left to lose." Elyasin smiled wryly.

"You have *me* left to lose, and I you." Therel pulled her close. "Adelaine is devious. She'll do what she can to split us like kindling. She's already got us fighting."

"We're fighting because we're both bull-brained." Elyasin lifted up to kiss him.

Therel laughed at last, though it was weary, and he held her close for a long moment.

"Therel." Adelaine's voice cut in, surprisingly gentle. "You two need me."

Elyasin supposed that the earnestness in her manner took Therel aback, for he blinked. At length, he gestured with his goblet to a high-backed chair near the fire. Adeline hesitated, as if she were uncertain he'd actually made the gesture, then claimed the seat. There was no offer of wine. Therel sat there, weighing Adelaine with a weary manner, as if he was still undecided whether he'd rip her throat out. Adelaine did not back down, but neither did she burst into a bitter tirade. Elyasin sensed that the woman was trying her very best to be civil.

At last, Therel spoke. "What is this urgency to which the King of Elsthemen must attend, Dremor?"

Adelaine responded to his highly formal speech with a demure nod. "My King. I fear you and your Queen are in danger. And, for once, your suspicion should not be placed with me."

"Speak, Dremor."

Adelaine took a deep breath, spreading her white hands over her furs. "It is said in ancient song, that in a time of great need, when war threatens the very fabric of all the nations, one will come to bind the people in a great and unprecedented unity, ushering in a golden age for all. The ancient Lay of Metholas, passed orally from Dremor to Dremor through hundreds of years, speaks this Unifier's title, the Rennkavi."

"This much Vhensa did tell me when I was crowned. Continue."

"The Lay also tells of the creation of your pendants." Adelaine nodded primly at Therel, then Elyasin. "At the hands of a Dremor and powerful Ascendant named Morvein Vishke. You have heard the tale in fire-stories of the Brother Kings. She is oft portrayed as a witch. But the Lay of Metholas speaks of her with high honor, as a woman with much power put to service for a greater good. It was Metholas' opinion, that Morvein yoked the Brother Kings to her purpose with those pendants. Apparently, she also made one for herself." She eyed Therel. "Which Metholas himself buried with her body at the base of the Plinth at Dhelvendale."

Therel quirked an eyebrow. "So someone's treasure-hunting her bones and I've had a vision of it. So what?"

"No." Adelaine shook her head. "The Lay says something else. That her grave was *sancriteni*, which in the High Alrakhan means *impenetrable*. Many have tried to dig at the roots of that Alranstone, and have famously failed. King Gruhne even sent to Cennetia for an iron urn of flash-powder to see if he could blow the ground open. Even that failed, though he managed to sunder the Plinth to nearly-useless pieces. And still, that ground remains intact. Not even snow remains long upon that hallowed spot."

Therel's eyes narrowed upon Adelaine, thoughtful rather than angry. "But I saw a woman digging there, the earth disturbed. Speak plain, Dremor. What do you suppose?"

"I think Morvein has come again." Adelaine whispered. Her eyes flicked to Elyasin. "May I share what you told me?"

"Yes." Elyasin nodded.

Adelaine looked back to Therel. "Your Queen has had a true dream of Morvein. She described Morvein to me *precisely* as she is described in the Lay, as a woman of dire pale beauty with long waves of white hair and oceanic blue eyes, with a white pendant beset with fire opal, onyx, and amethyst. And your Queen woke with Morvein's name upon her lips. That is no accident, Therel. Such dreams are portents. A spirit, announcing its presence in the world. And today, *both of you* had an annunciation from her. A summons."

Therel took a deep breath. "Even supposing what you say is true, why summon us?"

"It's these, isn't it?" Elyasin stroked her gilded keshar-claw.

Adelaine nodded. "Stories speak of the Brother Kings as the two most powerful men in Elsthemi history. Incredibly gifted. And Morvein used those pendants to yoke both of them to her influence, for good or ill."

"So you're suggesting we take them off?" Therel's half-smile was a snarl.

"I did not say it." Adelaine's eyes flicked away. "I don't even know if you can. Or if the yoke has already been set. You might remove the amulet but not be free of the bond."

Therel crossed his arms, scowling. "I'm sure you'd just love it if we simply removed them. Then you could worm all your little schemes right back into my brain. And Elyasin's. Tell me, Adelaine, did you suggest that my lady Queen remove her amulet?"

"Those days are behind me," Adelaine stared at her hands. "I am a wiser woman now than I was in my youth. You may never trust me again, Therel, but I implore you to have a care for what this could mean to your kingdom. Banish me again and then try removing the amulets to see if your double-seeings stop, I care not. You of all people know my mind-scrying reaches only a few leagues at best." She gave a wry smile.

"I'm not going to leave you near enough to find out." Therel crossed his arms, then eyed Elyasin. "And these pendants *stay put* until after Adelaine is long gone."

Elyasin nodded, knowing when a battle was not worth fighting. But she blinked suddenly, the visions renewing behind her eyes, as the scene changed.

"What just happened?" Adelaine glanced at her like a curious bird.

"It went from a view over the mountains to a small homestead in a valley," Elyasin murmured, seeing the vision fresh in her mind. "But the homestead is ancient, dilapidated. There's no one there. I think it's somewhere in Alrou-Mendera. There aren't any snows on the peaks ringing the valley."

Adelaine cocked her head, then glanced to Therel. "And you?"

"My vision is following the woman. She's left the dirt. She's upon the outskirts of the Dhelvendale ruins, headed southeast. And she has a white keshar-claw pendant around her neck now."

"The white claw was Morvein's." Adelaine hissed, her eyes enormous. "It's got to be her! Morvein's incarnation, the woman you are seeing! I'm certain of it. And if she's heading southeast, then she's coming here, to both of you. Do you see anything else, Therel?"

"I'm also…" Therel's lips quirked in a grimace. "Playing Ghenje matches. In my mind. I don't play Ghenje. I never learned it…"

Adelaine's eyebrows rose, almost off her pale face. "You two are connected to something *other* than Morvein! *Two* somethings, based upon the different visions! Or perhaps two someones."

"Two someones?" Elyasin crossed her arms. "You're saying that Therel and I are receiving thoughts from people? Living people? But my visions are floating *leagues* above the ground!"

"Dreams can do that." Adelaine shrugged. "If you are connected to someone else's dreams, you could be experiencing everything they do. But it's what happens when you both fall asleep tonight that concerns me."

"What do you mean?" Elyasin eyed her.

"I mean," Adelaine said with testy zest, "that if you are linked to someone else's mind, when you dream you may become more easily absorbed into their thoughts. When we go to sleep, there is a natural reduction in the barriers that keep the minds of others out. You may become more tightly bonded to whomever these someones are if you sleep tonight."

"So we never go to sleep again." Therel gave a bitter laugh. "That'll make planning a war easy."

"I could give you something to dull you," Adelaine suggested. "So you don't dream at all. So your mind goes too deep to be found by anyone while you sleep."

"And stop my breath and my heart while you're at it." Therel glared at her.

"They are not kind herbs." Adelaine shrugged. "They would leave you tired upon the morrow. But I know my dosages, Therel."

"You use them yourself." Elyasin was watching Adelaine, and the woman's twitch confirmed her suspicions.

Adelaine looked over, her pale eyes unreadable. "Sometimes having dreams night after night is worse than being a little fatigued by day."

"They waste you." Elyasin eyed Adelaine's bundles of furs, her skeletal appearance.

Adelaine's eyes hardened. "You know nothing of me. The cold wastes me more than herbs or dreams do. In any case, we were not speaking of me."

"I'm not taking your herbs, and I'm not taking off this pendant," Therel growled.

Adelaine surged to her feet. "Then suffer your curse in silence, Therel! But don't say I didn't warn you!"

"Wait." Elyasin held her hand out, forestalling Adelaine's departure. "Let us return to the original concern. Say we are linked to Morvein. What does she want of us?"

Adelaine fidgeted with her fingers and shrugged deeper into her furs, though she sank back down into the chair. "I know not. The Lay of Metholas speaks of a great duty between her and the Brother Kings, unfinished, connected to this Rennkavi. And that Morvein would return to finish it, that she worked some kind of dire magic to make it so. But the rest is simply not there. The Lay seems complete, but leaves far too many questions unanswered."

"So Morvein's coming here?" Elyasin asked. "Or this woman who is her incarnation?"

"Perhaps she feels the pendants and is drawn to them." Adelaine fidgeted.

"She called us by *name*, Adelaine." Therel's voice was soft, dangerous. "What are we up against?"

"I don't know." Adelaine blanched, trembling, scared.

Therel took a deep breath and set his jaw. He chewed his lower lip, then rifled a hand through his thick blonde mane. "I need some sleep," he sighed at last. Adelaine looked up, opening her mouth, but Therel cut her off. "No herbs. I'll take a risk. Elyasin?"

Elyasin understood that her choice was her own in this. "I will do as my King. No herbs. And I will not remove my amulet. Let us have these dreams tonight, whatever they bring, and we shall all breakfast upon the morrow before the war-council begins. Leave us, Adelaine. We must rest. All of us."

Adelaine stood slowly, but rather than her previous imperious nod, she actually gave Elyasin a courtly ladies' bow, sinking deep with her hands clasped at her waist. To Therel she merely inclined her head, and he did the same. Turning, she knocked upon the heavy ironbound door and was let out by Lhesher. Therel walked to the bed and sank down with a groan, his head in his hands. Elyasin went to his side, drawing her fingers over his hair. He sighed, leaning into her, his grimace pained.

"I don't know if I'll be able to sleep tonight," he said. "It's nothing but Ghenje, over and over. Aeon, how maddening! I hated the game when my father first tried to teach me, and I hate it now. But somehow…Somehow I find it fascinating. And I feel like I understand it. Which is absurd!"

"Would you like some wintermint and chamomile tea? I could send to the kitchens." Elyasin let her fingers play over his wayward hair.

Therel shook his head, then kicked off his boots and began undressing. "No. I'm tired. Let's just sleep. This has got to end sometime. What about you? Anything interesting in your head?"

"No. Just the homestead." Elyasin began undressing also, shedding her rabbit-shrug to the floor.

"Mmm… there's something better that I'd like to see." Therel reached out, pulling Elyasin's buckles, stripping off her jerkin. In moments, they were naked, though their lovemaking was brief and sweet with exhaustion. But as Elyasin lay in Therel's arms, she could feel his fingers still roving over her thigh, restless.

"Therel? Are you afraid?"

"Terrified." He sighed, blowing her hair behind her ear. "It's not easy for me, having someone in my mind again. Adelaine was predictable in her mind-ruses. They were always to trap me into lust with her, into being foolish and voicing something I couldn't take back. As soon as I had an inkling of what she was doing, Merra actually discovered it, I went to my father. He berated me severely, but as soon as I donned my pendant, it all came to a halt. Adelaine was exiled in disgrace by my father, sent to the northern tundra. The assassination attempt was later, after she'd gone."

"The two of you burn like phosphor."

"Gods, she crawls under my skin!" Therel gave a wry chuckle. "Sometimes I can still feel the sensations of her turning my mind, molding me like wet clay. But this, Elyasin…This is different. I feel no *reason* here. Like whomever is constantly playing Ghenje is absolutely unaware of me."

"I feel the same way." Elyasin gripped his hands where they lay around her middle. "Like I'm looking out of someone else's eyes. Watching them ponder. And it feels… so sad, Therel."

He gripped her closer, cupping one breast. "You feel their emotions, too? This isn't good. As much I hate to say it, I think Adelaine is right. Something is wrong with our pendants."

"Do we take them off?"

He paused. "No. Leave them on, for now. And we'll see what the morning brings."

CHAPTER 36 – JHERRICK

For seven days, Jherrick had sat in the Maitrohounet's rotunda, within the spokes of the Thirteen Tribes' emblem. The Jenner Sun, the symbol of an ancient unity, was his seat and solace. People came and went, joining the song, bringing instruments of every kind to sound their mourning, and taking them when they left. Incense burned night and day. Braziers were brought and massive bowls of water to steam the rotunda and all those within. Clothing were shed outside before entrance, and men and women danced or shook or genuflected or simply sat in prayer naked, sweating out their pain and sorrow.

Word had spread through Ghellen that the Olive Branch had come.

And word had spread just as fast that she had suddenly perished.

Now, the entire city mourned. Children sat at the edges of the space, wide-eyed in awe or fright at the spectacle before them. They were not permitted to play within the rotunda, but neither were they excluded. Jherrick saw elders teaching them the song in quiet voices, holding little ones in laps and whispering the music into their ears, rocking them to the pulse of the trance. Now and then a couple would be drawn together by the shedding of their inhibitions, and they would make love upon the floor, locked into the rhythm of the song and grieving. No food was taken within the rotunda, only water passed around by pitcher. And here or there men and women anointed each other's bodies with an ochre paste, covering their limbs in sigils not unlike their colorful Inkings.

Sweat streaming from his body, Jherrick rose at last from where he'd sat for so very long within the spokes of the Jenner Sun. Throat parched and head reeling, he walked to the edge of the rotunda, nodding his thanks to a woman who proffered a pitcher of water. With his back against the cool stone of the rotunda wall, Jherrick watched the mourning as he drank. He glanced to his left, noting Lourden, who still lay entangled with his wife near one wall. Jherrick had watched them grieve and fuck hard earlier, crying out their song through the rotunda, bolstered by a pair of thundering war-drums being beaten upon either side of their engagement. But they lay still now, Lourden's hand tracing slow circles over Thelliere's shoulder, her little body curled close. Jherrick could see his lips move as Lourden sung his song by her ear, and hers as she sung into his chest, kissing him occasionally.

At length, he felt a presence to his right. Jherrick glanced over as a sweat-streaked Aldris slid down the wall to a seat, elbows around his knees. Jherrick proffered the pitcher. Aldris accepted, drinking deeply, then settled his head back against the wall with a sigh. "Want to get out of here?"

"Yeah." Jherrick took the pitcher and had another drink. "Food?"

Aldris glanced over. "Fuck yeah. I'm goddamn starving." He clapped Jherrick on the shoulder with a tired, sweaty hand, then slid back up the wall to standing. "Come on. Plenty of food in the plaza. Gotta be something out there we haven't sampled yet."

Jherrick nodded, pushing with his legs to slide up the wall. His head spun and he blinked, not used to sweating or fasting for so long. They'd been in the rotunda from sunup to sundown each of the five days since returning from Khehem, and even some of the nights. Jherrick couldn't remember his last meal. The days had blended into each other for Jherrick, with the bliss of simply walking in to sit and cleanse and wring the sorrow from his soul whenever he felt he needed to.

Which was pretty much constantly.

But now, Jherrick's belly twisted, hollow and aching for food. Needing routine again, needing filling up to counter so many days of being emptied. Aldris was already walking to the reed door-cover, and Jherrick followed, ducking under it and out as more people ducked their way in.

Finally standing bare in the late-afternoon sun, a breeze of fresh air sighed over Jherrick's skin at last. He and Aldris found their clothing, boots, and weapons stored in the makeshift racks outside the rotunda, erected specifically for the purpose of this week's mourning. Nothing had been touched, an air of immense respect surrounding the proceedings of the past few days. The mourning would continue for a full week, but Jherrick already felt the fulfillment of its saturation. His muscles were long and languid, his breathing deep and calm, and his head was clear from the smoke of the incense and the fasting he'd done the past many days. He smelled spices upon the breeze and his stomach cramped anew, famished, as he finished pulling on his boots and stood.

Jherrick rifled a hand through his sweat-thick blonde hair, and accepted a wet hand cloth from a woman with a basket. He wiped his face, neck, and torso before winding his *shouf* about his shoulders. Aldris scrubbed the last of the sweat from his hair in a communal water-basin. Jherrick walked over and did the same before throwing up his *shouf's* hood.

His fingertips slipped into his belt-pouch, feeling the little clockwork still there. Relief rose in him, though for what reason, he couldn't say. And an ache in his chest, for Olea. It came and went through the incense and song and ceremony, but Jherrick had the feeling it would never really go away.

A part of him missing, that he could never reclaim.

Aldris nodded at a sprawling group of open-air tents in a plaza just beyond the rotunda's gardens. "Food's over there. I scouted it earlier. Some good pickings today. None of that goddamn lizard intestine they were serving yesterday."

"Fucking awful." Jherrick murmured, a slight smile lifting his lips.

"You said it."

They began to walk in a comfortable silence toward the sprawling silk tents. Groups of people cooked over coal-hot braziers in the center of the colorful conglomerate, serving those lining up at the periphery. Aldris and Jherrick took a turn around before they saw a few elderly women, brown and wrinkled as old leather, bending over meat on a grill and serving it up in a flatbread pocket stuffed with greens and a yellow sauce. They stepped up, hesitating at the periphery of the crowd. A gnarled little woman in line sensed their reticence to be rude. With a toothless smile, she shoved them into line ahead of her, and Jherrick jumped when his butt received a hearty pat.

Aldris grinned as his own butt received two pats from the feisty old crone. "My thanks, grandma."

The old crone cackled, then grabbed Aldris' butt, a hearty handful this time. Aldris laughed, gave a Guardsman salute, and faced forward, stepping up to receive a sandwich from the ladies behind the tent. He mimed trading money, lifting his eyebrows, but they shook their heads just like the past seven days and shooed him off. Jherrick stepped in and one tired old woman reached out to give him a pocket sandwich. He nodded his thanks, kissing the woman on the cheek in a friendly Ghellani gesture of honor. The homely grandma's eyes brightened, and she patted his cheek.

Aldris and Jherrick stepped out of the tent shade, meandering to an area of tall palms at the periphery of the plaza. Fountains burbled up here, forming a network between stepping-stones that sent runnels out to a garden area. There were plenty of places to sit and enjoy the shade, and watch the proceedings at the rotunda and food-tents. Aldris and Jherrick found a patch of tough grasses and had a seat. Communal water-pitchers went 'round to those eating, and Jherrick received one with a nod from a little girl who'd just filled it in the garden-stream.

"Spicy a bit." Aldris reached for the water pitcher after a bite of his pocket-bread.

Jherrick tried his, feeling his mouth burst with flavor and quite a bit of heat. He held out a hand for the pitcher and had a good drink.

Aldris poked through his sandwich, digging out the yellow sauce with his finger. He licked it, and his eyes watered. "Ha!" He wiped his finger off in the grasses, coughing. "That'll kill a man."

Jherrick's lips quirked in an unavoidable smile, digging out his own sauce. The result was edible, though his eyes still watered as some spice flared up his nose again and again. But it was deeply satisfying, the greens in the pocket crunchy and full of water, with sweetness from some tiny currant mixed in. At last, Jherrick leaned back on his elbows, belly full and tongue calming.

"Spice prickles up the nose fast, but doesn't stay," he said to Aldris.

"That's what we get for coming so far south." Aldris reclined on the wiry grass, his hands laced behind his head. "I've heard most

522

of the food in Ghrec is like that. Burn a man up from the inside."

Jherrick settled to his elbows, watching date-palms sway in the afternoon breeze. Sparkles of light revealed between the fronds, then hid, then revealed again high above. Movement at the entrance to the rotunda caught his eye. Lourden emerged, followed by Thelliere. He gave her a sweet kiss, and they exchanged a few words while they donned their clothing. Thelliere departed with a kiss, while Lourden went to a bench outside the rotunda, drinking deep of a water pitcher and leaning back upon the rotunda wall, eyes closed.

"Has he slept these past few days?" Jherrick nodded at Lourden.

Aldris shook his head, watching Lourden from across the square. "Not much. He's hardly left the rotunda. He lost a lot of people in Khehem. More than we did. I've seen him speaking with a number of folk, probably families of his spearmen, comforting them."

Suddenly, Jherrick recalled the herb-woman, the mother of the dead boy he'd deposited in the Kingswood. Her death-sobs raked his ears, wailing over her dead son. "I was never able to tell families what happened to their loved ones. I left a boy's body once, for his mother to find, so she could know… A part of me envies Lourden, that he can tell the families what became of their dead."

Aldris glanced at him, a strange light in his eyes. "You never got to make any of their deaths right. The ones Lhaurent killed. None of that was planned, was it? Olea's death. Lhaurent… back in Khehem."

A hard lump rose to Jherrick's throat. Rage was in it, a scream of agony was in it, and the oceanic sorrow of watching Lhaurent kill and kill again. "I wasn't forced to stand by this time, Aldris. What I was, was too slow."

Aldris' sat up. He reached out, settling a hand to Jherrick's shoulder. "You and me both, Guardsman."

Jherrick went to his place of stillness, a place so cold it burned. "When we find him, Aldris…"

"I know, kid." Aldris was silent as they watched Lourden. His hand slipped from Jherrick's shoulder and he settled back to reclining upon the grass. "Nothing you might do would be as much as that eel deserves. I might fight you for it, you know. The right to kill his ass."

"Do you think it was him controlling Oasis Khehem?"

Aldris eyed him. "Maybe. Was it coincidence he was there at that crystal Plinth? Knowing that bastard, not at all. Lourden said Khehem hadn't gotten bad until a few years ago. Maybe those places were left… primed, you know? Able to move on their own but not unless someone gave it a push. Someone like Lhaurent."

"Controlling the machine's *wyrria* not just in one city, but two. Fucking hells." It was a sobering thought. Jherrick crossed his boots, resisting the urge to touch the clockwork in his belt-pouch.

Aldris opened one eye, frowning at him sidelong. Jherrick weathered his gaze. "What?"

"Olea said you were a better man than I gave you credit for, Jherrick."

Jherrick pulled up a piece of grass, twiddling it between his fingers. "Guess we have something in common."

"No." Aldris came up to a full seat. "Captain-General Olea never minced words. If she said you were behaving like shit on toast, you were doing just that, and she wouldn't have it in the ranks. But she also gave praise where praise was due. If she said you were a better man than I gave you credit for, it means I was wrong. It means I need to look again. At the man beneath the Khehemnas."

Jherrick's fingers paused. He didn't dare meet Aldris' piercing gaze. "And what do you see?"

"I see a fighter who needs some purpose. I see a young killer who hates killing. I see a man ready to break from his lineage, who only needs a reason."

"To avenge Olea? Kill Lhaurent?"

Aldris was silent a long time. "You might think killing Lhaurent is your destiny… but I don't. You're not the blood for blood type, kid. The day of the coronation, you could have run back to your Khehemni Lothren. But you stayed, fought at Olea's side. Why? Because deep down you believed in her, just like me. You, me, Lourden. A people long ago split into three factions. Those who fled atrocity, those who followed on a meager hope of redemption, and those who stayed, losing hope while trying to survive another day."

Jherrick was still, his hands hovering over the grass. Aldris started to sing softly. The sweet, sad dirge of the Tribesmen. The one that had laved them in mercy and community when they had needed it most. Jherrick looked up, and Aldris came to silence.

Aldris' smile was wry. "Do you think it's any mistake we are where we are? A Kingsman and a Khehemnas?"

"So you think it's fate?" Jherrick asked. "Destiny the Alranstone chose for us when it let us through, to become part of some prophecy we don't understand?"

Aldris shook his head. "Destiny and prophecy don't concern me. Lourden's people can say all they want about the Olive Branch. But Olea's dead. None of us can change that. What we can change is how we keep her memory alive, her dream of peace. Olea was right when she reminded me that you didn't kill my family. Young men and women like yourself have been taught to hate on both sides of this ancient war, because hate was what their *parent's* generation did. Olea *believed* in us, Jherrick. Believed we can change that, heal it. I don't know how to do that, yet. But I'm going to find my way back to Alrou-Mendera and put a stop to this bloodshed, somehow. I owe Olea that. The question you have to ask yourself, kid, is are you coming with me or not?"

Aldris was more serious than Jherrick had ever seen him. Jherrick could see the strength of his belief, that he would somehow fuck Halsos and put a stop to an ancient war. It made something deep inside Jherrick stir, something that shook itself off from slumber and gave a righteous roar.

"The Lothren will hunt me if I join you." Jherrick spoke, tingling with this new sensation.

"And you think the Shemout won't?" Aldris raised an eyebrow. "How lightly do you think the Shemout deal with traitors? My marks weren't done in blood-Ink for no reason, you know. I'm forfeiting them, to follow Olea. To follow her hope in a greater unity the likes of which we've never known."

Jherrick tingled. Something was waking inside of him, something that had begun that night he left the dead boy in the woods for his mother, and surged when he'd watched Castellan Lhaurent kill Olea. After seven days of fasting and sweating, Jherrick found his emptiness filling. Filling with a feeling, that he didn't have to stand by in silence anymore.

That he could stand up, and roar, and make the world change.

Jherrick unsheathed one of Olea's longknives. Aldris turned, eyeing him. Holding Aldris' gaze, Jherrick drew the knife across his left shoulder. Fire seared Jherrick's skin like the passage of stinging ants. Tendrils of red wisped out from the cut. A stylized wolf and dragon blossomed crimson upon his shoulder, fighting in their ever-balance, surrounded by a circle broken into thirteen pieces.

Aldris' eyebrows raised. "The Khehemni Bloodmark. A Wolf and Dragon, just like in Khehem."

Jherrick wiped the blade on the grass and re-sheathed it, ignoring the throbbing pain radiating from his shoulder. "I'm with you, Aldris. We'll go back to Alrou-Mendera together, figure out how to put an end to this bloodshed. But we have to go back to Khehem, first."

Aldris stared at Jherrick like he'd gone insane. "Are you nuts, kid? We can't go back there."

"An overland route to Alrou-Mendera is impossible, Aldris," Jherrick argued, realizing he'd been thinking through this very issue for days as he mourned. "The oases are surrounded by arid mountains, a trek through to Ghrec would be death without aid. And caravans take months to cross as far as Cennetia, trading all the way. Taking a ship would waste weeks, and we'd be marked as Menderian with our blonde hair through Valenghian-occupied waters near Cennetia and Praough. The fastest and simplest way to get back to Alrou-Mendera is through a Stone."

"Lhaurent did something to block that crystal Stone against us and you know it." Aldris growled. "It wouldn't let us through after Olea's death, and it sure as hell won't now."

Jherrick gave a sigh and settled back upon the tough grass, thinking. Some part of him did know. Khehem was a dead-end. Part of him wanted to go, to see her body. To touch her, one last time. It didn't sit well with him that Olea would remain there, entombed forever like the rest of the dead Kingsmen. Jherrick's fingertips slid into his belt-pouch, fingering the clockwork.

"Then we'll try the Ghellen-Stone." He stated.

"And say it won't let us through?" Aldris argued. "What if the Ghellen-Stone only worked because we had Olea last time... and Vargen." Aldris' eyes went sad.

Jherrick's heart clenched. "It's a risk, I know. But if the Stone passed us through to get us to unite, a Kingsman and a Khehemnas, then it's got to pass us back to complete that reason."

Aldris snorted, giving Jherrick a withering glance. "And then what? You just want to run through Roushenn playing cat-and-rat with Lhaurent? Come on! Even if we had a thousand of Lourden's hefty spears to ram in the spider's web, he'll still be able to twitch his legs and bite. The only thing that would have made a damn difference is that clockwork of Olea's, and that got left down in the belly of Khehem."

Jherrick's fingers slipped into his belt pouch, feeling the clockwork, all its ridges and contours. Slowly, he pulled it out from the pouch. It glimmered in the dappled sunlight, precious metals and ores throwing color in the green of the garden. Rectangular with the Jenner Sun on the front, it fit in Jherrick's palm like a sundial. Jherrick could see all the minuscule parts, a painstaking interplay of components.

Aldris sat up, his gaze sharpening. "The clockwork! How... when...?!"

"It scattered into the machine," Jherrick could feel the weight of the clockwork, like a pull upon his essence. "But one piece stayed. I kept it. The rest came back to me, while we were at the dragon fountain that night."

Aldris gave a low whistle. Jherrick could see the Kingsman's mind spinning. "That clockwork stopped the machines. If it can control Roushenn..."

"... Then we control the man inside," Jherrick nodded. "Once the machine is off, Lhaurent is just as trapped in those walls as anyone else."

Aldris grinned, ruthlessly, from the shade of his palm tree. "Cut the spider's legs off and then see how easy it is for him to bite. To the Maitrohounet? See if she has a way to get us back to Alrou-Mendera?"

"I want to try the Ghellen-Stone first, Aldris. Tonight."

"If that's the way you want to play it," Aldris gave a nod. "It's a damn sight better than venturing back into Khehem. Let's get back to Lourden's. If there's even a chance of returning to Alrou-Mendera, I want my cold-weather gear."

"Agreed."

Aldris pushed up from the grass. Jherrick stood, settling the clockwork back in his pouch. Together, they strode from the plaza, moving through a bustling but still-grieving Ghellen.

CHAPTER 37 – ELOHL

They had broken camp two days after Elohl's recovery from his fever-dream. Or at least, Elohl thought it was two days. In the ice cavern with the black lake, time had no meaning. Ascending to the broken rift above to continue their journey had not been possible. Numerous times, Fenton had picked his way up the walls, trying every possible ascent. Only to have the ice crumble over and over, dumping him; once he fell more than twenty feet. But Fenton was hardy, and Elohl watched as he sat in deep trance yet again this morning, doing a rapid breathing that caused the bruising upon his body to fade fast.

They had packed up camp today with the silence of men mourning, after Fenton's meditation and a breakfast of stewed jerky. Moving on through a passage scouted the day before, their only route out of the ice cavern wormed deeper into the glacier, burrowing like a snake into frigid darkness. Pack hefted, Fenton made fire in his hand to light their way as they descended, a twisting flame of smelted gold and red that curled through his fingers. At intervals, he breathed rapidly to fan the flame, illuminating the tunnel and peering at the blue ice for cracks.

Elohl watched, fascinated, wondering about the Khehemni side of his bloodline for the first time.

"How do you do that?" Elohl asked as they traversed a decline, the tunnel slipping around a corner with a slick floor.

"Make fire?" Fenton shuffled down the patch of ice with careful bootfalls. Ice-walking, stepping down without pushing off, was a skill Brigadiers knew well. Both men wore ice-claws on their boots, but still. Ice was unpredictable, even in a cavern so cold and quiet as this.

"Can everyone of your bloodline do it?" Elohl navigated the decline after Fenton.

Fenton shook his head. The passage broadened and Elohl

stepped to Fenton's side. He glanced over, to see the Khehemnas grinning.

"What?" Elohl asked.

Fenton gave a low chuckle. "It's just something I never expected. The Rennkavi wanting to learn *wyrric* use from me. No, not everyone of my line can call fire, or lighting. It's actually quite rare. But the magic of Wolf and Dragon, the *wyrria* of *Werus et Khehem*, is not unique to my clan. Long ago, in stories that were ancient when I was young, it was told that Khehem was once a gathering-place for people from all over the continent who had the Wolf and Dragon wyrria. We were simply the first people to name it, for it ran strong in our tribe."

"So it can make fire." Elohl navigated another downslope, a blind twist to the left.

"It can. Among other things." Fenton stepped over a jagged stalactite, broken upon the floor.

"Like what?"

"The Wolf and Dragon *wyrria* is the essence of conflict, Elohl," Fenton stated. "It can create anything conflict creates, and is strengthened when a person has conflict within. The wyrria can call the conflict of air to combust, causing fire. It can move the conflict of water's currents to flow. The *wyrria* can pit plants against each other, growing gardens more lush than anything you've ever seen. Some of my line can twist minds, filling an enemy with the conflict of doubt or forcing an agenda into their thoughts. With each person, the aptitude is different. My own *wyrria* has a destructive flavor. It enjoys burning, fire and lightning. Heat, unrestrained fury."

"You've controlled it all these years." Elohl mused. "No wonder you're the calmest damn person I've ever met."

"My calm was learned out of necessity." Fenton glanced over, his gaze level. "Once upon a time, I was a raging animal, because of my *wyrria* and the things I experienced as a child, losing my mother as I did. You would not have wished to know me, then."

"You said your mother was the Prophetess. How did you know I was the Rennkavi?"

Fenton gave a smile as he slid between a tight group of stalagmites. "Even if you weren't gifted the Goldenmarks, I would have known you're the Rennkavi, to my very bones. I felt what you did when we fought the Elsthemi renegades, and again when your *wyrria* bested mine in that ice bubble. Both times, all you were focused on was *peace*, altruism. That was confirmation for me. Peace and unity are in your very fundament, Elohl."

"But isn't the Prophecy of the Uniter hundreds of years old?" Elohl pressed.

"One thousand thirty-seven years," Fenton spoke low.

Elohl halted, turning incredulous eyes upon Fenton. "But... how old *are* you?"

Fenton took a deep breath. His gold-brown eyes met Elohl's. "I'm one thousand thirty-four years. Those of us with the older magics of Alodwine live exceptionally long lives."

Elohl's mind spun. Fenton didn't look a day past forty. Elohl settled to a flat-topped stalagmite, resting his legs. "You're a thousand years old."

"Don't hate me for being beautiful," Fenton chuckled.

"How?" Elohl wondered.

"Strong *wyrria* was common in my time, Elohl, especially in the Thirteen Tribes," Fenton gazed down at his hands. "And the practices of the day made it more so. You think what I can do is impressive? It's nothing compared to stories I've heard, of the battle-mages of the Order of Alrahel and my Khehemni Alodwine kin. Among the Order, only those with the most accomplished *wyrria* could take the surnomme Alrahel. It became a royal lineage, the Linea Alrahel, the most accomplished *wyrrics* mating within the Order to produce children of exceptionally strong and unique talent."

"Like my gift." Elohl spoke, knowing how fast his body could move.

"Indeed. The part from your father. But through your mother, you're my kin," Fenton continued. "Alodwine. Royal blood of Khehem's ancient kings. As I've told you, the Rennkavi was foretold to come *of twinned blood*. From the Linea Alrahel, mixed with the Scions of Khehem. I've tracked you and Olea since you were born. Not only did you come *of twinned blood* from your father and mother, but you were twins, a twist to the Prophecy I'd not considered. When the Summons happened, I set myself to watch Olea. And had a watch set on you in the High Brigade, a man I could trust from my own line."

"Ihbram den'Sennia." Elohl startled suddenly, a realization hitting him. "He's of your clan. You set him to befriend me in the High Brigade."

"Ihbram's my son." Fenton confirmed with a small smile. But then his demeanor darkened, a slight knit of his eyebrows. "He was supposed to follow you when you were discharged. Obviously, something more important intrigued my inconstant lad than protecting our future Rennkavi. We will have words when next I see him."

Elohl's world reeled as it all fell into place. Ihbram's determination to befriend Elohl, right from the very first. The man had been dogged about it, putting up with all Elohl's brooding fury just after he'd been conscripted. Ihbram had stayed Elohl's hand on a few occasions, kept him from killing himself or drinking himself to death. That first year in the Brigade had been hell, but Ihbram had always been there with a laugh and a ribald joke and a quick smile.

And had been there for Elohl right up until the day Elohl left.

Resting upon his stalagmite, Elohl tried to take it in, to make sense of so much revelation. He massaged cold from his gloved hands, processing. "So you and Ihbram are not Shemout Alrashemni. You're Khehemni."

"We are *also* Shemout." Fenton said patiently, leaning his back to the wall of the tunnel to rest his burden. "My clan infiltrated the Shemout hundreds of years ago, taking Alrashemni oaths and Inkings so we could monitor both Khehemni and Alrashemni cities for the coming of the Rennkavi."

And then, Fenton told Elohl the story of the Khehemni and Alrashemni war, the true history of Khehem that Brother Temlin of the Jenners had only sketched. Fenton spoke of the tyrant king Leith Alodwine of Khehem, Fenton's own grandfather, who had razed the Order of Alrahel, engaging a horrible war that destroyed the Thirteen Tribes and caused Khehem's downfall. Of Leith's betrayal by his Queen, Maya, and of their daughter Alitha opposing her father. Of how Alitha escaped to the south of Ghrec before her father could harm her, protected by her battle-maids and the *berounhim* caravanserai, agents of the Order of Alrahel.

"Alitha Alodwine was my mother," Fenton continued. "I am

King Leith Alodwine's only grandson. My mother believed in her Prophecy of peace so strongly that she commanded her band to find the remnants of the Order of Alrahel as they left the Thirteen Tribes and traveled to Ghrec. She wanted to tell them the Prophecy, to make peace with them. To bring the Prophecy to fruition in her lifetime."

"They killed her, didn't they? The Order of Alrahel killed the Khehemni Prophetess. Your mother." Elohl suddenly understood.

Fenton nodded, his gold-brown eyes ancient. "When my mother's band found them upon the peninsular coast of Ghrec, now the southern coast of Thuruman, the Order of Alrahel attacked without parlay. It was a vicious battle, full of dire magic. Alitha Alodwine, the Prophetess, was killed. Some of the Order survived and fled. In rage, a number of Khehemni split off to pursue the Order and kill them for what they had done. And from my grandfather Leith's conflict of Khehemni against Alrashemni was born a new hatred, moved into new lands."

"Valenghia. Cennetia. Alrou-Mendera." Elohl realized. "Elsthemen. Your people brought a legacy of war wherever they went, chasing each other for centuries." Elohl could see it. Eons of hatred, spilling out in conflict after conflict between Khehemni and Alrashemni descendants.

Fenton took a long breath. "Ask the Twelve Tribes today why they call that area the *Shelf of Lost Hope*, and they cannot recall the reason. But I do. That battle was the moment we all lost hope. My mother named me against such war, Elohl. Fentleith means *Protector of Peace*. In the old tongue, *Leith* meant *peace*, and *fent* is the verb *to protect*. My mother named me against hatred, hoping her bloodline could do better. I believe as she did. That we can have peace. And so I created a curse to bind myself, and my Khehemni progeny, to the Rennkavi. Any who would swear by my blood would receive the benefit of my longevity. So we could keep hope alive. So we could find you. Protect you, when the time came."

Silent as the tunnel around them, Elohl stared at the man he'd once thought to be little more than a good right-hand sword. "So Ihbram is your son, cursed by your blood with your longevity. And you set him to watch me all these years."

Fenton gave a slow nod, watching Elohl cautiously, flames

flickering as they curled between his fingers.

"And Ihbram knew Olea was alive. Those eight years I thought she was dead."

Fenton gave another nod, his brown eyes filled with ancient pain.

"And you knew I was alive, and you never told Olea." Anger burned in Elohl, hot and wrathful. "For *eight years*, you let us twist, believing each other dead. And now she is dead. And I'll never have that time back."

Fenton settled to his heels with a heavy sigh, his pack braced upon the wall behind him. Massaging one shoulder with his free hand, his gold-brown eyes were sorrowful but honest as he met Elohl's gaze.

"Elohl. Those who have taken my blood-oath are *forbidden* to interfere with the Rennkavi's actions. Even a suspected Rennkavi. I couldn't interfere with Olea's life, just as Ihbram couldn't interfere with yours, except to keep you alive. You are my Rennkavi, Elohl. I will fight for you until death takes me from your side. As I did for Olea, for years. But no man can tell how the choices we make will affect the lives of those we love. I'm sorry. I truly am. Know that your sister was one of the most amazing women I've ever met. I was proud that she was a granddaughter of mine. And that you are a grandson."

A long silence filled up between them. Elohl stared at Fenton, grappling with the truth of everything Ihbram had kept from him. Of what Fenton had kept from Olea. The tense silence was crushing in the tight corridor. Needing space to breathe, to think, Elohl inhaled, then picked up his feet and moved on. The light followed. He heard the crunch of Fenton's ice-claws behind him. In a torpid silence, they navigated another downslope, then another. For long minutes, tension stretched between the two men, strained like climb-rope.

Elohl could almost feel it, his Khehemni legacy. Conflict boiled the cool lake he normally submerged his emotions under. Bitterness toward Fenton and Ihbram. Fury over his years without Olea that he could never get back. Aching woe that she was gone. The understanding that Ihbram and Fenton were good men, who'd made hard choices under desperate circumstances. A terrible love for

Ghrenna, that twisted his gut and clamped his heart, making his eyes prickle and his throat rasp.

All of it. Conflict.

Searing fire rose along his Goldenmarks. Biting like ants, Elohl could feel the product of his conflict limning his skin, diving deep into his flesh beneath his furs. And he realized with the coursing of that flame, that he'd been lying to himself all these years. Telling himself that he was calm. That his emotions could be submerged. That they hadn't defined him, shaped him, roiling under the surface as they always had. That they hadn't made him stronger, honed, capable. Made him into a weapon, an explosion of energy just barely contained with this overwhelming desire for peace consuming him.

All just to stop the pain of living, and loss.

They turned a corner, and the light's reach from Fenton's palm showed a blockage ahead. Elohl pulled up short, roused from his churning thoughts. Fenton stepped to his side, lifting his fire high to inspect the jagged cave-in. Huge chunks of ice had collapsed in upon the tunnel, creating a mess of cracked blue boulders. Broken ice shards were scattered underfoot, and their boots came to a halt in a crunching scree ten paces from the rubble.

"Damn." Elohl combed a hand through his hair, suddenly exhausted from so many unwanted surprises. "I thought this tunnel was too good to be true."

"Maybe." Fenton slung his pack to the ground. Doing a rapid breath through his open mouth, he brightened the flames in his fingers. Holding an in-breath, the flames expanded, filling his palm with a sphere of white-hot illumination, which Fenton lifted high as he approached the cave-in. He knelt, examining the ice, and then Elohl saw it. Between a triad of three massive sheets, there was a small opening, barely large enough for a man to slither into.

Fenton peered into the breach. And then huffed his air out, taking an inhalation at last. His fire's brilliance flashed back to a low simmer curling between his fingers.

"It goes through." Rising, Fenton walked back to Elohl. "About twenty lengths back, it opens into another cavern. Tight, but I think we can manage it."

Elohl eyed the pile. He slung his pack to the floor, leaning it against his knee. "That's a death-trap, Fenton. That block there," he gestured to the one leaning over the other two, buried beneath thousands of stones of ice, "jostle that one even a little, and the whole things comes crushing down on us."

"Then I suppose we'll have to move *carefully.*" Fenton's small smile held a subtle recklessness.

"Can't your magic do anything?"

Fenton laughed, wry. "I could melt it, I suppose. But then we'd be drowning like rats in this blind downturn, and the ice above would just keep sinking into our death-lake. I have fire-*wyrria*, Elohl. Great in some situations, terrible in others. Having magic doesn't solve everything in life."

Elohl thought about that, rubbing his short beard. He cast an eye over the broken blue rubble, his breath puffing in a cool steam. "Go through this or break our necks trying to pick up the sides of the that cavern we left." He said at last.

"Damned if you do..." Fenton began.

"...Damned if you do." Elohl finished. They shared a look. A Brigadier look. And just when Elohl thought he knew nothing about Fenton, he found he also knew much. The man was a fighter. He had frozen in blizzards and struggled to keep others alive. He'd fought in skirmishes upon the glaciers and lived to see another freezing night. He'd bled and suffered for his people, for the things he believed in.

He loved family with a ferocity not to be denied. Fenton had loved Olea, and it was wrong for Elohl to punish him with anger. They relied upon each other down here, and holding fury in his heart right now was likely to get them both killed. In the mountains, men lived by burying their emotions, and Elohl realized it was needed once more.

Elohl slipped his feelings away beneath his glacial calm, even knowing that somewhere deep, they still burned. He felt his Goldenmarks sigh out to nothing as he faced the cave-in and took a deep breath. Survival was first; everything else could wait.

"Let's do it. Before I change my mind."

Fenton gave a nod. With a flick of his fingers, he threw the *wyrric* fire from his hand. Giving good light upon the breach, it writhed like a coiled dragon in midair, folding in upon itself with a sinuous motion. Fenton knelt and began unclipping rope from his pack, getting a grapple-and-pulley set up.

"Packs first?" Elohl set to his own gear, mimicking Fenton's preparations.

Fenton nodded. "If the breach is big enough for the gear, then we should be able to squeeze through."

Tying a length of rope to his pack, Fenton threaded it through a pulley and gave it length, then affixed a stout grapple upon the pulley with a metal clip. Walking to the opening with pack and pulley, he knelt, grapple in hand. With easy grace, Fenton hucked the grapple into the opening. Elohl heard the skitter of the grapple and pulley, sliding through the breach. The lines of rope surged from Fenton's easy fingers, coils disappearing into the hole.

There was a clatter, and all came to silence.

Kneeling, Fenton peered in. He summoned the writhing fire back to his fingertips, illuminating the breach. "We're set. It went all the way." He pulled the ropes taught. Elohl heard the distant grind of the grapple digging into ice. Fenton gave it one more tug, then took up the slack. Clipping a second pulley to his pack, he threaded another rope, then clipped the far end to Elohl's pack.

Setting his pack in the breach, Fenton hauled on the head-rope until his pack began to scoot in. It disappeared, rope attached to Elohl's pack getting eaten up as it went.

"Here," Fenton handed the rope to Elohl. "Pull. I need to man the light."

Elohl knelt. He hauled the rope as Fenton peered into the breach, holding his fire out before him. Things went well for a long minute, when suddenly the rope pulled taught.

"The pack's stuck." Elohl noted.

"Damn!" Fenton cursed. "It's nearly at the end. Give it a haul. Maybe something on the outside just got snagged."

Elohl put his strength behind his pull. The rope tightened, resisted. And then with a grinding sound, the pack broke free and Elohl could pull again until he felt slack in the line.

"It's through! Dumped out the far end." Fenton handed Elohl the second rope. "Now yours."

They repeated the process. Elohl's pack got stuck in the same spot. He hauled on the rope, but this one was more resistant. Elohl had to set a foot to a massive slab of ice in the pile, bracing himself to pull hard. With a wrenching sound, the pack broke free. Elohl stumbled backward, taking up slack to keep from falling over. But as the pack slid on, the ice-rubble gave an ominous groan. A vast cracking sound emanated from somewhere deep within. Small shards of ice cascaded down with a clatter.

Fenton and Elohl leaped back. The showering shards ceased, but even to the naked eye, it was obvious the pile had shifted. Fenton approached warily, knelt to peer into the breach. "It's still clear."

"Fucking luck." Elohl said.

Fenton nodded. Elohl took up the rope again. In a moment, they had the second pack through.

Which left both men eyeing the pile, wary.

"Nothing for it," Fenton spoke. "All our gear's on the other side. Without it, we die."

"Trying to get it, we might die."

"Just so." Fenton was not grinning now. The *wyrric* fire writhed between his fingers, brighter than before. At last, he gestured to the pile. "Rennkavis first."

Elohl lifted an eyebrow.

"If the whole thing collapses, it's going to do so with continued disturbance," Fenton said. "I'm expendable. You're not. I'll be right behind you."

Elohl was about to argue, but the look in Fenton's eyes gave him pause. At last, Elohl nodded. Fenton had vowed to protect his Rennkavi, a vow that damned his soul to hellfire. The least Elohl could do was be gracious.

"See you on the other side." Elohl knelt at the breach. Shimmying his upper body in, he pushed in by the tips of his boots, their metal claws digging into the ice. The breach was narrow and utterly dark. Before he could say anything, a small lance of fire zoomed past his ear into the passage, curling into a writhing orb upon the far side. Elohl glanced over his shoulder, seeing Fenton slither into the breach behind him.

Fenton gave a wink.

Elohl took a deep breath to calm his nerves, then focused upon the distant light. Pushing forward, he realized it would be slow going. Pulling by his fingertips and pushing with his toes, he slithered over the ice, the breach too narrow to even crawl. He could hear Fenton's progress behind, measured breaths, the scrape of ice-claws. Claustrophobia gnawed at Elohl, the sides of the narrow tunnel damning. Pulling in slow breaths, Elohl fought off the fear of being trapped. Of a painful death, crushed beneath countless tons of ice.

Specters laughed at the edges of his vision. But fear was the mind-killer. Elohl breathed steadily, controlling his fear, focusing on that writhing fire at the end of the tunnel. Gradually, it came closer, until it burned just a few lengths distant. Elohl arrived at the tight spot near the end, where the packs had become stuck. Ice shards littered the passage, evidence of recent fracture. Squeezing breath from his lungs, Elohl tightened his shoulder blades to his spine. Using his toes, he pushed forward, wriggling through the stricture. Ice pressed in from all sides, cold, unyielding. Elohl sighed out the very last of his air. He wriggled, pushed, fear squeezing his mind as the ice squeezed around his shoulders.

Suddenly, his shoulders slid forward, through the restriction. But a horrible cracking sound came from the ice directly above. A shower of shards came down. Elohl's sensate sphere surged. Panic gripping him, Elohl moved on instinct, propelled forward by feverish toes and fingertips. He made it just in time. A shower of fist-sized ice chunks came down upon his legs and feet, and then he was through, slithering out to land upon the packs.

"Dammit!" Elohl shouted. He whirled, peering into the breach. The ice had settled again, ominous creaking ricocheting off dark cavern walls beyond the fire's light. "Fenton!" Elohl shouted through the breach.

"Here!" Fenton shouted back, his voice distant. Elohl could barely see him through the pile of white rubble. Only six or seven lengths into the breach, he was covered in chunks of glittering ice. "My legs are pinned! Nothing's broken, but I'm stuck."

"I'm coming to get you!" Elohl began to slither into the breach, but Fenton shouted at him.

"No! You'll be trapped! The ice is still shifting!"

A horrid crack came, groans. Scree littered down upon Elohl.

"Can you haul yourself out on the rope?" Elohl yelled into the breach, backing out.

A grunt came, then, "No! I can't get leverage through the tight spot!"

Hurriedly, Elohl picked up the grapple. With a tight throw, he heaved it into the breach. "Grab the grapple! Hurry!"

Fenton did. Elohl hauled on the rope, straining his entire weight behind it. But no matter how hard he pulled, nothing changed.

"No good!" Fenton called out. "I'm stuck! I have to melt some of this ice first! Hang on! Stand back with the rope and get the packs away from the pile!"

Elohl realized what Fenton was about to do. Fear raced through him, heightening his senses as he heard Fenton begin a heating breath inside the breach. A groan and crack came from the pile. Elohl's instinctual sphere tingled and he leapt aside as an enormous chunk of ice careened down where he'd been. Hastily, he seized the packs, unclipped them, and tossed them clear of the pile. Rapid breaths came from inside the hole. The entire pile shivered and shook, ice careening down around Elohl.

"Fenton!" Elohl roared. "The pile is coming down!" Seizing the rope, he hauled on it with all his might. *"Fenton!!"*

Suddenly, Elohl's Goldenmarks lit with a tremendous heat, searing his body like a bonfire burned within him. He heard a yell from Fenton. With a roaring sound, the pile collapsed. And as it did, a rush of hot water gushed from the breach. Elohl hauled on the line, praying to every god he knew. Fenton shot from the breach in a surge of water like a newborn seal, colliding with Elohl and sending them both careening backwards over the slippery ice. Illuminated by Fenton's writhing fire, the pile of ice rumbled, shuddered. Boulders of ice careened down, shifting, collapsing. And when it was done, skitters of ice still dusting down, the breach was gone.

Braced on his elbows beside Elohl, Fenton's breath heaved. His eyes were wide, filled with simmering flame and exhilaration. "Damn, that would have been a bad way to die!"

A relieved chuckle took Elohl. And then he laughed. The laughter wouldn't stop. He sat up to his elbows, giving into it.

And then he was crying. Sobbing, relieved and spent and twisting inside for Olea.

Fenton came to his knees. He seized Elohl in a fierce embrace. Elohl broke, giving in to it, letting his emotions erupt now that the danger was over. She was gone. She was gone, and there was nothing he could do. He and Fenton would probably die down here, trapped in a cavern far beneath the cold silence of a devil's glacier. And even if he didn't die, he held the burden of these fearsome marks, controlling some dire magic he didn't understand.

A responsibility he didn't want.

"Fuck me," Elohl gasped. "I can't do this! I can't do this alone…!"

"You're not alone, Elohl," Fenton murmured into his ear, fierce. "You'll never be alone, as long as I draw breath. You'll get through this. We'll get through this, together."

"I miss her! Fuck, I miss Olea so much…!" Elohl set a hand to his heart, pressing his chest as if that could stop the pain of his loss. His Goldenmarks burned, so hot and fierce he thought they'd set his clothes aflame.

Fenton's voice cracked. He gripped the back of Elohl's head, pressing their foreheads together. "I swear to you. I will avenge Olea's death. I will find whoever killed her, and I will make him pay for it."

Elohl's shoulders shook. He felt that knife across his throat, gasping as blood poured down. Unable to breathe, the last horrible thing Olea had felt before she died. Anguish filled him, making his Goldenmarks sear and writhe, that he'd not seen her killer. That he had no idea who had committed the murder, and perhaps might never know.

Lifting up his head, Elohl screamed to the black. Everything he was came pouring out in that one terrible howl, and his Goldenmarks flared until they burned him alive. As if he could feel Elohl's markings, Fenton suddenly broke from Elohl with a terrible roar of his own. Surging to his feet, he bellowed again, and then hurled a spear of lighting far into the dark cavern.

Fenton's lightning broke into a cloud of lancing electricity, illuminating the massive darkness. Elohl froze. Beauty was revealed in that so-sudden crackle of light. An incredible beauty, all around them, arresting Elohl's sorrow in a sudden wash of amazement.

"What in Aeon's fuck…?" Elohl rasped. Fenton shivered with rage, but by the way he stilled, Elohl knew he'd seen it too.

It wasn't a cavern that loomed around them, massive and dark.

It was a citadel, carven straight out of the glacier itself.

CHAPTER 38 – TEMLIN

Temlin was red-eyed from a week of sleepless nights. The taking of the First Abbey hadn't really been a taking at all. Temlin had seen Lhem's vile body shuttled off and sequestered in a cremation room. Lenuria had taken him promptly into private audience, asking if he'd gone completely mad and requiring proof of the Queen's survival. Temlin had taken Lenuria to the Abbeystone, and waited while Mollia had poured out to Lenuria everything she had seen about the Queen's position. At last, Lenuria had acquiesced, believing Temlin.

But then, she'd demanded that *if he was going to be a Dhenir, he'd better start acting like one.*

Today, Temlin was once again holding court in the Annex's enormous meeting-rotunda, the wide circular space with its soaring facades crowded with Brothers and Sisters nearly as red-eyed with lack of sleep as he was. A colored-glass window of a fighting lion poured golden and red sunlight down upon the low bluestone dais at the front of the hall where Temlin stood. Bread and cheese were being passed around on platters, as those in the hall listened. Temlin's dry throat screamed for ale, but he sipped only water, wetting his palate over and over to stave off the heat of two thousand bodies crowding the space every sweltering day.

A boom of thunder sounded outside, but it was dry, only a brisk heat-lightning flashing through the gathering clouds in the late summer afternoon.

"What you're proposing is madness!" Grey-haired Brother Lemvos from the orchards shouted, pounding his fist upon the table on the dais. He was a stout man with calloused palms, one who bore the Blackmark. "If we refuse trade with Roushenn, they'll starve us out by winter, Temlin! And then what do we have? Nothing. We don't have enough lamp oil, or fuel for the furnaces! Sure, we grow most things we need, but we're not fighters anymore! Those of us who were fighters to begin with."

A number of heads nodded agreement, Brothers and Sisters in the crowd shifting uneasily.

"We're not *talking* about a siege." Temlin said firmly, crossing his lean-muscled arms over his repaired black longjacket. Fully armored beneath and bristling with weapons as he had been the past week, Temlin scowled at Brother Lemvos. "We're talking about *withholding* from the King's City. How long can working men go without beer? How long will the populace tolerate inns without liquor? What happens when harvest-fest comes, which is next week, I might add, and there is nothing with which to *fest*? Not to mention the war-campaigns. We supply a full seventy percent of the alcohol at the fronts, gentlemen. What will soldiers do when they have nothing to help them relax? They'll get loud. And they'll want to know *why* we are withholding, which we'll tell them. And then they'll get pissed at the King's Chancellate. *Rioting* pissed. At which point, we can ply our cause."

"How do you mean?" Dark-haired and formidable Brother Sebasos, standing nearby upon the dais, asked only so Temlin could elaborate.

"When men are unsettled and begin to yell," Temlin continued, "they become angry, dangerous animals. Seed whatever objective you want during a protest, and the mob will do the rest for you. Flares will begin all over the city. The Chancellors will have no choice but to put such demonstrations down, severely. And when they do, they'll face a populace riddled with doubt and anger, believing the Abbey's side. That the wars against Valenghia and Elsthemen are a drain upon the nation and unnecessary. That Queen Elyasin lives and longs to come home. That the King's Chancellate has usurped her throne."

"So you'll risk a *severe* altercation between our Abbey and Roushenn?" Grey-hair scoffed again.

"No." Temlin held the man's eyes in his fierce gaze. "I intend to do no such thing. I *intend* to put out another rumor during the first demonstrations that anyone unhappy with the Chancellate may come here, and that we shall offer them food, shelter, and training."

"You're building a militia." Lenuria spoke from where she stood behind the stout table. The entire assembly turned to look at

544

her. Tiny-boned and regal, her cowl was pushed back to reveal her ornate braids of iron-shot hair.

"Yes." Temlin's gaze settled upon her. "It's time the Crown had a standing army once more."

Lenuria moved forward, every eye following her. "Once you declare throughout the city for Queen Elyasin den'Ildrian," she continued, "you're trusting that some of the older Guardsmen will defect."

"Some of them may yet remember me." Temlin nodded. "Some of the oldest, and some of those in retirement in Lintesh. I was in charge of the Palace Guard, once."

"You're hoping if things get bad enough during any conflicts," Brother Sebasos rumbled. "That we'll see a windfall of Guardsmen who aren't willing to debase the populace. Guardsmen who support their Queen."

"So say you're right." Lenuria continued. "Say we get, what? Perhaps fifty loyal Guardsmen?" She scoffed, but it was gentle. "That's not enough, Brother Temlin. Not for what you're trying to do."

"Not enough to fight an army, Abbess Lenuria, no." He shook his head. "But I'm not counting on that. What I'm counting on, is civil unrest *outside* Lintesh. Riots that spread far enough to damage the campaigns."

"So you want to fan the flames across our entire nation," Brother Lemvos scoffed. "Burn it all down. What's left? Nothing! Nothing for anyone to come home to."

Temlin sighed and growled, scrubbing a hand through his hair. He was about to open his mouth to address Lemvos' concern when suddenly, a breathless young Brother came pushing through the packed hall to the front, his face flushed and fear in his eyes. He staggered to a halt before Temlin, hands on his knees, almost retching he was panting so hard.

"Temlin… news!" The boy gasped.

"Catch your breath boy, for crying out loud!" Temlin poured the boy a glass of water from the pitcher upon the table and the lad downed it hastily. "Now. Tell me what has happened." Temlin commanded gently, setting a hand to the lad's skinny shoulder.

"Assassination!" The lad gasped, his breath coming more easily.

"The King's Chancellate!"

"Whom? Which Chancellor?" Temlin was aghast, his eyebrows raising in alarm.

"Not one." The lad shook his head. "All of them! Last night, in their beds. Throats slit."

"Holy sweet mercy!" Temlin's whisper was horrified.

"The city!" The boy gasped again. "Listen… can't you hear it?"

Temlin cocked his head, hearing a strange susurration upon the air through the open windows. Dry thunderclouds thickened the sweltering afternoon, but this sound he heard was not thunder. Striding through the throng as they parted like water before him, Temlin moved with fast purpose to a side-door, then ran up a set of spiral stairs that led to a roof-gable. Pushing through the stout ironwood door, he stepped out upon a high balcony of the Annex, gazing out over the Abbey grounds. Thin clouds choked the sky, flickers of lightning coming now and then, but that was not what arrested Temlin's attention.

Far out over the city, beyond the First Abbey's wall, the air seethed with noise. Voices like the rush of the ocean, raised in shouts and bitter with anger. Inhaling deeply, Temlin smelled tar and pitch upon the humid air. And burning, the acrid scent of fire. Temlin turned quickly, surveying the city. Far out over the Craftsman's Quarter, billowing smoke rose. Not just one column of it, but four, and as Temlin watched, five.

Heat-lightning flickered in the clouds, but no rain was coming from their wispy reaches. The city was going to burn tonight.

Turning back toward the open gable-door, Temlin saw frightened faces of Brothers and Sisters who had followed him up. Temlin began to command at once, the reflex innate. "All of you! Back down to the hall!"

Temlin pushed down the stairs towards the rotunda, the First Abbey beginning to erupt all around with fear. Temlin pushed back to the dais, then vaulted up to the stout table so all could see him.

"Brothers and Sisters of the First Abbey!" He roared. The room began to silence, fear turning to attention. "The city is burning! In the wake of this news that the King's Chancellate have been assassinated, we must prepare for the worst. I don't know what we will face this night, but we must prepare for all likely outcomes! Brother Lemvos!"

"Yes, Lord Temlin?" The man who had been arguing raised his brushy grey brows in surprise.

"You are in charge of keeping our Abbey from burning." Temlin gave him a hard smile. "I want everyone who works in the gardens and orchards to the go to the wells and ponds! I want buckets, and I want them moving! Organize a brigade! There is an old water-pump near the storm-grate by the men's dormitory. It accesses the river that flows beneath Lintesh. Use it! Dredge water up and keep the ponds full as the brigades go out! Every timber you can find near the walls, I want it soaked! *Soaked*! Lintesh will burn badly before this night is over and I'll not have the First Abbey burn with it! Spread the word! Water the gardens and the orchards and water them *thoroughly*. Move, man, move!"

Brother Lemvos blinked, then erupted into motion. Shouting for Brothers and Sisters of the gardens, he stepped into his role easily, summoning men and women to his side as he strode from the room.

Temlin's eyes scanned the crowd, fixed on the redheaded Sister near the dais who had bared Bloodmarks that day he'd killed Lhem. "You! Sister Alitha! Are you a fast runner?!"

"Yes, Lord Temlin!" She nodded, green eyes wide but ready.

"Find me fighters! If they can wield arms, if they've had *any* training, I want them up on those walls! Take this." Temlin pulled Lhem's keyring at his belt, and unsnapped an iron key. "There's an armory under the Abbey. Past the third brewery, it's accessed by a stout door framed in oak with the sigil of crossed swords. Go there. Bring Blackmarked and Bloodmarked, and any others who can wield a weapon. I want swords and pikes, bows and knives! I want mail under those robes, or cuirass and vambraces over them! I want helmets and stout boots! Send them to the Abbey's gates, and up to the wall. I will find you atop the first section by the main gate in one bell. Trade off your position in the armory to come make report to me. Go!!"

The Sister was fleet, hiking up her robes and tucking them into her belt, as she bellowed commands and strode from the hall. Temlin had chosen well, and her piercing shout pulled many

Blackmarked and Bloodmarked from the hall at her heels.

Temlin found one of the infirmary Sisters in the hall and barked at her next. "Sister Regina! Turn the Annex, the Cathedral, and any other large open space you find into an infirmary. Sacrifice bedding for bandages, find all the healing supplies you can, savage the herb gardens and start making salves and poultices! Expect blood. A lot of it. We're going to have wounded today, fleeing Lintesh. Knife-wounds, sword-slashes, burns, broken bones. Take the dormitory-keepers with you and have them prepare for masses to house."

"Yes, Lord Temlin!" She raced from the hall, beckoning white-robed Sisters from the infirmary as she went.

Temlin's gaze flicked to the lad who had brought the message, standing near upon the dais. "You. You're going to be my message boy. Find a flask of water and a pouch of food and keep them on your belt. You're going to be doing a lot of running today, lad. What's your name?"

"Brother Brandin." A terrified respect shone in the lad's eyes.

"Are you ready for this, Brother Brandin?" Temlin clapped him on the shoulder.

"Yes, Lord Temlin. You lead, I follow." The lad found some steel, straightening.

"Good lad. Brother Sebasos." Temlin turned to his stalwart supporter from the brewery, standing near. Sebasos' dark brows were set in a hard line. "You will organize our forces at the gate. The city of Lintesh will come flooding to our Abbey for protection tonight, from the chaos that is going to erupt out there. Be kind, but hold steady. Let in those who are peaceable, wounded, children. Hold the gate and the walls against threats. Watch for Palace Guard. We don't know yet how they will react, leaderless as they are right now."

"Yes, Lord Temlin." Brother Sebasos gave a rumbling growl. Setting an open palm to his chest and one to a longknife that now rode his hip, he bowed low.

"Stay a moment before you depart." Temlin stalled Sebasos with a hand. "I need you to be my First-Captain today."

Sebasos nodded, clasping his big hands behind him in a ready posture. Implacable, he stood at Temlin's side, dark-eyed and dangerous. He'd seen battle before, of that Temlin had no doubt.

There were more than a few scars beneath that robe, and Sebasos' calm in the storm bandied no misunderstandings. Temlin couldn't have selected a finer man for his First-Captain.

With a grim smile, Temlin surveyed the crowd. Shouts and confusion filled the rotunda. Over a thousand people still milled in the ample hall, tense. Men and women from the breweries, the kitchens, livestock-keepers. Masons and carpenters, historians and scholars who had yet to be given a duty. They gazed up at him with drawn faces, worried. Temlin realized suddenly that the high-gabled rotunda had become an impromptu war-room.

"Friends! Settle! Settle." Temlin eased open palms downward, and gradually the tumult of voices quieted.

"What's happening out there?" One frantic voice cut through.

"I can see little in the streets yet," Temlin began. "But smoke rises above Lintesh this day, and dry environs of the city will soon fan it to a torch. Today we must plan for two things: fire and flight. The city will burn, or at least part of it, and folk will come to us for refuge. We will see much chaos this day, but the orders I have already set in motion will save not only us, but also the people of our fair city."

Temlin surveyed the hall, found people beginning to settle into readiness. "For the rest of you, I need you where you have the most ability. Those who know herbs and poultices, go to the infirmary and the dormitories. Cooks will remain in the kitchens, for we will have a multitude to feed before the day is out. Fighters shall be with me upon the wall, divided into companies and watches. The bucket-brigade is already set, but if the Abbey begins to burn, I need *all hands* joining the buckets. Are we clear?!"

"Do you think it will come to that, Lord Temlin?" A gruff voice called out, stern and capable Brother Thenros from the brewery.

"We prepare for the worst, and hope for the best." Temlin regarded him, flint-eyed. "Steel yourselves, Brothers and Sisters. We shall see carnage before the day is out. Blood will soak our flagstones, even if there is no fighting. We shall see devastated refugees. And we shall help them."

Heads nodded all around, the idea of helping the dispossessed one that every Brother and Sister could support. It would make them strong when the time came, and these many who had never seen battle needed the strength of something they believed in to help them through.

"But do you think we shall see fighting on our grounds?" Brother Thenros called again, as if reading Temlin's mind.

"Consider this." Temlin began, eyeing the room. "*Someone* has cleanly implemented the assassination of not one, but *all* of our ruling Chancellate. And since the King is dead and our young Queen disappeared and presumed dead, and the governing body dead... who rules now in the Palace?"

Feet shifted, eyes darted. Few had considered the political implications of the news. But Temlin had. He'd been bred from birth to read such events.

"Ah... but there is someone," he continued. "In a time of crisis, when all governing bodies have been killed, the management of the nation falls to the King's Castellan. And under his command come the Palace Guard, the Generals, and the entire Menderian military. To be stewarded for one month and one day until a replacement Chancellate can be hastily elected or an heir to the throne found. But right now? The King's Castellan has not had a chance to send riders to the fronts, and we have no army in Lintesh save the Palace Guard. Will the Palace Guard follow the Castellan with their Guard-Captain and two highest Lieutenants missing? We don't know. So who protects the peace of Lintesh right now? No one."

"You do." Brother Sebasos' low growl was audible throughout the hall. He turned to Temlin, and took a knee. "Dhenir Temlin den'Ildrian. Uncle to the Queen. My liege."

Temlin blinked. His head jerked up, and he looked around the room. Thoughtfulness had crossed a number of faces. And then many began to kneel.

"No, Brother Sebasos——" Temlin put a hand to the man's enormous arm, urging him to come back to his feet. "I do not usurp the crown——"

"No." Sebasos was firm, and he budged from his knee not an inch. "Whether you hold the throne but a day for Queen Elyasin or a year or ten. You are blood-kin to the Crown. And the closest man to a King Alrou-Mendera has got."

"If the Castellan wants to fight you for the throne," Abbess

Lenuria was calm and cool, moving forward upon the dais to take up position beside Temlin, "he's going to get quite a surprise."

"Lenuria, I—" Temlin began.

She held up one regal little hand, forestalling him. "In the wake," Abbess Lenuria began, surveying the rotunda with her steely eyes, "of recent events, I am invoking two ancient Laws of the Order and one of the Realm. Those of you who adore history, you may peruse them at your leisure in those tomes there." She nodded to two hefty leather-bound tomes being carefully handled by scribes, who set them reverently upon the large oak table on the dais.

"First, I invoke the Right of Abbess," she continued. "In the event that the Abbot is not here to make crucial decisions when the safety of the Abbey is threatened, the Abbess may do so. Second, I invoke the First Law of the Order. In times of strife, the First Abbey of Lintesh may declare for a liege or a protectorate that it sees in its best interests to keep the Abbey safe. And so, do I hereby declare the First Abbey of Lintesh for Dhenir Temlin den'Ildrian, to protect our Abbey in this time of crisis."

Temlin eyed Lenuria, wondering where she was going with all this.

She gave him a small, secret smile.

"Thirdly, I invoke *Alhamrit den'Uhr*, the Chosen of the Hour, set down among the very first laws of Alrou-Mendera. In times of chaos, when the governing bodies are unformed, the people of the Realm may select a champion. A King-Protectorate to serve for as long as needed, who agrees by taking this role that he shall be slain should he not relinquish the throne to the proper liege when the time comes. And thus, do I act in service to the Realm and speak with the voice of the People, electing Temlin den'Ildrian as King-Protectorate of Alrou-Mendera, to act in stead of Queen Elyasin and do for the kingdom as benefits us all, until she can be rightfully returned to her throne. King-Protectorate, do you accept the fealty of the First Abbey, and your nominated station?"

Temlin's mouth hung ajar. "Lenuria…"

Slowly, Abbess Lenuria removed the ruby ring of the Abbess from her index finger. Her fingers found Temlin's and slid it in place. It barely fit his littlest finger. "Do you refuse?" She asked softly.

Temlin swallowed. Then shook his head.

Lenuria lifted his hand in hers, raising it up before the crowd. "Nominated and accepted this day as King-Protectorate of Alrou-Mendera, Temlin den'Ildrian! Long live the King!"

"Long live the King!" Brother Sebasos' booming voice flooded the hall. He began to chant it, and soon the room filled with it. Temlin's heart clenched in worry. He glanced at Abbess Lenuria. She gazed back, then winked at him. She faced forward again, imperious, as the chant filled the hall.

Temlin took a deep breath.

Lenuria believed in him. Mollia believed in him.

It was time he believed in himself.

"Enough!" Temlin roared. The hall fell to silence. "Pomp will waste lives today! Get to your stations! Lintesh burns, and I will not have it be said that King-Protectorate Temlin den'Ildrian did not make welcome those in need! I will protect this Abbey and the people of Lintesh like a lion for you, but I *cannot* do it alone! Help me save this city, and save our nation! For the people are her heart and soul, and a King is as dust to the grain of their wheat! Go, now! Save our city!"

A cheer went up. They were behind him now. Abbess Lenuria sidled close as the hall began to rush to task.

"Battle is coming, and it will be bloody because of what you've done today, woman." Temlin growled.

Lenuria raised her sharp chin. "And will it be any less bloody with Castellan Lhaurent at its helm? I would rather have options." She twitched a fold of her robes aside, and Temlin saw a girdle of longknives beneath. She smirked.

"You've created a hell, woman." Temlin sighed.

"And you're going to lead us out of it. Walk with me." Abbess Lenuria turned, striding quickly toward the main doors of the hall. Temlin was fast upon her heels. But they hadn't gone seven paces, when a man lingering in an alcove suddenly lunged straight for Temlin, blades flashing. Temlin whirled to counter, swiftly drawing his white-hilted longknives to match the weapons of the assassin. The resulting clinch brought him face-to-face with greying Brother Hender from the annals.

Hender's blue eyes were ferocious with hate. "Always knew you were a *rat*, Temlin!"

Hender growled as he vied for dominance in their clinch. He was larger than Temlin, but hadn't his youth anymore. Temlin pushed him off, upsetting Hender's balance as he pivoted to take the man's next blows. But Temlin didn't have a chance to engage when Hender cried out. Sagging to the stones, Hender's blades dropped from his hands. Abbess Lenuria casually wiped blood from her dagger upon Hender's black robes, gazing down at where she'd stabbed him cleanly through the side of the neck. He bled out, gurgling and twitching.

"You're efficient." Temlin sheathed his blades.

The Abbess' lips quirked. "When you're small and female, you learn to use your best attributes." Others watched, eyes enormous and mouths gaping to have seen the fighting, one of their own now bleeding out upon the floor. "An assassin!" The Abbess barked, surveying them with steely eyes. "This is the first blood shed today, but it shall not be the last! To your stations! Now!"

They hurried away, flooding from the hall.

"Temlin." The Abbess beckoned, and Temlin quickly followed. She led him on a winding route through the Annex complex, to an ancient ironbound door that led to stock cellars, then down further. Through cellars and catacombs, they finally came to a door of solid mahogany. She unlocked it with a key, then entered quickly. The room was small, nothing in it save for a door at the other end. But this was marked with a Kingsmount and Stars.

Temlin blinked. "Where does it go?"

"I haven't time to tell you everything, Temlin, but once even the Abbey served the royal house. The royal lineage was den'Alrahel, People of the Dawn, but the throne has long since fallen to other lines. This secret passage not even your brother Uhlas knew. But my people kept such secrets. My clan is long-lived, do not ask me how long, nor how old I am. Suffice it to say that I remember the First King of Alrou-Mendera, and I was there when he accepted the crown and took the throne."

"Sweet Aeon!" Temlin breathed.

"Listen!" Lenuria hastened. "One who can save us has come at last. The Rennkavi, Temlin. That young man who came to see you, Goldenmarked. Elohl den'Alrahel. But his coming means that we are indeed in dark times. Either we will stand or we will fall. The

Rennkavi's coming signifies vast upheaval, for the entire continent… *All* of us."

"Sweet gods."

"There is a man." Lenuria hurried on. "One of my clan, who haunts Roushenn. You may have heard him called the Ghost. I go to find him now. If there is anyone who knows of Castellan Lhaurent's true doings, it will be him. I will try to alert as many of the Palace Guard as I can, that a true den'Ildrian is acting as King-Protectorate, and that he is at the Abbey. Word will spread for you. Expect Guardsmen and others to surrender into your ranks. I must go. Take this. Lock this door behind me."

Abbess Lenuria pressed the key into Temlin's hand with a quick smile, then turned toward the door. Temlin reached out, snagging her by her black robe. "Abbess, why do you do this?"

She smiled, and laid a tiny hand upon his cheek. "Because I see a true King in you. And I did when you were boy, and when you grew into a man. But fate was cruel, and Lhaurent and his ilk have been crueler. I can no longer stand idly by, recording history. We are in desperate times. Be honorable, Temlin den'Ildrian. Save our nation."

And with that, she pressed a latch he didn't see, and the door opened. Abbess Lenuria whisked into a deep darkness, and the door boomed shut behind her. Temlin blinked, staring at the passage, wondering who the Abbess truly was and what was actually happening behind this slaughter of the Chancellate.

Gears were turning in Alrou-Mendera and beyond. Dire gears, machinations not of just war, but of something worse. Temlin could feel it in his bones, and Abbess Lenuria's words had struck deep fear into him. But Temlin did not have the time to luxuriate in fear. He squared his shoulders and took the single breath of his training. And then he turned on his heel and strode out, locking the door securely behind him, heading for the wall with battle-fury in his veins.

CHAPTER 39 – THEROUN

Morning dawned chill, an autumnal wind brisking through the valley. Rattling the canvas of the Elsthemi command tent, the gusts carried the peppermint feel of glacial melt. The braziers had nearly gutted out. Sitting up in his pallet of furs to the snapping of canvas, Theroun could see General Merra was already gone, the tent empty but for him.

For three days it had been thus, her waking before him, out the door and seeing to her clans before he'd even stirred. Merra was a true woman of war. Theroun had spent the past three days settling his men in with the Elsthemi clans, breaking up fights, working with Merra and her First-Captain Jhonen Rebaldi to get men and horses oriented to a new life. Theroun had led Jhonen and her group of cats back the first day to claim the cached poisons. All had been moved safely to a weapons-tent near the command pavilion and put under close guard.

Theroun came to the command-tent late after full days, but Merra always came in later. They'd said little to one another the past few nights, only sharing a cordial cup of telmen-wine before both collapsed to bed, Merra to her pallet of furs, Theroun to a separate pallet she'd had assembled for him. There weren't any guards on him, or on the pavilion. Merra was testing him, seeing if he was loyal. After their cups of wine each night, she trusted him to sleep in the same enclosure with her. And he had to show he trusted her back, even though they'd not yet had time for a formal parlay.

Especially since either could have slit the other's throat in the deep of night.

And yet, here he was, waking a third day to life in an Elsthemi war-camp. Perhaps there would be trust between them yet, Theroun mused as he rose from his pallet, stretching into his damaged side. He felt well this morning, rested and hale. His sleep had been deep, the pallet's cushions supportive. He could take deep breaths without pain this morning, his old wound only a stitching annoyance.

Theroun found himself smiling. He paced to the table, wearing only his leather trousers. A breakfast was laid out, cold meats, cheeses, dried fruits. Theroun helped himself, then drank from a pitcher and splashed his face, currying water through his greying blonde hair. Refreshed, he pulled on the Elsthemi shirt and jerkin Merra had thrown at him the first night he'd arrived. Theroun sat, pulling on his boots, then buckling on a tawny keshar-pelt he'd been given. He'd not been allowed his weapons about camp, but they sat nearby upon a chair in the command-tent, ready if necessary.

By the time Theroun strode from the tent, he felt like he had new life, dressed like a Highlands rogue as he'd been the past three days. The Elsthemi camp was awake as he emerged. Men sharpened blades, hurried through breakfasts of porridge, eggs, and roast meat. Clans joked raucously as the smoke of cook-fires drifted up. Women strode by, stout with thick muscle or lean like leather cording, tending battle-cats.

It was strange to see as many women in the camp as men. Rough and brutal, Elsthemi women were just as callous as any man, spitting and laughing or joining a sexual joke. Making lewd hand gestures, they were fast to their knives if any male soldier tried to go for a fondle. These women were every bit the warrior, and they walked by with swagger, just like General Merra Alramir and her fierce femininity. Theroun was about to stride off in search of his Captains, when Jhonen strode up with her brawny bravado.

"Yer awake!" Jhonen grinned, hands on hips. "About time! Merra wants me ta take ya 'round, meet the clans ye've not spoken to yet. Today yer mine, sweet cheeks."

Theroun's brows lifted at the pet name, but he let it pass. "Alright. But I'll check on my men and my Captains this morning also."

"'Course." Jhonen beckoned and Theroun fell in step. Proceeding around a line of tents, they moved off toward a red banner with a stylized white keshar's head laced between two white polearms. Jhonen eyed Theroun as they marched through the camp's early bustle.

"What?" He barked curtly.

"Did ye do her yet?" Jhonen grinned. "Merra, I mean. Did she ride ye?"

Theroun halted, giving Jhonen a severe eyeball.

"Well? Did she?" The keshari rider stood her ground, grinning.

"I can't see how that's any of your business."

"Ah, but it is, lowlander." Jhonen stepped close. "Me an' the boys got a bet, ye see. That Merra won't take another man to her bed until she sees her lowlander Fenton again. She's got it bad for him."

Theroun blinked. "Fenton? *Fenton den'Kharel?*"

"Aye, that's the one. Ye know him?" Jhonen cocked her head, orange braids cascading to the side.

"He's in the Roushenn Guard. Or was. How did he come to know your General?"

Jhonen winked. "No my story to tell. So. Here we are. These are Merra's lads and lassies. Her White Claws and Split Fangs. Aye, lads!"

Jhonen raised her voice as they came around the side of the tents. In an open space before the banner, the brothers Rhone and Rhennon Uhlki, Merra's Second-Captains, sparred with polearms against one brutishly-built woman with longknives. Jeered on by a ring of keshari riders, the brothers were breathing hard, while the woman was flush-faced from deflecting thrust after slice upon her knives. But she was holding her own, quite impressively, Theroun reflected. These were Merra's elite guard, after all, and they knew their sparring.

All action ceased, however, as Theroun and Jhonen came into view. More than a few pairs of eyes squinted at him. But these elite riders of General Merra's held their peace, many of them already familiar with Theroun. Breathing hard from sparring, the brothers Rhone and Rhennon gave Theroun a nod. They'd helped him settle the Menderian cavalry in two days ago, and he'd helped them break up a brawl yesterday. Jhonen strode in grinning, gripping Theroun's shoulder and tugging him along.

"So, lads! I win the bet! He's no done Merra! She wouldn'a have him in the place of her delicious lowlander Brigadier. So. He's mine." Jhonen nuzzled Theroun's neck suddenly, biting at his ear.

"Leave off, woman!" Theroun jerked away. But Merra's elite guard were grinning, the practice area ringing with jeers. Theroun suddenly realized Jhonen's act made the Elsthemi accept him more. Marking that he belonged to her, or possibly to the General, but that he was certainly not available.

"We saw yer sword, lowlander! Did ye no have enough girth on the blade to slit our General's leathers for her?"

"Ach, tripe! Ye better watch out, lowlander, Jhonen's got yer scent now! There'll be no dismissin' that cat until she's been ridden, aye!"

"Show us yer bollocks again, lowlander! Was yer Black Viper no big enough to help our General with what needs done?"

They erupted into laughter. Theroun didn't mind. The frank wit of the Highlanders was refreshing, and anything that would bind their armies closer was welcome. Humor could do that.

"She's a fine woman," Theron grinned, though he kept it hard, commanding.

"Cock too small, was it?" Rhone called out in a rolling laugh.

Rhennon punched his brother. "Nah. He's got a good wally. I saw it. Musta been those scars."

"Merra likes scars!" One woman named Elvia busted in. "He musta been too old an' creaky ta mount up properly!"

"So which was it?" Jhonen teased, now linked arm-in-arm with Theroun.

Theroun have a hard smile. "I think your General and I have too much in common. Fucking me would have been like fucking herself. And that's not as much fun as fucking someone else, now is it?"

The camp of the elite fighters burst into laughter. Jhonen made a few parting quips, then tugged Theroun along. When they were a decent way distant, she leaned over. "Well done. Ye'll no be knifed by any of Merra's best. But not all the clans are as forgiving as the White Claws and Split Fangs."

They walked toward an open space before a group of tents that bore a banner of a red hawk in a black field. Suddenly, Jhonen slipped a longknife into Theroun's hand. "Get ready. *Aye, lads!*" She raised her voice to a mean-eyed crowd watching from the tents. "We got a Menderian cunt for ye ta slice! A Black Viper! Do what ye will wi'im."

Jhonen suddenly kicked Theroun's knees out from beneath

him. He went down hard in the grass. The knife was up behind his forearm, out of sight as he stumbled. And in that instant of Jhonen's betrayal, all the old habits of battle woke in Theroun. Pure. Violent. Unstoppable. Someone lunged at him. He struck sideways, and knew he'd stabbed a throat when he was doused in blood. Another assailant closed from his left. Theroun rolled beneath the swipe of a polearm. His roll took him up into the man's groin, burying his knife, putting his weight behind it with both hands to slice upwards.

The man dropped, screaming.

Another assailant. His knife still buried in the man's thigh, Theroun splayed his fingers with a lunge. The man screamed as Theroun's fingers sank into the soft gel of his eyes. Pulling his knife from the thigh, he rolled away. Someone closed. Theroun slashed a forehead, and the man retreated, wiping blood from his eyes. A woman lunged for his wrist. Theroun dodged and she blocked, so he flipped his knife fast to his other hand, still lunging, scoring her deep beneath the ear. With a short scream, she clapped a hand to her neck.

Immediately, someone thick and heavy slammed Theroun from the right. Theroun sprawled. His left hand was dashed on the ground and he lost his knife. The massive brawler had him pinned. One meaty arm clenched Theroun's windpipe, another around the back of his neck, crushing, squeezing. Theroun gasped. The man roared behind him. Theroun shoved his fingers down the back of his pants and up his own ass, then stuck them in the brute's open mouth. The man choked, flinched violently away, losing his hold.

Theroun had him rolled in a blink, one hand searching the grass for his knife. He found it. Like a viper striking, he stabbed the man's neck, one, two, three. The fellow gurgled as his blood fountained up to spray Theroun's face in a red wash. He fell back to the bloody grass, limp.

Theroun rose, panting hard, covered in blood. All around him, warriors ringed his small field of battle. Keshari riders, their eyes agog. Clan-warriors with mouths grim. Jadounians with white grins, their dark eyes alight. Menderians pale and green at the gills.

"*Anyone else?!*" Theroun bellowed. He turned in a circle, breath heaving, knife pointing at the crowd.

"I think ye've killed them all." Jhonen's voice was astonished.

"Didn't even need a spot of help, did he?" Rhone's low rumble came nearby.

"He's the Black Viper, Rhone," Rhennon commented.

"Just so, Rhennon." Theroun saw the two brawny brothers now, arms crossed over their chests, grinning next to Jhonen a safe distance away.

"And that, gents," Theroun heard Merra's strong alto as she pushed forward through the throng. "Is what the Viper does to traitors! Anyone else fancy playing traitor to Therel and Elyasin by trying to strike down her Menderian General or betray either of our armies?"

A satisfied smile lit Merra's face. The bitch had set it all up. And suddenly, Theroun saw the genius of General Merra Alramir. It was a tactic worthy of adding to his own repertoire. She'd had Jhonen take him to the clan she thought would be the most hateful against Menderians, a clan probably full of Khehemni traitors just itching to gut Theroun. She'd had him fight for his life, out where all her clansmen would see. So they'd know the viciousness of the Viper. So they'd respect him.

So no one, Khehemni or otherwise, would fuck with him or the Menderians.

Theroun nodded to Merra, grim. She nodded back, level.

Still catching his breath, Theroun wiped gore from his knife upon one dead man before him. As he did, he heard a low voice rumble, "*Verouni*. You have brought the red rain. We honor you."

Theroun turned, to see broad-shouldered Duthukan touch his brow in a sign of respect. The rest of the Jadounians in the thickening throng followed, touching their brows. *Verouni* began to ripple through the Southrons.

"General den'Vekir. With me." Merra beckoned Theroun. She turned on her heel and strode off toward her white pavilion. Theroun gave one last eyeball to the clans, then with a flick of his wrist, flung Jhonen's knife into the nearest corpse. It stuck with a sharp hiss, like the fangs of a viper striking flesh. He strode off after General Merra. As soon as he ducked beneath the flap, Merra threw a fresh bundle of Highlander clothing at him. Theroun caught it with a quick reflex, making his side pull angrily.

"Clean up." Merra smirked. "Although yer nice ta look at with all those fierce scars an' lean-aged meat."

"My thanks." Theroun's bark was civil, knowing it was time to parlay at last.

"So." Merra shucked her baldric and weapons, tossing her gear to a stout oaken table. Unbuckling the top of her jerkin, she ripped off her white pelt. Reaching out to the carafe upon the table, she poured two stout measures of dusky telmen-wine into goblets, then extended one to Theroun.

"Drink?"

"After a fight? Always." Theroun had already stripped away his bloody garb, and was rinsing his face and hands in a nearby basin. Comfortable around Merra from the last few days, he paused to don the fresh leather breeches. They fit perfectly, and Theroun had the feeling Merra had been eyeing him the past few nights. Fit as he had ever been, his body was lean and trim from daily sword-practice and eating plain, despite lines now gracing his hands and wrists amongst old scars. General Merra's eyes were appreciative as Theroun stepped forward to receive his goblet. They clinked chalices, sipped. Merra reached out, her spear-calloused fingers brushing the mass of scarring upon Theroun's right side.

"These are terrible." Her pale blue eyes followed the path of her fingers. Her touch was seductive, and Theroun found himself shivering with a lust he'd studiously avoided for years.

"We're not here to discuss my scars."

Merra's fingers fell away. "But we are, General Theroun den'Vekir. I know who ye are. Therel's briefed me on everyone who was present for his Queen's negotiations in Alrou-Mendera. We suspected you of treason against her. You were one of the highest on our list. With yer history."

"My history slaughtering Alrashemni, you mean."

"Mmm…" General Merra's blue eyes were fierce, hooded, a look as tantalizingly brutal as her battle-cat. "I must say, the messengers ye sent through came as a surprise. And yer appearance when ye arrived…" Her eyes flicked to his crotch, and she gave a ruthless smile, "even more so."

"Glad I could amuse."

"Mmm." Merra stepped close, into Theroun's personal space. Lifting her goblet, she sipped while watching him, challenging him

561

as a woman dares a man. To be more, do more, take more.

"Don't think to tempt me with your charms, woman." Theroun growled.

"Temptation has nothing to do with it." Merra set her goblet aside. "Yer a fine piece of man, and I want to fuck ye. Now. I want to ride until ye scream my name."

Theroun did not back up, but neither did he allow himself to respond to what was stirring his groin. "No." Theroun lifted his goblet, had a sip, and set it aside upon the table. "I parley with my brain, not my cock."

A short laugh bubbled out of General Merra, and her blue eyes were suddenly merry, just like her name supposed. She stepped back out of his space and retrieved her goblet, proceeding to a pile of pillows upon the hide-stretched floor near one brazier.

"I suppose you're right!" She laughed, arranging herself into an artful slouch upon the pillows. Theroun took her lead, stepping over the thick bear hides and lowering to a seat. "Or are yer ridin' days over?"

"Hardly." Theroun gave a hard glower. "But I make a point of not confusing sex with war."

"So. A cunning old ronin-cat, ye are." A smile lifted her lips. "Rejectin' my offer."

"No less than you. Offering in the first place."

Her smile lifted further. "So. What would ye do fer our Queen in this war?"

"Much. I owe her father King Uhlas a great debt. For my actions upon the Aphellian Way and nearly every action I've taken since."

"I see." Her blue eyes were hard as she sipped again. "And are ye truly Khehemnas, then?"

"I have had a splitting of ideals from the Khehemni Lothren in the last few years. We have had a rather severe difference of opinion about the management of Alrou-Mendera." Theroun saw no reason to hide it.

"Only recently." Merra's blue eyes were stony.

"Sometimes a man is fool enough that he sees not the catastrophe of his ways until it is far too late."

General Merra held his gaze for a thick moment. The silence

weighed between them as smoke wafted up from the glowing coals of the brazier. "Ye've got a great, big sack, coming here to Alrashemni lands, Black Viper."

"My duty is to my Queen, General. And none other." Theroun was unflinching.

Merra narrowed her eyes. Tension filled her languid frame. Theroun suddenly wondered how many throw-knives she had hidden in those pillows. He was hoping he wasn't about to find out. He watched her take a single slow breath.

"So here we are."

"Here we are." Theroun echoed.

"An' ye will no take me?" She teased, lifting an eyebrow.

A short laugh escaped Theroun. "I don't think you want me to take you. It's just your way. Rule your men with sex and passion and blood, and they will follow you to the end. Righteous. Riveting. And absolutely committed to death. Both theirs, and their enemy's."

She blinked, and Theroun knew he'd read her right. Commanding on the field. Commanding in the sack.

"Besides," Theroun stretched out one leg, massaging deep beneath his ribs. "I should be put to pasture, as you said. My *riding* days are over."

She snorted. Then paused, really looking at him, at his fingers massaging out his old wound. "Ye mean it? Ye've no had a woman since…?"

"Since my wife died slaughtered by Alrashemni hands upon the Aphellian Way, and I was mutilated and consequently went mad. Yes."

Merra weighed him, as if seeing Theroun's heart for the first time. She lifted her goblet. "To yer wife. A love beyond measure. A treasure beyond count."

The simple sentiment stunned him. Theroun's hands dropped from his side. His eyes stung. He blinked unshed tears, face stinging, cheeks flushed. "Why would you say such a thing?"

"Because she inspired a man to greatness." Merra held his gaze with level purity. "Not what ye became upon the Aphellian Way. But what ye've learned since. That there is no greater ambition than honor. And no greater love than fealty. And no greater blessing than a righteous death."

Theroun's heart gripped. His side spasmed in an ancient ache as he raised his goblet. "To your husband. May he rest well wherever he lies."

A shine of tears lit Merra's eyes, and Theroun knew his guess had been right. Merra lifted her goblet and both drank back to the splutter and hiss of the brazier's coals. They didn't speak again for many minutes. Theroun took another sip of wine, and found his goblet empty. Merra extended the carafe, filling it again.

"Was he a man of battle?" Theroun asked.

"Aye." Merra settled into a soft silence. "So do ye truly repent yer actions upon the Aphellian Way?"

"Repent?" Theroun took a deep breath. "I don't think a man can truly repent for crimes only half-recalled in nightmares. They do not lie when they say I was mad. Fever had taken me, infection. And the drugs I used to staunch the pain and keep moving made my choices more and more abominable. I don't repent that I hunted Alrashemni at the time. I was livid at what they had done to my family. But I began to know unrest about it all when I saw my King's eyes afterwards. Saw what I had done to him."

"By harming his people."

"By losing my control."

Merra eyed him, her goblet idle in her hands. "An' now ye wear the mark of the Khehemnas."

"The Broken Circle, yes. The Shemout Alrashemni's hidden Inkings have a name also. They're called the Bloodmark, the mark of their true, blood-sworn intention. But this... though it is created by the same kind of ink, there are those of us who refer to it as the Deathmark. When Khehemni take this mark, especially those of us who belong to the Lothren's inner circle, we commit our death to the Cause. I will wear these marks until someone comes to kill me for the crimes I have committed."

"Murder?"

"Treason. I betrayed my liege, and his daughter, by joining the Khehemni. I didn't begin to see it, how the Khehemni Lothren were manipulating the throne, until it was far too late. With all my wit of strategy, I could not see Evshein and Lhaurent's vile strategy through my hate of Kingsmen. And I have come to repent it."

"An' do ye still hate Alrashemni?" Merra drew the lacings of her shirt open, bearing her Inking, stark upon her lovely white skin. "Do ye hate the army ye've come to join, Black Viper?"

Theroun drew a deep breath. "I love my family, and hate still rages within me at what was done to them. But let's just say I am coming to realize Alrashemni value, as I once did."

"Yer captains both trust ye. They're Alrashemni." Merra sipped her wine.

"I have given them reason to."

Merra's eyes went hard. "Walking here disarmed and butt-bare, all to avoid using those poisons yer false-king Chancellate gave ye against us, to kill yer army off just as much as mine."

"And that, I cannot allow. We are Elyasin's army."

"We are Therel's army." Merra's eyes glinted.

"Indeed." Theroun sipped his wine. "And Therel and Elyasin are wedded as one."

"So. Allies, then." Merra relaxed back against her ample cushions. "If ye no spit in my porridge, I'll no spit in yours, Theroun. I know a man of quality when I see one. Yer a rough old ronin, but ye've got the spirit of battle running to yer marrow. Ye led yer men naked and unarmed into ambush. Takes a low-hanging sack to do that, and takes a heart of iron to get them to trust ye. I've already sent a rider to Lhen Fhekran, to let Therel and Elyasin know what ye've done. It's their job ta pass justice on ye, not mine. In the meantime, yer my prisoner-of-war, so to speak. But here, in my tent, ye'll be my counsel. I want ta know—"

Suddenly, a baying of horns came from outside.

Theroun's head jerked up. Merra was already rising, buckling on garb and weapons, fast, and Theroun was right behind her. He slung on a black keshar-pelt over his new Elsthemi gear, and snatched his weapons from the chair. Pushing out of the tent after Merra, his gaze raked the hill and the camp, taking everything in at a glance.

A scout-guard of six keshari riders raced fast down the grassy knoll, horns busting frantic and repetitive from their retinue. The effect upon the Elsthemi camp was electric. With roars and curses, men and women raced for weapons, cinched on leather battle-gear. Women raced to paddocks, throwing open gates. Cats were liberated, streaking through camp for their riders. Hasty cheeks were rubbed. Men and women mounted up all around.

The scout-guard pulled up hard before the command tent and exchanged a few hasty words with General Merra as she cinched on white leather battle armor. Turning, she shouted orders to her Captains, including Rhone, Rhennon, and Jhonen, all mounting up on their cats. Theroun jogged up, Vitreal and Arlus galloping around the tent fast to meet him, already mounted upon their chargers and clad for war.

Lifting a keshar-skull steel helmet spiked with cat-fangs, General Merra turned to Theroun. "We're under attack. Menderian forces sweeping through the woods. Thirteen thousand strong, their entire army, by the look of it. Did ye know of this, Black Viper?!"

Theroun's gut clenched, icy. "As I told you when I arrived, den'Ulthumen's plan was for the main force to follow in a week. Enough time to send scouts and assess how badly your forces had been damaged before they mustered."

"Well, yer fancy-General didn'a wish to wait, it seems." Merra whistled sharply for her beast. The great snowy cat slipped around the edge of the pavilion with a rumbling growl.

"The Khehemni Lothren are behind this, I can smell it." Theroun growled. "This wasn't den'Ulthumen's strategy."

Mounting her great cat, General Merra eyed Theroun from the saddle. "Unless he was told ta lie to yer face. Can ye ride cat, lowlander?"

Theroun blinked. "I've never tried."

"Learn fast." Merra whistled. A massive black cat with dirty yellow fangs prowled around the command-tent, slinking to the side of Merra's snowy keshar. The black beast snarled, baring fangs, and the other keshari cats shied away, hissing, ears flat to their skulls. The nasty ebony beast fixed its mean golden eyes upon Theroun, the only person still on the ground. It paced forward, menacing. Opening its mouth wide, it snuffed Theroun's scent. Theroun stood his ground, staring the beast down. He lowered his chin, a viperous snarl coming to his own lips.

"Come on, then." Theroun spoke, soft and mean.

Lifting one massive paw, the lithe black male flexed claws big as raptor-talons. He snarled, swiping at Theroun's face. Theroun didn't budge. The tips of those claws sliced his cheek, scoring like razors.

Warm blood dripped to his collar. But Theroun knew a challenge when he felt one. He held the mean beast's gaze, letting it feel his true nature. Lifting its chin, it opened its mouth, scenting him with a rictus-smile. Rifling whiskers, its yellow eyes pinned Theroun. Suddenly, it lunged. Opening powerful jaws with fangs long as Theroun's forearm, it grasped Theroun's head in a vise-grip.

But did not bite down. Theroun's head was inside its mouth. Rank breath suffused him. Saliva covered his cheek as teeth grazed his temple. A paw thudded to Theroun's shoulder, nearly knocking him down. He bore the tremendous weight, tips of claws flexing into his back.

And just as suddenly as it had caught him, it released him. Rubbing one massive cheek against his, the mean cat marked him. It did not purr and it did not butt heads and it was not friendly. It simply marked him and moved back, eyeing him with those great golden orbs, cunning and evil.

"Lay the fuck down and let me mount up, then." Theroun snarled at it.

The cat lay down upon its belly. Watching him and flicking the tip of its tail, it allowed Theroun to mount up bareback and grip its long, swarthy fur in his fist. Mutters of awe sounded around him. A few low curses issued from the gathered commanders. It was clear that this creature had no bridle and saddle because no one could get close enough to touch him.

No one, at least, who wasn't equal in spirit.

"General Theroun the Black Viper," General Merra sidled her snowy cat close, respect shining from her pale blue eyes. "Meet Ronin the Black Bastard. Something tells me ye'll get along jes' fine."

"You trust this animal in war?" Theroun eyed the nasty beast beneath him, now ruffling the fur over his shoulders in irritation as if he wanted to shed Theroun.

Merra eyed the black beast, a brutal smile upon her lips. "Tha' one, ye can count on. He doesn'a do nothing but fight. He's mate to my Snowscythe, so he fights by her side. Which is where I need ye on the battlefield. But he's a wilder. He hides in the trees when we camp, slinks around Lhen Fhekran when I'm in residence. Leaps onta rooftops ta get into the paddock an' fuck my girl, then gets away before light. He's a menace, right an' proper. An' the only people he seems ta like are old, mean cusses who don't give a flying fuck if they live or die. Mean an' fang an' steel. Mark my words, Black Viper, ye'll be a match wi' that cat 'till the end."

Something inside Theroun went cold, ready. His hand nestled in the black ronin's fur, made a fist. Yanked hard. The nasty thing snarled beneath him, swiped with one ripping paw. It couldn't wait to disembowel enemies.

And neither could Theroun.

His gaze raked the camp. Cats were in ranks now, spreading in a long line away from the river onto the plain. Horse were arrayed in lines behind them, foot soldiers trotting into place behind that. A force of ten thousand covered a wide swath of the valley, leaving enough room for the Menderians to organize upon the hillside. Clan banners snapped in a brisk wind, like colorful flowers dotting the swath of golden summer grass.

Gold would be stained red today.

Theroun pulled his sword from its scabbard, weighing it in his hand.

His vicious black cat snarled beneath him.

CHAPTER 40 – KHOUREN

"The city is burning! Homes and lives are being destroyed! You've rolled a stone that's started an avalanche, and now there's no stopping it!"

Khouren advanced upon Lhaurent from the shadows of the Hinterhaft. He'd been out in the city today. It had taken four days for word of the Chancellate's assassination to spread through the Palace despite everything Lhaurent's agents had done to contain it. And now the news was a sweeping force, destabilizing the city in a desperate populace tired of war and famine.

Khouren had seen the chaos begin. A demonstration had gathered outside the palace gates, when rumor of the Chancellate's misfortune had leaked at dawn. An irate man had shoved another who'd gotten too close. The other responded with a knife. The seething anger had spread like lightning-fire in dry reeds. Rocks had been thrown at the gates and Guardsmen. Archers were ordered to fire into the crowd. Rocks were thrown into shops, torches lit, and fires had begun in the dawn. People fleeing, others looting as fires whipped down dry, crowded streets.

Accompanied by screams of people, burning.

Khouren advanced into the fey blue light. "The day has died, but fire yet chars the air and smoke poisons the wind. I can smell the death. You knew this was going to happen, didn't you?!"

"I did what I had to, to bring this city and this nation under our glorious Unity." Lhaurent was cool, controlled as he wiped a set of flechette knives clean from whomever he was torturing on the bed. "I have instigated martial law via the Roushenn Palace Guard to keep things from getting too far out of hand. I will address the populace soon, and quell their passions. But for now, destruction in the city reminds men of frailty, giving them fear. Fear makes men weak. And when a strong, persuasive leader steps forward, they will come together in unity beneath my banner."

"This isn't unity! This is *madness*." Khouren took another step forward. He didn't look at Lhaurent's victim. His Rennkavi's bloodletting was less important than the city burning.

"*This* is what is necessary." Lhaurent pointed the knife at Khouren. "The populace will be docile after the city burns, willing to acquiesce to strong rule. They will greet their new ruler with open arms."

"They will greet a tyrant!" Khouren surged forward, infuriated. A wash of silver filled his vision. Energy surged through his limbs, fueled by righteousness. Hardly knowing what he was doing, a knife was in his hand, and it was at Lhaurent's neck.

Lhaurent reached up fast, grasping his doublet and hauling it open at the neck, baring Goldenmarks aflame with ocean-deep light. "Have a care, *shadow*," Lhaurent's voice dripped with scorn, "whom you threaten. Or have you forgotten just how much ash you shall become from your Alodwine oath if you slay me?"

An anguished cry rent Khouren's throat. That light seared his eyes, into his very soul. He trembled, but quicksilver flared through his limbs, through his mind. Pressing his knife close beneath Lhaurent's chin, he forced the Castellan's head up.

"And so I'll die *relieved*," Khouren growled.

But he could not summon the will to slam his knife home in that white flesh. The penalty of his clan's oath was far worse than death. His soul would burn in torment, forever, should he disobey his Rennkavi. The thought filled Khouren with anguish. Rippling ocean light warred with silver in his thoughts, in his body. A battleground filled Khouren, fueled upon both sides by his indecision. He shivered, bitter rage and horror contesting against fear and righteousness.

Silver clashed with ocean light. At last, the silver ebbed back.

A low, chiding chuckle rolled through the room. "You still believe in your oath. You will always believe in it. You are of House Alodwine and I am your Rennkavi and there is only me to bring this world to the light of Unity. Olea may have borne the name of Alrahel but she was not marked, Khouren. She was not Goldenmarked to save our people. I was. Have a care, whom you kill."

Khouren made a strangled sound. Slowly, he stepped

backwards, releasing his blade from Lhaurent's neck. "You are *false*. Somehow... I'll prove it."

Lhaurent smirked, releasing his doublet's collar, the flaring Goldenmarks slipping from view. "Do that. But until then, you serve me. I have not released you from my service, Khouren. And if you go rogue, you will burn to ash, forever. So your ancient *wyrric* oath decrees, and so shall it do. Decide, Khouren. Decide to hate me or decide to live, and live to see the new Dawn of my continent's glorious Unity rise. But before you do, I have a task for you. There. Upon the bed. Interrogate her. Find out why she's here."

Lhaurent turned away, dismissing his lackey as he cleaned his blades. Broken, Khouren shuddered, breathing hard. He turned toward the bed, his heart gripping at whatever new odious task his Rennkavi had given him.

A woman was chained there, fae blue wisps swirling around her. And that petite frame, that tumble of salted hair beneath the blue globes, was far too familiar. Khouren stepped to the bedside in haste, his stomach falling though his feet. He cried out at the ruination of Lenuria's form. Manacled spread-eagled upon the bed, she had been severely tortured. Cuts slashed her naked body, blood everywhere. Limbs had been broken, bones cracked and exposed through her skin. Burns, branding. Entire sections of skin had been flayed. One beautiful eye was gone. So were four fingers.

With a strangled sob, Khouren stepped close, kneeling reverently by her side. The Rennkavi had no idea whom he was torturing. Lenuria had survived much over the years, healing herself by changing her visage and her body. A warrior to the end, she was stalwart and strong, and pain was no stranger. But the amount of blood soaking everything spoke of the vast damage this time.

She couldn't heal all this. She wasn't going to survive this time.

"Khouren. Unity's mercy I found you..." Lenuria's remaining grey eye rolled up. She twitched in a death-seize, before she blinked back. "Tried to change already, but I can't... lost too much blood..."

"You don't have much time, Lenuria," Khouren choked, tears flooding his vision as he pitched his voice low so Lhaurent couldn't hear. "The Rennkavi has cut you too deep."

Lenuria's eyelids flickered. "He is not my Rennkavi. My Rennkavi is Elohl den'Alrahel."

"Have you seen him?" Khouren rasped. "Do you know where Elohl is?"

"Go to Temlin," Lenuria breathed. "He knows. Find the other Rennkavi. Redeem yourself, Khouren…"

Her eyes rolled up in her head. Her body gave a swift shudder and she sighed her last. Khouren stared down, incredulous. Watching eight hundred years of life pass. Watching a woman of stalwart strength, undone by the cruelty of a man he'd once trusted. A man he'd once believed in. As Khouren stood there, gazing down at so much wreckage, he realized at last why he'd never spoken to Lhaurent of the others in his clan.

Some part of him had never trusted Lhaurent.

Silver washed through Khouren's vision. From a small thread in his mind, it woke to a raging torrent, flooding outward from the Kreth-Hakir's cursed gift all those weeks ago. Slowly, Khouren straightened, feeling that quicksilver blossom to life upon the tide of his own rage. Fury surged in his veins. Hot, wrathful fury. Quicksilver flooded his mind, his limbs, setting him to trembling in a vicious passion. Lenuria had come to give him a desperate charge, stepping into the eel's lair on a hope that Khouren would find her.

And find her he had. Too late.

When it comes time, will his power win you? Or will mine? The words of Khorel Jornath flooded back upon the tide of that quicksilver. Fed by rage, fanned by fury, the Kreth-Hakir's gift consumed Khouren, drowning out all fear.

"What did she say?" Lhaurent's voice cut through the silence.

Khouren did not answer. He bent to undo Lenuria's manacles with careful, honoring fingers. Her limbs fell slack. Slowly, Khouren bundled his half-sister's body in the bloody sheets, pulling her into his arms. He turned, his kinswoman's burden light, to regard Lhaurent. Silver burned in his vision. Silver seared through his heart. Silver rode his every sinew.

And as he faced his Rennkavi, Khouren suddenly felt strong.

"What did she say?" Lhaurent repeated, irate, setting a clean blade aside in his torture-hutch. Surging with fury, Khouren said nothing. Lhaurent's grey eyes went to steel. "Khouren. I order you to tell me what she said."

Tingling flooded Khouren, raced up his spine. That quicksilver flush suffused him. And suddenly, Khouren knew his choice was made. From indecision, his being sharpened like a lance, decided. His moment had come. The Kreth-Hakir had seen it coming, had known Khouren would eventually make a choice, to follow his heart or his Rennkavi.

And now, Khouren knew he'd rather die with his half-sister's body in his arms than perform one more atrocity for Lhaurent den'Karthus. He'd suffer an eternity of burning, rather than serve this beast of a Rennkavi even one more day.

The man didn't deserve the Goldenmarks.

So they'd been given to someone else.

Elohl den'Alrahel.

Heart pounding, Khouren turned his back. Fear flooded him, though it was buffered by the quicksilver rage. Anytime now, he would feel the scalding of his clan's ancient oath, which would consume him like phoenix-fire. The oath set down by Fentleith Alodwine that the *Werus et Khehem* wyrria burn their souls should they abandon the Rennkavi. Resolute, Khouren moved with deliberate steps toward the nearest wall, quicksilver pushing his muscles to contract and move. He would burn, and Lenuria would be cremated in his arms. It was fitting, for both of them to go in ash and flame, just like the rest of their ancient clan.

But would he burn for disobeying one Rennkavi in order to find another?

Khouren stepped forward. The wall was near.

"Khouren, stop! I order you to *tell me* what she said!"

Khouren said nothing. Fires would consume him now. He would burst into flame, his long and varied existence ended at last.

Khouren took one more step toward the wall.

"Stop! *I command you!*" Lhaurent roared behind him. A blaze of light illuminated the wall before Khouren, the force of Lhaurent's Goldenmarks overwhelming as he unveiled them. Khouren could feel the depth of that magic roaring all around him, pulling him with sucking tendrils back towards his master. His silhouette was cast on the wall in living light, stark black in the center of a luminous fury. But Quicksilver flooded Khouren, his vision lost to it, his mind devoured by a rage that tempered his fear. Khouren stepped forward again, now at the wall.

A whish of air sounded, a blade thrown at his back.

Quicksilver surged. Khouren lunged through the wall. Careening into a dark corridor upon the other side with Lenuria's body in his arms, he felt the silver thread in his mind snap suddenly. The quicksilver washed away like a dam breaking. His fear peaked as his rebellious fury flashed out, adrenaline hitting him in a rush. Khouren channeled that rush into movement, racing through walls, losing himself in the palace.

Halls rumbled behind him as he ran. Lhaurent was moving the bowels of the palace, searching for him. Heaving expendable and abandoned parts of the Hinterhaft and Unterhaft, though he would not dare move the upper halls of Roushenn to find Khouren. But the moving walls did not concern Khouren. Lhaurent could move what he wished in his rage at Khouren's disobedience.

Khouren feared only his ancient clan-oath. Any moment, he would feel the burn begin in the depths of his solar plexus, fanned outward until it consumed him. But as he ran, the burn did not come. He'd disobeyed his Rennkavi, abandoned him. And yet, Khouren's oath did not scald his flesh, did not burn him away in ash and flame.

A strange lightness took him as he ran. Arriving at king's crypt, Khouren knew his kinswoman would soon combust, all those who had taken Fentleith's Oath did after death. But her body held out long enough for him to place it upon an ornate slab of white marble, shoving aside bones to make room. He draped Lenuria in a swath of crimson silk, then bent to kiss her forehead.

A wisp of smoke rose from her body. Once it started, the fire caught quickly. A white-blue flame fierce as phosphor consumed her as Khouren shielded his eyes. Until there was nothing but white ash upon the scorched bier. Silence rushed through Khouren's ears in the catacomb, deafening. Khouren dipped his fingers in the hot ash and marked his face in mourning, down both cheeks and across the brow.

Emptiness hollowed his gut. The quicksilver in his veins was gone. The oath to his Rennkavi was gone. Lenuria was gone. From so much purpose, Khouren found himself suddenly purposeless. Uncertainty swallowed him as he heard a rumble somewhere nearby, of Lhaurent still searching for him. But this crypt was one of the few places in Roushenn that could not be moved, a hallowed place where the dead could rest.

If Lhaurent wanted to kill Khouren here, he'd have to come do it himself.

"I didn't die." Khouren spoke to Lenuria's ashes. "I should have burned… but Lhaurent's not the true Rennkavi. You knew it from the first, didn't you Lenuria? You knew the truth when Temlin told you. Lhaurent den'Alrahel is not our salvation. Elohl den'Alrahel is."

Khouren glanced to the bier where Olea was lain out in state. Then moved to her deathbed as the rumbles of Lhaurent's search moved away. Eyelids sunken and cheeks hollowed, she had begun to mummify. She was still lovely, even in death. Heaviness pulled Khouren's feet into the floor. He reached out, stroking the hollowed lines of Olea's cheek, her deepening eyes, her lips drying to smooth parchment. Silence rushed in his ears, overpowering like falling water. Absolute, it echoed in the cavern, feeding his emptiness.

"I had a glimpse of your brother, you know," he spoke to Olea. "First as a shadow visiting you in the dungeon, then standing guard for the Dhenra's wedding. I watched from the wall as he struck down the Elsthemi First Sword. He was so fast, like a heron. But our bloodlines come with their gifts, don't they? Gifts, or sometimes I think they're curses…"

Khouren stoked her beautiful curls, still lustrous, thinking about that day. He'd seen them, hadn't he? Upon the man's neck in that flash of movement. Sigils and trailing script.

"Goldenmarks." Khouren's murmur was lost to the silence. "I thought nothing of it at the time. Because I was still blind to the truth."

Gazing down, he suddenly felt something click into place, rise through his aimlessness. But even as it did, a deep uncertainty consumed him. Finding Elohl den'Alrahel would mean leaving Roushenn. For the first time, Khouren would have to travel in the open, where he could not hide.

"I'm afraid, Olea," he spoke as he knelt by the stone bier, stroking her curls. "For the first time in my life… I'm afraid of what might happen. Roushenn has been my refuge for centuries. Attired like a ghost, I… became a ghost after so long. A ghoul in these dungeons."

His knuckles smoothed her sunken cheek. "I would do anything for you. You know I would. Ask anything of me, and it is yours. What do you wish of me, Olea? Do you wish me to find your brother, protect him? Do anything I can to serve him? Do anything I can… to make certain he puts your murderer deep underground in tombs that will never see the light of day?"

A shivering vulnerability filled him, gazing upon Olea's corpse. "Where do I find redemption for the vast wrongs I've done?" He whispered.

And suddenly, an answer came, as if from across the Veil.

Your redemption lies not within these walls. Not as a ghost, but as a man.

With a hard in-breath, Khouren stood. Smoothing Olea's curls back from her forehead, he felt a tear come, then another. Breath shaking, limbs alive with tremors of fear and eagerness, he wiped his tears away with one sleeve. Leaning over, he kissed her upon the lips.

"I love you." Khouren murmured. "I will always love you. I will do you justice and I will right my wrongs. And when I see you again, when I come to the Veil at last, perhaps you'll smile for me. Just for me…"

Khouren's touch lingered upon her cheek.

And then he turned and walked through the wall.

* * *

Moving with quickening strides, purpose filled Khouren at last. Rumbling resounded through the bowels of the palace like earthquakes, Lhaurent still searching for a Ghost he was never going to find. Khouren angled left, heading into the heart of Roushenn. Stopping at a larder, he fetched an empty burlap potato-sack, in addition to bread and cheeses and cured meats for his journey. His next stop was a supply room beneath the barracks, where he stole a pack, bedroll, and sundries.

Moving swiftly through walls, Khouren came to his last destination. This room was impenetrable, one only Lhaurent could access by turning the walls. Impenetrable to all but a man who walks through walls. Peeking eyes through first, Khouren found the blind oubliette of Lhaurent's personal study empty. Glancing hastily around the octagonal space, Khouren crossed through the three-foot-thick byrunstone.

Wan blue globes clustered in the high vault like morose fireflies, lighting Lhaurent's study in shifting shadows. Maps curled upon tack-boards at every wall. Gilded tables sat laden with tomes and scrolls. A smattering of arcane items glimmered upon dust-heavy bookshelves. Khouren set to, tearing maps down from the walls, stuffing them inside the burlap sack. Anything that looked like it was in use went in. He raked tomes from tables, snatched up scrolls. Lists and ledgers were dumped in. He swept arcane items from as many shelves as he could, filling the potato-sack to the very brim.

It was nearly larger than he was.

But Khouren had the blessing of strength in his lean frame. He settled his rucksack of supplies on his back, then hucked the burlap sack across his shoulders like a dead deer. Turning, Khouren strode through the nearest wall, rumbling still resounding through the blue halls of the Hinterhaft. Walking swiftly, he was soon through the palace's depths and out an old watercourse gate to the streets of Lintesh.

It was chaos in the city tonight. Khouren halted beyond the iron gate, in the shadows of an alley. Eyes wide in horror, he took it in, then lifted his new black face wrap up over his nose and mouth to protect from the burning char that swallowed the air.

In all his years, he'd not seen Lintesh in such a state. Anarchy ravaged the streets. Screams echoed in his ears. Shouts rode the vicious wind that stirred firestorms into towers of black, twisting into the sky. The alley was choked with soot, falling like a devil's snow. Guardsmen rushed past the exit, backlit by red fire in the avenue.

A scuffle sounded nearby, behind a heap of empty crates. The muffled scream of a woman. Khouren strode forward, knowing that sound. A man had his pants down, a woman half-naked beneath him in the soot and the garbage of the alley. Her wrists pinned, he muffled her scream with his other hand as he fucked her, hard and merciless.

Khouren moved fast. His boot smashed the side of the man's head, sending him flying from his berth. He hit the brick wall of the alley with a sick crunch. Falling to the stones, motionless, blood oozed from his temple. The woman scuttled backwards behind the crates, trying to cover herself with her ripped dress. Breathing hard, she stared at Khouren, eyes wide, face sooted and animalistic with fear.

"Go." Khouren spoke. "Run."

She did. She picked up her skinny bones and dashed from the alley, into a night filled with chaos. Khouren strode after her, until his view opened up to the wide avenue. Destruction devoured the city. Death was all around. Women, robbed and raped, their naked bodies spreadeagled in the streets. Men in pools of tarry crimson, dead from sword-slashes and knife-wounds. Children running like packs of dogs through fallen buildings, others weeping near ashes still hot with glowing coals.

A beam of a burning inn tumbled from above. Khouren dodged as it hit, throwing up fire and sparks to the red night sky. Stepping quickly into the throng flooding the avenue, Khouren darted through townsfolk and Guardsmen like a specter of death. Laden carts had been abandoned, dead infants left in gutters. Khouren passed a cadre of desperate Guardsmen doing what they could to forestall brigandry. Vicious, they made arrests of anyone who attracted their attention with a boot to the face, a punch to the neck. Khouren had never seen the Roushenn Guard so violent against their own populace. His eyes went wide, watching a knot of Guardsmen spear down a fleeing woman who was clearly only a part of the rabble, not a looter.

And behind those men, Khouren saw a tall fellow in black herringbone leathers.

Khouren felt a surge of silver pass by him, urging the populace to riot. Urging the cobalt-clad Guardsmen to be merciless in their answering show of force. Bile surged in Khouren's throat. This was his Rennkavi's Unity. Chaos, so the city would be ripe for Lhaurent's strong lead when he stepped forward at last to fill a terrible void.

Pressing through the throng, Khouren headed down a largely unburnt avenue. Flanked by buildings of byrunstone, it had become a river of the dispossessed, shepherded by Guardsmen untouched by that silver from the Kreth-Hakir, wet cloths covering their mouths and noses. Eyes squinted against blowing ash, their hard gazes marked Khouren's passage, but they let him be. Until he flanked a stout Guardsman with fire-red hair, who caught him fast by his black garb.

"You! Are you one of Lord Temlin's fighters? Of the First Abbey?" The Guardsman coughed.

"Yes." Khouren lied smoothly as his mind raced through options, surprised at having been accosted.

"Is it true he's den'Ildrian? The Queen's uncle, living as a Jenner?" The Guardsman's eyes were hard, hopeful. "We heard it from the Jenner Abbess, on her way through the palace upon an errand two nights ago. I didn't believe her at the time, but... This martial law the King's Castellan has imposed against the populace, this isn't what we Guardsmen took our oaths to King and country for."

This was interesting. Clearly, the man didn't give two shits that Lhaurent den'Karthus was supposed to be in charge now that the Chancellate had been killed.

"Yes." Khouren answered. "Dhenir Temlin den'Ildrian is the Queen's uncle. He's at the Jenner Abbey."

The redheaded Guardsman glanced at his fellows, who had all heard Khouren's response. Nods came. The Guardsman released Khouren's garb. "Take us to him. We wish to swear fealty."

Something within Khouren soared, a spark he'd not felt in centuries. It made the Guardsman inhale, and Khouren knew his eyes had flashed red. It was a gift of his kin, of House Alodwine. A flash of fire in the eyes, a glimpse of the *wyrria* of war that lay within. But many tricks of the eye may be seen in a desperation-torn night.

Khouren stepped into this new role as easily as a specter sliding through walls. "Come. Follow me."

Khouren turned on his heel, his brusqueness summoning the Guardsmen into line behind him. They moved quickly through the crowd, men with swords making people shrink back. Khouren led them at a brisk trot despite his burdens, hearing the Palace Guard behind him shout to others, and shouted replies, more Guardsmen falling in as they went.

At last, they reached the gates of the First Abbey, rearing unburnt like a stalwart giant in the scorched night. The gates were thrown wide, cowled Brothers and Sisters ushering people in with soothing words and kind hands. Archers dotted the battlements, protecting the Abbey like the ancient stronghold it actually was. A bucket-brigade was running, dousing everything with water, the dust of the courtyard now a slurry. Armed men and women wearing the black robes of Penitents bristled by the gate.

Khouren marveled at the scene.

"Brothers and Sisters of the Light, taken up arms to battle," he murmured. It was one of the signs of the coming of the Rennkavi, that those dedicated to peace would take up arms only to fight for the Final Unity. Khouren could have cried in that moment, but there were Guardsmen waiting upon him.

He seized the hand of a Sister, a pretty little thing with honey-blonde braids, mail links glinting beneath her black robe. "Sister. Where can I find Dhenir Temlin den'Ildrian? These men wish to swear fealty."

Her brown eyes went wide. From the way she scanned the crowd behind Khouren, he knew he led a mighty force.

"Come with me. All of you." Nodding to others of her faith, she waved them back.

The Brothers and Sisters of the Abbey were about to permit passage, when Khouren felt a ripple go through the people around him. The Sister before him went blank. And then her hand whipped up with a knife, brandished to bar him passage. Khouren startled. The Brothers and Sisters before him suddenly advanced with snarls upon their faces, weapons bared.

And then, Khouren saw them. Two Kreth-Hakir Brethren, standing fifteen paces away in meditative trance, staring at the scene before the Jenner compound's walls. Each made a complicated sigil with his hands, one facing the Jenners at the gate, one facing the Guardsmen at Khouren's back. Khouren heard a rasp of blades drawn. The Guardsmen behind him had drawn weapons. Tension bristled upon the charred air, the kind of wrath that could only mean one thing.

The Palace Guard were three breaths from fighting the Jenners to the death.

"I don't think so." In one fast motion, Khouren threw down his burdens and drew his longknives. In a rushing charge, he came for the men in herringbone black, silent as a specter. They startled, seeing him. They dropped their silver weaves from the brewing melee, focusing upon him, pummeling him with waves of silver dominance. But those weaves washed through his mind and past, split down the middle by a silver spear that still caused Khouren chaos from Khorel Jornath.

Startled to have been deflected, the two Brethren balked, wide-eyed.

Their hands went to weapons.

But it was too late. Khouren was upon them. His longknives were thrust in a tight spin, one and two, right into the men's throats. Their silver weaves died as they went down, gurgling in shock, blood fountaining to stain the red night. Breathing hard over their bodies, Khouren spat his disgust, then wiped his blades clean upon their herringbone garb.

And looked up, to see shock upon the faces of the Jenners and the Guardsmen, though all weapons had been lowered.

"Inside the walls!" Khouren barked. "Now!"

Moving back to their lead, Khouren Alodwine, Ghost of Roushenn, strode into the First Abbey with a brigade of stunned Guardsmen upon his heels. He reached up and threw his cowl back as he entered the compound. The Abbey surged with motion upon every side. Lines of bucket-brigade ran in every direction, dousing buildings and orchards and silos and warehouses. Bedraggled dispossessed crowded courtyards, listless, as Jenners moved among them offering food and pointing direction to safe-houses for the night.

Khouren's guide marched his contingent through the chaos, up a short flight of stairs and into a long causeway that opened to a high-gabled meeting-hall. Jenners rushed in and out, and Khouren recognized an organized chain of command in action. His gaze strayed to the front of the hall, where a man stood, hands planted upon the top of a stout table carven with lions and grain.

Khouren knew Dhenir Temlin den'Ildrian the moment he saw him. Khouren had seen Temlin as a young man, had known his love for the beauty Mollia. Seen that love ruined when Lhaurent come for her through the walls. It had been his first taste of how his Rennkavi's cruelty could break a man, and a woman, and their love. He'd watched Temlin suffer, until madness and drink took him. Temlin's only option had been to enter the First Abbey in disgrace, pruned from the line of succession as if he'd never been born.

But something had changed. This man was not the Temlin that Khouren remembered. This man was not broken. And if there had ever been grey in that hair, there was not now. The lion of a man before Khouren sported a mass of red-gold waves combed back from his forehead. Wiry and trim, Temlin's green eyes bore the hawkish gaze of his niece as he glanced up, and then startled to see the mass of fighters entering his hall. Every line of his body was renewed, fit, in his prime again. His effortless stance screamed swordsman, and the set of his jaw reminded Khouren that Temlin had once been Captain-General of the Guard and Third General of the Realm.

"What's all this?" Temlin den'Ildrian barked in a gravel-rough voice, commanding and rich.

"My liege." The red-haired Guardsman who had snagged Khouren stepped forward and swiftly took a knee. All his men followed suit. Khouren moved aside, glancing behind. Cobalt jerkins filled the hall and extended out the door. All on bended knee, they massed perhaps two hundred good fighters.

"We wish to swear fealty to House den'Ildrian," the redheaded Guardsman stated, head bowed.

"Why?" Temlin barked. "In time of war, when the Chancellate and King are both dead, stewardship of the nation falls to the King's Castellan. So why swear to me?" It was a sharp question from Temlin's mouth, and the Guardsman clearly hadn't expected it. He glanced up uncertainly, then found his tongue.

"The King's Castellan imposed martial law and ordered the gates of Roushenn shut yesterday when the rioting began," the Guardsman answered. "To keep the Palace populace safe, he said. But the First Abbey's gates are open. You take the people in when the Castellan should have. Roushenn is byrunstone, it will not burn. It could have held everyone, saved the entire city, made his order of martial law unnecessary. Us Guardsmen would not have had to turn upon our own people. The Castellan's actions are not those of a true King. Yours are."

It was a simple answer, spoken from the Guardsman's heart. And it spoke of Khouren's vast mistake for years upon years. He'd served a man who had a black heart, who would let the people kill each other to unify the nation from weak leftovers. But this Guardsman disagreed with Castellan Lhaurent den'Karthus. And so had Temlin den'Ildrian. And so had Lenuria, bless her soul to ashes.

And now, so did Khouren.

Temlin drew tall, staring down at the Guardsman. Then, Temlin crouched before the man, reaching out to clasp the Guardsman upon both shoulders. "Swear not your fealty to me, sir, but to my niece, Queen Elyasin den'Ildrian. For she lives in exile in the north, I have it upon good confidence. I hold the throne until she returns, nominated as King-Protectorate by the old laws. Will you help me reclaim the throne, sir, for Elyasin, for our Queen?"

Khouren's throat clenched. Here was a true King. The Guardsman had seen it. The redheaded man's visage lit with fierce hope. He stood as Temlin did, then turned to his kneeling force.

"Elyasin lives!" He bellowed. "Elyasin lives, so swears her uncle! *Long live the Queen!*"

The chant was taken up in a rush, booming through the hall. Guardsmen stood, celebrating and embracing. Khouren saw Temlin glance to him, puzzled, before turning back to the Guardsman.

"Let us survive this night, with as many of Lintesh's people as can be saved!" Temlin barked. "Continue your peacekeeping, escort people here safely. Leave a portion of your men behind on the Abbey's gate to help settle the populace within our walls. If you encounter Guardsmen loyal to the Castellan, for Aeon's sake, don't engage them! And don't go shouting my name or Elyasin's outside these walls tonight. We don't want Guard fighting Guard in the streets! Your job tonight is *shepherd*. If asked, say you serve the Abbess, who has opened the Abbey this night to all who seek refuge. Go. Do your duty. Report to me here at dawn."

"Yes, King-Protectorate!" The redheaded man snapped a salute, then jogged from the hall, his ample force upon his heels.

Temlin's keen eyes snapped to Khouren. "I know you...don't I?"

Khouren did not bow. "Temlin den'Ildrian. Is there some place we can speak in private? Abbess Lenuria sent me to you. With her dying breath she bade me find you."

Temlin's green eyes snapped wide. Shock filled his visage. "The Ghost of Roushenn!"

Khouren gave a slight bow. "Sir."

CHAPTER 41 – TEMLIN

The Ghost of Roushenn stepped into Temlin's cramped study in the Annex, and Temlin closed the doors behind them so they could speak plainly. A lean man in ancient Kingsman greys, The Ghost wore his cowl down, showing blue-black hair done in lengths of braids. Glossy and well kept, they were pulled back from his temples and fastened with an ornate bluestone pin. His jaw was sharp and his posture held the relaxed readiness of a warrior. But no sooner had they arrived in Temlin's dusty, book-choked study when the Ghost upended the massive burlap potato sack over his shoulders all over Temlin's broad desk. Tomes tumbled out, flattened scrolls, papers, along with a jumble of arcane items that went jouncing all over the table, and some onto the floor.

Temlin blinked, his gaze flicking from the man to the mess he had just dumped all over the room. The Ghost's grey eyes seemed ancient, uncanny, as his gaze locked upon Temlin. A slight smile played about his lips. "Have you no words for me?"

"Should I have?" Temlin's tone was mild, but his body was tense with curiosity. "Are you certain you're not going to disappear like a phantasm when the torches flicker?"

The Ghost's smile was wry. "I am no phantasm. Just a man, I assure you."

"Legend says you disappear through walls." Temlin probed. "For some hundreds of years now. All you, this entire time?"

The man's lips turned up, a smile that did not touch his grey eyes. He spread his hands like he was about to do juggler's tricks, then walked backwards, directly towards a wall crowded with dusty bookshelves. When he touched the shelves, he suddenly seemed like mist or smoke. Temlin gaped even as his eyes lost focus, unable to pick the man out anymore. And then there was just books. And then the man's face returned, and then the rest of him.

"Aeon fuck me!" Temlin cussed, astounded. "What *are* you?"

"What I am is not under discussion, King-Protectorate." The man turned, contemplating the plethora of books, scrolls, and arcane items he had dumped upon the desk. He looked back, pinning Temlin with his eyes. "I am searching for something. *Someone*. Lenuria spoke of a man before she died at Lhaurent's hands a few hours ago. Elohl den'Alrahel. I seek him. She said he bears the Goldenmarks."

Temlin's heart sank. His knees gave out. He was suddenly sitting in his desk chair and didn't recall sitting down. He swallowed, his throat too dry. "Abbess Lenuria. She's... dead?"

The Ghost gave a small nod. His eyes seemed to flash with molten fire for a moment. "My half-sister spent the last breath of her vastly long life to impress upon me the importance of this man, King-Protectorate. The one with golden Ink. I must know of Elohl den'Alrahel's whereabouts. I need to find him."

"The Prophecy of the Goldenmarks." Temlin's voice grated. "The Rennkavi legend. That's what this is about, isn't it?"

"The coming of the Rennkavi is no legend." The Ghost had sunk to Temlin's threadbare couch. Fingers of one hand perusing his lips, he gazed at Temlin like he had just been handed a last goblet of wine before execution. "Where is this man? This Elohl?"

"I have no idea." Temlin stammered. "He went to Roushenn, posing as a Guardsman the day the Queen was nearly assassinated. I don't know what happened to him. I heard the King and Queen escaped, rode to Lhen Fhekran in Elsthemen. But whether Elohl was with their party—"

"They got out." The Ghost murmured, lounging upon the couch, his grey eyes faraway. "I trailed their party to the outer wall. They got out. The Elsthemi King, the Queen in his arms, and a few impeccable fighters. One was tall. And those blue-black curls... Aeon's darkness, I should have known! Den'Alrahel. He looks just like her..."

The Ghost's fingers perused his lips again. Temlin wondered if he were entirely sane, his grey eyes a thousand leagues away. At last, he rubbed both palms over his face, then up over his pulled-back braids, as if waking from a very long sleep. "I have to go north. Excuse me."

He stood and began to walk toward the door.

"Wait!" Temlin seized the man's arm, but found himself suddenly holding nothing as the Ghost casually pulled away. A sensation lingered in Temlin's fingers like he'd touched hot smoke.

"Why should I wait?" The Ghost's voice was empty. "I've already waited too long—"

"You can't just leave!" Temlin blinked. "You can walk through walls, for Aeon's sake! Castellan Lhaurent den'Karthus is behind this chaos in the city, I'm certain of it, and if anyone could get close to him in that fortress of his, it's you! For Lenuria's sake!"

The Ghost's sigh was like smoke on the wind, and his grey eyes were steady as he regarded Temlin. "You hated his cruelty as much as I, didn't you? Castellan Lhaurent…"

Temlin swallowed. "He ruined someone I love."

The Ghost stepped forward and reached out, placing a surprisingly smooth hand to Temlin's face. The Ghost gazed deep into Temlin's soul, his grey eyes ancient and haunting. "Mollia den'Lhorissian. I saw her torture, though I participated not. She was my first regret, you should know that. The first time I saw the cruelty of my Rennkavi. How he frightened her, took her, tried to bind her to his cause. All for the sake of a pair of healing hands and some visions. I have tried to look the other way, Temlin den'Ildrian. Tried for years to look past my Rennkavi's domination, all because of an ancient prophecy that says he will unite us and bring a golden age. I have never been a heroic man. But because of Lhaurent, I have become a monster. Lenuria's last thoughts were not for herself, but for me. For my redemption. I must go to find this other Goldenmarked Rennkavi, to save my very soul. Do you understand?"

Temlin's throat was dry. His eyes were wet. "Yes." He rasped.

The Ghost's hand fell from his face. "Goodbye, son of Kings. Take up your station. And do not falter. That which lies upon your desk is a gift for you. A gift from an old ghost who has lived too long for the wrong reasons. And beware this fight in the streets, for its instigation is unnatural. Have you seen the men in black herringbone weave armor?"

"Sweet Aeon!" Temlin blinked. "I thought I was just hallucinating them!"

"They bend minds and act as servants to Castellan Lhaurent," the Ghost spoke plainly. "Beware them. Let none come within these walls. Their effects diminish over distance, but once they bend a mind, they may leave their weaves within. Any refugee now among you may serve their will."

"Lhaurent's will." Temlin growled.

"Just so. Be cautious. In any case, I care not what happens to thrones. All I seek is my true Rennkavi, and to him I must go. Farewell…"

"Stop!" Temlin was desperate, grasping again at the man as he stepped towards the door, but again touched only smoke. "How do we kill Lhaurent?!"

The man paused at the door, then turned, his face thoughtful. "To kill the hydra, one does not cut the head. One stabs his heart. Or in this case… takes the focus of his power." He waggled the fingers of one hand. "Alas, I cannot assist you. I cannot lift a hand against even a false Goldenmark without damning myself. So look for the ring of white star-metal upon the eel's hand. And take that finger. Take his fortress from him. If you can."

The Ghost of Roushenn turned, then hesitated. "Will you do me a boon, son of Kings?"

"A boon?" Temlin asked.

"There is a girl," the man said, sadness in his visage as he glanced over his shoulder. "An innkeeper. She traveled with Elohl den'Alrahel. She was being tortured for information by your Abbott. Our Abbess saved her life. She is in the care of the Sisters. Will you watch over her for me? She is… special. But she has not yet woken from her ordeal."

Temlin's heart gripped his chest in a horrid spasm. "*Eleshen*?! She's alive! From the way Mollia spoke of her, I thought she had died!" Fury raged through his veins, hot as forge-sparks.

"She will need kindness." The Ghost's gaze was tender. "Look for a waif with raven hair, rather than a sun-bright beauty."

"What?" Temlin asked, but the Ghost had already vanished like so much smoke right through the door. An astonished shiver passed through Temlin. He watched the door a long moment, wondering if the man would come back through. He didn't. Temlin blinked stupidly, and then turned, gazing at the mess of maps, tomes, scrolls, lists, ledgers, and strange items that now choked his broad desk.

Dumped out from a burlap potato sack.

And suddenly, Temlin understood what it all was.

"That devious black-swaddled bastard...!" Moving to the table like a sleepwalker, Temlin un-crumpled a large map that had been hastily rumpled when the Ghost had stolen it from somewhere deep inside Roushenn. Temlin found he was looking at a map of the continent. A map with careful markings in red ink in numerous locations, with numbers and sums. Temlin's heart gripped hard, thinking of Lenuria, who had given her life for this.

A knock came at the door. When Temlin did not answer it, his runner-lad, Brother Brandin, popped his head in attentively. He came to the desk and shifted at Temlin's elbow. "Sir? I have news... what is all that?"

Suddenly, Temlin laughed, despite the heaviness in his heart. "The key to Castellan Lhaurent's empire, boy! And we're going to take it down, piece by piece! Find the Abbey Hawkmaster, Brother Gregor. I need to send a very special message to a very special friend. Have him fetch Fortuna, with the black jesses. She has a cunning way of avoiding archers."

"Fortuna?" The lad asked. "Who does the hawk Fortuna call her master? Whom will she return home to?"

"A Vicoute," Temlin grinned hard, ready for war, "by the name of Arlen den'Selthir, in Vennet. Finally! Something Arlen can go out and kill."

The lad gazed over the maps. "Who is he going to kill?"

"Mercenaries and lackeys," Temlin chuckled, reading the notes upon the map, done in a precise hand. "Lots and lots of Khehemni mercenaries and lackeys. Go, boy, get me that hawk! And on your way, tell Brother Sebasos upon the wall to not let any men in herringbone-weave leathers anywhere near the gates. Get the archers to shoot them on sight. Go, lad, run!"

The boy scuttled away as Temlin unrolled the next map, then the next. It was all here, movements of men, shipments of emeralds, payment lists for mercenaries and ship-crews. Signed documents of trade, all in the Castellan's impeccable hand. Enough to charge him with treason against the Crown. Temlin wanted to spend hours pouring over his ill-gotten gains from Lhaurent's fortress.

But there was another matter to attend first.

Briskly, he marched from his study and locked it. Temlin strode the halls of the Annex, descended the stairs, and trotted across the quadrangle through the gardens. Smoke still charred thick in the night. Tingeing the clouds red and orange, the Abbey was lit scarlet from the underbelly of Lintesh's destruction these past two days. Men and women hustled along the avenues, tending the wounded, shepherding the dispossessed, keeping the Abbey walls soaked with water. Temlin hurried up the steps of the Sister's quadrangle and pushed in the doors, marching to the women's infirmary.

It was packed. Refugees, coughing and hacking, burns being tended, broken bones being set. Screams issued from a partition to the left. Blood-soaked rags overflowed in baskets everywhere. Temlin snagged one doughy older Sister by her filth-stained white sleeve. "Sister Mitha! Where is the girl Eleshen whom the Abbess gave you care of?"

She blinked with glassy fatigue, then gestured out the doors toward the hall. "She has a private room, Brother Temlin. I mean, Lord Temlin. To the left, five doors down."

He exited, then made for the proper door, pushing in. An attending Sister within the plain bluestone cell stood hastily. But Temlin looked past her, his gaze resting upon the creature in the bed. He moved forward slowly, entranced. Astounded.

"Is this the girl Eleshen?" He murmured. "That the Abbess gave you care of?"

"Yes, Lord Temlin." The Sister nodded quickly. "She wakes now and then for a little broth."

"Give us the room." Temlin stood by the bed, then sank into the attending chair. The Sister slipped out, closed the door. Temlin stared down at the girl in the bed. Emaciated, wan, she had a haunting beauty that stunned him. An ethereal light, like starlight glowed from within her skin, though the room held no light but that of a single oil-lamp.

"How can you be the same person?" Temlin whispered. Not believing his eyes, he reached out to touch that sleek ebony hair.

Her eyes fluttered open. Two orbs of vivid violet gazed up at him, then focused. "Brother Temlin?" She breathed, her voice low with fatigue. "What happened? I remember sitting with Ghrenna at the Abbeystone, but after that…"

"Eleshen?" Temlin breathed. "Eleshen den'Fenrir?"

"Of course. Who else would I be?" Her dark brows knit, her full lips made a pout. Her tones were clipped like Eleshen's, irate even in her recuperation. Her fingers picked up a lock of her hair, fiddling with it in a sort of irritated exhaustion.

"Halsos in all his holy darkness!" Temlin breathed. His gaze raked her visage.

Eyebrows still knit in a very Eleshen-like frown, she lifted a weak hand, brushing long, wasted fingers across his short beard. "You look young! Twenty years younger than when I saw you last. How is that possible?"

Temlin brushed his knuckles across her cheek, completely amazed by her transformation just as she was his. "Ask me not, for I have seen more wonders in the past days than I have been privy to my entire life. And more horrors, too."

"Horrors?" Eleshen blinked, and then her gaze fell upon her hand. She blinked again. Her gaze strayed to those ebony locks, combed out over her shoulder, so long they reached to her hip. "What? My hair!" Lifting a section in trembling fingers, she held it before her eyes. A stricken look came over her. And then she lifted both hands up, touching her face, touching everything.

Tears filled her eyes, violets in the rain. "What has happened to me?!"

Temlin felt tears of sympathy fill his own eyes. "I don't know, girl. I'm so sorry…!"

"My face… my body!" Struggling up to sitting, Eleshen hauled the covers back. Wasted and narrow, her previously curvaceous frame was disastrously thin, though Temlin could still see good curves beneath her plain silk shift. But where she had been abundant, she was now fey, her bones finer and longer, everything more slender, her waist so narrow it pinched like a wasp. Eleshen brushed a hand down her body. Tears shed from her eyes, cascading down cheeks now flushed and pink. Those violet orbs were haunting in the lantern's light, and Temlin's heart twisted for her.

Without a word, he gathered her into his arms. She fought him for a moment, the raging fury of the Eleshen he knew. "What do you remember?" Temlin asked as he held her.

"I remember you and Lhem coming down the Abbeystone. I remember slapping you," she gave a soft laugh, "for being a bastard of a drunk. And then, I don't recall..."

Temlin gulped air, trying to halt the stinging of his own eyes. The tension of the past weeks flooded him. Transforming. Losing Molli. Stepping into his role as King-Protectorate. All eyes looking to him, to figure out how to fight for the nation. Eleshen pulled back, and Temlin realized she was staring at him, her face compassionate as if her own woes were nothing.

"Brother Temlin. You look distressed. What is it?"

"It's King-Protectorate Temlin, actually," he gave a hard laugh. "I'm den'Ildrian, brother to our late King Uhlas, or didn't you know? And our esteemed Abbess has recently named me King-Protectorate of our nation, before her sudden demise at the hands of Castellan Lhaurent den'Karthus. What a fucking cluster..."

Her dark eyebrows raised prettily, a very Eleshen look. She reached out, taking his hand. "That's a lot to swallow."

They stared at each other a long moment, feeling each other's sorrows and strangeness. Something stirred in Temlin, watching her. She was stunning, otherworldly. Eleshen had been lovely before, in a homey, bright kind of way, a woman who would swat you with the broom and then have a beer.

But now, it was all Temlin could do to not stare. His younger body had a younger man's urges, he found himself distracted from his sorrows. Lean, taller, Eleshen was without hardly any breasts at all now, and the overall effect was sylvan. But Temlin could still feel the punch in her, the battle and fire in her veins as she gazed at him. Her hair was sleek and black like an otter, a thick river that slid over her shoulder to her waist. Her skin was luminous, her veins pale with a haunting blue. Heart-shaped still, her face was sharper though still lovely. Black eyelashes curled above high cheekbones, framing her eyes. And what eyes. Vivid violet like the first crocus of the season, they were arresting.

As Temlin gazed at her, she gave a wry smile, and something about it was dark with a fantastic sense of humor, just like the old Eleshen. "Keep staring at me like that, old man, and I might just have to tell the Sisters."

Temlin gave a wry chuckle and pulled away. He spied a tray of food and tea upon the side-table and turned to retrieve it, settling it upon the bed. They were both silent as Temlin poured mugs of tea then gestured to a trencher of bread and stew. "You should eat."

"Only if you'll tell me what's going on. It sounds like war out there." Eleshen cocked her head, and Temlin could hear screams from the infirmary. Temlin handed her a mug, filling her in on all that had come to pass since he had gone through the Abbeystone. Eleshen's eyes widened, until they were enormous as Temlin described Lintesh's riots for the past two days.

She reached out for some bread, a rather hasty movement, and accidentally struck the trencher with her long, willowy fingers. "Dammit!" Eleshen cursed, flushing. "Damn this body! Everything is just in the wrong place!!" With an irritated growl, she focused on her fingers, and this time they made it to the bread. Ripping off a hunk, she dunked it in the stew.

"It's good to see you still have your spirit." Temlin smiled.

"Well." She eyed him, munching bread like a ravenous creature. "It sounds like nothing compared to what's been happening to you! And the city!" She gestured to her frame. "Besides. My spirit is really all I have that I recognize. Everything about this body is just put on all wrong. However it was done."

Temlin's gaze lingered. "I don't think it's on wrong at all. Whatever happened to you… it's not a loss, Eleshen. I'd say it was a gain."

She blinked at him peevishly, as if she would say something feisty, then suddenly sighed. Eleshen held a long-fingered hand up, examining it. "It just feels so… different! Halsos' Burnwater, I just wish there were something about it that was *me*, I swear!" She huffed, then picked up her stew and tucked in again.

"You have an appetite, at least." Temlin chuckled.

Eleshen mopped the last of the stew from her bowl with her bread. "I hate feeling like an invalid! Eating is the fastest way to recover from illness. And you! You don't look a day over forty! You don't even have a single streak of grey in your beard or hair. It just this fantastic copper color, like a well-made pot! You're fit and trim, and I never imagined you'd be so well-muscled! How did you feel when you…" she gestured at Temlin with her bread, "when *that* happened?"

Eleshen was giving him a very appraising eye. Temlin enjoyed it. His longjacket's buckled wool fit him like a scabbard fits a sword. Temlin put a boot up on the bed and leaned back in his chair, feeling not a single twinge of rheumatism.

"I feel like a man in my prime again." He chuckled, taking a piece of bread and eating also. "It's strange, really. Knowing that I had a chance at youth once and now I get to do it all over again. Mollia gave me a tremendous gift." His thought of her made him sad suddenly. Temlin gave a woeful chuckle. "I spent my younger years getting skunk-drunk, full of rage, Eleshen. And now I get a second chance. To be the man I should have been... the first time."

"A King." Eleshen gazed at him with her head cocked, alert.

"King-Protectorate." Temlin sighed. "For my niece."

"But many people must think the nation is currently without a leader!" Eleshen countered, leaning forward with energy in her wan frame. "If the King's Chancellate have been assassinated and Lintesh has erupted in riots... What do you think is happening out there?"

"People are leaving the city in droves, those that aren't coming here for refuge." Temlin slung his boot off the bed and leaned forward with fingers interlaced upon his knees. "But Castellan Lhaurent den'Karthus is planning something. He's already declared martial law, and set mind-bending men to move among the populous, causing chaos."

"Mind-bending men?" Eleshen blinked.

"It's a long story." Temlin waved a hand. "Let's just say I don't expect him to follow regular Menderian law. In these circumstances, he is supposed to order the lords of Alrou-Mendera to gather and nominate new Chancellate members. But that process takes months, to Darkwinter or longer. Castellan Lhaurent has the yoke of the Realm until then. He's got it neatly trussed up that he's in power right now, and I think he's going to try and keep that power rather than give it up."

"If everything you've told me just now about his atrociousness is true... wouldn't he be stepping quickly into the power breach?" Eleshen quipped, sipping her tea. "Making a formal announcement to the city?"

"No." Temlin shook his head, then sipped his own tea, feeling strangely comfortable discussing his inner thoughts with Eleshen and her cunning mind. "That's not his style. Lhaurent is part of the Khehemni Lothren, if not their leader now with the entire crooked Chancellate dead. He's got the palace, he's got Elyasin out of the way. And now, anyone upon the Chancellate who might have opposed him. My guess is he'll continue to be manipulative from the shadows rather than brash."

"So what are you going to do? How are you going to alert the populace that you've declared for Queen Elyasin? That the Abbey has? That you exist, her uncle, her King-Protectorate?"

"I'm not." Temlin eyed her over his tea. "I'm going to let Lhaurent make the first move. And that will be his undoing."

"What? Why?" Eleshen blinked those stunning violet eyes.

Temlin put down his tea. "Because he's comfortable in the shadows. But if he wants to take this country, he'll have to step out into the light, make himself known to the nation. If I make myself known *afterwards*, in support of the true Queen as her King-Protectorate, my rightful duty as den'Ildrian, he'll be outed as a Traitor to the Crown. Lhaurent is going to tell the populace Elyasin is dead. He's going to take a throne that's not his. And I'm going to let him do it, and then fuck him in the ass with the truth."

"Isn't that dangerous?" Eleshen sat back, cradling her tea. "Can't Lhaurent send armies to siege the Abbey? Once he's declared himself King?"

"Let him try." Temlin leaned back, gesturing expansively. "The Abbey is self-sustaining. We have been for centuries. The only thing we import are hops and grain to make beer for the city, but we grow enough of that for our own uses. Now imagine, what happens to a city when Lhaurent decides to siege us and the city's ale is suddenly gone?" Temlin chuckled, lacing his hands behind his head. "Men get angry when they don't have ale. And fighters... well. They get furious. And decide to turn on their lords."

"And come over to us." A pleased grin lifted Eleshen's lips.

"Indeed." Temlin grinned. "Lhaurent's going to have to up his Ghenje game to fuck me, my dear. And we have enough fighters to wait him out, with the Guardsmen that came to us during the riots."

"You'll need people to move through the city, quietly," Eleshen mused, "spreading word of you, of our Queen, of Lhaurent's treachery. In taverns, alehouses, places where the unrest is stirring."

Temlin watched her, seeing a side of Eleshen he liked. There was a brave ruthlessness to her, that her new body only accentuated. "You've got an arresting look now, my dear. Your presence in any alehouse would draw impeccable attention, I think."

She gave a satisfied smile. "Such a task is quite amenable. Once I'm a bit more recovered."

"But rabble-rousers will need protection." Temlin stood decisively. "Brother Sebasos knows a few of the Kingsmen here. I should take a jaunt to the walls to speak with him about all this."

Temlin rose from his chair with a buoyancy to his step that he hadn't felt in two whole days. Eleshen was good for him, her alert processing and wry humor a lightness unlooked-for in dire times. But as he stood, Eleshen swung her long legs from the bed as if to rise and follow him. She bumped her empty bowl with one slender hip, and it went careening off the bed towards the floor. Temlin made a grab for it, but Eleshen was already in motion, her slender hand snaking out like a whip, catching the bowl just before it hit the floor.

Their eyes met.

"That was tremendously agile of you." Temlin commented, impressed.

"I've never done that before. Caught something that fell." Eleshen's eyes were wide.

Temlin glanced at her hand, saw that it trembled slightly. "Have you ever had any special abilities?"

"Like Kingsmen abilities?" She looked down at her hand, shook her head. "Never."

Temlin's brows furrowed. He had a thought. Her body was different now in every way, from whatever had happened to her. *What if...?* Collecting his tea mug, Temlin quite suddenly threw it at Eleshen's head, hard. Her forearm whipped up, blocking, deflecting the mug to the floor where it hit and shattered, pieces of broken crockery skittering across the stones. Her violet eyes were enormous as her arm came slowly down.

She looked at her arm as if it were some unknown thing.

"You don't seem quite so left-footed as you used to be." A smile touched Temlin's lips.

She shook her head, mute. Slowly, Eleshen pushed up from the bedside. Though she trembled from long illness, she stood strong upon her elegant new legs. Tall and haunting like a gazelle in mist, she slid a step forward, and Temlin's eyebrows rose to see she'd unconsciously moved into a sword-fighter's stance.

Temlin paused. And then reached out, whip-fast, to slap Eleshen across the face. Her hand shot up effortlessly, seized his arm, twisted as she pivoted. Temlin was suddenly gathered into a neat throw over her shoulder, sending him ass-over-ears into a bookshelf with stunning force. Laying on the floor upon his back, Temlin stared up at the vaulted ceiling, re-learning how to breathe.

"Temlin! Oh, Halsos!" Eleshen rushed over, kneeling next to him. "Are you all right?! I didn't mean to, I mean I didn't think...! I just had this feeling, like I knew where to move...!"

"You've never trained in fighting, have you?" Temlin coughed, then chuckled himself up to a seat. His back ached like Burnwater from the impact, but his young body was otherwise fine. He pushed to his feet, and Eleshen followed. Her violet eyes were wide with concern. Standing close, her long fingers moved up, fussing at his jaw, his cheekbones.

Something sparked in Temlin. She was beautiful. Fierce, independent. Sane. Something moved in him and he put a hand to her waist, drawing her in. Her black eyelashes fluttered, surprised. Those red lips opened to say something, then stopped. Temlin's blood surged and he went with it, moving closer.

But she pulled back. Not out of his arms, but far enough, gazing up with those incredible violet eyes. "I can't..." Eleshen whispered. A flush of pink colored her pale skin. "I just, I mean..."

"You love someone else." Temlin knew it, and his chuckle was sad. He gave a sigh, moving his lips to her temple. "I know. I do, too... Forgive me. Heat and battle flood me again. I shouldn't have —"

But to his surprise, Eleshen settled her fingers to his ribs and leaned in close. Temlin gathered her in his arms, the both of them breathing in a silent comfort.

"Loving a man you can't have... it's madness." Eleshen murmured at last.

"I can relate." Temlin's chuckle was wry as he ran a hand down Eleshen's silken hair. "I loved a woman for decades who wasn't mine.

She went from being Uhlas' to being caged atop the Kingsmount, to being trapped inside the Plinth at the heart of this goddamn Abbey, by her own goddamn plotting. And now I'll never have her back. Curse my luck."

"Your luck?" Eleshen pulled back and looked up with a pretty pout. "Mine is just as bad, old man. I go from being named a traitor, to losing my family, to keeping an inn in the middle of nowhere. To meeting one man who was decent, who was smitten with that Aeon-damned seer Ghrenna ten years before he met me! And then I try to help her, because I feel obligated to, and I wind up——"

Eleshen stopped suddenly. She blinked.

"You wind up what? Did you remember something?" Temlin stroked her cheek with his knuckles. "From after I went into the Abbeystone and left you behind with Lhem?"

"Someone cared for me." Eleshen blinked up at Temlin. "I remember being held in his arms. Someone strong. A man dressed all in black. He gave me clothing to——" Her violet eyes went distant.

"Clothing?" Temlin prompted.

"To cover my nakedness." Her violet eyes had gone flat. "He cut me. *That bastard cut me!*" This last was said in a hiss so vicious, Temlin felt chills lift the hairs on his neck. Eleshen's gaze flicked to his, and what Temlin read there was brutal with rage. "The Abbott cut me. He chained me to a grate in a torture-chamber near the Abbeystone. He cut my clothes away, cut my hands, my feet…! Tortured me for information of Elohl and Ghrenna." She hissed suddenly, one hand reaching down between her legs.

"Lhem!" Temlin's gut dropped through the floor, and his rage whipped high. He clenched his fist, furious. "If I could, I would kill him all over again! Fucking Lhem and fucking Lhaurent! *How dare they!*"

Eleshen gripped Temlin's face, her violet gaze level, fierce. "The man in black saved me, from Lhem. Saved me before Lhem could try the things I saw seething behind his eyes. He wanted to use his blades in me, Temlin. I saw it. Cut me deep inside, then rape me while the blood flowed. He was a sick animal. Some people are rotten in places that never see daylight. And you say Lhem was working for Castellan Lhaurent? Did he… did he hurt your Molli that way?"

Fury shone in her violet eyes. A fury that yet had something vulnerable beneath it, something it had to lash out to protect. Temlin's heart broke for her, for Molli, for both of them.

"Mollia was tortured by them also," he rasped. "Long ago. She always asserted that Lhem and Lhaurent were in league together, both Khehemni Lothren. But I never truly believed her, until Lhem admitted it. And then I killed him. Gods know, Eleshen! If I had known he'd hurt you, too, I'd have made it last. Given you the blade and let you do whatever you might...!"

Eleshen's long hands cupped his face. Her violet eyes did not shed tears, and she did not crack into madness. Eleshen stood firm under the returning sluice of her horrors, and she held Temlin's gaze, her eyes clear.

"If Lhem and Castellan Lhaurent were in league," she seethed, "then I will do everything I can to bring the bastard down. Let Lhaurent pay the price of my maiming, and Molli's. Let all who shared in it come to ruin and blood. So I swear to the depths of my soul."

Staring into her eyes, Temlin saw nothing but strength. Wild courage, determination, fierce promise. And he thought suddenly that the young Kingsman Elohl had been a fool to let her go.

"So I swear it also." Temlin knelt before her, one palm to his chest, the other to his sword. "So swear I to Halsos and back. All who were Lhem's bedfellows I will make pay the Fifth Price. Again and again and again. For you, and for Molli."

Eleshen's hands caressed Temlin's copper waves, brushed them back from his forehead. "Teach me to kill, King-Protectorate. I will do it, for our nation and your niece the Queen. For your broken love. And for my own nightmares."

Slowly, Temlin stood. Unbuckling his jerkin, he pulled a dagger and nicked his chest. Crimson spread in searing flows, limning his Bloodmarked Kingsmount and Stars. Eleshen took the dagger. Putting it to her breastbone above her white shift, she did the same, though she had no Bloodmark to show. She did not wince. She stood firm beneath the blade, then handed it back to Temlin as blood slipped down her skin in a red line.

"Teach me the arts of war." Eleshen demanded. "And then teach me how to hunt Khehemni."

"With pleasure." Temlin growled, fire and battle surging in his veins.

CHAPTER 42 – GHRENNA

Ghrenna arrived at Fhekran Palace in the dead of midnight. Blackness showed through the colored-glass windows, a thick cloud cover swaddling the stars and moon. The palace had the quiet feel of slumber as Ghrenna was admitted by two female guards. Both raised eyebrows to hear Ghrenna call for an immediate audience with the Queen and King. They showed her to an attended alcove to wait, but before long rushed back, gesturing her deeper into vaulted halls. Making pace quickly through long passages and up a regal flight of stairs, they soon pushed through enormous carven doors with a boom of stout wood.

Ghrenna entered an octagonal war-room, blazing with lit fireplaces and ringed in high windows. In the center of the hall, she saw the individuals she sought, talking at a heavy map-table with goblets of wine to hand. Queen Elyasin den'Ildrian Alramir wore a blue embroidered night robe over a silk sleeping gown, her golden tresses loose as she brushed them back with her fingers. Her lovely green eyes widened, and she straightened, regal, as Ghrenna marched in.

King Therel Alramir wore a crimson jacket, buckles open over a rumpled shirt, standing next to a big guardsman with wild red braids. Lupine and graceful, Therel's tundra-pale eyes snarled as he set his goblet down upon the map-table, watching Ghrenna approach.

And yet, both monarch's gazes held awe.

Ghrenna could see herself through their eyes. Older, willowy but sinewed from years of climbing and stealth. Dressed in raw snowhare-furs like a vagrant, black Kingsman-gear underneath. The furs complementing her white cascades of hair, bound loosely at her nape, mussed from the elements and sleeping rough. Her visage pale like new snow, but with pink in her cheeks, lips blush-kissed. Blue eyes deep like snowmelt lakes under a cerulean sky, framed by long lashes.

Luminous. Exquisite. Beauty in its true natural perfection. Just like Morvein had once been.

"Morvein...!" Queen Elyasin breathed, one hand touching the golden pendant upon her chest.

"Send for Adelaine. Now." King Therel's voice was a harsh rasp.

The big guard with red braids nodded, marched to the door and murmured words to the female guards, who promptly retreated. Elyasin turned toward Ghrenna. Squaring her shoulders, she walked forward. Amazement was in her lovely face as she lifted a hand, lightly touching the keshar-pendant upon Ghrenna's chest. Her clear green eyes drifted to the grey and red fire-opal, then to the sigils of amethyst set with onyx that ran through the white claw.

"I dreamed of you, Morvein...and then you summoned us. And now you are here. How can it be?" Elyasin whispered.

"Ghrenna!" A hard shout startled the room. Ghrenna blinked, glancing over to see the last person she expected. Luc den'Lhorissian had just entered the hall, his golden good looks rumpled from sleep. Riveted to the spot, he stared, green eyes wide.

"Hello, Luc." Ghrenna smiled, her gut twisting to see him. She hadn't known Luc was here and a shiver of surprise lanced her. But as much as she wanted to go to him, to apologize and have him hold her, have him touch her and take away her pains and worries, she knew it could not be.

She was someone else now. Some*thing* else.

Luc still stared at her as the stunned silence of the war-hall pressed upon her ears. Ghrenna could feel the weight of King Therel's gaze, blistering. Everything within her told her to run, to turn and leave all this behind and search for Elohl. But the part of her that was Morvein held cruelly firm. She took a deep breath. Ghrenna fixed her drowning blue eyes upon Elyasin, then Therel. Her mind-penetrating power as a Gerunthane came as fluidly as breathing, Morvein's words upon its flow.

My lieges. I have been searching for you. You have both been claimed by my pendants. You are the chosen vessels, to finish what I began so many years ago, aided by my Brother Kings. I am Morvein Vishke, the Wind of Night. And to my command you will hearken.

Queen Elyasin and King Therel shuddered as Ghrenna's command knifed their minds. Part of her felt terrible to see such strong monarchs shudder at her cruel power. So it had been with Delman and Hahled, this shivering ferocity with which she could pierce minds. Morvein had seldom used such commands, knowing how horrible it was to subdue someone this way. But now was not the time for delicacy or decency.

The Path of the Rennkavi was all that mattered.

Ghrenna felt herself dissolving as Morvein's command thundered out. Some part of her quailed, knowing she was losing herself. But another part was strengthening. A part that had been there since she was born, waiting to take up Morvein's gifts, ready to live this dire path at last.

And yet, she was not truly Morvein. Ghrenna had lived a different life, loved a different man. She could make different choices. Softening her approach away from Morvein's jagged necessity, she addressed her King and Queen vocally, rather than knife their minds again.

"My lieges. I have traveled far to see you both. I come with news you will wish to hear. Privately."

The King and Queen blinked, confused at her sudden change in demeanor. Though pale, Queen Elyasin straightened with poise, as if she knew already what was coming. Her eyes flicked to King Therel. Pale also, Therel let out a slow, hard breath.

"Everyone. Leave us." Elyasin's quiet command echoed through the war-hall. All gawkers hastily issued from the room. Ghrenna watched Luc go, her heart twisting in agony. He gave her a pained gaze, so very handsome, so very Luc.

The doors boomed shut.

King Therel stepped down the dais to Ghrenna's side, his demeanor threatening. "Speak, woman."

"I come with news..." Ghrenna began, but the King reached out and gripped her wrist, crushing.

His eyes were pale blue fire, a cold snarl lifting his lips. "Not about that. About your words. *In my mind.* About that fucking Summons you pummeled through our heads!"

Ghrenna let her aching wrist be, and addressed him calmly. "I needed a response from you both to find my way to Lhen Fhekran from Dhelvendale. I sent a message strong enough to get the response I required. I've been following the threads of your thoughts ever since. That's how I knew to come here."

"Dhelvendale?" Queen Elyasin stepped forward, lovely in a ferocious sort of way. "I thought nothing exists there but ruins."

"It is so. I came through an Alranstone. It put me out at Dhelvendale."

"A Stone permitted you passage?" Though his grip on Ghrenna's wrist eased, Therel did not release her.

"I made it give me passage."

"You did *what?*" More fear than rage shone in Therel's wolf-blue eyes now. Ghrenna did not repeat herself. The silence hung, desiccating in the air.

"Who are you? Luc called you Ghrenna just now." Queen Elyasin stepped closer.

"I was born Ghrenna den'Tanuk. That's how Luc knows me. But now…I am something else."

The doors to the hall creaked open, and a sharp voice suddenly pierced the room. "Now Morvein surfaces within you, doesn't she?"

Ghrenna looked around to see a thin woman swaddled in furs enter the hall, her pale face sharp though comely. Her eyes were nearly white, shrewd as she stepped forward.

"Adelaine!" The King snarled. "Get out! You're not—"

"Patience, Therel!" She snapped back. "Let the woman answer my question."

"I recall Morvein's life, more every day," Ghrenna nodded. "Her memories, her losses, her duty."

The thin woman moved into the room, her eyes flicking to the King, then back to Ghrenna. "Her duty. For which she needs the unity of the Brother Kings once more…for which she needs those who wear her talismans."

"How did you know?"

"I am a Dremor. Adelaine Visek." The woman sank into a deep curtsy, which huddled her into her overwhelming furs. "And I am at your disposal."

Ghrenna's eyebrows knit, as the fur-swaddled woman rose from her adulation. "And why should I need you?"

"Because," the woman's eyes twinkled shrewdly. "I know

Morvein's history and her mistake with the pendants. Her Brother Kings are bound to them, and yet they cannot entirely come through, can they?"

Come through.

The words echoed in Ghrenna's mind. She had a vision suddenly, of Hahled and Delman Ferrian standing before her, waiting. One bright as the risen sun, the other cool as a moonlit night. "What do you know of it?"

"Enough." The woman smiled, a calculated lift of the lips. "I know the Brother Kings are tethered to those pendants but not entirely channeled *through* them, not like Morvein had planned. I know why my King and Queen suffer because of Morvein's handiwork. I know where you need to go to retrieve the Brother Kings, before you can call the Rennkavi."

"Tell me." Morvein's energy sharpened upon this woman like a lance.

The thin Dremor smiled, tight-lipped. "I haven't the information, precisely. But someone else does. And he's been most helpful in telling me what he knows."

Ghrenna's eyes flicked to a corner of the room. A lanky young man with straw-blonde hair hovered uncertainly by the wall. His eyes were wide, thoroughly terrified behind wired spectacles. They snapped between his King and Queen, then back to the fur-swaddled woman.

"Come here, Thaddeus." The thin woman commanded.

The bookish young man staggered forward a step, then moaned from the struggle of trying not to. Ghrenna could feel his mind overrun, even though he fought it. In her mind's eye, she saw tendrils of silver snaking out from Adelaine, wormed deep into the lad's thoughts. Webs strung from the Dremor's mind to the lad, dipping up through the base of his skull and mucking about in his mind. Infested, his mind was wrapped in weaves, strangled by them.

Controlled by them.

Ghrenna rounded upon the thin Dremor, furious. The full force of Morvein welled up from deep within her, rageful at what this woman had done to the lad. Ghrenna reached out without thought. With a ruthless flick of her mind, she sliced those cruel weaves. The lad stumbled, released. The pale Dremor staggered.

She fell to her knees, clutching her head, a cry escaping her. Relief surged across the lad's face as he came to one knee before his King and Queen, cheeks burning in shame.

"My lieges," he stammered hastily, "forgive me! I disobeyed. I sought her out! Please forgive me…"

But before they could answer, Ghrenna turned upon the fallen woman.

"*You!*" She hissed with the full force of Morvein's energy, buffeting the room with raw power. The Dremor's pale eyes were terrified as Ghrenna stalked near. "You have been cruel with your talents, Dremor. I should take your eyes, and make you ponder forever what it means to wield such *wyrria!*"

The woman shuddered, clutching her furs as if she could feel a wind. But then she straightened, eyes flashing fire. With an imperious lift of her chin, she struck out at Ghrenna, masterful mind-weaves silvered like frosted spiderwebs. The torrent ripped to Ghrenna, lancing her in a thousand places. Ghrenna startled, stepping back, overwhelmed by the intricacy of it, and the rage that powered it. For a moment, Adelaine coiled Ghrenna with her mind like a serpent, striking and striking again. But each lash of power was turned back by the white pendant upon Ghrenna's breast, Morvein's ages-old work still formidable, even if Ghrenna had little control over her abilities yet.

Adelaine lifted her lips in a snarl. Rage spiked in her eyes. Ghrenna took a breath, pressing her will toward the furious Dremor, seeing it lance out in silver streaks. But it was fractured, her true power still as inaccessible as Morvein's full memories. Using the breathing she had been practicing with Delman, she honed the silver into lances, but it was a crude thing compared to what Adelaine had done. The Dremor smirked, smashing Ghrenna's lances with casual flicks of her fingers and steady breaths. What Ghrenna had achieved so suddenly in a passionate fury, slicing the scribe's bondage, she found she could not replicate now.

Adelaine smirked as Ghrenna's attacks ceased. They both breathed hard, nostrils flaring from the exertion of what had occurred. It was plain they were at a stalemate, Ghrenna untrained in her new ability, the Dremor unable to overcome Morvein's pendant. Smoothing her furred hood back into place over her white braids, Adelaine lifted a chill eyebrow.

"Morvein. Indeed," she scoffed. "Break me first, and then I'll *consider* that you are what you say you are."

"I need not prove myself to you." The words dropped from Ghrenna's lips, cold. "You are strong, but harm another innocent, Dremor, and feel my fury."

Adelaine's pale lips dropped open. Ghrenna watched her hesitate, then shut her mouth as her eyes narrowed, considering. Ghrenna dismissed the Dremor and sank to one knee before her lieges.

"My Queen, my King," she spoke. "A great war is coming. Many lives will be lost, and this land cannot be saved by might of arms. We will fight until there are no men left. We will grind our bones to dust until there are none left to grind. Until the aged and weak take the field, slaughtering each other to annihilation. It happened in Morvein's time, eight hundred years gone, and it happens again now. The Brother Kings Hahled and Delman Ferrian gave everything to stop it once, and even then, disaster was not averted. Please. Help me. Our world is at stake and the only way we can bring peace is to begin Morvein's work anew. To open all the Alranstones, and let the Rennkavi come through in his true power to unite us all. I cannot do that without you. Both of you."

"Does it involve a ring of seven Alranstones?" The King had paled, his lupine eyes stricken.

Ghrenna blinked. Some of Morvein's memories surfaced at King Therel's words. In her mind's eye, she saw a circle of seven crystal Alranstones. Each with seven blazing eyes, somewhere deep underground, blue ice shining all around. "The White Circle. Yes. You know it?"

King Therel Alramir took a slow breath. He glanced at his Queen. They took hands gently, a tender love strong between them. "We know it. Let us adjourn and speak in more comfortable environs. I have the feeling we will get little sleep this night."

Therel moved down the dais, Elyasin at his side. Ghrenna followed and Adelaine stepped near, eyeing her like a snake eyes a mongoose. The scribe trailed as they boomed out of the hall. The big redheaded guard strode to his King. They exchanged a few words and the party departed from the throne hall as the retainer jogged off. Proceeding down a vaulted hall, they soon came to a sumptuous suite already being set with foodstuffs, steaming tea, and carafes of wine. The palace household bowed their way out, and Ghrenna saw the big man take up a guard position outside before the doors were shut.

Queen Elyasin motioned graciously for all to have seats as she poured tea, though she filled a goblet of wine for her King. Adelaine sank into a high-backed seat by the fire, Ghrenna taking one nearby. Elyasin and Therel prowled about the room, restless as a pair of winter wolves as they questioned Ghrenna about why she wore Kingsmen garb. They exchanged significant glances at mention of Elohl, pushing her into speaking of the visions, and of the Abbeystone and Mollia's valley. Again, Elyasin and Therel exchanged significant glances when Ghrenna spoke of Elyasin's uncle, Temlin. And both monarchs were astounded to hear that the Alranstones were alive, people trapped in stone. Ghrenna gave a brief summary of digging up Morvein's pendant, and her returning memories. And then she told of her long trek south, and riding with the Redbear clan as they moved south to the battle front.

Ghrenna came to silence. A small sound like a squeak came from Adelaine and Ghrenna glanced over. The Dremor's eyes were enormous, her thin hands shaking as she lifted her tea to take another sip. The lanky scribe was no less impressed, standing with lips open behind Adelaine's chair. Queen Elyasin poured Adelaine more tea from a silver rune-etched pot, then sank into a chair. King Therel came to stand behind her, hands resting upon his wife's shoulders, his brooding eyes faraway.

The Queen fixed Ghrenna with a hawkish gaze, not unlike that of Temlin. "So. Tell me of these." Elyasin touched the golden pendant hanging upon her chest.

"You must know, my Queen," Ghrenna murmured, "my mind has not settled completely into Morvein's. Much of what she could do, I cannot remember. Some memories come, others are resistant, like pulling millstones up from the bottom of a lake. I've tried to review her life as I came south from Dhelvendale... but some things I think she tried to forget."

Elyasin nodded, her lips pursed. "Tell me all you can remember of the pendants, we'll start there."

"Hahled, Delman, and Morvein, were three of the most powerful Gerunthanes, mind-scryers, the world has ever seen," Ghrenna spoke, memories flooding back like water as she focused upon them. "Like your Dremor, they had dreams and could manipulate minds. Morvein had two dreams that drove her and the Brother Kings. The first came to her when she was a young woman up on the tundra. A dream of ancient prophecy fulfilled, the unification of our continent under the Rennkavi. Ushering in a golden age and ending the curse of conflict that stalks us from the shadows, driving brother against brother, army against army. She traveled from her home to present herself to Hahled and Delman Ferrian, the Brother Kings of the Highlands, at their palace in Dhelvendale. But rot and ruin had already taken the Highlands from within, civil warfare between Khehemni and Alrashemni. At that time, the Khehemni had launched a vast purge against the Alrashemni, not only in the Highlands, but across the continent. Alrou-Mendera and Valenghia began to collapse, also, because of the in-fighting, and the subsequent war erupted over the entire continent. Morvein saw it coming, in a terrible fever after an avalanche, the second dream that drove her. A dream of carnage, of our world falling to ultimate destruction from a shadow-man of dire mind, unless the Rennkavi could rise.

"And so she made your pendants," Ghrenna stroked the white claw upon her breast, "and her own. And one more for the Rennkavi, to bind the forces together that could initiate the Rennkavi's rise. All four pendants were made impervious to mind-attack, to the best of Morvein's abilities, though they allow communication amongst each other to some degree. The gold pendant was made first, for the firstborn twin Hahled. Silver was made second, for the secondborn Delman. And then this one was made, with fire-opal to bind Hahled and amethyst to bind Delman. The onyx inset was to concentrate Morvein's own formidable power. And then the final pendant was made, for the Rennkavi."

"Why does the Rennkavi need a pendant?" Elyasin was shrewd.

"To bind not just Morvein and the Brother Kings to the Rennkavi, when he comes, but every Alranstone, in every land."

"In what way?" Elyasin's golden brows narrowed.

"In *every* way." Ghrenna took a deep breath. "Morvein bound herself and the Brother Kings by making these pendants, as tools for the Rennkavi to use. Utterly. Morvein didn't expect to live through the endeavor her dreams spoke of. That was what upset the Brothers so, why they fought so bitterly at the end. Delman eventually came to see what was necessary, Morvein's sacrifice for the sake of a great peace. But when Delman tried to convince Hahled, a bitter war ensued between them. One brother fighting for Morvein's right to do as she must, the other fighting for her life. She'd foreseen some of it, the conflict that took root, even in the heart of her resistance. And so she'd instilled barriers into both the silver and gold pendants, so the Brother Kings couldn't attack one another with their mind-abilities."

Therel snorted. "So they couldn't fight each other at the end, during the ritual? Binding men's minds. No wonder Morvein got such a bad reputation."

"Yes. But you must understand," Ghrenna continued. "Hahled and Delman Ferrian's gifts were formidable, and with Morvein's direction, they prepared the network to bind the Rennkavi, when he came through at last. Her dreams became reality. They built what had to be built."

"While war consumed their lands." Elyasin sat back in her chair, leaning into Therel's touch.

Ghrenna nodded. "Morvein heard a part of the Prophecy that said a powerful Gerunthane trapped in an Alranstone would recognize the Rennkavi and touch Goldenmarks upon his flesh. But as war consumed the continent like dry tinder, Delman, Hahled, and Morvein threw their minds so far into the Alranstones... and found no one who could mark the Rennkavi. Most of the Alranstones, even at that time, were slumbering, or mad from their long incarceration. The nations were already crumbling, being torn ruthlessly apart. As their time ran out, Morvein sought an alternative answer, a way to impart the Goldenmarks upon the Rennkavi herself. And she found it, deep under the mountains. I cannot recall those memories specifically, but Morvein came back with strange white Inkings on her skin, ones I bear now."

Ghrenna pulled up the sleeve of her jerkin, showing the white tattoos. "These have come back to me, as they were inscribed upon Morvein. And Morvein inscribed her Brother Kings with similar binding-magic, and made them learn the runes and sigils to bind the Rennkavi. But Morvein came to realize a problem. If a Rennkavi couldn't be found, only three people in the world knew the right runes to mark him, to open him to his purpose. And so Morvein made the Brother Kings swear a blood-oath with her. That they would let her trap them in Alranstones if their plan went wrong, to wait until a suitable Rennkavi could be found."

Elyasin gave a soft sigh. "She bound them into Stones. How awful."

"Where they still are today." Ghrenna stilled a shiver. "That's how I received these white markings. Delman Ferrian and I have made contact. He opened me to embrace the white runes once more."

Adelaine gave a violent startle, and had to place her teacup carefully aside upon a table. "You said they marked a Rennkavi in their time?"

Ghrenna shook her head. "They tried. A boy was found. One of the ancient line of den'Alrahel, the Line of Kings. Only fourteen, Theos den'Alrahel was their best hope of becoming Rennkavi. But Morvein had doubts. He was too young, too inexperienced. His gifts were a flickering thing, uncertain like his personality. She put him through tests, and he failed most of them. But they were desperate. As war decimated the continent, they took the boy to the White Circle and tried to impart the Goldenmarks to Theos. Their last-hour attempts failed. I do not recall that event exactly... but it was tragic. Many people died. And Morvein had no choice but to banish the Brother Kings into their Plinths right then and there. I know I... she... died after that, but I don't recall it."

"So the Highlands never saw their lieges again." Therel spoke, his tone scathing. "Our nation fell in battle, and Dhelvendale was ravaged into the ruin it is today. Abandoned in their hour of need. And fell into a dark age."

Ghrenna met Therel's lupine gaze. "Morvein did what she had to, to ensure a Rennkavi would be marked in the future. By a Gerunthane with enough strength of mind to withstand the rigors of time's insanity."

Elyasin reached up to clasp Therel's hand at her shoulder. "This vertigo. I'm seeing Hahled's vision, then, his mind-sight from within his Plinth. Since I wear the golden pendant. And Therel's seeing Delman's view."

Ghrenna nodded, an infinite sadness welling up in her. "Yes. As Gerunthanes, the brothers have the power not only to enter minds, but also to send their minds over the land. When they were alive, they surveyed battles this way, piercing the minds of their Generals to give strategy no matter where they were. After they were trapped in Alranstones, they watched as their beloved people fall to war, conflict, and pestilence. They watched their kingdom crushed, and could do nothing but wait."

"And Elohl," Elyasin continued with a soft sigh. "He has the Goldenmarks. He's this... Rennkavi you seek. Those golden Inkings, he was telling the truth that they were Inked upon him by Alranstone."

"Elohl has been marked in gold by Hahled. He has survived the Rennkavi's Mark. If the prophecies are true, then he is the one we must all fight for. The one who will bring us to a golden age. Or we shall fall into a dark time. Again." A shiver blew through Ghrenna.

King Therel drew up tall behind Elyasin, a thoughtful frown upon his face. "I had a report from Merra that Elohl evinced some very peculiar magics during a skirmish. Binding magics that flared upon his skin from the Goldenmarks like sunlight. It stopped a bitter skirmish that might have cost Merra her life."

Relief washed through Ghrenna, as an ancient worry she'd not known she'd carried suddenly eased. "So Elohl is truly the one. He's already demonstrating use of the gift without any attunement at all..."

A long silence pressed through the room.

"The Rennkavi has come." Adelaine's pronouncement slit the silence like a blade. "What does that mean for Elyasin and Therel? Morvein's pendants aren't working properly, are they? She intended them to create a mental link between a living host with strong enough blood and the two Brother Kings, didn't she? The Brother Kings need to occupy flesh during the ritual to open the Alranstones for the Rennkavi, don't they?"

"Yes." Ghrenna met her gaze, then glanced to Therel and Elyasin.

Therel's scowl was deadly. "If Elohl is already able to access his gift, why must we do anything?"

"Because his markings alone are not enough to challenge the curse that consumes our lands. He is the source, but the Stones carry ancient *wyrria* that can intensify and transmit his power through the land." Ghrenna sighed.

"Merra said Elohl was able to spread his magic by touch." Therel narrowed his eyes. "Compelling people to unify in peace."

"With all the Alranstones awake and lucid, and all under Elohl's yoke in a vast network," Ghrenna said, meeting Therel's stare, "he'll be able to unite the entire continent without touching anyone. The ritual in the White Circle can give him that. No more war, Therel. Peace and trade and mutual benefit for all. Consider it."

"But the Brother Kings need our flesh to step into. Mine and Elyasin's." Therel's voice was cold.

Ghrenna didn't have to nod. "Delman and Hahled are powerful, but they can't do what they need to, bound in stone as they are."

"And what if we take the pendants off?" Elyasin asked. "What if we choose not to assist?"

Ghrenna gazed back into the flames. "Even when I was Morvein, I wasn't entirely sure that Delman, Hahled, and myself would be enough to complete the ritual. And if we aren't, war will swallow this continent anyway, as the Alrashemni and Khehemni kill each other off. Yet again."

"And us?" Elyasin spoke again. "What becomes of you, me, Therel, Elohl?"

Ghrenna gave her a long look. "Binding magic has a way of burning the flesh up, so Morvein was warned by the one who gave her the white Inkings. I will be a focus for the Plinths, and the channel for all the awakening Alranstones to Elohl. Delman and Hahled will each only channel one-third of the burden, through to me. I don't expect myself to survive. But perhaps you both have a chance. I have made peace with my death. Like Morvein once had to."

"If we don't do this, the rising war will break us all." Elyasin whispered, her green eyes faraway as if she watched her country burn. "Alrou-Mendera. The Highlands. The Isles. Everyone. They'll be thrust into another dark age as all the kingdoms fail."

"So it was in Morvein's time." Ghrenna's words were soft.

Therel suddenly squared his shoulders and set his jaw. "I will not let my people suffer endless war, and Elohl doesn't deserve to face this on his own. I have been responsible for sending him to part of his fate. I will be responsible for the rest. I will do this thing. Let Delman Ferrian come into my mind. But he will not find an easy truce between us. Especially if the man doesn't give up the damn Ghenje." Therel gave a vicious chuckle as his fingers stroked Elyasin's neck.

"I will do this also." A hard light came to Elyasin's clear green eyes. "I must protect my kingdom, at all costs. I have seen war drain my nation and kill our spirit most of my life. If there is a way to prevent our continent from unraveling, I will do it. A Queen's first duty is to her people."

Ghrenna nodded, the part that was Morvein within her steeling for battle. "So be it. I will come for audience with you both upon the morrow, and we shall discuss what is to be done. I must spend tonight remembering as much of the Rennkavi's rituals as I can."

"You don't remember them?" Therel blinked at her, astonished.

Ghrenna stood from her chair, her rabbit pelt ruffling. "How easy would you find it to remember something from eight hundred years ago? The memories come when they come. Give me time."

Ghrenna did not ask her Queen and King's leave to depart. She simply left. As she strode from the royal chambers, she felt Delman's sad fingers smooth over her shoulder. Ghrenna pushed them away. Her heart choked, and her will broke with the weight of everything she was facing as she turned into a silent stretch of corridor. Ghrenna collapsed upon a bench in a blind alcove. Shivers rose. She bit her hand, but the shivers still came, unceasing.

Her first sob choked out. And then another. But even as Delman's fingers came smoothing at her shoulders, all she could feel was misery.

And all she could see were Elohl's grey eyes, shining in the dusky flickers of a nearby lantern.

CHAPTER 43 – ELOHL

Elohl and Fenton rose from the icy overlook in the black cavern, stunned in the wake of the citadel's illumination. As the crackling of lightning faded to nothing, Fenton resumed his rapid breaths until he was positively boiling with heat, steam rising from his drying clothes in thick clouds. When he was so crimson in the face Elohl thought he might pass out, Fenton suddenly clapped his hands together, slamming a massive shockwave of energy out from his body. Hands cupped, fingers gripping as if he held an orb, Fenton channeled all that energy back towards himself into a massive globe of fire that surged between his palms. Expanding his palms outward, shivering with focus in a fighter's stance, his brows knit and his breath heaved as he grew that globe to the size of a bear, enormous. A fire that twisted and writhed, white-hot, illuminating the space they'd come into.

Fenton blew out one last breath and pressed upward with his hands, lofting that burning globe high into the inky darkness. But suddenly, a change of air pressure around them sucked that ball of flame high, ripping it out of Fenton's control. Fenton cried out, staggering back, as his creation went careening far above, smaller and smaller.

It hit a surface far above with a concussion, rippling some substance that looked like a pool of water high upon the ceiling of the cavern. The fire was absorbed into the pool, muted like lava beneath thin obsidian. And then, ignited whatever was above them with tongues of blue flame that burst outward in a ring like burning lamp-oil. Shooting out, the entire ceiling of the cavern was lit with blue-white fire. If one could trap fire in a lake, Fenton's flames writhed and twisted through the strange oil. The ripples magnified the light a hundredfold, like mirrors, sending light into every crevasse and niche.

Illuminating a paradise within the glacier.

Elohl gaped, frozen with awe. Their position was up at an overlook, and the citadel spread out around them and then down in twisting staircases, all layered over and under in grand arches and colonnades. Domiciles and spires rose from the ice, palaces of grandeur carved in gleaming whites and chill blues. Fountain plazas burbled with water that ran through the cavern in rushing rivers. Clear staircases curled up from the cavern's floor, leading to enchanting bridges that tricked the eye. Everywhere they looked there were more twisting buildings, more spires, more domes. A thousand bridges, ten thousand buildings, all throwing the light from the vastness of the rippling lake of blue fire above.

Taking up their packs like sleepwalkers, they moved away from the collapsed rift and toward a staircase that wound down into the citadel. Elohl glanced back to see that their entrance had once held a grand arch, an egress millennias old from the city. Gazing around from their long balcony promenade, he saw ten, twenty, thirty more like it, gateways all burrowing away into the blue ice to destinations unknown.

The winding staircase carven straight from the ice led down from their vantage, into a grand plaza with three fountains in a triad at the bottom, surrounded by a ring of colonnades. Elohl and Fenton descended, the stairs strangely large and awkward, navigating carefully even in their ice-claws.

A maze surrounded them, a labyrinth of cunning and mastery, as they stepped down into the city. All of it was ornately carved like nothing Elohl had ever seen. Sigils decorated every surface. Runes and a curling script dotted with diacritical marks and underlined by a common level covered everything. All round him, the ice had been carved into birds and sylphs and satyrs of stunning variety. Plinths shaped to resemble women tall as three men, with long, flowing locks covering their nakedness. Fish so realistic they practically leaped for the dragonflies upon a high arch above. Herons lancing frogs, a whole flock of geese taking wing up the side of one column. Strong men in carven helms and armor covered in runes, making complex gestures with their hands, as if warding, or forbidding.

Following Fenton, Elohl headed toward the sound of flowing water, and they arrived at the nearest of the three fountains in the sprawling plaza. Water spewed from a fount in the center, carven with leaping fish. The ice was pristine, having not thawed nor even marred from the water that burbled into its wide bowl. Dipping in flasks, the water shocked Elohl's fingertips, crisp and cold. He startled to see a flash of silver in the fountain. Leaning closer, he spied a very long, narrow fish, almost like a small shark mixed with an eel, moving lazily through the water.

And where there was one, there were many. Silver streaks shone beneath the water, not only in this fountain but in the nearby rivers than ran like canals through the floor of the plaza. Peering closer, he saw the fountain's bowl was slick with a clear algae that gave off blue luminescence, which the fish hid in and ate.

"Look." Elohl pointed.

"I saw them. Look there." Fenton jostled his shoulder. Elohl looked up in time to see a lizard go scurrying up a nearby column of ice, so clear Elohl could see its organs pulsing faintly inside with pink blood. The lizard halted, flicked its tongue, and Elohl saw a blob like a clear leech disappear into its mouth.

"How in Halsos do they survive down here?" Elohl wondered.

"They have an ecosystem all their own," Fenton answered. He reached his fingers toward the lizard, and it took off, scurrying up the column. "I've never seen anything like it."

"In all your one thousand years?" Elohl glanced over, with a wry smile.

"In all my one thousand years." Fenton confirmed, sober. He looked up and around, admiring domes and turrets, carven in patterns that seemed to shift and writhe as one moved around them.

"Do you know where we are?" Elohl asked.

Fenton shook his head. "I have no idea. I didn't even know such a place as this existed. There are many secrets in our world, Elohl. Ancient secrets I'm not party to. It was rumored that my grandfather Leith unlocked a few, from which he drew his power. Our world is far older than anyone suspects, and we are but the most recent to inhabit it."

"So where do we go to get out?" Elohl asked, taking in the enormous labyrinth.

"Ready to leave so soon?" Fenton glanced over, teasing. "We could live like kings here. Explore for ages. Unlock vast mysteries. Maybe even draw power from them like Leith did."

"We don't have ages, Fenton. We have a duty to Elyasin and Therel, remember?"

Fenton sobered. His eyebrows knit. "I'm sorry. That was callous of me. Of course, we should focus on finding a way out. Getting our lieges the help they require is far more important than exploring old mysteries. I don't know what overcame me." He shook his head as if dizzy, then took a deep breath.

"Are you alright?" Elohl asked, concerned.

"I'm fine." But Fenton's gaze shifted away.

"Fenton." Elohl pressed. "If we are going to trust one another, we can't have secrets between us."

Fenton heaved a sigh, then met Elohl's gaze. "Forgive me. It's just... that accident I told you about. In Roushenn, after I battled the Khets al'Roch, I was badly injured. Dying. My grandson Khouren found me, took me to an ancient object of power my grandfather Leith once left inside Roushenn. The object of Leith's healed me, but ever since..." Fenton's eyes sparked red, then faded. "Ever since then, I feel... wild. Like the control I fought so long for is breaking down. Sometimes I find myself saying or thinking thoughts that aren't mine."

Comprehension dawned in Elohl. "Thoughts that are Leith's. His magic touched you, took root in you."

"Something like that." Fenton nodded. "And the more I use my power the more I feel his influence. Not like possession, not like his soul lives and is trying to take me over. But that I'm changing, because of the energy he left trapped in that object. I feel and sense... more from my surroundings than ever before. As if I can feel *wyrria*, flowing in the earth itself. And a part of me likes it. Wants it. I fear that I'm becoming like him."

"And Leith would stay to explore this citadel," Elohl understood. "To wrest secrets from it. Power."

"Exactly." Fenton's eyes had cleared, but there was still worry.

"I won't let you turn into a tyrant, Fenton." Elohl reached out, gripping him by the shoulder.

"Leith's *wyrria* is strong, Elohl, even dead as he is."

"Come on. Let's find a way out. The longer we stay, the more tempting it will be."

"Agreed."

They moved on, winding through the glacial space, admiring friezes and lattices of ice, fountains and palaces. But where once Elohl might have been tempted to explore, his worry about Fenton drove him onward. Fenton would halt now and then, gazing at a wall with a carven tableaux, or staring at a sigil upon a lattice, until Elohl prodded him. His gaze at those times would spark red, worrisome to Elohl. One time the red remained as he stood, transfixed before the image of a beautiful warrior-queen in full battle armor, riding a chariot pulled by six massive scorpions.

At last, they came to a place where eight roads of ice converged upon the points of a rose compass, surrounded by a grand ring of columns. An enormous amphitheater of ice sloped down in countless tiers to a central ring. At the center, a promenade as massive as the plaza where Elohl and Fenton had filled their flasks, arched a semicircle of ornate ice gateways, seven in all.

And before the gateways, sat a giant man. Hands palm-up upon his knees, he sat crosslegged in meditation, eyes closed. His padded red-ochre jerkin with its high collar was sewn with eye-smiting yellows and saffrons, and tooled in complex sigils. Short black hair curled at his temples, streaked with grey. Tremendous of stature, he was impressively broad through the shoulders with arms the size of tree trunks and legs even thicker. Muscled without a hint of fat, Elohl estimated the fellow to be three times a normal man's height, enormous.

Elohl could see his breath, heaving like bellows through his ribs. A thin mist curled from his nose into the cold air. But even as gigantic as he was, the man was small compared to the portals behind him. Looming high, the seven archways dominated the center of the amphitheater, forbidding. As Elohl and Fenton stepped beneath one of the arches in the external ring and entered the structure, the giant man's eyes opened. As if waking from a dream, his piercing pale blue gaze lifted to the intruders. But where Elohl thought the man might have been angry, a guard or a warrior to forbid them entrance, there was only gentleness in those eyes. Supreme patience emanated from the giant man, and his lips broke into a soft smile.

"Come." He rumbled in a smooth basso, peaceful like a lapping stream.

He lifted a hand, beckoned.

Elohl and Fenton looked at each other. And then stepped down the aisle, Elohl in the lead. The man watched them the long minute it took them to reach the central floor of the amphitheater. And when they arrived, he did not stand, simply beckoned them to have a seat before him. Towering over them, his kind eyes welcomed them as they settled. His smile grew broad, showing impeccable white teeth. Elohl could see alabaster tattoos curling over his cheekbones, up his temples, and down the sides of his neck. Dotted in the same elegant script found throughout the citadel, the tattoos looked like smoke curling upon a glacial wind.

And Elohl had the thought, that those tattoos looked startlingly similar to the golden script and runes written upon his own flesh.

"At last," the giant rumbled, his gaze moving between the two men. "The Uniter comes, with his Protector."

A surge of tingles cascaded through Elohl's golden Inkings. He shivered with tension, awed, yet feeling no threat. "Who are you? How do you know us?"

The gigantic man smiled. He gestured to the seven archways behind him. "The portals whisper many things, to those who listen. In my long life, I have learned that the seasons of the world turn and turn again. Many Uniters have graced this earth. Some succeed, some fail. One was a great hero, and saved the Many Worlds when all was thought lost, at a time when the Undoer pulled planets apart by the dozens. Agni was a servant of the Sacred Fire, and so are the both of you. For fire cleanses and renews just as it destroys."

The massive man waved one hand. Suddenly, Elohl's golden Inkings burned with a ferocious heat. With a cry, he tore his jacket and jerkin open, revealing his Goldenmark lit bright as day, no longer slurrying like they illumined from underwater. Elohl cried out again from surprise, but even as he did, he heard Fenton roar in pain at his side.

He looked over to see that Fenton had shucked his jacket also, and flung it away along with his jerkin and shirt. His entire torso was lit with crimson-gold flame, curling beneath his skin along the course of his veins. But unlike Elohl's markings, Fenton's curse was in his very blood. And as those veins of crimson surged, blossoming through Fenton in an unholy tirade, he roared from pain. His hands gripped into fists, his body arching into a tight, shuddering spasm, his eyes rolling up in his head.

"Cease! You're hurting him!" Elohl commanded the giant man.

"You know who you are, Uniter. But he must learn to be what he is." The giant man leaned forward, his arctic eyes intent upon Fenton. "He is the Cleansing Fire. He is the Destruction and the Regeneration. He is the Scion of Leith Alodwine. Unleash it, little brother. Let the fire cleanse you."

Head back in a terrible agony, Fenton screamed. His skin suddenly burst into flame, writhing with that smelted fire. Heat boiled from his body in shimmering waves that pummeled the chill air. As he howled out like beasts in torment, the fire expanded in a tremendous white-hot orb. Heat seared Elohl as that fire neared. It threatened to boil his bones. Heart thudding hard, Elohl twitched to rise and escape it, when the giant suddenly trapped him to his seat with a palm upon his shoulder.

"Stay. You shall not burn." The giant rumbled.

The rushing orb of Fenton's fire surged outward, engulfing Elohl. He cried out, thinking he was burning, but it was only a reflex. Where Fenton's flame passed, swallowing the center of the amphitheater and the seven arches, ice vaporized in a tremendous heat, surging away in a torrent of steam. But the men within Fenton's fiery orb did not burn. As Elohl watched, the floor of the amphitheater was transformed into a pure white stone like quartz crystal. The arches melted, turning into columns of the same entirely carven in luminous golden runes and script. And as Elohl watched, something flashed to life inside each arch, a sinuous, ethereal barrier. Music filled the amphitheater. Writhing, haunted, soul-breathing music. In voices Elohl had never heard, in a chorus no human had ever made, it wove its way through his mind, his heart, and his very essence, breathtaking.

Suddenly, Fenton's fire flashed out. Elohl looked over to see Fenton breathing quietly, face uplifted and eyelids fluttering as he took in that ethereal sound. Tears ran down his face, and he choked out a sob.

"There my small friend," the giant cooed, reaching out to touch Fenton at the heart with one finger, then again at the brow. "Be what you are at last. Find the balance within, and embrace that power."

"I don't want him," Fenton gasped. "I don't want Leith's horrible curse! I can feel its rage, its anguish… burning me alive from the inside out."

"Immense *wyrria* can do great things." The giant countered. "Embrace it. Feel the burn in your sinews and ask yourself, what would I sacrifice to make my world safe? For that is the question Leith Alodwine had to answer, and he gave everything because of it. He, and Morvein after him. And Agni and Chiron, Oni and Orasunne long before that. It is time you take your place among them, now."

"Morvein?" Fenton's eyes came open. "What do you know of Morvein?"

"Much." The massive man chuckled. "I taught Morvein binding-magic, and Leith before her. Those runes and script Goldenmarked upon your friend," he gestured to Elohl, "are of my people's origin. The Giannyk. We are portal-smiths, rune-makers, stone-shapers of old. Those particular sigils, as well as the ones writ upon your back in fire, are actually my own design. I am called Bhorlen Valdaris, Master Portalsmith of the Dhuvvin Giannyk. And I am the last of my kind, now that my half-brother Oslef in the Abyss has passed on."

The giant gestured, and Elohl's Inkings began to glow once more, but subtly this time. "Do you control them?" Elohl asked, wary.

"No, no." The big man chuckled. "Oh, no. They merely respond to me. They recognize the magic of their originator. I can make them flare, make them demand to be recognized, but it is your own power that makes them sing. Scripting and sigildry is a fine art. Binding a realm to another realm to make a portalway is difficult to master. But to bind a soul to dire power, that art is nearly impossible. Souls are many-splendid things." The giant gave a serene smile.

"So my soul is bound to these marks." Elohl murmured.

"Or are they bound to your soul?" The Giannyk countered with a sly smile. He winked.

"So Morvein had binding-magic," Fenton interjected, "given to her by you."

"Awoken in her by me." The giant corrected. "For the will to bind lies in every heart. What do humans do when they love? When they marry? When they fear? When they hate? They create a powerful bind upon another creature. My people simply learned how to master that bind, craft it, sculpt it. Morvein had the will, so did her lovers, Hahled and Delman. So did your progenitor, Leith Alodwine."

"You taught them all. You taught Leith." Fenton's tone was scathing, accusatory. "Why? Couldn't you see the evil in Leith, in Morvein?"

The giant clucked his tongue. He leaned forward, his gaze intense upon Fenton. "Careful, child of small thoughts. People judge actions as evil when they cannot see the larger framework. Great movers of the world make great sacrifice. Morvein sacrificed her reputation, indeed, her very life, for the enormity of her purpose. Leith was no different. And Morvein has come again, to sacrifice herself anew, her business as yet unfinished. Yes, I feel her in the winds of the Void once more..."

The giant turned, glancing over his shoulder at the portals, all of them now sliding and rippling with a vague film like oil upon water.

"Morvein has come again?" Fenton's whisper was dire. "What do you mean?"

"I mean she has resurrected herself." The giant still had one ear toward the portals. "She bound her soul to the mortal coil, to reawaken when the time was right. The Nightwind has returned."

"The Nightwind." Elohl glanced at the giant, then looked to Fenton. "That's the name I used for Ghrenna, in my vision just a few nights ago. When I had that fever."

Fenton's face was stricken, though Elohl did not know why.

"Have you been dreaming of a white tower, youngling?" The giant asked.

"You know of it?" Elohl looked back to him.

"I've been *calling* you with it." He smiled. "Calling you and her both. For upon that spire is where you shall work your mysteries, the great magic that will bind and open every Alranstone as it was intended to by Leith, all those years ago. And usher in the Great Peace."

"The Goldenmarks?" Fenton hissed. "The Unification? They

were *Leith's* idea? But I thought… the Prophecy!"

"Prophecy is a tricky thing," the giant commented. "Does it describe a future that is yet to be set in motion, or a future that has *already* been put in motion?"

Fenton closed his lips, ground his jaw. His eyes flashed red. "Leith was a tyrant. An Undoer."

"Leith was given knowledge that would twist any man into knots, trying to find the best way out of an impossible series of choices," the giant retorted, for the first time losing some of his impeccable calm. His eyes flashed back at Fenton, glacial. "You would be wise to open your mind, and consider that perhaps he did what he did out of love. A greater love than you will ever know."

"What do you know?" Fenton rose to his feet, shivering with anger.

"More than you can comprehend, young one." The giant rose to his feet as well, towering over Fenton, who only came up to his hips. "Test me not, Scion of Alodwine. Learn to trust in those you love, rather than bend events to your control. You have already done enough damage, cursing your bloodline as you have. There are ways of ensuring the survival of precious information that do not involve such ugly measures."

"Cursing your bloodline?" Elohl looked at Fenton. "Your Oath to protect the Rennkavi was a curse?"

"A blessing and a curse, carried through my *wyrric* blood." Fenton's voice strained as his dark eyes flashed red, bleak. "If I break the Oath, or if the Oath judges that it's been broken, then I burn in agony. My soul is cursed to burn from then on. To burn with pain every hour of every life I will ever live. It is the same for my Scions, those who have sworn upon my blood, ingested it, and benefitted from my strength and longevity."

"Sweet Aeon." Elohl sighed.

Fenton's gaze shied away. The giant stared at him, but Fenton could meet no one's eyes. With a sigh, he pulled a knife from a thigh-sheath and began walking it restlessly through his fingers. "I created my oath eight hundred years ago, Elohl, after Morvein and the Brother Kings disappeared. During a time when war ripped apart our continent, when all my clan's efforts to bring the Rennkavi were annihilated. My oath back then was a horrible thing. But I was desperate to preserve the knowledge of the Prophecy beyond so much death. *I am the forest that feeds the fire,*" Fenton's inflection suddenly changed, grim, as his knife walking ceased. "*I am the charnel upon the pyre. Should I fail my Rennkavi, my wretched blood no rest shall see. To the Undoer I will burn, as long as every world does turn. That is my Oath I swear tonight. That is my Curse, life without light.*"

The giant heaved a tremendous sigh at that utterance, as if fatigued. He glanced to Elohl. "Come with me. You need to see it. To feel it, the place where the great binding magic shall be wrought."

"Where?" But Elohl already knew where. Like the thought had been thrust into his mind, he saw the white spire, towering high into the clouds.

"Come." The giant smiled. The massive man turned, heading for the centermost of the seven arches. Elohl hesitated, then followed. He heard Fenton fall into step behind him.

Almost at the arch, the giant turned, his gaze fixing upon Fenton. "You are not allowed."

"I am blood-sworn to protect Elohl. Do not ask me to stay behind." Fenton squared his stance, grim.

The Giannyk considered him, head tipped. "Then you must let me bind you, until you are gone from that place. Untamed magics flow strong there. I cannot have you flare with the fear and rage you currently possess, spreading a pestilence through the world."

Elohl saw Fenton swallow hard. He dipped his chin. "Do what you must."

The giant lifted his hand, and then moved his fingers as if painting in the air. As he did, a rune of silver etched upon Fenton's forehead. Other runes flared to life upon his bare torso, at his heart, solar plexus, and abdomen. Fenton gasped, his eyes tight with pain. And then relaxed, as if a great weight had been lifted from him.

His eyes closed in bliss. "It's gone. The conflict of Wolf and Dragon inside me. Shaper be holy!"

"Not gone," the giant rumbled, "only tamed for a time. When you leave this place, your own nature will come roaring back, Fentleith Alodwine. I cannot prevent it. You must learn to unite the energies that war within you from your ancient bloodline, or they will tear you apart. Master the beasts, Scion of Alodwine, or be mastered by them. Such powers will not be tamed by breath work and meditation. Their roar will always be felt within you; a battle that must be used, not suppressed."

Fenton's cheeks flared in a flush, though his eyes narrowed, grim.

Glancing to Elohl, the giant gestured. "Come now. To the Spire." Turning, he strode through the center arch and disappeared like smoke upon the wind.

Elohl took a breath, then strode into the whispering light also, Fenton fast upon his heels.

CHAPTER 44 – JHERRICK

It was past dark when Jherrick and Aldris slipped away from Lourden and Thelliere's guesthouse. They'd decided it was better to leave without saying goodbye. Easier. Pacing quietly along Ghellen's labyrinthine avenues, back in their Roushenn cobalt garb and sword baldrics but with the addition of black *shoufs* drawn up over their heads, Jherrick couldn't help but note how Aldris moved like a trained assassin. Liquid and careful, he avoided patrols of Ghellani spearmen by slipping into deep nighttime shadows. The man was Alrashemni Kingsman, honed, and Jherrick found himself impressed as he moved through city at Aldris' side.

At last, they came to the break in Ghellen's western wall. They stalked through to a moon-flooded night, cool white sand shifting beneath their boots upon the broken causeway. Their walk to Ghellen's Stone was shrouded in silence, each closed in their own thoughts. The Stone stood tall in the tumbled plaza, stark white moonlight and black shadows swallowing all color in the night.

But as they stepped to the Stone, the desert moved all around them. Ghellani spearmen and women slid from the stark shadows of broken columns. Forming a ring around Jherrick and Aldris, they raised spears like desert vipers. Jherrick caught his breath. Of course, Lourden still had a watch on the Stone. He raised his hands, showing empty palms, and Aldris did the same. Someone tall approached, his face shrouded in a deep grey *shouf*. But when he lowered his hood and gave a tired smile, Jherrick smiled to see Lourden's chiseled face in the moonlight.

"Trying to escape without saying goodbye?" The spear-captain joked, though his eyes showed pain.

Jherrick and Aldris lowered their hands. "We have to get home." Jherrick stated. "Right these wrongs."

Lourden nodded, a sad understanding flickering across his

visage. "My heart wishes it had come to more. Your journey here, her presence among us."

Jherrick did not miss the fact that Lourden could not say her name. He wondered how much Lourden had mourned this past week for his *Rishaaleth*, and how much had been for Olea. Personally.

"Perhaps all may not be in vain," Jherrick murmured. "If a Khehemnas and an *Alrashem* can unite, because she was in our lives…"

"Then perhaps there is yet hope." Lourden sighed. He offered his arm to Jherrick. Silently, they all clasped wrists in the night. "Travel safe. And may hope come back to us all. Someday."

Jherrick nodded. There was nothing more to say. He and Aldris moved toward the Alranstone, entering its ring of sight with a cascade of shivers. They set their palms to its cool surface, stark white where the desert moon shone upon its smooth surface. Together, they closed their eyes and recited the Alrashemni words Jherrick had heard only a few short weeks ago.

Nothing happened.

Jherrick opened his eyes, glanced to Aldris. Aldris nodded at his belt pouch. Jherrick fished out the clockwork, holding it to the Stone.

Nothing happened.

"Dammit." Jherrick breathed.

Aldris gave a low chuckle. "Here." He slid a knife from his belt, pricked his thumb, handed the knife to Jherrick. Jherrick pricked his thumb also. Together, they pressed their blood to the Alranstone, like Jherrick had done at in Khehem's palace with the white line. Nothing. They anointed the clockwork with blood, pressed that to the Stone. Nothing.

"It sees you not." Lourden stood near, watching, hands on his hips.

"No fucking kidding." Aldris quipped. "Well, what now? Do you think your Maitrohounet knows another way we can get home, Lourden?"

The spearman tipped his head, his grey eyes thoughtful in the night. "There is an older way to travel, stories say. For those with the Blood of Khehem."

"Blood of Khehem?" Aldris glanced at Jherrick. "You mean if someone is Khehemni?"

Lourden shook his head. "No. Only if one carries the royal blood of Khehem's ancient line. A true Scion of Khehem."

"Scion? You mean a descendant of Khehem's kings?" Aldris glanced at Jherrick again. "You think Jherrick might be of their bloodline?"

Lourden shrugged, his eyes resting upon Jherrick with weight. "Perhaps. His touch affected the clockwork piece. He was the reason you were all transported to our land. Stories say the original *wyrric* magic of Khehem is conflict, the kind of conflict that tears the soul, that burns within the body like fire. Are you a Son of the Wolf and Dragon, boy?"

Something about Lourden's statement chilled Jherrick to his bones. He thought of the pale shine of the wolfpack, stalking him in the night. He thought of a dead boy's glassy eyes. Of a mother, screaming her anguish out like a howl in the forest. Of Olea's eyes, empty, gone. He shivered beneath the moonlight. Something inside him burned. Something inside him snarled, waking.

"If there's another way back to Alrou-Mendera, Lourden, show me." Jherrick demanded.

"Come." Lourden beckoned.

He turned from the Ghellen-Stone, walking briskly over the moon-drenched sand, gesturing for his spearmen to remain. Backtracking to Ghellen, they slipped through the shadows until Lourden stopped at a small building near the marketplace. Reaching up, Lourden seized a cord with a bone handle that issued from a hole in the wall. A bell rang, low and soothing, somewhere deep within the structure.

A man came to the door, rolled up the mat. Clad in a charcoal grey so flat it ate the night, Jherrick could see he bristled with weapons upon a black loa-leather harness. The loa-scales glittered in the moonlight, the same leather showing at the grips of the sickle-swords that rode his back. His *shouf* up, the man's flat grey eyes took them in, before he set a palm to his chest and nodded to Lourden.

Lourden stepped close, and they began a conversation in Khourek. Jherrick couldn't pick it all out, but he did hear *desert, escort, tonight, rift, Khehem's blood.* Lourden gestured to Jherrick. The man peered at Jherrick. At last, he nodded and ducked back through the entryway. Retreating through the shadows, he left the screen up behind him, but they were not invited inside.

"You want him to escort us tonight?" Jherrick sidled up next to Lourden. "What did he say?"

"Ghilos is *Berounhim*, a caravanserai. He will take us where we need to go tonight. He is waking Astaniia and Lhosos to attend us as well. Astaniia will take point."

They did not have long to wait. The man returned with two others, all three bearing long razor-tipped black spears, and one wearing a pack. Without a word, the three stepped out from the abode and lowered the mat. The woman, Astaniia, made Jherrick's instincts prickle. She moved close, into his personal space. She looked up at him from her petite height, and Jherrick's breath ceased, astounded. Like gold melting inside a ring of fire, her irises caught the light from the abode's windows and blazed.

"*Khehemnas ehla veh?*" She said in a lilting accent. Her eyes searched his. They showed doubt. At last, she turned to Lourden and spoke in Khourek, and Jherrick caught the phrases, *he is not, Khehem, it will reject.*

Lourden stepped to her, and they had a brief argument. The spear-captain made an exasperated gesture. She glanced at Jherrick, crossed her arms. At last, she sighed. Throwing up her hands, she bit words back at Lourden, then beckoned to her group.

They strode off down the dark avenue.

"Come," Lourden seemed tired, but his face showed relief. "They will escort us."

He moved off after the *berounhim*. Jherrick and Aldris fell into step behind. Suddenly, in the night, a sound rang out, like an enormous war-bell struck with a crystal chime. The peal rang out over Ghellen's midnight streets, and the *berounhim* and Lourden stopped in their tracks.

"The Alranstone!" Lourden looked to the west in alarm. "Someone comes through!"

Lourden broke into a hard run to the west, weaving through domiciles. The *berounhim* were fast on his heels, Jherrick and Aldris only steps behind. Taking steps two at a time, the party raced up a spiral stair upon the edge of Ghellen's western wall from the *berounhim* quarter. Hundreds of feet up, they raced to the parapet, gazing down over the moonlit desert.

"*Ghesha hakkni, al'kholouet nef shriai!*" Lourden issued a stream of harsh words that could only have been curses. Far below, Jherrick could see a black stain spreading out from the Alranstone they had left just an hour prior. An enormous force was pouring through the Stone, eating up the moon-drenched white of the plaza beyond the causeway. Fighting erupted at the rim of the causeway, Lourden's *Rishaaleth*. Lourden cursed again. The throng teemed, over two thousand strong and growing, glittering black dots notable in the mass like stars fallen to earth.

"Scorpion-riders! The eel sends his dogs through again!" Lourden spun, seizing the *berounhim* woman by her weapons harness. "Take them to the cavern! Now!"

Her eyes went wide. She gave a short nod, then barked orders to her kinsmen. They pulled away, beckoning to Jherrick and Aldris with their spears.

"We can't leave if Lhaurent has come through!" Aldris rounded upon Lourden. "This is our time to fight as much as yours!"

"No!" Lourden gripped Aldris by the shoulders. "No. The eel does not come himself tonight. I would sense it. He has a feel to him, like a dark ocean. His dogs and scorpions are Ghellen's to fight, and fight we will tonight. You must live. Go with the *berounhim*. Find a way home, and cut the head from the one who destroys our peace. Go!"

Lourden shoved Aldris backwards. Aldris opened his mouth to speak, but Jherrick seized his arm. "Aldris. We have to go. Lourden's right. We can't get through that Plinth, and we have to stop Lhaurent's atrocities at their source. The only way we help Ghellen is by getting back to Alrou-Mendera. The only way we avenge Olea's death, is by living tonight."

Aldris' eyes brimmed with tears. He set his jaw, raked a hand through his hair. Rubbed a hand over his stubble, pale beneath the moon. "Go," he rasped at Lourden. "Save your city. Make Olea proud."

Lourden clapped him upon the shoulder, then Jherrick. And then he was gone, rushing down the stairs as fast as the desert wind.

The *berounhim* beckoned again. "No time. Come." The woman spoke in broken Menderian.

Jherrick reached out and gripped Aldris, giving him a shake.

The man nodded, raised his *shouf*. The ring of battle could be heard now, clashing through the thin air. Trotting fast, they ran along the wall, spurred by that sound. Misery twisted Jherrick's gut that they couldn't remain and fight, as they neared the southern portal of the city and descended a long staircase.

Moving swiftly, they were soon out the oasis gate, slipping through the desert night as the sounds of battle faded out to nothing behind them. Like wraiths, they paced the desert, following their guide and her two clansmen. The *caravanserai* was adept, choosing the firmest paths over the hard-packed plain by sight, not even needing to test for shifting sands and sinkholes with her long spear. Their swift trot ate distance, the desert shrouded in midnight silence. At times they halted to Astaniia's upraised fist, and then Jherrick saw hunting things slither across the dunes, through the arroyos. Jherrick watched the moon rise through the hours as he ran, its sickle bright over the barren desert. His boots fell now upon sand-swept stones, an ancient roadway far from Ghellen.

Guilt gripped his heart, and his thoughts turned to Olea as the road angled down, twisting into a narrow canyon. It had been foolish, a boy's dream, thinking that someday he could have taken her in his arms. Pulled back those laces and buckles until he could see her Blackmark upon bare flesh, until he could kiss that skin. And now she was gone. And Jherrick couldn't even stay to fight a battle against the forces of the man who had killed her.

Who threatened Ghellen and all their peaceful ways that Jherrick had come to love.

Walls of a tight canyon loomed unassailable around them now, scroll-worked from wind and time. The stars were barely visible above, twisted walls of the rift arching overhead. At last, their guide stopped them with an upraised fist. Jherrick blinked, seeing no change in the depths of the ravine, sheer to either side. But then he saw it. A slim crack in one wall, a sliver of darkness so complete that it ate the night, riven through the stone to their left.

"*Khala khen'eya taliminae vhris khoum. Hemne sacri a Werus et Khehem.*" Astaniia glanced at Jherrick, her movement barely noticeable in the darkness.

Jherrick understood enough to know that this was where their road ended. This was the cavern that was sacred to the Wolf and

Dragon of Khehem.

"*Shouf'ne elimriae bith kii. Caravanserai.*" Jherrick set a palm to his chest, bowed with respect to her, then to her two attendants, giving them deepest honor.

"*Mitha devanii alith hemna. Ne lengii.*" Astaniia flicked her fingers to her clansmen. Ghilos stepped forward and gave Aldris and Jherrick each a torch and some phosphor matches, then two packets of food. And then they moved off, opening water flasks.

Jherrick turned to Aldris, pulling down his *shouf*. "The *Berounhim* will go no further. They will wait here until tomorrow's nightfall for us."

"And then what?" Aldris soured. "They go back to Ghellen?"

"I believe so." Jherrick uncorked his water flask, drank, then ran a bit through his hair. Aldris did the same, then pulled his hood up. His eyes sought Jherrick, pale like wraiths in the shadowed night.

"Back they go to fight while we fucking run. Goddamn it."

"You know Lourden was right."

"I know. Fuckitall, I know. This is our path, as much as it rips me up inside." Aldris gestured at the crack. "On to glory, Khehemnas. Let's get this done and shank Lhaurent's ass. For Olea."

"For Olea."

Jherrick took a breath and stepped into the emptiness of the rift. It was utterly silent. As if the wind of the desert simply died inside the black crevasse, a grave-like stillness swaddled the space. He and Aldris paused to light torches, then moved on.

Jherrick's eyes darted to the shadows, his neck prickling with the feeling of being watched, just like he'd felt at the center of Khehem. The jagged walls of the rift suddenly came together, into undulating scrolls of white sandstone that formed a barricade. An edifice of wind and time, the dead-end rippled in the light, making it seem like it writhed. In the center of the scroll, a massive spar of obsidian taller than a man blocked their way. Carven with sigils, the obsidian was set with an enormous fire-opal that bled into the black glass like a naked, luminous heart. The obsidian continued up to the darkness above, lost to the heights.

"What now?" Aldris' voice from the utter silence made Jherrick startle.

Jherrick's hand strayed to Olea's longknives at his belt, feeling that press of being watched more than ever. He reached out to touch the fire-opal. A thrum rippled through him, a primal, animal thing. He had an urge to snarl, to roar, to scream or maybe tear his clothes from his body and fuck something in fury. The ripple passed, leaving him shaken, his skin tingling with an unnameable dread.

"Blood." He said simply.

Aldris gave him an eloquent look. "Why is it always blood with magic?"

"Because both are primal forces, unknowable, uncontainable. Uncontrollable." The words poured from Jherrick's lips as the thought entered his mind. It was as if something called, speaking through him, from beyond the black glass. He shivered again, and his thumb slipped over Olea's blade where he clutched it.

Aldris cocked his head, gazing at the obsidian, but then his eyes flicked to Jherrick's hand. "You've cut yourself, kid."

Jherrick lifted his thumb like a dreamer. Blood welled from a gash, trickling in a steady stream. It didn't even hurt until he looked at it, so keen were Olea's blades.

"Blood of Khehem, huh?" Aldris gave a dark chuckle.

"Something like that."

Jherrick pressed his cut thumb to the fire-opal. He felt a tremble pass through the stone, and then a sliding sensation gripped him. Jherrick's vision dimmed. His head felt light, his ears rang. The dysphoria passed as soon as it had come, but when the world straightened, the obsidian was simply not there anymore. Gone was the fire-opal with its black glass, as if the whole edifice had simply slipped sideways out of time.

From the other side, a luminous cavern of crystal beckoned.

Jherrick stepped in through the portal-way. All around him, crystal sang and beckoned. The cavern's ceiling soared, jagged with stalactites of quartz that tore down like fangs of the gods. They were met by towers of crystal jutting up from the ground, plinths of gargantuan height that dwarfed the men now walking in their midst. Passing colonnades, Jherrick could see himself reflected again and again, edges sharp and facets sheer as mirrors. From every jag and spike, an eerie light glowed, like phosphorus burning underwater. It seemed sometimes white, then ruby-tinged like a drop of blood in a chalice of water. Jherrick's heart gripped him, his gut churning with tension. That ghastly hue spoke of death on the pyre, of bleeding out upon the battlefield, of ripped and torn flesh.

Aldris followed, silent. The quiet inside the cavern was as engulfing as the black rift. And as Jherrick rounded a hummock of flowing quartz, the center of the grand room was suddenly revealed.

Jherrick stopped in awe, and horror.

Below, the cavern collected into an amphitheater, stalagmites flowing down to a level floor. Like some long-lost ocean had been sucked down to Halsos, the floor rippled like dry sand in concentric rings, until they contracted at last upon a plinth of pure light. A monument to hell and heaven both, it rose like a leviathan from the deep, luminous and ghastly. Even from a distance, Jherrick could see plumes of blood drifting through those pure facets, as if the inside of the Plinth was blood the crystal had drank, forever trapped.

The source of that taint was obvious. Surrounding the base of the crystal pillar, like some horrible sea, was a pool of blood. Thick, wet, crimson, it was the kind of blood that never dies, that remains ever-lasting, sweet as it once flowed from the open vein of some expiring thing.

"Halsos' fucking halls!" Aldris' curse summed it up nicely. "That... *thing*... is going to send us home? That's not like any Alranstone I've ever seen."

"I wouldn't make any assumptions about what it is, or what it'll do." Jherrick moved forward, drawn by a subtle pull to walk down the smooth crystal to that bloody lake.

"Is that thing producing the blood pool, or consuming it?" Aldris asked as they came to the slope where the crystal floor evened out and the ripples began. One hand had slipped to his knife, his face bloodless in the eerie light.

"Drinking it, I think. Over eons." Again, the knowledge popped into Jherrick's mind as if from somewhere else. A sliding sensation took him again and he blinked hard, shook his head to clear it.

Aldris' keen gaze snapped to him, and the guardsman's hand arrested Jherrick's forward movement. "You okay, kid?"

Jherrick drew slow breaths. The dizziness was worsening. "I don't think so. This place... it's doing something to me. For now, I'm just dizzy. I'll tell you if it gets worse."

"Blood of Khehem." Aldris' green gaze was piercing. "We don't have to go down there, Jherrick. I'll be damned if I let that fucker drink your blood. We can find another way home. Maybe if that Stone near Ghellen opened up tonight for—"

"I'm alright. We can't go back, Aldris. That Stone won't let us through. You know that as well as I. Come on, let's just do this." Jherrick took slow breaths, fighting the sliding sensation. They moved forward over the rippled floor, Jherrick resting a hand upon Aldris' shoulder for steadiness. At last, their boots reached the rim of the blood pool. Slick, the crimson sea stretched fifty feet from the Plinth in every direction, glassy as death.

Jherrick hunkered, inspecting it, his fingers skating above the surface.

"Kid, I wouldn't—" Aldris began.

Jherrick thrust his fingers in. He didn't let himself think about it, he just did it. But his fingers hit bottom, only his last knuckles immersed in the blood. Nothing happened. A ripple spread out in the pool, but that was all. The liquid was cool. The towering Plinth looked the same, luminous, inert. Jherrick immersed his whole hand, pressing his palm flat to the crystal floor beneath the blood. Nothing. He slid his hand forward, submerging his wrist. Still nothing.

"I think we have to touch the Plinth." He murmured.

"Right. Lemme just make a boat and sail the fucker through all this blood." Aldris snorted.

"I don't think it gets very deep." Removing his hand from the blood, Jherrick stood. He slid one boot into the pool. With cautious steps, Jherrick moved in. Sliding his boots along the smooth crystal floor beneath the crimson lake, Aldris at his heels, he found it smooth except for the ripples of the concentric rings.

The blood pool was shallow, only just rising above the ankles of his boots as they reached the Plinth. Stretching out a hand, Jherrick touched the crystal. The unmarred surface was smooth and vaguely warm. This close to the monstrosity, he could clearly see runnels of blood inside it, blooming through the faceted depths like poisonous jellyfish in a luminous sea. Aldris' hand had come to the crystal, too, and nothing was happening. Everything was the same, a riddle without answer.

Jherrick pressed his cut thumb to the crystal. Nothing. "Did you feel anything?"

"No." Aldris' answer was terse. "I didn't even feel anything as we moved through the blood."

"Neither did I." Jherrick craned his neck, gazing up at the crystal's heights. "It's as if this Plinth is dead. Like it can't see us at all." He narrowed his eyes, searching the pristine surface. "I don't see any sigils or symbols or anything. Whatever this thing is, no one's ever touched it with a chisel."

Pressing his palms to the crystal, Aldris began to recite Kingsman words for passage, and Jherrick joined in, but the crystal remained inert. Aldris made a sound like a snarling wolf, and his fist connected with the plinth. He grunted in pain and sank to a crouch, cradling his hand.

"Damn you!" Aldris shouted, wrathful green eyes raised to the Stone. "Give us passage you fucking piece of rock!"

Aldris' temper was not solving anything. Jherrick flipped his belt-purse open and pulled out Olea's clockwork, settling it in his palm. He could feel it. Not the weight of it, but a thrumming vibration, as if it waited for something. Jherrick went with his instinct, pressing the clockwork to the crystal. He removed his fingertips, thinking it would stick in place. It didn't, falling with a clatter into the crimson pool. The viscous liquid held the clockwork suspended on top. Jherrick bent to retrieve it, but his fingers accidentally pushed the clockwork in, submerging it in the blood.

A horrible sound suddenly consumed the cavern. Like legions of shrieking demons, the Alranstone screamed, and woke. The clockwork hurtled up from the blood. The pieces scattered in a maelstrom of hot wind and flung red droplets, surrounding the plinth in a spinning fury.

"Shit!" Aldris cursed. He threw a hand to his cheek, ducking out of the way of flying metal and blood. Jherrick did the same. He felt a slap as a piece of the clockwork hit his jerkin, then slid toward the crystal, tearing at his wrap. Blood leaked from a gash across Aldris' cheek. They both watched, horrified, as the pieces whirled above their heads in a gory vortex. Wind wailed with the screams of a thousand dying things as the pieces shuffled into unseen niches, marring the crystal all the way to its summit with glittering ore and dripping gore.

Where each piece of the clockwork settled, orbs of golden light suddenly snapped open, the crystal staring at them with thousands of eyes in every direction. Blood ran down the sides of the plinth in weeping lines, dripping from each shimmering eye. There were far more eyes than there had been clockwork pieces, but it was as if the metal had simply woken a creature, a key to summon the demon within.

Now, that beast was awake. And it wanted its due. The Alranstone suddenly concussed in a wave of power, blasting them backwards into the blood pool, coating them with the Blood of Khehem. In a clap of thunder and a howling of wind, Jherrick felt the pressure of a terrible oblivion seize him like fanged jaws. His insides compressed, his eyeballs squeezed until they would burst. Threaded through a nowhere space, his flesh turned to water all around him. And when it seemed he could take no more, he was quite suddenly *wrenched*. In a space that had no space, he felt his midsection twist, felt his spine break, felt his innards ripped apart.

Torn through the fabric of time itself, Jherrick was thrust out into endlessness.

CHAPTER 45 – THEROUN

The tree line up on the hillside swarmed with men and horses. General den'Ulthumen had marched the entire Menderian army out at Theroun's heels. Just three days behind, the puppet-General for the Khehemni Lothren had brought the entire Menderian corps. Thirteen thousand men, eight thousand of those mounted.

Pennants fluttered as a chill Highlands wind curled around Theroun and General Merra's army down upon the plain. The sun was high, armies facing each other in a standoff so silent Theroun could hear an eagle's cry above the river. Horses snorted, cats growled in their throats. The Elsthemi army was ten thousand all told, half of that on foot at the rear of the blockade. But they had the fiercer demeanor, all snarling cats and bristling warriors, and with Theroun's two thousand, the odds were nearly even.

Except Theroun's army had the keshari.

As he watched, a group broke from the Menderian line. General Lharsus den'Ulthumen, proud as a lion with his golden mane and shining helm, rode down at a walk with his loyal Captains. General Merra caught Theroun's eye. She nudged her snowy cat and it ambled forward, Theroun at her side upon his mean black ronin, their Captains spreading out in a chevron from their flanks.

They met in a tense standoff at the bottom of the hill. Menderian horses snorted and stomped, wild-eyed before the cats. Cats whipped their tails, mouths open to breathe the scent of soon-to-be-prey. Theroun's mean creature surged beneath him, ready to kill. Theroun checked his nasty black beast with a severe fist in its mane. It snarled, displeased, but held the line.

"Theroun." Lharsus gave a nod. "I see the Chancellate's warning about you turning traitor was well-advised. The two of you, however," he nodded to Arlus and Vitreal, "I didn't expect."

"Then you don't know us very well, Lharsus." Arlus sat tall upon his black war-horse. "Nor what's Inked upon our hearts."

Lharsus blinked. He covered it well, but Theroun saw. He hadn't known that some of his best captains had been Shemout Alrashemni. Theroun scoffed internally. Lharsus was nothing but a golden-helmed pawn. Evshein had told the man less than nothing about the game.

"Kingsmen." Lharsus spat. His gaze fixed upon Theroun. "What's your excuse for turning coat, Theroun?"

Theroun's black ronin gave a sour growl, as Theroun gave a viperous grin. "Come now, Lharsus. You thought the Black Viper wouldn't sink fangs into the Lothren? I know what Lhaurent says about me."

Lharsus narrowed his eyes. "What is it between the Castellan and you, Theroun? You could have been useful to us…"

Theroun turned his head and spat, disgusted by how den'Ulthumen didn't even bother pretending anymore that he was loyal to the nation rather than the Lothren. But then, all his Captains in this parlay were Lothren themselves.

"You'll find out soon enough how well being used by Lhaurent den'Karthus turns out," Theroun growled. "You think you receive orders from the Khehemni Lothren, Lharsus? From Evshein? Think again. Lhaurent pulls those strings. You may take your orders from Evshein and the Chancellate, but those days are numbered. Wait and see."

General Lharsus den'Ulthumen shifted uncomfortably upon his war-horse. "I have my orders today from the King-Regent, Theroun, not the Chancellate. And I will see you hang for your treason."

"*King-Regent?*" Theroun snarled, shocked. A slipping, cold sensation gripped him. "Our nation's not had a Regent in nearly five hundred years. Check your history tomes, Lharsus."

Lharsus coughed uncomfortably. "When the direct royal line is deceased, and the Chancellate unable to govern, then the King's Castellan assumes the duties of the Crown, as King-Regent. You know that as well as I. Until an appropriate assembly of Peers are sworn in as a new Chancellate."

Theroun felt himself go very still. Wind snapped pennants. His cat shifted beneath him. "*What did you say?*"

Lharsus could barely meet his gaze. "Castellan Lhaurent is now

King-Regent, Theroun. Until the Peers can meet and nominate a new Chancellate."

"What the fuck happened to the King's Chancellate?" Theroun's words were barely a whisper, but they sliced through the chill autumn air.

For the first time, Lharsus' visage showed fear. "They're dead. Throats slit to a man. In their beds. We had a runner yesterday. You were lucky to leave the Chancellate when you did, Theroun."

Theroun's side gripped, his gut was ice. "And now Castellan Lhaurent rules in Alrou-Mendera. And he sends the full force of your army in against Elsthemi war-cats. You can't win, Lharsus. Lhaurent has fucked you, just like he tried to fuck me. Though we're slightly less in numbers, we have the superior force. You know that. And I already took your vile little toys from you."

"You shouldn't overestimate your forces, Theroun." Lharsus' face had gone stony.

"And you shouldn't take orders from a traitor, Lharsus," Theroun countered. "Elyasin lives. She's in Lhen Fhekran. Healthy. And pissed that her nation has turned against her."

Den'Ulthumen blinked. His Captains shifted upon their mounts, their eyes flicking to their General, faces uncertain.

"It's true." General Merra Alramir spoke up. "I've over a hundred clan-leaders an' cat-riders who have seen her with their own eyes, who kin tell ye the same. Yer Queen lives, and is here of her own accord, allied with her King my brother."

Lharsus' Captains were vastly disquieted. They shifted upon their mounts, their horses paced. "Is it true, Theroun?" Captain Khellus den'Fern of the Fifth Cavalry called out. "Does Queen Elyasin live?"

"Would it make any difference?" Theroun barked, his gaze upon Lharsus. "Would you stand down, Lharsus, if this was not Queen Elyasin den'Ildrian's will? If you could have proof of her here, alive before you, in three days' time? Would you camp your forces in the forest and wait to see your Queen before you attack the nation that defends her?"

Lharsus held Theroun's gaze for a flicker of a moment. And then his eyes shied to the side. It was all the answer Theroun needed.

"Bought and paid for!" Vitreal den'Bhorus' vicious sneer echoed Theroun's thoughts. The man spit. "Fucking traitor, Lharsus!

You and the Castellan and *anyone who's with you!*" Vitreal's voice rang out, clarion and cutting. Lharsus' Captains paced upon their horses, acutely nervous.

General Lharsus den'Ulthumen's gaze had gone distant. As if he listened to music no one else could hear, his jaw went slack suddenly, his lips parting and eyes unfocused. It lasted so long, Theroun thought the man might have had a stroke right there upon his horse.

But then he blinked. His eyes snapped to Theroun, and something about their clear blue was dead. There was no more fear, no more indecision in that gaze. Lharsus held up a hand, quieting his Captains. "The Black Viper is a traitor. The Elsthemi and the Blackmarked speak lies. Our Queen is dead. If you will not surrender your forces and King Therel Alramir, then prepare to receive Menderian justice."

And with that, the parley was over. Lharsus wheeled his big war-horse and walked it away up the slope. One by one, his Captains followed, some spitting back at Theroun, some simply turning with veiled mistrust in their eyes. Even Khellus den'Fern wheeled his horse, though he lingered to the last.

"You'll fall, Theroun." Khellus said, almost respectfully. "You think you have the advantage against Lharsus, but even without the poisons—" His words cut off suddenly. His eyes bulged. He made a gasping sound as if he was choking. A shiver went through his entire body, his face set in a rictus of pain. And just as suddenly, it was over. His gaze went blank. Khellus looked away, guiding his horse up the slope without a backwards glance.

"Fucking odd." Vitreal sneered next to Theroun. "It's like he was—"

Theroun held a hand up, cutting his Captain off. Far up the tree line, a man had ridden his black charger to the front of the Menderian forces. A man in black herringbone-weave leathers, his gaze piercing down the ridge like talons, his dark eyes fixed upon Khellus den'Fern as the Menderian Captain rode back up the slope.

"See him, there?" Theroun spoke low, as Merra sidled her cat close.

She gave a hiss of breath. "A herringbone fucker. One'a them has been picking off my hunting parties that supply the army these past weeks. I had a report passed on from a messenger of Elyasin's that snuck over the border. He saw one'a them riding a massive *scorpion* of all things, slaughter forty of my men. My outriders have seen them in the mountains now an' again these past ten years, clashed some. Never been able ta catch one, though. Whoever they are, they're a sneaky, vicious lot."

"I've seen two in the Menderian camp. They made men forgetful just by looking at them."

"What in blazes?" Merra growled.

As Theroun watched, four other men in identical herringbone-weave leathers moved through to the front, sitting tall upon muscled black steeds. And then a sixth came forward, riding a monstrosity of glittering black chitin. An enormous scorpion, tail arched high over the man who rode its back, claws clacking and shining like black diamonds in the sun. Fetishes had been braided around the scorpion's claws and tail, and as Theroun squinted his eyes against the sun's glare, he saw they were made of red, orange, and blonde human hair. Elsthemi hair. Horses at the front of the line shied away from the evil creature, but the men soothed their beasts with dead eyes.

"The scorpion rider!" Merra hissed. "Fucking *hells*?!"

Something horrible went sliding through Theroun as he surveyed those six men in herringbone leathers and the tall scorpion rider. As he watched Menderian men treat that scorpion like the most normal thing upon the battlefield, hardly worthy of a second glance. Gazing at the Menderian forces upon the hillside, he suddenly saw their army form up as one. Perfect, unshakeable. Every pair of eyes looked down upon the Elsthemi with a chill animosity that hadn't the look of men in war. A dominant snarl rode every face, a cold disdain. A look of utter destruction, a knowing that their enemy was already vanquished, was duplicated upon the faces of an entire army.

Theroun's gut turned to water. Instinct screamed within him, that he faced something far worse than he could ever imagine.

"Back to the line." Theroun spoke suddenly. "Form up. Quickly. Central faction retreats when they charge. Left flank will circle up and hem them to the east, cut them off from the woods. Drive them down to the river and the center faction will push. We

643

pin them in the Valley of Doors. And then slaughter the fuck out of them. Round up archers to pepper the men in black armor, and that scorpion, with arrows from a distance."

Merra nodded a quick approval to the plan, then barked to her Captains as to who would take which section. Before she could turn away, Theroun gripped her arm, making her sidle her cat close as he growled low. "If this battle turns, if you see it going sour for any reason, run. Don't think. Run. Gather as many clans as you can and head for Lhen Fhekran. Don't look back. And whatever you do, *do not* make eye contact with those men in black leathers."

General Merra's eyes narrowed. But whatever she saw in Theroun made her nod in silent understanding. Theroun saw her true now, fierce, capable. And aware that their army was perhaps already lost, though she had no idea why.

"Rhone, Rhennon, Jhonen!" Merra barked to her Captains. "Form up! We fight this day! But if you start to even see a *breath* of a rout, ride your forces immediately for Lhen Fhekran! My orders will not be gainsaid!"

"Yes, my General!" Jhonen barked, though her eyes whipped to Theroun.

"Yes, my General!" The brothers echoed.

As one, their group turned, riding back to the Elsthemi line. But as they did, Arlus and Vitreal sidled their mounts close to Theroun.

"Watch your men," Theroun spoke to them. "Pull them out if things go bad. Head up the valley to Lhen Fhekran. I can't say how, but I think we're about to fight for our lives, gentlemen."

"Yes, General." Arlus boomed softly. Vitreal echoed it, his voice holding no sneer for once.

Re-gaining the edge of the Elsthemi forces, there was a pause as they faced the mass of men upon the hillside. And then like a single organism, the Menderian soldiers drew breath, and screamed. Rattling shields, lofting swords, they screamed like they held a single mind. A vast organism, a surge like a furious hive of hornets.

And then they broke, flowing down the hill in a seething tide.

The clash was fierce at the base of the hill. One moment, cats charged Menderian horses, and then there was chaos. Blood slit the air. The sharp smells of shit and piss hit Theroun's nostrils.

Everything tunneled in as he fought like a madman at General Merra's side. Their cats were dervishes of death. Leaping, swiping, crunching necks of horses in their powerful jaws, Theroun's black bastard and Merra's white ghost held nothing back. They adopted a tight circle in the melee, continuing 'round nose to tail, Merra lancing out with her polearm, spearing with vicious precision, Theroun just as deadly with his sword.

Everything was a red rage. Theroun's heartbeat was fast, his breath heaved. He swiped with his momentum, controlling his energy, making this first flush of battle-fever last as long as possible. Some part of his commander's mind was aware of the larger movements as the battle raged. Merra and Jhonen's keshari had begun to subtly retreat, enacting Theroun's plan, enticing the entire Menderian army forward off the hillside. Rhone and Rhennon had run their cat-legions up the eastern flank, now penning the Menderian army in from the east and forcing them either down from hill or off the western cliffs, a sheer drop to the Valley of Doors below. The brothers were trying to take the Menderian's rear-guard and cut them off from the trees, get the entire Menderian army to flow down from the hill to the west and become trapped by the river.

It was working. Whatever mass-mind the men in herringbone leathers had created within the Menderian forces, they cared little about being hemmed in. Horses were flowing down the hill, hitting the river, getting pushed back now as Theroun and Merra and Jhonen began to press. Getting pushed into the blind-end cliffs of the Valley of Doors with its slippery shale footing. Pressing the Menderians deeper into the wide flats of the summer-low river, the Elsthemi army gradually hemmed the Menderians into that sundering chasm.

Fighting hard, covered in gore, Theroun's eyes darted between assailants to the cliffs. Raising high above in the gargantuan cul-de-sac, they cornered the Menderians in now, studded with thousands of doors carven into the rock. Theroun's arm ached. The old wound in his side screamed red misery. His body burned from blade-nicks as he clashed again and again beside Merra, as she used the strongest keshari riders in the center to push the Menderians back and back and back.

The cul-de-sac of the Valley of Doors was broad, the shale-flats of the gorge sliding beneath hooves and paws. Horses panicked, rearing upon that unsteady surface, but the cats crept onward by leaps and sure-footed bounds, pushing the Menderians into the cliff-blind. Ancient doors rose high upon the cliffs, all around the two armies that fought in their vast embrace. Doors with Ghreccan lintels stood strong down below. Doors of pyramidal shape were carven higher up, with no staircases to achieve their ingress. Five hundred feet up the cliff's sides, Theroun could barely make out doors of fantastic gargoyles and massive black runes that flowed like honey, impossible to the eye.

But Theroun had no time to ponder. He could only appreciate the ancient site for its tactical advantage. Shale turned red underfoot, bodies tainted the river's flow. Theroun could feel the rout starting. The Menderians had larger numbers, but Elsthemen had the stronger force. The Menderian army was pinned in the vast amphitheater with nowhere to run but fleeing across the river to the same shale-flats upon the far side, or tail it back down the chokepoint of the gorge with its precarious road.

Captains den'Pell and den'Bhorus barreled in upon their horses with Jhonen and her cat between them, taking down a knot of Menderian fighters. Giving Merra and Theroun a moment to breathe, Theroun surveyed the melee.

Suddenly, he saw an entire section of fighting near the river pause. Over two hundred Elsthemi horse-riders had suddenly ceased fighting. Like a nightmare, Theroun saw something he'd never seen in war. Five men in herringbone-weave leathers stepped to the front of that quiescent section. As one, all five raised their left hand and touched their smallest finger to their thumb. Elsthemi clansmen turned their blades. And in utter silence, buried their blades in their own necks.

Men went down, gurgling. Two hundred Elsthemi slipped from their saddles and plunged to the ground, blood spewing from their throats as their horses panicked and reared.

The line of herringbone-clad men advanced.

Theroun's gut turned to liquid. "Captains!!" He roared. Arlus and Vitreal killed their marks, turned. Theroun pointed with his sword at the Unaligned men. Horrific, the scene repeated in another section of his army, two hundred more men going down in a red wash of suicide. Theroun felt the battle turn, as countless Elsthemi near enough to see began to fear.

"RETREAT!!" General Merra's roar was deafening. Blowing three tones hard on a gilded battle-horn, she made a circling gesture with her polearm. Spattered in blood, her visage was furious. Her white cat was crimson with gore, and it leapt up to a mound of corpses so she could be seen.

"RETREAT!" She bellowed again.

Elsthemi horns blared among the keshari riders, sounding the retreat. Two hundred more Elsthemi went down, half of them keshari riders this time. They were losing the river. Menderians were pouring up the bank and circling around, pinning their flank. Hemming the Elsthemi into the Valley of Doors now, rather than the other way around.

Another wave went down, three hundred this time.

Theroun's cat followed Merra's as they streaked to the outlet of the amphitheater, Merra's keshari elite rushing in to forestall the Menderian maneuver. Men screamed, throats were torn. Theroun's cat was a demon, snarling and lashing out. Fighting for their lives, their knot of two hundred elite fighters nearly had the river secured.

Until the line of herringbones advanced again. Theroun felt an imperious command ease through his mind from their hard stares. Like a smooth line of silver spidersilk slipping into his thoughts, it made him suddenly doubt his purpose. His purpose as a warrior, as a man. Doubt himself as a fighter, doubt that he could make any difference here at all. Wonder what all this fighting was for.

Wonder, if it wouldn't it be nicer to simply die.

To kill himself.

Theroun went motionless, trapped in that idea. Two hundred keshari riders around him did the same. General Merra was quiet at his side, staring at the men in herringbone leathers, arrested by their mind-control. Cats snarled and lashed out, but without their rider's directions, they were only mean, not coordinated. Yowls of distress went up around Theroun. Cats circled, uncertain, riders upon their backs stock-still.

Theroun saw the four men raise their left hands.

And suddenly, rage surged through him.

He was the Black Viper, dammit.

"Not today!" Theroun roared. Taking his vicious ronin-cat by the mane, he hauled it to the side, close enough to seize Merra's battle-horn. Theroun blew it hard in a pattern of three, then again. Keshari riders jolted all around him. Already lifting weapons to their throats, their gazes broke from the herringbone-clad men.

"RIDE!!!" Theroun roared with all the fury in his soul. "Ride for the Highlands! Ride and live!!"

Eyes came alive, their wills returned. The cats felt that surge and knew what it meant. Turning tail en masse, the cats wheeled and ran. Like lightning streaking through storm clouds, they swiped and gnashed their way out of the Valley of Doors.

Catching up to the rear-guard yet upon the grasslands, Merra's elite had been saved, but all was devastation behind them. The Elsthemi horse-clans pinned in the Valley were lost. Only keshari riders had escaped, the cats three times faster than any horse. Hauling up foot-soldiers from the rear of the line, they rode hard. A force of three hundred keshari broke from the valley, a handful of horse-clans at the rear of the battle hard on their heels, perhaps a thousand fighters in all.

The rest were lost.

Theroun crouched over the back of his black ronin, feeling its rageful snarl, knowing that anguish. Merra rode hard at this side. Grim, her eyes raked their party, taking in who still lived. Jhonen rode to Merra's left. Rhone and Rhennon were not there. Neither was Arlus. Vitreal rode a dappled cat to Theroun's right, clinging behind a slight Elsthemi warrior-lass with grim determination, his horse gone.

Vitreal glanced over. His green eyes were pure fury.

Suddenly, something massive came thundering down from the hill. Slamming into the knot of riders, it carved a path straight for Theroun. Cats roared and hissed away from the chittering black monstrosity. The man riding the scorpion's broad back leveled his two-handed broadsword at Theroun's head. Cats broke around the scorpion, streaking away from it. Vitreal's cat shied away, and Theroun was suddenly face-to-face with the enormous scorpion rider in black herringbone leathers.

"Theroun!" He heard Merra's roar.

"Leave me!" Theroun bellowed back.

"Ride!" Merra's answering snarl was easily heard. "Ride ta Lhen Fhekran! Ride yer cat ta death!"

Keshari warriors bent low over their cats, streaking away with horse-clans following hard.

Theroun was suddenly left alone, face-to-face with the imperious bastard upon his clicking black beast. Theroun's ronin circled the clattering creature, hissing as silence settled around them. Theroun's cat roared, taking a swipe. The monstrous scorpion skittered sideways, Elsthemi hair-fetishes around its claws and tail rippling as it lashed out with a pincer. Theroun's cat dodged. Arcing its tail, the scorpion shifted, striking and missing as Theroun's cat darted back. That barbed tail flashed and flashed again, Theroun's nasty ronin cat anticipating each strike with uncanny speed.

The men upon their backs faced off as their creatures began a vicious dance, the scorpion chittering, Theroun's black bastard growling. A snarl rippled Theroun's visage, his sword ready, a longknife in his other hand. The scorpion rider in black herringbone leathers smiled, a gruesome leer upon his thick lips, his sword paused in his hands. His hood thrown back, his face was broad with high, cutting cheekbones like his comrades, and silver-streaked waves of brown hair. Broad-shouldered and tall, his manner was cutting yet elegant, and he guided his scorpion without reins or saddle. His armor was made entirely of studded leather with blackened iron buckles, its herringbone weave artful. Beneath heavy dark brows his gaze pressed Theroun, taunting, arrogant, an amused glint in his dark eyes as their creatures faced off.

You think I can be bested, General? The thought came knifing into Theroun's mind.

"I don't care if you can be bested," Theroun growled, "but I care how many of my fighters live today. The longer I keep you here, the longer they run."

Noble of you, Black Viper. An awful curl of dominance twisted the man's thick lips. *Yes, I know you, Theroun. Think back. Where have you seen me before?*

And like someone had turned Theroun's mind into a deck of cards, his memories were suddenly being shuffled through. They flashed before him, riffled, sorted, until one memory stood out from the rest. Theroun felt his raging fever once more. He saw himself, looking out through his own eyes, kneeling before the bodies of his slaughtered family in that bloodstained command tent. He felt himself stumble up, clutching his ruined side, blood and putrid fluids seeping through the filthy bandage as he swiped the tent-flap away, blinded by the scorching summer sun.

Men stood idle in the dusty camp upon the Aphellian Way, looking down, not meeting Theroun's wretched gaze. His Captains and Lieutenants paused around the map table, watching him. The table had been moved outside under a silk awning rather than keep it in the gruesome environs of the command-tent. Theroun had still not let his families' bodies be touched for burial, though three sweltering days had passed. Rot and shit and the copper tang of blood lingered in Theroun's nostrils, along with the putrefaction of his own wound, unable to heal because Theroun would not rest.

One of his best Captains, Aerundahl den'Behrn, stepped away from the command-table. Sweat-streaked and disheveled from fighting, he approached Theroun like one might a rabid animal, his blood-spattered jerkin and filthy shirt unbound in the heat of the day, his black Inkings plain to see.

"General Theroun, sir. Red Valor have broken the barricade of the Twenty-Fourth cavalry. They're routing us at Devil's Gorge. Captain den'Nerrae and I would like to send in the cavalry lancers." Aerundahl waited at attention, hands clasped behind his back.

"Trying to steal my army, Kingsman?" Theroun's voice was hateful, grating with pain and fever, as he heard it again in his memory.

"Sir?" Aerundahl den'Behrn startled, his eyes roving over Theroun, his black brows knit in concern. One hand lifted, raking sweat-thick black curls away from his face. "General Theroun, sir! We just thought with your wound, you should be—"

"No one steals my family from me! And no one steals my army!" Theroun's roar was a tainted thing. A longknife was in his hand. His hand trembled, spasmed from pain, from rage, from fever-heat.

The Kingsman before him shrank back. "No, General, I didn't —"

Over the man's shoulder, off in the dusty mirage of the afternoon, a motion caught Theroun's attention. A tall, robust fellow idled near one heat-rifled pavilion, arms crossed over his chest. He wore leathers in a herringbone weave, black as sin and studded with silver. No one seemed to notice his presence in the uncertain crowd now gathering. The man with thick lips and cutting cheekbones smiled. A thought went knifing through Theroun's fever-addled mind. *He killed your family. Him and all his kind. Traitorous Kingsmen.*

"Traitorous Kingsmen." The words fell from Theroun's lips.

Before he knew it, his hand flashed out, fast as a viper. Aerundahl's neck opened up, sluicing red over his stark black Inkings. His eyes were wide as he buckled to his knees. Theroun met the eyes of the man in herringbone leathers as his Captain went down. The man smiled a ruthless, dominant smile.

And then he was gone.

Theroun blinked, thrust back to the present moment. His black ronin still circled the scorpion, growling low, though they were no longer testing each other. The man in herringbone leathers watched Theroun, a half-smile upon his face.

"*You!*" Theroun breathed.

"Yes, I was there." The man's voice grated like gravel in a mill-wheel. "I began it all. Your glorious career. You should thank me, really. Now the name Black Viper is known far and wide. My people, the Brethren of the Kreth-Hakir, laud you as one of the most formidable warriors of the last Age. Men aren't made like you anymore. It's a shame the one we treat with wants you dead. I would have recruited you to our ranks myself."

"If Lhaurent den'Karthus wants me," Theroun snarled, "he should have come to get me."

"He is busy elsewhere." The big man upon the scorpion laughed. "I would almost like to bring you back alive! Watch the two of you fight it out. See who is the better master."

"I would best him." Theroun growled.

"Don't be so sure of it." The big man's eyes narrowed upon Theroun. "But I'm afraid that shall not come to pass, Black Viper. Your journey ends here. Savor it, your life. Take a final breath in upon your tongue and ready yourself for death. It was an honor to do battle with you. Lhaurent den'Alrahel sends his regards."

Theroun felt the man's mind slam into his. Like a battering-ram, it left no door in Theroun's mind closed. Flaying him open, it wrested his body from his control. His right arm spasmed, gripping the hilt of his longknife hard in his fist. The blade was up to his throat before Theroun could blink, piercing towards his flesh.

A vast rage blossomed in Theroun suddenly, that this was what his life had come to. That this was how he ended, not even in battle. Suicide, a death of ignominy, with no consequence and no honor.

A death ordered by Castellan Lhaurent.

Rage flooded Theroun, triggering his old wound. His entire body shuddered, spasming, muscles gripping and releasing. His hand missed its mark, slipping the longknife over his shoulder, gouging leather and shoulder there rather than his neck. Bright pain from the cut made Theroun's rage erupt further, a volcano of molten fury.

Before he knew it, something had slammed shut in his mind, smashing the Kreth-Hakir out.

With a roar, Theroun threw the longknife. It buried in the Kreth-Hakir's chest, that woven leather armor not strong enough to withstand Theroun's fury. The man's eyes met Theroun's, wide with surprise, as his thick hand went to the blade's hilt. Satisfaction blossomed in Theroun, nourishing his rage, feeding its forge-bright sparks.

"You can deliver *that* to Lhaurent," Theroun snarled. "With my regards."

The man slumped over his scorpion, coughing blood. The scorpion made a lunge for Theroun's cat. But the mean black ronin countered, swiping in, seizing the scorpion by one massive claw and crunching down with fangs in chitin. The black monstrosity made a shrieking sound like a lobster in the pot, stabbing with its tail as the cat darted sideways. The cat flashed in again, raking the creature's eyes, biting at the second claw, severing it.

The arched tail flashed down in a death-strike.

But Theroun was fast with his sword, lopping off the scorpion's tail with a mighty cut. The creature shrieked, shuddered. The man in black was tossed from its back to lay inert in the tall grass, tarry with the creature's black blood. Theroun's ronin gave a wicked scream, lunging in to savage the scorpion by the face, finishing it.

The glittering creature shuddered its last. The man in herringbone-weave leathers lay motionless in the grass, bleeding out. Theroun yanked his cat's mane, and they streaked away up the valley, towards Lhen Fhekran.

CHAPTER 46 – ELYASIN

Therel raged about the royal suites, pacing like a caged wolf. First to the fireplace, then to the table and back again. Elyasin's husband had been drinking too much these past days and eating little. He'd not touched his meal this morning, but had a silver goblet of wine to hand yet again. Elyasin watched him from the breakfasting table, her own eggs and roast boar barely eaten. Crisp autumn sunshine flooded in through the gabled windows, one open to permit a brisk breeze. Their suites held a war-council this morning. Comprised of the monarchs, Ghrenna, Thaddeus, and Luc, the council was more frustration than planning.

Just as it had been for the past three days since Ghrenna's startling arrival.

"My lieges. You *must* change your course of action, now." Ghrenna spoke determinedly. "As I've told you these past few days. You have no options. This war cannot be won by might of armies. Please. Set your most competent Generals at the front to manage the war for you. We must focus on moving immediately into finding Elohl, getting him back here, and unraveling where we all must go to work the Rennkavi's rituals."

Ghrenna sat at the breakfasting table with Elyasin, clad in her black leathers and a clean set of white snowhare furs. An exhausted impatience rode her today. Her cheeks were drawn as if she hadn't been eating, her lovely eyes darkened as if she'd barely slept. She had argued her point about turning over the war-campaign for three days, and Therel had raged against it, and still they were no closer to resolution.

Thaddeus hovered at the desk, the table piled with old parchments and tomes he'd found in the Lhen Fhekran vaults and crypts, anything and everything that mentioned the Brother Kings or Morvein. His slender arms were crossed, and he lipped at his spectacles, his eyes darting between his lieges. Thad had proven indispensable in the conversation about Morvein and the Brother Kings, recalling arcane scrolls he'd seen in Roushenn, determinedly unearthing everything that could be found pertaining to any angle of their situation, be it even the most obscure fae-tales.

Luc lounged against one wall with his arms crossed, watching Ghrenna with veiled eyes and a frightening intensity. Elyasin had noted how Luc had been undone by Ghrenna when she'd first arrived at court. She'd seen the ripple of anger in Luc's shoulders from Ghrenna's rebuff, the bitter twist of love lost in his every movement. Since then, he'd become guarded, watching Ghrenna's every move with flinty green eyes. When Elyasin had asked him about it, he'd laughed it off, saying *she's someone I once knew, that's all.* But he'd asked to be present at every negotiation, and Elyasin had granted it.

The tension between Luc and Ghrenna simmered. Him, hot and scathing, her cool and avoidant. Therel paced, enough frustration on his own to boil the entire room. Thaddeus fidgeted. Exhaustion filled Elyasin. Sighing, she rubbed her aching scar. Tumultuous dreams had plagued her, ever since Ghrenna's arrival. Of Morvein copulating with the Brother Kings by turns. One man fiery of nature, the other somber like a full moon night. Last night's dream cascaded over her skin, a creeping pleasure of sex, power, and lust she couldn't entirely shake.

Suddenly, Elyasin's vertigo tilted her again. Her view sharpened upon a tall man with owl-feathers braided in his white hair, with silver, purple, and white Inkings cascading over his lean body. Elyasin blinked, realizing she was looking at Therel but seeing Delman Ferrian bound to the silver pendant upon Therel's breast. The shock of seeing Delman superimposed upon her King was overwhelming. Elyasin had one horrible moment of feeling like she gazed at mirror after mirror in a trick-hall. She turned away and promptly leaned over her knees, gritting her teeth to keep her breakfast from choking up.

Luc den'Lhorissian came quickly to her side, fussing over her with his healing hands. Reaching out, he settled a palm to her forehead, then slid one behind her neck. Sunlight lit his golden waves and short beard ablaze as his mercy poured into Elyasin's skull. They'd found that Luc's ministrations could keep the vertigo at bay, and both Therel and Elyasin had been having five or sometimes six ministrations a day in order to keep their pendants on.

Elyasin opened her ears, keeping an ear on the raging conversation.

"You're asking me to abandon the campaign at the Menderian border." Therel turned to Ghrenna with a snarl. "Abandon my country, my clans, my own sister! What kind of King does such a thing?!"

"One who knows wisdom." Ghrenna argued, cold and dispassionate. "There is a larger fate befalling this continent, King Therel, and you either prepare for it or die upon the battlefield along with all your kin."

"But my clans hold the border." He eyeballed her with his ice-blue gaze, quaffed a large swallow of wine. "The Menderian cavalry are no match for keshari."

"Therel. Please." Ghrenna took a long breath. "In Morvein's time, the Elsthemi were fiercer than any fighters any land had ever seen. But when chaos swept our continent, even they began to fall. Even the might of the Brother Kings, the greatest warrior-mages in Elsthemen's history, was not enough to turn the battles to their favor. Something opposed them, something horrible…" Ghrenna rubbed her temples, as if she had a headache. "Something I've been trying to remember that decimated them battle after battle, until there was no hope left without the coming of the Rennkavi."

"So ask your precious Brother Kings." Therel snorted.

"I've *told* you." Ghrenna's voice was tense. "They are as ghosts to me right now. Wearing my pendant protects me from their minds. I feel vague sensations of them, but little more. I cannot speak with them right now, cannot ask them such questions."

"So take it off." Therel snorted, refilling his wine from a carafe upon the table. Elyasin's vertigo had waned, and she waved Luc off, who took up a post near her, his arms crossed.

"No." Ghrenna sighed. "You and I both know there is one in your palace I cannot trust. Adelaine is cunning. She has already tried thrice to re-weave Thaddeus' mind so she can keep her ears on every conversation we have."

Ghrenna rubbed her neck, twisted it. Her jaw was set, her cerulean eyes tight as if her head plagued her. Elyasin saw Luc shift.

Arms crossed, he rubbed his biceps with his hands. An agonized look haunted his eyes, as if he wanted to go to Ghrenna, though he kept his place by Elyasin.

"This choice you face was not dissimilar for the Brother Kings," Ghrenna continued. "They also found it difficult to leave their country behind, when the time came. But so the Nightwind calls, to all of us. I'm beginning to recall Morvein's life, more and more. She traveled hard through the Alranstones, collecting snippets of folklore and arcane verse about the Rennkavi. Even unto Jadoun and Perthe she went, searching for broken bits of the Prophecy. And the Prophecy is clear; without the Rennkavi, not only does the golden age not come, but *everything* falls to a dark and terrible ruin."

"The Nightwind." Thad cleared his throat by the desk. "Lhesher and I unearthed an interesting codex down in the Metholas Crypt beneath the palace yesterday. An entire box of them, really, written in High Alrakhan. They're poetic, but I believe they refer to Morvein. *Thus did the Nightwind sweep through the Stones and over the land, seeking her destiny. From the glaciers she returned in glory, the Mist of the Dawn binding her at last. And so she returned through the opened Heldim Alir, the Way Under the Mountain. And thence she brought her Sun and Moon, her Dragon, and the child of the Dawn, to wreck glory and destruction, for the Nightwind breaks all to make the world anew. There it was that she Bound her Beloveds, forever in the Ring of White. And now the Nightwind sleeps, until her time to unleash her storms comes again. I, Metholas Leifne, now commit the Lay of the Nightwind, here in its entirety. What follow are accounts of her Gale. For I was there, and I alone survived her destruction at the Ring. And now Scorpions gather upon Dhelvendale, and all fall prey to their strike. Shaper save us.*"

The whole room fell silent. Thad cleared his throat. "The rest of the codices contain riddles, diagrams, drawings, and writings in a language I cannot read. There are a few maps. I poured over them at length, but left them be down in the crypt. They were far too delicate to move. One crumbled as I read it. But I have them solid in my mind."

"*The Nightwind breaks all to make the world anew?*" Therel's gaze was cutting. "This Metholas didn't have a very high opinion of Morvein."

But Ghrenna had gone ashen. Her gaze was pinned to Thaddeus. Her unholy blue eyes teared, and when she blinked her lashes, tears shed down her cheeks. "Metholas! How you suffered, seeing it all burn! Forgive me...! Would that you had died with the rest of us..."

Prickles of wariness cascaded up Elyasin's spine as she watched Ghrenna, as if a specter had spoken from beyond the grave. Elyasin took up a wine goblet and drank. She was about to query Thad further, when the doors to their suite suddenly burst open. Elyasin had expected the belligerent Adelaine, not invited to this meeting, but it was Lhesher Khoum who hurtled in, grim. And just behind him, strode two warriors Elyasin had never expected to see side-by-side.

General Merra Alramir, filthy with blood and battle. Striding in next to Chancellor Theroun den'Vekir, the Black Viper himself. Blood coursed down Theroun's face from a nasty set of claw-scratches, his short iron-blonde hair thickened into a crest from sweat. His lightweight battle-leathers were ruined from not only blood, but also a tarry substance, and a shoulder wound had been hastily bandaged.

"Lhen Fhekran is under siege." Theroun barked curtly, his blue eyes piercing Elyasin, his battle-lined face set in a hard scowl. "We have hours before the entire Alrou-Mendera host comes swarming up over the palisades. And believe me, my lieges, you do not want to be here when they do."

"Chancellor Theroun!" Elyasin blinked in shock, rising from her seat.

"Merra! Our border? Our keshari?" Therel's words were harsh, his knuckles white as he gripped the back of a chair. At a bitter glance from General Merra, Therel sank into the chair, all fight taken from him. One hand came to his lips. "*Lost?!*"

"Therel," Merra's voice was tired as she moved forward. "General Theroun speaks true. We have to get you out of here. You and Elyasin. The Menderians have a weapon we cannot best. A cadre of men clad in foreign armor in a herringbone weave. Therel, you recall my reports that our scouts have seen them in the mountains these past years, but I did not truly know their purpose until today. They twist minds. They turned our fighters' blades against their own throats, Therel, two hundred at a time. If it hadn't been for Theroun, and for the cats, none of us would have made it home. As it is, we have only three hundred cats, and four hundred horse. The horse will be along, they're taking a mountain-route ta be safe. But our rear-scouts tell us Menderians are swarming up the valley as fast as they can gallop. They're killing their horses ta get to us, taking new mounts in every damn village, riding longer than the cats can run to make up the time. And the main body of their host is less than a day behind the riders. Maybe ten to twelve thousand in all. We have hours until the riders are at our walls. Maybe less."

Elyasin sank to her chair. A fell wind blew through her. Her eyes met Chancellor Theroun's. "Is all lost, Theroun?"

Theroun sank to one knee, wincing in pain, though he hid it well. "Not as long as you and King Therel live. We had a strong advantage, but we barely escaped with our lives. We have lost the border, my Queen. And we will lose Lhen Fhekran. Presently. This mind-power of the men in herringbone leathers... it is nothing we can best."

"Is it certain?" Elyasin breathed.

"It is." Theroun did not mince words, his gaze final.

"Sweet Aeon." Thaddeus spoke by the desk. Theroun's gaze snapped to Thad, and a slight smile lifted his lips to note his scribe there, before he was once again hard as a blade.

"Where can we take you, my lieges?" Theroun's gaze flicked from Elyasin to Therel. "Where is a safehouse no one would know to come looking for you, until this danger is past?"

"There is nothing." Therel growled. "Lhen Fhekran is sits upon an exposed hillside. Our only option is to break from the city and head south, into the mountains."

"Menderian forces would quickly follow," Theroun barked. "Something about these Kreth-Hakir, for that is what the mind-bending men call themselves, allow them to push horses nearly as fast as cats. You'd be soon caught in the mountains. Where else?"

Therel stared at Theroun, incredulous. "There is nothing else. Our palisade..."

"Will not hold their forces." Theroun growled, his blue eyes dire. "These Kreth-Hakir will break the minds of your men upon the gates. They will open the doors and let your enemies walk in, without any fighting at all. The same will happen if you barricade yourself inside the palace. *Think*, King of Elsthemen. There must be somewhere we can take you and Queen Elyasin."

A tense silence settled in the room. Elyasin saw her King and husband's eyes go tight, snarl and defeat in his ice-blue gaze.

"Tunnels lead out from beneath Lhen Fhekran." Thad spoke suddenly, shattering the silence. "Secret tunnels Morvein once used. The Heldim Alir, the Way Under the Mountain. Metholas mentions them in those codices I found. He mapped them. One leads out from this very foundation, my lieges."

"Tunnels?" Therel shot Thad a confused look. "You must be mistaken. I know this palace like—"

"The door of runes," Thad continued, holding the King's gaze, "in the southern wall down in the Heat Pools. Metholas was very specific. That wall leads to a tunnel, which connects to a vast network that goes deep into the Kingsmountains. Among them, is the way to this Ring of White Kenthos mentioned. Which I believe, is the place Ghrenna must go to work the Rennkavi's ritual."

Ghrenna shuddered, memories slipping into place with a terrible feeling of certainty as the scribe spoke. "Thaddeus is right. We must take these tunnels. They will lead us to the location of the Rennkavi's binding ritual."

"Ritual?" Merra's gaze sharpened upon Therel.

"From my dreams." Therel murmured, his visage bleak, tormented.

Merra's eyes went wide. And then she became fierce. "Therel. Take Elyasin and go. If all is lost here… then we need magic. Your dream has that. Vast, powerful magic. I was never the one with magic between the two of us. You are. Go do what you were born to do, brother. Go to the tunnels. Get us something stronger than these Kreth-Hakir. Find the ancient magic of Elsthemen, and save your people. For if you do not… we will surely fall."

Therel was silent. A long moment passed between brother and sister. At last, Therel took a deep breath, then looked to Lhesher Khoum. "Fetch Adelaine. Make preparations for a small host to travel through these tunnels on foot, quickly. We'll take no cats into the darkness. Thaddeus, gather these codices and anything else relating to this path under the mountains. Meet us down in the Heat Pools, by the southern wall. We go posthaste. Luc, you're with us. Lhesher, you too."

Therel nodded to the tense healer, then to his Highsword. Thaddeus gave a quick bow and shot from the room. Luc gave an elegant nod, like a courtier. Lhesher gave a growl of assent, a palm to his chest.

"I would keep your scribe Thaddeus with us in our exile, my General." Elyasin spoke to Theroun. "He has been a great help."

"Keep him close, my Queen." Theroun nodded, fierce pride shining from his gaze, a hard smile lifting his lips as he turned slightly to watch the lad go. "Thaddeus is more than he seems. That is why I sent him to you. His cunning mind may prove your most valuable asset in the days to come."

"We will remain behind, brother," Merra spoke to Therel. "Secure the city."

"Merra…" Therel's breath was soft. In it, Elyasin could feel so much love unspoken.

"Someone needs to give the bastards what-for," Merra growled. "And General Theroun and I make a passable team."

"You will not go needlessly into the fray." The harsh voice of Adelaine speared the room. The thin woman in her swaddling furs sidled in through the doors, her sharp white eyes narrowed. "Therel. If you would reinstate me as High Dremorande, I will remain behind. You'll need someone with a few mind-tricks to throw a burning wad of catshit in among these Unaligned men."

"You know these foreign men who break minds?" Elyasin blinked. "And how did you hear our council?"

"I know how to listen through servant's doors." Adelaine looked smug. "As for the Kreth-Hakir, in the oral stories of the Brother Kings, these men are spoken of as the Kreth-Hakkim Beldir, or sometimes as the Kreth-Hakk'ir, the Brotherhood of Annihilation. The ancient lays also name them as Scorpions, named for the creatures they often rode to battle. They can break any mind, sting their way into it with ruthless force, unless one has prepared accordingly."

"And are we to take it that you are prepared for these men?" Therel's voice was condescending.

"Therel." Adelaine raised her chin, defiant. "I am perhaps the only person in all of Elsthemen who is prepared for them. Ghrenna is strong, but her gifts have no finesse yet. She is unreliable. I am the only person who can bolster your Generals and give Lhen Fhekran any chance against what is coming. I was prepared by my lineage, and I stand by my people."

A long silence spread through the room. Ghrenna's gaze went long, eerie, as if she listened to music no one else could hear. Elyasin watched her, recognizing that look. Ghrenna was recapturing memories of Morvein whenever she went distant like that. Ghrenna shivered, looking sick, then rubbed her temple, then her neck, looking back to Adelaine. "Do you really think you have a chance against them?"

"Morvein was not the only person who studied mind-bending in other lands." Adelaine straightened, frosty, meeting Ghrenna's gaze. "All tundra-blood mingles with the raiders of the Unaligned. Your powers are still fragile like night ceanthus. How much of Morvein do you actually recall? Can you weave her vast magic yet? Do you think you have a chance of holding the off an entire cadre of Kreth-Hakir?"

Elyasin saw Ghrenna shiver. A ripple seized her, making her clutch her neck and set her jaw, her blue eyes deep with ancient pain. A choking sound issued from her. Elyasin saw a tear leak from her cerulean eyes.

Adelaine stepped forward, coming to clasp Ghrenna's hands in a surprisingly tender gesture. "You may keep your mind hidden by that pendant, but I know pain. The Kreth-Hakir broke you, sometime long ago. I know. I have felt their touch. I fought them when I was but a slip of a girl, in a raid on my home of Kithrassi. And lost to them, just like you did. But unlike you, I focused my life upon one thing: to be ready for them should we meet again. So I will stay. And you will go. Protect Therel. Remember Morvein. And then come, and avenge us all."

A moment passed between the two women, a deep understanding. Gazing at them now, Elyasin realized they could have been sisters. Both were tundra-pale like snowfields, tall and lean. But where Adelaine was pinched and wan, the very picture of harsh winters and deprivation, Ghrenna blossomed with strength, a sensual beauty that made everyone in the room stare. Clad in stark snowhare furs and leathers, Ghrenna was fierce, wild, an elder goddess of the north.

But one who did not yet know her true power.

Adelaine released Ghrenna's hands with a squeeze, then turned to Therel. She said nothing, merely lifted her chin, their ancient feud unvoiced. Therel set his jaw. But at last, he sighed. "Fine. Have your station. Adelaine Visek, I hereby re-instate you to your former position as High Dremorande of Elsthemen. Serve the Highlands. Die with honor."

"And so I will." Adelaine sank into a low curtsy, bowing her imperious head to Therel and staying down for a three-count. But as she rose, she flicked her thin fingers archly to Merra and Theroun. "Generals. With me. We must speak of strategy if we are to have any chance of surviving this onslaught."

Merra's lips fell open. Theroun scowled. Both looked to Therel and Elyasin.

"Go." Therel commanded. "Protect us. Hold the city, however you can. And we shall all pray to Aeon, that something of our people survives this night."

Theroun and Merra each gave a crisp bow, Merra with her palm to her heart, before moving out of the room after Adelaine's retreating bundle.

* * *

Lhen Fhekran was a hornet's nest, horns blaring commands, warriors dashing the halls to the armories, fetching weapons, readying supplies. But as Therel, Elyasin, Luc, Ghrenna, and Lhesher Khoum pushed through the doors to the underground Heat Pools, they found them deserted, cleared of people now rushing to fortify the city.

The massive space was eerie, silent but for the rush of water from fountains sending curling steam up into the vaulted reaches. Night had settled and lamps were lit, glowing with a fey light as the King's party moved through in a grim line. Packs hefted upon their backs, their bodies bristled with weapons, clad in winter-ready leathers and furs. It would be cold underneath the mountains, and they had dressed for winter's chill, with furred hoods, gloves, and wraps that left them able to fight.

Rounding a sighing fountain, they headed for the recessed

cupola and the massive arched door of rose crystal in the southern wall. Hasty footsteps were suddenly heard from behind. The party whirled, swords and longknives out. Only to face Thaddeus jogging up through the steam, a bulging satchel slung across his skinny body.

"My lieges!" Thad panted. "I have the codices, and all else that I deemed most important."

Elyasin slid her sword away. Therel, grim beside her, did the same. "Good lad. Lhesher. The scribe's gear and pack."

Lhesher Khoum, carrying two packs upon his broad frame, now unslung one, outfitting Thaddeus. Therel and Elyasin moved to a fountain, filling waterskins. Ghrenna stepped to the rose-crystal wall, Luc following at her side. In the enormous vaulted alcove of bedrock, the door looked like a blush dawn burning with twisted veins of white smoke. The onyx, gold, and white star-metal sigils glimmered in the lamplight, foreboding. Elyasin watched Ghrenna run her hands over them, tracing the unintelligible swirls and script.

"Do you think she'll be able to open it?" Elyasin wondered, capping a flask.

Therel glanced at Ghrenna. "I thought Lhen Fhekran was dead of the old magic. That Alranstone and this door haven't worked in living memory. This Stone was thought inert. It's never permitted anyone to travel through. And it's the only Plinth made entirely of crystal that I've ever heard of. This wall has an arcane beauty, but none of the sigils are even remotely Elsthemi. I can't help but wonder if it was made by an entirely different people altogether."

"It was." Ghrenna's voice cut through the mist. "Morvein remembers this Plinth and doorway were made by a people called the Giannyk. Enormous kings of men, twice or three times the stature of any man alive today. She learned their runes..." Ghrenna turned around. Walking away from the wall, she sank to a seat upon the lip of the fountain, staring up at the crystal wall.

"What's the matter?" Luc moved to Ghrenna's side, running his fingers over her hair, caressing her neck. Elyasin couldn't help but notice the healer's attention, his obvious devotion that made him war within.

"Morvein's energy remembers these runes." Ghrenna sighed, leaning into Luc's touch as if it soothed her. "But I don't. I have only the vaguest memories about them. A maddening dance of emotions… and the feeling of power."

"Can you decipher them?" Therel's gaze was hard. "Can you make the passage open?"

"Give me time."

"We don't have time, Ghren." Luc's murmur was soft by her side.

Thad moved to Ghrenna, pulling out a delicate codex, unfurling it. "Here. Take a look at this. In this codex, Metholas speaks of this entrance. He calls it *Ainaru Kitha Lhen Fhekresh*, though I have no idea what that means."

Ghrenna took up the delicate scroll, as Luc's fingers continued to stroke her neck. Perusing it, her pale eyebrows knit in a line, and she sat up straight. "*Kardesh a kandani, neth me a dir'rek…*" She spoke suddenly. "*He a mekani, drim Ainaru Kitha Lhen Fhekresh.*"

"You can read that text?" Thad leaned over the scroll. "I tried all the language compendiums in Lhen Fhekran's library to decipher that, but found nothing even close to it. What is it?"

"Giannyk. The language of the giants." Ghrenna spoke, her eyes far and haunted. "Ancient sigil-makers and masters of the Portalways."

"What in Aeon's fuck?" Luc blinked, eyebrows rising.

Ghrenna shook her head, her cerulean eyes still far-gone. "I don't know. Morvein searched everywhere to learn the Rennkavi's binding magic. She found an ancient place of power, a place revered as holy by the Giannyk. It was where she received these white markings, learned them. And with it is… the place where she could work the ritual for the Rennkavi? I… I can't recall…"

"So Morvein didn't build these tunnels." Luc nodded at the crystal wall. "Damn, I thought those sigils looked familiar! They're just like the ones in the cavern we called home in Fhouria, Ghren."

Ghrenna eyes had misted over, as if in deep trance. "I think that's why I felt so safe in that cavern, Luc, why I was drawn to discover it. Because the part of me that was Morvein was searching for this. Morvein rediscovered an ancient magic that used to live in this land. Giannyk magic."

Slowly, Ghrenna rose, walking to the wall and leaving Luc behind. Like a sleepwalker, she began running her hands over one rune and then another. Caressing them, she leaned in, whispering to them as if they were a living creature. Suddenly, the runes began to glow. Where Ghrenna's fingers traced, they gleamed with a silver light, then dimmed as her fingers slid past. Like she painted music upon the wall, Ghrenna's hands began to move in a subtle dance, touching here, stroking there. A soft, eerie song began to escape her lips. She began to sway, undulating with a pulse.

Elyasin was mesmerized, watching it. But her reverie suddenly shattered as doors far through the steam burst open with a boom. She whirled, blade out. To see a tight knot of keshari warriors rushing towards them through the curling mist, Adelaine like a fur-bundled wraith in their center.

"My King! My Queen!" Formidable Jhonen Rebaldi skidded to a halt before them. "Menderian forces have broken through the gates! They storm the city as we speak. Generals Merra and Theroun sent us to barricade you in."

"Therel. We'll buy you time. I swear it." Adelaine drew up tall, imperious in her swaddled furs.

"Jhonen. Adelaine." Therel's voice was tight as he regarded them. "Buy us as much time as you can. Ghrenna has yet to remember how the door works."

"She's close, Therel." Adelaine's eyes were enormous, watching Ghrenna. "She's very close. I can feel it. Magic wreathes her like some fell thing. We'll go. I'll hold the Kreth-Hakir off as long as I can to give you more time. I will give them a true wild keshar of the Highlands to fight."

Turning on her heel, Adelaine strode through the curling mist towards the doors. Lhesher broke from their group, kneeling his massive bulk before Therel. "My King. You need me at the door. Please. You and our Queen, Ghrenna, and Luc are accomplished fighters. Please let me hold off your foes in this hour of need."

Therel's hand settled to Lhesher's thick shoulder. "You were ever friend to me, Lhesher. In this darkest night, fight with the gods in all their glory. Fight the storm, Highlander. Fight for Elsthemen."

"My King." Lhesher's voice rasped. He stood, fierce, and clasped arms with Therel. Then bowed to Elyasin, one palm at his heart, the other to the sword at his hip. Turning, he jogged quickly off through the mist.

They heard the doors boom shut. Steam choked the cavern, lifting and curling in patterns from the vibration of the otherworldly music issuing from the door. A symphony of wraiths sang from the rose crystal, sighing out through the gloom. A dirge, Elyasin thought. A funereal weeping for all those who would die today. Who would be slain in a battle more terrible than any they had ever faced, against a foe who could not be matched.

Elyasin heard Therel choke.

She moved to his side. He twined his fingers in hers, his jaw set, fierce.

"I will kill them all for this." Therel growled. "For every Highlander who falls tonight. I will find the Kreth-Hakir and rip out their scorpion's nest from whatever black realm they call their home. And I will burn them all."

"Tomorrow." Elyasin murmured, gripping his hand. "Tonight, we survive."

"Tomorrow." Therel's wolf-pale eyes flicked to hers, absent of tears.

CHAPTER 47 – DHERRAN

Dherran, Khenria, and Grump spent another two days in Purloch's House, taking their rest as Purloch held counsel among his captains about aiding Arlen. Their days had been quiet, the calm before a storm they both could feel coming. The rancor of Dherran and Khenria's relationship had smoothed out into tenderness after Khenria's revelations. By day they hunted at each other's side, taking down bog-creatures with Purloch's archers. And back at the compound at night, they settled into hammocks around peat-fires in outdoor ceramic basins, listening to the bog-folk play reed pipes as frogs chorused in the darkness.

Dherran hadn't seen Elyria again. He asked Purloch about her, but Purloch had only shrugged, saying the half-wild Elyria often took to the forests alone for weeks. Dherran left it be, but he could still feel a tense energy within him at what the mysterious Elyria had said, like bees trapped in his nerves.

And this morning, it was finally time to leave. Grump and Purloch's negotiations had concluded, and they would be put through to Valenghia, though Dherran had yet to hear an answer about Purloch's men joining Arlen's banner. Sunlight filtered through the canopy, birds trilling adulations as Dherran's group assembled with Purloch upon a wide leave-taking platform. Mist curled up from the bog, writhing around massive trunks, slipping up nets of vines. Their escort of ten of bog-folk waited by the slung walkway that led down to the eastern river, checking gear, backpacks, and weapons for their trip to the Valenghian border.

Grump clasped Purloch's arm, and the two comrades shared a sad smile.

"Be careful, you old goat," Purloch rumbled. "The Bitter will not welcome your arrival upon her turf in Velkennish."

"I've got a few disguises left in this old bag of tricks," Grump chortled mildly. "Besides. Delennia will be intrigued with what I've brought her to bargain with. She may be more helpful to us that she'd care to admit."

"Don't be so sure about that." Purloch eyed Grump. "She's as much dragon as her sister is. Remember that."

"I always do."

An awkward moment passed between them. The Master of the Bog hesitated, then set a hand to Grump's face. Tenderness suffused the man's visage, and Dherran blinked to see it returned in Grump's demeanor.

"Be *careful*, Grunnach." Purloch admonished.

"Delennia can't hurt me. And her sister can't woo me, either." Grump reached up, taking Purloch's hand gently down from his face. Holding Purloch's hand, he gazed at it a long moment. "Can we count on you? Will you bring your contingent to Arlen's banner, if I can rally support in Velkennish?"

"You know I would do anything for you, you old goat." The big man's words were tender, haunted. "Arlen will have the men he needs, at least from me. We'll march as soon as we can get everything assembled, no longer than three day's time. I'll leave a small contingent here to await your return with Delennia's forces. Aeon-hope you can secure them."

"Thank you."

Suddenly, the big man growled, then stepped in close to Grump. Wrapping a thick hand around the back of Grump's neck, he pulled the smaller man in, bending his giant frame for a long, tender kiss. Dherran's eyebrows climbed his forehead. He knew his lips had fallen open, but he couldn't shut them. He stared, watching Grump kiss Purloch back. The bog-folk looked respectfully away, casual as if it were nothing, just not their moment to witness. Khenria tugged Dherran's hand, and he blinked, then looked away.

"Well! Shall we away, my friends?"

Dherran looked back at Grump's spry words, to find the man red-cheeked and beaming as he adjusted his weapons on their harness. "Old Grump is eager for a meal of real bread and butter down in the Tilthlands, not these endless courses of squirrel meat!"

Dherran shouldered his pack higher, still dumbfounded, and glanced at Khenria. She nodded and spoke. "Lead the way, Grump."

Dherran stepped back, letting the little grey mouse of a man move toward their guides. The ten bog-folk came to readiness with the silent alert of forest-cats. To the eye, they'd not changed their slouches in their moss-woven garb, but suddenly, they bristled with attention. A huntswoman named Yenlia and her partner Bherg stepped to the front, two that had led the hunting-parties these past days. Among Purloch's best, they and their regular company had been set as guides and protection for Dherran's group upon the watercourses.

Still mulling over everything he'd not known about his traveling partners, Dherran was lost in silent thought as Grump took the lead, striding down the walkway with his pack cinched tight to his spry frame. Dherran and Khenria came behind, and the bog-hunters fell into line. Their descent to the forest floor and the damp of the bog was silent, each hunter occupied in his or her own mind for the journey ahead. Dherran found himself wondering about death and life, love and loss. Wondering how much love Purloch and Grump had shared, feeling the ache of their ancient sundering and recent reunion. All the thousand little ways Dherran should have known about Grump that he had missed, too wrapped up in his own emotions. All the things he should have pieced together about Khenria, that Elyria had illuminated.

Wondering about himself. Wondering if his death would come today.

Wondering if there was anything he could do to prevent it.

They were soon down upon a watercourse, and the business at the dock interrupted Dherran's thoughts. Two long, shallow dugout-boats had been moored to a stout tree at the base of the walkway, and gear was being hefted in, arranged to balance the slender canoes. People were loaded in and seated at benches to row. Following the hunters, Dherran took up two paddles and settled behind Khenria, Grump in the other boat. Bherg soon had their dugout pushed off through the shallow muck, Yenlia doing the same with the other craft. Angling them from the sludge at the river's edge, they moved out from the shallows, deep into a channel of fast-flowing dark water.

The current caught their boats, pulled, and they were moving off to the east.

Talk rose as they sped along in their sleek craft. Jokes began, bawdy comments shouted from one craft to another. Soon, Bherg and Yenlia signaled a halt to the rowing. Letting the thick flow take them, they allowed everyone a rest except two men stationed at the rear of either boat to keep course with a paddle upon the water.

"So... Grump?" Dherran spoke low to Khenria. "Did you know?"

She shook her head, a slight smile playing out her lips. "No, but I suspected. He never goes to whorehouses, he immerses himself in cooking and foraging like a distraction. He's never had a woman that I know of, though I've never caught him with a man, either. I thought perhaps he was pining for someone. Now we know."

"Gods, I feel so stupid." Dherran ran a hand over his face and through his blonde mane. He glanced over to the other boat, but Grump was engaged in animated conversation with Yenlia.

"Don't punish yourself, Dherran." Khenria reached out and rubbed his back. "Grump was a mystery to us both. But I suppose it's only fair. I've hid enough from him, certainly."

Turning her attention to other things, Khenria rubbed a palm over the sleek, well-polished red wood of their craft. Their narrow wooden boats had been carven from a single tree, angled up at the prow and stern like a cupped leaf.

"These are beautiful." She commented as Berg stepped up with a pack of food.

"We do all our traveling by *bintha*, if we can." Bherg commented, handing around jerked meat, cooked spiceroot, and water flasks for a midmorning snack. "Going by foot is treacherous. The longer you walk the Bog, the more likely is death. See there. Look."

Bherg pointed toward the southern shore. In the gloom that rippled reeds beneath the draping moss, Dherran could barely make out grey ridges spiking the water, cold reptilian eyes watching the boats pass. A short row of ridges decorated the long snouts of the great lizards from blunt nose to the crown of their heads, something like rhino horn. Dherran watched as one of the thick-scaled creatures rolled in the muck, disturbing the water.

"Aelakir." Dherran said. He knew about the top predator of the Bog, though he'd not been out with the hunters when they'd brought a few home. Dherran could see the entire bank was lined with them, rolling in the black mud, massive clawed feet churning to get them into the water.

After the boats.

"Paddles!" Bherg and Yenlia barked fast.

Snacks were shoved into stow-nets lining the sides of the craft. Paddles were lifted, set to dark water. The boats took a brisk pace for ten minutes before Bherg and Yenlia signaled a halt. Dherran glanced behind, seeing a trio of the massive lizards turning around, giving up the chase. Food was procured once more, and the bog-folk began eating and jesting again.

"How long will aelakir chase a boat?" Khenria asked Bherg.

"They live in matron-clans along the waterline." He gestured with his hunk of jerked meat towards the shore. "Sometimes a clan is aggressive, and those might follow us for hours. Once I was chased by a big bull male for a full day. That's a good story. I had to track through seven watercourses, and still he'd not cease hunting me, the bastard. And then, after all that, once I was tiring and rowing slower, he attacked my boat!"

Dherran saw Yenlia glance over from the other boat cruising beside them. Concern was plain in her eyes, though masked by a warrior's calm as Bherg continued his story.

"The only way to deter an aelakir that attacks you," Bherg informed Dherran, "is to put your knife in its eye, or down its gullet." He demonstrated by pulling his bootknife, thrusting. "And even that sometimes doesn't work! A dying aelakir will latch on until it breathes its last, like a rabid dog. At a minimum leaving a massive wound." Bherg rolled up his sleeve to show a bicep riddled with ancient punctures and scars in the shape of triangular teeth. "But see here! I tore that big bastard up from the inside with my knife, then hauled it back for a feast at the House. He was good eatin'!"

But the veiled watchfulness in Yenlia's eyes told Dherran the truth. She'd almost lost Bherg that day, and they both knew it. Death was ever-present in the bog. But like a warrior, she spoke up, vicious and proud. "My Bherg could take six of the bastards. That big brute made a mistake, to his very last thrash."

"So he did, my lover!" Bherg laughed and saluted Yenlia in the other boat with his water flask. She saluted him back, and they both drank. Bherg chuckled, wiping his beard with the back of his hand. "She lies. I could maybe manage four. She could take seven of them."

Chuckles rose among the fighters. Their break was soon over, as a second clan of aelakir rolled into the water from the northern bank. All set to oars, but this time, the clan pursued. The fighters kept a steady pace, sweating under the humid sunshine filtering down through spreading canopy. Rounding a corner, Dherran suddenly saw a broad bank of stones rippling the bogwater. Yenlia called out and they angled the boats to put in at the stony beach. Leaping from the craft into clear shallows, they hauled the boats out of the current. Sharp, the red rocks of the beach were savage beneath Dherran's boots, and he cursed as he stumbled and went down, one knee driving onto what felt like volcanic glass.

"Careful!" Bherg clapped a hand to his shoulder as the fighters hauled gear from the boats. "We camp on the *roushenn* tonight. Aelakir do not come here. It tears their bellies, rips up their scales. We are safe here, but mind your flesh!"

"Roushenn?" Dherran accepted his pack to take to the shore. "Like Roushenn palace?"

Bherg nodded, taking up his pack, gesturing up the shore toward where the bog-fighters were already circling stones, getting a fire pit ready. "*Roushenn* means *cut-stone* in the old tongue. Fire-glass. A stone with much crystal or glass in its composition."

"Volcanic stone." Grump stepped up, marching towards the blossoming camp beneath the overhang of trees. "It's a very broad term. It can refer to any kind of granite, crystal, or obsidian. Stone that will slice your boots open, Dherran my lad!"

Grump clapped Dherran on the shoulder and moved ahead. Packs had been dumped near the fire ring, tinder and mosses were being fetched from the forest's periphery. One of the fighters was supervising getting a fire started. Another directed the stringing-up of hammocks from their packs upon the stoutest tree-branches that overhung the vicious beach.

"We're not sleeping on the ground?" Dherran slung his pack down with the others.

"Do you want to sleep on rocks that will cut your back open?" Bherg passed with a grin. "Be my guest. But my lover and I are

673

sharing a hammock."

"Don't be daft, Dherran," Khenria passed with a teasing smile. "Come set up a hammock to share with me."

She slapped him on the butt. Dherran grinned. He chased her up the rocks and she threw down her pack, squealing and laughing. Her dash to get away was halfhearted, and she let Dherran corral her and crush her close with kisses. Fighters laughed all around them.

But suddenly, a sharp alertness swept the fighters in a wave. With a fast clack of arrows nocked, they had their longbows unslung from their packs and drawn. Bows were trained, tense, at a certain spot in the dense foliage past the beach.

Yenlia nodded to Bherg. As one, the two of them loosed into the verge. An angry yowl was heard from the green shadows, like a keshar. The yowl dwindled to a growling rumble, then shifted. Moving away through the trees, the creature it had come from was still invisible in the underbrush. As one, the bog-warriors eased. But still they stood alert, watching the shadows.

"What the fuck was that?" Dherran asked Bherg.

"Keshar's smaller cousin," Bherg's grin was hard. "The tesh-tar. They're loners in the Bog, only meet them rare enough. Climb trees, stalk game both large and small, they do. Dappled grey-brown color just like the forest. You never see them coming, until they leap," he grinned wider. "And then you hope you have your bow or knife ready."

"Sometimes you don't see them coming at all." Yenlia commented as she stepped close, still scanning the shadows. "They like to leap when your back is turned. We'll set a watch tonight, both towards the river and the trees."

At Yenlia's signal, bows were slung across backs, arrows put away. Moving about their business once more, the hunters continued hoisting hammocks of woven vines into the trees. Then they began ripping down moss, padding the hammocks into wide sleeping-cocoons. Dherran moved to one, helping grab handfuls of draping moss and stuff a nest of a bed for him and Khenria. A roaring fire soon blazed in the fire pit. Mosses now padded the sharp river rocks to make seats around the fire. As the light died through the forest into the heavy gloom of dusk, their camp brightened, filling the night with life.

Midges came out, buzzing in Dherran's ear and sipping at his throat. Dherran slapped them away and soon learned to take up twists of a vile-smelling moss that burned green and waft it to keep the blood-suckers at bay. Aelakir drifted by in the black current, watching the beach with glittering eyes out in the dark water. But their camp was as good as its reputation, and none of the massive reptiles came ashore.

Four hunters came back through the trees, a dead *yempe* slung between them. Something like an antelope with webbed feet for pacing the bog, *yempe* was a staple of Purloch's folk. The small ungulate was soon trussed over the fire upon a spit, charring for supper. Before long, reed flutes had come out and the bog-folk lifted up their voices in a rousing roundel. Dherran smiled, his heart easy as Khenria settled by his side, leaning close so Dherran could wrap her in his arms.

"How are you?" He murmured in her ear, kissing her temple.

She took a deep breath, sighed. "Alright. It's strange, that you know my past, now. That you don't shun me for it."

"I would never shun you." Dherran nuzzled her neck.

She snuggled closer in his arms. "Dherran?"

"Hmm?"

"Do you think Arlen den'Selthir knows more about me than he's telling? And Grump, too?"

Dherran paused. "Do you?"

She shrugged. "It seems strange. Grump taking us to Vennet. Arlen there the very day I fought. That Arlen took us so suddenly under his wing. Trained us like his own son and daughter, grooming us for leadership. And then sent us for such an important mission into Valenghia. If he knew I'm Valenghian royalty, it would partly make sense. But he and Grump seem to feel I have... leverage, when we get there. Like they know what family I come from. Like they are certain it will help their cause."

Khenria fell silent. Dherran took a deep breath, troubled by her words. Unnerved that she had just voiced a dark part of him that had been chewing on the same thought for weeks. "Khenria. I want to help you find out. About your birth family. Once we get to Valenghia."

She stilled in his arms. "Why?"

"Because what if it's important? Who you are? Why you are the way you are? What if that's more important than anything else we're doing here?"

Khenria was very quiet. At last, she shifted in Dherran's arms. "I'm no one, Dherran. Just an abandoned Khehemni child with a bad past. I don't even know my birth name. Leave it be. Tonight, I just want to feel your arms around me and listen to songs. Eat, drink, and have sex... and forget."

It didn't sit well with Dherran. Something inside him prickled, certain Khenria's past was important, something she couldn't just abandon. But he held his tongue, knowing tonight was not the right moment to pursue it. Gripping her closer, he settled his cheek against hers as they watched the fire and the musicians. At last, she turned in his arms, lifting up to press him with a kiss.

"We're not fighting anymore." She said, a little smile playing along her lips.

"Because I'm holding my tongue." Dherran grinned a little.

"No," she kissed him again. "We're not fighting because I told you about me. Finally."

"Trust begets trust, Khenria," Dherran murmured. "I trust you more, because you trusted me."

"Do you trust Grump?" She whispered low, for Dherran's ears only.

Dherran paused. His gaze slipped to Grump, now at the roasting carcass, cutting off a hunk to put in his bowl. A slow rage stirred inside Dherran against his friend, something he'd never felt before. Grump was a spy. Secrets were his game. How many more did he have, and what would he use them to gain?

"I don't," Dherran admitted at last. "I don't trust him at all anymore. I don't know who he is, Khenria. And that scares me."

"Me too." She sighed. "What should we do?"

"Wait." Dherran breathed. "Wait until we get into Valenghia and see what he does. But stay by me. Don't let him separate us. I don't know what he's capable of. And I don't know why he needs us with him in Valenghia. It seems to make sense, but..."

"But then it doesn't." Khenria finished, pulling back, her gaze slipping to Grump.

Grump saw them both watching, gave a quick smile by the roasted meat. Then beckoned, calling out through the singing and music. "Khenria! Dherran! It's ready! Come get it while it's hot!"

Dherran and Khenria rose, but their gazes caught as they stepped toward the roasting meat. Indecision was in Khenria's eyes, and Dherran knew his visage spoke the same. Filing it away, Dherran approached the roast, putting a smile back upon his face.

* * *

They were on the water a total of three days. Travel was quick, letting the current take them, interspersed by occasional paddling to avoid aelakir. The party stopped for the night whenever they came to a rocky shoal, be it at noon or past evening's darkness. Fires were lit to keep midges and forest-cats at bay, and Dherran came to realize why Purloch's House was built so far up in the trees. At ground-level, where the midges bred in the slurried mud, they were thick like pepper-dust. The bog-folk wore a veil of moss tied before the face to keep from breathing them in while hunting beneath the trees, and Dherran soon did the same. But fifty feet up the bugs were picked off by birds and lizards that lived in the canopy, away from ground predators.

And predators there were. Numerous times, Dherran felt something stalking them from the draping moss at the edge of the watercourse. The boats were attacked not once but thrice by aelakir beneath the murk, surfacing strong enough to nearly roll the dugouts. Hails of arrows and strikes of swords did little, only drove them off until they became eager once more.

On the third day, their drinking water had become fouled somehow, and as everyone began to vomit, Yenlia had come around with a tincture. It had burned like whiskey and tasted like rotten straw, but the cramping and vomiting had ceased within minutes. Only later were they informed that they would have been dead within hours without that little elixir. Made of a plant harvested high in the canopy, such medicines were worth their weight in gold in the bog. Dherran didn't have to ask how many bog-folk had succumbed to such a death over the years. The grave quiet of their escorts was all too plain.

At last, the watercourse opened into a wide, fast-flowing river. The forest transitioned, the shores rockier, less moss coating the trees. The foliage had begun to change, the midges were nearly gone, and no drapes of hanging vines obscured the forest. The trees opened up, and something in Dherran breathed in relief that he could see through the undergrowth once more.

The boats were put ashore. Dherran and his group were gifted a fresh set of clothes and packs, dyed brown to look like wool so no one would know they had come through the Bog. Their garb was Valenghian, Dherran's a long split-panel jacket over a leather vest and soft white shirt, trousers tucked into boots. Their guides led Dherran, Khenria, and Grump on a short hike, when suddenly the land ended before them with a fantastic view, the river thundering over the rift in a magnificent waterfall. The land spread out before Dherran, thousands of feet down in a fertile green valley that stretched as far as he could see, and an old overgrown road moved from their overlook down through the forest to their right.

Bherg gestured out over the rolling hills and arable plains, to a city of white stone, far below upon the river's meandering edge. From this height, it looked like a white plate amongst all that ripe green, though Dherran could tell it was a massive city.

"Velkennish, the capitol. Welcome to Valenghia, my friends." Bherg then gestured behind them up into the trees. "We have a watch-post here, at the edge of Endless Falls. You can't see it from the ground, but know that we'll post men here to await you when your aims are done. Purloch looks forward to your safe return. The old road will take you—"

"I know where the road leads, lad!" Grump hefted his moss-woven pack.

"And you will remember to launder your items from the Bog without delay. We can't have anyone knowing you came through—" Bherg started up again.

"Yes, yes!" Grump grumped irritably. "I won't give you all away with a spot of mud on my trousers. Off you go, boy! And tell Purloch thank you for me. And also, that now he's the one who owes *me* money. Ha!"

"I shall, Grunnach den'Lhis." The man bowed low. "I have heard a tale or two of you, and you are a brave fighter, Greyhawk.

Luck be with you."

Grump snorted. "Tales can be misleading, lad. Be well. Dherran, Khenria! Hup, hup!"

And with that, he went striding along the overgrown ancient road, little wider than a deer-track. Dherran and Khenria clasped arms with Bherg and Yenlia, then set off after Grump, struggling to catch up to his ground-eating pace.

CHAPTER 48 – JHERRICK

Jherrick felt his body return, and he woke. Still far away, he felt smooth sheets slide over him, a thick pallet bed beneath. His body was dressed in a long tunic of silk beneath a coverlet. With eyes closed, he tested every limb. He wasn't restrained, though all his limbs were vastly weak.

Pain. He remembered it. Twisting, violent, screaming pain. He could recall being flung through the crystal Alranstone, out to nowhere. To a place so cold it burned as it froze. To a nothingness so vast, he'd not even had the comfort of a sense of self in all that emptiness. A place where flickers had raced around him, images of worlds, shuffling by like a pack of cards. And then he'd been flung through, his body returning in a rush of pain so diabolical, he'd been on the edge of death.

He remembered kind hands lifting him from a cold stone floor.

He remembered screaming at the pain.

Jherrick's eyes blinked open to candlelight in a vaulted space. The walls around him were made of some smooth stone with a soft opalescence, like white agate. Everything was carven with vines and flowers, starbursts and intricate scrollwork. Some walls had been carven through like the sun-shield at Khehem, appearing like lace and allowing his vision to roam beyond.

As if looking through time and memory, Jherrick could see into other rooms and halls, all lit with muted candlelight. He saw walls of glass and silvered mirror. Walls of crystal that emitted a soft-hued light, and walls made of twisting vines and tree roots. A candelabra made from an ancient willow formed a bower over his bed and wound the upper reaches of the room, white oil lamps like tiny flowers throwing shadows through its leaves. The lamps were otherworldly, licking with twisting blue flames that tinged green, then red or purple. That endless sinuousness held his fascination, his thoughts distant as he stared up into the vaulted dome.

Filigree had been carven through the ceiling of his bower, and the willow had sent tendrils up to the outside. Evening's gloaming shone beyond, prickling with stars like a high-north night. Jherrick thought he heard music, harps far away. Or voices twisting upon a subtle wind. But now it was reed flutes, and now it was drums beating the solid rhythm of a heart. And now, it was thousands of hearts in twisting unison, like a roll of thunder over the mountains.

Jherrick sank back into soft pillows, feeling that rhythm ripple through his bones. A great calm suffused him, a sensation of floating upon some vast, empty sea.

He took a breath. A woman stirred from dozing in a chair of twisted vines at his bedside, and Jherrick startled to note her. She was young and pretty, her skin the milky color of starlight, her hair a silver river that cascaded straight and pure from beneath her deep hood. Her garb was thin silk, a flowing robe that shone like an autumn moon. Her cheekbones cut across a face with haunting, immortal beauty.

But it was her eyes that arrested Jherrick. Entirely black with no white to them, her eyes were filled with the night sky, minuscule flecks of stars echoing in a vast, swirling emptiness.

Luminous. Endless.

She leaned over him with relief upon her visage. Mesmerized, Jherrick reached a hand up, though he trembled, weak. He brushed back her cowl to reveal long twists of luminous hair. She flushed prettily, pink coloring her cheeks as she drew her cowl back into place.

"There, now," she spoke in a lilting accent, "that's not a proper way to greet a Noldarum."

"Where am I?" Jherrick croaked, his voice raw.

"You're in our Sanctuary." She flushed again, smiling. "The Sanctuary of the Great Void."

"What...?"

She took his hand and pressed it back to the coverlet. "Rest. There will be time to answer all questions. But first, you must heal. Your journey was dire, and your body is weak."

Jherrick picked through her words, wondering who she was and where exactly this Sanctuary was that he'd ended up in. As he glanced around the room, he noticed no hutch or wardrobe and not a scrap of his personal effects, nor the clockwork key.

"My clothes? My weapons? My things?" He asked.

She shook her head. "As we are born, so do we come through to the Sanctuary. Nothing comes with us but our bones and our skin and our Essence."

Heaviness suffused Jherrick's heart. Olea's longknives, her curl of hair in his belt pouch. Her baldric and sword. Everything he'd had of her was utterly gone. Wanting to rise, to rage and scream, Jherrick lifted his head, but its weight pulled like a millstone. He dropped back to the cushions in bleak exhaustion.

"My comrade. Is he alive?"

Her face fell. Woe suffused her features. "I am sorry. We preserved his body in our Memorarium. But his Essence, I fear, was Scattered."

Jherrick's gut clenched, his body cold. "Aldris is dead?"

"The way through to us comes at a Price." The young woman murmured, stroking Jherrick's sweat-slick hair back from his forehead. "You barely made it. And the other... he was too Formed. The stronger one is Formed, the more vastly their being Concusses as they come through. But you were yet young and malleable, and thus survived the Concussion. Even so, you have been lingering for many days with fever."

Weariness and crushing sadness flooded Jherrick. Aldris was dead. He hadn't come through the crystal Plinth alive. Something horrible had happened to him. And now his blood was on Jherrick's hands. Along with the blood of all the others.

A sob wrenched Jherrick's chest. Guilt opened its maw and sucked him in, along with a tremendous, obliterating sorrow. Because of him, they were all dead. Vargen, Olea, Aldris. It had been his touch that had awakened the Alranstone in Lintesh, and now everyone who had come through that Stone was dead. A good Kingsman, loyal and brave. The woman who believed in Jherrick, whom he had loved and lost. And now, the one man who had given Jherrick a chance to prove himself a better man.

Olea's mission was sundered.

Her peace that had united them, had come to nothing.

Another hard sob hitched Jherrick's chest, but it was heavy. His limbs felt like lead, his body was crushed beneath a suffering weight.

Everything he'd thought he'd gained slipped away. All his fortitude that he could change the tides of time. All his newfound belief that he could change the world around him. He was just a pawn, again. And the crystal Plinth had used him, abused him, and spat him out.

Jherrick was alone, once more, in a world he could not control. And so far from home.

The woman attending him twisted to claim a pitcher from a table of woven branches. She helped Jherrick lift his head so he could drink. He fell back after he'd had enough, breathing slowly. Wherever he was, he needed to leave. Jherrick managed to struggle upright against the thick pillows. Swinging his legs to the bedside, he pushed up, head reeling, muscles shaking from exhaustion.

"You need to rest." The young woman watched his efforts with compassionate sadness.

"I need to piss." Vulgarity fortified him in his woe. And Jherrick's bladder did ache.

"I'll turn away." She gestured toward the sound of running water in one corner of the room.

Jherrick nodded, too tired to care. In his silk tunic, he stepped toward a vault of clear spring water burbling in a recessed hole in the floor. Keeping one hand against the wall for support, he lifted his robe and began. Leaning against the wall, he found it surprisingly warm. Jherrick gave in to that support, weary, as he finished.

He leaned there a long time, long after he had let his tunic fall. He heard a sound and looked back over his shoulder. The young woman arranged a tray of food upon the bed. She gave him a warm smile, gesturing invitation. Jherrick moved back to the bed and sat, his heart aching, his soul empty.

The food held no appeal, and he stared at it.

"Have something to eat, please," she encouraged. "When you are finished, I will take you to Noldrones Flavian, if you feel strong enough. He will have answers for you, about why you have come."

His mind thick with sadness, her words didn't seem to make sense. But Jherrick selected a piece of flaky pastry drizzled with honey to be polite. He bit it, chewed. It was of such quality and heady fragrance, like rosewater and telmen berries and peaches all rolled together, that he paused. His heartache eased back somewhat in a shock of bliss.

"This is good." Jherrick said, surprised.

"I'm glad you enjoy it." That pretty flush bloomed in her cheeks again.

"Who am I to see?" With every bite, Jherrick's heart eased. As if the flavors of honey and rose curried his sadness back. Though not able to take it completely, the heady taste of the food began to dull his sadness, to let it slip deep beneath other currents so he could breathe once more.

"Noldrones Flavian. He leads our Sanctuary, I suppose one might say."

Jherrick helped himself to more pastry, his appetite flaring. Ravenous suddenly, he finished four more pieces, then ate a large handful of pink berries the color of blush wine and tasting of pears.

"So I am in a monastery?" His mind cleared as his energy returned from the blessing of the food.

"Nothing so simple, I'm afraid. Though this is a place of study. And seclusion." Her gaze was endless as she watched him, offering no concrete answers.

Having eaten his fill, Jherrick rose, one hand against the bed for support. "Take me to him."

"Are you certain?" She cocked her head like a small bird, those uncanny eyes roving him. Jherrick knew he seemed weak. He felt weak. But he shook his head, putting dire strength in his movements, what little he could manage. He set his jaw and made his face hard. "Take me to him."

She nodded, blushing and flustered. Rising from her chair, she moved to the gnarled willow, then pressed a section of the bark. The live bark rippled away, knobs and all, revealing a compartment beneath. Jherrick eyes widened. Whatever *wyrria* this young woman had, it was like nothing he'd ever heard of. From the compartment, she removed a long robe of dark blue silk. She moved back to Jherrick, helping him into it. Rough-spun, thick and warm, the silk flowed down over his hands in draping sleeves, yet held a stiff high collar around his neck that kept away any chill. Set with knots down the front for closure, the young woman's fingers moved in to fasten them as she stepped close.

Jherrick set his hands upon hers, stilling her. "I can do that."

Something thrilled between them, a thrum like a

hummingbird. Jherrick's breath caught. Her cheeks flushed. Her eyelashes dropped, but she did not pull her hands away.

"You're feeling better." She murmured.

"Am I?" Jherrick mused, feeling her presence so close. Some perfume lingered about her, like honey and saffron. Her hands were warm beneath his. "How do you know?"

"I feel your Essence," she said, still flushing. "It burns hotter now. Your *wyrria* stirs like the slumbering dragon, strong. Dauntless. Your line will know you. And where once they feared, you will give them strength."

Her words gave him pause. Jherrick's brows knit, wondering what she meant, if she were some sort of prophetess. "What do you mean?"

She flushed more, pulled her hands away. "I may say no more. Come."

With one pale hand, she beckoned. Jherrick followed, still churning over the mystery of her utterance. As he moved, he was surprised to find his muscles stronger, able to support him. Following the woman around a lattice that shielded a vaulted alcove, he found a doorway beyond.

As Jherrick exited the room, his eyes moved through other lattices, seeing a graceful labyrinth in every direction. A mystery aching to be explored, welcoming to be lost in. Soaring buttresses revealed arches of agate that flowed with milk-white veins. Lattices opened to colonnaded halls cast of growing trees, arched limbs lost to unfathomable heights. Autumn leaves floated down like dying butterflies, to settle upon paths cut from a floor of white stone, below which a rushing river flowed.

Every vantage was more incredible than before. And as they walked, Jherrick saw persons of every variety performing strange feats. Here was a hall of crystal, staircases graceful as ocean waves curling up to an endless library, where a man with tusks protruding from his face imploded a scroll into being from nothing. In a hall of sigils, a group of five people clear as glass and filled with stars floated stones, sculpting a cool wind with their hands that etched the stones in a complex, effortless dance.

In a hall made of moss, a landscape of living green, strange people strolled or sat in meditation. Lounging in cups of green, men with long bodies thin as trees perused tomes with narrow, graceful fingers. Others had heads plumed with a crest of feathers that flowed like hair in bright shades of cerulean and royal plum, their airy bodies sleek with down, their hands and feet ending in talons. One man, though normal in appearance, stood five heights taller than the rest. A giant solid as the mountains, he stooped as he exited the chamber through a vast arch.

Every kind of wonder existed here. And Jherrick knew, suddenly, this was no place that existed in his world. Wherever he was, he'd been flung outside of things normal and known. Staring around in shock, he was too awed to blink or even breathe.

His guide beckoned up a spiral flight of stairs lit with tiny lamps, and Jherrick finally came back to himself. Mounting stairs was slow going, his limbs shaking. His guide waited patiently on each step, though she did not offer assistance. After countless turns, they reached a landing with a vaulted doorway. Jherrick stepped through, to find himself in a hall of living vines dotted with tiny white flowers, those same *wyrric* lamps casting a flickering light. A round recessed pool dominated the center of the room, smooth as glass. An oculus of vines had been knit above it, in a dome of liven green. Stars shone down from a violet-dusk sky, mirrored in the quiescent pool below.

A man stood before the pool, hands loosely clasped behind his back. Cowled in a flowing robe of pale silk like Jherrick's guide, he glanced over his shoulder as they entered. Jherrick felt strength emanating from him, in the way that the full moon holds court in the dead of night. Sharp eyes full of intelligence roved Jherrick.

At last, the man turned. Slender but muscled beneath his robe, he was without age. His skin was smooth, not a line edging those starlit black eyes. His profile was masculine but graceful, his jaw sharp and smooth, his lips full and nose aquiline. Gesturing toward the pool, he made a movement of his fingertips. A chair knit from runnels of vines that creeped over the floor. He nodded toward the chair. Jherrick took it, grateful. He'd not known how much longer he'd be able to stand, trembling with fatigue.

"Noldrones Flavian," Jherrick's guide held a palm to her heart. "Your charge has arrived. I withdraw." With an encouraging smile to Jherrick, she moved to the arched doorway. Then exited, leaving

Jherrick and the tall man alone.

Noldrones Flavian regarded Jherrick, his presence quiet, as if nothing existed in the chamber except empty space and haunting light. And then a teasing smile lifted one corner of his mouth. "You look terrible."

"Fevers do that to a man." Jherrick replied, having seen how awful he did in fact look at a fountain's reflection.

"Indeed. And I suppose traveling through a Portalstone does as well."

Jherrick kept his silence. He didn't know yet what game they played.

The man's eyes glittered. "Ah. You have secrets. Well at least tell me your name."

"Jherrick den'Tharn. Of Alrou-Mendera."

"Soon you will need no name. And you will come from no place but the Void's endlessness."

The man's words rattled Jherrick. He crossed his arms over his chest, so his fingertips rested nearer his longknives. Which he realized were no longer there, though the defiant posture gave him comfort.

"I need to return to my duties, sir. To my kingdom."

"Do you?" The man's endless black eyes bored into Jherrick. "Shall we speak plainly? I am Noldrones Flavian, Herald of the Noldarum. You have arrived at the Sanctuary of the Great Void. You are here because you chose to come, leaving everything you knew behind."

"Excuse me?" Jherrick blinked. His posture slipped.

The man gave a kind but stern smile, like an ancient scholar-king. "You chose to come through. You had a wish, a *desire*, for something only we can fulfill. Few portalways access our Sanctuary now, and the one you came through is unique. It operates upon the resonance of one's truest desire. So. What is it that makes your soul writhe in conflict and need, burning you cold from deep inside?"

"Olea." It was out of Jherrick's mouth before he could put it back.

"Indeed." The man eased closer, peering at Jherrick. Closing his endless eyes, he tipped his head back and spread his hands. Suddenly, Jherrick felt a smooth touch, like curls of autumn wind licking around him, *through* him. He couldn't touch it, couldn't stop it. As if every facet of his soul was being touched, explored, Jherrick found himself tasted by that gentle wind. Soothing and erotic, it was mesmerizing, until his every sinew was smoothed. His head tipped back. His eyes closed as he surrendered in bliss.

"Your oblivion calls," he heard the man whisper.

Jherrick opened his eyes, seeing Noldrones Flavian watching him.

"Something within you calls to wield Death, in the cold and the darkness. And yet, you've chosen something else. *Olea.* In some tongues, it means *olive* or *peace.* But in the most ancient tongue, the one that was old when the stars were born, it means, *resurrection.* Olea, Oliiya, Asiiya, Asya. A thousand ways to say one thing. When a star implodes after its life has been exhausted, it collapses. And then comes the rush as it involutes through itself and is born into being again, upon the other side. A *resurrection* of its life, as something other than how it began. You have named this thing. And the Portal you came through believes we can help you find it. So. Welcome, Initiate of the Noldarum. You are free to wander as you will. When you decide your training shall begin, it will begin."

The man moved forward. Lifting his hand, he touched a finger between Jherrick's brows. "Awaken, Initiate. See the Great Void for the very first time."

A spasm ripped through Jherrick's limbs. In a concussion of sound and energy, his mind suddenly opened, thrown to the far reaches of time and space. His vision of the room flashed out, expanding into an endlessness of stars. Expanding beyond all thought into a place of breathing, feeling, seeing, knowing.

Suddenly, he understood. Everything. Life, death. Beginning and ending. Transitioning from one form to another and back again, just as the stars are born and as they implode. Never to die, just to move *through.*

Nothing ever dies.

It only moves *through.*

CHAPTER 49 – ELOHL

Elohl stepped out on the top of the world.

Emerging from the white arch, he moved forward after Bhorlen onto a high platform of opalescent stone. Clouds misted around the platform, curling in a subtle breeze. The top of the white spire from his dreams was a cloverleaf, Elohl saw now. Three archways rose in a triad at the center of the structure, each arch facing one petal of the clover. Made of alabaster quartz, the stone was smooth like milk, run through with golden veins that caught the subtle, shifting light within the clouds. Mist curled and danced at the edges of the white stone, but did not obscure the platform itself. Swirled away by some ancient magic that also kept the platform warm and mild, the mist sighed around them without a breath of wind to curl Elohl's body.

There was no view, no time, no distance here. Only that swirling possibility of the clouds, easing around them in a sinuous motion. Fascinated, his heart pounding with an indescribable terror and elation to be here at last, Elohl walked to the edge of the platform they had emerged upon and looked over. Only white greeted him. Only clouds, skirling and dense, an eternity of nothing. An impossible feeling gripped him, that he could jump and just be carried away by all that pillowy white, rather than tumble to his death leagues below into a bottomless snowmelt lake.

"I saw this place once, from afar." Elohl's voice issued out muted and fey in this strange place. "And I've been here in my dreams, but I could see the world from this pinnacle. Dawn, rising over everything. Over the mountains, over so much land…"

"And so you shall," Bhorlen rumbled, coming to stand at Elohl's shoulder. "When the time is right, when you and your Gerunthane unite by the proper ritual, the world will open to you when all the Alranstones do. You will see the dawn of your blessing rise over the earth."

"The dawn of my blessing… the Rennkavi's Unity," Elohl

gazed into the swirling clouds, trying to envision it. "What does that mean? What will happen?"

"Truly?" Bhorlen's voice was subdued, thoughtful. "Who can say? Who can tell what will happen with *wyrria* that has never been attempted before? Leith Alodwine saw far. He saw a great need for this event, for it will turn the world to come. But what will that look like? How will it be Shaped? That is up to the hearts of those who wield love and hate, benevolence and fear."

"What did Leith see?" Fenton's voice was quiet at Elohl's left. "Why did he begin all this?"

"He saw a terrible evil unleashed upon our world," Bhorlen's voice was hushed. "As it was once, so shall it come again, that the Undoer rises among us. A time of trial, and sorrow, and destruction. The Many Worlds shudder with tales and legends, histories and myths. That the Undoer rises again and again, in epochs sometimes long, sometimes short. Leith saw that this fate would come, and he feared. And so he acted, building an empire, strength that could not be denied. Magic to last the ages, to foil this thing. We shall see."

Bhorlen trailed off. His dire words made Elohl shiver, as if a great black shroud had risen over him, a despair he couldn't shake off. Suddenly, he felt his own smallness, as if the world were a tremendous place, and he just a tiny speck of sand trying to push back a rising tide. One small human, trying to prevent a falling star.

"What is the Undoer?" Elohl asked with a shudder.

"There are two forces that govern the Great All, the natural processes of life," Bhorlen rumbled, "The Shaper and the Undoer. That which creates, and that which destroys. In our lives, we act their dance out everyday. We eat, destroying the flesh of plant or animal to create nourishment for our bodies. We sleep, destroying our consciousness to create rest and rejuvenation. We age, destroying our youth to create wisdom and perspective. As do we reflect the Shaper and the Undoer, so does the Great All. Stars are born and die. Galaxies expand and collapse. Energy is pulled in and through by the Undoer, and birthed upon the other side by the Shaper."

"Why did Leith fear the Undoer, if it's a natural process of life?" Fenton wondered.

Bhorlen turned to them, his blue eyes ancient. "When was dying something a man wished for? Hoped for, for his loved ones?

What about annihilation of your entire world? Long ago, my people succumbed to the presence of the Undoer among us. A time of terrible war, horrible sorrow. Of forgetting who we were and becoming no better than animals, scraping to survive. I am all that's left of the Giannyk, because the Undoer came among us. And my story is not unique in the Many Worlds."

A shiver passed through Elohl again. He could see it, some vast atrocity killing off thousands, hundreds of thousands. "What do you mean, the Undoer came among you?"

"The force became flesh." Bhorlen spoke. "It wanted a body and so it took one, to wreck its destruction among us. Personally."

"Personally." Fenton's murmur was dire. "That was what Leith saw, wasn't it? What he was trying to prevent? An incarnation of the Undoer in the flesh?"

"Yes." Bhorlen gave a tremendous sigh. "And yet, he worked tremendous atrocity with the power he was given. Would I teach him binding-magic again, if I could have seen how he would use it? I know not. The price was high. I only know I would do everything in my power to see that what happened to my people does not happen to yours."

"What happened to the Giannyk?" Elohl had to ask.

"Chaos and death. I do not wish to speak of it." Bhorlen rumbled to silence.

"Did your people create this place?" Fenton asked.

"No," Bhorlen picked up again. "My people did not create this Spire, not like the citadel of Heldim Alir we were just in, far beneath the glacier. This construct was wrought by a black-eyed people who once spread across this continent. The Ajnabi came to thrive after the fall of the Giannyk, when most of my kind were long gone to the Void. Builders of skill, they created marvelous works of gears and machinery, enormous cities with a clockwork science so tremendous it seemed magic. But the actual ability to harness the forces of the Shaper and Undoer into magical craft, they had not."

"But those portals," Elohl glanced behind him at the oil-slick shimmering between the arches, "if the Ajnabi didn't have magic, how did they create those?"

"They contracted with others who could harness *wyrria*," Bhorlen answered, "an ancient race of bird-folk called the Albrenni, who wielded formidable magic in this world long before my people came here. They were dying out, rare in my time, nearly extinct in the time of the Ajnabi. The story of the Albrenni is one even I do not know. But the Albrenni helped build this Spire, taught the Ajnabi what they knew. And yet, the Ajnabi came to ruin as their lands began to die in a massive blight."

"Blight?" Fenton said, "what do you mean?"

"Their green died. Every tree, every blade of grass," Bhorlen continued. "Sand and bare earth swallowed every plain, every mountain. Someone upon your world had let the Undoer into their flesh, and the Ajnabi were the first to pay the price. All that you now know, your Alrou-Mendera, your Valenghia, all was dead and barren here. So the Ajnabi sailed out from the southern coasts beyond the Twelve Tribes, to find someplace green. They did, far to the east. But the blight came there, too, and the Ajnabi fought the local dwellers in vicious wars over grain and green. The blight took that continent as well, took your entire world. But a group of people rose at the last hour, to fight, including the man Agni of which I spoke earlier. Finding the source of that destruction, the Undoer in the flesh, they sacrificed themselves to its transmutation. They succeeded, though it cost them. Green arose again upon your world. Though some blighted places upon your continent have been slow to recover, like Ghrec and the Twelve Tribes. And in those places, strife still reigns."

"So Leith saw this kind of destruction coming again," Fenton murmured, subdued.

"Something like it, yes," Bhorlen confirmed. "He would not tell me his vision, for it terrified him too much. But I could feel the strength of his conviction rolling from him in vast waves. I did not need to hear his horror, when he came to find me. I could feel it. So I taught him the magic he asked for. And when Morvein came to find me hundreds of years later, I felt the vision's echo in her. So I taught her binding-magic as well, to pass on to her Brother Kings. Which she did."

Bhorlen turned, eyeing Elohl as if seeing the entirety of his golden Inkings through Elohl's clothing. "The Goldenmarks you bear hold the signature of Hahled Ferrian. He was wise to mark you as the Rennkavi."

"But I was marked by a Plinth." Elohl spoke.

"Do you remember nothing of that event?" Bhorlen's smile was secretive.

Elohl scrubbed one hand through his ruff of black curls. "The man who marked me... he seemed like a King. A barbarian King with red and white Inkings over his chest and shoulders."

"Red and white Inkings... you *were* marked by Hahled Ferrian!" Fenton turned to Elohl, surprise and urgency in his manner. "Where was the Plinth you were marked at?"

"At a ruined fortress, on a ridge of mountains southwest of the Elsee."

"Haleth Tel. Shaper! I should have known!" Fenton rubbed both hands over his face. His eyes were far away, stunned. "I thought she'd killed them when the magic broke! But she didn't! Morvein trapped them in *Plinths*! Shaper! Was this her plan all along, if something went wrong? To make sure there was someone alive who could mark a future Rennkavi? Why didn't she *tell* me?! And now she's returned?"

Elohl reached out, touched Fenton's shoulder. Fenton startled, his eyes refocusing.

"You look like you're walking among ghosts, Fenton." Elohl observed.

"I am, Elohl." Fenton gave a sickly grimace. "You were Inked by a ghost from my life. Hahled Ferrian. One of the Brother Kings of Elsthemen. One of the strongest Alrashemni that ever lived, nearly eight hundred years ago. And died. Or I thought had died, killed by Morvein's machinations. But she sent them to Plinths! I should have seen it... she prepared everything to rise again. The Rennkavi, the Gerunthane, the Brother Kings to mark him when the time was right..."

"Gerunthane?" Elohl asked.

"The Rennkavi is supposed to have a woman who will channel power to him, massive power to aid his Unification. His Gerunthane, his seer-dreamer," Fenton said. "A woman who fills his dreams, who will be able to smash minds and break barriers to bring all under the Rennkavi's purpose. You have only one woman who fills your dreams, Elohl. And from what you've told me about Ghrenna... I am certain she is your Gerunthane."

Elohl's head snapped up. He could feel her suddenly, Ghrenna's nightwind perfume all around him atop the lofty platform. Elohl's fever-dream rushed back. A roaring sound filled his ears, and his vision was suddenly swamped by cerulean. "This platform. She and I have been here, together, in a dream."

"So you have." Bhorlen rumbled, a dark mystery suffusing his gaze. "For here is where it will happen. Here, your Gerunthane will open all the Paths of the World to you. For you to use, to touch every heart."

"What does that mean?" Elohl asked, turning to Bhorlen.

The giant settled a kind hand upon Elohl's shoulder. "The magic will act as it needs to. I do not know what that will look like, nor what the exact outcome will be. The Binding will come from your heart, and hers. Will it change the hearts of men? I do not know. I only know that Leith saw this element as imperative in avoiding a vast destruction. Something as terrible as what swept this land and killed off the Ajnabi eons ago."

Elohl took a deep breath. Responsibility weighed on him, more heavily than the giant's comforting hand. Fenton was silent at his side. Clouds skirled and sighed around the platform, moving to a wind Elohl could not feel.

"I must take you back," Bhorlen spoke suddenly. "You have much to consider."

Turning toward the archways, the giant beckoned. Elohl followed, Fenton a step behind. They were soon through the portal in a soft rush of wind, emerging back inside the amphitheater in the ice citadel without any of the pain and wrenching of traveling through an Alranstone. Elohl turned back, gazing at the whispering central portal of the seven. He was just in time to see Bhorlen reach out, touching Fenton at his silver runes. Like wraiths, they evaporated from Fenton's skin in curls of vapor. Fenton shuddered, eyes closing, brows knit as if in pain. When he finally opened his eyes, they were a calm gold-brown. Fenton stepped to his shed clothes, donning his shirt and jerkin, then his furred coat and sundries.

Turning, Fenton regarded Bhorlen with a wry grimace. "This fight inside me. Will it ever be gone?"

"Learn to love what you are," Bhorlen answered levelly, "and the beasts will be mastered."

"Easier said than done," Fenton laughed softly as he set his hands to his hips. "I've had nothing but hate for Leith all my life. My mother's handmaidens said he was a monster, that he tortured my mother. That that was why she ran from him..."

"Hate not the messengers of dire times." Bhorlen rumbled, setting a massive hand to Fenton's shoulder. "For men do terrible things when fate calls."

"How can I not hate him?" Fenton grimaced. "Leith, no matter his objective, was a tyrant. And Morvein... Aeon! Morvein..."

"Speak your ancient troubles, and they will weigh lighter upon you," the giant offered.

Fenton heaved a sigh, scuffed one boot upon the white stone floor that had been revealed by his fire earlier. "Eight hundred years ago, Morvein and I were in the middle of Goldenmarking the Rennkavi candidate I had found, Theos den'Alrahel, when everything went wrong. In the middle of the ritual, Theos couldn't hold the magic. One by one, the crystal Plinths of the White Circle began to explode. Ten of our guards were killed instantly. Our scribe, Metholas, was struck by a spar of flying crystal. Hahled and Delman snapped from the magical recoil as the Plinths exploded. They went insane, began to rage and fight each other. Morvein was bleeding from her eyes, her mouth, her skin...!"

Fenton took a shaking breath, his eyes faraway as if he watched the terrible event happen all over again. Elohl came over, resting a hand upon Fenton's other shoulder, giving it a squeeze. Fenton reached up, gripping Elohl's hand.

"Gods it was horrible, Elohl. I ran for the unconscious Theos, to get him out of the circle. Morvein screamed, casting her hands at me before I could get to the boy. The next thing I knew, I woke up on a beach, a warm tide licking my boots. Morvein had thrust me through the last surviving Alranstone, sent me a continent away. It was three years before I finally made it home. I returned to destruction. Dhelvendale, fallen. The Highlands in ruin. Alrou-Mendera, Valenghia, Cennetia, Praough, all without leadership, their cities burned and plagued with disease and famine. Morvein had disappeared. The Brother Kings had vanished, presumed killed by Morvein. I went back to the White Circle. It was destroyed. There was no trace of Morvein, nor of Metholas. But Delman and Hahled's bodies were there, mummifying, their dead Highguard littering the cavern like broken dolls. And in the center of it all, in the middle of the shattered ring, was Theos' body."

Fenton took a deep breath, let it out slow. "Our Rennkavi was dead. We were so close and it all fell apart. My anger turned to Morvein, blamed her. I raged... Aeon how I raged! I was certain that if she had not thrust me away, I could have saved the ritual, saved Theos, done *something*..."

"Morvein saved your life." Elohl replied.

"Some part of me knows it's true." Fenton heaved a sigh as a tear tracked down his face. "But some part of me still hates her. Blames her. Just like some part of me hates my grandfather Leith with a righteous fury, despite everything Bhorlen has spoken today. We were so close! And then it was madness. Destruction raging upon our continent for a hundred years before it finally gave out. I made my blood-oath during that dark time, for I was a man filled with darkness."

Bhorlen squeezed his comforting hand upon Fenton's shoulder. "Feel it, little brother. Feel the poison coming out. Consider this: if you had not gone through what you did, would you be the man you are today, dedicated to your Rennkavi, a stalwart fighter who has defied the wrath of time? Would you be a man who can protect those you love, in a night without stars?"

"I don't know," Fenton sighed. "I don't know if I am that man now."

"Patience," Bhorlen rumbled. "Patience."

Fenton closed his eyes. He took a deep, steadying breath as Bhorlen's hand lifted away. When he opened his eyes, they shone clear, their regular honey-brown, his features placid once more.

Bhorlen nodded, then turned to Elohl. "Are you ready for where you must go next?"

"I'm ready." Elohl said, feeling it, a steady ease spreading through him.

"Then take that arch there," Bhorlen gestured one massive hand at the rightmost arch of the seven. "That one will send you where you need to go. Directly. No more struggling in the mountains. No more fighting the snows and the glaciers. You will come out right where you need to be. And then your journey may continue."

Fenton stepped up beside Elohl, their packs gripped in his hands. Handing Elohl his pack, Fenton faced the arch as he shouldered his on. "Ready to go through to the bog? To find Purloch and raise an army of Kingsmen to support our Queen?"

"Is there an Alranstone in the bog?" Elohl wondered, facing the arch and hefting on his rucksack.

"No, but I get the feeling these things don't need an Alranstone."

"They do not." Bhorlen rumbled behind them. "These are older *wyrria*, far more subtle. Alranstones are crude totems of blood-magic sigildry. These were made by the Albrenni, here long before my people carved this vast citadel within the glacier. But all are gone now, the destinations of these arches lost to the winds of time just like their makers, all but two of them. Farewell, sons of peace. Safe journey, and do not fear the darkness."

Suddenly, a push of wind thrust Elohl off his feet and tossed him at the rightmost arch. With a rush of sound in his ears and a whisper of wind about his body, he was poured like liquid through a funnel. There was no pain or agony, not like traveling through an Alranstone. This was simply a feeling of *going*, of rushing through space and time in the blink of an eye. Visions shuffled before him, like a deck of fate cards rifled all around. Mountains, plains, a desert, a catacomb, and suddenly, he was out. He did not stumble, there was no shove that made him buckle to his knees. He was just suddenly out upon the other side, standing tall with Fenton to his right.

Elohl blinked, gazing around. They had come out in some vaulted underground chamber made of the same opalescent stone as the center of the amphitheater. Ringed in columns, the hall was a circle, expanding away from a crystal Plinth at its center, which towered up behind Elohl and Fenton. The Plinth shone with a vague light, a flickering luminescense that eased off streams flowing through the underground grotto. Burbling water created a network in the floor like a spider's web, stepping-stones leading from the Plinth to the encircling columns. Reflected up into buttressed domes that formed the hall's ceiling, the Plinth's light illuminated alabaster rock carven to resemble a forest of weeping trees. Fanciful gryphons snarled from ferns; writhing satyrs ate grapes in vaulted arbors. Actual moss dripped green from everything, emerald duckweed creeping between the floor-stones, while pale purple waterlilies bloomed in the streams, throwing the light from their saffron centers.

And before them, moving toward a vaulted exit, was a woman. She looked over her shoulder as if she felt their presence, then turned. Her lips parted in astonishment as she stared at Elohl and Fenton.

And for his part, Elohl stared right back.

She was beautiful. Lithe and elegant, a white silk-lace gown with a low décolletage dripped from her lean frame, embroidered with pearls that curled like vines up her body. Pale silver hair cascaded over one bare shoulder in a loose braid, shimmering in the shifting light. A thin silver circlet graced her brow, delicately set with pearls and small emeralds. Her eyes were almost white, yet Elohl spied the faintest hint of blue, as if a spot of blue ink had dissipated through a glass of water. Her lips were red, a luscious color like sex, her cheeks flushed. Dark and thick, her eyelashes made her eyes arresting, and Elohl found himself pinned by her gaze.

She was more than a vision. Elohl had thought Ghrenna was the most stunning woman he had ever seen. But this woman put Ghrenna's beauty to shame. Watching Elohl as she neared with dancelike grace, she gave a confused smile. She held out her hand, palm down, fingers together. An unmistakable gesture of those nobly born, for Elohl to be genteel and kiss her hand.

"Welcome, my lords," she spoke in a luscious alto. "I do not believe we have had the pleasure of acquaintance."

Elohl heard the sudden rasp of a blade drawn. Fenton's sword flicked out, the tip settling up beneath the lovely woman's chin. She froze with a slight inhalation, her chin lifting so she wouldn't be skewered, though she showed no fear and left her hand extended.

"Don't touch her, Elohl!" Fenton growled, bristling with a livid snarl.

"Fenton!" Elohl glanced at him. "Easy! She's unarmed."

And she was. No blade rode any belt. No impression of a dagger-hilt showed at her cleavage. And all that draping silk and lace would have gotten in the way of any thigh-sheath. Out of habit and because he felt a need to apologize for Fenton's rash act, Elohl reached out and took the noblewoman's hand, bowing and brushing his lips across those delicate fingers. She wouldn't try anything with Fenton's blade up beneath her chin, whoever she was.

At the touch of his lips upon her skin, the woman gave a rolling chuckle, then laughed like a tinkle of little bells.

"*Elohl!*" Fenton's cry was dire, stricken.

The woman's laugh rang like a chorus inside Elohl's mind. Wrapping him in a touch of gossamer, heady as a cloud of exotic perfume, Elohl suddenly had a thought that he would do anything for this woman. Her fey laughter was in him, moonsilver and ice tinkling over glass. Her warm breath slipped to Elohl like silver mist, as if she kissed him, parting his lips in a soft sigh, licking at his tongue. She beamed upon him, radiant as he straightened from his bow, and nothing in Elohl's world had ever been so beautiful.

She was life itself. She was what he had been waiting for, all his long years. She was the land, and the green fields. She was the peace of cicadas at noon and the chorus of peeper-frogs in the darkness. She was vines tangling him into an everlasting embrace; she was the tilth that grounded the roots of every forest. She was a mossy bower at midnight, she was sex by the light of the moon.

Elohl flushed, breathing hard. His groin stirred, a fire in his blood that had nothing to do with his Goldenmarks. Whatever she wanted, he would do. Anything at all. Only to touch her, to feel her blessing in his hands. To stroke that soft skin beneath him in the darkness. To smell the delicate perfume that sighed from her pores, heady like night-blooming ceanthus. His hand still lingering upon hers, Elohl brushed his thumb over her fingers and she smiled more, beatific, all for him.

Whatever she needed, he would do.

At his side, Fenton roared and surged to ram his blade home in her beautiful flesh.

"Fenton!" Elohl commanded in the underground grotto. "Stand down! She is not to be harmed."

With a wretched grown like a skewered wolf, Fenton lowered his blade. He trembled at Elohl's side from the effort of restraining himself. "Don't order me to do this, Elohl! She needs to die. You have no idea what this woman is capable of, who she is!"

"Put your blade away," Elohl commanded, stern. "You are not to harm this woman. I don't care who she is."

Fenton strangled. Rage boiled through him. Elohl saw crimson flash in his eyes. He snarled, but slid his sword back into its sheath. His Oath still held him, to do whatever his Rennkavi commanded, lest he burn in Halsos' fires forevermore.

And it was in Elohl's favor right now. Elohl turned back to the woman. He could never harm her. She was luminous. She was light. Her visage poured through his mind, nothing more excellent, nothing more precious.

"Tell me your name," Elohl found himself bending down to press another kiss to her fingers, lingering. "Please. And forgive my friend's rash action. He will not do it again."

"What a fascinating pair you are!" Her alto laugh was pure delight, a tinkling of bells. "What a pleasure to have you here in my palace, by whatever means you were sent. There will be time for us to discuss all. But for now, welcome! Welcome to Valenghia, to the White Palace of Velkennish. My name is Aelennia Oblitenne, but to my realm I am known as Vhinesse. I am the Vine that provides for my people. Come! Walk with me. Tell me how you are called as we walk, and how you come to be here."

With gracious elegance, she came to Elohl, tucked herself between him and Fenton. Reaching up, she caressed Elohl's cheek with one white knuckle, then Fenton's. Grasping both their arms with her light fingers upon their fur-padded jackets, she beamed, ready to be escorted. Elohl moved forward, knowing instinctually what she wanted, where she wished to go.

As they stepped from the Plinth, her perfume eased through Elohl's mind. Sweet like sighs of the night, it banished his inner conflicts. Her lovely laugh tinkled in his ears as all thoughts of Queen and country fell away. Gone were thoughts of Leith and Morvein, the Undoer and calamity. Bhorlan was sloughed away. Elohl's journey through the mountains and Fenton's struggle was erased from him as they exited the grotto. Even the woe of Olea's death evaporated as they walked, and Elohl's pining for Ghrenna disappeared, along with the image of the white Spire in his mind.

Everything washed out, like water flowing through a forest

bower. Until there was nothing but the touch of the Vhinesse's hand upon Elohl's arm, the sound of her voice in his ears, and the scent of her body in his nostrils.

Whatever she wanted, he would do.

Whatever she needed, he would do.

EPILOGUE – KHOUREN

Khouren paced the smoldering city in a red dawn. Hood up, soot-smirched, he looked like any of the wandering dispossessed, gazing up charred avenues with empty eyes. A barren silence ate the morning. Destruction loomed in every direction. Crows rode the breeze, diving down to bully away vultures settling upon dead horses and oxen. Mangled bodies in the gutter already attracted rats, who fought with the crows for the best leavings.

Lintesh was a city of charnel. Khouren had roamed the lower Tiers for a while, but the destruction of wooden hovels in the poorer quarters was absolute. His steps aimless, he now wound his way up a stairwell upon the outer wall of the Third Tier near the Central Plaza. No Guardsman halted his ascent, all of them busy in the streets below. Stepping out upon the wide parapet, he found it empty, silent but for the sounds of a ruined city wafting up from a hundred feet below.

Moving to a position that afforded a view, Khouren gazed out over the wide plains sprawling to the east and south of Lintesh. Dark clouds swallowed the morning sky, churning from a wind off the Kingsmount, hurried away over the plains in black channels that streaked the blue. People flooded from the city, a river of the dispossessed, moving through the gates of the First Tier. A shanty-town rose upon the plains, dust trailing from the passage of shuffling feet to further stain the soot-heavy air. The city below Khouren's vantage was charred, decimated. Fully three-quarters of Lintesh had burned over the past days, and smoke still seeped up into the sky from countless areas of smoldering rubble. The city was equipped with ancient water-pumps that dredged the underground river, intended for such calamity as this, and the ones that yet worked had been used, but still. Only the wealthy quarters had really survived, carven straight out of the blue byrunstone of the Kingsmount as they were.

Heaviness consumed Khouren's heart, gazing out over it all.

"So much ruin," he murmured, his words taken by the breeze and wafted away to nothingness.

Hearing a commotion building below, he looked down, then moved to the other side of the wall to better see the Central Plaza. A throng of the wealthy seethed in the plaza below, surrounding the fountain. Hundreds, perhaps thousands of lesser nobility, merchants, tradesmen of position whose homes had burned in the lower city. Many homes in the Queen's and King's Quarters had been spared, the avenues wide and the old mansions solid byrunstone, but warehouses of goods had gone up in smoke in the lower Tiers.

With shouts, the wealthy of Lintesh called for retribution from the palace. Wearing soot-stained finery, they slapped at the heavy iron portcullis lowered into place between the East and West Guardhouses. Khouren set his jaw in anger. If Lhaurent did not respond to this madness soon, he would have another riot, in addition to a razing of the lower city.

Suddenly, Khouren saw members of the palace household and those of greater nobility who lived in the palace being trooped out upon the Fourth Tier, shepherded by Guardsmen in cobalt. Maids, butlers, serving staff, kitchen-hands, laundresses. Hunters, foragers, young trainees of the Guard. Stable-hands, blacksmiths, cooks, tailors. All the various and sundry folk who lived in the palace and had for generations, that tended the needs of such a vast organism. They all came forth, hundreds of them, thousands, the vast army of Roushenn shuffling along the Fourth Tier in a wide arc.

Settling into silence.

For there was only one reason the entire palace had been called out this morning. Something was about to happen, for which all would bear witness. Highborn and low, they stood among each other, pushed back by Guardsmen from the central area atop the East and West Guardhouses, and kept from the parapet above the main gate.

Suddenly, a clarion call erupted from the central parapet between the guardhouses. Khouren glanced to the area above the main gate, watching ten palace heralds sound hunting horns in the clipped staccato that meant a member of the royal house was about to speak.

Tingles raced over Khouren, knowing what was coming. He watched the central parapet, alert, vibrating with tension. As the throng quieted and upon the Fourth Tier and in the plaza, he saw six men in black herringbone leathers step to the railing. Khouren set his jaw. His lips lifted in a snarl. The contemptuous visage of Khorel Jornath was not among these lesser Brethren of the Kreth-Hakir, but still, six of them together was a formidable force. Enough to sway the minds of every man and woman gawking below.

Enough to convince them of whatever Lhaurent wanted with this unprecedented show.

And like smooth mist, Lhaurent den'Karthus glided into view. Though impeccable as always in his grey finery, Khouren saw changes in Lhaurent's attire today. His silk doublet was chased with gold thread, patterns that even from this distance Khouren could see recalled his Goldenmarks as they caught the sunlight piercing down through the black clouds. His open robe was not his usual grey, but a soft white that blazed in the sun, true and pure. His hair had been carefully oiled, and he wore no silver chains of Castellan's office at the high collar of his doublet. Instead, he wore chains of gold that looped from two gold pins upon either side of his open collar, the pins set with rubies.

Each pin flared like a starburst, like the sun rising to a luminous dawn. Their gold flashed in the morning light, the rubies burning like fire. Khouren knew those pins. He'd last seen them upon a corpse down in the Alrahel Catacombs where Olea was entombed. Upon the desiccated garb of King Sophos den'Alrahel, the last Alrahel to wear the crown before his line fractured hundreds of years ago, and a non-Alrahel descendant had assumed Alrou-Mendera's throne. And now, Lhaurent had taken them up, ancient emblems of his birthright.

The horns called a fanfare again. The last of the murmuring died in the throngs below and above. Lhaurent spread his hands in a gesture of invitation, his face calm, serene.

"People of Lintesh, brothers and sisters of our city's beloved family," Lhaurent's voice was mellow and resonant, rolling through the plaza and over the Fourth Tier by a trick of Roushenn's acoustics. "We have risen this morning to find our city transformed. Indeed, our entire nation transformed. As many of you have heard, our most esteemed Chancellate were murdered just days ago, leaving our nation adrift in frightening storms. And the past days of madness were the product of that instability, of their abandonment of us when we needed them most."

Khouren took note of that, of how Lhaurent twisted his words, making people feel as if they had been abandoned. As if he was one of them, betrayed by recent events. His Rennkavi was silver-tongued, one of the many reasons he had ascended so far from nothing. Khouren's gaze flicked to the Kreth-Hakir flanking Lhaurent. He hadn't felt any pulse of power from them yet.

Not just yet.

"But I rise this morning to tell you," Lhaurent continued in his rich baritone, "that all is not lost. For in this time of devastation and sorrow, a new hope has emerged. From the devastation of a Queen murdered and a warmongering Chancellate slain, there is one who has brought order to this chaos. One who has never given up hope of what this nation can be. Of how it can rise, resurrected from the ashes of instability and carnage and ten years of unceasing war. Rise like the phoenix, and be birthed anew in strength, unity, and prosperity."

He had their attention now. Khouren could see the merchants, the lesser nobles considering his words, mulling them over. Those upon the Fourth Tier cocked their heads, ready to hear what was coming. Khouren's gaze flicked back to Lhaurent, watching his once-master ply his most skillful magic.

The *wyrria* of persuasion.

"As I was once your Castellan, to Kings of three generations," Lhaurent continued, "loyal servant to the Crown in times good and bad, I am now your servant. Your most loyal subject, people of Alrou-Mendera. The one who will serve you, help you rebuild what we have lost, regain what we have forgotten, re-claim what was once ours. For once, a people of power ruled this land. A people of skill and merit, who had gifts that could change the course of events, lives. A people who once held the surnomme of Alrahel, the People of the Dawn. Kings and Queens of old, they once held this very city in an age of glory. And today, we shall claim that glory again. We will make this city rise once more, better than before, with an ancient wisdom that should never have been forgotten! For today, my brothers and sisters, comes again the power of the Dawn. *Behold, the power of the Alrahel!"*

Lhaurent reached to his collar with a smooth motion, pulling open his silk jerkin and casting it and the white robe down from his shoulders to drape at his elbows. And through the red morning, his Goldenmarks suddenly blazed. Writhing with a furious light, they dazzled Khouren's eyes, smote his mind with surges of power no mortal could possibly comprehend.

Cries came from the throng below and from the spreading Tier. Astonished sounds, as hands clapped to mouths, to hearts. To weapons. And suddenly, Khouren felt what he'd been waiting for. The sneaking silver threads of the Kreth-Hakir moving through the crowd, seeking out those who were uneasy at this revelation, taming them.

Calming them.

Hands slipped from weapons. Those with hard eyes were dulled, smoothed, gaping at Lhaurent's revelation like the cowed of lesser minds. Khouren felt a tendril from the Kreth-Hakir seek him, lipping at his mind, trying to find a way in. But a barrier of quicksilver flashed up in his thoughts, barring them. And even as it brought relief to Khouren, it brought a shiver of horror.

Khorel Jornath's gift within him was not gone. Yet again, Khorel's influence had kept Khouren safe from mind-bending, but to what end, Khouren quailed to know. As the lesser Brethren's gifts slipped past, Jornath's curse within Khouren coiled away, slumbering once more like some devil of ancient sands. And there the demon slept in the shadows of his mind. Waiting.

Watchful.

But its presence had pushed back its own Brethren. And its presence had pushed back the thundering force of Lhaurent's unveiling, making his surging Goldenmarks with their obliterating illumination seem little more than a dazzling display of sun upon the sea. Khouren watched as the populace below and above cowered, as they surged with hope, as they bent to Lhaurent's will. To the determination that made Lhaurent what he was, that fed his Goldenmarks.

The domination of absolute rule.

"Together," Lhaurent continued, "we shall rebuild this city, this nation! Together, we shall rise, until our Unity of mind and purpose call other nations to our banner, to the glorious prosperity that we shall attain! And more than a nation, you will have a *world*, brothers and sisters, an entire world to call your home. An entire world to build in and prosper! An entire world, to call your own! And I, *Lhaurent den'Alrahel*, true Servant of the Dawn, marked by Prophecy, will bring this glorious golden age, this glorious Unity, for you!"

Cheering erupted in the throng, both below and above. Khouren could feel it, pushed and pulled by the currents of the Kreth-Hakir flanking Lhaurent, flamed to frenzy. Those who might have dissented were not silenced, but instead provoked to cheer and clap, to forget their concerns at this so-sudden unveiling. To forget a Queen assassinated, just months ago. To forget a Chancellate slain in their beds. To forget the atrocities that had screamed in the city for the past many days and nights.

The Brethren took inspiration and heightened it to roaring approval. Feet stomped, hands drummed in rhythmic clapping, screams of belonging and honed purpose engulfed the plaza and the Fourth Tier.

They were with him. They were all with him.

Unified.

And when Khouren thought it could get no more furious, Lhaurent suddenly raised his hands. With obvious motions so as to be seen below and to those upon the Tier, he danced his long fingers through the air in a sinuous weave, like eels twining around prey. And as that darkwater motion spun from his hands, the blocks of the guard towers suddenly wrenched.

With a groan of rock, the grinding sound of blocks lodged in place for hundreds of years, the central towers of Roushenn's Fourth Tier began to descend into the ground. The guard towers folded away from the rest of the Tier, pivoting as a section of plaza before the gates shifted, shuffling back with a rolling motion. The entire edifice moved downward, the iron portcullis gradually being swallowed by dark halls of the Unterhaft below.

People shied back from the palace gate, some with cries, though those were quickly stifled by the Kreth-Hakir. The parapet upon which Lhaurent and his Brethren stood descended with the rest, like a boat carried upon a slow wave, down into the earth. As it did, walls of the flanking sections of the Fourth Tier shuffled downward, forming long staircases that led down to the plaza. And when the central section finally neared the plaza below, Lhaurent halted the grinding descent with a dramatic flick of his fingers. With another flick, he caused the rampart retaining wall to split, blocks shuffling upon unseen tracks down into a spreading series of stairs.

An awed hush settled over the plaza. In that roaring silence, Lhaurent moved graciously forward, his step gentile and unhurried, down those stairs. And then he stood before them, level with them.

As one of them.

"Touch me." His smooth voice rippled through the air, carried to every ear by acoustics and the seeking tendrils of the Kreth-Hakir. "Know my power. The power of the Rennkavi. No longer do we need Kings. Kings only bring division, strife, and bitterness. A new era has dawned, my friends. A new era of power, stability, and most of all, *wyrria*. Know me. Touch me, and feel the power of our blessed Unity. Beneath a red dawn we rise, and we rise as One."

And like dreamers in a drug-addled haze, they did. One by one, they reached out, they touched his skin, traced those luminous curls of white fire. Men sighed to their knees after their fingers brushed Lhaurent, eyes wide and consumed with wonder. Some cried out in astonishment. Some fell, prostrate, weeping from the power that Khouren knew surged in those dire Goldenmarks.

From atop his height, Khouren shivered as he watched the crowd break, a fell wind rippling through him. With every touch, Lhaurent bound them. With every trace of fingers, with every lingering caress, he wrapped his sinuous coils around them, drowning them to the depths of a vast and evil sea. With a gesture to the Guardsmen above, Lhaurent invited those of the palace household to descend the stairs and come join the event below. Khouren watched in horror as Lhaurent began to walk among them, as he began to pass the poison of his Goldenmarks from hand to willing hand, aided by the compelling minds of the Kreth-Hakir.

As if Khouren's emotions had been felt by the tyrant, Lhaurent's gaze flicked up suddenly to Khouren upon the Third Tier. His gaze burned like brands, it scorched with triumph and scorn. Khouren trembled under the horrible, luminous grey gaze of his former master. But as before, Khorel Jornath's gift rose like a silver wave in Khouren's mind, swallowing Lhaurent's power.

Lhaurent's eyes narrowed upon Khouren. And then his gaze passed on, dismissing Khouren with cold purposefulness as more people moved in to touch his marvel with seeking fingers.

Their idol. Their Dawn. Their Rennkavi.

Lhaurent den'Alrahel.

Khouren choked. Lhaurent's meaning was absolute in that single pointed gaze. Khouren's services in the shadows were no longer necessary. And now, Lhaurent had dismissed him like so much trash. Like a cur, he'd been cast out from his master's grace for disobedience, for his betrayal. The light Lhaurent held, vile as it was, would never touch Khouren. That bliss the others felt would never be Khouren's again.

Stumbling back from the parapet wall, Khouren's gut clenched in a vast, unspeakable anguish. He turned from the scene, unable to face this horror he had wrought. Like a butcher with his favorite knife, Lhaurent had used Khouren to carve this awful path in silent dominance and bloodshed. Used like the tool he was, like the fool he was. Like an old ghost of the darkness, who had no further use now that his Rennkavi had been born into the light. Khouren was untethered in a rising storm, and there was no lighthouse to come home to, not even one flooded by the darkest ocean.

Lhaurent had stolen the Dawn, to Shape it as he willed. And now, a storm was coming.

And it would be terrible.

THE END

The adventure continues in GOLDENMARK, book three of *The Kingsmen Chronicles*.

Did you enjoy this book? Please leave a review for *BLOODMARK*

GET THE EPIC PREQUEL FREE!

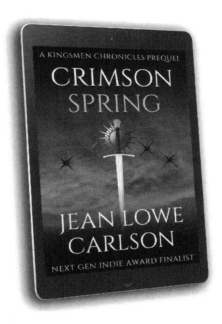

Join Jean's email list at https://www.jeanlowecarlson.com/crimson-spring-kc00 and get a free copy of *Crimson Spring,* the newsletter exclusive prequel novella to the Kingsmen Chronicles!

ABOUT JEAN LOWE CARLSON

Award-winning author Jean Lowe Carlson writes adventurous epic fantasy fiction with a dark twist. Her raw worlds remind one of Patrick Rothfuss, Clive Barker, George RR Martin, Robert Jordan, and Robin Hobb. Jean holds a doctorate in Naturopathic Medicine (ND), and has a keen awareness of psychology and human behavior, using it to paint vivid characters set amidst nations in turmoil or societies with riveting secrets. Exciting, challenging, and passionate, her novels take the reader upon dire adventures while exploring deep human truths. In 2016, she was the recipient of the Next Generation Indie Book Awards Finalist medal for her dark fantasy "Tears".

Find out more at: http://jeanlowecarlson.com/

APPENDIX 1 – PRONUNCIATION GUIDE

Word Beginnings:

Dh/Jh/Kh/Lh – Hard consonant, "h" is silent (Ex. Dherran [Dair-ren] like "dare", Jherrick [Jair-rick] like "jester", Khouren [Koor-en] like "kick", Lhaurent [Lao-rahnt] like "laugh")

Gh/G – Hard "g" sound (Ex. Ghrenna [Gren-na], Gherris [Gair-ris] like "good")

Ih – Long "ee" sound (Ex. Ihbram [Ee-brum] like "helium")

Th – Soft "th" combination (Ex. Theroun [Thair-oon] like "thespian")

Uh/U – Long "oo" sound (Ex. Uhlas [Oo-las] like "tulips")

O – Proper "oh" sound if begins a word (Ex. Olea [Oh-lay-a] like "ocean")

El – Open "eh" sound (Ex. Elohl [Eh-loll] like "elephant")

Il – Soft "ihl" sound (Ex. Ildrian [Ihl-dree-an] like "ill")

Middle of Words:

-i- If in the middle of a word, long "ee" sound (Ex. Elyasin [Ehl-ya-seen] like "do re mi")
Exception: Aldris [Al-dris, not Al-drees]

-ch- Soft "sh" sound (Ex. Suchinne [Soo-sheen])

-ou- Long "oo" sound (Ex. Roushenn [Roo-shen] like "frou-frou")

PHRASES IN HIGH ALRAKHAN:

Alran aenti vhesserin! Ahora! Ahora! Ahora!
Alran you are my vessel! Awake! Awake! Awake!

Alrashemnesh ars veitriya rhovagnetari! Toura Corunenne!
Alrashemni are the true protectors! Long live the Queen!

PHRASES IN KHOUREK:

Salish-te ah'khanek houret na hathne, ips hathne na houret salish-e, bithii.
We wile away the sundial's curve, as you while away your curves
upon the sundial, honored warrior.

Taile arabine welekhoum. (Welekhoum!)
You uncloak are welcome. (Welcome!)

Taile scherram Menderian, Maitrohounet. Ne Khourek.
Your guests speak Menderian, Maitrohounet. Not Khourek.

Taile elepsios sayan. Kirthe elim lhe'ghavanesh nhis Lhaurent den'Karthus!
They are traitors. We shall have them killed for being aligned with
Lhaurent den'Karthus!

*Ne, Maitrohounet! Taile ne elepsios sayenti! Ne elim! Ne ghavanesh nhis
Lhaurent den'Karthus. Taile Alrashemnari. Menderian Alrashemnari.*
No, Maitrohounet! They are not traitors! Do not kill them! They are
not aligned with Lhaurent den'Karthus. They are Alrashemni.
Menderian Alrashemni.

Taile fherroum lhis Alran-beihn?
They are all of the Alran-born?

Sahverya, Maitrohounet.
That is so. Maitrohounet.

Sei Olea brethan khoum tantha Alrahel! Sei Olea dihm Alrahel.

She is the Olive Tree that brings peace with the Dawn. She is the Olive Tree of the Dawn.

Titha dihm titha semna hahni.
The enemy of my enemy is my friend.

Elohl dihm Alrahel.
The Rising of the Dawn.

Fhekktir! Andüste!
Assemble! Let's go!

Ih tannaa. Gheme hehlia ahwei.
We cannot. Force us not to hunt. (Please do not force us.)

Khehemnas ehla veh?
Khehemni are you truly?

Khala khen'eya taliminae vhris khoum. Hemne sacri a Werus et Khehem.
Our spears venture onward no further. This place is sacred to the Wolf and Dragon.

Shouf'ne elimriae bith kii. Caravanserai.
I offer my deepest honor to you all. Caravanserai.

Mitha devanii alith hemna. Ne lengii.
My brethren will divine (linger) until the setting sun. No longer.

PHRASES IN OLD KHEHEMNI:

Thouliet dannoua Khehem, yethan chelis.
Remember you to Khehem, with your heart.

APPENDIX 2 — CHARACTERS

Elsthemen:

Elohl den'Alrahel — First-Lieutenant of the High Brigade, twin to Olea, Alrashemni Kingsman

Therel Alramir — King of the Elsthemen Highlands

Elyasin den'Ildrian Alramir — Queen of Alrou-Mendera, wife of King Therel

Merra Alramir — High General of the Highlands, older sister to Therel

Fenton den'Kharel — First-Lieutenant of the Roushenn Palace Guard

Lhesher Khoum — Highsword to King Therel

Jhonen Rebaldi — First-Captain to General Merra, Dremor

Luc den'Lhorissian — King's Physician, previously a thief in Ghrenna's Consortium

Jhennria Dhukrein — Keshar-Keeper and Master Trainer of Lhen Fhekran

Rhone and Rhennon Uhlki — Second-Captains to General Merra, twin brothers

Adelaine Visek — First-Dremor to King Therel

Irdi Lefri — A renegade keshari rider

Hahled Ferrian — One of the Brother Kings of Elsthemen

Delman Ferrian — One of the Brother Kings of Elsthemen

Mikka Khuriye — First Scout of the Bhorlen Rangers

Zhenaya Khehim — High General for Therel's grandfather, Bhorn

Harenya — A palace servingwoman

Erellia, Belumia — Keshari riders in the Split Fangs

Levva — A keshari rider, caught by Theroun

Morvein Vishke (deceased) — High Dremorande to the Brother Kings

Devresh Khir (deceased) — First Sword of Elsthemen

Martin Visek (deceased) — Brother to Adelaine

Rhugen Khersus (deceased) — Merra's husband

Born Alramir (deceased) — Therel and Merra's grandfather, King of Elsthemen

Ennalea den'Alrahel (deceased) — Elohl and Olea's mother

Elsthemi Clans:

Blackthorn – Outriders, patrol Bhorlen Mountains near Valenghia
White Claws – Merra's personal guard, her most elite keshari warriors
Split Fangs – Merra's secondary guard
Six-Tooth, Redbear, Redhawk, Khersus, Keth Malek – Elsthemi Highlander clans

Oasis Ghellen:

Olea den'Alrahel – Captain-General of the Palace Guard, twin to Elohl, Alrashemni Kingsman
Jherrick den'Tharn – Corporal in the Roushenn Palace Guard
Aldris den'Farahan – Second-Lieutenant of the Roushenn Palace Guard
Vargen den'Khalderian – A silversmith, Kingsman-in-hiding
Lourden al'Lhesk – Spear-Captain and host for ambassadors to Oasis Ghellen
Thelliere al'Lhesk – Lourden's wife, hostess for ambassadors to Oasis Ghellen
Gherlam al'Lhesk (deceased) – Thelliere's first husband, Lourden's brother
The Maitrohounet – Spiritual leader of Oasis Ghellen
Jhennah – Lourden's First-Spear
Ghistan – Lourden's Second-Spear
Ghilos, Astaniia, and Lhosos – *Berounhim* caravanserai

Oasis Khehem:

Leith Alodwine (deceased) – Khehem's last King (aka Leith the Red)
Alitha Alodwine (deceased) – Leith's daughter, the Prophetess of the Rennkavi
Ordeith Alodwine (deceased) – Grandfather of Leith Alodwine, King of Khehem, a tyrant

Roushenn Palace:

Lhaurent den'Karthus – King's Castellan
Theroun den'Vekir – A King's Chancellor, ex-General, Black Viper of the Aphellian Way

Thaddeus den'Lhor – Secretary to Chancellor Theroun
Evshein den'Lhamann – Head Chancellor
Rudaric den'Ghen – A King's Chancellor
Jhik den'Cammas – A King's Chancellor
Khouren Alodwine – The Ghost of Roushenn
Khorel Jornath – High Priest of the Kreth-Hakir (men in herringbone leathers)
Ihbram den'Sennia – High Brigade, Second-Hand to Elohl
Metrene al'Lhask – The Kingstone
Arthe den'Tourmalin – King of the Tourmaline Isles
Uhlas den'Ildrian (deceased) – King of Alrou-Mendera
Alden den'Ildrian (deceased) – Dhenir of Alrou-Mendera
Jhulia den'Lhorissian (deceased) – Mother to Luc

First Abbey of Lintesh:
Brother Temlin den'Ildrian – Second Historian of the Jenners
Ghrenna den'Tanuk – Alrashemni Kingswoman, a thief
Abbott Lhem den'Ulio – Abbot of the Jenners
Abbess Lenuria den'Brae – Abbess of the Jenners
Mollia den'Lhorissian – A Seer of the Jenners
Eleshen den'Fenrir – An innkeeper
Lamak den'Thun – The Abbeystone
Brother Sebasos, Brother Thenros – Jenner brothers in the Brewery
Brother Lemvos – Jenner brother in the Orchards
Sister Alitha – A Jenner sister, Kingsman-in-hiding
Sister Regina – A Jenner sister of the Infirmary
Brother Brandin – A young Jenner brother
Brother Hender – A Jenner brother in the Annals

Vennet:
Dherran den'Lhust – Alrashemni Kingsman, a prize-fighter
Khenria den'Bhaelen – Friend to Dherran
Grump (aka Grunnach den'Lhis) – Friend to Dherran
Vicoute Arlen den'Selthir – Vicoute of Vennet, leader of the Shemout Alrashemni
Whelan den'Yhenniman – A Kingsman, retainer to Arlen
Tristenne den'Hout – A Kingsman, retainer to Arlen
Lhuder den'Mhens – A Kingsman, top Captain to Arlen

Fhellas, Enthin, Fhennic, Valdo – Kingsmen, retainers to Arlen
Suchinne den'Thaon (deceased) – A Kingswoman, first love to
Dherran

Menderian War-Camp (Camp Lethia):
Arlus den'Pell – Captain of the High Brigade
Vitreal den'Bhorus – Captain of the Fleetrunners
Lharsus den'Ulthumen – High General at the Menderian front
Khaspar den'Albehout – High General at the Valenghian front
Herkhum den'Lhiss – Fleetrunner spy
Den'Bheck, den'Ferhn, den'Lennos – Khehemni-aligned Menderian
Cavalry-Captains

Purloch's House:
Purloch den'Crassis – Master of Purloch's House in the Bog
Elyria Kenthar – A Dremor
Finna – A fighter of the Bog
Bherg – Yenlia's husband, a fighter of the Bog
Yenlia – Bherg's wife, a fighter of the Bog

Valenghia:
The Vhinesse – Queen of Valenghia
Delennia Oblitenne – House of Oblitenne, once-lover to Arlen
den'Selthir

APPENDIX 3 — PLACES AND THINGS

PLACES

ALROU-MENDERA

Lintesh (The King's City) — City at the base of the Kingsmount
Roushenn Palace — The royal palace at Lintesh
Elhambrian Valley — Valley at the edge of Lintesh
Elesk (The Kingsmount) — By Lintesh
The Eleskis (The Kingsmountains) — Border of Valenghia and Elsthemen
Elsee — Lake in the Eleskis
Alrashesh — First Court of the Alrashemni Kingsmen
Dhemman — Third Court of the Alrashemni Kingsmen
Vennet — A city on the eastern bogs, home of Vicoute Arlen den'Selthir
Quelsis — A city in the foothills of Alrou-Mendera
Thalanout Plain — Where most of the fighting is against Valenghia
Aphellian Way — Site of the Black Viper's slaughter, on the Thalanout Plain
Lheshen Valley — In the mountains near Quelsis, has seen vicious fighting, now well-protected
Gerrov-Tel (Mount Gerrov) — Ruins in the Kingsmountains, site of Haled's Stone
Gerthoun — City on the border of Elsthemen and Alrou-Mendera
Southern Lethian Valley — Where the Menderian main war-camp is (Camp Lethia)
Long Valley — Valley on the Valenghian border just north of Purloch's Bog
Gerson Hills — Location near Vennet
Pallisade Fhen — Location near Vennet
Thickhole Swamp — Swamp near Vicoute Arlen's manor
Bitterwoods — Forest near Vicoute Arlen's manor
Khenthar Rhegalatoria — Respite of the Rulers, Molli's valley at the top of the Kingsmount
Heathren Bog — Enormous bog north of the Aphellian way (Purloch's Bog)

Purloch's House – Purloch's main city in the Heathren Bog

ELSTHEMEN
Lhen Fhekran – Capitol city of Elsthemen
Fhekran Palace – Therel Alramir's palace at Lhen Fhekran
Valley of Doors – On Alrou-Mendera border, has ancient ruins, on the Lethian Way
Northern Lethian Valley – Where the Elsthemi main war-camp is, and the Valley of Doors
Lethian Way – An ancient canyon-road up through the river-gorge in the Lethian Valley
Kherven Valley – The plains approaching Lhen Fhekran from the west
Bhorlen Mountains – Far up the Elsthemi-Valenghian border to the north
Mount Veldir – Elsthemi name for the Kingsmount
The Devil's Field – An immensely treacherous glacial crossing into Valenghia from Elsthemen
Lodresh Glacier – Glacier that holds the Devil's Field
Bitterrift Pass – The approach to the Devil's Field
Hokhar – City on the ice tundra
Mount Ghirlaj – Obsidian mountain to the south of the Devil's Field
Cannus Rift – Treacherous sheer gorge north of the Devil's Field
Fithri-Lhis – A lost city up on the ice tundra, home of Morvein

THE TWELVE TRIBES
Oasis Ghellen – An ancient city east of Khehem, capital of the Twelve Tribes
Oasis Khehem – A dead city west of Ghellen
Chiriit Crevasses/Oasis Chirus – North of Oasis Ghellen, protected by a vicious, secretive people
Oases Lukhaan, Niirm, Drashaan – Coastal oases of the Twelve Tribes
Oases Asyana, Vrenouhem – Northwestern mountain oases
Oasis Onaani – Far southeast mountain oasis
Oasis Aj Naab, Oasis Etrii – Eastern trade oases near the Ajnabiit lands
Oasis Revenhiim – Solitary central desert oasis

Oasis Bel'raa – Southern trade oasis to the Southern Desert (Ghistani lands)

VALENGHIA
Velkennish – Capitol city of Valenghia
Palace of the Vine – The White Palace in Velkennish

GHREC
Shelf of Lost Hope (Thuruman)
Sea of Ghrec
Ghreccan Desert

OTHER NATIONS
Cennetia, Praough – Nations annexed by Valenghia
Thuruman (Cape of Lost Hope) – Far eastern nation
Lhemvian Isles – Islands in the Archipelago of Crasos
Tourmaline Isles – Islands southwest of Alrou-Mendera
Crasos – Island to the west of Cennetia
Jadoun, Perthe – Southwest countries to Alrou-Mendera
Unaligned Lands – To the northeast, nomadic lands
Southern Desert – Lands south of the Twelve Tribes (Ghistani nomads)
Aj Naab – Ajnabiit lands east of the Twelve Tribes

THINGS
Aelakir – Like an alligator, a creature of the Heathren Bog
Aeon – God of the Air, like Zeus
Aeon's sack – A curse
Ajnabiit – A black-eyed people beyond the mountains east of the Twelve Tribes
Alahda – The tall native Ghellen date palm
Alran-keeper – One who knows the secrets of Alranstones
Alrashem (sing.), Alrashemnari (pl.) – Twelve Tribes name for Alrashemni = "Lost Ones" or "Engraved Ones"
Alrashemni Kingsmen – Elite fighters and peacekeepers sworn to the King of Alrou-Mendera
Avari – A long bladed pole-weapon used by the Elsthemi while riding keshari

Berlunid – Elsthemi battle-goddess

Berounhim – Caravanserai for the Twelve Tribes, their most elite warriors

Bhuirn – An enormous Highlands bear, like a kodiak

Bitterwood – A stout desert tree, used to make Ghellani spears

Blackfoot stag – Like a moose

Blackmark – A derogatory slur used for Kingsmen, refers to the mountain and stars Inking upon the chest

Bloodmark – The hidden inkings of the Shemout Alrashemni, written in blood-ink

Box-elder, sing-leaf, Lhugard's Pine, strongoak, leatherleaf – Highland trees, mountain elevations

Brenner's Fire – A cuss in Elsthemi

Byrunstone (Bluestone) – Common bluegrey stone in Alrou-Mendera

Cendarie – Like a cedar tree

Chandria – Yellow mushrooms, edible, grow in woods

Chellis – An edible plant with wide, waxy leaves, like collards

Chiriit – A secretive people of the Twelve Tribes' northern crevasses

Chiron – The Growing Vine, Twelve Tribes god of knowledge and green land

Chirus Alrashemni – Mountain and Stars Inking "Dedicated of the Land"

Claw-feet – Like crampons for climbing

Cliffs of Khosh-Nianti – Unassailable se-cliffs in the Unaligned Lands

Der Skerrzen – The lance in Old Valenghian, nickname for Arlen den'Selthir

Devil's Breath – Asphyxiating powder

Diamantii – Great black sand-scorpions of Twelve Tribes, Ghrec, and the Unaligned Lands

Die Berkzat – The bitter one in Old Valenghian, nickname for Delennia Oblitenne

Dourienne's Cap – An edible mushroom

Dremor – A True Seer, with accurate visions

Dwelven – A large Highlands wolf

Fennewith – A drug that is smoked, like opium, seeds can also be chewed, like fennel

Fiirhen – Ghellani alcoholic beverage made of plums
First through Eighth Seal – Rites of passage for the Alrashemni,
start at age 14, end at 21
Fithrii – The white-haired people of the ice tundras
Galhuk – A guttural pidgin language spoken in the Unaligned Lands
Gerunthane – A person who can touch minds and command them
Ghellani – People of Oasis Ghellen
Ghistani – Nomads of the Southern Desert
Green chacao – Like cocoa
Hagsgill – A poisonous mushroom of the Heathren Bog
Halsos – Lord of the Underworld, like Hades
Halsos' Burnwater – Like Hades' Hell
Hathnou-tusk – Tusks of a vicious Jadounian mammal, like a giant
wild boar
Hazelfern, winterbloom, snakeroot, laurel-urn – Medicinal herbs
near Vennet
Henroot, basalm, mint, chennery – Elsthemi healing and cooling
herbs
Hesh-ti – A spiky crimson fruits of the Twelve Tribes, tasting like a
juicy pear
High Alrakhan – Ancient Alrashemni language, originated in the
Twelve Tribes
High Vouniete – Language of Chiron, god of the Twelve Tribes,
mostly forgotten
Highsummer Tithe – A woman ceremonially gifted to the Kings of
Elsthemen by the tundra people
Highsummer, Darkwinter – Summer and winter solstice in
Elsthemen
Hopt-ale – Like beer
Hopt-blume – Like hops
Horsewhip frond – Stimulating herb, like coca
Jenner Sun – A flaming golden circle like the sun, with thirteen
spokes, emblem of the Jenners
Jenner's Penitent – An order of monks in Lintesh at the First Abbey
Jherra-style – Ancient Alrashemni fighting-style with two curved
daggers, of Twelve Tribes origin
Keshar – A large battle-cat/saber-tooth cat, like a cougar but huge
Khehemni – A shadowy faction in opposition to the Alrashemni

Khehemni Lothren – The elite secret ruling group of the Khehemni, one exists in every nation

Khets al'Roch – A massive black beast, lean with razor claws and fangs

Khourek – Native language of the Twelve Tribes, a bastard version of Ghrec and High Alrakhan

Kingskinder – Children of the Alrashemni, not yet 21

Kotar – Elsthemi god of sexual stamina

Kreth-Hakir – Mind-bending monks from the Unaligned Lands

Lace palm – A shorter, fringed palm tree in Ghellen, often in pots on porches

League – Mile (measurement)

Leavonswood, bairn, ironwood – Different kinds of trees

Lheshoni – Elsthemi goddess of the hunt

Loa-leather – Leather made into flexible armor from a scaled desert lizard

Maitrohounet – Spiritual leader of Oasis Ghellen

Majiyenou – Term for a sorcerer (person with wyrric ability) in Jadounian

Mehrkordiat Desik – The tableaux of Wolf and Dragon forever locked in combat

Mherkhet – A nation over the sea from Elsthemen, bronze-skinned foreigners

Miner's cabbage, thimbleberry, mherrl – Edible plants near Vennet

Mocktarn-root – A sedating herb

Moruhaine – A people who live in the far northern tundra - Adelaine's kin

Nightbloom – A Twelve Tribes flower, like night-booming jasmine

Olea-gishii – Branch of the Olive Tree, a symbol of peacekeeping, what Lourden calls Olea

Order of Alrahel – Order of the Dawn, wyrric high priests and priestesses who governed the Sun Tribes

Pay the Fifth Price – An Alrashemni Kingsman threat, killing five people you know for a transgression

Pythian-resin – Flesh-eating resin

Reghalia – A poisonous Highlands incense, stops the breathing

Rishaaleth – Lourden's elite warriors, protect the Alranstone near Ghellen

Shakha-tassel – Long crimson bristles in a tassel, adorn Ghellani warrior spears

Shouf – A face-wrap of the Twelve Tribes, covers the mouth and nose

Skunked to the Crasos Canals – An expression of being so drunk you swim in shit

Summons of the Kingsmen – Historical event ten years prior

Teller-wort, thorough-bottom, lanceola, thuma, heatherfern, deathstool - Herbs for opening Seeing abilities, focus, and vision-travel

Tesh-Tar – A tree-hunting cat in the bog, like a jaguar

The Lothren – High council of the Khehemni

The Sun Tribes – Ancient name for the Thirteen Tribes before the War of the Sun Tribes (Khehem War)

Thellas Alri – An old term for the people bound into Alranstones

Threllis – A drug that is smoked, like marijuana with cocaine

Trundle-Bell – A poisonous mushroom, brings paralysis, looks like Dourienne's Cap

Union of the Sun Tribes – The Thirteen Tribes unification under the Order of Alrahel's leadership

Verouni – Truth Warrior in Jadounian - term for a elite warrior or wise man

War of the Sun Tribes (Khehem War) – Khehem's rebellion from the Union of the Sun Tribes, led by Leith Alodwine

Werus et Khehem – The Conflict of the Wolf and Dragon, ancient battle-wyrria of Khehem

Wyrria – Magic - a term originating in the Twelve Tribes

Wyrric – A magic user

Yempe – A bog-gazelle

Alrou-Mendera Ranks of Lords (Least to Greatest):

Dhepan – Mayor of a town/city

Vicoute/Vicenne – A lower Viscount, manages a moderate area around cities/townships

Couthis/Couthenna – A higher Count, manages large areas including multiple cities

Duchev/Duchevy – A Duke/Duchess, manages major sections of the nation

Chancellor (King's Chancellor) – Advisers to the King

Dhenir/Dhenra – Prince/Princess of Alrou-Mendera
King/Queen – Monarch of Alrou-Mendera

Alrou-Mendera War Brigades:
High Brigade – Operate in the highest mountains in the Valenghian
border
Longvalley Brigade – Operate in a well-protected valley on the
Valenghian border
Fleetrunners – Messengers at the Valenghian border
Stone Valley Brigade – Special tactical unit, fierce fighters, called in
where necessary

Made in the USA
Las Vegas, NV
06 June 2021

24294545R00400